LEGACY
OF STEEL

By Matthew Ward

The Legacy trilogy
Legacy of Ash
Legacy of Steel

LEGACY
OF STEEL

MATTHEW
WARD

www.orbitbooks.net

ORBIT

First published in Great Britain in 2020 by Orbit

1 3 5 7 9 10 8 6 4 2

Copyright © 2020 by Matthew Ward

Map by Viv Mullett, The Flying Fish Studios, based on an
original illustration by Matthew Ward

The moral right of the author has been asserted.

A CIP catalogue record for this book is available from the British Library.

HB ISBN 978-0-356-51338-6
C format 978-0-356-51340-9

Typeset in Minion by M Rules
Printed and bound in Great Britain by Clays Ltd, Elcograf S.p.A.

Papers used by Orbit are from well-managed forests
and other responsible sources.

Orbit
An imprint of
Little, Brown Book Group
Carmelite House
50 Victoria Embankment
London EC4Y 0DZ

An Hachette UK Company
www.hachette.co.uk

www.orbitbooks.net

For Mum & Dad.

Home isn't just where you live.
It's where you are loved.

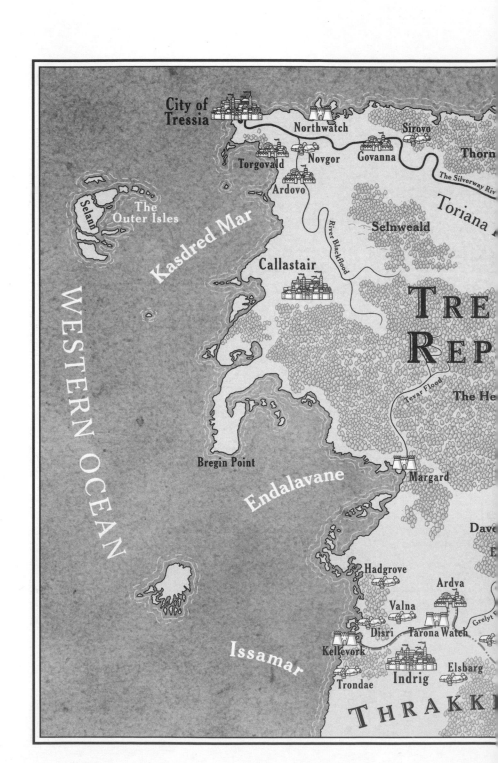

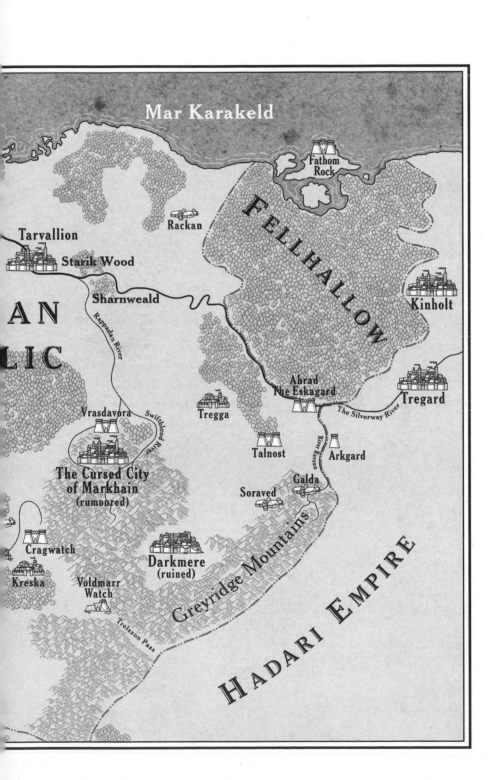

Mar Karakeld

Fathom
Rock

Rackan

FELLHALLOW

Tarvallion

Starik Wood

Kinholt

Sharnweald

Rappadan River

AN
LIC

Vrasdavora

Swiftblood River

Tregga

Ahrad
The Eskagard

Tregard

The Silverway River

The Cursed City
of Markhain
(rumoured)

Talnost

Arkgard

River Ravona

Galda

Soraved

Cragwatch

Darkmere
(ruined)

Greyridge Mountains

HADARI EMPIRE

Kreska

Voldmarr
Watch

Trelazon Pass

Dramatis Personae

In the City of Tressia

Josiri Trelan	Member of the Tressian Privy Council
Malachi Reveque	First Councillor of the Privy Council
Stantin Izack	Master of the Knights Essamere; Member of the Tressian Privy Council
Anastacia Psanneque	Definitely *not* Lady Trelan
Vladama Kurkas	Captain of the Trelan Hearthguard
Lilyana Reveque	Tressian Noble, wife to Malachi Reveque
Sidara Reveque	Daughter to Malachi and Lilyana Reveque
Constans Reveque	Son to Malachi and Lilyana Reveque
Altiris Czaron	Fugitive
Vona Darrow	Captain of the Tressian Constabulary
Hawkin Darrow	Steward to the Reveque household
Leonast Lamirov	Member of the Tressian Privy Council
Erashel Beral	Member of the Tressian Privy Council
Messela Akadra	Member of the Tressian Privy Council
Elzar Ilnarov	Tressian High Proctor; Master of the Foundry
Konor Zarn	Peddler of wares and influence
Sabelle Mezar	Member of the Grand Council
Adbert Brass	Sergeant of the Trelan Hearthguard

Dregmeet

Apara Rann	A vranakin, a cousin of the Crowmarket
Inidro Krastin	Pontiff of the Parliament of Crows
Karn Athariss	Pontiff of the Parliament of Crows
Endri Shurla	Pontiff of the Parliament of Crows
Erad Nyzad	Kernclaw
Koldra	Vranakin Rogue

In Defence of the Border

Roslava Orova	Knight of Essamere; The Council Champion
Sevaka Psanneque	Captain of the Tressian Fleet
Riego Noktza	Castellan of Ahrad
Emilia Sarravin	Commander of the 7th regiment
Indro Thaldvar	Borderer captain
Zephan Tanor	Shieldbearer of the Knights Essamere
Halan Gavrida	Lieutenant of the 11th

Of the Hadari Empire

Kai Saran	Hadari Crown Prince, King of Rhaled
Melanna Saranal	Hadari Princessa, daughter of Kai Saran
Sera	Lunassera; a devoted servant of Ashana
Kos Devren	Rhalesh Warleader
Aeldran Andwar	Prince of Icansae
Naradna Andwar	Prince of Icansae
Haldrane	Spymaster; Head of the Emperor's Icularis

Elsewhere

Viktor Akadra	Champion of the Tressian Council
Armund af Garna	Thrakkian outcast
Ardothan af Garna	Thane of Indrigsval
Inkari af Üld	Ceorla of Indrigsval
Arlanne Keldrov	Reeve of Ardva

Gone, But Not Forgotten

Malatriant	Tyrant Queen of Old, known as Sceadotha in the Hadari Empire
Ebigail Kiradin	Disgraced member of the Privy Council
Aelia Andwar	Princessa of Icansae
Anliss af Garna	Thrakkian outcast; sister to Armund af Garna

Divinities

Lumestra Tressian	Goddess of the Sun, known as Astarra in the Hadari Empire
Ashana Hadari	Goddess of the Moon, known as Lunastra in Tressia
The Raven	The God of the Dead, Keeper of Otherworld
Jack o' Fellhallow	God of the Living Lands
Astor	Lord of the Forge, Keeper of Skanandra
Tzal	The Unmaker
The Nameless Lady	Inheritor of Mantles Past
Endala	Goddess of Wave and Wind
Elspeth	Daughter to Ashana
The Huntsman	Ashana's Equerry

Six Months Ago

Lunandas, 28th Day of Frosthold

Of seven, six sprang from Dark of Old.
One drowned. One sleeps. One waits.
The fourth sets blood awry with gift of self.
The fifth bargains all to ruin.
The last yearns for treasure lost.
Gods do as they please,
never knowing their roles are set.
But it is a poor story that changes not in the telling.

Excerpt from The Undawning Deep

The moon blazed in the field of stars and the royal city of Tregard reached up to embrace her. Filigree patterns laid into flagstone and wall glowed bright with whorl of root and branch, supplanting the blocky buildings of day with a silver forest whose limbs offered worship to regal Ashana.

A goddess who no longer spoke to Melanna Saranal as once she had.

Melanna released her grip on the balcony and strove for joy amidst melancholy. No room for sorrow this night. By dawn, everything for which she'd striven would be hers. No longer a mere princessa of the Silver Kingdom of Rhaled, but recognised heir to the imperial throne – the first woman acclaimed so.

But the cost ...

Storeys below, crowds gathered beneath skeletal birch trees. Tregard had emptied for this moment. Despite the hour. Despite winter's lingering cold. Thousands upon thousands of citizens gathered beneath Mooncourt Temple's alabaster walls, standing vigil until the toll of twelfth bell proclaimed a worthy soul had claimed the imperial crown.

Gentle hands bound the last black tress of Melanna's hair with jewelled chain.

"Ashanal. The hour is upon us."

"Thank you, Sera." Melanna gazed out across the shining city to Ravenscourt Temple's brooding spires. The black stone lay ever in shadow, unyielding as the promise of death, and implacable as the embrace of Otherworld's mists. "I wanted to see the city one last time. We'll never be quite the same, it and I."

"You will bring it only prosperity, Ashanal."

Ashanal. The title that marked her as a daughter of goddess as well as Emperor. Fit for one who'd walked with Ashana since her earliest years. But no more. Not since Melanna had allowed a scion of Dark to escape her grasp. She longed to hear Ashana's voice. She'd begged. But the silence in her prayers had stretched through the turning of leaves and the harsh bite of winter.

Melanna set her back on Tregard's splendour. Always so hard to read Sera's expression behind the silver half-mask that left all but her eyes and the olive skin of her jaw concealed. Melanna couldn't even be certain of the handmaiden's age. Sera's ready vigour spoke to youth, perhaps as brief a tally as Melanna's own nineteen winters. Indeed, in complexion and build they were twins. But the poise Melanna envied belonged to a greater span.

What would Sera say if she knew the truth? She was lunassera, hand-maiden to the Goddess, driven to serve Melanna by faith more than friendship. But Sera remained inscrutable, and Melanna found, once again, that she couldn't raise herself to the confession.

A bright peal rang out. The eighth bell of coronation ritual, welcoming dignitaries into the temple's heart. The ninth would call Melanna to her father's side. The eleventh would invite the Goddess to grant her blessing. It had gone unanswered for decades out of mind.

Sera stepped aside in a swish of close-fitting white robes and drew aside the balcony's drape with graceful precision.

"Come, Ashanal. Even for royalty, punctuality is politeness."

Melanna returned Sera's smile, though she shared little of its warmth. She crossed the threshold, exchanging the crisp silver of the midnight sky for the glow of torchlight. Sera followed with soundless tread, pulling closed the drapes and the etched glass door.

Two mannequins waited between hearth and changing screen. Melanna traced fingertips across the golden scales of the nearest, the scars of battle long since repaired. The armour alone was challenge to tradition, but not so much as the sword belt laid alongside. Though they were otherwise equal to men in all things, women did not fight wars. They did not bear swords – not even a divine gift, as was the Goddess' silvered blade – and because of that, could not rule. On the second mannequin, the threads of a golden gown shone like sunlight – as different from the black cotton dress she currently wore as night from day. Armour of a different sort, worn to draw attention to the wearer's body, and thus guard her thoughts.

The warrior or the courtier. Wearing armour to her father's coronation would be affront to tradition and the pride of jealous men. The dress was conciliatory – proof that the upstart Saranal had not completely forgotten her place.

Her father would prefer she don the dress. Soothe the feathers of a Golden Court ruffled by his wary acceptance of peace overtures from the Tressian Republic. The panelled gown was entirely beautiful, crafted from Ithna'jim silk, and radiant with a magic of a type not practised in the sprawling kingdoms of Empire.

The armour bore old memories of rash decisions poorly made. Its presence beneath the last night of full moon would sour events.

Chimes broke out high above. Ninth bell, calling the heir to the sanctum.

The warrior or the courtier. As Empress, she'd one day have to be both. Today, the path was clear. She reached for the gown.

Brash trumpets split the air. Melanna began her descent of the long, marble stair towards the grassy mound and the triad of birch trees. Anticipation shivered bare skin at the base of her neck, quickened by the air's crisp, sweet scent. Only the stoniest heart roamed the cloister's open skies and felt nothing.

Beneath the largest tree, a simple stone block sat bathed in moonlight. The first altar at which the Goddess' praises were intoned, or so legend told. Simple too was the circlet atop it. The first Emperor, Hadar Saran, had died in the Sceadotha's dungeons, but the crown endured. Flesh withered and blood faded, Emperors came and went, but the crown abided. It *was* the Empire.

And it was all Melanna had ever desired. The crown, and what it meant for her to wear it.

A knot of Immortals stood on the root-woven path to the sunken sanctum gate, resplendent in emerald silks and golden scales; swords drawn against those who would disturb the meditations of the

Emperor-to-be. Nearer, on the shore of the pool that made an island of the sanctum mound, a ring of temple wardens, garbed in brilliant white, and their long spears held at guard.

Melanna pressed on, neither too hurriedly nor too slow. She strove to ignore the murmurs and widening eyes from balconies set in concentric tiers above the cloister. Kings, princes and clan chiefs called from across the league-strewn Empire to acclaim one among their number more equal than the rest. Men of Rhaled, Corvant, Britonis, Silsaria and others. Representatives of the Gwyraya Hadar, the great kingdoms of Empire, and the client realms under their sway. In garb and feature, they were as varied as fallen leaves in autumn. But women had no place here, save as servants or celebrants.

Certainly not as heir.

How many murmured with awe at her splendour? How many with disgust because she wore her sword at her back, the woven links of its belt crosswise at right shoulder to left hip? Melanna stifled a smile. She hadn't left the warrior behind entirely. Better to remind her peers who she really was. That despite the soft promise offered by silk and the gossamer chains binding her hair, she was their equal. No, their better.

The chimes of tenth bell swept the courtyard. Conversation fell silent. The bare branches of the birch trees rippled gently in the cool breeze.

A second fanfare heralded Melanna's arrival at the base of the stair. Head bowed in respect, she awaited the high priestess' approach.

White robes brilliant in the moonlight, the old woman made stately procession over the narrow latticework bridge. Wardens crossed spears behind her, barring Melanna's final approach to the sanctum mound.

"Why have you come?"

The priestess' words were ritual. Scowl and unfavourable tone were not. Disgust that the heir was a woman, or because that woman bore a sword?

"To guide my Emperor out of Dark, and into Ashana's light." Melanna let her voice blossom, acoustics folding echoes beneath the words. "As a daughter will one day do for me."

Fresh murmur broke out on the balconies. To the Golden Court, the Dark was ritual and history. An enemy overcome long ago, first by Ashana's radiant sister, and once again – in the form of the

Sceadotha – by Hadar Saran's allies. But Melanna had walked within it. She'd carried the Goddess' fire against it. And at the end, she'd failed.

None of the sourness left the priestess' tone, but she persevered. "May the Goddess walk with you in the Dark."

She stepped aside. Spears parted.

Melanna crossed the bridge. She gave ritual bow to the Immortals, and their golden wall split apart before her coming. Beyond, the stone pathway diverged, the upper fork arriving at altar and crown, the lower at the sanctum's birchwood gate. Offering a bow to the former, Melanna took the latter, passing beneath the woven arch.

Once the double leaves of the gateway were behind, and Melanna deep in the sanctum's gloom, she allowed the mask of unconcern to slip and her stride to quicken. The soft, damp fragrance of soil thickened as breathing shallowed. White crystals glimmered in the root-woven ceiling, shaping passageways and revealing shimmering insects scurrying across loose soil.

At last, the passageway widened into a broad chamber, dominated by a statue of Ashana – though the likeness little matched that of the Goddess who had guided Melanna since girlhood. Two Immortals flanked the Goddess. And before the statue, Kai Saran, Prince of the Silver Kingdom of Rhaled and scion of Emperors past, stood in silent contemplation, eyes closed and expression unreadable above a neat, greying beard.

Melanna knelt. "My prince. You are called to coronation."

He spoke without turning. "And who calls me?"

"The one . . . " She swallowed to ease a throat suddenly parched. "The one who will follow."

Though the words were part of the ritual, they felt impudent. Presumptive. Had her father felt thus addressing her grandsire? How would she feel to one day be reminded that her fate was to die so that another might rule? Proud, or resentful? What governed her father's humours? They'd argued too often about this day for Melanna to be sure. She was the one to break tradition, but he'd made it possible. He'd be as notorious as she if affairs went ill.

"And will you serve me until that day? Will you guard my life with your own?"

"To my dying breath, my prince."

Dark robes whispered against emerald-set golden scales. Dark eyes met hers. Expression rigid, he bore down, a mountain to her willow. The slight limp, a reminder of wounds that should have taken his life, little besmirched his grandeur. He swept back the dark folds of his woollen cloak and drew Melanna to her feet. Cheeks the colour of weathered teak cracked a smile. Then, uncaring he did so in full view of his Immortals, he drew her into an embrace.

"I shan't ask you to obey, for I know you won't," he whispered. "But wherever the path leads from here, know that I am proud."

Melanna sighed as her worries melted away. "Thank you, Father."

"*My prince*," he corrected. "Ritual must be observed."

She pulled free and bobbed a rare curtsey. "Yes, my prince."

"Better." His lips twitched a smile. "Dagan? I am called to coronation. Announce me."

The leftmost Immortal offered a deep bow and strode towards the passageway.

"Tell me," said Melanna's father. "How appalled are my peers?"

"Does it matter?" she replied bitterly. "They're swine. Those who sneered to see me with a sword would gladly have entertained me without my gown."

He grunted. "There are honourable men among them. And you will have to find one you can at least tolerate if this day is to mean anything."

Could he not enjoy the moment without borrowing strife from the future? "A discussion better left for another hour, my prince."

A rolling *boom* shook the chamber.

"The gates!" Dagan broke into a run and vanished into the root-woven passageway.

Melanna grasped at racing thoughts. "Tell me again of the honourable men in your court, Father."

"They'd dare?" Her father drew his sword. "In the heart of the temple? In the Goddess' sight?"

"Why not? They believe they do her work. They believe—"

A new sound rose in crescendo beneath the roots – a chorus of screeching crow-voices and thundering wings, growing ever louder. A sound she'd first heard months before at Tevar Flood and almost died for the privilege.

Kernclaw. She'd not known the name then, but she'd taken the trouble to learn it. An assassin lured from the shadows of the civilised world.

"Dagan!" she shouted.

A wet, tearing sound and a bellow of agony from the passageway cut through the squalling. The thump of a falling body. Harsh voices redoubled in fury. The chamber drowned in a rush of talons and beating wings.

The second Immortal vanished, overcome by the shadowy flock. Fresh screams rang out.

Across the chamber, corvine fragments coalesced into a hooded figure. One steel-taloned hand at the Immortal's ravaged throat. The other against the torn and bloodied armour about his waist. Green eyes blazed beneath the ragged hood.

Melanna drew her sword. The Goddess' sword. White flames sprang to life along the silvered blade. The shadow-flock parted with strident cry. Crows peeled away in panic.

Her father bellowed in pain. Melanna lunged to his side, bringing him within the safety of the firelight. She ignored the talons ripping at her hair, blotted the shrieking voices from her thoughts. Steel glinted within shadow. Metal scraped on metal. The weight vanished from her sword. Melanna's flailing hand found soil and tangled roots.

Should've worn the armour. Not that armour had done Dagan or his fellow much good. And for all Melanna's bitterness, she'd believed the temple safe ground, and the quarrels over the succession settled.

Honourable men. She'd teach them honour.

"What's the matter, kernclaw?" Melanna shouted. "Afraid?"

Cruel laughter shook the chamber. "What a lioness! We should have charged more."

Teeming bodies swamped everything beyond the sword's light. The kernclaw could have been three paces away, or fled entirely.

Melanna glanced behind. Her father stood with his shoulder against the chamber's roots. His sword-hand shook. His other pressed against the mess of torn scales and rushing blood at his flank. Already his robes were dark with it. His face was pale above his beard, tinged with greyish-green.

Poison?

"Go," he breathed. "Leave me."

Melanna's throat tightened. "No."

"You can't best him. Save yourself."

"I guard your life to my dying breath." A booming chorus shuddered through the gloom. Fists and shoulders thumping against the timber gate. "Your Immortals are coming. We need only reach them."

And if that wasn't enough? Better to face the kernclaw in the cloister. The confines of the sanctum only made the shadow more oppressive and the clamour deafening. In the open, those advantages would fade. Theirs would grow, swollen by loyal blades.

Her father's face twisted. He lurched into the passageway. Melanna gripped her sword tight and followed.

The sanctum gate emerged from shadow. Barred from within, and with two temple wardens crumpled at its foot.

Crow-voices blossomed anew.

Melanna spun about and lashed out at a shape half-seen. Talons gleamed. She struck them aside. Her wild backswing slashed at green eyes. The kernclaw shrieked. Eyes vanished into shadow.

"Father?"

She found him slumped against the wall, blood speckling his lips and the sword at his feet. Gasping for breath, he allowed Melanna to brace her shoulder beneath his, the mountain borne forth by the willow, stride by staggering stride.

The shadows of the passageway thickened with crow-voices.

The chorus of hammer-blows gave way to a crash of abused timber. A tide of Immortals trampled the ruined gates. They flooded past with swords drawn, plunging into shadow without hesitation. Screams vied with the thunder of wings.

Back arched beneath her father's weight, Melanna lurched for the open air.

"Melanna . . ."

He slid away as the first moonlight touched Melanna's face. She lowered him beside the altar. His fingers slipped from hers, leaving bloodied trails on golden silk.

"Father!"

She knelt and clutched his hand. Skirts clung to her legs, warm with his blood.

Uproar overtook the balconies as kings and princes descended into confusion. Some scrambled for the stairs, swords drawn and outrage on their lips. Others stared, frozen by events. One alone, resplendent in scarlet silks and the serpent of Icansae, reached the far neck of the bridge, steel naked in his hand, and two of his own Immortals at his back. Too distant to offer aid. The priestess who had so meanly welcomed Melanna stood immobile a few paces beyond.

Eleventh bell tolled, the distant bell ringers unaware that the ritual of coronation lay savaged beyond repair.

The last scream faltered. The sanctum's empty gateway filled with shadow.

"Is this how the line of Saran fades?" The kernclaw's mockery billowed. "In desperate flight? With wounds behind to mark its cowardice?"

Melanna let her father's hand fall. She stood, her sire's shuddering breaths to her back and the Goddess' sword steady in her hands.

"You will not take him." Her body shook to the words. Not the cold of fear, but anger's searing flame. "Not while I live."

"The commission was always for both."

There it was. A truth known from the first. Her father died for loving her more than tradition.

She levelled the sword. "Dead men claim no coins."

"And slain princessas no crowns." Was his breathing at last ragged, or did Melanna hear only her own wild hopes? "I am of death, and you are nothing but a girl who clings to moonlight."

Melanna drew up to her full height. "I am a princessa who *commands* it."

With a screech of triumph, the crow-flock spread like monstrous wings.

A horn sounded. Not a trumpet, but the deep, breathy notes of a hunter's salute, strident and sonorous. Then hoofbeats, quickened to the gallop.

Mist spilled beneath bare branches, and a shape coalesced behind. A rider with an antlered helm, and a cloak streaming like smoke. The white stag he rode as steed was more suggestion that substance, flesh and blood only when moonlight brushed its flanks. The head of his long spear blazed with starlight.

Melanna's heart skipped.

The crow-flock screeched, shadow scattering before starlight. The spear-point ripped into the kernclaw's chest and pinned him screaming to the bloodied soil.

The rider released the spear and wheeled about. His eyes met Melanna's, green as the kernclaw's were green, but vibrant where those of the crow-born promised only death.

He winded his horn once more. The thickening mist blazed. A pale woman in a shimmering gown stood beneath the trees. Another, a stranger to Melanna, stood close attendance, her skin shining silver.

Eleventh bell had sounded, and the Goddess Ashana had come.

The sword slipped from Melanna's hand. Fire faded as it struck the grass.

Moonlight ebbed. The cloister fell silent at a sight lost to living memory. Kings and princes who would have died rather than pay homage to a woman knelt in silent reverence.

The Huntsman twisted the spear in the kernclaw's chest. Shadows parted at the accompanying scream. All was moonlight and mist.

Ashana strode past the corpse without a glance and enfolded Melanna in embrace.

"Forgive my lateness. I have been away too long."

Shame and joy mingled in Melanna's heart. Shame for what had driven them apart, and joy at beholding her once again. "I failed you. I'm sorry."

Ashana stepped away and bowed her head, straw-blonde tresses falling to frame her face. "The failure was mine. I have been timid, too afraid of taking action. No more. Do they still call you my daughter?"

"Some do, Goddess."

"Ashana." She delivered the rebuke with a soft smile. "Always Ashana."

Melanna scowled away discomfort. The Goddess seldom enjoyed being named such. Indeed, she sometimes claimed not to be a goddess at all. "I beg you, save my father."

"Those who would rule should never beg."

"Then I ask."

The smile faded. "Elspeth?"

The attendant drew close. Lustrous silver complexion turned dull as she slipped into the shadow of the trees. A slender woman, she was in aspect no older than Melanna, and like to the Goddess in all ways save ash-blonde hair cropped close.

She leaned near, her cold grey eyes but inches away.

"You'd have done better to guard him closer," she whispered. "Such a disappointment. How can my mother love a failure so?"

Elspeth knelt beside Melanna's father, her fingers dancing briefly across his brow before she straightened. "His wounds are bitter with poison. I need silver. I need the crown. And soon."

Ashana's sapphire eyes bored into Melanna's. "The choice is yours. What is more important? Your father's life, or his crown? *Your* crown?"

Melanna stiffened and faced the altar. The imperial crown. The heart of Empire. Their family's history. Everything for which her father had fought. Everything she'd thought to claim. Her past and future were bound to it.

She stared at the latticework bridge, where the Icansae prince knelt. He and his kind would never forgive. Her father would never forgive. If she sacrificed the crown, there could be no throne. She'd become the wrecker of tradition in truth, as well as jealous whisper.

Melanna tore her eyes from the bridge, her gaze touching briefly on Elspeth's. Her eyes held only contempt, as one bored with a performance that had overstayed its due. Only the Huntsman offered any solace. Or she thought he did. A slight dip of the head that might have existed only in her imagination, urging her to make a decision.

"Take it." Melanna raised the silver circlet from its bed of ivy and held it out. "No woman can be worthy of a crown she chooses over those she loves."

"The correct answer."

Melanna barely heard Ashana's soft-spoken words. She felt sure no other had.

Elspeth snatched the crown. "About time."

Corrosion crept outward from her fingers as patina and tarnish, faster and faster as the rot spread. Black dust rushed away, and the crown was gone, reduced to twisted fragments. White light danced about Elspeth's fingers, her hands once again silver as they had been in moonlight. Rent armour crumbled at her touch, and she set her hands to Kai Saran's wounds.

His scream echoed across the cloister. His body convulsed on shoulders and heels. Melanna clenched a fist – her one concession to weakness as her sire writhed.

At last, the screams faded. Elspeth stepped away. Her bare arms were black to the elbow with charred skin, her expression dark with caged pain. Melanna's father lay motionless in the drifting mist, his tan skin no longer marred by poison's taint.

"He will live," Elspeth said tautly. Her blackened fingers scratched at a charred palm, scattering dark flecks and revealing pale skin beneath. "If he so chooses."

A final spasm and a rasping cough brought Melanna's father to a propped elbow. A welter of dark blood spilled across his lips and dribbled into the mists.

"Charming," Elspeth murmured.

Melanna fell to her knees. "Father?"

Eyes cracked open. A breathy voice hailed from a distant place. "Melanna?"

Wary of the eyes upon her from around the cloister, Melanna forewent the embrace she longed to offer, and instead held out a hand.

"Can you stand, my prince?"

She stuttered the words, barely able to speak for contrary emotions. Those emotions soared as his hand closed about hers. Not yet the strength of the mountain, but better than she'd dared hope. His breathing rasped more than she liked, but such things would improve while life thrived.

He rose, and at once bowed his head as he realised in whose presence he stood.

"Goddess." A flicker of eye and lip betrayed a nervousness Melanna had never before witnessed. "I owe you my life."

"You owe your daughter, not I." With some surprise, Melanna noted that Ashana didn't quibble her father's use of the title. "Her sacrifice saved you."

"Sacrifice?" His eyes sought Melanna's.

She glanced away. "The crown is gone."

His face tightened. "Then there can be no coronation. I cannot be Emperor."

For a heartbeat Melanna wished she could undo the decision already made. But only for a heartbeat. A corpse wore no crown. If her father hated her for what she'd done, he'd at least be alive to do so. She could bear that burden, even if she spent the rest of her life seeking to atone. A life that love for her father had cast far adrift.

"No coronation?" Ashana shook her head and spread her arms wide. "The bell chimed invitation, and I am here. If I'm a goddess, and the Goddess comes only for coronation, then a coronation there must be. You owe your daughter your life, Prince Kai, and I owe her a crown. Only one of us need make good on the debt today."

Reaching high above the mists and into the rays of the moon, she wove the brilliant light like thread. A shape coalesced. A circlet of silver that was not silver, for it shone even when gathered down into the shadows beneath the trees. Ashana held it level with her waist and tilted her head, her lips moving silently as one struck by a failure of memory at an inopportune moment.

"Prince Kai," she said at last. "This crown is for your daughter, who led you out of Dark and into moonlight."

Though the words were spoken to Melanna's father, the sudden force in Ashana's voice made them plain for all to hear.

"But you may bear it, for her and for me, until I call you to the gardens of Evermoon and all ephemeral burdens fall away. Do you accept this responsibility? Will you be my hand upon this world?"

His eyes met Melanna's in question. Her mouth was ashen, so she nodded instead. Eyes still averted, he knelt at Ashana's feet.

"Yes."

Elspeth peeled another strip of charred skin from her arm and edged closer to Melanna. "A sword," she hissed. "He cannot be crowned without a sword."

And her father's sword was lost in the sanctum. Melanna glanced at the trampled grass where her own had fallen. It caught light anew as she took it by the blade, but the moonfire made no mark upon her skin.

"For you, my prince." She paused, savouring the words. "My Emperor."

Melanna felt a pang as her father took the sword, as if she'd given up a piece of herself.

Ashana nodded. When she spoke, it was not with the wry warmth Melanna knew so well, but tones cold as ice and hard as glass. They carried across the cloister.

"I will not ask whose coin brought a vranakin to my temple. But from now on, a hand raised against the House of Saran is a hand raised against me. And among my many questionable virtues, patience cannot easily be found. You might seek it the rest of your brief lives and never catch a glimpse."

She paused. The Huntsman ripped his spear free of the kernclaw's corpse. The *thud* of its butt against the grassy mound was that of a stone casket falling closed.

The courtyard, already drowning in quiet, fell utterly silent.

"You name me Goddess, and as she I call upon you now! Dark is returning to this world! Will you bicker as it takes your children? Or will the Hadari Empire stand as one, and bring light to those who have squandered their own? The road ahead requires sacrifice and offers glory. Will you follow your Emperor to its end?"

Ashana's expression shifted, the regal mask of an eternal goddess slipping to reveal a younger, unsteady soul beneath. But the moment passed, and Ashana was once again as unknowable and ageless as the heavens.

"Ashanael Brigantim! Saran Amhyrador!" The Icansae prince rose to one knee, his sword point-down on the bridge's timbers. "For Goddess and Emperor!"

"*For Goddess and Emperor!*"

The cloister boomed with sound and fury as other voices took up the cry. Swords offered salute from balconies. The Huntsman watched unmoving, inscrutable; Elspeth with grey-eyed resentment. And Ashana, the Goddess who sometimes claimed not to be a goddess at all, set a circlet of moonsilver upon the brow of a man delivered from delirium to rule.

Thus Kai Saran – who had knelt a prince – rose an Emperor, and swept a sword swathed in moonfire to the heavens.

And Melanna Saranal, who had longed for this day all her life, wondered why she shivered.

Lunandas, 28th Day of Ashen

The past is not dead.
It slumbers, the custodian of our follies.
A moment's waking brings all to ruin.

from Eldor Shalamoh's "Historica"

One

One

Dawn stumbled across Tressia's crooked rooftops, Lumestra's radiance as reluctant as Josiri's blood. No. Not Lumestra's. The goddess was gone, dead perhaps even before his birth. The sunlight was her legacy. And in Dregmeet every scrap of light counted.

Tressia had been founded before the Age of Kings, a labyrinth of townhouses, mansions and churches reaching into the sunlit sky, white stone agleam and stained-glass windows rich as gemstone. A place of industry and guilds, where farmers and millworkers jostled beneath bright market canopies, soldiers drilled to perfection on muster fields, and gold-frocked priests preached to the bright carillon of bells. At least, that was so of the wider city. Dregmeet was Tressia's most ancient quarter – or the oldest not to have been torn down and built upon across passing centuries. Decaying wattle and timber buildings that were the last refuge for those who had nothing.

Even on the district's fringes as Josiri was that morning, far from where ancient walls held the western sea from sunken streets, mist muffled the sounds of the wider city. The further one descended into Dregmeet's slums, the deeper one trod another world. Or so nursery rhyme and folk tale insisted.

Stifling a yawn, Josiri brushed a tangle of blond hair from his eyes, and clung deeper to the alley's shadows. A year ago, he'd lived a life of broken hours, sleep snatched wherever it could be found. Today, rising before dawn had almost destroyed him.

Captain Kurkas scratched beneath his mildewed and curling eyepatch. "Pardon me for asking, sah, but you're sure about this?"

Josiri stared across the empty street, past the crumbling spire of Seacaller's Church to the dilapidated manor house. Decades before, Crosswind Hall had served as the portreeve's home and headquarters. Then, its windows had shone with light, bright heraldic banners of council and family streaming to welcome guests and petitioners. Now, sagging timbers covered broken glass, and the overgrown garden was caged only by the iron railings at the boundary. The roofs were sunken, weatherworn expanses shed of tiles.

"Quite sure, captain," Josiri replied. "And I've told you before. It's *Josiri.*"

"Right you are, sah." The gruff accent remained steadfastly neutral. "Still, I can't help but wonder if the First Councillor ... "

Josiri frowned away his annoyance. "We can't wait for the Council's approval. If the Crowmarket move the captives, we might not see them again."

"Not 'till we find them floating in the Silverway." Kurkas sighed. "And I suppose it's too late anyway, what with half the constabulary lurking hereabouts."

True. Little went unnoticed in Dregmeet. Eyes would be watching.

"Glad to have your support, captain."

"I just don't want this turning sour on you, sah."

Josiri tried to read his mood. A wasted effort. The captain had been too long a soldier, and far too accomplished at misdirecting superiors' questions.

Kurkas had parted with his right eye and most of his left arm on the battlefield, and what remained never seemed terribly concerned about parting ways with the rest. Or appearance. The eyepatch was the least of it. Nothing crumpled a uniform so swiftly as surrendering it to Kurkas' care. Even in Dregmeet's gloom, the Trelan phoenix on his king's blue tabard should have glittered – gold thread giving shape to white feathers. Instead, it more resembled a guttershrike's filthy plumage. Taken alongside a shock of black hair that surrendered but reluctantly to the comb, and Kurkas looked more suited to a life in Dregmeet than as captain of a noble's hearthguard.

But he'd come with the highest possible recommendation. Besides, Anastacia liked him. That placed Kurkas on a very short roster indeed, and brought forgiveness for less esoteric flaws. And without Kurkas, they'd never have known about the vranakin nest at Crosswind Hall. Beneath the crumpled respectability of his hearthguard uniform, he was still a son of Dregmeet, with contacts who'd never consider speaking to a constable, far less a Privy Councillor.

Footsteps heralded a woman's emergence from the alley's depths. Like Kurkas, she wore a blue tabard belted tight about her waist, and a captain's star at her throat. But she was otherwise his opposite; watchful, heavyset and controlled.

"Are we ready, Captain Darrow?" asked Josiri.

She nodded, one hand on her sword's pommel and the other about the stem of a muffled hand bell. "My lot are in place. Unless you've kraikons coming, it won't get better than this."

Even one or two of the bronze giants would have made the morning's work faster and safer, but borrowing kraikons meant approaching the proctors, and approaching the proctors meant gaining the Council's blessing. And the Council's blessing took *time*. Scaring up a score of constables had been hard enough.

And then there was the other problem. Kraikons weren't reliable in Dregmeet's mists. As in the Forbidden Places Josiri had trespassed as a boy, and later relied upon as a wolf's-head outlaw, unhallowed magic brought the foundry's constructs to a creaking halt.

Josiri shook his head. Too late to worry about that now. "Let's get to the morning's business."

"Yes, my lord. I'll send word once it's safe."

"Thank you, captain, but I'll be coming with you."

Her lips twisted in the expected scowl. "I don't think that's—"

"These are my people."

She stiffened. "Mine too."

Her voice held enough pride and resentment that she probably meant it. That made Vona Darrow something of a rarity, and a nobler soul than her predecessor. But better the blame fell on his shoulders than hers if matters went ill. His past created an expectation of rashness. His rank offered forgiveness for it.

Ever since the Council had passed the Settlement Decree – finally annulling the old laws of indenturement, and freeing thousands of

Josiri's fellow southwealders – there had been disappearances. Freed from their slave's bridles, too many had simply vanished. Officialdom had never cared much about the fortunes of those who bore the rose-brand upon their wrist, save to ensure that they weren't taking unearned liberties or passing themselves off as "decent" folk.

Again and again, Josiri had heard the same tale: that the missing had been taken by the Crowmarket, dragged down into Dregmeet. It didn't take much imagination to determine the rest. A welter of unwholesome trade transacted in the city's shadows. And beyond the walls? Plenty of unscrupulous merchants who'd spend coin on workers no one might miss. Cheaper to pay the local reeve to look the other way than part with fair wages.

"Then let's waste no more time arguing," said Josiri.

Darrow exchanged a brief glance with Kurkas, found little in the way of support, and offered a stiff-armed salute. "Right you are, my lord."

She slipped woollen muffler from clapper. The bell rang out. Others answered through the mist. Constables emerged from alleyways and bore down on the portreeve's manor, a circle of king's blue tabards to seal its secrets tight.

Josiri advanced, Kurkas at his side. Darrow pushed on ahead, her long stride eating up the roadway's mismatched and sunken cobbles. The gate's sagging hinges yielded to the strike of her boot. The rusted bars crashed back into tangled bushes.

"This is Captain Vona Darrow of the city guard!" She ploughed on down the choked pathway. "Anyone within these walls is bound by law. You'll come to no harm, unless you want it otherwise."

"Maybe there's no one home," muttered Kurkas.

Josiri tugged the tails of his coat free of a bramble's snare and peered about. "No. Someone's here. Too many snagged and trampled branches on the path. Plenty of visitors, but hiding their numbers. Some veteran you are."

Kurkas sniffed. "'Course I noticed. Wasn't sure you had, that's all."

"Once a wolf's-head, always a wolf's-head."

He'd never thought of those as happier times. And they weren't, not really. But they'd been simpler.

"Sah!" said Kurkas. "But you're a councillor now. Stay back and let me take the lumps in your place, if any are in the offing. Matter of professional pride."

Josiri glanced down at his waistcoat, shirt and trews. Practical enough in the morning chill, but they wouldn't turn a blade. Not like the leathers and chain Kurkas wore beneath his tabard. "Yes, captain."

The manor erupted. A knot of men and women in patchwork garb and the ragged cloth masks that were a vranakin's only uniform burst from the front door and ran headlong for freedom.

Bells chimed, rousing the constabulary to pursuit. Darrow tackled one fugitive, captain and quarry striking the weed-choked gravel with bone-crunching force. Another shoved a constable and bolted for the undergrowth. Dark shapes crashed through tangled branches. Cries of alarm and the dull smack of truncheon on flesh rang out. The clash of steel upon steel. A scream, and the crunch of a body falling onto gravel.

It was over by the time Josiri reached the manor itself. Constables led living fugitives to the clogged fountain and forced them to their knees beside a growing pile of confiscated weapons. The dead, they dragged by their heels. A scruffy bunch, but then the vranakin were seldom otherwise – crow-born with tattered wings. The desperate, the poor and the hungry rubbing shoulders with the thuggish and malevolent. Society's left-behinds. No one chose a life in Dregmeet.

Darrow broke off from conversation and hurried over. "We're secure, my lord. I've set watches on the exits. No sign of anyone yet, but I'll wager we'll find a few rats inside the walls."

"Let's take a look, shall we?"

Darrow's scowl deepened, but she nodded and turned away. "Sergeant Marzdan? You're in charge out here. Drag this rabble to the cells. I'll want a long talk with them later."

Josiri ascended the weatherworn steps. The archway keystone bore the ever-present rays of Lumestra's sunlight, and also a tide motif. An oddity, but he supposed it made sense that the portreeve would offer deference to Endala, if only to ensure safe passage for his ships. For all the church liked to pretend otherwise, Lumestra was not the only divine power worshipped in the Republic.

He reached for the door.

Kurkas grabbed his arm. "Hold up."

"What is it?"

The captain pointed at the arch, where the upright began its gentle curve towards the keystone. There, concealed by the dawn's shadow, was a bundle of black feathers, bound with woollen thread and topped with a corvine skull. Nailed into the mortar at shoulder height, its eyeless gaze cut across the threshold. It gave the impression of something waiting to pounce.

"Crow charm," said Kurkas. "Used to mark territory and warn away the curious. Give the Raven a coin, he'll hear you. Give him a feather, and he'll guard you."

"Is it dangerous?"

Kurkas shrugged. "Plenty of folk'll tell you they bring bad fortune."

"And you?"

"Do I look like a man smiled on by fate?"

The captain's face held a measure of wariness, but it was a rare day when it did not. Might have been a trick of the eyepatch, but superstition was a fickle thing. Priests and crowmarketeers alike grew fat off it. But just as all lies held a grain of truth, superstition coalesced about fragments of the divine. Harmless, until it killed you.

"Not often, no," said Josiri.

"Too late anyway." Kurkas snatched the charm from its nail and crushed it beneath his heel. "Crossing the Crowmarket *is* bad fortune. Don't let anyone tell you different."

Josiri stared down at the fragments, shook away a pang of dismay and eased the door open. Darkness loomed beyond.

"I'll need a light."

"Typical highblood. Never prepared." Darrow unclipped a small iron-bound firestone lantern from her belt and handed it over. "Can't have you falling down a hole and breaking your neck, can we?"

Josiri nodded his thanks and twisted the knob at the lantern's base. Quartz blazed to life behind the glass as captive magic roused. Fitful light granted shape to cracked and peeling walls, to collapsed stairs and a bowed ceiling.

He edged into the entrance hall. Somehow it felt colder inside than out, the mist thicker about his feet than before. A filthy chandelier hung from a twisted chain, the glass of its firestone housings shattered and its crystals smashed. Water-stained portraits stared down from the walls like weary vigil-spirits. And the smell. Musty and cloying, with a sour, metallic tang. Forgotten years and old death.

He pressed on across the hall. Lanterns bobbed as constables pressed after him.

"You want upstairs, or down?" asked Darrow.

Josiri peered at the rotting staircase and the equally uncertain ceilings. "Down."

She offered a crisp nod. "Right you are. Kressick? Treminov? You're with me. Jorek and Narod, you keep his lordship from getting into too much trouble. And that goes double for you, Vladama. Still can't believe you talked me into this."

Kurkas shrugged. "Can't help my silver tongue, can I?"

Darrow shook her head and stormed away towards the stairs.

Kurkas relieved Narod of his lantern. "You two see to what's left of the kitchens and the service quarters. His lordship and I will take the rest."

The constables withdrew. The glow of Jorek's lantern bobbed along the kitchen passageway and out of sight. Josiri gripped the pommel of his sword, fingers clenching and unclenching without conscious bidding.

He followed Kurkas through the great hall's mouldered furniture. Marks in the filth betrayed recent travel, but such was hardly proof of illicit business. The wretches outside might simply have needed a roof over their heads – even when that roof was more open to the sky than not. But of the spent fires and refuse that went with such habitation, Josiri saw no sign. Strange, given the downpours of recent days. Sommertide was but a memory, and Fade had its cold talons tight about the city – even the leaves of the Hayadra Grove were curling.

"Now here's a thing."

Kurkas stumbled past the fireplace and out into what had once been a wide stairway, now clogged with debris from the upper landing's demise. The lower stair was clear of rubble. At its foot, a wooden door practically gleamed among the decay, unsoiled by mould and lichen as it was. The heavy bar set across its jambs and a second crow charm all but demanded investigation.

Josiri started down the stairs. Kurkas' hand fell heavily on his shoulder.

"Now you've not forgotten our little chat about lumps and the taking thereof, have you, sah?"

Instincts screaming reluctance, Josiri allowed Kurkas to pass him on the stairs. The captain reached the bottom and dealt with the second crow charm much as he had the first.

"Who knows," he said conversationally, as bone splintered under his boot. "Maybe if you break enough of these things, bad luck comes good again. You know, like a wheel turning. Can I trouble you for a hand with this bar?"

Josiri set down his lantern. Taking a firm grip on the bar, he hoisted it aside. A soft chorus reached his ears. Muffled. Barely more than whispers, and readily lost beneath the creak of timber floorboards.

Caution demanded he call for Darrow and her constables. Impatience insisted he press on.

Impatience won.

Josiri drew his sword and eased back the door. Wooden stairs and cracked plaster gave way to bare stone and deepening mist. The sounds, no longer muffled, betrayed themselves as soft whimpers and hurried breaths uttered by those hoping to escape notice. Josiri reclaimed his lantern. Kurkas set his own aside in favour of drawing his sword.

With a last, shared nod, they continued their descent.

The stairs opened into a vaulted cellar, heavy with the rank stench of sweat and bodily waste. Corroded iron cages lined the walls. Most stood empty, though trampled straw and other detritus suggested they had not always been so. As Josiri approached the foot of the stairs, a handful of gaunt, filthy faces turned away and shuffled back into the darkness. All save one, belonging to a red-haired lad. Where his neighbours shrank away, he pressed close to the bars, eyes widening at Kurkas' tabard.

"The Phoenix ..." A grimy hand reached through the bars, the dark whorls of the rose-brand stark against a pale wrist. "Are you here to free us?"

Crouching beside the cage, Josiri took the lad's hand. The fingers were cold and thin, but he took encouragement from the strength of his grip. "We are."

"Did Lord Trelan send you?"

Josiri ignored Kurkas' soft chuckle. Another unwanted reminder of his changing circumstances. Traitors, however high-born, didn't merit the statues and portraits by which common citizens might recognise their betters. But for Kurkas' phoenix – long the symbol of the Trelan line – there'd have been no clue at all. The lad looked barely old enough to have been born at the time of Exodus, some sixteen years before. To him, Lord Josiri Trelan, the duke of vanished Eskavord, could only ever have been a stranger.

"In a manner of speaking." Josiri pulled free and turned his attention to the cage's iron lock. Too sturdy to force, and he lacked the skills for anything subtler. It would have to wait for Darrow. "What's your name?"

"Altiris. Altiris Czaron."

Josiri cast about the cages. Fewer than a dozen captives, and all save the lad reluctant to meet his gaze. A drop in the ocean to the hundreds still missing. That cellar alone could have held two or three score. "Where are the others? There *were* others?"

He nodded, hesitant.

"How many?"

Altiris stared past him to a slatted iron door behind the stairs. "I don't know. Couple of dozen, perhaps? They took them in there. One at a time. They don't come out, not ever, but we all heard the screams. It was my turn next. The woman with the feather-cloak told me so. Said it was necessary. She smiled. That was the worst of it."

"Feathers?" asked Josiri. "Black feathers?"

Altiris bit his lip and pinched his eyes shut. "Black as nightmare."

A chill brushed the back of Josiri's neck. He'd no memory of seeing a feathered cloak among Darrow's prisoners. Which meant the woman was still here. And if she was what Josiri suspected . . . ? He stared at the iron door, his fingers closing again on the grips of his sword.

"Captain?" he murmured.

"Might be a good time to fetch Captain Darrow, if you take my meaning?" Kurkas sounded no happier than Josiri felt.

Josiri glanced from Altiris to the iron door. "Feel free. I'll wait."

Kurkas shook his head. "Oh no. I'm not falling for that. Not again. But if you get me killed, I'm never speaking to you again."

"Noted."

Josiri's doubts resurfaced as he approached the door. Kurkas was right about fetching Darrow and her constables. But what would that do, except drive others onto the kernclaw's talons in his place?

The door whispered open on the oiled hinges.

The smell hit Josiri first. Death. Not the old death of the rooms above, but the iron tang of blood recently spilt. The rough stone floor was dark with it, and never more so than where glistening grooves led towards a large, open grate at the room's far end. In the chamber's centre sat a low stone altar, its worn flanks etched with effigies of carrion birds with glittering gems for eyes.

The strangest feature was the lone, empty archway between altar and grate. Like the altar, it was made of older, rougher stone than the room in which it sat. Like the altar, it was covered in bloody smears – the print of many different hands visible against pale grey stone.

But of the kernclaw – or indeed, any other living soul save Kurkas, Josiri caught no sign.

They don't come out, not ever.

A couple of dozen, Altiris had said. Depending on how long he'd been here, the true tally was likely higher.

"Blessed Lumestra," breathed Kurkas.

"Have you ever seen anything like this?"

"On my old mother's soul, I have not. Never even *heard* of anything like this."

Josiri set the lantern down on the altar and put a hand to his mouth in a vain attempt to blot out the smell. No bodies, but that didn't mean anything. Not with the sound of water rushing somewhere beneath the grate. A sewer, or one of the Estrina's tributaries.

They don't come out, not ever.

Indenturement was bad enough. This was worse. Whatever "this" was.

"I think it's time you fetched Captain Darrow," said Josiri.

Two

Josiri's mother had once insisted that the Privy Council chamber was the Tressian Republic distilled to its purest form. For years untold, weighty decisions and momentous events had played out in that austere chamber, shepherded to fruition by representatives from families of the highest rank.

He'd been only a boy, easily impressed by Katya Trelan's descriptions of the great stained-glass windows and stone visages of councillors long dead. Where history clung to every breath, filling the lungs as readily as the dust. Such an impression had her stories left that they'd survived Josiri's turbulent passage into adulthood. For all the woes that had flowed south from that room – for all that the deaths of his parents and the oppression of his people had been plotted at that gilded table – it retained a status almost divine.

Or perhaps the deaths were part of it. Perhaps the Privy Council reflected not the citizenry below, but the divinities above. Of all the gods and goddesses, only Lumestra showed compassion for her ephemeral children.

Nine chairs beneath the golden map of a Tressian Kingdom now shrunken to a beleaguered Republic. Four counties remaining of a continent-spanning realm. Royal Tressia, spiritual heart of the nation. The rebellious Southshires – once Josiri's home, and his family's domain. The embattled Eastshires. The Marcher Lands that bound them all together.

Five men. Three women. One chair empty. And the latter often the most productive of the lot. The Privy Council was home to much talk, and little action. Still, better to be there than among the irrelevant multitudes of the Grand Council in the chamber below.

"Why ever did you take it upon yourself to get involved, Josiri?" Elbows braced against the table, Lord Lamirov leaned forward in his chair. Combined with hairless pate and leathery, wrinkled skin, he resembled a turtle striving to escape its shell. "It's not becoming to embroil yourself in ... squabbles."

Josiri counted silently to five, partly to instil the false impression that he'd given the words weighty consideration – which he hadn't – but mostly to quell a temper worn thin. He hated the austere, tailored suit seemliness required he wear to council; the silk cravat and the high-necked waistcoat. They constricted and confined, made him feel something other than himself ... which he suspected was the point.

"Squabbles, Leonast?" Using the personal name was a conceit of council – the pretension of familiarity and shared purpose where too often none existed. "Dozens of my people tortured and killed at vranakin hands?"

"You didn't know that at the time." Lord Lamirov's eyes gleamed. "Intent matters in all things, and it troubles me that a representative of this council indulges his ardour by seeking cheap thrills. Especially a councillor of your ... reputation."

He leaned back, content to have landed a telling blow – though to what end that blow had fallen wasn't immediately obvious. Such was often the way when Lord Lamirov spoke in council.

It had bothered Josiri at first, for the woman who'd previously occupied that very chair had revelled in verbal fencing to further wicked ambition. But as the months had passed, and no such ambitions had flourished, Josiri had realised that Leonast Lamirov had few aims beyond cleverness for its own sake, and of burnishing his own ego to the detriment of others. If the Privy Councillors were indeed to be likened to gods, then Lamirov was Jack o' Fellhallow, ensconced in his thorny fastness; offering torment and bargain to those within his orbit for no other reason than because it amused.

It didn't take much imagination to conjure the spectre of Ebigail Kiradin laughing at her successor with disdain. No one could ever have accused her of being without grand design – however cruel and misjudged her attempt to seize control of the Republic had been. The memory of the horrors Ebigail had unleashed usually gave Josiri the strength to tolerate the withered old man's fussiness. But not today, with the horrors of the portreeve's manor still uppermost in memory. Patience – never Josiri's most abundant asset – began to slip.

"My reputation . . . ?"

A hooded glance from the head of the table warned Josiri that his voice held entirely too much growl. But Malachi Reveque simply turned his filigreed paper knife over and over in his hands and made no move to intervene. By nature a conciliator, he wore the rank of First Councillor lightly. Gracious Lumestra, holding court over her quarrelling siblings . . . no matter how little he looked the part.

In a city where fine cloth and golden thread so often heralded status, the drab greys of Malachi's waistcoat and tailored jacket marked him out more as a merchant of the middling sort, rather than the holder of authority unprecedented since the Age of Kings. Authority that had taken its toll. Dark hair fought a losing retreat against the grey of still-distant middle-years.

Josiri took a deep breath. "You can speak plainly, Leonast. We're all friends here." The lie came easily, born of practice. "What has my reputation to do with any of this?"

Lord Lamirov glanced away. A terror to those who laboured on his estates, he soon tired of confrontation with those who snarled back.

"Your reputation has everything do with this, *your grace*."

Erashel Beral had seen barely half Lord Lamirov's sixty years. She seldom spoke without purpose, or without care. There'd be no accident in her use of the ducal honorific.

Erashel's father had fought and died for Katya Trelan's rebellion. The following Exodus – the Council's punishment for the failed insurrection – had scattered her family, just as it had done so many other southwealders. The Settlement Decree had unshackled Erashel from a Selanni farm, and restored to her a portion of the estates and property stolen after her father's death, but calloused hands and weatherworn skin would for ever set her apart from sheltered peers. As did her chestnut hair, worn short and without the plaits and ribbons customary for noblewomen. She bore her past as proudly as Josiri sometimes wished to forget his own.

"May I be blunt?" she asked.

"By all means," said Josiri.

"That I am free, let alone that I sit at this table, comes as a direct result of your actions last year. Others present were spared from the gallows by those same deeds."

With an effort, Josiri kept a motionless expression. Tressian history was a fluid thing, sculpted by those in power. Josiri hadn't fought for the Republic, but for friends. For Malachi, and for ... A name surfaced. One he strove to forget just as diligently as the Council's historians strove to erase Ebigail Kiradin from history, lest another find inspiration in her treason.

Josiri scarcely recognised the official record of that day. It placed him in the forefront of the battle that had wrested supreme power from Ebigail Kiradin's grasp. His own memory recalled a more modest contribution. But Malachi had insisted. Easier to sell the idea of ending the Southshires' occupation if its most notorious son was known to have redeemed himself.

And it had worked. At Josiri's inauguration, the Grand Council had cheered him as one of their own. Him. The son of Katya the Traitor. He'd have laughed, but for a heart heavy with grief for a sister slain and a home burnt to ashes. He'd saved his enemies, but failed those who'd trusted him. Erashel's use of the ducal honorific was a deliberate barb to remind him of that, even if she didn't know the whole truth. The fate of Eskavord and its dukedom was one painstakingly concealed. Or at least the *cause*. The fate was known by all. A vibrant town become a haunted and forbidden place.

"Too much is made of that," he said. "Others fought far harder than I."

"The herald who greeted me at the docks didn't believe so. There was I, fresh off the ship in a borrowed dress – because I could hardly be presented to the Grand Council in a farmer's rags, could I? Do you know what he asked me? Was it true that my father had fought beside the great Josiri Trelan?" She laughed without humour. "I said that your mother had gotten him killed at Zanya. He didn't know how to reply. Lessons in etiquette have their limits."

"I am not my mother," Josiri bit out.

"Are you not? You attend council only when it suits you. You otherwise embroil yourself in matters better left to others. Settling guild disputes. Interfering in constabulary business. And now this morning, you provoke the Crowmarket? That sounds very like Katya Trelan."

"If I hadn't, more of our people would be dead."

A little of the fire slipped from Erashel's eyes. "I know. But this isn't about individuals. We can't afford it to be. The Crowmarket's actions are reprehensible . . . "

Lord Lamirov nodded sagely. "Indeed."

" . . . but this council must be seen to act as one. United. The Grand Council worries at what you might do next. Yesterday, they loved you. Today they tolerate you. What comes tomorrow? How long before they see only an upstart southwealder to be put in his place? Your mother's recklessness nearly destroyed our people. Don't repeat her mistakes."

Josiri opened his mouth but found no voice with which to offer reply. Erashel's onslaught, precise and considered where Lord Lamirov had offered only hollow cleverness, strayed close to uncomfortable truths. If Lamirov was Jack, all directionless, self-satisfied malice, then Erashel was the Raven. Remorseless, methodical . . . and above all resentful for a life spent in shadow, toiling to another's purpose.

Strange to think of Jack and the Raven embracing shared purpose – as embodiments of life and death, no two could be more different – but no stranger than finding accord between the landed and wealthy Lamirov family and the near-destitute daughter of Beral. A shared enemy made common cause faster than friendship.

Again, Josiri heard Ebigail Kiradin's disdainful laughter, this time directed at him.

Still an outsider, even now.

"What would you have had me do?" he asked softly.

"No one doubts your intentions, Josiri," Erashel replied. "But if our people are to have any chance at all of regaining their place in the Republic, they need you and I to set an example. To respect how things are done, and in so doing prove we are not our parents."

Josiri didn't miss the subtle shift in language that bound them back to common purpose. *They* need us. *We* are not our parents. Erashel was far better at this, and Josiri wondered how she'd honed the knack while tilling crops on Selann. Rhetoric and wheat fields made for an unlikely combination. Or perhaps it was simply that the father she so plainly disdained had done a better job of preparing her for the future than she'd likely admit.

Maybe it would be better to back down. Mend bridges. "What if I can't do that?"

A chair's creak marked Lord Lamirov rejoining the fray. "If the last year has proven nothing else, it is that a place on this council is no longer a birthright, but a privilege." He gestured to the empty chair. "We have two worthy candidates for the one seat that remains. If you were to step down, it would save us all a difficult choice."

"Would it indeed?" asked Josiri.

The twitch of Erashel's left eyelid might have suggested she'd not intended matters to escalate as they had, but could equally have been a tell-tale of satisfaction. Malachi looked pensive. Were the matter set to a vote, he could of course overrule the result – the position and power of First Councillor had been created specifically to serve as a brake on infighting – but doing so would undercut the neutrality he strove to present. As for the others, conspicuously silent as they'd been throughout the exchange . . . ?

Lady Messela Akadra sat apart as she always did, eyes downcast and shoulders drawn in – the epitome of one seeking to draw no attention. A vain hope, for she'd have been beautiful if only she didn't always look so worried. As it was, the silver ribbons plaited into her black hair did little to shake the impression of a woman mourning a lost husband – if one rather too young to be so beset, as indeed she was not. At seventeen years old, she'd barely come of age when the family seat had fallen vacant following her uncle's disappearance and her cousin's self-imposed exile. No one – least of all Messela herself – had expected the responsibility to fall as it had. And so she attended every meeting, hearing everything but saying nothing. The goddess Endala, too cowed by her peers to wield her influence, save in secret ways?

Lord Evarn Marest and Lady Rika Tarev were scarcely better prospects for support.

The Tarev family owned dozens of farms across the Marcher Lands. Farms whose workforce – and therefore whose profits – had received a dolorous blow since the Settlement Decree. By nature distant and calculating, Rika was a force for good or ill as the mood took her, and ill more often than not. Much like Ashana, Goddess of Evermoon and patron of the Hadari Empire.

As for Lord Marest, though an heir by adoption rather than blood, he'd famously inherited his great aunt's piety along with her estate and council seat – though rumour suggested that piety arose more to meet the terms of said inheritance than out of any great love for Lumestra. So like cruel Tzal of myth, who never did anything for anyone save himself.

That left one other.

"Bugger that."

The speaker wasn't so much sat in his chair as draped across it, a wiry, blond man taking his ease and very much bored to be doing so. In his way, he was as much an outsider as Josiri, first for his tan skin, which belonged more to the eastern borderlands than to the paler flesh common in the city, and second for his dress. Council was a place for respectable attire, not chamfered plate, steel circlet and a knight's surcoat of hunter's green. To Josiri's knowledge, no one had broached the topic with Stantin Izack, Master of the Knights Essamere. He suspected no one ever would. No godly mantle suited Izack better than that of Astor, the bellicose and plainspoken Forge-God.

"You've something to add, Izack?" asked Lord Lamirov. Even in council, no one addressed Izack by his first name. No one felt they knew him well enough. "You might observe the niceties of—"

"You keep talking like Josiri sneaked off and did something unmentionable behind the Council's back, but I knew. We discussed the matter, and concurred that we needn't bother the Council's valuable time with . . . " Izack turned his grey gaze on Erashel " . . . matters better left to others. I wanted to go in with a brotherhood of Essamere's finest and crack a few skulls. His lordship talked me out of it. Still think he was wrong on that, mind, but I'm just a simple soldier."

Josiri shook his head. "Hardly that, Izack."

He was a liar, for starters, and as smooth-tongued a rogue who'd ever worked a hustle. There'd been no prospect of the Knights Essamere joining the raid, because there'd been no conversation. But even Josiri, who knew Izack's corroboration was entirely false, found nothing in voice or expression to offer contradiction.

"Then your judgement is every bit as suspect as Josiri's," said Lamirov.

"Wasn't aware I needed your permission to give a bunch of scoundrels a good thumping." Izack drummed idly on the table and hoisted himself upright. "Tell you what. Next time the Hadari are clamouring at the crossings of the Ravonn, the gates of Chapterhouse Essamere and those of its vigils scattered up and down the Silverway will stay shut until ordered otherwise. Just remind me. Does that need a two-thirds vote, or a simple majority?"

Lord Lamirov levelled a scowl. "That's hardly the same thing!"

"Right enough. We've the prospect of lasting peace with the Hadari, if the First Councillor's to be believed. But the Crowmarket? There's no peace there. Vermin under-bloody-foot, stealing whatever isn't nailed down and slipping their knives into all kinds of uncomfortable places."

"No one's arguing the vranakin aren't a problem," said Erashel. "But we must act together. The people need leaders, not restless souls with something to prove."

"Perhaps we should put the matter to a vote?" said Lord Lamirov.

Josiri bit back a scowl. There it was. Now Erashel had done all the work, Lord Lamirov was closing for the kill. There had to be a way of recovering the situation. "I don't think—"

Izack's fingers ceased their drumming. "You want a vote? I've something we can all get behind." He raised his right hand. "Here's my proposal. That we take advantage of the lack of mischief on the border and go into Dregmeet mob-handed. Turn over every stone, pull down every rotting building and arrest or stab anything that scurries for cover, depending on how the fancy takes us."

Josiri's pulse quickened. Izack's suggestion went far beyond what he'd hoped to achieve. It would drive the Grand Council to apoplexy, fearful of retribution from the vranakin whose bribes lined their pockets, and whose favour ensured that secrets remained closely held. But it might just break the Crowmarket's power for good.

"You're talking about half the dockside," said Lord Marest. "We'd need hundreds of soldiers. Thousands!"

Izack tugged at the neck of his surcoat. "You need the troops, I'll find you the troops. All you need do is raise your right hand, and say 'aye'. Maybe offer a prayer to Lumestra, if you can find it in you. That can't hurt." He slapped the table, provoking a flinch from Lady Tarev. "What do you say? Josiri? This morning give you a taste for plucking feathers?"

He raised his hand. "Why not? Aye."

"Good man. What about the rest of you? Evarn? Rika? Leonast?"

Izack twisted in his seat. Each looked away in turn. "No? What about you, Messela? Viktor would have jumped at the chance. Show us some of that Akadra fire, eh?"

Josiri winced back the flood of mixed emotion at the name. Messela didn't move a muscle. She, at least, had learnt that the best way to keep one's dignity in the face of Izack's stare was to make no attempt at contesting it.

"I vote aye." Erashel offered a lopsided shrug. "I've no objection to actions, when preceded by the proper words."

More likely, she'd concluded that Izack was a more valuable ally than Lord Lamirov. Which was true enough. Lord Lamirov could empty his vaults of every last golden crown and still not purchase the loyalty of Essamere. Josiri's mother had attempted much the same, and lost a war for it.

"Three in favour," said Izack. "Care to join the sortie, First Councillor?"

Malachi remained silent, the forefinger of his left hand tapping silently against the armrest of his high-backed chair. His expression gave no clue to his thoughts. To Josiri's mind, it had been increasingly so of late – a consequence of too much time spent shepherding the Republic's twin councils. Politics was too often about masking one's intentions until they yielded advantage. Josiri understood the principle, even if mastery escaped his grasp.

"I vote 'aye'." Messela raised her right hand, the tremulous motion growing steady with increasing confidence. She even raised her eyes from the table. "You're right, Izack. My cousin wouldn't have hesitated."

Izack grinned. Lord Lamirov paled. Neither Lady Tarev nor Lord Marest looked any more at ease. No wonder. With one chair still empty, Messela's vote tipped the balance, four to three. The Grand Council wasn't the only place the Crowmarket concealed influence. The older the family, the more secrets to protect.

"This council is no place for proxy votes," said Lady Tarev. "And certainly not for those cast on behalf of disgraced kin."

Lord Lamirov nodded agreement.

With a scrape of chair against flagstones, Malachi rose.

"Messela has made her decision," he said mildly. "I for one am very glad that she has at last found her voice, and look forward to hearing more of it. Which makes *my* decision all the harder. I'm afraid, Izack, that I don't concur with your reading of the situation. While Lord Krain's missives certainly hold encouragement, lasting peace with the Hadari remains a long way off. I'd rather we didn't find ourselves fighting the Hadari and the Crowmarket at the same time."

Josiri gaped. Messela aside, the vote had brought no surprises, but this? Unwelcome thoughts surfaced. Malachi had treated with the Crowmarket in order to bring down Ebigail Kiradin. Did he remain under their shadow? "You're annulling the vote?"

"Consider it more a stay of execution," Malachi replied. "Until such time as we can be certain of Emperor Kai's intentions. You're free to involve yourselves in Captain Darrow's efforts, under my *personal* authority. I trust that will temper your disappointment, Josiri? Izack?"

Josiri nodded, ashamed at his rushed conclusions, born of frustration though they'd been. Politics. It was always politics. He only *wished* it something more tangible.

"I daresay it will." Izack leaned back, a man well-content with his prospects. "And even if it doesn't, I've learned plenty today."

"Concerning what, pray?" said Lord Lamirov.

"Concerning who among us is pissing their pants at the prospect of upsetting the Crowmarket. Always nice to know where everyone stands. Even if it's in a puddle."

"How dare you!" Lord Lamirov reached his feet with a speed Josiri hadn't suspected he possessed, finger jabbing across the table. "I'll not be spoken to like that by some . . . some . . . "

Malachi cleared his throat. "I think we might call the session concluded. I had entertained hopes of seeing my family before this evening's ball, and I think we'd all welcome a chance for tempers to cool and tongues to regain a measure of courtesy."

Lord Lamirov tore his eyes from Izack. "And the vote concerning Lord Trelan's conduct?"

"This council can hardly censure him for taking the self-same actions I've just authorised, can it? We'd look ridiculous."

Lord Lamirov cast about the table for support. Finding none, he lapsed into silence.

Malachi offered a wintery smile. "I'm glad that's settled. Please, remember that each of you is on this council for a purpose. After tomorrow's vote, the ninth seat will be filled. Let's try to set a good example for the newcomer." Ice thawed from voice and expression. "That will be all. Josiri? Stay a moment, if you would."

Josiri sat in silence as his peers filed out.

Malachi exchanged a few hushed words with Messela, then set the double doors closed at his back. The posture of First Councillor gave way to the altogether humbler man who'd once welcomed a travel-stained and adrift southwealder into his home.

"Can I offer you a drink?" he said. "Whatever her other sins, Ebigail maintained a stash of excellent brandy. I found it just last week, and there's still a little left."

Josiri snorted. "Knowing Lady Kiradin, it's probably poisoned."

"If so, it's a very slow poison, for it's not killed me yet." Malachi shrugged. "Her claw marks are on the decanter, but that's about as far as it goes."

He crossed to the north wall, dominated by the great golden map. *The Ancient and Honourable Bounds of the Kingdom of Tressia.* Other realms had long since claimed much of that land. The Hadari Empire to the east. The quarrelsome Thrakkian thanedoms to the south. Enclaves of other, stranger folk about whom Josiri knew little save rumour. And yet the map remained, an echo of the distant past, and perhaps aspiration for the future. On the one hand, reassuring; on the other, depressing.

Malachi prised open a section of wooden panelling beneath the map and produced a crystal decanter and two glasses. He set the glasses down on the table and poured.

"What shall we drink to?"

Josiri took his glass and glanced up at the map. "The Republic?"

Malachi smiled. "What a long way you've come. I think I hear your mother wailing her horror from Otherworld's mists. There are so many old voices in this room. And too many mistakes besides." He shook his head, the maudlin tone retreating, and offered up his own glass. "No. I thought to absent friends, may they never be forgotten."

"To absent friends."

So many of those, slipped away beyond the mists. Among them a sister, who'd proved herself twice the leader he was. Josiri wondered what Calenne would say of him now. Likely she'd have laughed. He could have borne that, if it meant seeing her again. But Calenne was gone, lost to the same fires that had consumed their ancestral home.

Crystal chimed, and Josiri took a sip. Sweet, smooth and with a hint of vanilla to betray liquor lain long in the very finest of barrels.

"Are *we* still friends?" he asked. "I see so little of you outside of council ... "

"You sound like Lily."

"Your wife has a sweeter voice."

"But I doubt she'd top Izack's little performance," said Malachi. "You owe him a favour."

"The man's a whirlwind."

"He is. And you need to be careful. This won't be the last time someone tries to dislodge you. I can't protect you for ever."

The brandy lost its taste. A rebuke was still a rebuke, even delivered in private. To have it delivered by a friend made it all the worse, for it hinted at disappointment, rather than anger.

"You're like Erashel, then? You think I should have sought permission?" Bitterness crept into Josiri's tone. "You saw how quickly they backed away from conflict with the Crowmarket. If I'd sought the Council's blessing, they'd have refused, and then—"

"And then you'd have done it anyway, and things would be worse." Malachi sighed. "Better to seek forgiveness for a deed done. You're more like Viktor than you admit."

Josiri twisted away to hide a scowl. "You think I did the wrong thing?"

"Hah! Let me turn that back on you. Do you think I resent you for saving lives?"

"Of course not."

"Then you have your answer. How bad was it?"

Josiri turned back to face him. Crosswind Hall's cellar danced before his eyes, the memory vivid enough to smell the blood. "Darrow thinks we stumbled onto a maniac's lair."

"And you?"

"I don't know. I just want to find the others while there's still chance. I wish you'd voted with us."

Malachi swirled his glass and stared into the dancing liquid. "It's not as simple as that."

The old, rutted argument beckoned. "It never is."

"We've been over this. I'm not always as free to act as I wish. A balance must be struck."

"You mean Lamirov's vanity must be eased."

"You see the position of First Councillor as a bludgeon, power to be wielded. But power wanes with use, Josiri. Rely on it and people stop listening to *why* you cast your weight about, and remember only that you *did*. I can do nothing to settle the Republic's inequities if folk think me a tyrant." He stared pointedly at Lamirov's chair – the one that had lately belonged to Ebigail Kiradin. "And tyrants do not end well."

"You don't have it in you to be her."

"It's not you I have to convince. This Republic is built on the shoulders of its oldest families, and those families hoard influence jealously. They see what I've done to unmake past mistakes, and they worry at what I might do next. If I too often favour your wishes over traditionalists like Leonast? It won't end well for anyone."

Games. It was all games and posturing. "I understand."

"Good."

"But that doesn't mean I like it."

Malachi emptied his glass and poured himself another. "You have to see things in the long term, Josiri."

"In the long term, the Raven takes us all."

"Yes, we've opportunity to achieve something before that happens. Fresh blood. A council that represents *all* its people. I confess, I'd hoped for better from Rika and Evarn, but they're too shrivelled up inside. Their habits have solidified with age."

Josiri chuckled. Both were younger than he and Malachi by several years. "And Messela?"

"She shows promise. And for all that you and she don't get along, Erashel at least follows her principles and not her pride. You were right to recommend her."

"We needed another southwealder. Better someone like her than another former rebel. A wolf's-head on the Council? That *would* have upset the old guard."

Malachi smiled. "You see? You can think like a politician when you try. Would it be inappropriate to ask which of our two presumptive candidates you'll be voting for tomorrow?"

"Probably. But I'm only an upstart southwealder. I don't know any better." He shrugged, as if the subject were unimportant, though in truth he'd given the matter a great deal of thought. "Konor says all the right things, but there's something behind his eyes I don't trust."

"He *is* a merchant," said Malachi. Konor Zarn was a merchant in the same way that Izack was "merely" a soldier. Half the merchantmen plying passage of Endalavane and down into Thrakkia did so under his flag. Two centuries back, his wealth would have elevated his family to the first rank. Nowadays it was regarded as gaudy and envied by bloodlines whose own coffers ran low. "So you prefer the Lady Mezar? I'm surprised."

"I can set aside the past, when I have to."

"Sabelle's father signed the warrant for *your* father's execution."

"So did yours. I've not yet tried to kill you for it."

"Father-in-law, actually. One of the benefits of being a Reveque by marriage is that the sins of the kith don't stain my hands so deeply."

Josiri took the correction in his stride. "Lady Mezar has done more than any to make reparations with the Southshires. I'd acknowledge that even if I didn't like her personally."

"But you do? Like her, I mean?"

"She's direct. She doesn't hide behind tradition and protocol. I doubt I'll ever be certain what Konor thinks, but I've no doubt that Sabelle won't hesitate to speak her mind."

"And at some volume. I'd vote for her too, if I could. Alas, a First Councillor must remain dispassionate in these matters. But she'll pass easily enough without my support." One hand on the back of his chair, Malachi gestured at each empty seat in turn. "Messela. Erashel. Izack. Sabelle. I doubt they'll always agree with you, but you have to admit it's an improvement on how things were when you first arrived."

Josiri nodded his concession. The average age of the Council was a good twenty years younger, for starters. Lamirov aside, only Izack was older than Josiri himself, and then by but a few years. Even adding Lady Mezar to the roster wouldn't skew things much closer towards the grave.

A far cry from the grey heads and entrenched attitudes that had seen the Southshires crushed. Still, Malachi had missed a name off the list.

"What about you?"

Malachi dribbled more brandy into his glass. "Cleverness will only get me so far. Sooner or later, I'll have to throw my weight around and I won't be forgiven for it. I only accepted this position in the hope of convincing Viktor to take the burden from me, but fate had other plans."

Josiri thought back to the last time he'd seen Viktor Akadra, unrepentant and alone, with the charred fields of Eskavord at his back. The anger still smouldered, even now. A family broken. A home destroyed. And all of it Viktor's doing. "It did."

"Now, I just want to leave things better than I found them, Josiri. I doubt I can do that without your help. So please, be more careful. And remember that I am your friend, even if it's not always possible for me to play the part."

Josiri nodded, regretting he'd ever thought otherwise. "Go home, Malachi. See your family before your house fills with strangers chasing patronage."

"I intend to." Malachi rounded the table and held out his hand. "But I *will* see you later, won't I? And Anastacia too? A few friends among the favour-seekers?"

"She's looking forward to it," Josiri lied.

He clasped Malachi's hand and left the stultifying air of the council chamber behind.

Malachi sat heavily in his chair. Truths and lies were exhausting when told apart. Carefully mingled, they drained a body like nothing else.

"Well?" he asked the empty chamber. "Are you satisfied?"

For a moment, Malachi allowed himself to believe that he *was* as alone as he seemed. Then the shadows shifted in the far corner, beyond the revelation offered by afternoon sunlight, bringing with them the cold scent of Dregmeet's mist-woven paths. The scent of Otherworld.

The Emissary approached the table, eyes cold and green beneath the hood of her feathered cloak. Even in sunlight, the edges of her form blurred and shifted, as if she wasn't truly there.

"My cousins won't be pleased. You should have stopped him."

Malachi closed his eyes and suppressed a shudder. There was an edge to the Emissary's presence. Something not entirely human. The threats were bad enough, but to hear them uttered with what would otherwise have been a pleasing, sultry voice? No amount of brandy taken could prevent his blood turning to ice.

"He'd only have become more determined. This will keep him contained."

"You should have done more."

Was that a new note he heard? In another, Malachi might have taken it for uncertainty. Even regret. But while this Emissary lacked the open malice of her predecessor, he wasn't ready to assume she was any more compassionate. But still, perhaps a little defiance was called for.

"I agreed to turn a blind eye to much, but abduction and slaughter? I won't conceal that."

"You'd rather my cousins took matters into their own hands?"

Again, she distanced herself from the threat. Interesting.

"Your cousins should instead consider returning those they've taken. Remove his motivation."

She hesitated. "My cousins will not be dictated to."

"I saw the reports of what was done to those people. What possible benefit can such cruelty bring?"

"That's not your concern."

"They're my subjects," he snapped. "Of course it's my concern."

"And your children? Are they your concern?"

Malachi reached his feet without conscious decision. He grabbed at the Emissary's throat. She parted in a storm of rippling crow-shadows. Buoyed aloft by anger and the brandy's aftermath, he barely felt the icy cold of her passage. As she reformed beneath the window, he spun about, finger stabbing at the air.

"If any harm comes to them, I—"

Her hand closed around Malachi's wrist and twisted it up behind his back. Dark spots danced before his eyes. "What will you do, Lord Reveque?"

"I'll set Izack loose," he gasped. "And it won't be Essamere alone. The other chapterhouses will join the hunt. Those of you they don't burn, they'll cast into the sea."

The pressure increased. "Malatriant couldn't drive us out. What makes you believe you can?"

"The Crowmarket of the Tyrant Queen's time is gone. Your Parliament is only a shadow." Malachi swallowed. "Why else would you need me? Why else be so worried about what Josiri might find?"

The pressure about his wrist vanished. A shove sent him sprawling.

Malachi grabbed at the table for support. Despite his throbbing arm, he swelled with elation. That the Emissary had made no direct concession didn't matter. He'd won. His first such victory in many months. The Crowmarket *had* grown weak. Or else the Emissary had realised she'd overstepped.

"My cousins have another request," said the Emissary. "They believe it would be in everyone's interest if Konor Zarn ascended to the Council, and not Lady Mezar."

Which meant Zarn was in thrall to the Crowmarket ... or perhaps even a cousin himself. At best, he'd be an obstacle. At worst, he was being groomed as Malachi's replacement. Either would be disastrous.

"No."

The Emissary's eyes glinted beneath her hood. "No?"

"I won't do it. When the Parliament of Crows helped me remove Ebigail, I promised a sympathetic ear on the Council. But I am *not* their plaything."

She held his gaze. Silent. Unmoving. Malachi held his breath. This was it. Had he imagined the Emissary's reluctance before? Did his threats truly have purchase? If he was wrong, then the best he could hope for was that he alone would pay the price, and that his family would be spared. But if he was right, there might just be a chance of getting out from under a fool's bargain.

The Emissary sighed. "Oh, Malachi. We're all their playthings."

She stepped into shadow and was gone. Loosing a sigh that stretched all the way to his boots, Malachi reached for the brandy.

It was only when the glass was halfway to his lips that he realised that was the first time she'd addressed him by name, rather than title.

Three

Everything of value flowed into Dregmeet, sooner or later. Coin. Goods. Life. Love. Hope. Tokens of trade, borne down through the crooked, sinking streets by those in need of a favour. As a girl, Apara had watched petitioners from the rooftops, sifting the proud from the desperate, the rich from the poor. Judging with a keelie's practised eye those fit for plucking if bargains were refused. All were fair game as soon as they crossed from the sunlit city and into the unfading mists. All save those to whom the Parliament of Crows granted protection.

She pressed on through the narrow, cobbled alleyways. Vranakin watched from the shadows, peering through the gaping eyeholes of filthy cloth masks. Watching as she'd once watched, though in idle curiosity more than predation. The inky, ethereal feathers of the raven cloak marked her as a quarry beyond ready ambition. No one of any sense provoked a kernclaw.

All the more ironic, as Apara had never sought to be one.

She still remembered her first glimpse. No more than eleven or twelve years old – the year of Apara's birth being somewhat nebulous, even to her – and still a lowly rassophore, a fledgling too young to be proclaimed full cousin to the vranakin. She'd done a grand trade along Lacewalk, dipping the pockets of bawdyhouse patrons, and them never the wiser. But she'd been too flashy with her pickings, and earned a jealous beating.

She'd tried to fight, but she'd always been wiry rather than strong. After the first snapped rib, she'd begged to be left alone. Even with her stolen coins in his pocket, Czorn had kept punching her. He'd been three years older, on the cusp of becoming a full cousin, proud and vicious with it. As he'd forced her face down into the gutter-filth for a third time, Apara had known with utter, paralysing certainty that he meant to steal away her life.

The beating ceased in a chorus of screams and a scuffle of desperate feet. The next Apara knew, a ragged cousin had hauled her upright.

You're not cut out for this. Leave while you can.

The woman's words had lingered. Apara had never decided if the cousin had meant them as instruction, or challenge – only that she'd taken them as the latter. What else could she have done? Dregmeet was her home, the Crowmarket her family. And so, her filthy face stiff with dried tears, she'd limped down to the shore. There, she scratched Czorn's name onto stone, buried it with her last coin and a scrap of feather, and begged the Raven to settle her score.

Czorn had broken his neck two days later, scrambling out of a townhouse window. Just bad luck, many had said, to fail a jump any four-year-old could have made. Apara had known different. She'd spent the rest of her life paying off the Raven's debt.

Shaking away old memories, Apara quickened her pace. It was always cold so deep into Dregmeet, even at Sommertide. And a part of her felt the chill deeper of late. The part of her that wasn't really part of her at all, but had gripped her soul ever since Viktor Akadra had set it there. The echo of Dark that made her a puppet to his will.

She skirted the clogged fountain of Tzalcourt, suppressing the familiar shudder at its statue of a moulder-winged angel – half woman, half serpent, and with a frame of rotting crow-feathers for wings. The lopsided gate of the Church of Tithes yawned wide from amidst a field of moss-wreathed gravestones. Uneven, squared-off towers loomed above, and beyond them the jettied walls of timber-framed houses held aloft by buttress and chain. Just as the Dregmeet slums were the lowest part of the city, the Church of Tithes was the lowest part of Dregmeet.

There were no guards – or at least none readily observed – and no petitioners. Both would come later, when evening came, and the empty streets filled with those in search of food and fleeting comfort. For that was the bright truth among the cloying shadows: the Crowmarket brought sustenance to all who desired it ... for whatever price they could pay.

The shadows of the archway drew together into a man's form, raven cloak swept back and hood lowered to reveal nondescript garb and an equally unmemorable face. Lesser cousins might hide their identity, but kernclaws revelled in notoriety. Notoriety and fear. "Cousin. How does the life of a noblewoman suit you?"

Jealousy rippled beneath the mockery.

"Erad. I've business with the Parliament."

He nodded. "As, I'm told, do I. But you may want to wait."

They'd run together as children, learning their trade beneath old Inbara's watchful eye. A strange pairing, what with Erad being vranakin by birth, and her come to the nest by abandonment. But the bond struck in tender years had endured.

"There's a problem?"

Impassivity gave way to a knowing smile. "Depends on where you stand. For you and I, not so much, for Nalka ... ?"

Nalka, who'd ruled over the nest at Crosswind, and had barely slipped the veil into Otherworld before the constabulary had descended. Who'd through negligence exposed a sacred site to the Council, and lost valuable offerings alongside.

Offerings. Apara scowled away the word. Old rituals, practised anew out of growing desperation – hoping to draw an ancient eye with gift of blood and spirit.

She glanced past timeworn bas-reliefs to the church's heavy black door. "What do you reckon to her chances?"

"Who knows? Used to be that a kernclaw could do little wrong." Erad shrugged. "Now? With the mists receding and the Raven deaf? She'll be fortunate to walk away. *Unless* you've tidings to warm withered hearts. That might save her."

"I've no words to help Nalka."

A familiar rush of guilt. One that wasn't hers. It sprang from the shadow shackled to her soul. The price of old failures. Bad enough it existed at all, and with it the promise of servitude if Viktor Akadra crossed her path again. But even quiescent, the shadow wouldn't let Apara be. Without its master's guiding hand, it couldn't dominate her will, but it delighted in sparking empathy where none was appropriate. Empathy was seldom appropriate for a kernclaw.

Erad grunted. "The only salvation is that which you steal for yourself. Is that it?"

Apara winced at the snatch of prayer-cant. The words underpinned all that the Crowmarket did. Nothing for nothing, and take from others whatever you desired. "That's not how I meant it."

"This morning went that badly?"

Apara closed her eyes, once again in the Privy Council chamber. "Enough that I'll end in the mists alongside Nalka if things continue. Lord Reveque is stubborn."

"I warned you not to take the position."

"I didn't have a choice."

"There's always a choice, cousin."

Was there anything less useful than advice after the fact? Erad didn't know the whole story. He was ignorant of the shadow shackled to her soul and the bargain that bound Apara closer to the Parliament than ever. "I hope you've never cause to learn how wrong you are."

He shook his head. "Whatever happened to the Silver Owl and her ready smile?"

Apara scowled at the old nickname, lost alongside the thief's vocation she'd loved so dearly. "Everything has its price, dear cousin. Even a smile. I've no longer any to give away."

A woman's scream washed over her, shrill even through the mists and the intervening stone.

The door creaked open. A ragged figure filled the space. Garbed in grey wool-cloth, and all but its green eyes hidden by the folds of its hood, its form was broadly that of a man, but was as much something else also. As if its raiment were not the only thing fraying at the edges.

Elder cousins were nameless, interchangeable, with only the barest variance of form and voice to tell the women apart from the men. The Raven's gift, by whose grace Apara walked Otherworld's paths and commanded the restless spirits of her cloak, flowed like a millrace through their veins. A reward for service to the Crowmarket and its Parliament. Or it should have been. Now they seemed somehow shrunken, frail. As if the Raven's distance diminished them. Not for the first time, Apara wondered how old they were.

The Parliament invited no such conjecture. They'd been ancient when Apara's parents had been young. Grandsires-in-shadow, feared and respected. Let the citizens of the sunlit world consider the pontiffs' endless existence the stuff of woven myth; Inidro Krastin, Karn Athariss and Endri Shurla – names handed down as title to deceive the credulous. Echoes of the crowfathers and crowmother of old. Apara knew better. You couldn't stand in their presence and claim otherwise. Centuries clung to them like shrouds.

"Greetings," breathed the elder cousin. "The Parliament of Crows calls you both."

They followed, footsteps swallowed by the mist. The light of the outer world fell into cloying gloom. Thick, waxy candles guttered greasy radiance more green than orange, the tallow-scent thick with dust and old memories. Rotten pews framed walls of crumbling plasterwork and bare brick. Crooked pillars braced a sagging roof.

And at the end, where a triad of preachers' pulpits clung to a bowing wall, and a feather-strewn altar sat silent beneath a vast, boarded window, a moaning woman knelt among the rubble, hands clasped to her eyes. Five elder cousins stood in silent semicircle about her, tattered robes writhing in a non-existent breeze.

The darkness within the centremost pulpit shifted about a cowled face and grey-mantled shoulders edged with faded gold. "Nalka." Krastin's voice held none of its usual kindness. "You have failed your cousins."

"You have broken our first law," Athariss added from the rightmost. Disdain and cruelty sought balance within his tone. As ever, disdain edged ahead.

"You have allowed us to be seen," said Shurla from the left, her voice taut with a zealot's disgust. "Heresy."

Behind the altar, the discoloured planks across the window faded into white-green mist, and thence to nothing at all. Listless etravia spirits – their pallid forms clad in mockery of mortal dress, but their bodies vaporous beneath the waist – drifted through the space beyond, for ever searching for the path that would bring them to paradise. A broad, dark road gave way at either side to raised terraces, edged with tiles and hung with unfamiliar heraldry – all distorted by the curling mist and Otherworld's greenish light.

But it was empty. The Raven had not come.

Athariss leaned closer. Even with his face hidden by the folds of his gold-edged robes, there was no mistaking his anticipation. "The debt must be paid."

"You will wander the mists in penance until he finds you," said Shurla.

"Farewell, cousin." Only Krastin's voice held any regret.

Two elder cousins hauled Nalka to her feet. Hands pulled clear of her face revealed mangled flesh where her eyes should have been. As a kernclaw, Otherworld's paths were no secret to Nalka. Sighted, she might have escaped into the Living Realm before the Raven found her. But not blinded. Even if she evaded the Raven, her mind would fall to madness as her soul ran thin. Just one more flesh-hungry prizrak roaming a realm where all else was spirit.

Apara stifled a shudder as they led Nalka to the archway.

The first law that Nalka had broken wasn't really a law at all. *The light creates us; it does not reveal our purpose.* It spoke to the conceit that the Crowmarket was a hidden force. Perhaps that was true in the eastern Empire or the quarrelsome south, but not in Tressia where, even in the Crowmarket's waning days, a goodly portion of the city was overrun by Otherworld's mists. Nalka met her fate not for sharing a secret that was no secret, but as caution to those who might yet fall short of expectation.

With a final wordless sob – Apara wondered bleakly if the elder cousins had taken tongue as well as eyes – Nalka was cast onto the dark road. The mists faded, and the uneven boards of the window returned to sight.

"Erad Nyzad," said Krastin. "Step forward."

Erad bowed low. "How may I serve?"

"A ship is due into Sothvane tomorrow from Selann," said Shurla. "A vessel of the Fallen Council that nonetheless serves holy purpose. The *Amber Tempest*."

"You are to see that its cargo is secured," said Krastin. "And taken to the Westernport nest. The rituals are to continue."

More death. All to draw the attention of the Crowmarket's wayward deity.

"It shall be as you command," said Erad.

"See that it is," said Krastin. "You may go."

Erad bowed and withdrew. He passed Apara without a glance and departed the church.

"Apara Rann. Step forward."

Apara obeyed Krastin's command and tried not to think about the bloodstains on the rubble. Worse were the unblinking gazes of the elder cousins, now arrayed in semicircle about her.

"Tell us of the Council, cousin," said Athariss.

"What do they know?" said Krastin.

"I cannot speak to what they *know*," Apara replied carefully. "But they seem unaware of Nalka's true business. A matter of imprisonment and slavery, nothing more."

A strange life where the disposal of folk as goods and chattels could be considered ordinary – even preferable – beside the truth. Then again, wasn't that the way of the world? Especially in the Republic, where life was cheap, save where backed by good name and firm coin. Was there ever much difference between ritual murder in the Raven's name, and in the pursuit of the Council's false justice?

"Then the matter will be forgotten?" asked Shurla.

"Not by Lord Trelan. He worries for his fellow southwealders. He sought the Council's authority to purge the dockside and give us all to the pyre."

Silence reigned, and with it the first suggestion of wariness. The Crowmarket had flourished during the Age of Kings – had survived even the tyranny of Malatriant's rule and her overthrow at the hands of Konor Belenzo and his fellow champions of the divine – but that had been with the Raven's patronage. Without it, the outcome of open war with the Council was far from certain.

"Which of the heretics voted for this?" asked Shurla.

"Izack, Lord Trelan, Lady Beral and Lady Akadra," Apara replied. "Lord Reveque overturned the vote, but granted permission for them to assist the constabulary, if they wished."

"The upstart Trelan is becoming a problem," said Krastin.

Shurla snorted. "That family was never anything but. Ingrates and idolaters all."

"Alas, Katya Trelan died before her time." Anticipation returned to Athariss' voice. "It might be that young Josiri follows her example."

Shurla joined him in wheezing laughter.

"And what of Lord Reveque?" Krastin cut short the shared mirth. "Did he accede to our request concerning the empty council seat?"

Apara fought a wince. "He ... did not."

"I trust you communicated our dismay?"

"He insists the matter falls beyond the original bargain."

Pale fingers steepled on the edge of the centre-most throne. "Konor Zarn will sit on the Council, and Lord Reveque must learn his place," said Krastin. "An example shall be set. His daughter, perhaps."

This time, there was no containing the wince. "If we harm any member of his family, Lord Reveque will reinstate the vote. He'll empty the chapterhouses against us."

"Bravado," snapped Athariss. "Men often make such claims until the future closes about them like a fist. Let Lord Reveque cradle his daughter's body. His priorities will shift."

Apara's raven cloak cawed delightedly at the prospect of murder, but the thought of killing a child – even one as far from defenceless as Sidara Reveque – awoke disgust. "She wields Lumestra's light."

"We have every confidence in your abilities," sneered Athariss. "Light cannot bar the determined blade. If you fail, we can always send another."

"Take from him that which he loves most and our hold weakens," said Apara. "No threat will ever hold the same weight."

"Is this cowardice I hear, cousin?" Athariss gripped the edge of his throne and leaned closer, his voice full of threat. "Do you fear the girl's light?"

Of course she did. She'd seen it, where no other present had done so, and counted herself fortunate to have survived. But saying so would end poorly, especially with Athariss in typically intemperate mood.

"I fear failure," she said instead. "There are other ways to show our resolve."

In the darkness of the pulpit thrones, green eyes flicked back and forth in silent consideration.

"Very well," said Shurla. "You may proceed as you judge appropriate."

"But do not fail us, cousin," said Krastin. "Failure is weakness, and we can afford neither."

"Nor can you," said Athariss.

Apara bowed low, but felt little relief. Ever since becoming a kern-claw, she'd convinced herself that she was merely the weapon, not the mind that guided it. No longer. Whatever deaths followed would belong to her.

"And if I may," she said without rising. "What of my request?"

Athariss' green eyes dimmed to a smoulder. "You come to us in failure and demand payment?"

"She means nothing by it," said Krastin mildly. "A bargain *was* struck."

"And it will be fulfilled," said Shurla. "At the proper time. When she has proven her faith."

Apara held her pose, lest the bitterness welling up in her heart leak into expression. The same answer she'd heard a dozen times since she'd parted ways with Viktor Akadra. Since she'd begged the Parliament of Crows to excise the Dark he'd planted in her soul. But they hadn't. All she'd done was grant them the power to bind her with hope, as well as fear. The more she strove to be free, the more a puppet she became.

Some thief she was.

"Thank you," she said at last. "I won't fail."

Four

The fortress of Ahrad had commanded the passage of the Silverway River since the Age of Kings, its foundations laid down in wars long ended, fought by heroes and tyrants long forgotten. As history turned and the Tressian kingdom fragmented, Ahrad had endured, a bastion of the shrinking Republic holding firm against the sprawling Empire to the east. As long as the fortress stood, the deep waters of the Silverway brought warships and troop transports to its walled harbours, ready to contest any advance.

But to take Ahrad by force? To breach the warding enchantments and storm its walls, all in the face of the defenders' fire? Roslava Orova, Knight of Essamere, the Council's Champion and storied Reaper of the Ravonn, would have wanted no part of that. One thing to face the foe in a clash of shields or astride an armoured destrier. Siege-work was different, a machine of murderous overlapping fire that ground all to offal and cherished memory.

Every time Rosa stared out across the three concentric walls she felt a strange frisson of dismay for the besiegers she'd be called upon to kill.

"Commander Orova? If I didn't know any better, I'd say you weren't listening."

Rosa detected more amusement than rebuke in Castellan Noktza's tone. For all that Ahrad was a storied command, he hewed little to pomp and ceremony. He seldom even wore the scarlet heraldry of the Prydonis chapterhouse, preferring the simple king's blue uniform of a common soldier.

Likewise, Noktza forsook grand musters of his officers and underlings in the citadel hall. Come rain or shine, he favoured quieter, informal discussion on the broad turret adjoining his quarters, whose worn stones screamed like a mournful cyraeth whenever the Dusk Wind blew from the west. Fortunately, both rain and wind were in abeyance that day, the waters of the Silverway River blazing like fire in the glow of the setting sun.

Rosa tore her eyes from the outer barbican, and the rushing weir gates that fed the moat, and offered a nod of accession.

"I'm sorry, Riego. After the first couple of petitions, they all began to blur."

Noktza chuckled and joined her at the parapet, his back braced against the crenellations. Behind him, a mile or so beyond Ahrad's northern wall, the plains gave way to a sheer, root-worn cliff and the brooding, leafy expanse of Fellhallow.

"When I was your age I'd have given my right arm to be so feted."

Rosa scowled. "I don't know what they want from me."

"Yes you do. You're a hero. Let the regiments wine and dine you as such. There's really nothing to it. Some polite conversation, a rousing speech and drink them dry of the good stuff." Noktza tugged at a goatee more white than grey. "I honestly don't see why it bothers you so."

No, he didn't. That was the problem with those blessed of a garrulous nature. For Noktza, every gathering was an opportunity for revels. For Rosa, who held her words close and her feelings closer, to stand in a crowd of strangers, drunk or sober, was a tortuous prospect. And not just because she was doomed to remain steadfastly clear-headed throughout, regardless of drink taken.

"I'm the Council's Champion," she said instead. "I should be out there. Fighting."

She cast a hand to encompass the Ravonni Plains and their sparse forests. Running from the foothills of the Greyridge Mountains to the south before boiling away into the majestic depths of the Silverway within Ahrad's curtain wall, the River Ravonn served as a natural border between the Tressian Republic and the Hadari Empire. A border she'd spent much of her life defending. A border upon which she'd lost too many friends and shed too much blood.

"Fighting who?" asked Noktza. "Three months since a shadowthorn trod within sight of the walls, and if there are any scoundrels within a dozen leagues, they're cowering so deep in their caves that you'll never find them."

"I'll dig them out. It's my duty."

"It's also your duty to set an example to the soldiery. I could make this an order."

She snorted. "Just like a Prydonis. All reason until you can't get your way."

"And it's just like an Essamere to hide behind chapterhouse rivalry to avoid an uncomfortable truth." *Now* the bite of authority surfaced. "Ahrad is my command, so you're my responsibility. And you concern me. A year ago, I thought you felt you'd something to prove. Your predecessor was a difficult act to follow."

Rosa made play of straightening her surcoat. Yes, Viktor was certainly that. He'd looked the part more than she, a mountain of a man whose black hair and brooding countenance struck disquiet even in those who knew him well, where her own wiry figure and straw-blonde tresses seldom worried anyone. At least until steel was drawn, and the killing began.

And there had been so much killing in the wake of last year's invasions. Wars seldom ended as tidily as history recounted. Where Kai Saran's doomed invasion of the Southshires had drawn readily to conclusion, skirmishes had raged along the Ravonn for months after. Never enough to truly threaten the Eastshires, let alone the wider Republic, but enough that Rosa's blade had found employment.

And then, six months back, the fighting had simply ... stopped. Cessation had left Rosa with a void she'd struggled to fill, and a growing fear that what had once been vocation now owed more to obsession. When Rosa had first earned her spurs, she'd proudly proclaimed she was never more herself than when filling Otherworld with the vanquished. Lately, she'd come to worry that the reverse was true – that each death lessened who she was. And yet that fear never eclipsed the longing to draw the sword, to feel its bite shiver her arm and see the light leave an opponent's eyes.

She met Noktza's appraising stare. "I'll talk to the regimental commanders."

An eyebrow twitched, betraying Noktza's awareness that her promise lay some way short of the concession he'd sought. He planted his hands upon the rampart and stared eastward across the middle bailey and its tangle of barracks, warehouses and armouries.

"Do so," he said. "Who knows? You might even enjoy yourself, and it'll do you no harm to polish the societal niceties. If the Hadari share Lord Krain's enthusiasm for peace, the duties of the Council's Champion are likely to become more ceremonial, not less. You may even find yourself called back to the city. Or worse, to the Council itself."

Rosa stifled a wince. "You really think there'll be peace?"

"You've met the princessa. You tell me."

Rosa cast her mind back to those last, dark days of Eskavord, before mists had swallowed the fire-blackened fields. To the unlikely alliance with Melanna Saranal. She recalled an earnest, defiant young woman who offered no apology for what she was, or what she'd done, but nonetheless wore old ghosts like a cloak. Much like Rosa herself.

"We didn't talk much. And I asked first."

He grunted. "The Hadari invade, and no sooner have we sent them packing than some fool on the Council hurls armies across the border to recapture lost ground. Round and round, back and forth, and only the Raven is laughing." He shrugged. "But who knows? Maybe this time *is* different. It *feels* different. There's something new on the wind."

"Late pollen from Fellhallow," said Rosa. "I wouldn't breathe too deep. You'll sprout blossoms."

"Yes, commander," he replied drily. "I don't know. Perhaps Lumestra's finally shaken sense into that sister of hers, and she in turn has brought the shadowthorns into line. The First Councillor must think so, to send an envoy to Tregard, rather than an army."

Tregard, the stolen city, captured by the Hadari when the kingdom of Rhaled had spread its bounds two centuries before. "All the more reason to remain watchful. Lord Reveque has been wrong before."

"And we shall. The watch-forts east of the Ravonn are fully manned. We'll have plenty of warning if the Hadari attempt nastiness."

"Even so, I should—"

"Take advantage of the lull and live a little?" said Noktza. "That's exactly what I was thinking."

She glared at his back, uncaring that Noktza likely knew what was in her expression. "I meant I should inspect the watch-forts. Drill the garrisons."

"But you're on leave," he said with mock surprise. "By order of the Castellan of Ahrad, whoever he is. A shifty sort, I'm sure, and not to be trusted. But unflinching, too."

So that's how it was? Rosa bit back a reply that, despite long years of comradeship, would only have made things worse. "I thought we agreed that wouldn't be necessary if I allowed myself to be . . . what was it? Feted."

"Simpler to find the time for that if you're not shackled by duty, surely?" said Noktza. "And we both know you agreed to no such thing. Two days, Rosa. Put aside the colours of Essamere and wear the champion's mantle lightly. Be yourself."

"Yes, Lord Noktza," she replied stiffly.

"You'll find the 7th barracked in the North Quarter of the inner bailey. Lady Sarravin expects you within the hour. I thought you might start among familiar faces." At last, he turned about. "And because I'm not the malignant old man you've not quite accused me of being, I thought you'd like to know that the *Zephyr* tied up at the inner dock this afternoon."

"The *Zephyr*?" Rosa's cheeks warmed with surprise and pleasure. "I didn't know."

"You were busy, I'm sure."

Yes and no. A patrol to the north under Fellhallow's eaves, chasing rumours of smugglers. All for nothing, as it had turned out. Maybe all this *was* for the best.

"Riego . . . Thank you."

He waved her away. "Enjoy yourself. Should the Hadari attack, I promise not to cede the fortress without your express permission."

Rosa hurried along the harbourside, every other step punctuated by a sibilant curse as the skirts of her sleeveless gown conspired to trip her. She'd always been fonder of practical clothes – to Rosa's mind, a dress could never be *truly* practical – and even now wore soldier's boots rather than the lighter, softer shoes fashion demanded. The roadways of Ahrad, well-dunged as they were by draught horses and the garrison's destriers, rewarded firm grip and punished fripperies.

Other than three shallow-keeled corpse-barges, only two vessels graced Ahrad's inner dock – an artificial harbour, fed by sluices and joined to the Silverway River at either end by stairways of huge lock gates that were small fortresses in their own right. One, a supply hulk sitting low in the water, had travelled as far east as the river permitted. Beyond the fortress, the Silverway's majesty narrowed sharply, barring passage for such wallowing vessels.

Not so the single-masted caravel silent in the hulk's broken-backed shadow. Had its master wished, the *Zephyr* could have made passage of the eastern lock gates, ghosted out beyond Ahrad's walls and sailed all the way to the Hadari capital of Tregard. Not that such a course would have been advisable. For the *Zephyr* too, Ahrad marked the last stop before favourable winds and the Silverway's current carried her back to Tressia. Where the supply hulk bore the heavy burdens of the garrison's rations and armaments, diligently unloaded by straining crewers and towering bronze kraikons, the *Zephyr* carried something altogether more precious: word from home.

Leather satchels bearing the wax seals of great families carried orders from Council and chapterhouse. Larger, rougher sacks were filled to bursting with letters penned by loved ones and tokens from sweethearts sundered by distance. When the *Zephyr* slipped her moorings and headed home, she'd bear the frontier's tidings to the Council's ears – written in plain language, but couched in coded phrases known only to the author and to the Privy Council to ensure authenticity. She'd perhaps also bear one or two of the garrison's officers who'd no patience for making the journey by conventional steed.

Rosa ducked away from an oncoming dray cart and approached the caravel's gangplank. Anticipation blurred with awkwardness she knew was misplaced but could never entirely banish. A slight woman in a drab naval coat and cocked hat stood at the head of the gangway, deep in conversation with a crewer. As Rosa approached, the woman dismissed her underling and turned about.

"Lady Orova." A broad smile beamed beneath dancing grey eyes.

Rosa fought a smile of her own. "Captain Psanneque. Permission to come aboard?"

"Always."

Gathering her skirts, Rosa picked her way along the gangplank and onto the *Zephyr*'s foredeck. As she found her footing on tar-stained timbers, Sevaka's gloved hands brushed her cheeks, cradled the back of her jaw, and drew her in for a kiss.

Rosa tensed, her shoulders prickling, aware that at least three pairs of eyes were upon them between wheelhouse and bowsprit – to say nothing of onlookers on the harbourside. Overt affection, while not exactly frowned upon by the nobility, was neither fully approved of. But Sevaka, who was as open about her feelings as Rosa wore them close, was long past caring about such things. Try as she might, Rosa could never quite emulate her candour. A different kind of courage to the one she knew so well.

Ignoring the soft wolf-whistle somewhere to her left, Rosa fought back panic and closed her eyes, slipped her hands about Sevaka's waist, and lost herself in the warmth of a reunion too long in arriving.

Sevaka drew back. "Miss me?"

Rosa wondered what Sevaka's brother would have made of it all. She'd loved Kasamor, though she'd lacked the courage to say so until it was too late. She shook the thought away. Kas was gone, and life was for the living. The living, and whatever she was.

"Yes."

"Your hair's different."

"You said you liked it longer."

"I do." Sevaka spoke matter-of-factly, but with an impish gleam. Without turning away, she raised her voice. "Mister Alvanko?"

"Captain?" said a weather-beaten crewer to Rosa's left.

"If you ever again whistle like that when I'm having a private moment, I'll find a needle and thread and stitch your mouth shut. Do you understand?"

Alvanko grinned. "Yes, captain."

"You see what I have to put up with? And the others are no better. Rogues, all of them." Blonde plaits glinted in the dying sun as she swept off her hat. Her next words were wistful. "Then again, look at the captain."

Rosa waited for eyes to wander elsewhere before speaking. "What is it?"

"Nothing. It's just ... " She patted the gunwale. "She's fast enough to chase corsairs out at Selann, or slip the Hadari blockade lines. I've pleaded with Admiral Tralnov, but the orders don't come, and I'm stuck plying the Silverway as a glorified herald."

A little more than a year before, Admiral Tralnov would have fallen over herself trying to please Sevaka's influential mother. But Ebigail Kiradin was gone, and Sevaka had given up the family name as a last act of spite against a woman to whom family and continuity were everything. Twice a pariah, once through circumstance and again out of choice, she'd little prospect of being trusted with responsibility. Psanneque, the name she'd taken upon orphaning herself, meant "exile", and carried bleak connotations.

"At least this way I get to see you." Rosa laid a hand on hers. "Selann's a long way off."

"Come with me. I'll smuggle you aboard."

The prickle returned to Rosa's shoulders. Sevaka had spoken lightly enough, but joining her on that particular course of conversation would only lead to argument – and Rosa had even less enthusiasm for overt discord than she did unseemly affection.

"I didn't know you were coming," she said instead.

"I thought to make it a surprise," Sevaka replied. "Seems I failed."

"Lord Noktza told me."

"Ah. And how is Riego?"

"Insufferable," said Rosa. "He's instructed me to play hero for the 7th this evening. Speeches. Wine. More speeches. Over and over until I slit my wrists out of boredom."

"For all the good that'll do," said Sevaka. "Sounds ghastly. Would you like me to come along? If you can bear to be seen with me, that is."

Rosa passed over the barb and seized gladly on the rest. "I'd hoped you might."

Sevaka looked herself up and down, taking in the weather-stained shirt and coat, the cracked and peeling sword belt. "I'm not exactly dressed for it."

"For carousing with soldiers? You're fine. They're not worth making the effort."

"You did."

"But not for them," Rosa said. "For you."

Sevaka's smile made all worthwhile. The murderous skirts. The *Zephyr's* voyeuristic crew. Maybe even the silent confession that Noktza had been right, in perhaps a small way.

"Well that's different." Sevaka shot her a quizzical look. "Wait a minute. Dockside. Dress. The spectre of drink. You're not planning on killing anyone tonight?"

Rosa blinked. How had she forgotten? Their friendship had begun that bitter night on the Tressian dockside. The night of Kas' wake. She'd settled one of his old quarrels and saved Sevaka's life in the process. Not that she recalled much of it. She barely remembered Aske Tarev's skull breaking beneath her fists. How many things had changed since then? How many had remained the same? She stared down at her hand and flexed her knuckles. The blood was long since washed away, but the anger had never really faded.

Could she ever really let it go? Did she even want to?

Uncaring of intrusive eyes, she leaned in and kissed Sevaka.

"No promises. But I'll try not to."

Five

Firestone lanterns and torches flickered among the tents and squat stone barrack-blocks bounding three sides of the muster field. Amber tongues leapt from firepits towards the night sky, as wild as the fiddle and fife that goaded crowds to dancing and carousal.

The music took root in Sevaka's soul, rousing blood made sluggish by the boredom of travel.

Beside her, Rosa went taut in that way that she so often did, and that Sevaka pretended so often not to notice. "I'm going to kill him."

Sevaka smiled wryly. "And so easily the promise is broken."

The victim's identity took little sleuthing. At full strength, which the losses of war and the complications of leave seldom allowed, a regiment numbered a thousand men and women under arms, plus as many as a dozen companies of wayfarers, pavissionaires and other auxiliaries. Easily twice that was gathered across the muster field and beneath the overhang of the wall-ward buildings. Despite Noktza's words, the 7th were not alone. Sevaka spotted tabards of at least three other regiments, as well as the plainer, rougher garb of borderers and the bright surcoats of knights. And that was before she tallied the array of spouses, children, traders, courtesans, craftsmen, and servants.

Five regiments held Ahrad – plus perhaps another thousand knights – but the soldiers were outnumbered at least three times over by their hangers-on. The luckiest had quarters within the inner bailey – most lived in ramshackle houses beneath the western walls.

"I don't think you have to talk to *all* of them."

"That's not the point."

Rosa's arm, crooked through Sevaka's since leaving the *Zephyr*, slithered free. Her expression grew guarded as she tugged her dress into place. Sevaka knew the ritual. The donning of armour and the raising of ramparts ahead of battle. She didn't resent it, not as such. She even found it endearing, in its way. What she hated was that when the walls came up, she invariably found herself on the wrong side.

A voice rang out. "Who goes?"

Two sentries approached, a lieutenant at their head. All sober, to Sevaka's eye. She wondered what infraction had damned them to be thus on a night of celebration.

"Lady Roslava Orova, Knight of Essamere and Champion to the Council." Rosa's voice held not the uncertain tone of moments before, but a battlefield's authority. "I believe I'm expected."

The lieutenant saluted, expression stiffening as perceptions shifted. "Yes, lady. And your companion?"

"My friend, Lady Sevaka."

Sevaka kept her dismay hidden. She'd thought they were past this, but in four simple words, Rosa had concealed both her identity and their closeness.

The lieutenant spared Sevaka barely a glance. "If you'll both follow me?"

He set a brisk pace across the crowded muster field. Sevaka fell into step beside Rosa "Your *friend*?"

"We *are* friends. If we weren't, we couldn't be anything else."

A sterling reply, for it was true enough. Had Rosa's tone been warmer, Sevaka might even have believed her. "Embarrassed to be slumming with a kinless exile? Half the officers will already know. Or does soldiering knock the gossip out of a highblood?"

"Kas and I served with the 7th for years. And this is hard enough without fending off half-baked innuendo about your lineage." The rampart of Rosa's public face cracked. "I really *don't* want to kill anyone. But if someone starts hurling slurs about us – about *you*—"

"A champion for my honour. How romantic." Try as she might, Sevaka couldn't help but feel mollified. "All right. But your promises about the wine better hold up."

"They will. The Sarravins own half the farmland along the Tevar Flood, and Emilia has a reputation for generosity."

They walked the rest of the way in silence, though one a touch more companionable than before. It wasn't that Sevaka didn't understand Rosa's reluctance. In fact, she sympathised, having striven to conceal more than one past relationship from her mother's judgemental eye. She'd shared her passions freely, and seldom with those equal to her family's once-imposing rank. Now situations were reversed.

She breathed deep of the swirling smoke. Soft fragrance betrayed that more tinder had been gathered beneath Fellhallow's eaves than was entirely wise, but it soothed away hurt. Yes, she understood. But understanding was the domain of the mind, not the heart, and the heart hung heavy with every reminder of the gulf between pragmatism and desire.

Fortunately, a lifetime as Ebigail Kiradin's daughter had taught Sevaka how to keep such burdens from touching her expression. By the time they'd threaded their way through the fires to the long, bottle-strewn table at the muster field's heart, her smile was back in place.

"Lady Orova . . . " Emilia Sarravin, Commander of the 7th, broke away from a knot of her junior officers, hand extended in greeting. Sevaka knew her to be on the cusp of her fortieth year, but she looked older – worn in the way folk were by military life. Her uniform – king's blue, and bearing the Tressian hawk – was crisp, and closely tailored. "So glad you could join us. I told Riego not to trouble you, but he said you'd insisted."

"Did he now?" Rosa shook the proffered hand, her expression unread-able. "I was glad to be invited. It's like coming home. Do you know . . . ? "

Lady Sarravin glanced in Sevaka's direction. "Sevaka? Only by name. But her mother sought to send my father to the gallows." Her expression flickered. "But that's all done with, thank Lumestra."

But it wasn't, was it? It'd never be done with, or else why offer reminder? "I have no mother," said Sevaka. "I am myself alone."

"Well said." Lady Sarravin's expression lightened. "You're welcome at my table, of course."

One wave dismissed Rosa's escort. Another summoned a servant bearing goblets and a bottle of wine. A whirl of introductions followed, an array of majors, captains, lieutenants and squires, all of whom offered either handshake or salute, according to their family's relative standing with Rosa's own. The Orovas were not of the first rank – although their star was said to be on the rise – so even the lowest squire could have treated her as an equal, had lineage justified it.

Sevaka, who had so recently and loudly reinforced her status as a Psanneque, received only nods of acknowledgement, despite the captain's saltire on her faded epaulettes. So she ignored the litany of names and ranks, and instead focused her full attention on the wine. Which was, as Rosa had promised, quite excellent.

She'd finished her second goblet by the time introductions were complete. As she snagged a bottle for a refill, Lady Sarravin shot her a glance.

"Drink your fill. There's plenty more. We may be on reduced rations, but there's wine enough to run the Silverway red."

Sevaka nodded. Between the invasion of the previous year, the burning of much of the Southshires' croplands and the Settlement Decree leaving too many farms short of workers – which in turn had seen many grumbling soldiers and unwilling prisoners assigned to pick up the slack – shortages were rife. Easy enough to manage when you'd a crew of a mere dozen to tend – and when duty took you to docksides famous for cargo going astray for the right price. Feeding a regiment was a different matter.

"I'm told the Council are working to resolve things," said Rosa.

"Which means Thrakkian traders are filling their purses with our coin," grumbled a heavyset major. "Probably selling us our own stolen grain."

"It is what it is," said Lady Sarravin. "I can't keep food in their bellies, but I can at least give my lads and lasses drink enough to take their minds off their pangs. If only for one night. Let others watch the walls."

Sevaka stared out across the muster field. "You supplied all this?"

"Why not? This '73 would be wasted on them, but the estate cellars run deep and to some variety. What use is privilege if it cannot spur one to generosity? Or to toast one's friends?" She raised her goblet high, and her voice a fraction higher, cutting through the hubbub. "To our guest. A daughter of Essamere – which we shall forgive her – and also of the 7th, which makes her dearer than kin. To Lady Orova!"

"*Lady Orova!*"

Sevaka readily joined her voice to the chorus.

Rosa, face expressionless but spots of colour high on her cheeks, pulled out a chair, used it as a stepping stone to the table top, and raised her own goblet up to the moonlit skies. "To Tressia's finest, even if their commander's a preening Sartorov." The words drew unabashed grins from around the table, betraying chapterhouse allegiances buried beneath the regular army's king's blue. "To the 7th!"

"*To the 7th!*"

Cheers rippled outward, gathering momentum as common soldiers took up the cry. They redoubled as Rosa emptied her goblet at a single pull and did the same with the refill. By the time she returned to ground level, there was enough vigour to her expression that she'd pass for human. None of it, Sevaka knew, was to do with the wine. Angry mob or drunken throng, crowds lost their terror once you were among them.

Lady Sarravin smiled. "Preening or not, this Sartorov thanks you."

"For drinking your wine like it's farthing ale?" said Rosa.

"For giving them something to aspire to. Soldiers need exemplars, and you've certainly been that . . . even before you were chosen as the new champion."

She cast surreptitiously about, and led Rosa a pace or two from the table. Sevaka, uninvited but scenting the whiff of gossip, followed.

"A shame about Lord Akadra," Lady Sarravin murmured. "I've heard the rumours, of course – and in all their contradictory splendour – but I don't know what really happened. You were there, weren't you?"

For the first time, Sevaka realised that Lady Sarravin, who had supposedly been carousing since sundown, had eyes as clear as Sommertide skies.

Rosa shrugged, though she looked little relaxed to Sevaka's eye. "When the Hadari retreated, the southwealders started fighting among themselves. The council charged Viktor to bring it to an end, and he did. But when the rebels murdered his betrothed . . . It didn't end well."

"And the burnings? I understand he killed thousands."

"The fields of the Grelyt Valley are still black. Nothing grows there now. And Viktor just . . . walked away from it all."

"You didn't try to bring him back?"

Rosa shook her head. "The Council would have punished him. Maybe even hanged him. Better it's all forgotten."

"And we do forget so well in the Republic. Our mistakes, our families and even our purpose." Lady Sarravin tilted her goblet. "To Viktor Akadra, may he find what peace he deserves."

"Viktor Akadra."

Sevaka murmured the toast's reply and examined Lady Sarravin's face for any hint that she knew that Rosa's tale was, if not a pack of lies, one that strayed far from absolute truth. Personal embellishment aside, it was official history approved by the Council, and laid down forevermore in the Republic's archives. Sevaka knew better. She knew about the Dark that had risen to claim the Southshires, and the price paid to defeat it. A truth shared by few others, and some of those had been posted to outposts so distant that their knowledge would trouble no one else.

"Still," said Lady Sarravin, "it need not all be to the bad. I understand Messela Akadra is hardly comporting herself well. Where one family fades, another burns bright. Perhaps your family, Rosa."

"My family?" Rosa said warily. "I don't follow."

"Don't be so modest. I know your uncle Davor's working to see that your efforts are properly recognised, and it's hardly unknown for the Council's own champion to sit among its ranks. But if that's to happen, you need to be more than a name and a body count. Come along with me. You really must meet . . . "

Sevaka took another pull on her goblet. Whatever Lord Noktza had intended from Rosa's attendance, Lady Sarravin sought to profit by being remembered as the one who'd brought her together with the scions of influential families. It was everything Sevaka had hoped to put behind her: whispers, conspiracy, jockeying for position – a game played to its own purpose and the Republic's detriment.

Ignoring Rosa's pleading glance, Sevaka hitched her sword belt a fraction higher, plucked a bottle from the table, and strode towards the nearest firepit.

"You ladies enjoy yourselves. I'm of the mood to dance."

A long, tedious hour passed before Rosa finally extracted herself from Lady Sarravin's social hurricane. Lumestra alone knew what they'd made of her. After three exchanges of platitudes and one insubstantial conversation, she felt certain her face had set solid and cold as ice.

Enough of the officers she'd met – especially those of the 1st, who'd seized on the chance to broach Lady Sarravin's wine stocks – would remember little, but still the worry remained. In all cases save one. The upstart major of the 10th – who'd jumped to the entirely wrong conclusion of her profession before introductions could be made – had a sprained wrist to remind of the perils of wandering hands. Rosa had earned more grins than scowls at furnishing him thus, which made her suspect the major's was a luck pressed too far, too often.

An hour to escape, and the better part of another without sign of Sevaka, who'd gone from the fire where Rosa had seen her last. As the search wended far from Lady Sarravin's entourage of pressed uniforms and ribboned hair to the frayed cloth and filthy faces of the common ranks, Rosa grew suspicious that Sevaka had abandoned her entirely.

Finally, after receiving direction from a sergeant as lamentably sober as Rosa herself, she found her quarry. Not amidst the music and dance of the muster field, but on the ramparts of the inner wall.

Shoulder wedged in the jamb between drum tower and battlement, and wine bottle propped between the crenellations, Sevaka was lost in conversation with a tall fellow of tanned complexion whose neat, dark beard and watchful eyes lent sardonic cast to his features. He straightened as Rosa approached.

"Lady Orova, is it? Your reputation precedes you."

Rosa eyed him warily. Too many platitudes over too short a period had left her with a tin ear. "And you are?"

"Indro Thaldvar. I'm an unforgivable ruffian, by which I mean to say I'm a borderer."

That much Rosa had already guessed from Thaldvar's garb: rough, practical leathers and a cloak the colour of winter skies. No two borderers' tales were exactly the same, but most hailed from the ravaged villages of the Eastshires, or else claimed lineage from the lost lands beyond the Ravonn. Though not officially part of the Republic's army, they were invaluable to its operation, able to walk unnoticed where a column of soldiery could not.

The common soldiery resented the borderers their freedom; the nobility disdained them as uncivilised. Rosa could never have lived as Thaldvar and his kind did, always on the move and with no real home to return to.

"He kept me company while you played hero," Sevaka slurred. "All exiles together."

"Are you drunk?" asked Rosa.

"No." A pause. "Little bit."

All exiles together. Now Rosa thought on it, there *were* a great many borderers on the battlements, clustered together in ones and twos, offering the occasional stolen glance at the noblewoman who'd stumbled into their midst. Rosa felt like an intruder.

"You don't care for Lady Sarravin's hospitality?" she asked.

Thaldvar's lip twitched. "I care greatly for her wine, but less so for the attitudes of her soldiers." He cast a hand out over the battlements. "And it *is* a magnificent view."

The wall on which they stood was Ahrad's innermost and highest – the curtain wall that defended the citadel and its inner harbour. To reach it, an attacker would have to breach two others, or else storm offset gates thick with sentries and bell towers. Their broad abutting ramparts were patrolled by sleepless kraikons – bronze statuesque constructs that stood twice the height of a man, and were armoured with the finest steel the forges could produce. Even in the dark, Rosa saw them making ponderous circuit of the defences, golden magic crackling from their eyes and through rents in their armour. Should danger threaten, the kraikons would be joined by the blades of whichever regiment held the duty watch, then the soldiers of the ready garrison, and by others soon after.

Further out, past Ahrad's walls and crowded baileys, the dark ribbon of the Silverway snaked across the Ravonni grasslands and into the forests, shining brilliant beneath the moon.

"The land of my fathers. *Domis everan unmonleithil.*"

Thaldvar's use of the old, formal language caught Rosa so off-guard that it took her a moment to parse it into low tongue. A wistful prayer that would most likely never come true. Even if peace reigned, Thaldvar's home would never again be what it once was. At best, it might command a seat on the Privy Council, but the thought of even Malachi inviting a borderer to the highest court struck Rosa as fanciful.

"A home lost, but not forgotten?" translated Sevaka.

"Something like that. You're surprised a borderer speaks so well?"

"I try not to judge."

He nodded. "There are borderers and there are *borderers*. Some of us are quite civilised." He stared down at a muster field strewn with inebriates. "Though I suppose that's relative."

Heavy footfalls on the stairs preluded the arrival of a lieutenant of the 7th, his face florid from drink. Rosa tried to recall the name from the flurry of introductions and promises sought. Stasmet, that was it. And he'd not come alone.

Half a dozen soldiers trailed in his wake, none the better for the evening's festivities than he. All moved with the distinctive purpose of folk with malice in mind, hands close to weapons not yet drawn.

"Borderer!" Stasmet was as boorish in voice as appearance. "I told you to move on."

"And I did," Thaldvar's brow creased in polite surprise. "From down there, to up here. You see how that works, lieutenant?"

Stasmet growled and started forward. Along the rampart, the hubbub of conversation deadened to nothing. Hands slid beneath cloaks. Eyes narrowed. Rosa stepped in front of Thaldvar.

"Is there a problem, lieutenant?"

Bloodshot eyes flicked from Rosa to Thaldvar and back again. "Cheated me at jando. A marked deck."

"The very idea," said Thaldvar. "He was drunk. Couldn't tell the Queen in Twilight from the Court of Kings. A child could have cleaned him out."

"You think I'm a fool?"

"Well—"

"Enough," snapped Rosa. "Get some sleep, lieutenant. Your pride's hurting."

Stasmet's sword scraped free of its scabbard. "Not until he pays up, or moves on."

Rosa watched the point of Stasmet's sword bob back and forth and despaired at finding this conversation one of the more enjoyable of the evening. Small talk left her adrift, but bellicose threats . . . ?

She drew forth her best parade-ground voice. "Lieutenant Stasmet, you do know who I am?"

Several of Stasmet's would-be threateners exchanged glances, their hands retreating from their swords. Stasmet either missed the threat in her voice, or was too far lost to anger and wine that he didn't care.

"The Council's high and mighty Champion?" He snorted. "I know all about you."

Sevaka pushed away from the wall. "Not enough, or you'd put that sword away and apologise."

Stasmet stared as if seeing her for the first time. "You? Shouldn't be surprised, always a Kiradin hanging around you, isn't there, Lady Orova? Working your way through the whole family, are you? Who's next, another sister?"

Rosa's enjoyment melted beneath a red rush of anger. "What did you say?"

She took grim delight in a flinch that betrayed Stasmet's faltering confidence. Clearly rumour had told Stasmet a great deal. She and Kas had made no secret of their friendship, and plenty had seen how his death had ripped her apart. But did Stasmet know the rest, or was he simply craven? Perhaps he needed to see that part first-hand. She'd not need a sword to make the point.

She stepped closer.

Sevaka moved between. Her hand found Rosa's shoulder and she stood on tiptoes, bringing her lips level with Rosa's ear. "Remember your promise."

The red fought, but it receded. Rosa met Sevaka's gaze, nodded and received a slight smile in return.

"Thank you," said Sevaka.

She spun about, naval cutlass sweeping free and striking Stasmet's sword from his hand. A stomp of boot on instep set him howling. Then Sevaka had a handful of grubby shirt twisted between her fingers, and Stasmet up against the ramparts. All to the horrified stares of the lieutenant's accomplices, and the borderers' laughter.

"Lady Orova's right," said Sevaka. "You're drunk. I think you should sleep it off, don't you?"

Stasmet spluttered and nodded as frantically as her stranglehold allowed.

"And since you asked so politely," Sevaka went on. "I *do* have a sister. But I'm the nice one."

She brought her knee up between Stasmet's legs. He howled, and she let him drop.

"Always good to see an accord between wetfoots and dry," said Thaldvar.

The words provoked a ripple of mirth from fellow borderers. It drew filthy looks from the soldiers but, with their erstwhile leader gasping on his knees, what little fight they'd started with was long gone.

Sevaka retrieved her wine bottle from the wall and drained its dregs at a single pull.

"You shouldn't have done that," muttered Rosa.

"And what would you have done?" When Rosa found no answer – at least, no answer that would help her cause – Sevaka sheathed her sword and cocked her head. "See?"

Behind her, Stasmet bellowed like a wounded ox and staggered to his feet. A dagger shining in his hand, he lunged at Sevaka.

Rosa shoved Sevaka aside. The dagger meant for her spine instead slipped between Rosa's ribs.

She felt no pain. She seldom did, unless silver was involved. Just the rip of tearing cloth, the tugging sensation in her chest, the tooth-rattling judder as the dagger's blade scraped across her rib. The rasping, sucking sensation as steel punctured her lung. That was the worst part, reflex gasping for a breath that wouldn't come, and every fibre of her being screaming that death was coming for her.

"Lady!" cried Thaldvar.

Borderers started to their feet, expressions twisted in shock.

Rosa clubbed Stasmet down and kicked him hard in the head. Thaldvar's horrified expression provoked a rasping laugh. He at least hadn't heard all the rumours. One in particular had escaped him: that the Lady Roslava Orova, who fed the Raven so readily, could not herself be killed. A goddess' curse. The Raven's blessing. Rosa didn't know which had made her thus, only that she was.

Aware she had the full attention of everyone around her, Rosa fumbled for the dagger's hilt. A dribble of black blood became silver vapour as she dragged the blade from the prison of her flesh. She hurled it away, and sought a leader among Stasmet's soldiers.

"Corporal?" The word bubbled with black spittle that turned to mist on her lips. "Take the lieutenant away, lock him up and I'll forget I ever saw you here tonight, agreed?"

The corporal gulped, nodded and seized the fallen Stasmet's shoulders.

Rosa coughed, the rasp fading as her wounded lung reknitted. She cast about the surrounding faces. Borderers and soldiers alike bore curiously similar expression, men and women afraid to speak as if in so doing they'd break some terrible spell.

Only Sevaka's was different, frozen in concern and distaste that presaged a difficult conversation.

But despite it all, Rosa found herself laughing.

At least, until she raised her eyes past Sevaka's shoulder to meet those of a pale, dark-suited man in a feathered mask. A man no one else saw, and whose polite applause no other heard.

Six

Awash in tangled feelings, Sevaka closed the door to Rosa's quarters and dragged the heavy curtain into place.

"So you're not keeping it secret any longer?"

Worry made the words more accusatory than she'd meant.

Rosa's fingers brushed the firestone lamp above the crackling hearth. Soft moon-shadows retreated before the blaze of enchanted crystal, bringing shape to sparse furnishings more suited to a penniless carpenter than a knight of good family. A champion's chamber should have been opulent of cloth and possession. This was a shell – the bare timbers of a house after a hurricane.

Halting in front of the dresser, and its simple wood-framed mirror, Rosa teased apart the torn cloth level with the spur of her sternum, and peered mournfully at the reflection.

"Another dress ruined."

"A dress?" Sevaka started forward. "That's all you can talk about? What if the church's provosts come for you? You know what they'll say."

The Lumestran church was technically forbidden to marshal soldiers of its own – even the kraikons and simarka crafted by its proctors fell under the Council's authority, rather than that of Archimandrite Jezek – but it wasn't entirely toothless. The provosts were tireless in their search for spiritual corruption, and ruthless when their quest bore fruit.

"That I'm an abomination? Some hideous Dark-tainted harridan to be burned on the pyre?" Rosa unfastened the gemmed clips holding her plaits in place and tugged the ribbons free. Straw-blonde hair brushed her shoulders. "The time for that would have been three months ago, when that Immortal nearly took my arm."

"What?"

"I was careless, and ended with my left arm hanging by a scrap. The physicians wanted to amputate. I had them stitch it back on." Her back still to Sevaka, Rosa raised her left hand and wiggled her fingers. The bare flesh bore not a scar. "All mended."

Winding the ribbons tight, Rosa set the clips to hold them closed and arranged them on the dresser with methodical care. Her fussiness, like her social reserve, was sometimes appealing. Not at that hour.

"And then there was the ambush at Ranadar," she went on. "That was a bad one. A dozen of us, and fifty of them hiding among the trees. My horse took an arrow in the throat and kicked me in the head on my way down. I awoke in darkness with a mouthful of soil. Buried in a shallow grave by the shadowthorns, would you believe? Once I stopped screaming, I clawed my way out. Half of them fled when their arrows couldn't put me down. I don't remember much of what came after."

Sevaka swallowed to clear a claggy mouth. Death was a soldier's fate, but to hear it described thus ... "You never told me."

"It's not the sort of thing one puts in a letter."

"You could've told me last month, at Tarvallion."

Tarvallion. Three days without the burdens of vocation, or the lingering threat of the empty border. Just the elegant spires and vibrant gardens of the opaline city, reviving memories of early days together, before diverging duties brought the separation of distance. Laughter and dancing, and sometimes nothing at all save the quiet of company well-shared – contentment that went deeper than the moment, and into a promise that it could always be so. But secrets soured the memory. Lies always did, even lies of omission, rather than intent.

Rosa shrugged. "I didn't think it was important."

"Not important? Rosa, you could have died. Still might, if word reaches the wrong ear. The provosts—"

She spun around, lips pursed. "Don't care. That's what I'm trying to tell you. The garrison's proctors all know. They think I'm a miracle, blessed by Lumestra. That I'm doing holy work. The high proctor himself once even suggested as much."

"But you don't think that, do you?"

Irritation gave way to wariness, eyes hooded and suspicious. "What do you mean?"

"You talk in your sleep."

Sevaka folded her arms. Rosa slept barely at all. Those brief hours where she did were seldom peaceful, but the muttered words of nightmare seldom made sense.

"I see," said Rosa, her voice low and dangerous. "So is this about what the church provosts might think, or what *you* think? Do you believe I'm a creature of the Dark, hungry for souls?"

"Don't be ridiculous. *I* think you don't trust me. I think a part of you's embarrassed by me, and that's why you keep me at a distance."

"I'm sure you'll find consolation somewhere else," snapped Rosa. "A girl in every port, isn't that the way?"

The words hurt, the weight of old truths driving them deep. Companionship sought as solace for an unhappy life, rather than its own joys. All done with.

"Is that really what you believe?"

Rosa glanced away. "No. I shouldn't have said it. And you don't embarrass me. I love you."

The rare confession should have ended the argument – would have, had Sevaka's temper not already slipped its moorings. "You only love me in the darkness, where no one can see us. It's not enough. I know that sounds selfish, but it *can't* be enough. Don't you understand?"

The emotion swirling in Rosa's eyes was as uncertain as Sevaka's own. Through seething thoughts, Sevaka swore she wouldn't be the first to look away, only to prove herself a liar immediately after. Rosa let out a pained sigh, crossed to the bed and sat down.

"You know I don't do well with letting my feelings show. You know the mistakes they've led me to." Hands on her knees, she stared at the threadbare rug. "I'm the Council's Champion. I'm only free to be myself in the darkness. The rest of the time, I have to set an example. When others look at me, they need to see the warrior, not the woman. And certainly not a woman who lowers herself to embrace a Psanneque."

Not for the first time that night, Sevaka wondered if she'd erred by casting off the family name. That in a moment of vengeful spite, she'd blighted herself for ever. But no. To keep the Kiradin name would have been worse, and not for its legacy of treason. It would have proved her mother *right*, even in some small way.

With a sigh, she sat on the bed beside Rosa. "So you *are* embarrassed by me."

"No. Not that. Never that. But your name ... your choice. It makes things difficult."

"It doesn't make things difficult for Josiri Trelan," said Sevaka. "His Anastacia's even more of an outcast than I am, but he doesn't hide her away."

"That's different. He's a southwealder. No one expects better from him. I'm daughter of Orova. A knight of Essamere."

"And too good for me?" Sevaka fought to contain bitterness. "You should at least admit it."

"That's not what I meant."

"It's not what you mean that's the problem, Rosa. It never is. It's what you say. And what you don't. I love you, but I won't be some backstairs consolation, ushered in and out of your chambers when it suits your fancy or your reputation." She hesitated, the next words leaving her heartsick even before they were spoken. "It has to be more than that, or it's nothing at all."

"Then what do we do?" said Rosa. "What would you have me do?"

"We could marry." The audacious words slipped free before Sevaka realised she'd intended to speak them. "Few care that I was once a Kiradin now I'm Psanneque. Fewer still will care about either once I'm an Orova. The betrothal might ruffle a few feathers, but it won't last. We'll finally be free of it all. Together in the darkness and the light."

Excitement gathered pace as the idea gained purchase. Hope rushed to fill emptiness.

Rosa frowned. "My uncles would never approve."

"Who cares? You're a grown woman, Rosa, not a child."

"They're the heads of the family. I have to respect their wishes." She clenched her fists. "The star of Orova is on the rise. Davor and Gallan won't want me to jeopardise that by joining my future to a Psanneque's."

The flame of hope flickered and died. "It's yours to jeopardise. Or do you suppose it's Davor's work in the treasury that sets hearts aflutter at your family name? Or does the Grand Council cherish Gallan's prize-winning roses so highly they consider them grounds for acclaim?"

"But that's just it," snapped Rosa. "My ascension isn't mine alone. It's theirs, and that of all my cousins alongside. It will raise up the whole family to new heights. I *can't* throw that away. Could you do different if the situation were reversed? If you were still a Kiradin, and I the Psanneque? Would you have defied your mother for me?"

The words sucked away the room's warmth. Sevaka closed her eyes. They both knew the truth. Even before Kas' death had proven the horrific extent of Ebigail Kiradin's desire to control her family's future, Sevaka had been terrified of crossing her. She'd joined the navy to escape, and still never been free. The past swallowed the future and left only ashes behind.

Blinking back tears, Sevaka stood. "Then I guess it's nothing at all."

Rosa grabbed her hand. "Please. Don't go. Not like this."

"What would I be staying for?" She made no attempt to hide her bitterness now. What was the point? "A future that will never come?"

It took every scrap of resolve to pull free of Rosa's grip. The chamber's heavy door was nothing by comparison. Sevaka barely felt the cold night air on her tear-stung cheeks.

"Goodbye, Rosa."

The door slammed. The fires of the hearth sank to a dull glow, and Rosa stared at the wall. The wall demanded nothing. It didn't call her a liar, or a coward.

Or a fool.

And so it shouldn't, Rosa told herself, for she wasn't a fool. She'd responsibilities beyond her own desires. Sevaka didn't understand. Sevaka was selfish. Sevaka . . .

. . . was gone, and the room left colder and darker for her passing.

Unable to bear accusing silence any longer, Rosa dulled the firestone lantern and swept out into the night, her feet finding old patterns of patrol along the inner wall's ramparts. The warmth of day had long since faded from Ahrad's walls, but the wind's kiss lingered little on the bare skin of her arms and face. Cold, like pain, seldom troubled her any longer. Just another ephemeral feeling stripped away. Only her heart ached.

Sentries – used to her walking the walls at this hour – stiffened to attention at her passing. Their expressions offered only deference, with no hint of question or mockery at unbound hair in disarray, or a stride almost at a run.

As she reached the ballistae of the northeast bastion, the skies split. Cold, heavy rain lashed the battlements. The frustration that quickened Rosa's stride spread to fill her soul. With a strangled cry, she slewed to a halt and slammed her fist into stone.

Knuckles split. Birds scattered from the parapet, their voices thickened by corvine amusement. Further along the rampart, a pair of sentries cast curious glances towards the sound, and turned quickly away.

"Would you like me to talk to her?" said the Raven. "I can be *very* persuasive."

He stood a pace distant, elbows propped atop the wall and black-goateed chin resting on his hands, to all appearances staring off into the distance. The black-feathered domino mask was familiar, as was the long-tailed coat. The hat was new. High-crowned and narrow brimmed, it lent imposing height to an already tall figure. And about him ... that sensation that what she saw was but a fraction of what *was*. A presence. A pressure that tempted the mind to flights of bleak imagination.

Rosa glanced at her knuckles. The skin had already healed. "What I want is for you to stay well away from her."

A dry chuckle matched gravelly tone. "Oh, that's not going to work. Sooner or later, I'm close to everyone."

A pair of sentries drew near. A giant kraikon lumbered on their heels, footfalls setting the wall atremble. The flesh-and-blood soldiers offered Rosa a clasped-fist salute as they passed; the foundry-born automaton ignored her. Neither party acknowledged the Raven. No one ever did. He was her burden alone.

"Would you like to continue inside?" The Raven's tone flirted with solicitude but never wholly committed. "That gown wasn't made for this."

In point of fact, the dress was already sodden through, and clung to

Rosa like a second skin. But she'd never asked anything of the Raven, and wasn't about to start. "I'm fine. Don't you have anything better to do?"

Strange to talk to a god thus, without fear – even without respect – but nothing about their relationship struck Rosa as normal. Raven-worship was the province of scoundrels – vranakin and other desperate souls who'd reason to court the Keeper of the Dead. And yet he constantly sought her out – she, who seldom prayed even to Lumestra.

"Quite possibly," he replied, still hunched over the wall. "A stream of petitioners, plaintive and shrill. They don't realise that in matters divine, less is definitely more. You can't imagine what it's like to have unwanted admirers chasing after your coat tails. I confess it was flattering to begin with, but that was *such* a long time ago."

"Yes, I've *no* experience of that," she said sourly.

Lips twitched in a wry smile. "Oh, don't be embarrassed. All the souls you send me, and yet expect nothing in return? That's flattering. All this other business?" He waved a hand, shooing an imaginary petitioner away across the Ravonn. "Flensing. Torture. Dismemberment. It's so tedious. I'm the God of the Dead, not the God of Spite and Cruelty. Another wears that crown and he's very welcome to it, let me tell you."

"I meant you. Petitioning *me*."

"Ah. So that's how it is." The Raven drew up to his full, ungainly height. "This really isn't how it's supposed to be. You're to cower pitiably and beg indulgence, not take me to task for imagined slights."

"Imagined? Whenever I draw a sword, you're there, watching. Why? Why am I so important?"

"I've told you many times. I admire your work."

"If death alone was all that mattered, a dozen others could satisfy you. A hundred."

"Who says they don't? But you're different." He tilted his head, lip curling in thought. His affect, usually careless, grew guarded. "I want you to be my queen."

Rosa felt the laughter build but was powerless to contain it. Her guffaws echoed across the ramparts, incredulous and uncaring that mocking a god seldom ended well.

"This seems to be a night for inappropriate proposals."

"Ah, but you turned her down, didn't you?" If the Raven was offended, it lay hidden beneath his mask, along with most of his expression. "Otherwise you'd still be inside, living love's young dream and not out in the cold with me."

Rosa wiped rain-mingled tears from her eyes, aware that any onlooker would think her a madwoman. Was the Raven even serious? During their reluctant association, he'd proven himself the master of peculiar humour, and seldom spoke plainly. His words too often framed not the truth, but the boundaries of a road he wished her to walk.

"The Goddess of the Dead?" It sounded no less ridiculous now than before.

He wagged a finger. "Queen of the Dead. There's certain hierarchy to be—"

"Why?"

He shrugged. "Because I'm bored. Otherworld's dreary and grey. I've no one to talk to but the departed – who want nothing except for themselves. There's certainly no one to dance with. I'd leave it all behind, but someone has to keep the clock ticking. Otherworld must have its Raven. So it's either a queen, an heir ... or both. But I don't see any need to rush into everything at once."

He *was* serious, Rosa realised, or at least determined to spin out the jest. Possibly he meant to rouse her spirits, if in habitually roundabout manner. But that he even cared to do so ...

"Moments ago, you offered to speak to Sevaka on my behalf."

"Oh, I'm not the jealous type." He shrugged. "Sevaka's stronger than she appears, but sooner or later, she'll be gone, the spark of happiness suffocated by endless grief. You and I will remain. Moments are simply moments. Eternity is for ever."

Stronger than she appears. As was so often the case when the Raven spoke, Rosa glimpsed a truth among the pedantic rambling.

She'd accused Sevaka of lacking the strength to stand up to her tyrannical mother, when in fact she'd done precisely that, saving not only Rosa's life, but many others besides. More than that, Sevaka Kiradin would never have been called upon to embrace Rosa Psanneque, because Rosa would never have had the courage to disown her own family. Sevaka had spent her whole life being told she was weak, but by her actions made those words a lie. What Rosa had taken for Sevaka's weakness was but a mirror of her own. Her failure to fight for what was truly important.

She stared at the Raven, vainly seeking a clue to his intent. He seemed genuine – which horrified her in ways she couldn't adequately express – but then, he always did.

"This is your idea of courtship?" she said. "It may pass for that in divine circles, but ephemerals are different. People are different."

He chuckled. "You're not a person any longer, Rosa. My sister Ashana made sure of that when she snatched you from my grasp. Tampering with the dying never goes how you might want. You're not ephemeral, but eternal. More than mortal – stronger, certainly – but not quite divine. To be eternal is to be driven by obsession, and haunted by loss." He went back to staring into the night, pale fingers pattering restlessly on stone. "But still, I take your point. You've proved yourself to me many times over, and what have I done in return? Words are nothing without actions. I stand suitably chastened."

His tone, both contemplative and worryingly cheerful, sent a shiver down Rosa's spine. "What does that mean?"

"I confess I don't know." His eyes flashed. "I'll think of something."

Then he was gone, a shadow in the rain, leaving Rosa with no answers, a sense of foreboding ... and one other thing besides. A fleeting truth, delivered by divine messenger, and now impossible to ignore. Actions *were* more important than words.

But words had their place, if chosen well.

Sevaka jerked awake at the knock on her cabin door. Ignoring it, she pinched her eyes shut against the heavy patter of rain against the stern window, and sought sleep.

The knock came again, sharper and more impatient than before.

With a growl, Sevaka rolled blearily from her cot. She padded across the deck, swearing ferociously as her knee banged into the chart table as it always did. Still limping, she pulled a coat on over her nightgown to provide semblance of authority, and eased open the door.

A bedraggled figure stood on the rain-lashed deck, pale and shivering in the light of the masthead lantern. Rosa, and soaked through. The sight awoke sailor's stories of weeping rusalka spirits who drowned those who'd wronged them in the waters of a black, glimmerless river that flowed between worlds.

"Rosa?" Anger and concern fought for command of Sevaka's wits. "Who let you aboard?"

"Your watchgirl. Can I come in?"

Alith. She'd have to have words with the lass. That was how they got you, by looking vulnerable and begging for shelter. And not just the rusalki. But what to do now?

"All right, but try not to drip everywhere."

She withdrew into the cabin, leaving Rosa to follow. "Couldn't this have waited until morning? Nothing's changed."

Rosa set the door closed. "Moments are only moments. They pass, and we've already lost so many. And something *has* changed. Not much, but maybe enough." She went down on one knee, her skirts a sodden puddle on the deck. Her eyes never left Sevaka's. "Sevaka Psanneque, you already have my heart. Will you join your family to mine, to share my life and my future?"

"I . . ." Sevaka swallowed. "Is this real?"

For the first time since the *Zephyr* had come to Ahrad, Rosa offered an unguarded smile. "As real as you want it to be."

Seven

Only the most suspicious soul would have guessed Malachi loathed playing host. Coloured lanterns lined Abbeyfields' long driveway, sparkling stones to guide lost children through the gardens' dark. Others shone bright beneath the trees, beside ornamental ponds and marble statues, patches of light about which guests gathered in conversation while servants ensured no stomach bore the burden of hunger, and no throat went dry.

The world beyond the carriage window was still strange to Josiri, not least because the character of the Abbeyfields estate had changed so much so swiftly. On his first visit, the gardens had been ... not exactly overgrown, but certainly unkempt.

The statues of the glades too were peculiar to him. While a few were the crude, hunched guardian statues born of superstition and said to protect against evil spirits, most were noble statesmen and martial heroes, rendered in clean, classical form. Statue-haunted dells were common enough in the Southshires, but there they were of rougher make – tributes to the divine, raised in places where old magic held sway.

Such images were hardly suitable for gatherings of quality – and often-times terrifying into the bargain – but Josiri missed them, all the same. Tressia was a city where the old ways were scrubbed away or hidden deep, where Lumestra held supreme sway. Radiant Lumestra, who had fashioned the world from primal Dark as a haven for ephemeral children. A goddess of infinite patience and compassion, or so it was said.

Josiri had his own reasons for doubting *that*. After all, how different could mother and daughter be?

[[If it transpires you dragged me from the house at sword-point merely so we could sit and stare at a different house, I shall be greatly displeased.]]

The echoes of their not-quite argument clung to Anastacia's hollow, sing-song voice. Swords had not been involved, only words. Anastacia was impervious to the former, and unyielding to the latter.

Josiri opened the carriage door, stepped down to the gravel and extended a gloved hand. "My lady has only to command."

With a soft, musical flutter – the approximation of a sniff from one who no longer had need to breathe – Anastacia took his hand. A flurry of brocade skirts, gold thread glinting among shimmering cream, and she stepped lightly onto the driveway.

[[If only that were so.]]

Her gaze shifted to the front door's wide flight of stairs, where servants waited in silent attendance. And not just servants. A pair of bronze lions sat motionless at the crest. Foundry simarka – magical constructs cast in mortal metal – and, to Josiri's certain knowledge, more watchful than they appeared.

Anastacia issued a hollow sigh. [[The things we do for love.]]

Josiri *thought* he heard more wryness than annoyance in her tone, but even after all their years together, she delighted in being a mystery. The smooth, gold-chased samite porcelain of her face never altered expression, save when interplay of light and shadow lent the branch-like patterns a hint of sardonicism.

The body hidden beneath the dress was the same, gilded and unyielding limbs jointed by thick leather, a doll-like form as proof from sensation as from harm. Life breathed into clay as surely as when Lumestra had created humankind in the Light of First Dawn. Beautiful, certainly, and every bit as unnerving if her gleaming black eyes dwelled too long upon yours. Even clad in the finest cloth and her white hair bound with golden ribbons, Anastacia could never have passed for human. Nor would she have wanted to, for it was no ephemeral soul bound to that body of clay and golden leaf, but that of an angelic serathi – a daughter of Lumestra.

Seldom did a day pass when Josiri went unhumbled by the knowledge that she'd chosen to share his life – which was almost certainly part of the reason she'd elected to do so.

"Who knows," he said. "You might even enjoy it."

[[We'll see.]]

Josiri turned his attention to the driver. "Come along, captain."

Kurkas made no move to clamber down from the coachman's bench seat. "Actually, sah, reckoned I'd stay out here and watch over the horses. Been a lot of thefts and—"

"The First Councillor's estate is as safe as anywhere in the city."

"As you say, sah," said Kurkas. "But I can't, in good conscience, be so remiss in my duties as to take the chance."

[[If I have to suffer through tonight's platitudes, Vladama, so do you.]]

Kurkas scowled. "As you say, plant pot."

He dropped to the driveway, leaving Josiri to once again speculate on why Anastacia – never blessed with overabundant patience – permitted Kurkas to address her so.

A pair of pages hurried forward to lead the carriage away. Kurkas still an unhappy presence somewhere to his rear, Josiri took Anastacia's arm and made his way up the stairs, towards the strains of music and the burble of conversation. A frock-coated servant met them at the door and guided them smoothly into the grand hall.

Murmured conversation and a quartet's lilting strings vied for dominance. At the chamber's centre, a dozen couples whirled a waltz beneath the gilded chandelier that was the sole source of light. All with fashionably pale skin, though no few owed their appearance more to powder than natural complexion. To a certain sort, bloodless skin was a mark of superiority. To Josiri, it spoke more of inbreeding and the most suspect and isolationist of ideologies.

At the chamber's far end, a low balcony overlooked events. Malachi stood atop it, his back to the room and his head bowed in conversation with a gold-robed priest.

"Lord Josiri Trelan and Lady Anastacia Psanneque."

Reactions to the steward's announcement were an education in themselves. Which eyes drifted towards the door. Which stared pointedly away. And the stolen glances that pretended disdain but were really fascination. The southwealder wolf's-head and his mistress. The traitor and the heretic. Josiri suspected half the folk in the room would have gladly led him to the gallows and Anastacia to the pyre. All the more reason to stand among them in defiance.

Kurkas, of course, didn't rate announcement.

A servant threaded his way through the crowds, and presented a tray of crystal glasses, brimming with ruby wine. "Refreshment, my lord?"

Josiri glanced at Anastacia, and shook his head. "No, thank you."

Anastacia glided between them and snagged a glass. [[His lordship would love refreshment. Please see to it that his glass is never empty.]]

The servant nodded and withdrew. Anastacia held out the glass with one hand, and propped the other on her hip.

"Ana ..."

[[I appreciate the gesture, Josiri, really I do, but just because I *can't* indulge doesn't mean you *shouldn't*.]] She offered a lopsided shrug. [[I promise not to stare.]]

Josiri took a sip, only to break off at Anastacia's soft, keening whimper. He stared, aghast. The whimper ceased, and she cocked her head – shorthand for a mocking smile her immobile lips could no longer form, just as the rich, dark fruits of the wine were no longer hers to sample. For a creature who'd once revelled in all the pleasures life had seen fit to offer, to be trapped in a body of unfeeling clay was the coldest cut. That Anastacia so often made a joke of it little disguised her sorrow.

"Don't do that."

[[Do what?]] The sing-song chimed with the innocence of a spring morning.

Josiri glared. He raised the glass again, only to break off as the whimper began anew.

"Ana!"

The whine faded. [[If you're to be like that, I think I'll take a turn on the terrace.]]

In other words, away from as many of the other guests as possible. "And leave me all alone?"

[[I agreed to accompany you. I didn't agree to be stared at.]]

"No one's staring at you."

[[They will, once they find their nerve. They always do.]] Her fingers closed around his, rigid and yet somehow warm. [[Drink. Mingle. But don't enjoy yourself too much. I see a lot of pretty and inviting faces here tonight. Remember that I can crush every bone in your body to powder.]]

"Yes, dear." Josiri stooped to kiss her forehead. "Maybe you'd go with her, captain?"

"Gladly, sah," Kurkas said feelingly.

As his reluctant companions retreated, Kurkas ducking awkwardly beneath the chandelier's mooring rope, Josiri cast about for familiar faces. He found a few. Grand councillors with whom he'd exchanged words both fair and foul. One or two captains of hearthguard, their loyalties proclaimed by the colours and emblems of their uniforms, and none of them looking much happier to be present than the departed Kurkas. And somewhere between those strata, guests of less certain rank. Churchmen, artists and actors – merchants not yet rich enough to ease passage to a councilman's chair. The good, but not yet necessarily *great*.

"Josiri!"

An enthusiastic wave heralded a train of ruby skirts and a trail of chestnut curls.

"Mistress Darrow."

"Mistress Darrow?" Green eyes sparkled. "We're very formal tonight."

"We're overcome by mortal terror. Anastacia gave stern warning about flirtatious behaviour."

"Then we've something in common, my bonny. Vona gave me the same lecture. Manacles were mentioned, along with losing the key thereof. I *had* taken a fancy to one of the servants – they're always so grateful – but if you've a better offer ... ?"

Josiri laughed. Hawkin Darrow was about as different from her wife in build and manner as could be imagined, with a dancer's grace and a generous nature. She was also something of an oddity that evening. A steward had no place among the finery of her betters, except as a servant.

"Incarceration for one and pulverisation for the other?" he said. "I've no desire to end up as a tragic fable."

Hawkin shook her head. Slender, musician's fingers plucked a wine glass off a passing tray. She clasped it tight and gave a rueful shake of the head that would have been convincing but for the wicked grin.

"Woe is me. This is why I'm only a poor steward. I can't even arrange a simple assignation with the most notorious man in the room. I might tell Vona you made a pass at me, just for appearances."

"Please don't."

The smile faded. "She told me what you found this morning. I'm sorry."

Memories of mist and a bloody archway flashed back. "We saved some. That will have to do."

Hawkin nodded, her eyes glassy. "Last year, when the vranakin took me . . . I thought I was going to die. I woke from a wonderful dream, and they were there, at the end of my bed. Waiting. I didn't even have time to scream." Her voice tightened. "I hope you find them."

"I intend to. And with Vona's help, I might actually succeed." He shook his head, the better to dispel unhappy memories. "Where is our gallant captain of the constabulary?"

"She and Izack are making military assault on the buffet. I pity the bystanders."

"And the children?"

"Constans is banished to his chambers. I didn't ask why. Sidara's around somewhere. Dressed prim and plain as you can imagine. Lady Reveque's hoping no one will notice her."

"It's the nature of mothers to worry after their daughters." A grey-haired woman appeared at Hawkin's shoulder, swelling the conversation circle to three. "And the nature of the Republic to make those daughters old before their time."

Hawkin smiled. "Lady Mezar, the cynic."

"A realist, if you please." She delivered the rebuke softly, sea grey eyes betraying no offence. "Malachi's the closest thing we've had to a monarch in a great many years. Those looking to share in his power will set their hopes on arranged marriage to his heir."

Josiri scowled. "Sidara's fourteen. She's still a child."

Lady Mezar laughed. "And when has that stopped anyone? It's not the marriage that's important, but the promise of it. The rest will wait. The Republic was built upon such traditions."

Those traditions *were* responsible for Lilyana Reveque being guarded with her daughter – but unflattering dress was only part of it. Where her ten-year-old younger brother often left the estate – albeit in the company of parents or servants like Hawkin, Sidara seldom did. A pious recluse, whose studies held sway over youthful enthusiasms, so the official word went. The unofficial truth, to which Josiri was privy and Lady Mezar was not, was that

Sidara was confined to Abbeyfields. For all that Josiri had readily sworn himself to secrecy regarding Sidara and her ... unusual talents, he'd nothing but pity for a girl he'd seen perhaps a handful of times in the past year.

"The Republic was built on a great many traditions," he said. "Some do far more harm than good."

"But are we a Republic any longer?" said Lady Mezar.

Hawkin's eyes lingered on expensive gowns and tailored coats. "Most people in this room would say so."

"Most people in this room are fools," Lady Mezar replied.

Josiri sipped from his glass to conceal a smile. "But not you?"

She shrugged. "I leave that for others to judge."

"You prefer to judge Malachi?" said Josiri.

"Someone should, don't you think? I promise you this, Lord Trelan. When I'm on the Council, I'll do everything I can to annul the position of First Councillor."

"Because you think Lord Reveque's in danger of becoming a tyrant?" The gleam in Hawkin's eye might have indicated amusement, or could equally have hinted at offence.

Lady Mezar shook her head. "From what I've seen, he's an honourable man. But life does strange things to honourable men. Especially when they learn that all the power in the world has its limits. Think on that, Lord Trelan, I beg you."

With that, she withdrew into the crowd.

"Very sure of herself, isn't she?" said Hawkin.

Josiri drained his glass. "She has reason. I wonder how she'd feel if she knew the tyrannous Lord Reveque supports her claim to the Privy Council seat?"

Hawkin arched an eyebrow. "Truly?"

He nodded. "He's not alone. She speaks her mind, and for the most part, it's good sense. Malachi as First Councillor? That's one thing. His successor might be something else entirely."

"You just don't want to be the only troublemaker in the room."

"Harsh words, from a woman who tempted me to indiscretion only minutes ago." Josiri cast a surprised glance at his glass, which had been refilled without his noticing. "But there may be some small truth to that."

*

The veranda was empty, the night breeze having driven guests to seek the gaiety of the house or the shelter of the trees. Kurkas was well content that it was so, protected as he was by the thick cloth of his uniform. But he worried about the heaviness of the air and the promise of rain. He'd been too long a soldier not to know when a storm was in the offing. He stared across the treetops, to the clouds looming above the skeletal ruins that gave Abbeyfields its name, and decided that the storm would hold off for a time yet.

That storm, anyway.

He crossed to the veranda where Anastacia stood, hands braced on the balustrade and expressionless eyes staring at the ruins of Strazyn Abbey. As ever, she gave Kurkas the impression that what she saw was not what he beheld, and he wondered if her ageless eyes had fallen on those stones before their humbling.

"We could take a turn around the gardens?"

[[Are there people in the gardens?]]

"One or two."

[[Then no, we couldn't.]]

A sharp *clink* drew Kurkas' gaze to the balustrade, and the spidery crack where Anastacia gripped the stone. Yes, a storm was coming. A sensible man would have sought shelter, battened down the windows and offered a prayer for those caught without.

"Right you are, Lady Psanneque."

[[Don't call me that.]]

"Right you are, plant pot."

She turned from contemplation of the distant ruins. [[You're insufferable, you know that?]]

Kurkas kept his eye fixed straight ahead. "Yes, ma'am. Not fit to stand in your shadow or breathe the same air. If you want your shoes licking clean, you've only to say. Haven't eaten since midday, and it'd be something of a treat."

The baleful stare dissipated into musical laughter. [[One of these days, I might say yes.]]

"And won't that be a day?" He chanced a smile. "You have worse, growing up in Dregmeet. And as for army rations—"

[[Have you really not eaten since midday?]]

First laughter, now concern. Weren't many folk who rated one, let alone the other. "Been busy. Be a while before your hearthguard will be anything like real soldiers."

[[There's food inside. Don't let me stop you.]]

"Orders is orders," Kurkas replied. "Besides, you've the look of one fixing to cause mischief. I wouldn't want you to happen to anyone."

More laughter. [[You really think I might?]]

"Why don't you tell me?"

With no reply forthcoming, he stared back at the half-glassed doors and the simarka standing sentry to either side. The bright lights and soft pastel cloth of quality folk whiling away the night in comfort and gluttony. For a moment, he was a child again, face pressed up against the glass, wondering at what it must be like to live in such a world. As hearthguard captain to a family of the first rank, he teetered on the threshold, but he'd never truly belong. Dregmeet was more a part of him than it was not.

[[*Ephemerals.* So certain of their place. So busy chasing after things that don't matter and ignoring things that do. If I still had my wings, my flesh – if I was still as my mother made me – I'd break every heart in that room, shatter every marriage and bring death so horrific and indiscriminate their grief would darken the sun . . . Yet still they'd crawl to me, begging for a word, a blessing.]] Anastacia stared down at her hand and flexed her fingers. [[A touch. Instead, I'm an outcast. A freak tolerated because of the bed I share, and pitied when they think my attention's elsewhere.]]

The words resonated more than they should. Or perhaps not. Fifteen years and more had flown past since Kurkas had lost eye and arm on the battlefield, and yet each time a gaze lingered on leather patch or folded sleeve he felt the loss anew.

"I didn't think it bothered you," said Kurkas. "It's not like you go chasing approval."

[[It didn't, and now it does. I can't explain.]]

"For what it's worth, I reckon you could still kill 'em all, if you put your mind to it."

The idea seemed to cheer her, for she stood straighter. [[That's right, I could.]] She sighed theatrically. [[But Josiri would never let me hear the end of it.]]

Kurkas chuckled. For all that Anastacia's humour teetered on the homicidal, he found it refreshing. And he clung to the uncertain hope that such words *were* spoken in jest.

"You know what I think?"

[[Honestly, there are days when I'm surprised you even can.]]

"Glad to have your sympathy, milady." He hesitated. "I think you're more human – more ephemeral – than you let on."

She glared. [[That's a horrible thing to say.]]

He grinned. "How long is it you've been stuck among us now?"

[[It feels like for ever. And this conversation longer than all the rest.]]

"We're rubbing off on you. Or Lord Trelan is, at any rate. A piece of you wants to be accepted, otherwise none of this would bother you."

[[Vladama? Your lips are flapping and making a distressing noise. You should put a stop to it before I take the decision out of your hands ... *hand*.]] She growled. [[You really think I seek acceptance from those *creatures*? All that squirming delusion driven by selfish appetite?]]

More than ever, given that Anastacia languished in self-delusion and appetites that differed only in scale and subject. However, Kurkas elected for discretion. Reduced in stature though Anastacia considered herself, a grip that cracked stone was not one to lightly offend.

"Not all. Just one or two. The ones that matter. You're not seeking worship, but friends."

Her posture shifted, the tilt of the head and the crook of her arms suggesting thoughtfulness. Kurkas found her easier to read than many of his flesh-and-blood betters. She'd honesty others lacked – while the language of her being made for challenging translation, it offered little deception.

[[And are we friends, Vladama?]]

He stiffened to attention. "Appalled you should even ask, milady. Dregmeet scum, me, and unbecoming of such hallowed company."

She turned away, returning to contemplation of the distant abbey. [[See you remember that.]]

But all the hauteur of her words couldn't disguise their warmth.

Kurkas stiffened further as the door opened a crack. A tall, waifish girl with loose-bound golden hair slipped onto the veranda. She set the door softly to, turned about, and jumped in startlement.

"I'm sorry." She averted her eyes. "I didn't mean to intrude. I just wanted some air. It's so stuffy in there."

The lie was smoothly enough told, but she'd much to learn about controlling her expression. The twitch of the cheek betrayed the deception as surely as golden hair and sharp features made plain her identity. Sidara Reveque was very much her mother's daughter – in appearance if not character. A dowdy grey dress could no more hide that than it could conceal the sun, and would likely struggle all the more as she left the last years of childhood behind.

"Not enjoying the party, miss?" asked Kurkas.

"Not really. It's like I've been glazed in honey and left out on a butcher's stall. I'm offered plenty of sweet words, but I don't think they're really for my benefit."

Kurkas grunted. Clever, too. Still, given her parentage, that wasn't really a surprise. Lord Reveque was canny, and Sidara's mother was said to be shrewder still. Not that Lilyana Reveque had ever bothered to speak with him. A keen proponent of charity she may have been, but her largesse seldom extended to speaking with the lower orders.

[[Then you should make them so, child.]] Anastacia turned in a swirl of gold and cream skirts. [[Even insincere flattery betrays desire for *something*. You don't have to appreciate the attention to make it serve you.]]

"You're Lady Psanneque?" The words were more statement than question. "Mother says I'm not to talk to you."

But she made no move to leave, and her expression remained more curious than worried.

[[Really, child? Why's that?]]

"She says you're a demon. A creature of the Dark that pretends to be a daughter of light."

[[And she invited me anyway?]]

"Father invited you. He trusts Uncle Josiri, and Uncle Josiri says you're a serathi."

[[He told you that?]]

"Not . . . Not exactly."

Kurkas stifled a smile. So Sidara had a knack for eavesdropping too? She'd take to politics like a natural.

[[Your mother hates me. Your father trusts me by proxy.]] To Kurkas' surprise, Anastacia's tone held no hostility, only a curiosity that mirrored the girl's. [[What do you think?]]

Sidara swallowed, but didn't look away. "I ... I think I should go back inside."

[[Because that's what your mother would want? And you never disobey your mother, I'm sure.]]

The first trickle of unease crept in. Kurkas cleared his throat. "Perhaps—"

[[Hush. Didn't you just berate me for unfriendliness?]] Anastacia stepped closer to Sidara. A fisherman linked to the fish by the line, except the more Kurkas lingered on the scene, the less certain he was of which was which. [[You have a brother, don't you? I imagine he never misbehaves.]]

"He never does anything but." The words came out in a breathless spill, tinged with pent-up defiance. "Escaping the grounds to go exploring the city, avoiding his lessons. And he's seldom punished. The only reason he's not allowed to attend the party is because he was missing for the better part of a day, crawling about in the catacombs, and never once a word of apology. Yet I'm stuck in this house, and they talk of letting him attend one of the church colleges next year, and perhaps join a chapterhouse after that! I never see anyone, and when I do it's for being my father's daughter and not for myself, and—"

She broke off, suddenly cognisant of speaking such in front of strangers – one of whom might well have been a demon and the other of which was a commoner, and therefore worse. She glanced at Kurkas, at Anastacia, and back again. "I have to go."

But again, she made no move.

[[Family is always difficult,]] said Anastacia. [[You should see mine. I've two uncles in particular who need only the slightest excuse to cause trouble. Tell me, do *you* think I'm a demon?]]

Sidara hesitated, eyes on Kurkas.

[[Oh, don't mind him, child. Even a soldier knows how to keep a secret, don't you, Vladama?]]

More and more, Kurkas was of the unhappy mind that he stood only partial witness to whatever was playing out before him. "Yes, milady."

He didn't try to sound convincing, but apparently Sidara had heard all she needed.

"I think you're beautiful. Your wings. Your hair. I saw you once before, I think. When Uncle Josiri first came to stay. You were watching over him."

[[You can see my wings?]]

Sidara nodded, transfixed. "It's like there are two of you, standing in the same place. One like the statue on grandfather's tomb, and the other the part that everyone else sees."

[[You know what I think?]] Her sing-song voice flooding with rare warmth, Anastacia cocked her head. [[I think you're the most intriguing person I've met in a very long time.]]

Sidara beamed, and bobbed a curtsey. "Thank you, Lady Psanneque."

[[Please, call me Ana.]] Her fingers brushed Sidara's brow and tucked a strand of golden hair back behind her ear. [[You'd like to show me something, wouldn't you?]]

"I'm not supposed to. I'm to keep it locked away, and not even think about it."

"Not to be impolite," said Kurkas to Sidara, "but what in Raven's Eyes are you talking about, miss?"

Anastacia turned a quarter circle and slid her arm across Sidara's shoulders. The frozen lips of her mouth pressed close to the girl's ear. [[Show him. He won't tell anyone. I won't let him.]]

Sidara giggled, a spark of youth breaking deportment's façade. With a conspiratorial glance at Kurkas, she knelt before the nearest simarka. She looked this way and that, peering carefully through the door before returning her attention to the lion. The construct stared back, unflinching and motionless, as they always did until roused by a proctor's command or an intruder's presence. Her fingers traced the stylised curves of the leonine mane and smoothed its jaw.

For a moment, nothing happened. Then, to Kurkas' astonishment, soft, golden light began to play about her head. Speechless, he looked on as the same glow awoke within the simarka's eyes. Swallowing hard, he reached Anastacia's side.

"Plant pot, this ain't—"

[[Hush.]] The sudden, insistent pressure of Anastacia's hand about his wrist lent urgency to her murmur. [[No one else can see.]]

She was right. From any distance at all, Sidara's light would be swallowed by that of the veranda's firestone lanterns. The house's drapes were closed, and the girl was kneeling well below the level of the door's glass panels. He'd just about remembered that discovery wasn't what concerned him when the simarka began to purr.

Kurkas had no other way to describe it. A deep, guttural rumble betraying profound contentment. And as if to dispel all doubt, the construct then leaned into Sidara's hand, guiding her fingers to the desired spot.

"I'll be damned," muttered Kurkas.

So much now made sense – not least Sidara's reclusiveness and Lord Trelan's oblique explanations as to why that should be so. Sidara had a proctor's magic, blazing with light and possibility. Fourteen was more than old enough to serve in the foundry, sharing that light with new-forged kraikons and simarka. Was necessary, even, as fewer and fewer were born to the light with every passing year. In fact, Kurkas couldn't think when he'd last seen a proctor with less than twenty-five years behind them. That Sidara wasn't already in the foundry meant that her parents hoped to keep her gift secret.

"Everyone thinks they're just machines," said Sidara, "but they're not. There's a spark of something else, but it's buried deep. It calls to me. Just like you called to me, Ana. Sometimes I can feel them clear across the city. I see snatches of what they see."

The house bell tolled for a quarter to midnight. The purr faded as her hand slipped away, the simarka growing silent and motionless.

"I have to go." She rose to her feet and dusted herself down. "I'm to be there when Father gives his speech."

With a glance torn between exhilaration and embarrassment, Sidara slipped back inside.

[[Don't worry, child,]] Anastacia said softly. [[I'm sure we'll speak again.]]

Kurkas looked from the simarka to Anastacia, her skirts fluttering in the southerly Ash Wind but the rest of her stock still in contemplation. He stifled a shudder. One storm had passed. Another was building. Anastacia had found her mischief.

*

Malachi stared down from the balcony as the midnight chimes faded, taking in guests arrayed for his speech. The clock's chimes had brought stragglers in from the gardens, servants had furnished them with dark wine for the toast, and all stood shoulder to shoulder. Waiting on him.

How things had changed. Little more than a year before, most wouldn't have accepted an invitation to Abbeyfields, fearing that to do so would be to show unwelcome allegiance. Now they feared refusal. A strange power to wield, and Malachi hoped never to grow comfortable with it.

Thin fingers found his and squeezed. He offered Lily a sidelong smile and glimpsed its reply beneath a veil worn to hide her scars. Such were the moments that made it worthwhile. The long hours. The interminable disputes. The Parliament of Crows' Emissary as an intimidating presence at his shoulder. For the first time since marriage had bound him to the Reveque family, his wife had reason to be proud of him. The Republic was changing, perhaps just a little, but maybe enough.

Footsteps on the stairs heralded Sidara's flustered arrival on the balcony. Squeezing past Captain Kanda, she took position at her mother's side. Late, but at least she was there. Unlike her brother, who showed no signs of growing into the responsibility that would one day be his. A problem for another time.

"My lords and ladies. Honoured guests." Malachi found his rhythm as nervousness faded. "Lily and I would like to thank you for sharing tonight with us. Life too often brings us together in moments of opposition, or sorrow. We forget that each day can be a celebration – a reminder of all the Republic has endured, and the struggles we've overcome."

He paused, letting his eyes touch on those he'd not yet had time to greet: Josiri Trelan, standing among the knot of guests beneath the chandelier. High Proctor Ilnarov, a quiet, dignified presence at the back of the room. Izack, Rother and Mannor, the masters of the city's foremost chapterhouses. Friends, or at least allies, and pushed to the back of the list because of it. Too many others needed a firm handshake and kind word to keep them true.

"Look around," Malachi continued. "Whatever our quarrels, whatever has happened in the past, we are all of the Republic. We all serve its prospects and its people. Remember that, as we continue to heal the wounds that sundered our southern kin. As we seek a peace with the Hadari Empire that has eluded us so long ... "

A few unhappy growls sounded, as was only to be expected. Until Jardon Krain sent word from Tregard, there were no facts to quarrel over, only concessions and humiliations to conjure. It would change soon enough.

"But let us never lose sight of what lends the Republic its greatness: the courage of its soldiers, the strength of its bloodlines, and above all, its unfaltering allegiance to Lumestra's light. My lords and ladies. Honoured guests. My friends." He raised his glass, the motion mirrored all around the room. "Our glorious Republic, may its light—"

A whip crack sounded. The mooring rope thrashed like a wounded serpent. Lantern light scattering mad shadows, the chandelier plunged. Malachi glimpsed Josiri falling clear, his arm tight about Hawkin's waist as he dragged her aside. Glass shattered and darkness drowned the hall to rising screams.

Malachi twisted on his heel. "Lily?"

She was already gone, running down the stairs, Kanda on her heels, her tone strident in instruction. The screams below turned to the commotion of vying voices and hurried footsteps – the slam of doors thrown open to the night. Malachi turned to Sidara, who met his gaze with wide eyes and a hand pressed to her mouth.

"Go to your room. I'll send for you."

She nodded blankly and departed, leaving Malachi alone in the dark.

By the time he looked out over the balcony once again, wan light gave shape to events. A floor covered with glass. The twisted wreckage of the chandelier watched over by horrified faces. And the bodies pinned beneath: a proctor, his gold robes already dark with blood; one of the maids, her body so mangled that only her uniform offered clue to her identity; and pinned beneath the chandelier's fluted stem, Sabelle Mezar stared blankly at the ceiling.

Malachi's blood ran cold before he felt the whisper of movement at his shoulder.

"You pushed us to this," murmured the Emissary. "Have a care you do not push us any further."

He spun around, but she was already gone.

Eight

"First night out on patrol, and the skies open," muttered Dvorad. "Queen's Ashes, but I get all the rotten luck."

Haval pulled his cloak tighter. Dvorad was indeed blighted by poor fortune. Everyone in the 2nd knew that, because he seldom ceased complaining. Poor rations, unfaithful women, feckless comrades, medical complaints that mystified physicians ... the litany went on. And would do so for some time, if left uninterrupted.

No one wanted that. Not Haval, and not the cluster of studiously blank faces sharing the shelter of the rocky hillside. Midnight was past, the patrol done. Ten bedraggled men and women in sodden uniforms and rain-slicked plate longing for the limited comforts of Arkgard. Krasta would have been better, but Krasta lay to the east, not the west, and had been abandoned the year before during Maggad Andwar's attempted invasion.

The watch-forts weren't exactly civilisation. They weren't meant to be. But their palisades kept out the wind, and their campfires held the promise of a hot meal, thin rations or not. If a body was to be stuck on the wrong side of the Ravonn, with Hadari lurking behind the eastern hills, better to be so behind walls and at garrison strength.

"Could be worse, sarge," he said. "And I reckon it's easing."

Dvorad peered suspiciously out from under the rocky overhang. "You might be right."

No sooner had he finished than Haval's words, spoken more in hope than truth, became prophecy. Hissing rain eased, the bright silver of moonlight broke through murky clouds. Even the wind, whose fingers had long ago pried beneath armour and rain-soaked cloth, faded to nothing.

And away to the west, its lights just visible through a strand of trees, the walls of Arkgard. Two miles that would have been nothing but misery in the rain now seemed no distance at all.

"That's good enough for me." Dvorad straightened into some semblance of soldierly appearance. "Move out."

The soldiers shuffled to their feet, as glad as their sergeant to be on the move.

"I don't like this."

Predictably, the objection came from Calarin. If Dvorad was the patrol's whinger, she was its alarmist, always seeing portent in the fall of shadow or the shape of spiderweb. But then she'd been born within sight of Fellhallow's eaves. Hallowsiders were strange folk.

Dvorad glared. "No one cares what you think."

"The air's not right," Calarin replied.

Now she mentioned it, there *was* a strange smell on the breeze. Not perfume as such, but a taste. Crispness beyond that which normally followed rain. If fond memory had a scent, it would be that. Haval shook his head. Nonsense, like everything Calarin spouted.

"Nothing's ever right for you," growled Dvorad, seemingly unaware of the irony. "Think old Jack's stalking out of the deepwoods to make mischief? You're welcome to stay and greet him, but I'm heading back."

Dvorad at the fore and Haval at the rear, the patrol headed briskly out through the rising mist.

No one spoke as their scattered line picked its way across the muddy moorland. Not even Dvorad about his ill-fitting boots, nor Calarin concerning the night's ill omens. Haval was as glad of the latter as the former. For all the church preached that Lumestra's light was supreme among the divine, it was hard to take solace in such promise when the sun was down. If Jack o' Fellhallow really was abroad that night, a prayer would be too long reaching Lumestra's ears to be worth the breath.

It was therefore with some relief that Haval reached the strand of trees. Halfway, and with no greater ills than skin chafed by sodden cloth, and flesh both hot and clammy from exertion after rain. Or at least, what Haval *hoped* was halfway. The mist had thickened. The sparse trees were shrouded by it, dark shapes half-hidden by a luminescent, vaporous grasp, as if the moon herself had reached down to embrace them. The scent of old memories was thicker than ever.

"I told you I didn't like this."

Calarin slid a hand beneath her tunic, fingers closing on the sun-pendant she always wore against her skin. The rest of the patrol were lost in the eerie splendour of the mist, figments of fleeting shadow. All too easy to imagine shapes moving where they shouldn't. Easier still to worry about having strayed from the path.

"Sarge?" The mist swallowed up Haval's shout as readily as it had Calarin's complaint. "Meskin? Daskarov?"

No answer came. Fear wormed along Haval's spine. By unspoken accord, he and Calarin picked up their pace. Boots snagged on root and fallen bough.

He'd drawn his sword even before the singing began.

The notes danced through the mist, borne aloft by a chorus of women's voices, and bore in turn sharp-accented words in a tongue Haval couldn't speak, but recognised from the close-fought horror of border skirmishes. Not Jack o' Fellhallow.

"Shadowthorns," he hissed.

Calarin let go her pendant and drew her sword. "Their women don't fight."

That was true. At least, true at the Ravonn. But Haval had heard rumours that things were different elsewhere. That women had ridden at the fore of Kai Saran's invasion of the Southshires. Tales of pale-witches, moonlight swords and victories pledged to faithless Ashana, whose silver burned away sunlight. With that cold, clear hymn echoing all about, such tales were easier than ever to believe.

A scream split the air. Not from ahead, where the rest of the patrol should have been, but away to Haval's right. He spun about, but the shadow-shrouded mist offered only uncertainty.

"We can't stay here!" Calarin's face was pale, her voice taut. The point of her sword twitched back and forth, challenging every shadow.

Instinct told Haval to run. Duty demanded he stay. "What about the others?"

Another cry. This one more whimper than scream.

Calarin shot him a harried glance. "Do you really want to find out? Or do you . . . "

The woman did not so much step out of the mist as coalesce from within it, her close-fitting white robes dancing in harmony with the drifting vapour, and the silver traceries of her wooden half-mask writhing. A dagger of angular, silver light flickered in the pale-witch's hand. Calarin fell, dying hands clutching at a ragged throat.

Through it all, the pale-witch didn't stop singing.

Haval bellowed to drown out the song, to drive back the fear clutching tight his chest. He hurled himself across Calarin's corpse, sword two-handed and swinging wild.

The dagger shimmered like glass. The blow that should have beaten down the shining blade and split the wooden mask instead scraped aside. Haval staggered, balance thrown, and cried out as a cold, searing spike slipped between breastplate and pauldron to jar against bone. The woman whirled away, untouched.

Blood slicked an arm suddenly numbed. The sword fell away into undergrowth.

Haval stumbled away. The pale-witch advanced, her white robes splotched scarlet.

The mists parted to a wild bellow. The pale-witch's song faltered as Dvorad's armoured shoulder thumped into her chest.

Down they went with a crunch of breaking bone. The shard-dagger skittered off the sergeant's breastplate as he kneeled above her. His sword thrust down, and the pale-witch's song ceased.

"Shadowthorns," Dvorad growled. "Bloody hate shadowthorns."

The mournful chorus heightened through the billowing mist. Three more pale-witches coalesced, daggers wicked in their hands.

Dvorad's shoulders dipped, then came up straighter with a sword levelled in challenge. His eyes met Haval's.

"Get to Arkgard! Warn them!" He rounded on the nearest pale-witch, sword alive in his hand and defiance in his voice. "Death and honour!"

Good arm cradling the other, Haval ran.

He drove hard for where he'd last seen Arkgard's walls, praying that the mists hadn't scattered all sense. He didn't look back as Dvorad's scream sounded, but forged on through mist and shadow, his desperate pace a match for a ragged, thundering heart.

The trees' oppressive shadow passed away to suggest clear skies overhead. Still Haval ran. The cruel, aching song faded behind, and still he ran.

He stumbled at the brook, ankle turning as rushing waters clutched at his boots. Muddy ground slipped away into a rain-soaked ditch. A palisade loomed dark through the mist.

"The shadowthorns!" he shouted. "The Hadari are coming!"

His words vanished into the mist without reply. Gasping for breath, Haval stared up at the walls, hoping for a sign he'd been heard. None came. Between mist and the diffuse glow of firestone lanterns upon the battlements, all was opaque.

The brook gave Haval his bearings. His course had run too far south. The gatehouse lay to the north. Lungs a fiery ache, he stumbled about the ditch's perimeter.

The drawbridge was down, without sentry in sight.

Relief rushed cold. Not a soul seen, when a dozen men should have offered challenge. Haval edged across the bridge, the crackle in his skin growing. The song might have faded to the east, but the scent of the mist remained. Memory and longing, all bound together.

He passed beneath the gatehouse, leaving bloody palm print as proof of passage. Still no challenge. No voices. No bodies.

The courtyard spread before him, vaporous tides ebbing and flowing about barrack house and stables. Horses champed and whinnied in their stalls. But there, at the base of the beacon tower . . . a shadow in the mist – a hint of king's blue cloak and steel armour.

He wasn't alone.

"The Hadari are here. They—"

The shape shifted and fell with a clatter. Not as would a body cast down or struck, but one who simply no longer wished to stand. Haval glimpsed Captain Bandar's bearded face, eyes closed and lips slack in a contented expression.

"Do tell." The young woman who'd let Bandar fall was unlike any Haval had ever seen. She wore no robes, nor mask to conceal her wistful expression and close-cropped ash-blonde hair – only a pale shift dress worn over skin shining silver. What beauty she had was not so much cruel as disinterested. A cat waiting to unsheathe claws, but uncertain of making the effort. "Which would you prefer, the dagger or the dream? It doesn't matter to me, but I am to give you the choice. Mother insists."

The mists ebbed, revealing bodies strewn beneath the walls. Some lay in pooling blood, weapons yet clutched in their hands. Others seemed untouched, their faces beatific amid slaughter.

Haval stood transfixed as the woman drew closer. Her left hand, which he'd thought empty, nursed a wicked blade.

Green eyes blazed into Haval's soul. The pressure of her being stole his breath. He'd never felt so small, so insignificant. For all her slightness, the woman felt vast, as if she filled all the space between the palisade walls, and more besides. He never even thought to regret the loss of his sword, because every fibre of his being screamed that she wasn't his to kill – that he'd never be worthy of offering her harm even if steel could threaten such.

"Well, ephemeral?" Her voice turned playful. "Shall I choose for you? Would you like that?"

Haval's answer fell dry on a dusty mouth. Somehow, he found the strength to tear himself away. As he lurched for the gatehouse, the archway crowded with pale-witches. Their song crashed back as if it had never left.

Breaths short and shallow, he stumbled for the battlement stair. His foot caught on the uppermost step. He sprawled against the rampart. And there, among the thinning mist and moonlit field, bore witness to the Republic's doom.

A great, golden column approached Arkgard from out of the eastern hills; serried ranks of scale armour and tower shields marching beneath banners of emerald silk and silver owl. Some led caparisoned horses by the bridle. Others bore great axes and war hammers. The Emperor's Immortals – the finest warriors of a realm that birthed little else. Behind them came archers and outriders in drab leathers; spear-bands and creaking wagons. Thousands of men, marching west beneath the cover of mist with bloody purpose in mind.

And without even turning his head, Haval saw three others just like it.

A hurried glance away south towards Sargard confirmed his horror. There, on the open meadows, a fifth column, and lagging behind at the eastern hills, a sixth. At the head of each, walking a dozen paces before the foremost banner, a woman of silver like the one he'd fled in the courtyard below. And in the spaces between, the alabaster robes and mournful song of the pale-witches.

Three such columns could have ringed Ahrad tight. Six would set the Eastshires burning. In that stark, terrible moment, Haval was seized by certainty that what he beheld was but a part of the whole.

"Glorious, isn't it?"

Haval grabbed at the wall, heart in his throat. The silver woman had reached his elbow without sight or sound to betray her approach.

"I don't understand Mother's reluctance." She spoke as one puzzling over a mystery. "Certainly it's gaudy, and crude beyond words. But the anticipation. The resolve. I'm certain it will only get better once the killing begins."

Purpose returned to Haval's sluggish thoughts. The beacon. It might not penetrate the mists, but it had to be tried. Ahrad had to be warned.

Shoving away from the palisade, Haval ran for the beacon tower's winding stair. With every step ascended, he left a piece of himself behind, trickling away with his blood. But the gold glinting in the dark drove him on, one faltering step at a time.

As he reached the top, he risked a glance behind. The silver woman stood on the battlements, her expression twisted as one puzzling at another's inscrutable deeds. Did she not grasp the beacon's purpose? Bleak mirth forced back fear. The oil-soaked logs waited in their geometric stack. The brazier burned close by.

One last effort.

With his good hand, Haval reached for a burning brand.

"Death and honour," he gasped.

He felt a featherlight touch at his neck. The world rushed warm and red.

Silver hands caught him as he fell, the embrace gentle, almost kind. Warmth faded before a creeping chill.

"Hush now," she breathed. "Secrets are sacred. But though you chose the dagger, you shall have the dream anyway. Because it pleases me. Forget this life, and let wonder carry you off."

Bloody fingers brushed Haval's brow. When they withdrew, they took with them pain, cold, fear, sight – all sensations save one. For that last, longest heartbeat he knew nothing but joy.

Lumendas, 1st Day of Wealdrust

Magic is neither merciful nor cruel. It serves only the purpose to which it is put. Such is true of all power, mortal or divine. A beneficent deity is merely one who has not yet found wrathful cause.

from the sermons of Konor Belenzo

Nine

While Sevaka's snores challenged the *Zephyr*'s creaking timbers, Rosa lay awake. Troubles loomed forth from days to come – the outrage and disappointment of family – but would wait. What mattered was the moment, and in the moment Rosa found only happiness.

Happiness, and numbness in her fingers. Sevaka wasn't without weight.

Rosa slid her arm free of the embrace and slipped from the master's cot. An indistinct murmur spoke of a departure not wholly unnoticed. Rosa missed sleep, or at least the sleep of which she'd once partaken. Her nights now were full of blurred nightmare.

Barefoot, she padded to the stern window and wiped away condensation with her palm. Beyond lay a wall of roiling white. All beyond the mooring rope was lost.

She froze, one hand still on the glass. Mist wasn't uncommon during the months of Fade, especially at Ahrad, and the confluence of its twin rivers. But strange things happened when the mists came down. She'd lived through such moments, if barely.

And then there was the scent on the air. Old days and old friends, bound together.

She shook Sevaka's shoulder. "Wake up."

Bleary grey eyes cracked open. A hand scrabbled for the edge of the cot. "'sa matter?"

"Something's wrong." Rosa clenched a fist, frustrated by unease without clear definition. "Or it might be. I'll be back when I can."

A brief kiss, a clutch of fingers, and Rosa reached for her dress.

*

"It's time," said Ashana.

Melanna tore her gaze from the Ravonn, from golden lines waiting ready in moonlit darkness. The watch-forts that guarded the bridges and fords had fallen without a fight, silenced by the daughters of Ashana and the lunassera. No warning. No beacon fires. Ahrad slept in thickening mist. This wasn't the way of war to which she'd been raised. No volleys of arrows to proclaim intent. No formal declaration at all. A rush of blades in the dark belonged to brigands, not to Emperors . . . or goddesses.

"Is there no other way?"

Ashana ceased her pacing through the rushes and halted beside the pool's thorn-tangled statue. Restless hands tugged at glimmering sleeves and smoothed hair that was in no way out of place. "How long has this fortress defied your people? How many thousands of your sons has it cast into the mists?"

"When did the Goddess stop answering direct questions?" said Melanna.

Ashana stared into the statue's eyes. Though time had taken its toll on the smooth, white stone, the crescent moon in her hands was recognisable as such. The woman's features shared little similarity with those of the Goddess. But then, Ashana claimed not to be the first of her name.

"Perhaps she never started," she murmured.

"Then start now." Melanna winced. That was *not* how one addressed a goddess.

Ashana turned from the statue, her lips holding a smile. Or perhaps it was an illusion of the mists, and uncertainty of the heart. "The Dark has taken root in Tressia. You've seen it. We can afford no half measures. No mercy. No regrets. It must be driven out and destroyed, or this world of Aradane will become one in its grasp."

Aradane. It wasn't the first time the Goddess had called it that, though to Melanna her home was one of vying nations, not single identity. She thought back to Eskavord. To citizenry and soldiers fallen to the Dark. Hundreds – thousands – bound to a single, malevolent will, their individuality extinguished. To skies choked with empty darkness, with neither sun nor moon to light the way. A place where names meant nothing, and inevitability smothered hope. Her heart ached to think of her own people thus conquered, to imagine the glories of the Silver Kingdom suffocated by unfeeling blackness. And yet . . .

"We could have warned them."

"Would they have listened?" Ashana asked wearily. "To a shadowthorn princessa who brought slaughter to their lands?"

Melanna winced at the hated slur. "Some might."

"And of those, how many are already touched by the Dark?"

A harder question. Those who'd showed Melanna kindness or deference were too close to Viktor Akadra, the man-of-shadow – the Droshna – in whom the Dark had taken root. They couldn't be trusted. Likely, they were already corrupted, even if they didn't know it. Even Josiri Trelan, who'd held Melanna's life and honour in his hands, but set her free.

"You see," said Ashana softly. "They don't recognise the rot. My divine siblings are blind to it, and will not offer champions as they did before. It falls to us to cut it out. Are you afraid?"

"Yes, Godd . . . Ashana."

"You should be. We should all be."

"Then let me take my place at my father's side, as an heir should."

"Soon. This is your father's hour. Don't resent that. For now, your place is here."

"Why?" Melanna flung a hand towards the mustered army, to the white robes among the golden scales. "You have an entire priesthood to serve you. A sisterhood of lunassera. I'm a princessa, forged in battle. I should be there. I should—"

"Because they are not my daughter."

The answer was no answer at all, for Ashana had no shortage of daughters shining silver along the grasslands. She drew closer and took Melanna's hands in hers. "Even necessary deeds have price. I need you to see for yourself. To understand."

"Then this is a lesson?"

"Not everything is a lesson, Melanna. Some things, simply . . . are."

Melanna found little comfort, and nothing in the way of answer. Only a reminder of duty. She was both Saranal and Ashanal, daughter of Emperor and goddess. She'd been born the first, and had chosen the second. On that bitter morning, she couldn't be both.

"Yes," Melanna hesitated. " . . . Mother."

This time, there was no imagining Ashana's smile.

The war horse champed restlessly, mirroring Kai Saran's own frustrations. For all that patience was the highest of virtues, he'd never mastered it – in great part because he'd made scant effort to do so, and never less than in recent years.

Crowns were not claimed by patient men. Nor was the glory of legend merely given to those who desired it. One was now his, but the other? And he wanted a legend. He needed one. For himself, and for those who would come after. The dichotomy of Empire: that it was ruled with wisdom and compassion, but the right to do so was earned and reaffirmed by the horror of the sword. And for all that Kai's blood burned with vigour he'd not felt in a decade, he felt the passing years keener than ever.

Twice in recent memory he'd almost died. A third brush with the Raven might be his last. He hoped only that if that were so, it would be from wounds suffered in victory or defiance, for those would cement his daughter's claim and thus ease his own passage into Otherworld.

Until then, the waiting. The fraying patience and the urge to thrust back one's spurs. Five hundred cataphracti Immortals silently at his back, the horses' scales as thick as the riders'. Beyond, a thousand more waited on foot, the renowned Tavar Rasha at their head. Behind them, men of Rhaled who paid tithe of fealty with spear and bow, or goaded the horned, leathery grunda into war from atop creaking wagons. Clansmen tithed from village and town, mustered beneath their chieftains' banners and awaiting the order of the havildars and sorvidars who led them. And further still, white robes and ghostly grace of their horned chandirin steeds lost to the mists, the sisterhood of the lunassera – the women who were the Goddess' handmaidens, and thus exempt from tradition that forbade women to fight.

Near eight thousand in all, and more behind, all come to usher their prince – their Emperor – to glory. A fraction of the might marshalling along the Ravonn. He wouldn't dishonour that service through display of weakness. And especially not with Elspeth Ashanal close by, side-saddle on a horse as white as the mists. If one did not show weakness to one's subjects, one certainly did not do so before the divine.

And so Kai Saran, Prince of Rhaled and Emperor of the Golden Court, ran a gauntleted hand across his steed's neck, and soothed its impatience to distract from his own.

Muffled hoofbeats closed. Mist parted about Kos Devren's wiry form and bear-pelt cloak. Guiding his horse across the column's face, the warleader tugged his helmet free and rested it across the horn of his saddle.

"Dawn's close, my Emperor. We should go now."

Elspeth glared, but held her tongue.

Kai stared into a grizzled face he knew as well as his own. Devren was a worrier. He never threw lives away out of eagerness, and spent them only in need.

"We wait," Kai replied.

"The ladders are ready. The catapults are ready. Your warriors long to close with the foe." Devren hesitated, the greying stubble of his jaw twisting. "If we wait for the dawn, the mist will burn away. Crossbows will fill Otherworld with our dead long before we reach the walls. But if we go now . . . "

Kai shook his head. Dawn remained at least an hour away. And as for the mist? It had come for the Goddess. He doubted it would retreat before the sun, unless Lumestra contested her hated sister. "Calm yourself. If Ahrad could fall to such an assault, it would have done so long ago. Better men than you and I have thrown their lives away for nothing on its stones."

Devren narrowed his eyes. "But not today?"

"Not today." Kai raised his voice and wheeled his horse about to face his cataphracts, trusting that the mists and still air would prevent it carrying to walls barely half a league to the west. "Today we come not just as warriors of Rhaled, but of Icansae, Silsaria, Demestae and others . . . " *That* was technicality more than truth, for Demestae had sent barely a hundred spears, its princes ever watchful of the hungry desert beyond their southern border. Others had sent even fewer, a tithe that expressed loyalty but served as reminder that the Empire could never truly stand as one against a single foe, lest a swarm of lesser enemies pick clean its lands. "Today the Empire fights as one. We will take recompense for our dead, and claim stolen lands for our own. We will drive out the Dark.

This is not pride. This is not vengeance. This is Avitra Briganda – a holy war, and a holy duty. And the House of Saran will see it done."

He raised his arm in salute and was repaid a thousandfold. Enough had seen. Enough had heard. He hauled on his reins and again stared west, and willed his words to truth.

"A fine speech." Elspeth's tone lay on the border between praise and mockery. The silver hand that gripped her horse's reins was dark with dried blood, as were her shift dress and the dagger tucked beneath her belt of silver cord. A feral creature, for all her composure. "Harbour no fear. Your destiny is to break Ahrad. I am charged to make it so, and I do not mean to fail."

Kai had been father to a daughter long enough to hear the brittleness in the promise, and to recognise the tension in her thin shoulders. Though she strove to conceal it, Elspeth was as impatient as he, and nervous besides.

"Have you been in battle?"

"I am of my mother's dream," she replied archly. "I have seen sights of which you cannot conceive."

Kai chuckled. Yes, so very like Melanna. Perhaps all daughters were thus, ephemeral or divine. "Then I'm certain you'll bring her nothing but honour."

"*That* was never in doubt."

But her shoulders eased, all the same.

Castellan Noktza was already above the outer gatehouse when Rosa arrived, a pair of young heralds at his back, and Major Tsemmin of the 4th in close attendance. Despite the hour, he managed a clear-eyed stare. Not a crease in his uniform was out of place. His *scarlet* uniform. The colours of Prydonis, seldom worn, did more to portray concerns than any cast of expression.

"Commander Orova . . . " A wry flicker of his eye accompanied the greeting. "An eventful night?"

Rigid self-control held Rosa from glancing down at her uniform, hurriedly donned and without armour. She knew it to be in disarray, having tarried in her quarters as short a time as she could manage.

"You tell me."

She passed beneath the gatehouse's limp flags and took position beside a sentry. The mists were thick beyond the wall. Past the Silverway-fed moat, the sluices of the outer barbican were barely visible. Everything beyond lay drowned in white.

"It came down about an hour ago. Swept in from the east." He shrugged. "I don't know why it bothers me so."

"Any word from the watch-forts?" asked Rosa.

"None." Major Tsemmin had the look of a man suffering strained patience, but not wanting to challenge his superior's judgement. "It's mist. A warm day and a cold night. Nothing mystical about it."

Rosa suspected the reasonable argument was buttressed by Tsemmin's reluctance to drag his immediate superior from beneath the covers. Commander Davakah took his sleep very seriously, and woe betide any underling who disturbed it without good cause.

Noktza scowled. "Then why are my thumbs pricking? Rosa?"

She glanced along the battlements. Golden sparks marked krai-kons on patrol or at sentry, and sparse braziers where flesh-and-blood sentinels held bitter night at bay. A score or so humped pavissionaire-silhouettes dotted the mists, the crossbowmen's outlines misshapen by the heavy willow pavissi shields upon their backs. Few enough, if mischief abounded.

Setting her back to Noktza, Rosa peered east, towards the hidden Ravonn. Beacons would have glowed orange, even through the mist. Maybe Tsemmin was right. A warm day, a cold night and nerves on edge. But it was a poor soldier who never trusted her instincts.

"Call out the guard. Get blades on these walls."

Noktza nodded. "Thank you, commander. I concur."

Tsemmin frowned. "I must object, my lord. To rouse a regiment over fancy ... "

"They're soldiers, major, and accustomed to a superior's whimsy." Noktza waved at the nearest herald. The girl bobbed her head and scurried away towards the gatehouse's bell tower. "If it's nothing, we'll call it a drill. If it's not? Well, we'll have more to worry about than Commander Davakah's beauty sleep, won't we?"

Rosa hid a vicious grin. As she did so, her eye fell on dark shapes closing from the barbican. Five figures. Four in a loose square, advancing with the marcher's gait of common soldiers. The fifth walked at their centre, the mist stealing all clues to identity.

A scuffle of feet on stone presaged the arrival of a flush-faced herald.

"My lord, there's a man at the gate." The boy clasped his fist in salute. "Claims urgent tidings from Tregard. Captain Vorrin sent him through, under escort."

Rosa glanced back at the barbican approach, though interplay of height and distance now obscured the group beneath the walls. "Urgent news" could have meant anything. Communication from the Hadari capital was almost unheard of, but then so much Hadari behaviour of late defied usual pattern. One of the Council's spies? A defector? A fugitive? One of Lord Krain's entourage?

"Did he now?" Noktza raised his voice. "Major Tsemmin, the battlements are yours. Commander Orova, would you be so good as to join me? And perhaps round up a handful of knights, in case of nastiness?"

"Gladly, my lord," said Rosa.

With a last glance out into the mists, she made for the stairs.

The mist muffled Ahrad's bells, but couldn't disguise them entirely. Devren rose in his stirrups, vainly peering into the murk for some clue of what had come to pass.

"They know we're here," he said. "It must be now, my Emperor, or not at all."

Kai glanced at Elspeth. The daughter of the moon shook her head.

"No," she said. "Trust my mother. Wait for the sign."

Devren shot a pleading look. "My Emperor . . . "

Kai waved a hand. "Have faith, old friend."

Devren lapsed into silence. Kai gripped the pommel of his sword and stared off into the mists, praying the Goddess had not erred.

Rosa and Noktza met guard and escort beyond the twin gates. Three armoured and wolf-surcoated Knights Sartorov of the ready garrison stood at their backs. Above and behind, bells chimed out. Ramparts shook to the scuffle of feet on stone. The outermost gate stood ajar. The innermost was barred shut at Noktza's command, the intricate mechanism of cogs and gears driving steel bolts deep into the foundations.

The messenger, if such he truly was, stood in the middle of the drawbridge, his guards a little behind. A man of unimpressive height and average build, he was clad in a green cloak and studded leather armour of unfamiliar type. That alone would seem to have placed him as denizen of lands far to the south and east, but for fair skin and dirty blond hair which spoke to Tressian descent.

"You are the master of this fortress?" His voice was deep, the words sharp-edged.

Noktza ignored him. "Was he armed?"

"No, sir," said the sergeant of the escort. "He had only this."

Another guard stepped forward with a silver box. Measuring roughly a foot in each dimension, its sculpted curlicues and whorls dizzied the eye.

Noktza shifted his gaze to the prisoner. "Who are you? What is this?"

"I am a bearer of tidings from the Emperor Kai Saran; from Queen Ashana of Evermoon and Eventide. *That* is accompaniment to those tidings."

Noktza's cheek twitched. His eyes didn't leave the messenger. "Rosa?"

She approached the box. The hasp was simple enough, without artifice or obvious trap. She unfastened it and creaked back the lid.

A severed head lay on emerald silk, eyes closed peaceably in stark contrast to the violence of the death.

She knew the face, with its neat, grey beard. Its eyes had shone with prospect and possibility but weeks ago, before setting out on what she'd considered a fool's errand. So much for dreams of peace.

She glanced away, a muscle twitching in her throat. "It's Lord Krain."

Noktza's sword cleared its scabbard. Knights pressed forward.

"And the message?" Noktza snarled. "Answer swiftly, for a box of your own beckons."

The man snorted, his reply gaining in pace and volume until the words rippled like thunder. "It is simply this: that there can be no peace for those who kneel to the Dark."

He held aloft his hand, and what had before been empty now held a starlight spear. The form of man bled away, and a dark knight stood tall, inky black cloak billowing behind. Green eyes blazed beneath an antlered helm. He strode into the knot of blades, growing in stature until his antlers brushed the archway keystone.

"Demon!" howled Noktza. "Bring it down!"

The spear flashed out. The castellan collapsed in a pool of his own blood. A Sartorov vanished over the side of the drawbridge and into the moat's murky waters. Another crunched against the gatehouse wall. The third struck the outer gate's timbers with a sickening thud and collapsed into the roadway.

Rosa drew her sword. "With me! With me!"

One of the demon's erstwhile guards dropped to his knees, hands clasped in prayer. The others charged with her, screaming to dull their fear.

The demon turned. The spearhead arced out.

Rosa's world rushed red. Wet, meaty thuds echoed beneath the arch. Those screams that didn't fade entirely turned mewling. When sight returned, she lay among the dead and dying, sucking for breath that wouldn't come, bones grating in her arm.

"Close the gate."

Her words were little more than a gasp, speckled by rush and pop as ribs reknit.

The demon bore down on the outer gate.

Rosa hauled herself up onto her good elbow. She strove to ignore Noktza's accusing, sightless stare and the whimpers of the dying.

"Close the damn gate!"

Her second shout was louder, driven by a whooping gasp from healing lungs. The rattle of chainways joined to the commotion of the reveille bells. The outer gate creaked inwards.

Gears bit. Bolts locked into place. The way was closed.

The demon halted, stymied by the gate.

Sensation returned to Rosa's left hand as bones scraped back into place. She clambered to her feet and flexed her fingers. A voice at the back of her head told her to run, to beg forgiveness – anything but rouse the demon's ire or draw its notice.

But it was a champion's duty to stand.

Rosa's left hand snagged Noktza's broadsword. Heavier than hers. A butcher's blade. But that was good. Heavy was good. Anger was better. She let it rise, fire filling veins that felt so little. Better the demon was trapped outside the walls, and she with it, than both inside.

Unaware of her approach, the demon took his spear in both hands and raised it aloft.

"The declaration has been made!" he bellowed. "Honour is satisfied! Let there be war between the Republic of Lies and the Silver Kingdom!"

The spear slammed down with a hollow *boom* and a flash of searing white light. The ground shook, and the walls of Ahrad screamed.

Ten

The screech of dying stone reached Melanna a heartbeat before the mists boiled apart. Stalwart of untold decades, Ahrad's outer wall did not yield easily, but yield it did, the stones of its gatehouse – and much of the adjoining wall – hurled upwards and outward. As the mists rushed back in, masonry and the dark specks of bodies plummeted from the skies to dam the moat.

And there, where the gatehouse had once stood, a vast, antlered figure brandished a starlight spear to the sky.

A clarion sounded on the hillside to challenge the watch-bells' chimes. The hillside shook to the thunder of hoofbeats and drums, the owl banner and her father's moonsilver crown at the fore.

Without her.

Melanna fought the urge to seek her steed among the reeds. Her father would triumph. The way was clear. Near half the eastern wall had toppled with the Huntsman's strike. Ragged wounds gaped in the towers. What had once been a broad moat was now an uneven causeway of wreckage, strewn with corpses. The outer bailey would fall, and then . . .

And then . . .

Melanna stared at the Huntsman, already stalking away up the bailey's rise, bathed in light that somehow seemed . . . wrong. What should have been pure silver bore a reddish tint. She gazed up at the moon and saw that its majesty had darkened.

"Ashana?"

She turned. The Goddess stood motionless beside the statue of her former self, eyes closed and hands clasped in imitation of devout prayer.

Melanna drew closer. The Goddess' pale skin was lined, her flaxen hair shot through with grey. Melanna gazed again at the slighted moon and wondered at the price of victory.

"Ashanael Brigantim!"

Kai Saran held the Goddess' sword aloft so that all might see its flames, and rowelled his steed to the charge. Quarrels hissed from the north as the outer barbican's marooned garrison shook off their horror. One tugged at his cloak. Another skittered across his armoured shoulder.

Melanna would never forgive him for riding into battle without a helm, but in that moment, with the cold air stinging his cheeks and his blood rising to the thrill of battle, he didn't care. How long since he'd felt thus? Years? Decades? Young again. Invincible. Unstoppable. With each galloping stride, the burden of years sloughed further off, swept away by the promise of the drums.

His steed balked at the mass of part-submerged masonry that had been Ahrad's moat. Kai drove on into the clouds of stinging dust. The Goddess had promised triumph, and so triumph there would be. A lurch, a shudder. A scrape of hoof on stone. Then the ground was firm underfoot once more. His horse strained to the gallop through shattered ballistae, ruined kraikons and the mangled bodies of the garrison.

A thin line of king's blue shields waited on the rubble crest. Two-score men and women clad in the overlapping, segmented steel plate that was the pride of the Tressian forges; pale, horrified faces all but hidden by close-set helms.

Kai allowed a moment's admiration. Few stood long before the golden thunderbolt of his Immortals. To do so now, and in such paucity of number? In the face of divine wrath and disaster? Remarkable. Worthy of the highest praise.

"Ashanael Brigantim!"

Shields buckled as his steed crashed home. Kai struck aside a halberd's blade and leaned low to split the fellow's helm. Devren struck to his right. The warleader's long spear cheated a shield's steel rim to find flesh behind. Then came the screams of men and horses, the killing weight and the press of bodies. The hot stink of death and fear that clogged the throat and roused the senses.

A sword grazed the scales at Kai's waist. Another clanged off his golden shield. He sent fire to take the attacker's throat. Then the pitiful shield wall was broken, panicked cries drowning out the moans of the dying. There was only the open ground of the bailey and fleeing foes.

"Ashanael Brigantim!" Kai bellowed at the top of his lungs, and wondered if the Goddess saw his deeds.

"Saran Amhyrador!" Devren shouted the wild rejoinder, claiming victory not for the Goddess, but his Emperor. A thousand voices took up the cry.

"*Saran Amhyrador!*"

To north and south, the bailey was full of proud gold and fleeing king's blue. To the west, a new line of shields formed before the Huntsman's advance.

Elspeth rode past, musical laughter wild behind. With dancer's grace, she slipped from side-saddle to one hand about the saddle's horn and a foot in a stirrup. A fleeing woman fell to the dagger's kiss. Then the daughter of the moon was atop her steed once more, away in search of fresh victims.

"*Saran Amhyrador!*"

The bellowed salute rippled beneath the open sky, and a moon whose silver face bled crimson.

And Kai Saran, to whom the Goddess had promised a victory no other had won, spurred anew.

Sevaka staggered onto the *Zephyr*'s deck, sleep scattered by the onslaught of watch-bells, drums and the clash of battle. The mist that worried Rosa so had gone, replaced by swirling dust.

The inner harbour was a streaming mass of bodies. Soldiers ran for the walls, some still pulling on armour. Families and servants milled about, lost to panic and confusion. Haggard, exhausted expressions matched Sevaka's own sleep-deprived mood.

Alith met her at the gunwale, face taut in an attempt to conceal fear. Sixteen summers old, or so she'd said to escape Dregmeet. The claim had never looked more a lie.

"Captain? What's happening?"

"What's *happening*?" said Sevaka, incredulous. "The war has found us."

She fought pirates, not the Empire's golden legions; aboard ship, the contest of arrow and ballistae. The brawl of boarding action. Blessed Endala, but she'd no place on solid ground and serried ranks. She belonged to the sea.

Alith knotted her fingers in the Sign of the Sun. "Maybe it's Last Night."

Last Night. The Reckoning of the Gods. One final bloody conflict to split the world before Lumestra raised the faithful into the light of Third Dawn. "Don't talk nonsense. It's just the shadowthorns come to die on the walls. This is Ahrad, the Eskagard. There's no safer place in the Republic."

She hoped Alith's inexperience blinded her to all that was wrong with the assertion. The blood moon was only part. The stone dust on the air. The screams and clamour of swords closer than they should have been. The milling dockside that spoke to failing leadership. Where was Noktza? Where was Rosa?

"Wake the others." Sevaka started towards the gangplank. "I'll be back soon."

The girl hurried away just as the sky lit to flame.

The darkness was a vice about Rosa's body. Each breath drew down bitter dust. Each sonorous heartbeat pounded like a funeral drum. And beyond the darkness, muffled sounds she knew so well. The strike and the parry. The wet rip of torn flesh. Hoarse bellows of fear and command. The thunder of hooves.

She pressed down outspread palms. Stone scraped on stone. Her back strained. Shoulders screamed. Something rumbled above her head. The vice tightened, crushing her down. She snarled, and regretted it at once, for what little air lingered in the darkness pricked a thousand needles at her lungs.

Memory rushed back. The demon. The falling gatehouse. She was trapped beneath the rubble. Helpless while the Hadari brought death to Ahrad.

Anger returned. The anger she'd known all her life, but which had never been worse than in the months since her "death". The anger she fought to control lest it bring her to ruin.

Not this time.

Fury galvanised strength. The Raven had named her true. She wasn't ephemeral any longer. She was different. Stronger.

Rosa braced anew, and heaved. Again, the scrape of stone on stone. Again the feeling of the darkness pressing close. Again the impossible pressure across her spine and shoulders. Limbs that ordinarily felt so little trembled and screamed. She ignored them.

Degree by degree, she forced elbows straight. Weight shifted. Rubble clattered away. Fresh air filled starving lungs. Light bled through, and darkness fled. The sounds of battle reached murderous crescendo. With a ragged, wordless scream and masonry spilling from her shoulders, Rosa staggered into nightmare.

The curtain wall fallen, and the gatehouse gone. Ladders against the barbican's walls. The outer bailey overrun by shadowthorns and the garrison's bloodied dead. Silver women striding beneath a crimson moon. The sky screaming with fire as catapults rained death behind the middle and inner walls. Scattered knots of blue shields and hawk-banners shuddered. Golden light sparked as war hammers cracked a kraikon's outer shell and left the brute inert.

Of the demon, she saw nothing. But beyond the moat, a second wave of Hadari gathered – Immortals advancing in lockstep with tower shields held high.

"Saran Amhyrador!"

A cataphract closed at the gallop, sword flashing down. Rosa flung herself aside, the wind of his passage tugging at her tattered uniform. She cast around for a weapon as he wheeled about. Her sword was lost beneath the rubble. Noktza's too.

She scooped up a hunk of masonry and hurled it overarm at the cataphract. Stone crunched against scale. The shadowthorn twisted in the saddle, his charge awry.

Rosa leapt. Her shoulder thumped into his waist. They fell, she atop and he below. The impact of the ground scattered the sword from his hand.

Rosa's first punch buckled the metal of his helm and split her knuckles. Her second struck him cold. Those that followed, born of frustration and failure and fuelled by ragged breath, hammered home until her fist was slick with blood.

She lurched upright, gasping for breath, eyes darting between her bunched fist and the mangled corpse. The first time she'd killed that way, she'd been overcome by horror. Now she yearned for more. She stooped to claim the cataphract's tasselled sword and golden shield, expecting to see the Raven laughing at her. But of Otherworld's master, Rosa saw no sign.

Trumpets sounded. Hadari shields advanced across the stone-clogged moat. Hundreds. Thousands. More than enough to sweep aside the outer bailey's lingering resistance. An army out of myth, with a demon for its herald and treachery as its clarion.

Rosa cast her gaze to the nearest knot of Tressian soldiers: a thin score trapped against a tower's jagged stump as golden infantry hacked and hammered at failing shields. Doomed. Fleeting. Like all ephemerals. But the Raven had been right. She wasn't like them.

She wasn't a person, wasn't ephemeral. She was eternal. She *was* myth. Let the shadowthorns see how an eternal fought.

"Essamere!" The fury of the battle cry bore Rosa over the gatehouse rubble and down towards the ruined tower. "Essamere!"

Warned by her howl, the rearmost shadowthorns spun about. An Immortal took the rim of her borrowed shield in his throat. Another screamed as her sword pierced scales. A third hacked down. Rosa staggered as his blade bit through flesh and cracked against her skull.

Pain flared black, but pain too was ephemeral. Rosa screamed to speed its passage. Red wrath rose in its place. The third Immortal died with his throat torn away. Beyond, king's blue shields rose taller as the pressure against them slackened.

"*Death and honour!*"

The cry went up from within the ring of shields, a growl of hope rekindled rising beneath. The Hadari, caught between a woman who could not die and the valour of Tressia reborn, faltered.

And Rosa lost herself to the red.

The shout rang out as Sevaka reached the battlements.

"Get clear!"

A dozen men hurled themselves aside as the fireball roared over the parapet. It snatched one from the rampart and bore him screaming into the inner bailey. Flame crackled across tents and outbuildings. Horses whinnied distress. Even as Sevaka regained stolen breath, another fireball crashed home against the northern bastion, setting wooden hoarding and ballista alight. In the smoke-strewn slaughter of the outer bailey, isolated soldiers dwindled and perished as Hadari spears pressed forward across the rubble-choked moat.

Sevaka forced her way along a rampart crowded by pavissionaires of the 7th. They parted reluctantly. Word of a Psanneque had spread. Even with the walls shuddering and the outer bailey crowded with shadowthorns, prejudice held sway.

"Captain Psanneque!" The ranks that had parted so sluggishly for Sevaka showed no such impediment for Lady Sarravin. "What brings you to my wall?"

On the tower behind, a kraikon heaved a last mighty crank of a ballista's windlass. A bolt the girth of a tree shot away and ploughed a bloody furrow in the outer bailey.

"I'm supposed to make my crew available to the ready garrison's commander."

Lady Sarravin snorted. "Major Tsemmin? No one seems to know where he is. Nor the castellan." Pulling a lieutenant aside, she took his place on the rampart and stared towards the ruin of the outer wall. "Likely they're beneath all that."

If a night's carousing retained any embrace on Emilia Sarravin, nothing showed. Her uniform was crisp as ever, her back arrow-straight. Only a wisp of hair, escaped from a plait, suggested anything other than the pinnacle of composure. Sevaka, in her weatherworn naval coat and with her disarrayed hair hidden by her cocked hat, felt shabby alongside.

Sevaka's throat twitched. "And Ro ... And Commander Orova?"

"Raven only knows."

"Then who's in command?"

"In here? I am, until someone tells me otherwise." She shrugged. "Out there? I've sent a herald. Until then, we hold the line until we can't hold it any longer, and hope the shadowthorns wear themselves out."

A fireball shattered against the upper rampart. Flame spattered across the battlements, the hot rush of burning oil bitter. Soldiers screamed as the fires took them. Others rushed forward with spread cloaks to smother the flames.

"What are they playing at?" murmured Lady Sarravin. "They need stone shot. Fire won't breach these walls."

Maybe so, but it was doing a fine job elsewhere. Half of the middle bailey was ablaze, and the inner in dire likelihood of following suit. "What brought down the wall?"

"I didn't see, but we've two left." A shadow of doubt crowded Lady Sarravin's eyes. Talk all she might about Ahrad's strength, the outer wall was a sore loss. "And surprise is a flighty bird. Once flown, it's gone for good. The shadowthorns have shown their hand. Now they'll feel our fist."

Pavissionaires thickened on the middle bailey's wall, volley after volley of quarrels hissing away to join the inner wall's ballista-fire.

"Last I heard, the shadowthorns haven't even approached the cross-walls," Lady Sarravin went on. "If they're content to die in the east, I'm happy to oblige. And I've had the bridges cut, just in case they change their minds."

Sevaka nodded. The cross-walls split the outer and middle baileys along the north-south line, effectively dividing them into two separate east and west expanses, each served by its own set of gates. The cross-walls were connected to the curtain walls by narrow bridges – once cut, an attacker faced an uncertain climb across smooth stone through a storm of crossbow fire.

"And in the west?" she asked.

"Clear for now," Lady Sarravin replied. "Your crew ... are they steady?"

Sevaka forgot Alith's tender years. "As stone."

"Then I'll borrow them and you, if I may? I can always use more eyes in the west."

Sevaka nodded assent, though it wasn't a question, despite the phrasing. Strange to feel resentment, even among so much death. She didn't *want* to fight from Ahrad's walls, but to be sent away? That smacked of the Psanneque curse at work. At least Lady Sarravin had tact enough to make it a suggestion of usefulness, rather than outright dismissal.

"Of course, commander."

"Good. I'm very grateful to ... " She stared past the middle wall. "Queen's Ashes, but I don't believe it."

Sevaka followed her gaze to the outer bailey, to a swathe of dark blue amidst the carnage – Tressian soldiers, shields levelled and hoving a bloody path across the corpse-choked field towards an embattled shield ring. Even as Sevaka watched, the advancing shield wall ground to a halt; a cataphract charge broke apart on its hedge of blades. As the Hadari assault crumpled, the shield ring of erstwhile victims broke apart and ran headlong to bolster their rescuers' formation.

Between smoke and the eerie moonlight, it was too far to recognise faces, but Sevaka didn't need to see to *know.* Savage glee mingled with heartfelt relief. "It's Lady Orova."

The lieutenant so lately displaced from his position on the walls shot her a contemptuous look. "Could be anyone."

Lady Sarravin glowered. "Your superiors are talking, Lieutenant Borgiz. Have a care they hear nothing unfortunate."

Borgiz flinched and stared away.

Lady Sarravin's lips twisted apology. "You're sure, captain? My eyes aren't what they were."

"I know what she's capable of," Sevaka replied. "And anyway, does it matter?"

It mattered greatly to her, of course, but to Lady Sarravin it was a balancing act. Were a few score survivors worth the risk of a sally?

Lady Sarravin's brow set in determination. "Captain Psanneque? The walls are yours."

Sevaka blinked. While it was true that a naval captaincy – even for so small a vessel as the *Zephyr* – meant she outranked everyone on the walls save Lady Sarravin herself, the reversal from moments before set her head spinning. "I beg your pardon?"

"I'll leave you my pavissionaires, but I'll need the rest. You boy!" She hollered this last to a herald crouched in the shadow of the drum tower's stairway. "Lord Strazna's down below. Tell him I'm calling in his debt from Talnost. I want his knights at the gatehouse. All of them."

The herald bobbed his head and scurried away down the stairway.

"You mean to sally out?" Sevaka still couldn't quite believe it. "Into that?"

Lady Sarravin nodded. "It's mostly cavalry out there at the moment and no archers to speak of. If we go out hard and locked tight, they'll back off. Might even get some lost lambs back into the fold. The 7th does *not* abandon its own."

The cataphract's sword hacked down. Rosa caught the blow on her shield and lunged. The shadowthorn slipped from the saddle and his horse bolted, dragging the dying man away across the churned ground of the outer bailey.

Cheers rang out behind as the cavalry wheeled away, their bloody lesson learned.

"On!" Rosa shouted, her voice thick with blood and dust. "If their spear bands catch up to us, we're dead!"

The shield wall shook apart and resumed its march to the middle gate. Even in the drifting smoke and blood moon's uncertain light Rosa made out pavissionaires on the battlements.

"Banners high!" she shouted. "I don't want to get shot!"

A backward glance confirmed the tattered company flags of the 2nd stood tall above helm and halberd, the spear-points bright atop their banner poles. It also revealed the gleam of gold, and spears lowered to the charge.

"Shadowthorns behind!" cried Captain Ragda. "Shields!"

The formation shuddered to a halt, steel rims clashing as shields locked anew. Rosa itched to leave her position, to stand against this new charge as she had so many others, but knew better than to succumb to temptation. The double circle of overlapping shields held only as long as it went unbroken. And Ragda knew his business – even if he *were* a Prydonis. What she'd have given for a hundred like him at that moment ... Or fifty Knights Essamere.

Dark rain hissed from the wall, the vast shadows of ballista-shot flanked by a swarm of quarrels. Screams split the air. Fresh cheers shook the shield ring.

The cataphracts spurred away, leaving dead behind.

"Are we clear, Captain Ragda?" said Rosa.

"As a spring morning! Courtesy of the 5th's shooting."

Rosa's neighbour spat. "The 5th? Probably aiming at us and shot wide."

She stared up at the looming cliff of the middle wall. How far to the gate? A hundred yards, maybe less. Hard to tell with the gatehouse drowning in smoke from the bombardment. For all that, safety was in sight. Or the illusion of such, for there was no telling if whoever commanded would dare risk the inner bailey by their rescue. It didn't matter. Dead was dead, whether at the gate or beneath the walls. Better to seek salvation than assume it lost.

So why the hesitation?

"We've shadowthorn spears marching straight for us," called Ragda. "We've outstayed our welcome."

That settled it. There was no future in being caught between the anvil of infantry's shields and the hammer-blow of a cataphract charge.

She opened her mouth to issue an order and closed it again without a word. The pavissionaires were still shooting. Not *behind* Rosa's pitiful shield ring as before, but to her front. At the billowing smoke where the gateway should have been.

The Dusk Wind gusted. The smoke twitched but didn't wholly clear. It wasn't smoke at all, but the folds of the demon's cloak, pierced in a dozen places with crossbow quarrels. His mantle bristled with them. The starlight spear shone in his hand. Intent blazed brighter still.

"Queen's Ashes," breathed Rosa's neighbour. "What *is* that?"

Dark liquid gushed from hidden openings in the overhanging rampart. Steam rose from shoulders and antlered helm. The demon roared and staggered, one hand clutching at stone. Then he held aloft the starlight spear that had already humbled Ahrad once that day.

"To the gate!" Rosa shouted. "Bring him down!"

She broke ranks and ran headlong towards the demon, already knowing she'd never reach him in time.

The spear struck with a voice like thunder.

Eleven

Ashana cried out, her knees buckling. Melanna caught her and lowered her gently beside the pool. The Goddess weighed no more than a child, her once-youthful body withered and shrunken. Her hair, no longer blonde but ash-white, hung lank against her skull.

And in the sky, the moon throbbed deep and wrathful crimson.

"Help me stand." Ashana's voice was a parched echo. "Moonlight is finite, and so am I."

"It's killing you." Melanna's certainty was that of the dawn, already paling eastern treetops. "You must stop."

Ashana shook her head. "A bargain was made, and a bargain between ephemerals and divine binds all parties. I give of myself to empower him."

The Huntsman. The light he wielded wasn't his own, but that of his mistress. But the price? Melanna stared up at the statue of Ashana that was not Ashana, wreathed in thorns. The goddess of yesterday. How had she passed?

Melanna shivered, her thoughts thirteen years in the past. The night after her mother's fall from horseback, when fussing physicians had done little save bar a weeping child from the bedside, and sent riders to a campaigning father fated to return too late. As Melanna had cried herself hoarse in her bedchamber, moonlight had banished the darkness. A hand had found hers. At six winters old she'd lost one mother and gained another. And now . . . ?

"What if I strike a new bargain?" She fought the tremor in her voice. "Two walls have fallen. Trust to our warriors for the third."

"How many more lives will that cost?" said Ashana. "How much time? You know what's at stake. The Dark must be driven out of the Republic, or all will suffer. Your father plays his part. I must play mine. And when the time comes, so must you."

"Then I was right before," Melanna said bitterly. "This *is* a lesson."

Withered lips framed a sad smile. Ashana stared down at her reflection in the still waters of the pool. "Everything's a lesson if you allow yourself to learn. For the longest time, I never thought it possible that I might age. I yearned for the furrows that spoke to years lived and wisdom garnered. Anything to dispel the illusion of one too fragile to go unguarded in a wicked world; a treasure set on a pedestal but never really *seen*. Now I resent every wrinkle."

Was she any longer speaking of herself? The words reflected too much of Melanna's own life, and her struggles against the traditions of the Golden Court.

A crooked finger tapped the water. The reflection rippled apart. "What would Inga say if she saw me now?" Ashana murmured. "What would any of them?"

Melanna glanced away, embarrassed to intrude on private contemplation. "Mother ... "

"Help me stand." Determination blossomed. "One last effort."

Weighed down by heavy heart, Melanna obeyed.

The distant shield ring had stood firm where so many others had crumbled, a tide line of golden dead testament to the murderous work of the warriors within. Of the black-headed maces and wicked claymores that made mock of armour. Kai had learned not to underestimate the valour of the Knights Prydonis, whose emblem of a fiery drakon claimed descent from the Age of Kings.

"*Saran Amhyrador!*"

The distant Icansae column reached the gallop, serpent banners streaming above narrow helms. Elspeth's laughter billowed above the drums. "How glorious!"

Devren, his spear lost to the fortunes of battle and his cloak torn, regarded her morosely. "There's no glory in needless death, Ashanal."

Kai nodded, his sentiments torn. Glorious death was a man's final currency before disaster, a reckoning that settled all debts. But the Icansae prince sought only to forge a name, and the corpses about the Prydonis shield ring already spoke to the price.

Even robbed of their walls and dismayed by the Huntsman's fury, the Tressians fought like cornered rats. Elspeth's sisters walked the captured ground under lunassera guard, bringing their healing touch to those who could be saved while the lunassera brought final mercy to those who could not.

Elspeth's sisters, but not Elspeth herself, who'd shown no inclination to matters of life since she'd plucked him from the Raven's grasp six months before.

And as for the Icansae prince? Better he live to earn his name than die with glory.

Kai drove back his spurs, the moonfire sword blazing to challenge the new dawn.

"Ashanael Brigantim!"

A gauntleted hand reached down out of the swirling dust. Rosa grabbed it and clambered to her feet. Her whole body felt like a fading bruise. She nodded her thanks to Captain Ragda, whose moustachioed face was pale beneath his open helm. The backwash of the demon's strike had hurled her away like a toy.

"Blessed Lumestra," he breathed. "That's what happened to the outer wall?"

Rising sun gave shape to shadows beyond the drifting dust. Like the outer before it, the middle gatehouse was gone, and the wall over which it had commanded passage naught but a rubble mound and buried bodies. Beyond, banners flew dark against fires raging behind the third and final gate.

Antlers rose out of the dust, silhouetted against flame. Buccinas sounded, and a storm of quarrels burst from the walls. Hadari trumpets flared. Immortals and cataphracts, drawn from across the carnage of the middle bailey, hurried to form up around the demon, silk banners shining in reflected firelight.

Muttered prayers rippled through the smoke and dust, fervent even through the whine of bombardment and the juddering thunder of hooves. Rosa took measure of the soldiers gathered about her and found little encouragement in bloodless expressions and wide eyes. She shared their horror, but couldn't afford to surrender to it. She'd a duty to Essamere. To the Republic. To those she loved.

Sevaka . . .

Rosa set her back to the carnage and held aloft her sword.

"We've family beyond that wall, and friends upon it. The demon can be hurt! And if it feels pain, Otherworld has a claim. I mean to send it howling to the Raven. Need I do so alone?"

Too late, she regretted a form of words that made offering of the demon's death. But gazes once averted now met hers with determination renewed. Colour returned to filthy faces. Swords returned her salute.

Rosa turned again towards the inner gate, and broke into a run.

The knight screamed as Kai's moonfire sword split steel helm, her claymore falling from nerveless hands. Spears splintered on shields. Others punctured steel plate and weary flesh. On the shield ring's far side, beyond the fluttering drakon-banner, the Icansae charge crashed home in perfect mirror.

Elspeth vaulted the faltering shields entirely, wild laughter in her wake. Her horse slewed on the muddy ground before the Prydonis banner. What should have been an ungainly sprawl became lithe dismount. Armour rushed red as her dagger did wicked work to knights who'd thought their danger ahead, not behind.

Kai's shield shuddered under a mace-blow. His backswing sent another knight into Otherworld's mists. Cataphracts forced the gap wider with spear-thrust and armoured bulk.

"Close up!" roared a grizzled knight at the shield ring's heart. "Drive them out!"

Elspeth spun about. A mace-blow meant to split her skull merely grazed it. She dropped, no longer an unstoppable shard of the divine, but a defenceless, huddled shape.

"Ashanal!"

Kai slammed his heel into a shield and spurred forward. Knights scattered before moonfire, and the way fell open. The mace-wielder readied another blow and died with steel in his spine.

Elspeth lay unmoving, black blood oozing beneath ashen hair. Prydonis knights closed in.

Kai dropped from his saddle and stood astride her, weathering blows on shield and armour. A claymore's strike scattered scales from his right sleeve. He roared defiance and sent the wielder sprawling with a strike of his boot. A mace clanged off his shield. Another struck wide his sword.

And then Devren was there, keening like a man possessed as he hacked at shield and helm. And behind, vengeful cataphracts and thirsty spears. The grizzled Prydonis fell, a spear in his open mouth. An Icansae Immortal hoisted the stolen drakon-banner high. What had been a bastion of flesh and steel became rout and vengeful pursuit.

Kai let his weapon fall and stooped at Elspeth's side. Was she dead? How would he face the Goddess thereafter?

An eyelid fluttered.

Kai forced himself to breathe. "You should be more careful, Ashanal. Arrogance is more dangerous than a sword. And never more so than in battle."

Awarding his concern a filthy look, she ignored his proffered hand and propped herself to a sitting position among the dead. Pale fingers probed her scalp and came away black. She stared at them a long moment, studied disinterest failing to conceal trepidation. Then her jaw set – her eyes with it – and she scrambled to her feet.

Yes, so very like Melanna had once been, before the years had honed her.

A cloth-caparisoned war horse halted at Kai's side, golden serpents bold upon red silk. The rider bowed low in the saddle and held a notched Tressian sword out by its blade.

"Their captain's weapon, my Emperor. Offered with thanks by your servant, Prince Naradna Andwar of Icansae."

The lightness of the voice spoke to youth, its enthusiasm to blood afire with battle. Robes and scale armour – by tradition of lighter, closer make than that Kai himself wore – suggested a slight figure, though one wiry enough to wield the heavy war spear, and to wield it well. The helm too was of traditional Icansae design, close set and framed by a silver halo. Beneath it gleamed a mask of gold, forged in beatific likeness.

Kai searched his memory, but the name Naradna eluded him. He was tempted to offer rebuke, for putting personal acclaim above all else. But brashness was the prerogative of the young, and he'd been little better at Naradna's age.

"Keep it, as a trophy hard-won."

"Yes, *savir.*"

Naradna withdrew the sword and spurred away. Kai turned his gaze south and west to where the final gate lay lost to smoke. Yes, he'd have been wrong to rebuke Naradna, when he himself had veered so far from purpose. Ahrad had to fall. All else would wait.

A cataphract cantered close, leading Kai's steed by the reins. The Emperor thanked him, and regained his saddle. Behind, the survivors reformed their double line, Kos Devren a moody presence at their head. And in front, Elspeth stared eastward, her expression cold and distant beneath the smear of dried blood.

"You are tired of battle, Ashanal?"

Yes, screamed her expression.

"No," she said. "But my horse is lost."

Kai leaned down from the saddle and spread his hand.

"You have leave to join your sisters if you wish, or you may ride with me. I suspect you're a slight enough burden."

She stared for a long, baleful moment. "My mother bade me not leave your side until your destiny is met."

Her fingers closed around his.

"Loose!" shouted Lieutenant Borgiz.

The volley hissed down. The demon stalked on through the smoke, on through the storm of quarrels, crossing the rubble crest and plunging into the raging fires of the middle bailey. Green eyes blazed beneath the helm and the starlight spear arced out, scattering bodies. The Immortals and cataphracts of its escort trampled survivors to offal. Sevaka railed at the uselessness of it all. At her fear of the creature come straight out of myth to kill her. And at the deafness of fools most of all.

"Ignore the shadowthorns!" she shouted. "Aim for the demon's eyes! Its eyes!"

Wood smacked against the stone walkway. Winches rattled and

clacked as the pavissionaires wound back drawstrings. Bolts were set in place. Crossbows presented above the parapet.

"Loose!" shouted Borgiz.

The pavissionaires of the 7th ignored Sevaka's command as they had all others before. Instead, they sent another worthless volley into a body shielded by armour no ephemeral bolt could pierce, and against cataphracts who'd no hope of taking the walls alone. A ballista shot might have stopped the demon. It would certainly have staggered the brute, but too many of the siege engines were ablaze. Assuming any would have obeyed Sevaka's orders.

It was one thing to be placed in command of the wall. Another to make a Psanneque's voice count. Gazing west towards the inner harbour, Sevaka saw the masts of the merchant hulk blazing against blue skies. Was her *Zephyr* burning also?

She stared across the muster field where the bulk of the 7th formed up alongside the ochre shields of Lord Strazna's Knights Fellnore, and the ragtag array of banners and shields Lady Sarravin had assembled. What had begun as a sally looked more and more like Ahrad's last hope . . . assuming she could bring order to the ranks. To depart the gate as a mob would only invite slaughter, and leave the citadel bereft.

Another volley hissed out, this one sharper, whistling. The demon raised a gauntleted hand to shield his face. Spent arrows scattered away from darkened steel. Another followed, and another. Faster than the crossbows of the 7th. Grey cloaks and yew bows atop the drum tower south of the gatehouse, Thaldvar with one foot braced on the rampart as he directed his borderers' shots.

The demon shrank back into the smoke. A cry of victory went up from the battlements.

Sevaka cheered with the rest. In a day of disaster, small triumphs counted as never before.

A kraikon loomed out of the smoke, a sword taller than Sevaka in one massive hand and a shield like a fortress door in the other. It shouldered a trio of cataphracts aside, scattering men from their horses, then swung at the demon's head.

Starlight checked steel with an ear-splitting screech. Molten metal hissed and spattered. Undeterred, the kraikon lumbered on, golden light sparking from its armour. Still shielding its eyes from the borderers' arrows, the demon thrust. Spear's strike raised a great molten gout across the kraikon's shield. The heavy sword came about in response, too fast for the demon to evade. An antler shattered. The demon staggered. The cheer from the battlements redoubled.

Before the construct recovered, the spear punched through steel plate and bronze beneath. Sunlight flared across the smoke and the kraikon toppled sideways, lifeless with the flight of its animating spark.

The cheer faded. The demon surged on.

Sevaka glanced behind the ramparts. The 7th weren't ready. The spear would come down. The last wall would fall, and half of the Eastshires alongside.

Then the dancing smoke parted, revealing warriors forgotten in the horror of the moment. A motley wedge of soldiers and knights, filthy from battle's fortune. And at their head, a woman who could not die.

"Essamere!"

Rosa screamed the challenge at the top of her lungs as she crossed the rubble of the middle wall. Let the shadowthorns hear. Let them turn. Let them ready shields and form ranks to face her, so long as the demon turned also.

Even as her breakneck stride closed the distance, cataphracts broke apart and wheeled to face the enemy at their rear; the Immortals' rear ranks turned and locked shields. The demon swung about, green eyes blazing beneath a scarred and broken-antlered helm.

Bolts and arrows hissed out from the wall, aimed at the demon no longer but into the backs of Immortals whose shields now faced away. Men slumped. Gaps opened up in the lines. Rosa aimed for the nearest. Shields clashed together to bar her path. Casting her own aside, she lowered her shoulder to the join.

She heard the wet ripping sound as a sword sliced her flesh, felt the shuddering scrape as steel struck bone. Then her blade was between an Immortal's ribs, and Ragda at her side, a wordless bellow on his lips, and his mace unstoppable. Ragda fell, a sword in his belly and another in his spine, but others flooded into the gap he'd made, swearing and howling like damned souls.

The way was clear.

Rosa struck down an Immortal's blade and ran for the bronze husk of a fallen kraikon. Boots skidded. Momentum drove her on. She reached the construct's shoulder and hurled herself at the demon, sword gripped two-handed above her head, point levelled at those blazing green eyes.

At the last moment, the demon twisted. Rosa's sword buried itself in mantle and armour. His deafening bellow swept the middle bailey. A hand dashed Rosa to the ground. Ribs snapped. Then he was astride her, knee planted against the mud, and a hand larger than her head splayed across her chest.

"She saved you." The sour steam of his breath rose from beneath his helm. "She blessed you with new life. Look what you do with it. Have you no shame?"

"I . . . never . . . asked for this." Rosa twisted, struggling to break free.

He leaned closer, eyes blazing and voice thunderous. "You should fight for her. Instead, you side with the Dark."

Rosa didn't know what he meant, nor did she much care. She saw only that her sword, its blade still buried in his shoulder, was within reach.

"I fight for Essamere," she gasped. "For the Republic. For my friends!"

Straining fingers closed about the sword.

The demon howled and reared up as the sword came clear. Autumn leaves bled from the wound, gold and amber dancing on invisible winds. The starlight spear struck the sword away. He seized Rosa about the throat and hoisted her high into the torrent of leaves, the bones of her neck grinding beneath his grip.

"Then die with them!" he roared.

The spear blurred. Rosa's world turned to fire.

Sevaka clutched the rampart, helpless to do anything but watch. "Rosa!"

The demon drove his spear clear through Rosa's chest and into the trampled mud at the bailey's eastern edge. She lay silhouetted against the flames, back arched and body held upright on heels and on the impaling spear. Stillness among the raging battle.

Sevaka drew her cutlass and ran for the stairs.

The rampart shuddered to the rattle and boom of the opening gate. A chorus of buccinas rang out.

Lady Sarravin's sortie was at last on the move.

The demon turned about in a swirl of umber leaves. A flurry of bolts rent the air. He fell to one knee, his flailing hand sweeping a luckless cataphract from the saddle.

"Death and honour!"

The Knights Fellnore led the charge, banners raised. Lances swept cataphracts from saddles and bit deep into embattled Immortals. Others thumped home against the demon's smoke-wreathed body. Still he staggered on, scattering knights from destriers and trampling them underfoot. The flood of leaves thickened, their colour dark as rotten mulch.

The demon's abandoned spear turned dull where once it had shone like the heavens. Mocking laughter mingled with the boom of drums as that same light gathered about his upraised fists.

"For the Queen!" he cried.

Sevaka froze, the wrath of moments before now cold as ice.

"Get off the walls!" she shouted. "Get—"

The demon's fists came down in a flurry of black leaves.

Twelve

Sevaka's eyes cracked open. The remnant of the inner gateway loomed through a storm of black leaves and bitter smoke, broken teeth in the wall's shattered jaw. Where the demon's blows had sundered the outer walls for much of their span, it had barely broken the gatehouse of the innermost. Already, king's blue and ochre surcoats filled the gap, smoke-stained and bloodied.

"Captain."

Lady Sarravin's greeting barely pierced ringing ears. She offered a dust-streaked hand. Sevaka took it, ignoring creaking bones as she stood. Her eyes fell upon the rubble and the patches of king's blue cloth that spoke to buried bodies. Hundreds more dead, and she lucky not to be among them.

"Borgiz didn't listen. No one did."

"Make them listen. Your mother would have found a way."

"I don't have a mother. I am ..."

" ... yourself alone, I remember. But if you refuse to let one name define you, why allow the other to do so?" Lady Sarravin shook her head. "Can you fight?"

New sounds gathered as the muted whine faded from Sevaka's ears. The thump of running feet. The faltering hymn as a gold-robed proctor sought to rouse the shield wall to fervour. Even the crackle of flames seemed muted. She glimpsed a battered helmet half-buried in the rubble, antlers broken and remembered the demon scattering to drifting leaves in the moment the walls shook. And before that ... Rosa.

Could she fight? "Yes."

"Good. They've fallen back, but they'll come again. I mean to buy all the time I can. Even if it's tallied only in minutes."

Sevaka's heart sank further. "Then it's over?"

"The citadel stands, but it's not enough. I've ordered the west gates opened. The civilians are already on the move, and I've ordered what remains of the 11th to keep the shadowthorns off their backs. The rest of us? We spit defiance ... " Lady Sarravin brushed a hand against a hunk of stone – the remains of a pillar somehow come intact through the gatehouse's fall " ... and we give this grand old lady one last place in the histories."

Sevaka gazed back across the inner bailey, at the drifting cinders of a muster field where so many had celebrated the previous night. How quickly the world turned, and fate with it.

"You don't have to stay," murmured Lady Sarravin. "Your ship can't leave, for there's no one left to work the locks, and your crew have gone with the rest. But you might find a horse."

A bright spot on a dark morning, but not enough to quash the insult, kindly though it had been offered. The same insult Sevaka had endured for months as a Psanneque. The same insult her mother had levied at every opportunity. Psanneque or Kiradin, no one expected any more from her than the least she could give.

And besides, Rosa was still out there, somewhere in the smoke.

She gripped her cutlass tighter. "I'm not going anywhere."

Kai Saran distrusted the quiet. And not just the quiet. There he stood, on the cusp of a victory that overshadowed any won by his sires, and yet where was the joy? That he already knew the answer only made matters worse.

Devren cantered out of the west. Blood caked the warleader's right arm, and his shield was battered and scarred. But beneath his narrow helm, his eyes held all the satisfaction Kai's own lacked.

"The Goddess' equerry has fallen ... "

Elspeth sniffed disparagingly from her perch behind Kai's saddle. Devren offered her an unfavourable glance and pressed on.

" ... but the wall is humbled. The breach is no more than four hundred paces wide, and held at the crest. I've already ordered archers and catapults brought up to end matters." A smile gleamed beneath the helm. "It will take a few hours yet, but the fortress of Ahrad is yours."

Kai looked back across the thinning smoke of the outer bailey. At the shieldsmen scouring the last defenders from the eastern walls, and the Immortals mustering beneath their banners. Ahrad was his, and yet he'd never thought so great a victory could ring so hollow.

"No."

Devren stiffened in his saddle. "No?"

"Most of the victory belongs to the Goddess, and you'd have me yield the rest to peasant arrows? Where is your pride, old friend?"

He felt Elspeth's hand on his shoulder. Her breath warm on his ear. "This is what my mother wished for you. The destiny of the House of Saran. The triumph is yours to claim. You need only reach out your hand."

"And what do you know of triumph?" snapped Devren. "You should be tending the fallen, *savim*, not playing at battle."

"I might say as much to you," she replied. "You've clearly lost your taste for it."

"My Emperor—"

Kai raised his fist. "Enough!"

"I hear the old way calling you, *my Emperor*," said Elspeth. "How would you look back on this day? How would you wish your heirs to recall your deeds?"

The old way. The charge. The offering of blood and steel that honoured the foe, and in turn honoured the gift-giver for his sacrifice. The tradition by which crowns were earned and stolen, and which Kai had flouted in allowing the Goddess to aid the fight. For all that Ahrad was but the first step on a road without obvious end, those traditions held power.

In embracing that truth, Kai felt hollowness recede from his heart.

"Rouse my spears, warleader. Let the drums roar. One last charge."

Trumpets sounded through the smoke.

"Here they come!" shouted Lady Sarravin. "Show them how the 7th fights!"

Shields locked across the uneven crest of fallen masonry. A wall of flesh and willow to stopper the gap in stone. The 7th didn't hold the gap alone. Ochre surcoats of the Knights Fellnore dotted the line, survivors of the demon's last blow. The rearmost rank of the line was full of mismatched uniforms and no uniforms at all. Church provosts in their drab greys. Citadel constables. Even a few proctors in flowing gold, sun-staves readied like spears above the line of shields. And at Sevaka's side in the centre of the line, where Lady Sarravin stood and the 7th's banners challenged the skies, the grey cloaks of borderers.

"Should've taken my winnings and gone." Thaldvar's bow was slung, and he leaned on a borrowed halberd as though it was his only support. "Bad fortune always follows the good."

The quarrel over cards. Last night and a lifetime ago. So much had changed. From broken-hearted to betrothed, and now broken-hearted again. Because for all that Rosa claimed she couldn't die, that claim needed only to be once a lie to make a lie of all. And if a demon's spear could not unmake that beautiful illusion, then what could?

Sevaka shook away her sorrow. It would wait. All the way to the mists of Otherworld if it must. Living or dead, Rosa lay beyond her reach. She clung tight to her cutlass, and to the unlikely promise of Third Dawn.

"I'm surprised you're not on the walls with what's left of the pavissionaires."

Thaldvar grunted. "The thing about arrows – the truly *important* thing – is that they're finite."

"So are the shadowthorns," said Sevaka.

So were the borderers. As she glanced about, she realised their numbers in the breach were thinner than on the walls. Had they suffered so badly in the gatehouse's fall? The tower from which they'd taken their shots had lost most of its outer face, but it still stood, its crumbling rampart dotted with pavissionaires. For all the resentment flung their way by the garrison, the borderers had given their all.

The ground shook. The rumble that spoke of horses goaded to the charge. The golden thunderbolt of Empire flung forth from a merciless hand.

"Death and honour," murmured Sevaka.

"Honour I leave to others." Thaldvar hooked an eyebrow. "And I've no intention of dying today."

"Steady!" Lady Sarravin tugged on her spread-winged helm and pushed through to the fighting ranks. "Keep your shields tight and trust to your neighbours!"

To the east, smoke parted in a blaze of gold.

The Icansae cataphracts pulled ahead, borne on by swifter horses and the banners of an impetuous prince. Men and horses fell screaming into the mud, cast down by volleys from the slighted wall. Those who survived reached the rubble crest not as a conquering fist, but splayed fingers, further prised apart by waiting blades.

Cataphracts perished under halberds' axe-blades, or were thrust onto their spear-points by the impetus of their own onset. War spears splintered against shields, or lodged so deep that they were abandoned in favour of the sword. And all the while, quarrels rained down from vestigial ramparts, bleeding the charge of the bodies needed to break the wall of shields. The wall buckled all the same, leaving a tide mark of blue among the gold and scarlet of the Icansae dead.

As Naradna's trumpets sounded the retreat, Kai spurred his horse to one last effort and came to finish what the prince had begun.

"Ashanael Brigantim!"

Elspeth's whoop of joy ringing in his ears, Kai crashed home.

The line shuddered. A halberd shrieked against Kai's shield. The moonfire sword jarred against a steel pauldron. A twist, a swing and the knight whirled away in a spray of blood. A woman in the second rank took his place, cursing and screaming even as Kai sent the alabaster flame to claim her.

To Kai's left, halberds hooked a cataphract from his saddle and dragged him down behind the shields. To his right, a dismounted warrior in Icansae scarlet battered madly at painted willow until a sword took his throat. Others came forward, keening the wordless hymn of men driven to victory or death.

Inch by desperate inch, the king's blue wall edged back.

"Death and honour!"

The woman, new-come to the bloody work, screamed her challenge. Kai checked her thrust and swept it aside. Her helm bore the brunt of his counterblow, and she rammed her shield up at his horse's jaw. As Kai fought for command of the rearing beast, the woman tugged free her ravaged helm, revealing an expression bereft of fear.

"Death to the shadowthorns!" she cried.

The Tressian line, so close to breaking, came forward. Kai's opponent wasted no effort on florid sweeps, but threw her all into short, stabbing thrusts. Kai parried one, felt another scrape his armoured thigh, then leaned low in the saddle and hacked down.

The woman's pauldron yielded where her helm had not. The moonfire sword bit deep and she went back with a thin cry.

Tressian valour stuttered. Another thrust, another scream, and it crumpled entirely. A gap formed as shields split apart. Suddenly there was nothing between Kai's sword and the regimental banners upon the crest. And beyond that, Ahrad's inner bailey and a victory hard-won.

Sevaka was in the third rank as Lady Sarravin's body was dragged away, the 7th's banner beside her and her cutlass untested. She saw the shadowthorn Emperor rearing high in triumph, the pale woman behind his saddle laughing even as she clung to the flanks of his emerald-studded armour; the backward steps as all heart went out of the men and women around her. Suddenly, she was in the third rank no more, but on a rubble slope thick with dead and thinning shields.

"7th!" she shouted. "To me! To me!"

The cry went unanswered.

Trumpets blazed brash triumph, and the cataphracts surged like storm-driven seas. One breach, and all would be washed away. One sword alone couldn't hold back that tide.

"7th!" she cried once more. "To me!"

The battle swallowed up the words. Fear of shadowthorns. Distrust of a Psanneque. The weariness of soldiers who could give no more. Did the reason matter?

Sevaka cast about for an officer of the 7th whose voice might carry more authority. Even for Thaldvar, but caught no sign of either.

White flame shattered the last shield in the Emperor's path. He spurred forward, the moonsilver crown brilliant against the smoke. At Sevaka's side, the banner bearer moaned in dismay, and stumbled back across the rubble.

Make them listen.

Sheathing her useless cutlass, Sevaka ripped the banner free of its bearer's grasp. Gripping the ash pole as tight as the Raven ever clutched a purloined soul, she levelled it like a lance and flung herself into the Emperor's path.

In one moment, the crest was clear of living warriors. In the next, a lone woman charged headlong across the dead, screaming like a cyraeth torn straight from Otherworld, the pennant of the regimental banner ripping and snapping behind her.

Kai twisted in his saddle, sword blurring to turn the pole's spear tip aside.

Driven by headlong impetus and desperate strength, the tip scraped past his guard. Golden scales shrieked. A wet, empty *thump* hurled him back in the saddle. The world shuddered and slipped away into murk.

The last thing he saw was a thin arm reaching past his to seize the reins.

The Emperor's horse wheeled about, ripping the banner pole from Sevaka's grip. Boots skidding on the blood-slicked rubble, she fought for balance. In the moment before she fell, a heavy hand grabbed her arm.

The slope filled with a rush of king's blue and cheers. Soldiers stoppered the gap, shields uneven and ragged, but growing less so with every passing moment. The shadowthorns rode away, their Emperor a limp bundle held atop his horse only through the efforts of a woman half his size.

Sevaka stood slack-jawed, stunned amid cheers, as the middle bailey thinned of riders. As blades brought mercy to dismounted Hadari too slow to flee. Her rescuer, whom she tentatively recalled as a Captain Varnaz, nodded grimly and offered salute. To her. A Psanneque.

"That was well struck," he said. "The 7th thanks you."

Lost for words, she stared out over the mended shield wall. A bare rank remained where three had once stood. That the breach approach was choked with blood and gold did nothing to alter a bitter truth: when the Hadari came again, as they surely would, there were no longer enough bodies to hold the line.

"What now?" she asked.

"We do our duty," said Varnaz. "We fight on."

He walked down the slope towards the sparse shield wall. Retrieving the 7th's fallen banner, he hoisted it aloft. "Death and honour!"

A new chant rose up across the slope. "*Varnaz! Varnaz! Varnaz!*"

They called the captain's name as if he'd ridden out with the light of Third Dawn and a host of serathi at his back. And more than that, Sevaka realised, for her victory. For her "well struck" blow. Disbelief soured with spoiled pride, and she hated herself for feeling thus when so few had survived to feel anything at all. But to so soon be again alone in a crowd was a bitter, black weight upon her thoughts.

"Don't . . . take it to heart," gasped a thin voice. "It *was* well done."

Lady Sarravin sat propped against the rubble. Her armour was rent and bubbled at the shoulder; her once-splendid uniform sodden and dark. As Sevaka knelt beside her, the proctor tending her wounds gave a surreptitious shake of the head. Lady Sarravin waved him away.

"He thinks I don't know the Raven's coming for me," she wheezed. "But he's here. See?"

She extended a bloody finger to the east. Sevaka saw nothing remarkable.

"You should run," gasped Lady Sarravin. "There's no duty here any longer . . . only a fool's death. The daughter of Ebigail Kiradin shouldn't be a fool, whatever kinship she claims."

Sevaka shook her head. "I can't."

No reply came. Lady Sarravin no longer had ears for any words save those spoken by the Raven.

Sevaka rose. It *was* a fool's death to remain. It might even be too late to flee. But duty remained. Not to the 7th, now the only officer who had showed her respect and comradeship lay dead. Not even to the Republic, that had courted her as a Kiradin and disdained her as Psanneque. No, only one duty remained, and there might yet be time to see it done before the Hadari came again.

Descending the slope as one in a dream, Sevaka pushed her way through the thin shield wall, crossed the rampart of dead, and went in search of Rosa.

*

The gasp drowned Kai's world in red. Lesser agony than that awful breath taken beneath moonlight and birch trees, but not so much as to offer meaningful solace. Lungs emptied of air as soon as it was drawn in a howl that reached down to his toes. Spasm jack-knifed him upright. Fingers found handhold on stone.

"Don't be a child." Elspeth, kneeling level with his chest, threaded charred fingers and glared at him as one might a wayward pet. "The pain will pass. If I can bear what I have taken, you can most definitely endure what remains."

A second breath. The pain receded. Stiffness remained. Senses took in the surroundings. A ring of lunassera around him, their backs inward, and their weapons outward. The rent scales, and the torn cloth beneath. And not just above his heart. A dozen tiny harms, unregistered before, now screamed for attention. Yet the pain was distant, numb, compared to the great draining horror of that first breath.

Kai spread a hand across his breastbone. "I should be dead."

"Do you feel alive?"

The last of the pain dissipated. The vigour of recent days returned. "Yes."

She rose, and held out charred fingers. "Then rise, my Emperor. You owe my mother a victory."

He took her hand, marvelling at the strength of her grip, and wondered why there had been no blood.

Sevaka found Rosa fifty yards beyond the breach, held aloft by the demon's spear and her own rigid body. Her smoke-blackened faced was set towards the rising sun, eyes closed and expression oddly peaceful, and her hands hung limp at her side.

Sevaka closed the distance at a run, unheeding of ramparts crowded with golden armour and the emblems of eastern kings. She clasped Rosa's hand tight and stared blankly through the clearing smoke as a Hadari shield wall formed beneath the brilliant sun, and a moon that was little more than a hazy shadow.

"My life joined to yours," she murmured. "For however little is left."

She swore silently that she'd not die alone. Maybe she'd even make the Raven an offering so great that he'd permit them to walk Otherworld's mists together until Third Dawn.

Fingers tightened about hers, the pressure so slight she first thought it wild imagining.

"Rosa?"

Sevaka stared anew, her thoughts racing. Rosa wasn't impervious. Harm passed as her body healed. But how could she heal with a spear through her heart? Hope took strength from anger and burned away sorrow.

"I'll have you down from there. I will."

Though how was she to do so alone?

Hoofbeats thumped. Sevaka spun about, cutlass drawn. Thaldvar slowed to a halt, hands upraised in surrender. His grey cloak was torn ragged, and his cheek crusted with dried blood. The horse was plainly not *his* horse – nor any other Tressian's either – for it wore barding of golden scales.

"I saw you leave the wall. Thought you'd gone mad." He slid from the saddle and stared at Rosa. "Now? Now I understand. But you can't stay here."

"She's alive," snapped Sevaka.

"I know what I saw last night, but there's being stuck with a dagger and there's . . . this." He shot a hurried glance east and stepped closer, his weary expression a poor job of masking incredulity. "My fellows have snagged horses. Lumestra knows there's nothing more to do here but die. Come with us. The walls have emptied. Half of Varnaz's lot have already turned heel, and the rest look like they mean to as soon as his attention's elsewhere."

"I'm going nowhere without Rosa."

The Hadari lines, so distant when there had been no hope, now seemed close enough almost to touch. And in the centre of the front line, beneath banners of emerald silk, a bear of a man beneath a moonsilver crown. Sevaka's gorge thickened.

"That's not fair. I killed him."

"Not well enough, it would seem," Thaldvar replied.

She turned away, more determined than ever. "Help me get her down."

"And if she's dead?"

"Then I'll stay with her." Sevaka clenched a fist and cast about for something – anything – to convince him to help. "You owe Rosa for last night. Or is it true that borderers don't settle their debts?"

He stiffened. "I've paid my debts and more this morning."

"Not to her."

"All right. But as soon as the first shadowthorn takes a step this way, I'm off – with or without you."

Sevaka cast her cutlass aside and looped her arms about Rosa's waist.

"Stay out of the mists just a little longer," she whispered. "For me."

She took her weight while Thaldvar dug the silver spearhead free of the ground. They laid Rosa, who made no sound through it all, on her side as gently as circumstance allowed. Sevaka could only imagine the pain it set her to, and the insidious fear that her love's spirit had fled returned full force.

No amount of hacking at the spear staff would split its timbers, no matter how Sevaka swore or struck. In the end, half-mad with desperation, she whispered Rosa an apology. Then she tipped her onto her front, planted a foot on her chest and hauled for all she was worth.

With a wet tearing sound, the spear at last came free. Sevaka cast it away and fell to her knees. Rosa spasmed and rolled onto her back. Eyes flickered once and closed, but her chest rose and fell.

Thaldvar clenched his fist in the sign of the sun, and tapped it to his brow. "Queen's Ashes."

"So you finally . . ." Black blood coughed across Rosa's lips and dissipated as silver steam. " . . . finally got around to saving me."

Sevaka wiped her cheeks free of tears. "Ingrate."

Trumpets sounded to the east.

From her hillside vantage, Melanna watched as her father's distant shields ground across the inner bailey. Only a thin scattering of Tressians remained. They fought to the last, a knot of defiant blue amidst the embers, but the outcome was never in doubt. She watched until the first owl banners stood proud above the inner walls, then turned away.

"What do you see?" croaked Ashana.

The shrunken goddess sat among the rushes beside the pool, lost in contemplation of a lined and withered reflection. Silver dust spilled from ashen hair, turning lifeless and dark where it touched the water.

"Victory," said Melanna. "My father's triumph."

Ashana nodded jerkily, and returned her gaze to the pool. "I don't recognise myself any longer. Maybe that's fitting. What I've done this day ... But the sacrifice will be worth it, in the end." She looked up. "Remember your promise."

"Yes, Mother." Kneeling, Melanna threw her arms about the Goddess' thin shoulders. "I won't fail you. I will see the Dark destroyed."

Wind gusted. When it passed, Melanna was alone among the rushes, and the waters of the pool thick with tarnished silver dust.

Thirteen

Dawn found Malachi too exhausted to sleep. The chandelier's fall had spawned a score of thankless tasks. Guests ushered home and servants steadied. The grim matter of attending to the dead. He could've left these things to others, as was expected for one of his rank. But for all that the deaths had come at vranakin hands, the blood stained his also. And so, he saluted the dawn from the terrace, a glass of Selanni brandy in one hand.

"Is my husband crawling into a bottle? Didn't we agree to discuss weighty decisions?"

Lily stood in the doorway, still in housecoat and night-robe. The silken veil remained in place, muting her golden hair and hiding the scars granted by a kernclaw's talons.

For all she pretended otherwise – for all her wry inflection – Lilyana Reveque hadn't quite been the same since that day. Her wit had grown harder, her tongue harsher. Strange then, that husband and wife were closer than ever. Or perhaps not so strange. Of all Malachi's friends and allies, only Lily knew of his crooked bargain. Knew of it, and had agreed its necessity.

Malachi swirled the dregs. "I burn it off too quickly for that. Nervous energy."

"You should have come to bed."

"I wouldn't have slept, and I didn't want to keep you awake. One of us should greet the business of the day rested. Especially as you're petitioning the Grand Council on behalf of Saint Tremare's Convent this morning."

"As if they'll listen. They hear my name, not my words." Measured, graceful steps drew her closer. "How much of the business of the day is the business of the night before?"

"Not much and too much. Josiri helped with the other guests. I had a free hand elsewhere."

Lily's left eye twitched beneath the veil. "You're fortunate to have him as a friend."

You, not *we*. "He's practical. He sees every insurmountable problem as a throng of trivial obstacles to overcome, one by one. I needed a little of that. I sent a herald to Sabelle's brother, though I'll offer condolences in person before the day is out. I haven't done so for Dathna yet. I understand her mother lives in Sothvane. We'll pay for the interment, of course."

"We'll pay for more than that. She leaves two children. The father died in last year's ... unpleasantness."

He winced. Consequence rippling ever outward. "Of course. We'll see their needs are met."

She laid her hands on his lapels. "A strange councillor you are, Lord Reveque, to worry over a maid's orphans. A strange councillor, and a good man."

"It's my fault she's dead."

The words should have occasioned guilt, or grief ... maybe even fear. But he was too worn away by a sleepless night and the promise of a long day.

Lily's eyes narrowed. "Explain."

"The vranakin asked me to ensure Konor Zarn rose to the Council. I refused. This was their response."

"Removing Sabelle from this world, and thus the running?" She gave an unladylike snort. "It's clever."

Lily had never warmed to Sabelle Mezar, claiming that the other woman was too self-assured with too little reason. In another person, Malachi might have thought it jealousy, and perhaps it was. After all, Lily could've been councillor in his place – *should* have been, but for her father's old-fashioned notion that she be a mother first and a woman second. Truth told, Malachi hadn't much cared for Sabelle. But she'd been an honest soul, and a necessary piece in the puzzle.

He scowled, disgusted by the callousness of his own thoughts. "They've always stopped at threats before."

"Before, you always gave them what they wanted." Fearless blue eyes met his. "Why not on this occasion?"

"Because this isn't just slackening patrols around Dregmeet or shifting tariffs to favour their enterprises. This is the Council. It's the Republic's future. That's what we agreed, you and I – that the vranakin wouldn't have the Council, and they wouldn't take our children." He stared off into the dawn. "I just need a little longer. Then the bargain can die with me, if it must."

It shouldn't have been necessary at all. When he'd convinced the Parliament of Crows to abandon Ebigail Kiradin, he'd offered himself up as the prize. No easy trade, even with Lily's reluctant support, but one Malachi had been prepared to live with. But then he'd been one councillor among many – one voice alone that could benefit the Crowmarket little – and his push to create the position of First Councillor would have diminished his own influence further.

If only Viktor had taken the position. If only circumstance hadn't forced Malachi to step up in his stead. If. If. If. Cleverness counted little when fate was laughing.

"Viktor's not coming back." As ever, Lily read his thoughts with accustomed ease. "You need to let him go."

Malachi braced his palms on the balustrade and hung his head. "I know."

"Then who would you have take your place?"

"Josiri."

"Josiri." She spoke flatly. "You've promised him this?"

"No. He'd refuse. I have to choose my moment."

And shape a council that would back such a decision. Setting a south-wealder in the First Councillor's chair might prove the work of years. But it would be worth the effort. For all his faults – impetuousness high among them – Josiri had adapted to his role better than Malachi had expected. On a Privy Council too long obsessed with marking the passing years, Josiri got things done. He understood the necessity of change. Which was, Malachi supposed, precisely why Lamirov disliked him. But it had to be Josiri. No other would build on the hoped-for peace with the Hadari.

"Perhaps you shouldn't choose it at all," said Lily. "Josiri's no less compromised than us."

"Josiri has nothing to do with the vranakin. You should have seen him yesterday. He and Izack would have ridden into Dregmeet and toppled it back into the mists if I hadn't put a stop to it."

"I don't mean the vranakin," Lily said sourly, "but the demon he flaunts as his consort."

So that was it? "Anastacia has done nothing to deserve your accusations, Lily."

"She *claims* to be a serathi," she snapped. "What is that, if not the highest blasphemy?"

There was no arguing with Lily on matters of the divine. Though duty to family had waylaid her from a serene's chaste and reverent path, pious lessons of girlhood were burned into her being. Admirable, on most occasions, for it underpinned generosity of spirit unusual in a woman of her rank. Confronting it head-on only brought woe.

And then there was the problem of Anastacia's inhuman nature. Even at her friendliest – an increasingly rare state of affairs – she made for an unsettling presence. Too often, Malachi felt as though he were the butt of a joke only Anastacia understood. He suspected Lily did also, which only fed her imaginings of idolatry. A strange thing to yearn for proof of the divine, and then reject it because it poorly matched your ideal.

"We've been over this, Lily. Anastacia has Josiri's trust, and Josiri has mine."

She joined him at the balcony's edge. "And if you're both of you wrong?"

He offered a smile. "Then if she wends seductive wiles about me, I can rely on you to put matters right."

"You shouldn't joke about such things, Malachi." She shook her head, but the fight had gone from her voice. "Very well. Have Josiri as your heir. You trust him, and for all your myriad flaws, I trust you. The Council and our children. I will tolerate Anastacia's proximity to one, but not the other. Am I understood?"

"Always, my love."

"Good." She rested her head against his shoulder. "Then we should discuss our exposure."

Malachi nodded. Even a hint of skulduggery invited scandal. "Captain Darrow ruled it all an accident. A restraining hasp pulled clear of the wall. No suggestion of anything suspicious."

"She's convinced? You're sure?"

"With Hawkin almost among the dead? Our good captain isn't one to hide her feelings."

"True, but that isn't what I meant by exposure. The vranakin came to our home, Malachi. Our *home*. They could've murdered Sabelle in the street, or in her bed, but they did it *here*. This was a warning."

Further proof that his relationship with the Crowmarket was shifting, and not for the better. "I know."

Malachi ran the tally in his head. He'd been the last of the Satanra line even before marriage to Lily. There were none left alive for the Parliament of Crows to threaten. On the Reveque side of the union? Lily's parents had passed away some months earlier – her mother to illness, and her father to a broken heart. That left an array of cousins distant in both proximity and fondness. No leverage to be had there.

It came down to immediate family. Perhaps a few friends beyond. Josiri, Rosa and Viktor. Try as he might, Malachi couldn't conjure a circumstance where the Parliament of Crows would pursue any of them. Josiri had lived a life of secrets, and was far from complacent. And besides, he had Anastacia – serathi, demon or something else entirely, Malachi understood her to be formidable in every sense. Rosa had already proven herself more than a match for the Crowmarket's kernclaws. And Viktor? Malachi almost wished the vranakin would try, and thus learn a pointed lesson of their own.

No. It would be Constans or Sidara.

Now the fear came.

"Sidara should go to the convent," he said. "She'll be safer in Lumestra's sight than in this house."

Lily straightened. "You know that's impossible. Her eyes too often shine with the light in her blood. For all she claims to keep the rest locked away, I don't know that I believe her. She's too much like her mother. Clever and defiant." She shook her head. "She'll not keep her secret cloistered among serenes, and then the church will have her for the foundry."

Malachi scowled, but allowed that she was correct. Magic was too rare a gift, and the constructs it granted life too valuable. It was selfish to keep Sidara from the foundry, but if a father couldn't be selfish with his daughter, when could he?

"Then she must at least learn to defend herself," he said. "And she must learn to keep her light hidden. Perhaps High Proctor Ilnarov would be prepared to tutor—"

Lily rounded on him. "You'd reveal Sidara to the head of the foundry? After all I've said?"

"The man is not the position he holds, Lily. He kept Viktor's secret for years. Why would Sidara be any different?" He sighed. "And what would you suggest otherwise?"

"We will pray together, she and I. Lumestra will guide us."

Malachi touched his eyes closed. "All right. But I hope for Sidara's sake that Lumestra is forthcoming. You'll permit me to arrange tuition in more . . . practical arts? For her and Constans both?"

Lily's glare didn't waver, but here Malachi found himself on firmer ground. Lily handled a sword rather better than he did – the dividend of girl-hood lessons – and would be unlikely to oppose tuition for her own children.

"I won't have Sidara be a knight any more than I will a foundry drab," she said. "She's a Reveque. She's meant for better than war and filth."

"Only if she lives." Malachi bit back a frisson of dismay. "Vranakin or not, it's a dangerous world. You can't keep her at Abbeyfields for ever, and Sidara needs to know how to defend herself when her mother's not there to protect her."

Lily looked away. "You'll assign one of our hearthguard?"

He took a deep breath. "I don't trust the hearthguard. Not with this. That trick with the chandelier? That took preparation, which means we've vranakin among the household." He'd borne that realisation some hours. Time had only soured it further. "If someone's to spar with our children, I need to be sure of them."

"Then who?"

"I'll think on the matter." He ran a palm across stubble and scowled. "But first, the business of the day. The Council beckons."

Lily leaned in, lifted her veil, and kissed him. "Go. I'll attend to things here. But carry one thought with you. Last night was *not* your fault."

Malachi held his wife close, and wished he believed her.

Fourteen

Apara jerked upright, breath frosting and blankets clutched to her chest. Dust motes danced in a shaft of light cast through drapes improperly closed. Green eyes shrouded by grey robes regarded her coldly from the foot of the four-poster bed.

"Crowfather Krastin requires your presence."

Apara swallowed. She never felt entirely at ease around elder cousins. It wasn't just the cold, but something . . . else. Something harder to define. Still, *some* asperity was required, if only for appearances' sake. She wasn't any longer a rassophore, to be commanded and bidden. She'd duties of her own – duties the elder cousin's presence jeopardised.

"You shouldn't be here."

Her tone fell short of intended reprimand, but remained steady. A victory of sorts. Her fingers closed about the pendant – the Parliament's gift, and their charge. It hummed under her hand.

Though she'd decreed her bedchamber off-limits to staff, Apara never slept without the pendant. She never removed it while within the house's bounds, even in the most intimate of company. Such moments were few and far between, for whatever joy lay in the deception was insufficient to douse the loss of not truly being the object of desire. Or perhaps that too was the work of the shadow in her soul, draining the joy even from such trysts?

Thus every gilded mirror held the face of a stranger – the councilwoman whose likeness granted Apara fine living, and a seat at the highest table. The pendant's spark of enchantment ensured that servants and guests saw what she wished. What they expected. What did her cousin behold?

If only she were permitted to indulge old skills practised as the Silver Owl. By day, the face she wore was a passport into so many highblood households, their secrets and defences laid bare. The woman she'd once been would have revelled in that knowledge, and cleaned them out of all that was valuable by night. But that was before the kernclaw's mantle had been forced upon her.

"You remain uncompromised." The elder cousin's pronouncement was bereft of uncertainty.

Would her cousin have spoken differently *had* he been seen, and maintained secrecy by disposing of the witness? *That* had consequences, if not so immediate.

"I'm to attend the ceremony at the Hayadra Grove," she said. "And the council meeting thereafter. My position—"

"Is for the Parliament to grant, or to take away." He drew close to the foot of the bed. "Have you grown too comfortable, cousin? Are you so used to playing a lady of sunlight that you've forgotten your loyalties in the mist?"

The room grew colder. Dust prickled the back of Apara's throat. "No. Of course not. I will do as they ask."

"Well," said Sergeant Brass. "This has turned into a shadowthorn wedding, hasn't it?"

"Never you mind what it is or it ain't," Kurkas replied. "Eyes on the crowd. Or are you fixing to have another lord vanish under your watch?"

Brass stiffened and again gave his attention to the seething masses in the Hayadra Grove.

Kurkas drummed fingers against thigh, and conceded that Brass had a point. It *was* a touch extravagant. Thousands had flocked to the space beneath the alabaster trees – enough that the grassy mound and the ruins of the old temple were all but hidden. Young and old, rich and poor. The rough garb of farmers and labourers mingling with the silks and velvets of the middling classes. Knots of hearthguard marked the positions of the lesser nobles. All held at bay from the podium at the grove's centre by a double line of constables.

Barely a tenth the number had come for Lord Lamirov's ascension. Lady Tarev's had drawn even less. Only Erashel Beral's confirmation had come close to challenging the size, and that by dint of her reputation having drawn southwealders from far afield. But that had been an austere and weighty occasion.

This ascension had the feel of the Reaptithe carnival whose wagons and bands had thronged the streets just weeks before. The crowd had drawn a swarm of hawkers, their candies and sweetmeats competing for spare pennies. Priests preached to inattentive listeners. Masked jesters capered hither and yon, bells ringing from their curled cloth horns. Swazzlemen had erected ramshackle booths about the grove's perimeter, eliciting childish shrieks of delight with every clack and scream as wooden puppets battered out brutal morality plays.

At the highest point, hearthguards formed a second line of defence against celebrants with more than entertainment in mind. The sky-blue tabards and lion badges of the Lamirov family dominated, with the stylised arch and wine-dark uniforms of Reveque a close second. The Trelan phoenix was pitiful by comparison, numbering a mere eight – Kurkas and Brass included.

Beyond the hearthguard, a garlanded podium had been raised beside a great tree – the last survivor of the central grove, her shimmering green crown turning umber with oncoming Fade. Shaddra, she was called in the old tongue, named like her sisters for a queenly serathiel – a keeper of dreams beneath whose boughs the pious often slumbered, and whose sprawling roots enfolded the gate to Tressia's burial catacombs. Those sisters were all gone, fuel for Ebigail Kiradin's pyres a year before, and now the venerable Shaddra ruled over her court of trees alone, granting Lumestra's blessing to the councillors upon the podium.

The absences among the Privy Council were striking. No Izack. No Messela Akadra. No Rika Tarev. The Lords Lamirov and Marest bore impassive expressions little removed from scowls. Lady Beral's folded arms suggested defiance. And Kurkas knew for a fact that Lord Trelan attended out of duty alone. Only Lord Reveque smiled as he spoke, head bowed, with Lord Trelan and soon-to-be Lord Zarn.

"I guess Konor Zarn's not a popular fellow with the highbloods," said Kurkas.

Brass offered no reply. Kurkas, never one for unnecessary contemplation, nevertheless regretted his earlier harsh words. Like him, Brass had served in the Akadra hearthguard. Difference was, where Kurkas had been recommended – and even courted – to transfer allegiance, Brass had found himself adrift following the disappearance of Lord Hadon Akadra. Though Kurkas had no real regrets about accepting the Trelan phoenix, he still felt a pang with the sable surcoats and silver swan of the Akadra hearthguard so close. Brass undoubtedly felt the loss keener.

"Look," murmured Kurkas. "I spoke out of turn. Nearly lost Lord Trelan when that chandelier came down. It's making me jumpy."

Brass grunted. "I heard that was an accident."

"Yeah, I heard that too. But we do have so many *accidents* in this city, don't we?"

"True." Brass paused, the ebb and flow of his features speaking to weighty consideration. "He's a good 'un. When that fever came for my Kandrinne last Wintertide? He paid for a physician. Probably saved her life."

"Then we'd better keep him out of the Raven's grasp, hadn't we?"

A blare of buccinas drowned Brass' reply and silenced the crowd. Lord Reveque approached the podium's edge.

"Citizens of the Republic. Today is another milestone as we rebuild that which had fallen into decay." Lord Reveque spread his arms. A supplicant speaking to a master, rather than a ruler speaking to sub-jects. "The Council has too long been dominated by those who have put their own advancement over that of this city, and this Republic. When I accepted the position of First Councillor, I swore I'd fill empty seats with worthy souls. That our nation would be guided by honest debate and shrewd minds, rather than selfishness and petty interest. Today, I fulfil that promise."

Applause rippled across the hilltop. Even a few cheers. Kurkas refrained from either, his eye skipping from one adulating group to another, seeking trouble. The old Lord Reveque had been well-meaning, but walked as if he at any moment expected the ground to swallow him up. Full of good intent, but lacking resolve. The man on the stage was another matter entirely.

Brass grunted. "Looks like he wants to scarper and never come back."

Kurkas frowned, but saw nothing of the claim reflected in Lord Reveque's expression or posture. "I don't see it myself."

"It's the eyes," said Brass. "Prey's always like that. Hackles up, a firm stare and a snarl on the lips, but the eyes always tell the truth."

Poacher's knowledge? Brass had been a blight on the Akadra estates before he'd been put to honest employment. "Don't let his hearthguard hear you say that. Nor Lord Trelan."

"You reckon I blame him?" Brass spat on the grass. "Me, I'd rather swim with sharks than witter at council. At least you know what you're in for."

Lord Reveque at last broke his spread-armed pose, and gestured for quiet. "Friends. Citizens." He lingered on the latter word. "In the name of the Council and the Republic, I welcome Konor Zarn to the service of the Privy Council, and his family to the first rank."

Lord Zarn joined him at the podium's edge. The crowd's joy crashed back full force, cheers drowning out applause in a raw, almost frantic bellow. Fists punched the air. Old soldiers hoisted scabbarded swords high in salute.

Kurkas chewed thoughtfully on his lower lip. Viktor Akadra had earned such a response when he'd been named the Council's Champion. But he'd been a war hero. The vanquisher of rebellion and shadowthorns. The Raven's right talon, bloody to the knuckle. Zarn had done nothing save amass a small fortune through trade. And yet the cheers grew louder as he offered a deep and florid bow.

There was little denying that Zarn was handsome – black hair, oiled and brushed back from his brow, combined well with narrow, aquiline features. His dark green suit was trimmed with gold brocade, and clung tight to his wiry frame in a manner that suggested the tailor's skill had been every bit as expensive as the cloth. Gold also trimmed the white velvet cloak – a garment so short and narrow-cut it served no purpose other than an excuse to wear the opal-crusted clasp holding it in place.

It was an appearance to bewitch and beguile, to set hearts a-fluttering, or otherwise earn their envy. And yet Kurkas found himself beset neither by tremor nor jealousy. For all that Zarn seemed the perfect match for the lustful dreams of his youth, the man's manner was somehow amiss. Even as Zarn straightened and gazed out across the Hayadra Grove, Kurkas had the peculiar sense that he didn't see the assembled citizenry, but his own reflection.

"I don't have the First Councillor's way with words . . . " Zarn's voice was perfect complement to appearance – warm with promise, but lacking depth. "So I'll restrict myself to two pledges. The first is that I shall do my utmost to live up to the responsibilities of this great office. And the second is that I shall not forget my friends."

He spread his arms, not in supplication, as Malachi had done, but as a showman. The crowd cheered again, though on the podium, only Lord Lamirov seemed pleased, no doubt counting himself among Zarn's nebulous "friends". By contrast, Lord Trelan's expression was a study in stony neutrality. Kurkas wondered – not for the first time – why his master expected anything different.

Archimandrite Jezek made careful procession up the podium's steps, the foot of his sceptre thumping and his scarlet robes pooling behind. A black-clad serene followed, bearing a time-worn copy of the second book of Astarria.

As Zarn placed his hand on the book, Kurkas turned his back on the podium, and set his attention on the crowd once more. He'd heard the oath more times than he cared to remember. He'd even spoken it himself, back when he'd first enlisted – though like most he was entirely ignorant of the old, formal language and had merely parroted the sounds.

The crowd listened with rapt attention, although by now the outer edges were dispersing as folk lost interest. Still, Kurkas was content to embrace a morning bereft of violence, rare as it was.

"El, versas cala te tremar . . . " intoned the archimandrite.

A disturbance broke out downhill. Drawn steel betrayed a constable seeking to send a message. Kurkas sighed. Inexperience everywhere. Nothing incited a mob to violence like the promise of a brawl.

He tapped Brass on the shoulder. "I'm off for a wander. Keep an eye, would you?"

Without waiting for confirmation, Kurkas ambled downhill.

"I'll not tell you again," said the constable with the drawn sword. "You're not coming through. Now back off."

The ragged, red-haired lad balled his fists. "I have to speak to the duke."

"Then you request an audience at the palace. But clean yourself up, first. This ain't the Southshires. We've standards here."

The lad flung himself forward, only to be intercepted and borne to the ground by a sergeant. In height, the two were evenly matched. In terms of bulk the lad was at marked disadvantage, though that didn't stop him wriggling free and regaining his feet. A peal of laughter went up from the onlookers.

The lad broke again for the line. Two constables seized his arms and held him fast. The sergeant bore down on the lad with fists clenched. The crowd's jeer darkened into disapproval.

Enough, Kurkas decided, was enough. "There a problem?"

"No problem," the sergeant spoke without turning. "Just a south-wealder brat getting a lesson in manners. His sort always did need a slave's bridle to keep 'em quiet."

"That's 'no problem, sir' or 'no problem, captain'," said Kurkas equably. "Or do you need a lesson in manners too?"

The sergeant glanced behind, winced, and unfurled his fist into something that might have passed for a salute. "Sorry, sir. Like I said, there's no problem."

"Of course there's a problem. Always is when there's a southwealder around. But it's not always them that starts trouble, is it?" Kurkas squinted at the lad. "Met you yesterday, didn't I? You miss the chains so much you're picking fights?"

"I have to speak to the duke." It was hard to look defiant when dangling from the grasp of two constables, but the lad gave a fair effort. His whole body was tense as mooring rope. "It's important."

"Everything's important." Kurkas shrugged. "Tell me, and I'll pass it on."

"No." The refusal came hurried and frantic. "I have to speak to the Phoenix."

Kurkas rubbed at his brow and glanced at the podium. "Free piece of advice, lad. Don't call him that."

"Altiris. My name's Altiris."

"Doesn't change the advice." He sighed. "Let's have the message. Then these fine gentlemen can let you go, and we can all go back to enjoying the archimandrite's droning voice."

Defiance and desperation fought for control of Altiris' features. And underneath it all, fear. "If I tell you here, now, people will die. It has to be the duke, and in private."

"Ignore him, sir," said the sergeant. "Just another southwealder dreg wasting everyone's time."

Kurkas frowned. An urgent request, a hint of mystery and peril. Just the thing to convince a soft-hearted soul like Lord Trelan. Might even get a body close enough to cause mischief. But leaving Altiris to the sergeant's displeasure meant a beating, and ugliness in the crowd warned Kurkas how *that* would end. It would have felt like a betrayal, and not just of the lad.

"Finest woman I ever knew was a southwealder," he murmured. "Let him go."

The sergeant's brow creased. "Sorry, sir, I thought I heard you say—"

"Let him go." Kurkas leaned close. "You don't want me to ask again."

The constables, faster on the uptake, let Altiris drop. He scrambled away and came to a halt as Kurkas' heavy hand found his shoulder.

"Come along," said Kurkas. "But you remember what I said about phoenixes. And don't even think about causing me any grief. You hear?"

He set off uphill towards the podium. With a last glance at the constables, Altiris fell into step.

As they approached the ring of hearthguard, the archimandrite muttered his way through the last syllables of the oath.

Zarn repeated them in a booming voice. "Te magnis cala nomaris, magnis vratis!"

Altiris shook his head. "The power of justice is power indeed?"

So the lad had an education? Lucky him. "The world ain't perfect," said Kurkas. "Still, the crowd likes him."

"Of course they do. Half of Dregmeet got drunk on Zarn's purse before midnight. They're hoping for the same again."

Kurkas grunted his surprise. Not at the bribery, which was as common as breathing in the Council's rarefied orbit. But it seemed Zarn wanted to be loved – or at least be *seen* to be loved – so badly he'd stooped to muckying his boots in Dregmeet.

"Not you, though?"

"Oh, I took his coin, but I won't cheer him." Altiris laughed bitterly. "Just because I've nothing doesn't mean I can be bought."

The archimandrite withdrew. Zarn's eyes dipped from his audience to rest on Kurkas and Altiris. Distaste, no doubt, for the two dishevelled creatures making oblique progress towards the podium. Then he returned his attention outward in final address, arms spread wide once more.

"My friends, I thank you all. I promise you, we will see the Republic restored! We will, every last one of us, get everything that we deserve!"

With a final bow, Zarn descended the stairs to the podium's rear, followed by newfound peers. Only Lord Reveque remained as the brash buccinas marked the ceremony's end, head bowed in hushed conversation with the archimandrite.

The first carriages were already pulling away along the tree-lined colonnade of Soldier's Mile as Kurkas approached the back of the podium. The name Soldier's Mile was new, bestowed in honour of the patriots Viktor Akadra had led to end Ebigail Kiradin's treason a year before. It hadn't stuck. Sinner's Mile, folk called it, linking as it did the squalid business of the council palace and the Shaddra's piety. As crack of whip and rumble of wheel bore Lord Lamirov and Lady Beral down the hill to strike fresh sins in politics' name, Kurkas climbed aboard the Trelan carriage, gestured for Altiris to follow, and awaited his master's arrival.

Lord Trelan showed no surprise at Altiris' presence, but then he *was* getting better at keeping thoughts close. He took a seat opposite and pulled the door to. "Altiris, isn't it? And in something of a state. I thought you'd been granted sanctuary."

"In the workhouse? It's just a different sort of slaving. I'll take my chances in the gutter." He leaned closer. "Your grace, I know where they are. Some of them, anyway."

Lord Trelan's eyes flickered in a wince at the reminder of his old title. "You're not making any sense."

Altiris glanced left and right before pressing on. "Our fellow southwealders, your grace. I know where the vranakin have taken them. A warehouse down in Westernport. I've seen the carts. Scores have gone in, but no one comes out."

"Have you told the constabulary?"

"Look at me. Do you imagine they'd listen? They'd just send me on my way. If I was lucky, they'd skip the beating first. If I was really lucky, they'd not tell the vranakin."

"You might be surprised. Things are changing."

"Maybe if you've a name," Altiris said sourly. "And money."

Kurkas gave a warning tug on the lad's shoulder. "That's enough."

Lord Trelan waved a dismissive hand. "It's all right, captain. It's nothing I haven't said. You're certain of what you saw?"

"I've been inside. Only over the threshold. Didn't dare go further." Altiris clenched his fists and stared down at the carriage floor. "They're killing them. Please, your grace. You have to do something."

The shallow nod. The tightness about the eyes. Signs Kurkas had come to know too well.

"Have you heard anything about this?" asked Lord Trelan.

"Not had much chance to ask around," Kurkas replied. "And after yesterday? Won't be many tongues flapping. But I'll give it a go, if that's what you want."

"How long will that take?"

"Couple of days. Maybe a week. Like I said, lips'll be tight after yesterday's raid."

"Not good enough."

Kurkas cleared his throat. "The portreeve's manor was one thing, sah. Westernport's another. Right in the thick of Dregmeet. I can round up Brass and the others, but we don't have the numbers. I've been telling you for months that you need a larger hearthguard."

"So I'll speak to the Council. Malachi can't ignore this."

"Ignore the word of a dregrat?" said Kurkas. "Nothing easier."

"He'll believe *me*."

"And if the lad's wrong?"

"You'd have me gamble lives against my reputation, captain?"

Kurkas stared past his shoulder. "'Course not."

"As for the size of the hearthguard . . . Altiris, can you handle a sword?"

"Not well."

Lord Trelan nodded. "Then you'll learn. You'll have lodgings, a wage and a purpose . . . if you want it. Otherwise, there's always the gutter."

Altiris' mouth hung open. "I'd be honoured to serve the Phoenix."

"Then you can start by never calling me that again, nor your grace. Those titles . . . " For a moment, Lord Trelan was far away, amid the ruins of an ashen, mist-wreathed home. "They don't belong to me. I don't think they ever did. 'Lord Trelan' will serve."

"You sure about this, sah?" asked Kurkas. "Not exactly the done thing, filling your hearthguard from the gutter."

"And where did you start out?"

Kurkas shot him as baleful a stare as propriety allowed, but said nothing.

Lord Trelan offered a dry chuckle and shook his head. "Then it's agreed. I've every faith that the captain of my hearthguard will make something of the boy – he's quite formidable, so I hear. Get Altiris cleaned up, give him a uniform, and meet me at the palace. We've work to do."

Fifteen

Green-white mist drowned the uneven flagstones beneath Apara's feet, and grasped at her knees. It billowed thickest about the crumbling archway, remnant of an ancient temple upon which the warehouse had been built. The cages along the walls belonged to another world, the stream of mournful sobs and ragged breaths distant and faded. Above all, it was *cold*. As chill as an elder cousin's presence. Ice under the skin, prickling at bone.

Erad's talons flashed. The mists rushed red. His victim passed, her whimper lost beneath the sonorous chant of masked vranakin concealed about the low rafters. She hung heavy a moment in the arms of two grey-robed cousins, body bound in black ribbon and garlanded with tokens of feather and bone. Then she was gone, flung past the elder cousin's crouched form and into nightmare streets beyond the archway; all crooked architecture and strange shadows beneath a viridian sky.

Apara wondered who she'd been. Another stray southwealder? A cousin who'd displeased the Parliament? It was unwise to know. Did the maid concern herself with the log given to the fire, or the butcher with the hog? All were fuel. All served grander purpose. The shadow within her disagreed, and set her gorge rising.

The elder cousin remained motionless through it all, rag-bound hands on his knees. Lost in meditation. Or what Apara assumed was meditation. He seemed *realer*, the frailty of recent months washed away by blood. By death. As if he feasted alongside the Raven when an offering was made.

"You feel it, don't you?" Even so close, Krastin seemed more shadow than shape, the flesh beneath his gold-trimmed robes a mystery save for the withered hand about a soot-black walking stick, its head sculpted in the form of a spread-winged raven. "Otherworld embraces us once more. The Raven is appeased. Even Athariss is smiling. Shurla mutters her nonsense about scripture and holy purpose, but it's a small enough price to pay if it stops her complaining."

"I feel nothing," Apara lied. Better that than admit the empty sensation in the pit of her stomach. Like pieces of her were melting into the mist. "Cold, perhaps."

A thin laugh. "It's natural to worry, but unnecessary. The long decades of our dwindling are ending. As the mists rise, the Council will learn why even Malatriant fled us. No more hiding. No more frailty. And you? The shadow preys upon your weakness. The mists will strip that weakness away and leave only strength. Perhaps an elder cousin's strength? Time will tell."

An elder cousin. How Apara had yearned for that while still a child – to have the influence of one steeped in the Raven's blessing. And yes, the fear. No one commanded fear like an elder cousin, save the three pontiffs. For all that Krastin pretended affability, his presence gnawed her spirit. Still, better him than his siblings; Athariss' bleakness and Shurla's fervour were each more unsettling in their way.

Now? The prospect brought uncertainty. Or perhaps it wasn't her uncertainty at all, but the shadow twisting her instincts. Half the problem was that Apara could no longer separate her own reservations from those forced upon her. The other half was that it was sometimes stronger than she, and held her back from the deeds required of a kernclaw. What use was an assassin incapable of bloodshed? She was fortunate the Parliament of Crows indulged her. Such largesse would not last.

Two vranakin dragged another captive to the archway. The old man offered no resistance as black ribbons were bound about his limbs, nor as the jagged eye-rune was smeared on his brow in the blood of past victims. He barely blinked as the talons stole his life. Then he too was cast through the arch into Otherworld's crooked streets, an offering to he who drew sustenance from all that perished.

Pallid etravia coalesced about the arch. Empty-eyed, they drifted past

Erad and the elder cousin. Gasps rippled as younger vranakin in the rafters made sense of the sight. Apara had walked Otherworld's time-lost streets too many times to feel more than a pang of unease. The etravia lacked the awareness to offer malice.

"You see?" Krastin breathed deep of the cold air, a man savouring the finest spring blossom. "Otherworld rises. The Raven's blessings will follow. See that nothing disturbs the work."

Apara shuddered as another piece of herself peeled away into the mists. "Yes, Crowfather."

"Again, Josiri? Can we not go a single day without re-treading old ground?"

Lord Lamirov's theatrical weariness drew a thin smile from Evarn Marest. Malachi's and Erashel Beral's discomfort differed only in degree. Konor Zarn's attention was given over to the statues looking down from on high, the lint on his jacket or the polished grain of the table top – in other words, anywhere save on the matter at hand. No help anywhere, but Josiri had long ago grown used to standing alone.

"I've neither the time nor the inclination to play games, Leonast," he said. "Lives are at stake."

Lord Lamirov leaned forward, wrinkled features approximating concern. "Then take the matter up with the constabulary."

"Captain Darrow's on the road to Torgovald, as well you know." The request that she lend expertise to the food riots had come directly from Lord Lamirov. And her deputy refused to support a foray into Dregmeet without approval from the Privy Council. "She's not expected to return today. This won't wait."

Lord Lamirov shrugged. "You're still free to act as you wish, and without wasting the Council's time, I might add. Set your hearthguard loose, if it matters so much."

Rising temper swirled to a heady brew. "I haven't the numbers for this. Some of us don't have decades of peculation and corruption lining our pockets—"

"My father was exonerated!" Lord Lamirov lurched to his feet, face ruddy and knuckles braced against the table top. "I won't have my name dragged into disrepute by a southwealder!"

Josiri regarded him with polite confusion. "... unlike the Kiradin family."

Lord Lamirov wobbled like a child's top, smoothed a hand across his bald pate and retook his seat. Josiri held his satisfaction close. Putting Lord Lamirov off-balance – pleasant though it was – wouldn't solve the issue at hand.

"Please," he said, now addressing the room entire. "I must have this council's support, either to mobilise the constabulary or through pledge of your own hearthguards."

"You're certain your informant isn't leading you astray?" asked Erashel.

Josiri hesitated. Altiris could be mistaken, or even lying. Desperation was easily faked, and it wasn't hard to conjure reasons why someone might want to lure the upstart Lord Trelan into Dregmeet. "Certain enough that inaction represents greater risk. These are our people, Erashel. Help me bring them home."

She nodded. "Of course."

A victory, but one that was both the easiest won and carried least weight. Alone of the Council, Erashel had no hearthguard at all. As for the others ... Lord Lamirov had made his position clear, and Lord Marest would follow his lead. Messela Akadra and Rika Tarev had each excused themselves from the day's business. If only Izack had been present. He'd have gleefully offered vote, hearthguard and a body of knights. But Izack had ridden for Northwatch at dawn, not on council business, but because he'd "no bloody intention of being a dancing bear at Konor Zarn's ascension".

"How many prisoners are we talking about, Josiri?" Lord Zarn asked.

"It might be hundreds."

"Or only a handful?"

"Is there a magic number at which the moral course becomes the proper one, Konor?"

"Of course not." He swatted the words aside. "But you know Dregmeet. Full to the brim with rumours and lies. Half the Crowmarket's power comes from this council's failures. The vranakin feed so many of those we can't. What happens if they're seen to lead us a merry chase through the mists? And today of all days."

Josiri bit his tongue. Was the man so vain he'd put his ascension ahead of saving lives?

Erashel scowled. "Afraid it'll sour your party, Konor?"

Lord Zarn smiled. "My party, Erashel, will proceed in glorious fashion, regardless. But if we're to deal with the Crowmarket, it must be at the proper time, and in the proper way."

Lord Tarev and Lord Lamirov nodded sage agreement. Two votes for. Three absent. Three against. Only Malachi remained. A tie would be as good as a victory, for it would bring the substantial Reveque hearthguard into the matter.

"Well, Malachi?" said Erashel.

Malachi started as if woken from a dream and brushed a greying fringe back from his brow. His gaze swept the table before settling on Lord Zarn. Watchful. A man lost to appraisal, and uncertain as to what his labours uncovered.

"I'm sorry, Erashel, Josiri," Malachi said at last, "but I fear Konor is correct. This is the perfect bait. If we're seen dancing to a vranakin drum, many will be tempted to accept the Crowmarket's promises in place of this council's authority."

"Then we should do nothing?" demanded Josiri.

"Not without cause." He rose and spread his hands, as if hoping to pull a more palatable answer from the chamber's stuffy air. "Can your informant testify? So we can hear the claims?"

Josiri hesitated with the lifeline in reach. Altiris would likely agree, little knowing the verbal mauling to follow. Would a homeless south-wealder not yet of age convince where Josiri himself had not? Unlikely.

He glanced around the table, at allies and opponents, and at the man he increasingly struggled to think of as his friend. What if Lamirov's attitude wasn't mere bluster? Or if Zarn's was owed to something more than laziness? Did they speak their own concerns, or parrot the will of the Parliament of Crows? Were that the case, putting Altiris on display invited a slit throat.

"No. She'll speak only to me." A little misdirection never hurt.

"A pretty face, is it?" murmured Lord Zarn. "Sounds more like a snare all the time."

Malachi scowled. "Konor, please. In Captain Darrow's absence, I'll direct Lieutenant Raldan to make enquiries. If your informant has a change of heart, Josiri, I'll be pleased to speak with her. Otherwise, I'm afraid the answer must be 'no'."

The slam of the door against the wall and the accompanying trickle of plaster told Kurkas everything. Lord Trelan's low-shouldered stride only reinforced the message, leaving his thunderous expression a necessary aid only to the very slowest of wits.

"The Council didn't see things your way, sah?"

Lord Trelan lurched to a halt, so blinded by anger that he'd made it halfway across the carpeted landing and well past Kurkas.

"The Council—" He cast about at the curious expressions of clerks and petitioners on the floor below, their attention drawn by his shout. He lowered his voice. "The Council wishes to take no action. So we will."

Not that there'd been any prospect of a different outcome, but a man could dream. "As you say, sah."

Lord Trelan straightened, the colour receding from his cheeks as he gathered himself. He stared over the banister. "Are the others outside?"

"Every last one, sah. And a surprise."

"I've had enough surprises today."

"You'll like this one."

Lord Trelan's eyes narrowed. Kurkas stared straight ahead and pretended not to notice as the Privy Council filed past.

"Josiri!" Lady Beral hurried over. "I was afraid I wouldn't catch up to you. Is there any hope of getting the Grand Council involved?"

Lord Trelan's basilisk stare slipped away. "With Malachi urging caution? None."

"Then we'll make do with what we have." Her expression hardened. "It was always the case that southwealders should hang together."

Malachi drained the glass and stared bleakly along the empty council chamber. The brandy did nothing to warm the chill about his heart. That last look of betrayal Josiri had shot him . . . The temptation remained to follow, to plead change of mind and do the right thing, consequences be damned. But temptation didn't blaze bright enough to burn away foreboding.

Worse was the betrayal of self. Josiri didn't make demands without cause; *that* truth left Malachi scant shelter from his own scorn. From the moment Zarn had spoken against the venture, he had known he'd have to. For if he didn't . . .

In his mind's eye, he saw again the fallen chandelier, and the bodies beneath. Only this time, it wasn't Sabelle, Dathna and the luckless Proctor Sadrianov, but Lily, Sidara and Constans. In saving them, he doomed Josiri – Erashel also, if he read her mood right. The Parliament of Crows wouldn't lightly suffer another affront in their own territory.

Have a care you do not push us any further. Was the Emissary laughing even now?

Malachi glared at the shadowed corner of the chamber. Her favourite lurking point.

"Are you happy?"

No answer. No green eyes. And yet Malachi felt her mockery all the same.

"Answer me!"

A flash of anger sent the empty glass spinning into shadow. Shards glittered in the lantern-light as it shattered against the wall. Malachi stared blankly. What would he have done had the missile struck its target? What punishment would such an offence have elicited?

The outer door creaked open behind him. "My lord, is all well?"

"An accident, Moldrov. Nothing more."

Somehow, he divorced the words from rising elation. But elation there was. Because if the shadows were empty, then his watcher wasn't there. Her absence brought freedom, if he was clever enough to make use of it. Possibly even enough to buy back a sliver of his soul.

"As you say, my lord," replied Moldrov. "I'll instruct one of the maids."

Malachi nodded, the words only half-heard as he considered timings and the layout of the city's tangled streets. Yes, it would work, for only a little risk. Friendship was worth a little risk.

"Please do," he said at last. "But first, call for a herald, would you? I've a message needs sending."

Sixteen

The slaughter had become rote. A whimper. The wet rip of steel on flesh and the daub of rune. A ribbon-bound corpse cast through the warehouse arch into Otherworld's distant fields. The muttered prayers, calling upon the Raven's favour. The icy cold of the mist, and the iron tang of blood. Even the drifting etravia. Unremarkable, save for the shadow pulsing ever more unhappily in Apara's gut.

With each new death, the shadow called on her to do something, *anything* to prevent the killing. It whispered that the ritual was not as it seemed, that the deaths were meaningless. It railed as if she herself stole the offerings' lives, and called upon her to take action.

Only the knowledge that the shadow strove thus out of fear gave Apara strength to resist. It knew the mists were its doom. That she'd be free.

If the Raven paid heed to the labours, he offered no sign. Apara was thankful for that. One encounter with the Keeper of the Dead was sufficient. Not that he'd been cruel, or even unkind. She'd been but a mote in his disinterested sight when her cousins had pledged her to his service. Better to remain unremarked and unnoticed, lest he collected on her debt this side of the grave. Apara had seen how that ended. The darker domains of the Otherworld were thick with such fallen souls, faces gaunt and eyes burning with hunger.

But still Apara wondered why, if the Raven desired tribute – if he had to be coaxed to fulfil age old-pact – why had he not come? Again, the pressure in her gut warned her that the deaths were meaningless. And, for the first time, Apara wondered if that was so.

*

Josiri peered at the bodies in the gutter. Skeins of mist clung to patched and faded garb. Masks twitched to unconscious breaths. So much for the watchfulness of vranakin. He stared across the narrow alleyway to the vast dockside warehouse, now bereft of guardians.

"I'm impressed," he murmured.

Kurkas let go the heel of a fifth body and scratched at his tangled black hair. "I have my uses. Besides, it wasn't me alone, was it? Begging your pardon, sah, but I've never seen a highblood move so fast."

Kurkas had been impressive enough, threading the mist-cloaked streets to take out both patrol and watchmen on the warehouse cause-way with a flurry of violence. A timely reminder that the captain wasn't defined by missing parts and pieces. Erashel had been something else. One-armed as he was, Kurkas would never have reached the sentries on the opposite rooftop, not without notice. Erashel had navigated the tiles like a cat. Only one vranakin had seen her coming, and she'd not had time to scream.

"It'd seem there's more in Lady Beral's past than toiling over crops," said Josiri. "I'll be more polite when next we quarrel."

Erashel appeared in a patch of mist he could've sworn was empty moments before. The close-fitting traveller's garb suited her far better than the dress she wore to council, a perfect match to boyish figure and a pauper's cropped hair. Dark and dangerous. As if the formality was worn as a disguise. Josiri had played a similar game himself for many years. Perhaps they were more alike than they were different...

"See that you are," she said. "I'd hate for us to fall out again so soon."

The joke provoked grins from nearby hearthguards. Himself and Erashel included, Josiri's small force tallied a round dozen. Enough to attempt a raid in the civilised streets beyond Dregmeet, but down in the mists? The constabulary didn't come so deep without an army, and every one of his phoenixes knew it. But none had shirked their duty. Falteringly old or desperately young, they'd followed him onto Crowmarket territory, drab cloaks worn to hide the heraldry and muffle chainmail's clink.

Kurkas leaned close. "You want to do this, now's the time. I know these streets. We linger, they'll close tight about us and squeeze us dry."

Josiri nodded. He'd never been so far into Dregmeet, and had been prepared for neither the cold nor the emptiness of the place. Save for a huddle of beggars further up the alley – a group swathed in rags so worn and filthy as to occasion the very widest of berths – there wasn't a soul in sight. Nor had he been prepared for the thin voices dancing on the edge of hearing. He saw unease reflected in the faces of his companions – even Erashel's, though she laboured to hide it.

Only Kurkas remained unaffected. No. That wasn't quite right. The one-eyed captain was still wary, but it was the wariness of knowledge more than ignorance. For better or worse, Kurkas had taken the measure of foolishness, and resigned himself to its completion.

"We're not here to fight a battle." Josiri let his voice carry as far as he dared, and infused the words with every scrap of confidence at his command, and a little that was not. "Thanks to Altiris, we know that there are prisoners in that warehouse. I'd rather get them out quietly, and without bloodshed. If the vranakin choose otherwise? Then it's a fight."

"And if that doesn't work?"

Altiris' fingers were wound tight around the pommel of his sword, but his voice was steady. The strange balance between fear and resolve.

"Then we do as the church teaches, don't we?" Kurkas shot a glance at the beggars and lowered his voice. "We put our bloody faith in the divine."

The words provoked more grins, though Altiris' was tinged with confusion.

Josiri turned to Kurkas. "How do you recommend we do this, captain?"

"Two groups, sah. You take half round the front, I'll take the rest in along the dockside."

Josiri pulled Erashel aside as Kurkas set about dividing the hearthguard. "One of us should stay here. I doubt Leonast will shed a tear if we both vanish."

"Then stay. I won't think less of you."

Her words left Josiri with the sense she'd purposefully misread his meaning, but he supposed the time for argument had been at the palace. Any doubts he'd had about Erashel's ability to look after herself had vanished when the first sentry's skull had cracked against tile.

"Then do me a favour. Stay close to Altiris," he muttered. "He wouldn't let me send him away either, and I worry more for his safety than I do yours."

"Orders, is it?" Sharp scowl melted into wicked smile. "At your command, Lord Trelan."

Kurkas was already on the move out of the alley's mouth, four cloaked hearthguards slipping through the greenish-white mists alongside. Altiris waited with the two that remained. Merisov and Taladan, both of them grey-haired veterans of the 12th regiment, recruited at the start of Kurkas' tenure.

Josiri set off across the grimy cobbles, feeling more than ever that a hundred eyes watched his every move. But he heard no cries of alarm, only the uneasy, distant voices trailing through the mists.

A smear in the grime marked where a vranakin had fallen to Kurkas' fist; a scattering of black feathers and shattered bone where a crow charm had disintegrated beneath his heel. With a last glance over his shoulder at uneven rooftops and brooding grey skies, Josiri eased the warehouse gate open and slipped inside.

Nothing at Crosswind Hall had prepared Josiri for what lay within. He'd expected the steel-barred cages, but not so many. The greenish-white mist was thicker than outside, opaque to the level of his knees and scarcely less dense above. The dark stacks of crates and cable spindles were islands floating upon a sombre sea. A cluster of vranakin gathered about a bloodied archway, greys and blacks against spattered scarlet, their chant echoing beneath the empty rafters. And all about, pallid, translucent spirits, their flesh and faded clothes little different in colour to the mists in which they stood.

"Raven's Eyes," breathed Erashel, open-mouthed.

Josiri dragged her behind a stack of mildewed crates. Altiris crouched beside him, lips working fiercely in silent prayer.

Half a dozen paces off, Merisov and Taladan crouched behind another crate. Both wore aghast expressions, but then Josiri supposed his own made interesting viewing. A hurried glance caught sight of the nearest cage, and the ragged folk within. Josiri raised a finger to his lips, warning against cries that would draw vranakin attention. He needn't have bothered. Of the six or seven captives, only one even seemed to notice him. Seemed to, for there was little recognition in those hopeless eyes. A dozen cages. Perhaps a hundred captives, all waiting for the knife.

The first spark of anger caught light in Josiri's gut.

"I've changed my mind." Erashel's cheeks were pale, her hazel eyes lacking habitual confidence. "I think I should stay outside."

The air didn't taste as air should. It lacked the mustiness of the harbourside, the decay that seemed inevitable in the rundown warehouse. Blood, yes – too much blood – and the stale foulness of men and women caged without respite. But beneath it all, a subtle, pervasive scent that defied precise definition. Forgotten recollections stirred to conscious recall, or the contentment that came with the weariness of honest labour.

Josiri felt as though he were again in the company of his mother, his sister – kith and kin long lost to the Raven's clutches. He fought the longing to embrace that feeling, to cling to a dream of the faded past, and felt himself slipping all the while. In desperation, he bit down on the heel of his hand.

The world reshaped about the flash of pain. The memories retreated. He took another breath, shallower this time. But whatever enchantment lay within the mist had lost its grasp.

All the tales of the Crowmarket and their Raven-worship, and he'd never truly believed. Not until that moment. An age too late.

Taladan jerked her head at the far wall. A pair of vranakin in mismatched garb made procession through the swirling mists, angling for the cages. Josiri pressed his shoulders against the crate and sought a fruitless glimpse of Kurkas.

What to do? Pragmatism demanded he withdraw, return with Izack and the glory of Essamere. But *was* that pragmatism, or fear? There were only a dozen vranakin in sight. The odds were equal, maybe even in his favour once contingency was invoked. Retreat, and he risked abandoning Kurkas. He guaranteed that others would die beneath the archway. All hope would be lost. But open the cages, rally the captives . . .

He was moving before conscious decision, dagger eased from its sheath. He kept low behind the crates until the jailers had passed, then ghosted in behind, grateful that the mist deadened his footsteps. Merisov drew level and nodded understanding.

One pace. Two. Josiri sprang. His hand muffled the vranakin's cry, even as his dagger took the woman's throat. He staggered under the corpse's weight, dragging it down and out of sight. Merisov inched back, burdened by his own victim. As he did so, his foot caught something hidden by the mists. It clattered away with a metallic, hollow chime.

Over by the archway, the kernclaw's head snapped up.

The chant dissolved into screaming birds.

The warehouse lurched from horror to madness. The screeching of crows shook the rafters, joined by the voices of men and women raised in wild imitation. Vranakin plunged from the ceiling with short, wicked blades flashing. Kurkas parried a lunge, then lashed out behind with his elbow. A vranakin flailed through an unseeing etravia and vanished over the quayside.

Another parry. A thrust. A second vranakin fell gasping. A third barrelled out of the mist. A shoulder struck Kurkas in the gut. His feet shot away. He howled into vapour as his head struck stone.

Above, steel glinted as a vranakin came for his throat. Eyes glazed over beneath the mask as Jaridav hacked him down from behind. She shook as she helped Kurkas rise. Only sixteen summers behind her. Never seen more action than clearing drunks from Stonecrest's gate.

"Thanks," gasped Kurkas.

He cast about the chaos. A hearthguard lay slumped beside the door. The two who remained fought back to back close by. No sign of Lord Trelan, but sounds of battle from the far corner told a tale all their own. He ignored the drifting etravia, put childhood tales to the back of his mind. He could turn to jelly later.

Two more vranakin circled close, wary now of chancing his blade. Jaridav backed up, her eyes as often on the drifting spirits as living foes.

"So much for doing it quiet," said Kurkas. "You stay close to me, lass."

Jaridav swallowed. "What do we do?"

"We make some bloody noise, that's what." He raised his voice to a roar. "For the Phoenix!"

"For the Phoenix!"

Kurkas' bellow ripped through the mist. Elation swept away Josiri's annoyance at a battle cry he hated. But elation had little purchase on that moment.

Once-level odds slanted heavily in the enemy's favour. Two vranakin for every phoenix. That they weren't overwhelmed already was because so many crow-brethren hung back beside the archway where the ragged grey figure knelt in meditation.

Josiri caught a flicker of motion and hurled himself aside. A dagger clattered off the wall. The thrower reeled away as Erashel's thrust ripped into his leather-clad arm. She pursued, and another vranakin dropped from the rafters.

"Erashel!"

Josiri struck the vranakin's sword aside. The blow meant for Erashel's spine instead scraped across her ribs. She hissed and fell to one knee. As the vranakin rounded on Josiri, Altiris came screaming out of the mist.

"For the Phoenix!"

What Altiris' artless, two-handed haymaker lacked in precision, it compensated for in raw power. The vranakin spiralled away, the vengeful southwealder in pursuit.

Josiri knelt. "How bad is it?"

"Barely a graze." Erashel winced through the lie. "I'm just glad *they* bleed. I was starting to wonder."

Taladan staggered into view. The left side of her face was masked in blood, her cloak ragged and torn. "This would be a good time for that divine favour."

"Wouldn't it just." Josiri grimaced and admitted defeat. "For the Phoenix!"

"*For the Phoenix!*"

Voices hammered out of the mist in reply.

Taladan thrust her sword high. "For the—"

The space between them came alive with a torrent of crow voices. Raking talons snatched her screaming into darkness.

Josiri spun on his heel as Taladan's body fell. A man's form took shape among a storm of shadowy wings. Then it dissolved, seething like smoke through the mist.

Josiri shoved Erashel clear. The kernclaw boiled towards him, a nightmare given form, but Josiri had nightmares aplenty. The eyes mattered. Only the eyes.

With the shadow but a pace distant, a flicker in its green eyes betrayed intent. Steel scraped as bloodied talons met Eskagard-forged steel. Josiri's riposte flowed from shoulder to wrist. The kernclaw flinched away then whirled about, talons slashing at eye-level.

Josiri jerked his sword to parry, though he knew it to be too little, too late.

The kernclaw shrieked and whirled away. Erashel stood behind. Blood oozed between fingers clasped to her side and gleamed on the edge of her blade. A nod of breathless gratitude, and Josiri dived in pursuit. The kernclaw collapsed against a stack of crates. Screeching, shadowy flock boiled away, and then he was merely a man in a feathered cloak, heels kicking as he struggled to stand.

With a growl of triumph, Josiri closed the last distance and levelled his sword like a spear at eyes that no longer glowed.

The air came alive with crow-voices once more.

This time from behind.

Apara bore Josiri to the ground. His sword skittered into the mist, and then she was atop him, the tips of her talons against his throat.

"Enough!" she shouted. "Lay down your swords or Lord Trelan dies!"

She met his gaze, daring him to call her bluff. The shadow wouldn't let her kill him in cold blood. Even now, certainty bled away beneath its disapproval. And she didn't care for the way Lord Trelan regarded her. Fear, certainly. Fear was good. Anger was expected. But . . . recognition? Had she erred in coming so close? Had some quirk of mannerism or voice betrayed her dual life?

"I know you," he said. "Sevaka's sister. The thief. We wondered what had become of you. I told her I'd look for you, but I never found you."

So her position on the Council remained secure? "I have no sister, only cousins." She raised her voice. "Weapons down! I won't ask again!"

The hearthguards complied. The one-armed captain – the man whose onslaught had left three dead cousins in its wake, and as many wounded besides – obeyed last of all. Only Lady Beral refused. Even though her face was taut with pain, the steel in her hand remained second to that in her eyes.

"You'll kill him anyway."

"Dead men are of no use to the Parliament of Crows, Erashel." The use of the personal name was a mistake, born of one-sided familiarity, but there was no taking it back. "The Crowmarket is rising from the shadows. You can both be part of that."

Erad staggered upright. Parting the ring of cousins about Erashel, he ripped the sword from her hand. "What are you doing, Apara?"

"It never hurts to have more voices on the Council."

Erashel's eyes touched on the bloodied archway. Josiri laughed. Talons at his throat, and his pitiful band dead or ringed with blades, and he actually *laughed*. Anger mingled with admiration for a strength she lacked. The raven cloak murmured discontent. The shadow hissed.

"We're southwealders," he said. "Threats don't buy our allegiance."

Admiration faded. Defiance was one thing, idiocy another.

"Fine." Apara dragged Josiri upright and pushed him to Erad. "Give him to the Raven."

"Gladly, cousin."

Erad's shove propelled Josiri through the dead-eyed etravia. He walked backwards, eyes never leaving Apara's. "It's not too late. You can be free, as Sevaka is free."

Erad's talons goaded him towards the archway, and the silent elder cousin kneeling alongside.

The raven cloak's voices blossomed in discomfort, and Apara wondered why. The shadow squirmed in her gut. But stopping her from landing a deathblow was one thing; it lacked the strength to compel her to prevent another's.

"So like a councillor," she replied. "Always bargaining with something not yours to offer."

Erad set his talons at Josiri's throat. Fresh blood trickled along the steel. Still Josiri gazed defiantly back.

"You forget," he said. "Before I was a councillor, I was a wolf's-head. And if you learn anything as a wolf's-head, it's to never show your full hand until you must."

The warehouse door exploded inwards.

Seventeen

Anastacia seldom looked more unreal than in that moment, framed by the shattered warehouse door, and mists coiling about the rags of her beggar's disguise. The gold and white of her doll's mask conspired to fury without expression, and her sing-song voice held bleak promise.

[[Crawl away, Raven-sworn.]]

The lack of a weapon in her gloved hand little diminished the words' threat. Silence met Ana's demand; vranakin and hearthguard alike frozen in transient expectation.

All save Josiri, who grinned like a madman. "I'd do as you're told. My offer stands."

Sevaka's sister stiffened.

A half-dozen newcomers pressed in behind Ana, swords and cudgels ready. Erashel's men.

What the impoverished Lady Beral lacked in hearthguard, she compensated for in influence with the scattered southwealder community. They'd come without question, setting aside duties and labours to join Anastacia's disguised vigil. The signal phrase had been Kurkas' idea. *For the Phoenix.* A battle cry Ana knew Josiri would countenance only in direst circumstance. He forgave them both.

The male kernclaw shoved Josiri into Sevaka's sister's grasp and split apart in a storm of inky feathers. Silence drowned beneath the maddened screech of birds.

Beating wings dragged Ana into darkness. Sparks flew as steel talons sliced through soiled rags and chinked against samite porcelain beneath. A choked cry. A hollow thud.

The crows scattered. The kernclaw thrashed with Ana's hand tight about his throat – a grown man suspended a foot off the ground by a figure slender to the point of fragility. He gave a small, stuttering gasp, talons slashing uselessly at her arms.

[[I won't ask again.]]

She cuffed him about the head and cast the unconscious body aside.

Josiri drove his elbow into his captor's gut and dived for his sword.

Ana's companions charged. Anarchy overtook the warehouse for the second time. As Josiri's straining fingers found the grips of his sword, Altiris flung himself at a vranakin.

The clash of swords chimed through the mists. The first screams followed.

Expecting at any moment to feel talons in his spine, Josiri rolled to his feet, but found no sign of his captor. Only the archway, and a drab-robed figure kneeling beside.

The knife flashed past Kurkas' ribs. Fresh tinder for future nightmares. Then the vranakin was within reach. He clubbed her down and kicked her twice in the head. To his right, Jaridav slammed a heel into a vranakin's knee. The howl of pain gurgled as her sword finished the job.

Good lass.

Kurkas scooped up his fallen sword and loped for the cages. A ragged figure spiralled overhead and crashed into the caravel's sunken timbers, courtesy of Anastacia's throw.

"Took your time, didn't you, plant pot?"

She drew back her hood, revealing a chestnut wig with plaits askew. A white face flushed with golden sheen. *That* was new. [[I can always leave.]]

Kurkas grinned. "Ain't no point now you're here, is there?" He took in the cages, and the weary, desperate eyes within. His grin slipped away. "We got a key?"

Anastacia followed his gaze. Her shoulders drew back.

[[Yes.]]

Vranakin scattered from her path. One withdrew too slowly, and died with Kurkas' blade between his ribs. Gloved hands closed about a cage's hasp and twisted. Metal screeched. Anastacia dropped the remains at her feet and ripped open the barred door.

[[Key.]]

"Show off," muttered Kurkas, but she was already on her way towards the next. He raised his voice. "Look lively, you lot!"

Disbelieving eyes regarded him from inside the cage, and then the prisoners moved for the threshold. The third – an old woman – stumbled across the rusted doorway. Kurkas held her upright.

"Jaridav? Brass? Lend a hand, would you?"

"I have her." Wiping filthy blond hair back from his eyes, Lord Trelan propped his shoulder beneath the old woman's. "See to the others."

"Yes, sah!"

Another crash of steel echoed as Anastacia ripped open another cage. Further along, Altiris set purloined key to another lock. A vranakin lunged, and reeled away as one of Lady Beral's militia swung at his head.

A new scream split the air, a shriek so mournful and soul-struck that it stole the breath from Kurkas' lungs and set goose-bumps racing across his skin.

He stared across the warehouse to the archway. The grey-robed figure was on his feet, cloth-wrapped hands about the wrists of one of Lady Beral's militia and his cloak streaming behind like the wings of some vast, tattered moth.

The scream faded. Released, the militiaman fell away, withered lips drawn tight across a rictus grin. Dust scattered from brittle hair and sunken cheeks. Pearlescent, sightless eyes gleamed in reflected light as the body slid into the mists.

Kurkas licked dry lips. He knew about the elder cousins, of course – you couldn't grow up in Dregmeet and not – but there was knowing, and there was *knowing*. In that mist-shrouded warehouse, the etravia retreating from the grey figure as readily as the living, he caught a glimmer of just how far short that knowledge had fallen.

"Blessed Lumestra . . ." murmured Lord Trelan.

Gasps and terrified sobs came not only from the captives – not only from his lordship's mishmash of soldiers – but from vranakin also.

Kurkas kindled the scraps of his fleeting courage. "Hearthguard! To me!"

An insistent hand fell on his shoulder. [[No. Get everyone out.]]

Too often, Kurkas found Anastacia's voice hard to read. Not now.

Loathing. Concern. Disgust. She strode past, arrow-straight through the mists.

[[You do not belong in this world.]]

"Nor do you." Robes hissing and snapping, the elder cousin lunged.

Anastacia caught his rag-bound hands at her throat. Fingers interlocked. Boots scraped on stone. Slowly, impossibly, she slid backwards.

Her hollow cry, frustration tinged with pain, echoed through the mists.

Kurkas gaped, the empty feeling returning to his gut. He'd seen some of what Anastacia could do. He'd heard more – not least that she'd stood square in the path of a charging grunda and not lost an inch of ground. To see her overmatched?

"Kelver? Get this woman outside." Lord Trelan started forward. "Kurkas? Merisov? You're with me."

Anastacia slipped another inch. Dark-carapaced insects scuttled beneath the elder cousin's robes, rushing across linked hands and Anastacia's grubby sleeves.

Kurkas tried to tear his gaze away. "She said 'no'."

"I don't care," said Lord Trelan.

Lady Beral drew closer, her eyes glued to the contest. "Don't be a fool, Josiri. Remember why we're here."

Anastacia's gloves disintegrated into dust and desiccated cloth. Her legs buckled. Her knee hit mist-cloaked flagstones. Her shoulders heaved as one labouring to breathe, though she never did. Her arms trembled.

[[I said LEAVE!]]

The air howled with a sudden, furious wind. Kurkas flung up an arm to shield his eyes as Anastacia vanished in a flash of searing, golden light.

Josiri staggered upright, blinking to clear dark spots from his eyes. Fire raced across walls and rafters, filling the air with bitter, choking smoke. Righted by a spluttering Altiris, he stared back towards the archway.

"Ana?"

She was on her feet, a pair of translucent wings spread behind; vaporous golden feathers black as soot at the edges, her rags charring as fire took hold. Her hands were still clasped to those of her grey opponent, but her stance was subtly different. No longer was she holding him at bay, but locking him in *place*. Insects skittered away across her arms, shells crackling in the flames. Horrific, but for the laughter spilling from frozen lips.

Actually no. The laughter made it worse.

[[I am a serathiel! A daughter of Lumestra! Guardian of Astarria's golden towers! I do not kneel to the dead!]]

Altiris stared, awestruck and open-mouthed.

The mists parted to Josiri's left. A coughing Kurkas lurched to his feet. "You know she could do that?"

"No."

The crash of a falling beam dragged Josiri back to reality. Already the smoke was as dense about the roof as the mist was the floor. The cages were empty, the path to the door full of fleeing souls, some running, some hobbling and a few carried. Erashel chivvied them along with barked command and shove.

Heat blossomed. Josiri joined the etravia in staring blankly at the shifting contest between serathi and ... whatever the grey figure truly was.

Concern for Anastacia battled fear. But more than ever, Josiri had no idea how to help. He'd seen so many sides of her over the years, but there was always more lurking behind the veil. Friends, lovers, partners in conspiracy ... From their first meeting, he'd known she was more than he'd ever be. Never had their differences been starker. Was this how an ant stared at the sun?

The grey figure screeched as the flames took hold. Golden wings, alabaster skin and tattered grey robes vanished in a maelstrom of blazing timber and spiralling smoke.

"Go," Josiri told Kurkas.

"Sah!" He frowned. "What about the vranakin?"

"Let them burn." Josiri tugged at Altiris' arm. "Come on, lad."

Kurkas set off for the warehouse door. Skin prickling with sweat, Josiri followed.

Half-blinded by the smoke, he never saw the kernclaw's approach. There was only the maddened shriek of a raven cloak, the thick wet scrape of its talons, and Altiris' scream. Josiri spun around in time to see the lad fall, his belly torn apart. Beyond, bird-shapes swirled in the thickening smoke.

"Altiris!"

Josiri knelt beside the wounded boy – still alive, though that was little mercy. The kernclaw would have done kinder to cut his throat.

"He came between the Raven and his promised prey." The kernclaw's voice lacked its earlier strength, his posture its earlier certainty.

Josiri struck the first slash aside. The second scraped past his guard and split the skin on his right cheek. He circled away from Altiris' fading gurgles. Blazing wattle peeled from a nearby wall, scattering flames through the mist.

Claws made a dizzying dance, swirling ephemeral smoke and divine mist. With each scrape of steel, Josiri lost ground. Every slash ran him closer than the last. Every parry inched closer to disaster.

Raven's Eyes! Where was Kurkas?

The kernclaw cried out and spun away. Josiri caught sight of a dagger's slender hilt protruding from his shoulder. A storm of black wings, and the kernclaw was gone.

Josiri gasped down stinging breath and blinked smoke from his eyes. Kurkas and Brass stumbled into sight. "You cut that fine, Vladama."

"All part of the service, sah!"

Ana, her clothing charred and the samite porcelain of her face smudged black, staggered out of the smoke. Of the golden wings – of the light she'd wielded – he glimpsed no sign. With every step, her feet caught as one on the point of complete collapse.

"Go, lord." Brass gathered Altiris beneath shoulder and knees. The lad moaned, eyes wild and unfocused. The phoenix tabard he'd worn so proudly was torn and bloody cloth. "I have the boy. See to your lady."

Sheathing his sword, Josiri slid an arm about Ana's waist. She sank into him, the exposed clay of her arms warm against his skin.

[[That was fun.]]

A blazing rafter crashed through the smoke. Tiles followed suit, stone rain shattering on the floor.

Apara clung to the rafters as the warehouse burned. So many cousins dead. The Raven's offerings taken. And through it all, she'd kept to the shadows, forbidden to act by the sliver of darkness Viktor Akadra had set in her soul. But the strangest thing was ... she wasn't certain she'd wanted to.

And as for the elder cousin ... Was that revolting abomination of an existence to be her reward for faithful service? Were they all like that? Decay clothed in tattered robes? Neither dead nor alive? She gagged – a mistake in the acrid air.

A portion of roof gave way, burying the mass of burned flesh that had once been an elder cousin. Past time to leave. Erad had already fled, nursing wounded pride and shoulder both. She should do the same. Let others lead the pursuit.

The main body of the warehouse collapsed as Josiri reached the alley. The roof gave way with a screeching rumble, the rear slope shedding tiles and generations of accumulated filth into the harbour. Flames flickered through the mist in their race to find fresh fuel, but the easterly Dawn Wind dissipated their fury across the water.

"Yeah," said Kurkas. "We did that nice and quiet."

[[Hush, Vladama. I've warned you about making that horrible noise.]]

Josiri sank against the alley wall. The mists felt colder than ever away from the flames. Scores of filthy, blackened faces stared back. He'd come to Westernport with fewer than twenty, and would leave with three times their number and more. He took in the sight. Hope shone in weary eyes. Filthy bodies tangled in embrace. The tears of joy. A worthwhile exchange, and a duty done.

A piercing, croaking cry split the gloomy skies. It was answered a dozenfold across the crooked rooftops. Bells tolled, joined to the rush of running feet. Along the alleyway, murmured conversations fell silent, and expressions turned to panic.

"Word's out," said Kurkas. "Every vranakin for streets'll be on our heels."

Josiri nodded bleakly. A brisk walk and they'd be at Drag Hill, and beyond Dregmeet's mists. Easy enough under most circumstances. But now, with a mob of weary, terrified people and fewer than a dozen soldiers scarcely less hale to guide them?

"Listen to me! Listen! My name is Josiri Trelan, Duke of Eskavord. Son of Kevor and Katya Trelan ... "

Faces tightened in recognition. He hated using the title to which he'd proven a poor heir, but he needed them to listen more than he needed to salve his shame.

"I've brought you this far. Stay together – stay calm – and I'll get you the rest of the way. Lady Beral?" He used the formal title deliberately. "If your militia will lead the way, my hearthguard will bring up the rear."

"Gladly, Lord Trelan."

Of course Erashel understood.

Another shriek wracked the air. Another clamour of bells. Neighbouring alleyways shook to quickening footsteps. Then the haggard procession lurched away uphill, Erashel at their head, Brass carrying the dying Altiris close behind.

Josiri glimpsed drab figures in alleyways and side streets; the gusting mist revealed others pursuing in their wake. They grew closer with every shuddering step up the cobbled incline, scavengers snapping at the heels of wounded prey.

Others followed the crooked skyline, boots clattering on tiles and leaping from rooftop to rooftop. Children lined windows, balconies and the summits of uneven walls, hurling jeers, pebbles and rancid waste. Josiri staggered on, one arm about Anastacia's waist to offer her support, and told himself that there was no evil behind their malice, that it was just the cruelty of poverty.

"Keep going!" he shouted. "We're almost clear. We cross Drag Hill and make for the Hayadra Grove. They'll not follow us there."

A fresh jeer rang out above. Josiri's head snapped back beneath a stone's glancing blow. He clapped his free hand to his brow and swore.

[[So much for the Council's authority.]]

Anastacia's remark, which would ordinarily have been sharpened to a razor's point, was distant and languid. Signs of an exhaustion seldom seen. Josiri forced a smile. "At least you're feeling better."

[[I'm fine. Truly I am.]] She made no effort to pull away. [[For a moment, I was myself again. My *real* self, not this shell of spirit and clay. I could smell the smoke. I felt the fire's heat on my face. It was . . . oh, it was wonderful.]]

"How? How did it happen?"

[[I don't know.]]

He'd known her too long to not recognise the lie, but lacked the energy to offer challenge.

The first suggestion of open sky clawed its way through the jettied roofs, not yet the blue of a sun-graced afternoon, but the first mellowing of mournful grey. Drag Hill. So named for the cargo incline used before more accessible harbours were cleared further north.

Almost there.

Josiri only hoped that Kurkas had been right about the vranakin halting at Dregmeet's border. His own legs shook from the steep climb – the starving and wounded were immeasurably worse off.

The familiar chorus of crow-voices echoed across the rearward rooftops as they left the mists behind. Jeers from the buildings fell away into raucous, bloodthirsty cheers.

"Pick up your feet!" bellowed Kurkas. "Move it!"

Josiri glanced back over his shoulder. On the right-hand side of the street, a kernclaw clung to a bell tower's sill, then dissolved into a torrent of sable wings to continue pursuit. Two more ran full tilt across the sunken rooftops to the left, effortlessly vaulting a broad alley.

On the threshold of Drag Hill a new problem loomed. The barbican in the old wall; a defence against pirates and Thrakkian raiders of yore. The gate itself hadn't closed in decades, and the dilapidated wall was half its former height, but the choke point of the narrow archway would give the kernclaws all the time they needed to close the distance.

Unless someone stopped them.

Josiri drew to a halt where Drag Hill opened into the barbican approach. "Enough left for a defiant gesture?"

Ana pulled free and nodded. [[With you? Always.]]

But she tottered, an arm outflung for balance. Josiri strove not to notice, and drew a sword heavier than it had been before. "Captain Kurkas!"

"Sah!"

"Get everyone home, captain."

"Certainly bloody won't, sah! Lady Beral and her lot have that well in hand." Kurkas limped to take position between them. "Hearthguard! This is the line. Time to earn your pay."

One by one, they formed up. A thin line of king's blue, blazoned with the spread-winged phoenix. Jaridav. Kelver. Merisov. Only Brass went on with the rest, Altiris a limp bundle in his arms.

A district emptied onto the hillside. Urged on by crow-voices and ringing bells, the mob drew on through the mists, knives and cudgels ready. The poor and hungry come with expectation of rich pickings, the vranakin in search of revenge.

"Death and Honour, captain," said Josiri.

Kurkas shrugged and gave an experimental swipe of his sword. "I prefer 'For the Phoenix.'"

"Shut up."

"Sah!"

On the rooftops, a kernclaw threw back his head and screeched. The mob roared in answer and broke into a ragged, stumbling run. The kernclaw spread his cloak wide and cast himself to the winds. Talons glinted.

Josiri staggered in the backwash of something heavy. The gleaming shape blurred over his head. It caught the kernclaw mid-flight, and bore him to the cobbles. The simarka landed rather better than its victim, sculpted forepaws braced against the kernclaw's chest and noble, leonine brow gazing intently down at its prize. The kernclaw's scream died as metal jaws tore out his throat.

The mob's fury ebbed as more simarka loped to join the first, skirting Josiri's thin line of phoenixes to form one of bronze a dozen paces to his front. Others scrabbled for purchase on the crumbling wall and bounded down to join their fellows.

The mob juddered to a halt. As the line of simarka thickened to a full dozen, the mob dissolved back into the mist, leaving a handful of resentful vranakin to stand witness from the safety of the rooftops. A single simarka, more enthusiastic than the others, pursued too far and shuddered to a halt as the mists overcame its light. Others halted just short and prowled back and forth.

Kurkas wiped his brow. "All right, plant pot. How'd you manage that?"

[[I might ask you the same.]]

Revelation arrived when congestion about the archway slackened. Three riders passed through the arch: a pair of gold-robed proctors and an aged, wiry man in altogether humbler attire who wore salt-and-pepper stubble and a wry smile. High Proctor Ilnarov was of that rare breed who mined amusement from even the most overworked seam.

Josiri blinked. "Elzar? What? Not that I'm not grateful, but you can't be here. The Council—"

"The Council, in the form of our beloved Lord Reveque, had me spend the better part of the afternoon ushering cohort after cohort of simarka from the foundry to Lord Zarn's estate to add spectacle to what I suspect will be a gathering already drowning in the same. And I will *not* have my simarka sit idle when there's mischief afoot." He sniffed and swung down from his saddle. His two companions pressed on into the mist to retrieve the frozen simarka. "Lumestra's teachings about mischief are very clear."

It all sounded too convenient for truth, but what was done was done. *And* forgoing death and glory for another day among the living suited Josiri very well indeed.

"Then I'll impose further. We need physicians for the wounded."

"I've sent an apprentice to fetch them. Lady Beral was insistent. Southwealders always are, I find." Elzar crouched beside Altiris and his expression turned cold. "Poor boy."

One last defeat from the unexpected victory. "Without him, I'd be dead."

Elzar's hand brushed Altiris' brow. He shook his head. "He's all but gone. We'll make him comfortable and pray that Lumestra grants him peace."

[[No,]] Anastacia said flatly.

"Ana, this isn't the time." The last thing Josiri needed was an argument about the fate of Elzar's storied goddess.

[[That's not what I meant. You want to save the boy? There *is* someone in the city that can help him. We both know it.]]

She was right. Malachi would be furious, but did that matter any longer? He'd done nothing while people suffered and died. While others had fought, he'd spent his efforts ingratiating himself with Konor Zarn. He'd forfeited his stake in all this, and any respect owed his wishes.

Let him be furious.

"Elzar. I need your horse."

Eighteen

Afternoon wore into evening before Melanna rode for Ahrad. The hours since the fortress' fall had passed in a wrenching blur. How did one mourn a goddess? How even did one convey tidings to others? Should she even try? What right had Melanna to remove hope? Did she have a duty to the truth? A noble sentiment, to be sure, but what if all she sought was solace? Another with whom to mourn?

Perhaps her father could offer that solace. He at least lived, for the owl banner flew free atop Ahrad's keep, rather than furled to mark his passing.

No gateway remained along Ahrad's eastern walls, but a perimeter guard of Silsarian shieldsmen held vigil on the bank. The rubble slope and choked waters were thick with labourers tending the dead.

No, there was grief enough that day. The Goddess' fate would wait.

"Saranal." The havildar of the guard was a thickly bearded brute. His bare forearm wasn't flesh, but a bindwork limb of wicker and woven metal, animated by a glimmer of moonlight, and crafted to replace one lost in battle. A rare and expensive gift that spoke to a history of loyal service to his chieftain. "I am to tell you that the Emperor awaits you within the keep."

He stumbled over the formal phrasing, and the Silsarian accent – which many likened to a slow, grumbling avalanche – lent roughness. But his greeting was sincere. How far she'd come. No longer an outcast. No longer the distaff heir.

"Have the Tressians given any trouble?"

He offered a wolfish grin. "The lunassera have the living in hand."

There was no finer keeping. The healing skills of the Goddess' hand-maidens transcended the efforts of other ephemerals, bringing peace to seething wounds and speeding recovery through precious salve and soothing touch. A worthy tribute to the defeated, to have the lunassera tend the enemy. A small gesture set against the dishonour of unheralded assault, but small changes rippled outward. The people of the border-lands would not be enemies for ever. Mercy would speed transition. If they were free of the Dark. There could be no clemency for those afflicted with the Sceadotha's curse.

"And the dead?"

He shrugged and thus revealed a deeper truth. The Tressian fallen would be given to the worms, there to languish in darkness until a Third Dawn that would likely never come. Melanna had never understood that. The promise of tomorrow superseding the passage of today. But it was the Tressian way, and would be respected. Glory in victory, fortitude in defeat, and honour always. The warrior's mantra.

She thanked the havildar and spurred through the sentry line.

Long hours after the battle's end, there was still work for the lunas-sera. They drifted like ghosts over the broken ground, bearing biers to pyres already burning in the innermost courtyard. Men walked with them, heads bowed and helms removed out of respect. Others knelt upon the rubble where brothers and sons had fallen, and wept for their loss.

In the middle bailey, where damage to the wall was less pronounced, men erected a palisade of new-felled timber to span the gap. The air was full of groaning wagons, the bellows of straining work crews. Whenever the wind dropped, a foul stench rose – death, soured further by sweat and the aroma of dung.

Only in the bailey's absolute centre was there peace. The Huntsman's spear lay untouched in a ring of smooth stones, cold and alone. When Melanna slid from her saddle and crunched across the autumn leaves, she understood why. The air within the ring was cold, in defiance of the sunshine. It crawled across her skin, neither wholesome nor entirely unpleasant. It simply . . . was.

Melanna knelt among the brittle leaves and closed her eyes. The Huntsman had set her on this path as surely as his mistress. He'd defied

Ashana to do so. And yet Melanna realised she'd never offered thanks or prayer. Now he too was gone, and the chance was lost.

Realisation brought forth tears held too long. Brimming heart couldn't say whether they were offered for Ashana, her Huntsman or the hundreds who joined them in death. The Tressians wouldn't have understood. They couldn't comprehend that a warrior's tears were her greatest gift, save her life.

"Ashanal?"

Melanna opened her eyes. Sera stood on the ring's edge, another lunassera waiting in close attendance – a bright, calm presence among the drab bustle. More surprising was the sight of Melanna's own outstretched hand, fingers spread, less than a span from the spear.

"That weapon is not for you," said Sera. Both lunassera trembled with unease, their eyes ever upon the spear. "Leave it be."

As Melanna let her hand fall, she noticed green shoots among the russet leaves.

"Not everything is for ever," said Sera.

Melanna stood, comforted, though she knew not exactly *why*. It was only then she noticed uneasily how Sera's white robes glistened with fresh blood. "Are you hurt?"

Lips twitched beneath the silver half-mask. "No, Ashanal. The prisoners."

Unease returned. The prisoners. Taken in battle that had come without warning. "I would see them."

Sera offered a fluid bow. "Of course, Ashanal."

Melanna turned to the other lunassera. "Would you go to my father, and tell him where I can be found?"

The lunassera glanced at Sera for confirmation, then bowed and withdrew.

They headed north, Sera on foot and Melanna in the saddle. As they travelled, they overtook a column of prisoners, hands bound and heads bowed as lunassera goaded them on. Crusted blood upon brow and tunic spoke to wounds taken. But none were tainted by Akadra's curse – by the deathless Dark that hung like a cloak about those it corrupted.

The morning's dilemma returned. Did Sera not deserve to know the Goddess' fate? The lunassera were Ashana's handmaidens, the keepers of her temples and her mysteries. They, more than any, deserved to know of her passing. But something held Melanna back.

Unease redoubled as they drew near to a broad, squat building tucked inside the middle wall. A truncated tower marked it as a Lumestran church, though the pedestal beside its door was empty, its statue dashed to rubble. A ring of lunassera guarded the entrance. Cold, clear song danced about the walls. Not moribund Tressian hymns, but sweet praise offered to Ashana.

As Melanna drew nearer, a wagoner lashed his grunda to motion. Melanna peered over the dray's timber side. A corpse wagon, laden with Tressians. More than ever, Melanna felt the burden of her own, unbloodied armour.

The lunassera parted without challenge, and Melanna dismounted before the church's door. She stumbled on the ridged and rutted mud. The corpse wagon had not been the first, just as it was unlikely to be the last. She'd seen outriders dragging Tressians back to their abandoned fortress.

The iron stench hit Melanna as she passed beyond the gateway. Death from a gushing vein, hot, rich and pungent. Subtler notes drifted above: sweet incense, and the faint perfume of burning heather. Soft, stuttered moans drifted beneath soothing song.

She crossed the vestibule, passing through the six veils of silk and one of cotton strung from archway stones to mark the lunassera's domain. Seven steps of purity by which sins were driven out and shelter provided.

By the time Melanna reached the final veil, her throat was thick with blood, her soul weary with the sounds of dying. It reminded her too much of the stockade after the Battle of Davenwood, her father's life ebbing away, and despair so thick she'd almost choked. But there had been kindness, too. Freedom offered at the hand of Josiri Trelan. A man bound close to Akadra, but not corrupted by him. Melanna hoped he remained so.

She parted the final veil and walked into nightmare.

The sanctum's pews had been pushed to the chamber's sides to clear space beneath the bell tower, the windows covered with black cloth stripped from the lunassera's sanctum tent. What light penetrated ashen incense sprang from the guttering white flame of silver braziers set on altar and tomb. Scores of Tressian soldiers stood in uneven lines, wrists bound – their eyes glassy, unseeing. A lunassera waited behind each, a glinting, translucent shard dagger pressed at every throat. Others knelt about the perimeter, voices raised in a song that had long since lost its beauty. And bodies, so many bodies. Enough that the floor was slick with blood.

Elspeth stood halfway along the furthest line, wearing what Melanna took for a red dress, until she realised the stain went far beyond the cloth's extent. Her skin was smeared with it, even to her lower cheek. A soldier stood before her, back arched and her hand about his throat. A silver dagger gleamed in her other – though it, like her dress, was slick with gore.

The grin of the Silsarian havildar. The disturbed ground beyond the gate that spoke to the departure of many wagons. Disgust and shame boiled free. The cotton veil slipped from Melanna's hand, and fell closed behind.

"Stop!"

Elspeth started. The song faded. Lunassera stared, unabashed. Not one Tressian responded, their wits far afield. What sounds they made were those of sleepers lost to the darkest of dreams.

"What is this?" Melanna demanded.

Elspeth barely glanced at her. "What we came to do."

The silver slit the Tressian's throat.

"No!" shouted Melanna.

The soldier gurgled his last. No cry. No struggle. He simply fell forward into Elspeth's arms. The wrinkle of his expression might have been a smile.

Elspeth held the convulsing body as the tremors faded, her grey eyes glinting as if she sought to memorise every detail. How many other such details had she witnessed? Melanna stared, numbed by the barbarity. The lunassera held their positions, daggers at Tressian throats.

"All is as it should be, Ashanal."

Melanna spun around. Sera's masked face was suddenly a stranger's. "How can you say such a thing?"

"How can I not? She is the Goddess' daughter."

"So am I."

The twitch of Sera's lips spoke volumes. Ashanal wasn't a title of equality. A daughter of Ashana's heart was nothing to one sprung from divine essence. Cold shivered Melanna's spine. The lunassera had followed her when no other would. In the fury of battle, she'd felt safe in their company – even loved. Now, surrounded by them in that place of slaughter, she was alone.

"I am still the Emperor's daughter. You *will* obey my command. This horror ends. Now."

Sera's eyes twitched beneath her silver mask. "It is the old way, Ashanal."

The old way. A bloodier time. Without mercy, and without honour. Hearts offered in tribute beneath a waxing moon. Melanna knew the stories well, but the Ashana who had revelled in those tributes was not the Goddess she'd known, but another deity whose name and trappings the successor had claimed. A deity that was *not* Elspeth's mother any more than she was Melanna's. Expediency and half-truths. Old religion roused to justify deed.

"They feel nothing. This is kindness. It is necessary." Elspeth stepped over a seeping corpse. "All who bear the Dark must die."

Melanna gazed at the prisoners. In her haste, had she overlooked the taint of the Dark? But no, there was nothing. No bleak and writhing halo. No abyssal mantle seen more with the soul than the eye.

"The Dark has no claim on these people," she snarled.

Elspeth shrugged. "Why chance that you're wrong? They are your enemies."

"We kill on the battlefield, with honour! Not . . . Not this!"

Elspeth leaned close. "My mother foresaw the Republic overrun with the Dark and a populace under its sway. Have you forgotten so soon?"

Her presence swelled in unspoken demand, hidden corners of divinity scratching at the world Melanna perceived. Somehow, she met the stare without flinching. Fear shone in Elspeth's eyes. It wasn't alone. Outrage enough for three women, and plenty of anger alongside – even the echo of the curiosity with which she'd beheld the dying Tressian. But a child's fear bubbled beneath, nameless and nebulous.

"Prophecy is a word by which we justify our deeds, or excuse their lack." Sorrow rushed cold across Melanna's anger. "Ashana feared the rise of the Dark and acted to prevent it. She wouldn't want this. We march into death. We don't carry it with us."

"You dare speak for my mother?"

"Someone must."

Elspeth's expression set hard as granite. The fear in her eyes drowned all else. "What do you mean?"

She already knew. At least in part. Was this slaughter as much directionless grief as misguided zeal? Did it even matter, now the truth was halfway in the open?

"Our mother is dead. I held her as she passed."

"*Our* mother?" Elspeth hung her head. Bitter laughter spilled free. "You'd match your loss to mine?"

She sprang, the motion so swift and savage Melanna barely caught her wrist. The dagger's point trembled inches from her eyes. The world spun. Melanna gasped as her back struck bloody flagstones. Then Elspeth was atop her.

"You did this!" she keened. "Your weakness!"

Pale fingernails slashed Melanna's cheek, then closed about trailing black hair and cracked her head against stone.

"Sera!"

Never in Melanna's darkest dreams had she feared she'd die surrounded by Ashana's handmaidens. But now?

The dagger ripped free. Through blurred vision and ringing ears, Melanna batted it aside. Silvered steel scraped across golden scale, then slid beneath to slice flesh.

Melanna rode the flash of pain – harnessed it to desperate strength and flung Elspeth clear. Armour crunching, she rose up on one knee, and drew her sword.

"Enough!"

All froze at the thunderous bellow. The lunassera, Sera among them, stared at the ground. Elspeth went still, fists at her sides, her whole body aquiver.

Melanna's father stood beneath the sanctum arch, the grizzled Tavar Rasha leading a quartet of helmed and armoured Immortals at his back. Melanna strove to read the storm clouds in his face. Was he part of this madness? Her heart, already sore, creaked at the prospect.

"I have lived long and seen much I would rather forget," he growled. "But this?"

Melanna bowed her head. Her voice shook with rekindled anger. "She's killing them, my Emperor. She claims they are Droshna, steeped in the Dark, but they are not."

His eyes took in the rows of sightless, witless Tressians. "You are sure of this?"

"As certain as of my love for you."

"They are slighted," Elspeth's tongue was edged with glass, "as all in this land are slighted."

The Emperor's expression gathered to fury ill-concealed. Disappointment and distrust. Emotion Melanna had too often seen directed at her, but now . . . ?

"Handmaiden?" His brooding gaze fell upon Sera. "I will have the truth."

"I . . . " Sera swallowed, her eyes still fixed on the ground. "Your daughter speaks it, my Emperor."

"This was my mother's command!" said Elspeth. "You've no right—"

"The heavens are Ashana's domain. This is mine." He set his back to the scowling daughter of the moon and addressed Sera once more. "The prisoners. Will they recover?"

"The enchantment will pass with the memory of our song. Their wits will return."

"Daughter?"

Melanna rose, her veins coursing with relief. "Father."

"You will arrange shelter, and food." He addressed the whole sanctum. "The lunassera will tend their wounds as they would our own kind, or I will dig a hole in this place and bury every last one of them within it, wrath of the Goddess, or no. Am I understood?"

Fear rippled through the assembled lunassera. All save Sera knelt, shard-daggers dissipating into wisps of moonlight.

"No!" Elspeth flew across the chamber, eyes wild and dagger yet in her hand. "How dare—?"

Melanna barely saw her father move. The strike of his fist drove Elspeth to the bloody floor. The dagger skittered away. Sera flinched. Rasha started forward, sword drawn. Melanna's father checked him with a shake of the head.

Elspeth spat a stream of black blood and propped herself up on one hand. The other cradled a grazed cheek. Her voice shuddered with disbelief. "You . . . You struck me."

Uncertainty graced the Emperor's brow, and vanished so soon Melanna was certain no other had seen it.

"If you insist on behaving like a rabid cur, I will treat you as one. Struck you? Had another come at me with drawn blade, their head would be forfeit." He took a deep breath. "If your mother finds fault with my actions, she need only strike me down in turn."

"I saved your life."

Her defiance was gone, replaced by raw, ragged hurt that yearned for sympathy. Melanna had none to offer.

"As I recall saving yours when we took this fortress," Melanna's father replied. "If you've quarrel with the trade, take up your dagger, and we'll settle it now. But this? This is not our way. I pledged to fight this war, but I will cast aside honour only out of direst need. If you cannot respect that, Elspeth Ashanal – if you cannot serve your Emperor's will – you have no place at my side, or with this army. You may howl all you wish, but you will do it in the wilderness, where wild things belong."

The daughter of the moon stared down at the floor, legs curled beneath her and shoulders shuddering. A cur she'd been named. In that moment the insult fitted all too well.

Sera started forward.

"Leave her. Let her think on the path ahead." He looked out across the prisoners' sightless ranks. For the first time, sorrow touched his brow. "As for the rest . . . ? Daughter, let us unmake this horror."

Melanna rose, heart swelling. A mother was lost, but her father remained. And whatever of herself she owed Ashana, she owed to him all the more.

Kai found Melanna hours later, hunched over the empty rampart of Ahrad's citadel. Her gaze stretched across the Ravonn and away to the forested eastern hills. Stern of feature, as Aethal had so often been in adversity. Worn down, but not yet overcome. Like mother, like child.

"Daughter. Am I intruding?"

"Of course not." She stood straighter. "You taught me better than to worry over what I cannot change."

Kai fought the guilt. Each year brought regrets, but the day's tally thrust all others into shadow. "I didn't know. Even an Emperor cannot see all within his realm."

"Never say so within earshot of the Corvanti. It will be sad surprise for them to learn that their Emperor is no god."

A slim, humourless smile accompanied the words. He returned one warmer. "The opinion of the Corvanti is of little account. Yours, I value more than gold. I swear I knew nothing of Elspeth's labours. Whatever I must do to prove the truth of that, I shall."

Melanna's smile broadened to genuine warmth. "You already have, Father. Or should I demand the throne?"

"Do you desire it?"

"In proper time, not sooner. Let that day be long in coming."

For all the softening of her manner, still there was reserve. So often she was a stranger, not quite the inheritor of her mother's character, for all she'd inherited her silken black hair and watchful eyes. That Kai knew the fault to be his alone little eased frustration. Too many years wasted trying to mould her to mistaken ideal. Too much selfish anger that Aethal had not lived to bear a son. Only when he'd mustered the strength to step outside the strictures of tradition had Kai realised their daughter was a gift greater than he deserved. Melanna had been a stranger for many of her nineteen winters, and he less than a father.

He joined her at the rampart's edge, and stared out across the ruined walls. The inner and middle baileys were already thick with encampments, the cold air heavy with smoke from funeral pyres. Yet despite the glorious sight, Kai felt only weariness deeper than the labours of the day. A part of him indescribably adrift. Stark contrast to the vigour of the morning.

"Are the captives attended to?" he asked.

"Yes, Father. I had the north gatehouse turned into a prison." Her voice was as bitter as pyre-sent wind. "The lunassera watch over them as they should have from the first."

And Kai's icularis – his "eyes" – would watch the lunassera, just as they had already forewarned much of what Melanna had said. An Emperor had more than the eyes in his own head.

"Should I send the lunassera away?" asked Kai.

"Who then will tend our wounded? They have their role, and their place."

He grunted. "And Elspeth?"

"That's for you to decide."

"Indeed. But an Emperor's wisdom often lies in minds other than his own. Where better to seek it than in a daughter who is the very best of him?" He sighed. "But I fear Elspeth is the very worst of her mother. Elise, Elene, the others ... Her sisters more closely match my expectation. Perhaps the Goddess can offer a mother's chastisement?"

"And if she can't?" Melanna scowled and turned away. "Ashana is gone."

Finding no reply of worth, Kai offered none. Gone. The Goddess of Evermoon. The guardian of the Hadari people since before Empire was Empire. He clasped his fists tight against sudden tremor, and was glad of the rampart's support. He'd dared Ashana to strike him down. When the blow had failed to fall, he'd assumed her favour. How foolish that now seemed. He stared to where the ailing moon – no longer bloody, but somehow discoloured – fought the brightness of the day.

"Are you certain? What did you see? What does your heart tell you?"

Melanna twisted about, her voice thick. "All that she had, she gave to us. And when nothing remained ... "

Glad to have insisted his bodyguard afford a moment of privacy, Kai drew his daughter into an embrace. "Who else knows?"

"Elspeth, so I assume her sisters must. And the lunassera. But they didn't see. She didn't fall apart in their arms." A measure of solidity returned to Melanna's voice, and she stepped back. "What are we to do?"

For that, at least, he'd answer. He swept a hand across Ahrad's battered defences. "See what we have wrought, daughter. Ashana gave everything. How can we give less? The Dark must be excised. The war goes on." He set fingers beneath her chin, and raised her eyes to meet his. "Will you fight it with me?"

At last, defiance returned to Melanna's eyes. For a wondrous moment, she was again Aethal reborn to youth and vigour, the best of her, and of him – and perhaps also of a departed goddess.

"Yes, my Emperor."

Nineteen

Scarlet and gold gleamed through close-set trees. Four miles away, perhaps five. No distance at all for men on horseback. Serpent banners and bright silks. A sight for which Sevaka could no longer spare emotion. Not with smoke spiralling high above the northern trees. Even though her naval coat faded into the forest as well as anything could, she squatted closer to the oak.

"You'd think they'd be celebrating," she muttered. "Or mourning their dead."

Thaldvar dropped to his knees in the rain-soaked mulch. "Not the Icansae. Maggad lusted after the imperial throne his whole life. His grandsons won't be any different. Any chance to prove themselves worthy, they'll take."

"How many?"

Stubbled cheeks twisted into a scowl. "Perhaps a thousand. Mostly outriders, but there are cataphracts too."

Good news and bad. Outriders meant boiled leather rather than golden scale, but it also meant bows. Worse, while the cataphracts would be weary from the morning's assault, the outriders would be fresh to the pursuit.

"They'll ride right over us," she said. "Where's the worthiness in that?"

"Maybe they're pursuing the woman who laid low their Emperor."

For all the good that had done. "So this is my fault?"

"Worthiness lies in the eye of the beholder. Glory is as much tale as truth. Whatever happens, Aeldran and Naradna will spin a story worthy of their grandfather's crown."

"You know them well?" Sevaka asked.

"Tempting me to rash admission?" A smile softened offence. "Icansae lies far south of here, and they've never fewer than two or three Thrakkian thanes glowering across the border. Maggad paid well for sellswords, and a few years back my people were hungry enough that I took his coin. I'm a pragmatist. I can't afford to be anything else."

Sevaka spread her hands. "This is pragmatism?"

He snorted. "The Hadari won't forget I took to the walls. You and I are bound, and all because I believed Ahrad the Undefeatable was truth, not tale." He shook his head, the smile fading. "But to answer your question? Aeldran has a reputation for bravery and generosity. Naradna? Never met anyone who knows him well. Wears a golden mask to hide scars. But I saw him fight once. Like a rat trapped in a sack with a cat. Hacked his way alone through a thane's circle of vanaguard and took the fellow's head. If it comes to a choice, cross swords with Aeldran."

Sevaka grunted. Thrakkian vanaguard cultivated hardiness as merchants cultivated coin. The only one she'd seen – during a shipboard skirmish at Bregin Point with a reiver's black flag snapping in the wind – had killed four men before a cutlass took his throat. If Naradna had bested even one, that was caution enough. Aeldran's bravery or Naradna's ferocity. Didn't sound like much of a choice, but Sevaka was growing used to a losing hand. Ignoring the creak of weary bones, she clambered to her feet.

"Let's get back."

Thaldvar pressed crooked fingers to his lips. At his high, fluting whistle – as close to the cry of a duskfowl as made no difference – a handful of grey-cloaked figures broke concealment.

No one spoke as they made ascent to Soraved, cutting through the undergrowth to avoid the worst of the road's winding course. The village itself was a jumble of wattle and thatch whose north, south and east boundaries lost themselves in gentle, tree-choked slopes. The western extent clung to a sheer face of crumbling, weatherworn earth as the hill slid away into Draneback Gorge. What passed for the outer wall had long since decayed or been picked apart to feed expansion. More proof that no one expected Ahrad to fall.

Lieutenant Halan Gavrida met them at the gate, two muddy, scuffed soldiers of the 11th at his back. Gavrida looked little better than his men.

What would have been a face handsome enough to melt any heart had grown haggard across a desperate day. They'd found each other on the road south from Ahrad, Sevaka with her exhausted band of borderers, and he with a mismatched company of wounded soldiers and desperate civilians.

"What news?" he asked.

"They're maybe an hour behind," replied Thaldvar. "We leave a trail a blind man could follow."

Gavrida nodded sourly. "We'll get moving."

"There's no time," said Sevaka. "Get everyone together."

She caught the glimmer of objection in Gavrida's eyes. The familiar resistance to a Psanneque's order. Then he nodded. "At your command."

'Everyone' was already assembled by the time Sevaka reached the village square. Three companies of the 11th, reinforced by scattered knots of soldiers from the 7th, 3rd and 10th stood clustered about the statue of Lumestra. Bloodied tabards and haggard faces were poor companions for the harvest garlands about the Goddess' outspread arms. Captain Dlevera and a dozen other knights Fellnore stood aloof and apart, ochre tabards dulled by the stain of travel. A score of half-plate wayfarers – counterpart to Hadari outriders – tended restless steeds in the shadow of the ivy-clad church. Thaldvar's borderers huddled beneath the creaking tavern sign of the Headless Shadowthorn.

There were others, of course. The villagers. The wounded who'd survived the journey – Rosa among them – who rested in the tenuous comfort of the village hall. Soraved had its own handful of militia, but Sevaka had no faith in that collection of threadbare tabards and rusted swords.

With a generous eye, perhaps six or seven hundred souls. Numbers to match those of the Icansae. But numbers lied. Discounting the wounded, Soraved had fewer than five hundred fit to fight. And those were weary. A dozen miles travelled by blistered boot drained a body more than the same journey by saddle.

Sevaka hauled herself onto the statue's plinth. What the extra height did for her confidence, Lumestra's graven presence stripped away. Sevaka's head barely came up to the Goddess' belted waist.

"The Hadari are on our heels," she shouted. "They'll be here within the hour."

Hubbub faded into the predictable. Shock. Fear. Weariness. Anger.

The headman's chain of office shook as he thrust an angry finger in Sevaka's direction. "You led them here!"

"They'd have come anyway." Scorn dripped from Thaldvar's reply. "This is an invasion, you old fool. The road would have brought them had we not."

"Then we keep going to Vrasdavora," said Lady Dlevera. "What time we have, we use."

Vrasdavora was deep in the mountains to the west, guarding roads abandoned since the disintegration of the Tressian kingdom. Even if they outmarched the Icansae, there was no guarantee there'd be a garrison left to offer shelter.

"We've too few horses, and too many wounded," Sevaka replied. "They'll catch us before we're halfway there."

"We can't fight them," growled the headman. "We're not soldiers."

Gavrida growled. "You're *supposed* to be. That muster field's for drills, not grazing cattle. Raven's Eyes! You've carried on like there's an uncrossable ocean between you and the shadowthorns."

"You were supposed to protect us!" The shout came from the crowd's anonymity. "Ahrad was supposed to protect us!"

The square descended into uproar. Sevaka's heart sank further. Rosa would have known what to say. But Rosa was delirious, her mutterings filled with the Raven's name. Unable to do more than hold her hand, Sevaka had made reconnoitre as much to escape the makeshift sickroom as out of duty.

"You're right." The crowd fell silent at her shout. "But Ahrad is gone. So now we do the best we can."

Gavrida folded his arms. "What do you propose, captain?"

Sevaka hesitated. "We fight. We've high ground and dense woodland, neither of them friends to cavalry. Banners on the crest might make the Hadari think twice about pressing the charge. If Lumestra's feeling generous we can slip away at nightfall without having drawn a sword." Heads nodded, Gavrida's among them. Others levelled unwilling stares, resentful of the risk. She took a deep breath. "And it's not a proposal. It's an order."

"I do not take orders from a Psanneque." Ice crackled beneath Lady Dlevera's words.

"I will." The speaker was a sergeant of the 7th, between beard and bandage, little of his face was on display, but his eyes were steady. "Saw her put a banner-spike through the Emperor's heart. What's a name next to that?"

Lady Dlevera scowled. "I am a Captain of Fellnore, a daughter of a noble house. You'll follow my orders, *sergeant*."

"Begging your pardon, my lady. But if you can choose to set aside rank, so can I."

"The lay of the land won't favour us further west," said Gavrida. "I'd prefer Hadari spears on my shield than in my spine."

"Then do so," growled Lady Dlevera. "Die with this outcast. I'm riding south."

Gavrida's cheek twitched, the reluctance mirrored around the square. Thaldvar had already agreed the course, but a borderer's support was worth nothing. Again, Sevaka wondered what her mother would have done, what threat or cajolement she'd have issued. But the truth was that Ebigail Kiradin would never had let matters go so far unchecked.

"I'm staying."

The new voice was quiet, with steel beneath. Every head in the square turned to stare at the tavern doorway, and the ragged woman who stood with one hand braced against the lintel. Sevaka felt a grin steal across her face.

"Captain Psanneque has the right of it," said Rosa. "The Hadari are as weary as us. We only need give them a reason to pause."

"And if they don't?" said Lady Dlevera.

"I'll fight. Maybe I'll die." Rosa stepped across the threshold, gaining solidity with every pace. "But if I don't? You'll be running from me as well as the shadowthorns."

Lady Dlevera fell silent.

"11th!" shouted Gavrida. "Form up at the north gate!"

The sergeant of the 7th added his voice to the growing tumult. The square dissolved into a rush of bodies as soldiers and villagers hastened away. Then Rosa stood before the plinth, and Sevaka had no more attention to spare the commotion.

"Did you really kill the Emperor?" asked Rosa.

So close, she looked paler and more unsteady than ever. Sevaka consoled herself with the knowledge that she shouldn't even be breathing, let alone walking. Dropping from the plinth, she flung her arms around Rosa and held her tight for a long, wondrous moment.

"It didn't take."

Rosa untangled herself. "There's a lot of that about."

"I thought I'd lost you." The words brought grief flooding back. How fickle was the heart that it couldn't allow joy to last?

"You nearly did. That spear ... I'm still not ... " A shadow passed across blue eyes. She nodded. "But I will be. Where are we?"

"Soraved."

The corner of Rosa's mouth twitched. "You've done well to get this far."

The praise soured in Sevaka's gut. Part irritation at the Psanneque's barbed mantle, part resentment that Rosa had turned the tide so easily. "You saw what happened when I tried to do more. If not for you ... "

Rosa squeezed her shoulder. "You'd have handled it. I just hurried them along."

Sevaka nodded, but her smile was more for Rosa's benefit than it was born of agreement.

"Brother."

Aeldran Andwar, Prince of Icansae, hauled on his reins at Naradna's greeting, and fell into step. Behind, a file of cataphracts waited in silent attendance. A quarter mile further up the road, a line of gold and scarlet spread through the trees. Further still, a string of mismatched banners and shields sat formed and ready on the crest.

"They've found their courage."

"Good." Naradna's horse champed. Gold-clad fingers soothed its braided mane. The eyes of the mask stared at the distant hilltop. "One more triumph before nightfall."

"Perhaps one better left for a new dawn," Aeldran replied. Oblique suggestions always went over better. "Our warriors have been long in the saddle. The horses are tired."

"I want their banners, brother. Saran spurned my trophy at Ahrad, so I will lay others at his feet. Tonight. Before the campaign divides us, and our peers no longer stand witness. He will recognise my worthiness. They all will."

Aeldran winced at bitterness that seemed only to grow bleaker. The whispers of disease-scars and a ravaged face so at odds with the handsome, kingly brow of the mask only made matters worse.

For Aeldran, the war was a chance to restore Icansae to the Golden Court's trust. Too many of his peers looked upon him without true recognition, seeing instead the shadow of his grandfather Maggad – a man whose paranoia had thinned Icansae of many a rival. Valour on the battlefield, pledged to the House of Saran, would go a long way towards ending the whispers.

Naradna's ambitions were personal, and burned like fire; less about Icansae's reputation, and more concerned with proving worthiness for the kingdom's empty crown. In the months since Maggad's death, Naradna had earned a reputation for being driven, and for indulging that drive on those foolish enough to chance the crossed swords of an honour duel.

Aeldran hadn't approved at first, for so many of Naradna's desires went against tradition. And yet those same traditions demanded obedience, for Naradna was the elder. Even had they not, it would have changed little. The bond of blood held pre-eminence.

The simple truth was that Naradna inspired him. Courage. Determination. Aeldran had never lacked for those traits, but Naradna burned incandescent with them.

Aeldran drew his sword. He held the curved blade high, so that its moonsilver-etched runes gleamed in the dying light. The blade had been his father's gift, twin to that carried by Naradna, as they were twins.

"If it is trophies you seek, it is my honour to fetch them for you."

He made to spur away, but Naradna's hand closed on his wrist.

"No, brother. We will take them together."

The Hadari drums thundered as the first raindrops fell.

"They're doing it," murmured Rosa. "They're actually doing it."

Her mismatched shield wall was anchored at one end by the precipice of Draneback Gorge, and at the other by upturned wagons. A concerted charge *might* have broken the line, but the trees and the slope would rob the Hadari of momentum and unity long before they struck home.

"Shields up!"

The bellow scraped tender muscles against her ribs. The worst of the pain was a memory, but still it overshadowed anything she'd suffered since fate had made her an eternal. Some enchantment of the demon's spear, or the simple fact she'd no business walking about having taken steel to the heart? It didn't matter. Nothing mattered now but keeping the borrowed shield tight. To hold the line.

"Death and honour!"

Rosa didn't notice who started the cry. The line shuddered with it as voices hammered out. Militia, soldiers and villagers, standing as one. Tressia as it should be. United.

"*Death and honour!*"

Bows sang to Rosa's left as borderers spent their last arrows. Crossbows rattled from the right, where Lady Dlevera was a sullen presence beneath a tattered ochre pennant. A cataphract plunged into briars, thrown by his dying horse. Another slumped in his saddle, a shaft between gorget and helm.

"*Andwar Brigantim! Icansae Brigantim!*"

The shadowthorn battle cry drowned out the drums.

"*Death and honour!*"

This time Sevaka led the shout. Rosa gritted her teeth and leaned into her shield.

A blast of trumpets hurled the shadowthorns to the charge. The heavens burst.

A cataphract slewed on the road, the screams of man and beast indistinguishable in the hissing rain. Brambles snatching at the silk skirts of its caparison, Aeldran's horse leapt clear and slammed into the line of shields.

A rusty sword skittered across his shield. Blue cloth and steel plate gushed red beneath his own blade. The Tressian line buckled.

"Fellnore! Drive them back!" A woman in ochre flung herself into the gap. Her mace crunched an outrider from his saddle. "Hold the line!"

A thicket of steel pressed forward through the hissing rain. A cataphract fell to the cobbles. The reforming line swallowed him up, hungry blades hacking at throat and spine. Aeldran's horse shied from a halberd's swing.

Then Naradna was at his side, screaming as one possessed, hacking and snarling with no thought to defence. The woman in ochre died in the breach she'd sought to close.

Aeldran spurred past the falling body. His sword took the banner bearer's throat. Letting go his shield, he snatched the stave high into the rain.

"Naradna!" he howled. "Naradna Brigantim!"

The Tressian line crumpled.

"Behind! Enemies behind!"

Gavrida's warning was the first Rosa knew of disaster.

An eastward glance showed gold and scarlet where blue shields should have held, routed militia and the Fellnore pennant raised high in a shadowthorn's grasp.

Hadari trumpets blared. The anarchic mass to Rosa's right dissolved into screams. The soldier at her side crumpled. An Immortal spurred his horse through the gap and hacked down.

Rosa rammed her shield forward. "On me! Form on—"

An outrider's spear-point scraped across her shield's rim and lodged deep in her shoulder.

"Shield ring!" Sevaka's voice rose high above screams of flesh and steel.

Twisting about, Rosa hauled hard on the spear, tugging the tip free of her shoulder and the outrider from his saddle in one painful motion. She stamped on his throat and lunged for the emptied saddle. The rain glimmered gold.

Her desperate parry checked a cataphract's blade, and then he was gone, borne through the wreckage that had been the shield wall's centre and onwards to the pitiful ring Sevaka mustered at the gorge's edge.

The cold mist of descending clouds gathered about the bloody ruin of the right flank. Shadowthorn riders hurtled through the veil, triumphant cries muffled as they hunted down the survivors.

The mists parted. Two Hadari, armour too finely wrought for mere Immortals, galloped into view. One held the captured Fellnore pennant aloft. The other's helm bore a stylised silver halo above, and a golden mask beneath.

No time to reach the shield ring.

Nothing to do but fight.

A fanfare shook the hillside. Not the harsh cry of trumpets, nor the mellower note of buccinas, but a deep, fibrous roar born of days long sundered.

A cold wind parted the mists. Shadows gathered beneath the trees and at Soraved's gate. Shadows with the barest likeness of men, their forms boiling like smoke as mist rushed back in. Only their helms offered substance – silver death masks of leering skulls. Silver too were the hilts of their swords. Their blades burned like dark fire.

The Hadari charge faltered. Cries rang out. Horses circled as riders stared hither and yon.

And Rosa felt . . . nothing. Not fear. Not confusion. Guided by sudden, pressing instinct, she glanced to her right and saw a thin figure watching the commotion with sardonic amusement.

"Oh, hello, Rosa," said the Raven, as if he were surprised to see her there. "I've been thinking."

The breathy fanfare sounded again. Shadows writhed.

The black sword passed through the outrider's chest without finding hindrance in flesh or armour. There was only a murky hiss of rising smoke, and a scream that jolted Aeldran from his fug of terror.

He wheeled his horse. A shadow rippled out of the mist.

Steel drove black flame aside and lunged to the riposte. Living shadow parted before Aeldran's blade, dissipating into the mist. Masterless, sword and silver helm tumbled to the ground.

With a cry of triumph, Aeldran rowelled his horse, only to turn as instinct prickled.

Behind, the silver helm rose from the ground, tendrils of shadow crawling from eye socket and rictus grin to weave a body beneath. A coalescent hand closed about the fallen sword.

Aeldran's triumph died on an ashen tongue. His pulse quickened to deafening pace. Letting the Fellnore pennant fall, he spurred away.

"Naradna!"

Muffled screams sounded. Vapour danced with swirling shadow and parted beneath falling bodies. Trumpets blared for the retreat, and thundering hooves joined the cacophony.

There. A gleam of gold. A clash of steel.

Aeldran clung tight to his sword, and urged his horse on.

Naradna stood beside a dying horse, crowded close by three shadows, sword ablur in desperate parry.

Somehow, Aeldran found the steadiness of hand to hack one down before it turned. The others dissipated beneath Naradna's quicksilver blade as the odds shifted.

Aeldran sheathed his sword and flung out a hand. "Climb up behind me!" Terror lent the words ragged pace. "We cannot fight this."

Naradna levelled a cold, flat stare. "There is no glory in retreat."

Already, tendrils of shadow reknitted beneath the silver helms.

"Please," begged Aeldran. "Glory is no use to the dead. Bring word to the Emperor. Let that be your trophy."

Naradna gave a curt nod but, instead of grasping Aeldran's hand, snatched a sword from a shadow's re-coalescing hand. That prize clutched close, Naradna at last joined Aeldran atop his restless steed.

"Yah!"

Aeldran flicked his reins. His horse sprang away downhill, leaving horror far behind.

The screams faded. The mists ebbed, rolling gracefully back across the hilltop – a retreating tide leaving grim bounty upon the shore.

"Queen's Ashes," murmured Thaldvar, "but what just happened?"

Sevaka swallowed to clear a dry throat, and willed fingers to slacken about her sword. They refused. All had been a shadow play within the mists, dark shapes and screams. Now, where the village approach had been full of blades and charging steeds, there were only bodies.

"I don't know," she said softly. "I don't think I want to."

The mists continued their retreat, revealing Rosa riding tall on a Hadari steed. For a moment, Sevaka glimpsed a dark stranger beside her, head shaking softly as one enjoying a rare and splendid joke.

The last of the mists pulled away. The stranger went with them. And Sevaka, whose blood was already awash with ice, felt a cold hand about her heart.

Twenty

"I'm sorry. Lord and Lady Reveque aren't home."

Aided by the fading dusk and shadows cast by his outstretched lantern, Sergeant Heren made a masterful job of concealing his suspicion. But after a year's practice with Kurkas – undisputed master of letting an expression say only as much as he wished – Josiri knew better. What hearthguard would greet such a sight with equanimity? A Privy Councillor, his mistress and captain of his hearthguard – all filthy, one of them charred – and with what increasingly resembled a corpse clutched tight across the saddle. Elzar's makeshift bindings were already sodden through. Minutes remained, their passage marked by Altiris' stuttering breaths.

Josiri grasped for patience. "This boy needs help. He'll find it nowhere else."

Heren's lip twitched. "I can't let strangers have the run of the house, my lord."

[[Let me persuade him.]]

Josiri winced. There'd be trouble enough to come without borrowing more via Ana's notions of diplomacy. "Do you really think Lady Reveque will be pleased if you send us away and the boy dies?"

Giving the low exhalation of a man recognising the impossibility of his position, Heren nodded. "This way."

Malachi had always known Konor Zarn's ascension party would be extravagant, but expectation paled before opulent truth. The gardens blazed with firepits and lanterns, setting elusive shadows fleeing across the lawns to escape their brilliance. Canopies filled the space between

the brooding silhouette of Woldensend Manor and the sculpted wood-
lands that hid the city streets, a dizzying array of shapes and colours
with some small semblance to a market – fitting, perhaps, given Zarn's
beginnings. Beneath, guests reclined upon chaises and armchairs,
surrounded by gilded statues and easel-set paintings fetched from the
house. The indoors, outdoors.

I shall not forget my friends. Judging by attendance that evening, Zarn
had a great many friends to remember. A sea of tailored suits, flattering
dresses and plaited hair. So many, that Malachi was hoarse from greetings neither delivered nor received as warmly as they pretended. All of
them dancing, gossiping and conspiring beneath the darkening skies,
surrounded by enough food and drink to feed the city's empty bellies.

Gluttony and waste, pride and preening. Everything Malachi hated
about the Republic.

"Father would have loathed this." Lily steered him adroitly away from
a merchant whose eyes gleamed with hopes of patronage. "Barbarians at
the gates, he'd have called it. Look at them. They lust for the trappings
of responsibility, but care nothing for its burdens."

Such had been the case Malachi's whole life, and for much longer
besides, but he'd never said as much to his father-in-law, and knew better
than to say so to his wife.

"It's expected that we at least show our faces. Konor is my equal at
council ... "

"Equal? He's nothing. From nowhere."

"So was I to your father." Then again, Andor Reveque had judged
all Lily's suitors so, regardless of rank or character. "We can manage a
little grace."

She shook her head, setting her veil dancing. "Even when he's a
vranakin?"

Malachi froze. Fortunately, the nearest guests were lost in laughter
at a pair of harlequins in black and green motley fighting over a branch
carved in grotesque likeness of a woman. One wore a cloak of leaves and
a smooth, blank mask; the other a coat of black feathers and a crooked
hat. Jack and the Raven, at war even in theatre.

"You mustn't say that," Malachi hissed. "Not here. Not ever."

She glared. "Because they'll come for me?"

"Because they'll come for our children."

Something broke behind her eyes. "We can't allow this to go on, Malachi."

"I know."

Malachi's gaze fell on a simarka sitting at silent attention – one of fifty fetched from the foundry to lend official sanction to the celebration. What had become of Josiri? Was he even now a "guest" of the Crowmarket? Or maybe he was dead, sacrificed in place of Constans and Sidara. Or maybe – just maybe – Elzar had intervened.

"Jack" struck his opponent's hat away. As the Raven stooped to reclaim it, Jack snatched the birchwood stick and made capering flight across the lawns, chased on by laughter and the Raven's shaking fist.

Lily was right. Something had to be done, but try as he might, Malachi saw no path beyond the bars of a cage he'd set so neatly about himself.

"Malachi! So delightful that you could join us."

Konor Zarn made stately procession along the path, his smile too broad to be genuine, and his tone unsteady with drink. In one hand, he held a glass of sparkling wine. His other rested about the waist of the snow-blonde woman at his side, her inky gown perfect accompaniment to his suit of black velvet. Laughing eyes glimmered a vivid shade of blue-green. She looked barely older than Sidara, and scarcely of decent age.

Was she bought and paid for, as were so many of those present? The line between arranged marriage and transactional liaisons of a briefer sort was subjective. And it wasn't as though Malachi counted himself any less a hireling, bought as he was by hope and fear. Thus the question became whether or not she wore the gown and sparkling smile out of choice.

Malachi offered a slight bow, one equal to another. "I never thought to be elsewhere. May I introduce my wife, Lilyana?"

Lily bobbed a stiff curtsey. "Lord Zarn."

"Konor, please." He gathered Lily's gloved hand and pressed it to his lips. "I abhor formality."

Lily's gaze rested on his companion. "So I see."

Again, Zarn seemed wholly ignorant of her veiled hostility.

"Of course, where are my manners? Kasvin, may I present Lord and Lady Reveque?"

Kasvin's curtsey was more fluid than Lily's had been, but her apparent lack of family name went a long way to confirming Malachi's earlier suspicions. Seemliness held no more sway with Zarn than formality.

"She cleans up well, don't you think?" said Zarn. The hand that had so lately held Lily's now brushed Kasvin's jaw and tipped her chin a fraction higher. "Such a waste to leave her in the gutter. And so eager to please. After all, we none of us wish to go back to how we were, do we?"

Through it all, Kasvin's smile remained steady. Malachi wondered what it cost her. A better man would have called out Zarn's boorishness, but Malachi was fast losing illusions about himself.

He offered Kasvin the same bow he had Zarn. "A pleasure to meet you, Kasvin."

The smile flickered, gaining warmth and perhaps gratitude. "Thank you, Lord Reveque."

Malachi straightened and cast about for something – anything – to distract from his galloping discomfort. "I must say, Konor, I'm impressed. This must have cost you a fortune."

Zarn drained his glass and stared out across the crowds. "Coin is for spending, and if one can't lavish wealth on one's friends, why bother chasing it?"

"Perhaps to help others less fortunate than ourselves?" said Lily.

"Ah yes, the poor. I know your work with the hospices, of course. It must be exhausting."

"It's a duty privilege demands."

He nodded equably. "Privilege demands so much, doesn't it? Still, we soldier on." A twist of the lips, and his attention returned to Malachi. "My thanks for your gesture, by the way. The simarka are splendid."

In point of fact, the verdigrised bronze lions looked tawdry alongside the luxuries fetched from within Woldensend's walls.

"My husband has always been generous," said Lily. "It's one of his faults."

Zarn smiled. "But what a fault to have. What we give to others is always more valuable than that which we keep for ourselves, don't you think?"

"Such as service?"

"I was speaking of friendship, but I suppose friendship is a kind of service."

At last, Malachi realised what was unusual about Zarn's manner. It wasn't the slur of intoxication, or the threat so easily read into his words. Rather, it was that whenever he spoke to Lily, he displayed none of the awkwardness her veil provoked in others.

"You might say so," said Lily. "I consider friendship second only to love, and love should never be given in service, or else can it ever truly be love?"

Kasvin's smile flickered. Zarn's handsome features darkened. "Kasvin, my dear, can I trouble you to find me another glass? This one seems to be empty."

She nodded and withdrew, empty glass in hand.

"I'm surprised you let her go so easily," said Lily. "Those I care about, I fight for."

Appalled, Malachi turned his back to Zarn and set his hand on Lily's shoulder. Beneath the silk, her muscles were taut. "Enough," he breathed.

She gave a small, curt nod. Malachi turned about, thoughts racing as he considered how best to soften his wife's rudeness. That he'd little desire to do so made the search harder.

"Konor—"

Zarn waved a dismissive hand. "It's forgotten. A man shouldn't be held accountable for a wife's overindulgence, and the wine *is* splendid. I joke, of course. But Lilyana. You leave me with the distinct impression we've been talking at cross purposes. I seek only prosperity for all, especially those without the good fortune of noble birth. I like to see folk get what they deserve. Kasvin deserves better than your scorn. And your assumptions."

Malachi didn't have to see Lily's face to know there was a scowl beneath the veil.

"Then if you'll excuse me," she said, "I'll tender my apology in person."

"Of course."

Malachi didn't know that he believed her – Lily's apologies tended towards the infrequent – but was nonetheless glad when she strode away. Affairs were bleak enough without offering insult to the vranak-in's chosen representative on the Privy Council. Or rather, their *willing* representative. "Speaking of apologies—"

"Do I seem a man given to thin skin, Malachi? Your wife has a repu-tation, and doesn't disappoint. So few people in this city wear their true faces, save in private." He spread his arms wide as if to encompass the grounds and everyone within. "Look at them. All busy pretending to be something they're not."

"Does that include us?"

"That remains to be seen. But you might counsel your wife to caution. Not everyone has my forgiving nature."

"Lord Reveque. Lord Zarn."

Malachi was spared the need to respond to that not-so-guarded threat by Elzar's arrival. The high proctor looked as one worn away by a busy day, spurring brief regret at having set the man to so much trouble. But what did that mean for Josiri? He could hardly enquire, not with Zarn standing right there.

"High Proctor Ilnarov," he said. "The simarka look splendid tonight."

Zarn nodded. "Very majestic."

"Kind of you to say," Elzar replied. "I'm only sorry I couldn't bring the final cohort here on time. We got caught up in this afternoon's nastiness."

Malachi's pulse quickened. "Nastiness?"

Elzar blinked. "Why yes. Lord Trelan and Lady Beral brought dozens of southwealders out of Dregmeet. Had half the district on their heels. The simarka settled things down." He shrugged. "I'd have been here sooner, but Lord Trelan asked me to ensure the southwealders were looked after."

"Why am I only just hearing about this?" Malachi saw none of his own surprise mirrored on Zarn's face. But then, *of course* Zarn already knew.

"Lord Trelan said he'd bring the matter to your attention," Elzar replied.

Then why hadn't he? Did Josiri suspect the cause of Malachi's reticence? Suddenly, the ground beneath Malachi's feet felt less than firm. "I've heard nothing."

"To be honest, there's little to tell," said Elzar. "Apart from that lad, of course."

"What lad?" asked Zarn.

"One of Lord Trelan's hearthguard, I think. Ripped open. Nothing to do for him but pray, but Lord Trelan wouldn't hear of it. Took my horse and rode off." He rubbed at his bristled chin. "I admire determination, but that boy . . . Take a miracle to keep him from the Raven's clutches."

Zarn clapped Elzar on the shoulder. "It's done with now. You've had a busy day, master proctor. Let's see if we can ease its passage into night."

Malachi scarcely noticed their departure. The puzzle pieces were coming together, and not in a manner he liked. Not the skirmish at Westernport, of course. By the sound, that had gone better than he'd dared hope. But the rest? Josiri needed a miracle. Of course he'd break a promise to find it. Especially with the bond between them so frayed.

"Malachi?" He looked up to see Lily staring at him. "We need to leave."

Josiri set Altiris down before the entrance hall fire and bundled his coat beneath the boy's head. Only the twitch of sightless eyes and the shallow, febrile flutter of the lad's chest gave any clue he still lived.

Heren, still lurking beside the outer door, winced. "I can ring for a maid to fetch blankets, but he doesn't look like he'll last that long."

Josiri glanced at Kurkas, who slung his arm about the sergeant's shoulders. "Tell you what, why don't we just leave them to it? Unless you reckon this is a ruse to make off with the family silver?"

Heren frowned, but allowed Kurkas to lead him outside. The door slammed shut.

Josiri ran for the stairs. "Stay with him."

Anastacia sank to a crouch. Josiri looked back from the first landing to see her regarding the dying boy as one might regard a hound struck by a runaway cart. Sadness without loss.

"Sidara!" he shouted. "Sidara! Where are you?"

A door opened onto the landing. A swirl of dark skirts and chestnut curls.

"Josiri? Queen's Ashes, but what's all this noise?" Hawkin Darrow's thin features creased. "Lord and Lady Reveque . . ."

He held up a hand. "They're fine. I didn't expect you to be up."

"I'm the steward." She hooked a lopsided grin. "And let me tell you, the power goes all the way to my head. So if you're after an illicit rendezvous you'll have to ask *very* nicely."

"Where's Sidara?"

"Probably in the chapel."

"Fetch her. Please. It's important."

She stared over the banister, a hand at her mouth. "Blessed Lumestra."

Josiri took her by the shoulders and drew her back onto the landing proper. "Hawkin, listen to me. I need you to fetch Sidara. Right away."

"Why? I don't understand."

"You'll have to trust me." The words soured as he spoke them. "Can you do that? Please?"

Hawkin nodded and took the stairs two at a time. "Sidara!"

As Josiri began his descent, a small voice hailed him from a half-open door. "Uncle Josiri? Are the vranakin coming for us again?"

"No, Constans. No vranakin. I promise."

The boy nodded, though he looked more disappointed than reassured. It was always hard to be sure with Constans. Sidara wasn't exactly an open book, but in the past year Josiri had at least learned enough of her mannerisms as to glean where to start reading. Constans remained a mystery. Ten years old, and possessed of Malachi's inscrutability as well as his dark hair and hooded eyes. His temper came very much from his mother.

Constans, guided by the ever-present instinct that drives children to seek things their elders wished they wouldn't, ducked beneath Josiri's restraining hand, rose up onto tiptoes, and peered over the banister.

"Is he dead?" Excitement gave way to suspicion. "You said there were no vranakin."

"There aren't. I think you should go to your room."

"*I* think I should stay," he said airily. "I'm to be a knight. Dead bodies don't bother me."

Limited reserves of patience exhausted, Josiri admitted defeat. "Then stay, but stay *here*. Agreed?"

"Yes, uncle."

Constans threw an unsteady salute. A small rose-hilted dagger no larger than a table knife gleamed in his hand. Josiri couldn't imagine where he'd found it, nor Lilyana approving.

"I need to borrow that," Josiri lied.

Constans narrowed his eyes, glanced guiltily at the dagger and reluctantly held it out. "I keep it under my pillow. In case—"

"In case the vranakin return. I know." Josiri took the weapon. "I'm here to do that now."

Leaving Constans peering over the balcony, he threw a worried – and unfruitful – glance after Hawkin and made his way to the ground floor.

"How is he?"

[[How should I know?]] said Anastacia. [[Have I ever struck you as one with a healer's touch?]]

"No. But it's been a day for surprises."

Too many to credit. Enough that Josiri wished to write it off as a bad dream. The mists he was accustomed to. The kernclaws he'd come to accept. But the ghosts? The grey demon who'd withered living flesh and matched Anastacia without effort? And as for Anastacia herself...?

[[Things are stirring, Josiri. Things that should be left sleeping.]]

"And what about you? I've never seen you do that before."

[[A touch. That was all it took. A wall fell, and the light rushed through.]]

"You're not making any sense."

The char-smudged mask of her face regarded him without offering clue to thoughts beneath. [[Nor are you. Why does this boy matter so much?]]

"Shouldn't he?" Josiri knelt and took Altiris' hand. "He was there because of me. He took wounds that should have been mine. If I can't honour that, what am I?"

Anastacia gazed past him to the stairs.

"Uncle Josiri. You called for me?"

Sidara stood halfway up the steps in her grey dress, golden hair gathered in a fraying ponytail. She shared nothing of her brother's fascination with the dying Altiris, and held her gaze averted. Hawkin stood behind, hands on the girl's shoulders and eyes alive with suspicion.

"Sidara." Josiri rose and held out a hand. "He's dying. He needs your help, as Sevaka did last year."

She stared at her feet. "Mother says I mustn't. She won't even let me mend her scars."

"If you don't, he'll die. I know that's a horrible burden to place on you, I do, but it's the truth."

"Josiri!" Worry fled from Hawkin's eyes, replaced by anger. "If the boy needed help, you should have taken him to a physician. Sidara can do nothing they cannot."

Josiri ignored her. "Sidara. Please. Your parents will understand."

Her blue eyes met his, crystal clear and piercing. "You know they won't."

He winced, embarrassed to be caught in a deception by a girl less than half his age, and more so for having made the attempt. "You're right, I'm sorry. But I still need your help. *He* needs your help."

Altiris shuddered. His lips parted in low, tremulous keening. Constans stood higher on his tiptoes, straining for a clearer view over the banister.

"Sidara . . ." Josiri began.

Anastacia glided past on filthy skirts, her black eyes locked on Sidara's. [[The question is not whether or not your mother will disapprove, but whether or not she is correct to do so.]] With grace at odds to her tattered appearance, she knelt before the girl. [[Don't listen to Josiri. Don't dwell on your mother's scolding. Look inside. Look into the light. What does it tell you?]]

Sidara chewed her lower lip, eyes never leaving Anastacia's immobile features.

"Josiri!"

Malachi flung open the front door and staggered back, arm upflung to shield against a rush of golden light. One hearthguard turned his back entirely. Another cried out. Lily shoved Kurkas aside and forged on, splayed hands braced against brilliance.

Dark figures drowned in light. One knelt beside a huddled shape. Another stood behind, hands on the shoulders of the first, an echo of feathered wings spread wide. Dazzled, Malachi stumbled. His foot caught on the threshold.

Light faded, and all that remained was fury. At Josiri's broken promise. At his intrusion. At exposing Sidara to a world from which her parents had striven to keep her safe. But Malachi's anger paled before that of his wife's, who bore down on Sidara with all the fury of Lumestra banishing the Dark.

"Sidara!"

Lily dragged their daughter up and away from Anastacia. Away from the filthy, bloodstained huddle beside the hearth. Malachi's anger ebbed, sapped by insidious guilt. Life and death were easier balanced in the abstract than the present.

Sidara, never more gawky and willowy than at that moment, tottered and missed her footing. Malachi gathered her up as she fell, though not without effort – one more reminder that his little girl was growing beyond him.

"Are you all right?"

Eyes fluttered. " . . . tired," she breathed. "Did it work?"

Malachi glanced at the boy. He lay still, but with the peace of sleep, not death. "I think so."

"I'm glad."

The last of Malachi's anger slipped away at Sidara's proud declaration. Not yet grown, and she'd a clearer sense of things than he. The boy had found his wounds in Dregmeet. He was victim of Malachi's own refusal as much as Josiri's reckless endeavour. Sidara had balanced the scales.

Lily jabbed an accusing finger at Anastacia. "Guards! Drag this abomination out of my house!"

Three hearthguards crossed into the hallway, Sergeant Heren at their head. They lost all enthusiasm when Anastacia folded her arms.

[[Do try.]]

"Ana, please," said Josiri. "Wait for me outside?"

She rounded on Lily. [[Your daughter bears the greatest of gifts. It is not yours to cage.]]

Sidara rose unsteadily. "Mother . . . it was my choice."

"Demons always have you believe it so," snapped Lily.

"Should I have let him die?"

"Mistress Darrow." Lily seized Sidara's hand and bundled her towards the stairs. "Take my children to their rooms. We will discuss your part in this later."

Hawkin nodded, her face pale. "Sidara, come along. Quickly now."

Sidara stumbled. Hawkin slipped an arm about her waist and led her away up the stairs. For a wonder, Constans fell into step without whisper of protest. He, at least, knew better than to argue with his mother.

"Now." Lily crossed to the hearth and took up a poker. "Will someone rid my house of this demon, or must I do it myself?"

[[A demon?]] Anastacia drew closer, joyless laughter spilling from her frozen lips. [[You should be careful hurling such names about, lest you make them true.]]

"Ana ..." Josiri stepped between them, arms outstretched. "Altiris' wounds are closed. He's breathing steadily. We've done all we came to do."

[[Step aside, Josiri. She wants a demon, she can have one.]]

The hearthguards closed in, swords drawn.

"Back away!" shouted Heren. "Now!"

"Enough!" said Malachi. "What is done is done. Are we really to compound our errors by brawling like Thrakkians over coin?"

The hearthguards froze. So did Anastacia. Lily glared, though he suspected more in surprise than anger. Josiri looked on with approval. That might have meant something at another place, or another time. But not there. Not then.

"Lily, our daughter needs you," said Malachi. "Trust me to attend to this."

Even through the veil, he recognised the struggle between worry and wrath, a mother's instincts torn between shelter and retribution. Retribution lost. The poker clanged to the floor and Lily stalked away up the stairs.

"Sergeant Heren," Malachi continued, the words low and soft out of fear that speaking any louder would be to lose all control. "You and your men will take the boy to my carriage."

Heren glanced at Anastacia. "My lord, I—"

"Do as I ask, sergeant."

"Sir."

With one last glance at Anastacia, Heren gestured to the other hearthguards. Swords were sheathed, and Altiris borne out into the gathering night.

"Anastacia Psanneque," said Malachi. "You are no longer welcome in this house, or in the company of my kin. You will depart, now."

Her dark, hollow stare met his, no less threatening for the lack of accompanying words. Cold sweat curled across the base of Malachi's spine. Somehow, he held his gaze unblinking until she turned and left.

Josiri grimaced. "Malachi, I—"

"You broke my trust, Josiri. You swore on your sister's soul that you'd not speak of Sidara's gift, and now—?"

"Ana already knew. I don't know how, but she knew."

"And now so do Hawkin, Constans and a number of my hearthguards."

Constans had likely known already, of course. As for the hearth-guards, their presence could not reasonably be laid at Josiri's door. But reason was poor company at that moment.

Josiri's grimace tightened. "You'd rather Altiris was dead?"

"It isn't that simple."

"Of course it is." He sighed. "As simple as a broken promise. Don't you even want to know what happened in Dregmeet?"

No. At least, Malachi didn't want to ask. Not with the possibility of hearthguards or servants listening at the doors. Not when at least one was likely reporting his every move to the Parliament of Crows. Not when Josiri's actions were sure to have consequences long after a new dawn.

"Elzar told me."

Josiri shook his head. "Not all, because I didn't tell him. What the vranakin are doing . . . it's worse than we thought. We need to–"

"No!" snapped Malachi. "I will not entertain another word. Not now. You have dominated the Council's precious time with this obsession for weeks on end. I will at least have refuge from it within my own walls!"

"What's happened to you?"

Suddenly weary, Malachi turned away. He picked up the poker so recently abandoned by Lily and returned it to its rightful place beside the scuttle. "Go home, Josiri. I'll see Elzar's horses are returned. Things will be different in the morning."

"If that's what you want, *First Councillor*." Josiri growled out the reply. "But I have one last gift before I leave . . . on the topic of refuges and safety."

Malachi turned to find a small dagger in Josiri's hand, the pommel extended in offering. Taking it, he turned it over but found no hint to the workings of Josiri's mind.

"I don't understand. You took this off a vranakin?"

"I took it off Constans. He sleeps with it under his pillow in case the vranakin come for him in the night. You may see this house as a refuge. Your children see it otherwise."

Twenty-One

Drunken song hammered out beneath the funeral pyres, stark contrast to the solemn observances as Ashana's priests ushered the dead into the Raven's care. A Last Ride made glorious by triumph, for they would walk the mists of Otherworld attended by those their efforts had conquered – and of the Tressian dead there was no shortage. It should have been a night for celebration, and yet Melanna's unease held her apart.

She found little to cheer. A goddess she knew not how to mourn. A sister in moonlight for whom she conjured no affection. A just and necessary cause founded on slaughter to glut ravens both ephemeral and divine. And to underpin it all, the slighted moon, its light somehow colder and darker than it had been in all the years before.

"Saranal."

A man approached out of the crowd, his swagger born of ale not yet taken to excess. Midnight blue silks marked him as a son of Corvant, the golden trim as a man of rank and the dark chiselled features perhaps as a man used to taking women for granted. Melanna eased her hand to her sword. Princessa or no, a woman alone in a field of drunken men brought hazards.

"My heart grieves to see you wander without joy, *savim*," he continued. "Please, share the poor comforts of our fire. Compliments of Prince Haralda Jardur, offered one warrior to another."

Instinct warned her to refuse. That the invitation concealed hopes of more intimate entertainments to follow. "And Prince Haralda? You are he?"

He bowed. "For good and ill, *savim*."

Still hesitation prickled. But how could an Empress rule such men if she'd only ever been a stranger?

"Then lead on," she replied.

Haralda led her through raucous clamour to a firepit ringed with Immortals. There, at least, existed watchful sobriety to guard against rivalry goaded to violence by demon drink. Deeper, where dancing flames crackled with dripping fat and tantalised the tongue with the rich scent of roasting meat, sat a gathering of silks and scale armour, some tarnished and stained by the business of the day, others gleaming in the firelight.

Melanna recognised a few among the dozen, though names escaped her. Young and old. The inheritors of thrones not yet emptied, and others whose sprawling families denied them elevation. Men whose houses had clawed and gouged at one another for generations; others whose alliances were the bedrock upon which the Empire was built. Brought together by her father. By her.

And by a dead goddess.

"Brothers!" Haralda spread his arms. One by one, the princes fell silent. "I welcome Princessa Melanna of Rhaled to our circle."

"About time," grumbled a grey-haired man beyond the flames. "I was starting to think her a myth. Does she have a tail? A myth should have a tail."

He raised a tankard to bearded lips, only to have it dashed from his hand by the younger man. "Hush, cousin." The speaker shifted his attention to Melanna. "You'll have to excuse Maradan. No manners. It's why I speak for Britonis at the Golden Court, and he doesn't."

Laughter rippled about the flames, much to Maradan's scowling disgust.

A space cleared beside the fire. Still not wholly at ease, Melanna sat atop the bundled blankets, expecting someone to pass comment at the novelty of a woman in armour, or issue guarded slight. None came.

In fact, once the blur of introductions ended – few of which held lasting purchase – no one spared Melanna even a curious glance. Instead, the night wore on as it presumably had before her arrival, with stories of battles old and new, coarse banter and jokes that would never again be as funny as when eased along by ale.

Thus when Melanna at last felt stiffness slip from her shoulders and burdens from her heart, it was little to do with drink taken – of which she'd indulged only sparingly – but owed to a stranger sensation. That of being unremarked and unremarkable. Accepted without concern for tradition, rather than shunned for her aspirations. A curious sensation in which to revel, especially in the company of men whose lives were dedicated to standing tall among their peers. But to Melanna it was an unlooked-for delight, and she held it close.

Before long, her laughter flowed freely, and faltered only when she cast eyes skyward to the slighted moon.

Melanna's neighbour – a thin-featured prince of Silsaria named Thirava – took a pull on a wine bottle and passed it on. "Can't help but notice the brothers Andwar aren't with us."

"Surprised they show their faces at all," replied Haralda.

"Naradna never shows his face anywhere," grunted Maradan. "So what's the difference?"

"I keep hearing rumours about their grandfather," said Thirava. "That he didn't meet the Raven through natural means."

"Never known you to be short of rumour, Thirava," said Haralda. "Nor slander."

"Maggad was rotting long before he took his Last Ride. Explain that."

"I don't have to, because I don't care. Doesn't matter to me who warms the Icansae throne, so long as they stand with us when called. Maggad seldom did. Maybe Naradna will."

He offered a bottle to Melanna. She took a swig – the full-bodied red wine washing away the bittered ale of before – and passed it along. She knew a little of Naradna's situation. The reclusive crown prince was not well-liked by his cousins, all of whom could leverage slighter claims through victories won in battle. Thus Naradna had to prove himself their better through the flexing of his own sword. Melanna empathised, for her father had been forced to similar lengths only the year before – ironically by Naradna's grandfather, whose claim would have been laughable, had it not been backed by so many spears.

"I heard they fought well today," she said.

Maradan laughed. "Have you not heard the troubadours? We all fought well today. Even those who didn't fight. That's what troubadours are for. Tell me, whose honeyed words extolled the House of Andwar's virtues?"

She shot him a cold stare. "My father's. He's not given to sweetness."

A mirthful rumble accompanied Maradan's sudden silence, a sound more suited to children mocking a playmate for transgression than grown men.

"Then the Icansae must have fought well." Maradan hoisted his tankard high. "To the Emperor! May he walk ever in moonlight."

"*To the Emperor!*" cried a dozen voices.

Melanna raised voice and bottle to the toast, but faltered as Maradan raised tankard anew.

"And to his princessa. A herald of victory in this fallen land."

"*To the princessa!*"

The second chorus was quieter than the first, spoken with hesitation in some quarters. Still, Melanna inclined her head to hide a blush of pleasure that risked being taken for weakness.

"Pay no attention." Haralda's grin undermined his dismissive words. "He's hoping for a few honeyed words of his own. That maybe the Emperor will carve him a kingdom from the conquered lands where his family refused. Or does your father intend to claim the Republic's lands for himself?"

"Neither," said Melanna. "Tressia will be a kingdom of Empire, with its own voices in the Golden Court."

Thirava frowned. "He'd make a Tressian our equal?"

"You can put a dog in a dress and teach it to dance," said Haralda, "but it'll never pass for a wife."

Others joined his ribald laughter. The warmth of moments before slipped away into anger.

Melanna sprang to her feet. "Where is your respect? Glory in victory, fortitude in defeat, and honour always. That is our way. How did Corvant come into the Empire? With razed fields and chains about its daughters' throats? No. My grandfather's grandfather forgot the blood of old, and named you equals. We've not come to break these people, but to free them from the tyranny of the Dark."

Laughter stuttered. Thirava flinched. Others glanced away or stared into the flames.

"It's an honourable cause," said Haralda, all mirth gone from his voice. "But honour doesn't put food in hungry bellies. It doesn't pay for spears when Thrakkians come howling over the border, nor walls when the Ithna'jîm send zaifîrs sweeping in from the desert. Nor does it weave tales for my kin to remember when Ashana calls me to Evermoon. I fight for these things. The honour I leave to my Emperor, and to his daughter."

"Do you care nothing of the Dark?" she bit out.

"For all your father's warnings of corrupted souls and possessed warriors – for all the claims of a warlock to rival the Sceadotha's Droshnas – I've seen nothing but the same faithless warriors I've fought all my life. They deserve only what respect I afford, and what scraps of mercy the Empire can spare."

Melanna strove to bring anger to heel. Words could never convince Haralda. They could never convey the horror of Davenwood, where the Droshna had blinded an army and scattered it in defeat. Nor could they truly recount the stygian malice of Eskavord's populace shackled to a singular, malevolent will.

Some things, you had to survive.

"They're people. Like us. If they are to die, we should at least—"

"But they're not, Saranal." Even now, Haralda's voice held no conde-scension. Somehow, that made it worse. "They're Tressians."

Melanna cast about the fire but saw only strangers. Minds closed as steel traps. They saw not the Dark, nor the humanity of those they fought. As lost as Elspeth, in their way. And she'd sought to be their equal?

Snarling, she dragged her sword free of its scabbard and thrust it into the flames. The blade bit into ashen soil beneath.

"I say otherwise. And so does my sword." She stepped back, and let her gaze sweep the circle. "To press your claim is to challenge us both."

Haralda narrowed his eyes. "Your father—"

"Knows better than to involve himself in my honour. What of you?"

He found no more support about the circle than Melanna had before. Likely, most agreed with him, but wished no part of what might follow. Peers they had acclaimed her, but no man of Haralda's thirty winters would look the better for duelling a woman who had yet to see her twen-tieth, no matter the outcome. Or maybe they recognised what Melanna clutched close as unbreakable truth: that there could only be one victor in that contest, and it wasn't he.

"Sister."

The soft, musical voice cut through the silence. Melanna held her gaze on Haralda for one heartbeat, two, and then turned about to find herself staring at Elspeth.

No. Not Elspeth, but similar enough in build and aspect that she forgave herself the mistake. Ashana's daughters were of common cast, with little to choose between them save in manner. Where Elspeth was all hard edges, this woman was diffident.

"Elise." Melanna strove to keep the guess from sounding like a question. "What is it?"

"The Emperor requests your presence."

"Of course. Lead the way."

Elise's pale brow creased in confusion. "But . . . your sword?"

Melanna glanced back at the fire and its circle of resentful silence. "They need its example more than I."

"I don't understand. They lack for weapons?"

"Something like that."

Ahrad's great hall struck Kai as excessive. The vaulted ceiling was too high, designed to accommodate towering statues whose stone could instead have buttressed the walls.

It wasn't as though the statues were pleasing. Too austere, in the way that Tressian art often was, with neither Lumestra nor her attendant serathi properly displaying the beauty for which they were fabled. Hardly the faces or forms fit to tempt a hot-blooded soul, though at that moment Kai was anything but, his skin prickling and fingers beset by creeping numbness that the hearth's fire did nothing to hold at bay. He told himself that this too was the fault of the architect, but in truth knew it to be the price of a long day wedded to advancing years.

Despairing of feeling truly warm, he bent over the table and let his eyes roam the map, mulling the interplay of distance with reports from his icularis spies. The unseen algebra of campaign that made victory or defeat faster than the fall of any sword. He knew it by heart, and yet had the feeling of something unseen creeping to undo all he sought to achieve. That was the problem with growing old. The closer you came to becoming a ghost the more you saw them in every shadow.

The door creaked open. Earlier than expected.

"Daughter, I didn't expect you so soon . . ."

Not Melanna, but Elspeth. The daughter of the moon stood with the closed door at her back, her hands behind, and all traces of the afternoon's bloody business washed away.

"What has become of my guards?"

"What makes you think anything has become of them?"

"They know who I wish to see, and who I do not."

She pushed away from the door. "And they always obey, because you are their Emperor?"

"Because they are my Immortals," Kai replied, wishing he could read motive in her brittle tone. "Their service is a gift I strive to earn. So I ask you again: what has become of my guards?"

A frown touched her brow. "I haven't harmed them. I knew they wouldn't let me in, so I set them dreaming."

Elspeth trod lightly, skin shimmering silver as moonlight from the windows fell across it, and growing pale when she crossed into shadow. A reminder that however much she looked an ephemeral waif, she was something entirely other. She drew hands from behind her. A dagger glinted.

How easy to recall the wild, cornered creature of the afternoon, snarling up from a floor slick with blood she'd shed. "Have you come to kill me, Ashanal?"

She sank to her knees, head bowed. The dagger she extended in trembling, cupped hands. When she spoke, her voice shuddered and cracked. "My mother is gone, and I am lost beyond words. All I know to do is what she bade of me, and I cannot do that if you send me away. I will take any vow you demand, but please, let me stay by your side until your work is done."

Kai blinked, taken aback by the unexpected turn. "You're a daughter of Ashana. Is there any vow I can demand that will hold you?"

"A bargain with the divine binds all parties," said Elspeth. "Or else it is not a bargain at all."

"So priests proclaim. What if I refuse?"

"I beg you not to."

Of all the words he'd envisioned spilling from Elspeth's lips, "beg" wasn't among them. Was this genuine, or some game to which he did not know the rules? What if he accepted? Would she strike as soon as his back was turned? What if he did not? Could he prevent her shadowing his every move? The creature he'd beheld in the chapel had been unworthy of his sympathy, but the huddled shape before him reminded more of the lost child he'd rescued from battle's fury. Which was the true Elspeth? Was there any way to know?

"You will kill only to defend others, or at my order," he said at last. "You will comport yourself in a manner that does honour to your mother. Abide by these conditions, and you may stay by my side until this war is done."

She shuddered, and craned her neck to regard him. "I ... I accept your bargain."

As simple as that? "What more must I do?"

"It is already done. I'm told ephemerals like to shed blood to mark a bargain." The first smile crept across her face, more unsettling than reassuring. "I have a dagger."

"But it isn't necessary?"

She pursed her lips. "No."

Her disappointment was palpable. Or was it all just an act? Either way, the decision was made. Kai gently closed her fingers around the dagger's blade and pushed it away.

"Then rise, Ashanal. You are divine and need not kneel before me, nor anyone else."

Twenty-Two

"What remains of Ahrad's defenders scatter like rats before a watchman's torch." Melanna's father reached across the map and tapped each coin stack in turn. "They're making heaviest retreat towards Tregga, picking up garrisons from villages and watch-forts as they go."

"Heaviest?" said Melanna. "What about the others?"

Haldrane stirred himself from the shadows by the great hall's mantlepiece. The head of the icularis sought out darkness as other men sought out food. Other than Kos Devren and herself, the spymaster was probably the only other who commanded her father's trust.

Certainly not Prince Cardivan of Silsaria, whose ancestral claims to Rhaled's throne remained suppressed, rather than settled. Nor King Raeth of Corvant, whose open venality explained much about his son's manner. And nobody trusted King Sard of Britonis, for he did entirely too much trade with the Ithna'jîm. But they were also her father's peers and held sway over the army's largest contingents. Rulership, as Melanna had been so often reminded, was as much about the appearance of consultation as command.

As for the daughters of Ashana waiting patiently at the room's perimeter? After Elspeth's display that afternoon, Melanna was little inclined to trust any of them. Why Elspeth alone was permitted to come so close to the table – to stand behind the Emperor's chair, no less – was a mystery she swore to unravel and, if at all possible, unmake.

"I hear whispers of scattered forces in the Greyridge foothills," said Haldrane. "Never more than a few hundred souls, but if they gather as one, it could prove problematic. I understand King Sard's outriders are having some trouble with the Knights Sartorov a little to the north."

Sard bristled. "My son has the matter in hand." The heavy, resonant vowels – seldom heard so far north and west – reminded just how far much of the army had travelled. "By nightfall tomorrow, he will lay their banners at the Emperor's feet."

"I'm sure he will," Haldrane said smoothly. "Or at least, he would, if not for the garrison mobilising from Fathom Rock. And don't discount the citizenry. They breed them feisty in the Eastshires. Your son may discover that the hard way."

Sard glared at Haldrane, but offered no retort. Folk who crossed the spymaster had a tendency towards unfortunate accidents.

Melanna's father gestured at the table. "Your estimates as to the rest. Do they stand?"

Haldrane clucked softly under his breath and made slight alteration to the positions of three coin stacks, added a pair of copper pennies to another, and removed a fifth entirely. Though Melanna wasn't certain as to how denominations scaled, the scope was clear: sizeable garrisons at Tregga, Tarvallion and Fathom Rock in the north, and at Margard and Kreska in the south; an array of forces retreating south and west from Ahrad; in the west, a towering stack of silver and copper coins atop the city of Tressia itself. The prize.

"We go on," said Melanna's father. "Straight for the throat. Tregga, Tarvallion and then Tressia itself."

"Are you sure, my Emperor? Perhaps now is the time for a methodical approach. Remember the Siege of Hasmarere." Devren grinned wolfishly. "Prince Sallan paid dearly for his haste."

"He did indeed." The Emperor nodded, the curl of his lip a sign he was lost in old memories. "We taught him caution, you and I. A shame he lost his head."

"No shame, *savir*. My pleasure."

Cardivan shook his head. Snow-white hair made it look more struggle to stay awake than objection. "Tregga alone might stall us for weeks. They've rebuilt the walls since your father's time ... "

"And manned them with avaricious fools," said Haldrane. "I've had

six *months*. A tenth of the garrison do my bidding. The gates will spread
wide in welcome."

"Then Tregga will wait until we've secured the border."

Melanna shook her head. "Delay gives the Tressian Council time to
shake free of complacency. If we take the capital, we're halfway to victory.
If we delay, the shirelands will muster against us."

Raeth snorted. "Let them. Farmers and militia?"

"I've learned not to underestimate farmers," said Melanna's father.
"The Tressians have no shortage of pride, and pride grinds mountains
to dust. We keep to the plan. Nothing has changed."

His voice held steady. How, when so much *had* changed? Ashana and
her Huntsman were gone, though most of the war council were ignorant
of the fact, and deliberately so. Ashana had brought the kings of Empire
together in common purpose. Word of her death threatened to break
them apart.

But what choice was there? With the Goddess gone, surprise was their
chief weapon, and it faded by the hour.

Kos Devren gave a stiff bow. "If that is your wish, my Emperor."

"I wish none of this were necessary, old friend. All war is risk, but we
must cleave to the course. We owe the fallen nothing less. The Dark must
be driven out before it overtakes us all."

Sard and Raeth nodded. Cardivan shook his head. Haldrane smiled
a thin, sly smile and slunk back to the shadows.

"The Dark is upon us already!"

Flanked by watchful Immortals, two silver-haloed warriors in Icansae
scarlet strode into the chamber. The earthy stench of hard travel came
with them; scuffed armour and tattered cloaks told a bleaker tale. The
taller of the two was every inch the royal son, with dark eyes and rugged
cheekbones beneath oiled black hair. The shorter carried a narrow, cloth-
wrapped bundle. His golden mask gave no clue to intent.

Melanna moved to intercept, already regretting that her gesture
beside the fire had left her weaponless. Devren beat her to it, the folds of
his bear cloak shifting as he laid hand on his sword.

"Prince Naradna! You will address your Emperor with respect."

Naradna halted, unflinching though Devren was near two heads
taller and twice as broad. "This morning, I offered the Emperor a sword

in victory. I do so again in defeat. I trust he will heed this token where he ignored the other."

The bundle thumped across the table, scattering coins before it. The cloth covering fell part open. Sard leaned across the map and twitched the rest aside. Smoke curled up from a sword's blade.

"We pursued the Tressians to Soraved," said Naradna, his eyes on Melanna's father. "The trees filled with shadow. Silver helms and swords that burned like fire. They slaughtered my warriors. You say the Dark will soon overtake us? I say it is already here."

Melanna stared at the sword. At the hair-thin runes etched across its single-edged blade. Uneven metal spurs stretched from pommel and guard, but never met. Thick black tarnish lay between worn ridges that might once have been sculpted design.

Elspeth approached the table, her fingers tracing the runes along the steel. White fire and black danced at her touch, but left no mark on her skin. "This is not of the Dark." She looked sharply up at Naradna. "Tell me, how did you offend the Raven?"

The room went deathly still, the shadows longer than before. The men in the chamber, kings, would-be kings and warriors all, shared a common caste of expression. Men who felt the call of the pyre before their time and knew not how to answer.

Melanna grabbed at the table and closed her eyes against sudden dizziness. There were legends of the Raven's revenants walking the living realm. There were legends concerning *everything*. The Dark and the Raven. One to command you in life, the other in death. To fight one was horrifying enough. To fight both . . . ?

Soft, soothing light penetrated the darkness behind Melanna's eyes. Dizziness receded, a little of the fear alongside. Enough that she could open her eyes. The daughters of Ashana had left their posts about the chamber's edge in favour of new stations about the table. Silver to drive away darkness.

"We brought battle to the foe," said Naradna. "Nothing more."

Melanna wondered at the rumours of the firepit, and the claims of a grandsire who had met unnatural end. Had Maggad cursed his grand-children with his final breath?

"Perhaps this is nothing more than bleak happenstance," said Melanna's father. "Divine children are as apt to rebellion as any other."

Elspeth threw him a sour look. "The Raven has no children. His revenants are pieces of himself. They obey absolutely, as do fallen ephemerals who offer souls in trade for fleeting gifts. There is no rebellion in them."

Interesting that she spoke of the Raven as a man, as the Tressians did, rather than the grim matriarch Melanna had been raised to fear.

"Have the Tressians fallen so far that they beg aid from the Keeper of the Dead?" said Cardivan.

"It should surprise no one," Haldrane said tautly. "Tressia is built on tombs. They worship their dead as fervently as they do faithless Lumestra. No wonder the Dark has taken root in their souls. Who is to say which lapse caused the other?"

"Does it matter?" said Aeldran. "We cannot fight what we cannot kill. These 'revenants' reform within moments of being struck down."

"There are ways." Haldrane rubbed his chin. He, at least, had overcome his fear. Just one more problem for the spymaster to solve. "At least, if the old tales are true."

"And if they are not?" demanded Sard. "We cannot fight the Tressians and the Raven."

"Blessed Ashana," said Devren, "but we cannot fight the Raven alone."

"We must find a way," snapped Melanna's father. "I will not yield. Not to the Dark. Not to the Raven. And not to fear."

He was losing them. Melanna saw it in hooded glances and the twitch of cheeks. Devren would follow unto death, as would Haldrane. But the others? For all its strength, Rhaled could not seize victory alone.

Elspeth smacked her palm down on the sword. Cold, black fire rose to meet it, only to be smothered by her own white flame. Her lips curled in disdain.

"Do all men so easily lose heart?"

Naradna stiffened but said nothing.

"Whatever drew my uncle out of Otherworld will not hold his attention," Elspeth went on. "Do not allow him to distract you."

"Forgive me, Ashanal," said Haldrane, "but a moment to the divine can pass as an age elsewhere. What if we cannot outlast his interest?"

Metal hissed and spat beneath Elspeth's hand. Pale steam rose up between her fingers. "You have my mother's blessing. You have the lunassera. And you have us, her daughters. Otherworld's shadow can no more prosper beneath moonlight than beneath the sun."

She raised her hand. Of the revenant's sword, no sign remained – only its silhouette on the map's charred parchment.

One by one, the war council bore brooding thoughts out into the night. Kai didn't resent their worries, for he shared them. When still a boy, he'd watched in stark terror as his grandfather had taken his Last Ride. Not the pale imitation that greeted the battlefield's dead and carried them to the pyre, but the grand and terrible pomp beneath the Temple of Ravenscourt, where body and bearers journeyed into the mists, never again to be seen. For a week after, he'd dreamed of a dark shape half-seen through twitching vapour. A beckoning hand, and a promise whispered without words.

Yes. He shared their fears, deeper than they knew. But a warrior could not surrender to fear and remain a warrior.

"Daughter. Stay."

Melanna halted at the door. "Father?"

"We should speak."

She approached, suspicion glimmering. How easily she read him now. How long before he'd no secrets at all? "Do you believe Naradna's tale?"

"I believe the sword. As to the rest? I've heard whispers of patricide. It may be the Raven's interest is *very* focused."

Kai grunted his surprise. "Let us hope so. If not, we must trust that Elspeth can keep her promises."

Melanna scowled. "It concerns me to see her at your side."

Kai sat heavily in the chair, already wishing the conversation done. "She prostrated herself and swore to serve."

"And you believe her?"

He drummed his fingers on the table to conceal a sudden spasm. Melanna would see through a lie. "A bargain with the divine binds all parties. Her words."

"Ashana once told me the same thing," Melanna replied. "She called it the thread that linked divine and ephemeral."

"So I should believe her?"

"That would depend on how much the daughter is like the mother.

My doubts are inked in the blood of her victims." She shook her head. "But you've made your choice, so perhaps we should speak of the other matter, my Emperor."

"The other matter?"

"The one you're avoiding."

Kai brought his hand to rest. No. No secrets at all. "Tomorrow, I ride for Tregga—"

"*We* ride, you mean."

"No. You will go south with Haldrane, and what remains of the Icansae. You will have two warbands of our shieldsmen, a cadre of Immortals, and whatever outriders I can spare."

"I see." Betrayal ran thick beneath the words. "How many times must we do this, Father? How many times must I prove myself? You promised. You swore we'd fight this war together! That we would face the Droshna together." She brought her fist down on the table, setting coins dancing. "And now you're sending me away. How could you possibly think I'd agree?"

He rose and met her glare with one his own. "That would depend on how much the daughter is like the father."

"Now you make jokes?"

"I seek to remind you of your duty!" he roared.

He breathed deep, less to soothe his wrath than to replenish aching lungs. Where others would have shrunk away, Melanna stood firm, dark eyes flashing. Defiant. Pride and fury, and he the wellspring of both.

"Haldrane worries of forces gathering in the mountains," said Kai. "I believe he is right to do so. If Naradna's ambitions become a problem, I need someone I trust holding his leash. If the Raven's interest in the south is not as fickle as Elspeth believes, then I need someone I trust to teach him to mind his own affairs. You think I'm sending you away? I'm giving you an *army*. Tell me I make no mistake in doing so."

She blinked, fury fading. So he could yet surprise her, given opportunity? It wouldn't soon happen again. Melanna had misread his mind only because she'd been so intent on a single dead tree that she'd missed the glory of the forest.

"But . . . I'm a woman. The others—"

He laughed, his own anger forgotten. "And when did that bother you before, *essavim*? You are my heir, named and presented to the Golden Court as such, but we both know that is not enough. You must prove yourself, and cannot do so if others think you hide behind my shield."

"And who will protect you if I am not at your side?"

"I have an army for that. My Immortals. Perhaps even Elspeth. And I am not so old as to be borne easily into the mists. You will fight at my side again, I promise. But not now. I need a trusted warleader more than I need a daughter's company. Scour the hills of resistance, then ride to join me. Not before." He paused. "Will you obey me in this?"

After seeming eternity, Melanna nodded. "Yes, my Emperor."

Twenty-Three

For all his exhaustion – for all the luxury of the former castellan's quarters – Kai found no sleep. He told himself it was always so before momentous days, but knew the solace for a lie. The coming days held little excitement, and a great deal of logistical drudgework from which an Emperor was exempt. A momentous day had come and gone. Others would follow, but were yet distant.

As Kai dragged his weary bones onto the balcony and stared out across the dammed Ravonn, he wondered if the sleeplessness sprang from guilt. For the lie told to Melanna. A warleader he'd made her, and for all the reasons stated, but also to send her from his side.

So much could yet go awry. He'd known that even before Naradna's tales of revenant spirits and black flame. With the Goddess gone and the prospect of armies marshalling from Otherworld . . . Well, if victory came, Melanna would share in it, as an heir should. But if matters turned sour, distance would shield her from the shame of defeat. The House of Saran might endure, and an Empress yet claim her throne.

Kai's left hand shook in sudden tremor, the sensation kin to that of the early evening, but far greater. As he clenched his fist to bring it under control, the shudder raced along his arm, the spasm spreading, squeezing and tearing deep inside his chest. His pulse thickened, slowed.

He doubled over, consumed by coughing. Air that should have been cold and clear was sweet with decay, and thick with the peculiar fragrance of soft, wet soil. At last, tremor faded from his limbs, and the pain from his chest. As he steadied himself with an outflung hand, a westerly gust of wind sent mist rushing across his feet, though the skies beyond were clear. Curling leaves gathered in the crannies of the balcony wall. As the Dusk Wind ebbed, a rush of soft, scraping noises rose to prominence, sharp footsteps on stone.

A memory stirred. Half-believed tales, rousing hope in the dark. "Goddess?"

{{No.}}

The voice crackled like leaves underfoot, buzzed like a swarm of angry flies. Grating yet soft. Sharp yet resonant. A cold hand closing about his heart, Kai turned.

The castellan's quarters lay overrun. Brambles coiled across wall and ceiling, the curling fronds woven to discordant design – a bower fashioned by drunkard's hands or madman's decree. The floor lay lost beneath a carpet of writhing vines, with petals shed from black roses barely visible in the gloom.

And beside the bed in which Kai had so lately taken ease, a hunched and gangling figure. Man-sized, though sharing only fleeting resemblance to man's shape, he was garbed in a rough robe and tattered hood the colour of decay. A wooden mask that lacked all features save the dark hollows of eyes concealed his face. A likeness borne on the stones of overgrown temples, or by crooked statues guarding forbidden paths. Jack o' Fellhallow. Lord of the Living Land.

The hand about Kai's heart closed tight. The Raven was a secretive figure, feared from a distance; Jack was entirely something else. Tales of Fellhallow ran rife across the western Empire, and never more so than in Rhaled, whose border vanished for many leagues beneath sombre eaves. It was said to be a capricious place of shifting paths and tangled dreams. Where day and night mingled like the confluence of streams. *Said*, because few who trod beneath its boughs returned to speak of what they had seen. Those who did returned with minds riven and tongues wild. Yet still a handful of travellers slipped beneath the trees each year. Warriors in search of challenge and poets dreaming of inspiration. The lovelorn and the lacking. The curious, the reckless and the desperate.

Wherever Fellhallow's eaves darkened the horizon, villagers wove protective garlands about wells and fashioned wicker sentries to stand as watchmen at ditch and wall. Mothers warned children against the honeyed words of thornmaidens who walked summer fields shrouded in pollen-bloom. And when harvest nights fell, and the whispering ones came a rat-tat-tatting at the windows, all clung close to their fires and strove not to think of overgrown villages standing testament to crumbled vigilance.

Tressians often named Jack, *Jerack;* Thrakkians, *Livasdr.* Both meant "God of Life" – a granter of bountiful harvests and strong children. A profound misjudgement. Jack was life and death, and all things in between. At once generous and miserly, and never to be trusted save where his own interest reigned.

And yet it was common belief also that Jack never crossed the Silverway, as he had that night. Another reminder that the Goddess was gone, and her protections spent.

Kai glanced at the chamber door, half-hidden beneath the vines. His sword – the Goddess' sword – made for a better prospect, its belt hanging from the bedpost, barely touched by the thorns twitching across the sheets.

"What do you want?"

{{Is that how an Emperor greets a guest?}}

Kai forced himself to meet the mask's empty gaze. "It is how he greets an intruder."

Buzzing laughter filled the room, a swarm of bees about its hive. {{These lands were mine, and will be again. Your brief hour is not mastery.}} Jack paused, his head tilting this way and that. {{But if I have given offence, I seek pardon. Can one king not hail another in friendship?}}

Eyes ever on Jack, Kai circled towards the bed. "The legends of my people are littered with unhappy souls who thought themselves your friends."

{{Friendship is barter. I do only as the bargain demands.}}

Kai took another step. "And a bargain with the divine binds all parties?"

{{Indeed.}}

Kai glanced at the sword. Still out of reach. "If it is friendship you wish, then friendship you may have."

Jack drew closer, the sound of his stride like old trees beneath the wind. The scent of decay swirled with the sweet fragrance of heather after rain.

{{Friendship is better forged through gifts exchanged, is it not?}}

The pressure about Kai's heart grew cold. "I've no need of your gifts."

{{Have you not? Young Ashana opened so many doors, for ever turning this way and that. Always looking ahead, and never behind. And now things are different. Old days are done, and despair creeps in with the dawn. Already, my preening brother tests his freedom. He will render your dreams dust to claim his desire, and shed not a tear.}} Jack leaned close, the black hollows of his eyes dizzying, mesmeric. {{I offer aid. A pact of war between the might of Fellhallow and the Empire of the Fallen Moon.}}

The Fallen Moon. The name reminded Kai of his helplessness, as Jack had surely intended.

"Against the Dark?"

Jack crackled with laughter. {{Against the Raven.}}

The legendary hatred between Raven and Thorn. Did it really run so deep that the brothers would claw at one another even as the Dark rose to claim all?

"And the price? There's always a price."

{{You're better at this than your grandsire.}} Amusement graced the buzzing words. {{I will fill the void my sister has left behind. I will grant armies of bone and briar to strive alongside those of flesh and steel. And in exchange? When the war is done, you will give me your future.}}

Kai's fingers closed around the Goddess' sword.

"You seek my life? My service?"

Jack straightened. {{Your future for your present. How do you answer?}}

Kai gritted his teeth. "I answer thus."

The sword came free. White flame banished shadows from the room and set the carpet of briars seething. Black petals fell like rain. Jack spun about. Mist spilling from his shoulders, his gangling form drew in until his hood brushed the ceiling – a withered scarecrow looming with fell promise. The eyes of his mask came alive with brilliant green flame. Crooked fingers hooked like claws.

{{I came to you in friendship!}}

His wrath tugged at hair and set robes dancing. Kai held his ground and stared up at the blazing eyes, the sword at guard between them.

Though the Goddess was gone, her grace remained, and her fire brought solace even in the dark.

"And you may leave the same way," he said. "I walk in moonlight, as my fathers before me. As my daughter will after. But you will have nothing of me, Jack o' Fellhallow. Not one drop of my blood, nor one hour of servitude. And if your brother crosses my path, he will have the same."

To his surprise, Jack shrank away, tattered robes ravelling back in until he was again but a hunched figure before the flame. Thorns ceased their thrashing and went still.

{{As you wish, proud Saran. But when you change your mind, you need only call my name.}}

The mist swirled, and he was gone. Kai stood alone in the chamber's heart, the sword in its sheath, and the sheath hanging from the bedpost. Only a floor strewn with black petals and withered fronds offered any proof that Jack had ever been there.

Astridas, 2nd Day of Wealdrust

When war calls, answer in kind.

from the saga of Hadar Saran

Twenty-Four

Vapour danced across a pond purpled by morning's approach. A reminder that Sommertide was passing into Fade, and that the months ahead would grow colder before warmth returned. Neither borrowed hearthguard greatcoat nor brandy held the chill entirely at bay, but wasn't that always the way? Never a simple answer to all life's challenges.

Malachi sipped from his glass and stared up at the moon. Would Ashana bestow wisdom, if asked? A heretical thought, but tempting. Lumestra had never offered succour, despite his prayers. Was it simply that his troubles were beyond even the divine? Certainly, a night's pacing had brought no answers, just weariness that clawed at his eyes and buzzed through the blood.

What if Anastacia was right about Sidara? That her gift was too important to conceal? Lily didn't see it thus, but Lily's judgement on spiritual matters was shaped not only by faith, but also by the strictures of a church that had been her parent as much as any kith. Like law and justice, religion and faith were infrequent allies more than close kin.

One thing was undeniable: events had proven that secrecy would not keep his daughter safe. Magical or mundane, talent found expression.

Long, midnight hours spent pacing the gardens had gleaned no insight in what to do otherwise, much less how to convince Lily to change tack. And come the day, the business of city and Republic would once again dominate his time, the father's mantle set aside for the duties of First Councillor.

It might perhaps have seemed necessary – even honourable – but for his utter failure at both.

A flash of temper sent the glass spinning away. It cracked off a nymph statue and vanished forlornly beneath the lily pads.

"Temper, temper, Lord Reveque."

Malachi bit back a scowl. So the business of the Republic wouldn't wait even for the day? Or at least the business of the Crowmarket, which was increasingly the same.

"I know why you've come," he said without turning. "Lord Trelan had the *temerity* to interfere."

The Emissary plucked the near-empty brandy bottle from the stone table and tipped it towards the wan light.

"You shouldn't drink so much, Lord Reveque. A man in your position can't afford false courage." She set the bottle down and joined him in staring out across the pond. "As for Lord Trelan, he did more than *interfere*. My kin slain, an elder cousin among them. Our property taken."

Property. Southwealders. Malachi tamped down rising anger. She was right: false courage would only do him ill. "You think I should care?"

"I think the Parliament of Crows grows tired of your failure to bring him to heel."

Even through tiredness and burden of liquor, Malachi caught an unfamiliar note. Reluctance? Resentment? Disdain?

"You can't bring a Trelan to heel, it's in the blood."

"Find a way, Malachi. Or they'll have him killed. If he's fortunate, he'll be a groom of the grave. If not, they'll give him to the mists."

Buried alive or cast into Otherworld? Not much to choose between those fates. He stared at her, though couldn't say for certain if it were the threat or the use of his given name that had seized his attention. More than ever, her tone was amiss, though with her features lost in the hood's shadows, he'd no clue to determine exactly what.

"Can you really afford the attention that will bring?"

"It will matter little to Lord Trelan. Dead is dead. I know how the Parliament works. The order will come."

Malachi blinked. He'd misread the warning, which came not from the Parliament, but from their Emissary. How many similar warnings had he confused?

"Why do you care?"

She sighed. "I . . . I don't know."

He regarded her in silence, the candour an unexpected chink of light amid the gloom. All these months, he'd allowed himself to think of her as a thing. An obstacle to overcome. Never a person. One mistake among many since his rise to First Councillor. Politics was the art of finding common ground. He'd once considered himself accomplished at it. Had he, this past year, made the mistake of treating the Crowmarket as a single, unified body? What if the Emissary wasn't his jailer, but merely the woman who minded the key?

"How long have you served the Crowmarket?" he asked softly.

She snorted. "All my life. My mother gave me up to spare her reputation."

"That must be hard."

"Perhaps. I've seen enough of her since to think it might have been for the best."

"Still, to put your own prospects before those of your child . . . Do you ever look at the path you've walked and wonder how you've strayed so far?"

"My path isn't your concern."

She turned abruptly away. In anger? Or out of fear that the shadows might shift, and reveal more of her face – and her thoughts – than she wished? "Forgive me. A rhetorical question, aimed inwards."

"Did you find an answer?"

"Not yet."

"Only a man with the luxury of choice would even ask," she replied bitterly.

The chink of light widened, more of the Emissary's thoughts on display than ever before. A crack in the expressionless wall that was the Crowmarket. "Then you *do* have regrets."

"I breathe. I sleep. I have regrets." Her voice hardened. "Don't mistake them for weakness."

There it was. Beneath the steel, beneath the defiance – the plea to be understood. "Only a man who never experiences doubt would do so. I'm hardly he. It takes courage to grow beyond the past."

The Emissary gathered herself to the pounce. Green eyes glinted beneath the hood. Malachi stumbled back, hands upraised in what he knew to be a forlorn attempt at defence. His hip jogged the table. The brandy bottle shattered against the pondside flagstones.

The Emissary went still, her eyes darting past Malachi to the gardens beyond. She drew herself upright, hands falling to her sides, and shook her head in disdain – though at him, or at herself, Malachi was far from certain.

"If you've any love for Lord Trelan," she said, "stop him."

A heartbeat later, she was gone, lost in a pall of crow's wings and squalling voices that bled through the trees towards Strazyn Abbey.

Malachi let his hands fall and took a deep breath. A first step. His first truly *proactive* step in his dealings with the Crowmarket. Perhaps there was hope. *If* he stirred himself to courage. *If* the Emissary was truly as conflicted as she seemed.

Back through the gardens, he glimpsed the approaching lantern that had startled the Emissary to flight. Three silhouettes, two upright and one stumbling. Had they seen the vranakin? Unlikely, and if need be any one of a dozen lies would conceal the truth. More concerning was why anyone would seek him at such an hour.

Malachi propped himself against the stone table and waited. Though he was no closer to solving the twin problems of Sidara and Josiri, the future seemed less bleak than before, and alive with possibility.

The lantern reached the pondside, giving shape and colour to two hearthguards and a filthy woman in the uniform of the 7th. She swayed and forced herself to a semblance of attention, the salute uncertain and imprecise.

"My lord." Her hand shook as she held out the sealed envelope. "I bring grim tidings."

Given the circumstances of their parting, Josiri had assumed that when Malachi had spoken of discussion "tomorrow", he'd meant in the wake of the Privy Council's mid-morning meeting, and within the austere neutrality of the council palace. It was therefore a surprise to find himself back at Abbeyfields before dawn was fully in the sky, summoned by herald, and without explanation. Stranger still to be ushered into the darkened house via the servant's door, coming to one of the smaller sitting rooms via the kitchens.

"If you'll wait here, my lord?"

The hearthguard withdrew and closed the door behind, leaving Josiri swamped in gloom. Though the drapes were drawn back, purple-grey skies offered little more illumination than the smouldering fire. Or perhaps it only seemed that way. The carriage ride had done little to stir the cobwebs of sleep.

"Josiri?" Erashel turned from her vigil at the window. Dark-ringed eyes spoke to thoughts scarcely less gummed than Josiri's own. "You look worse than I feel."

He grunted. "Ana and I were . . . talking . . . until quite late."

Explanation undersold truth. Worn away by the day's events, he'd made the mistake of pointing out that – however noble their reasons – they'd overstepped their bounds with Sidara. He remembered little detail of what had come after. It had drowned in the red tide of his own flaring temper after Ana refused to admit even the *possibility* of wrongdoing. Harsh words had yielded to stormy silence, and thereafter separate rooms. And all the while that gnawing, creeping uncertainty that Ana had been right. But then, she was always right, even when she wasn't.

"About what we saw at Westernport?"

"Among other things."

"I know what *I* saw," Erashel replied. "I've met Anastacia once or twice, of course, but I didn't know what to make of her. I suppose I never really *believed*. I imagine it can be quite challenging, you and she."

The words awoke memories of the burning warehouse. Challenging. Yes, that was a good start. The distance between them had never felt so great, even before the argument.

"It has its moments."

She took the hint. "And Altiris. Is he . . . ?"

"Alive. And better rested than us, I suspect. He'll live."

A frown touched her brow. "He should be dead. How did you manage it?"

The inevitable question. One for which he'd meant to have a credible answer. Events had crowded out such practicalities. But the truth? That remained beyond the pale if he ever again wanted Malachi to speak to him in friendship.

"I can't tell you. Consider it a miracle."

The frown blurred into suspicion. "Anastacia. It's something to do with her."

"After a fashion." Josiri chided his sleep-deprived tongue for saying even that much. Erashel was too canny to pass up even oblique hints. She and Ana were so alike, strong without and vulnerable within; compassion tempered by fierce intelligence. Admirable and infuriating. "Please, let it rest."

To his relief, she nodded. "Keep your secrets. I owe you that much for yesterday."

This, at least, was safer ground. "You owe me nothing."

She shook her head. "They're my people too. But for you a good many – perhaps all – would be dead." Her voice stirred with passion. "I was wrong to fight you. We're stronger together than apart. For the good of our people, we have to be."

Josiri waved towards the door. "And does that include when Malachi delivers the lecture he's spent the small hours preparing?"

To his surprise, Erashel nodded. "Let him believe I persuaded you to take action. That you were only in Dregmeet at all to recover the situation."

"It isn't true."

"At this moment, I suspect I'm better placed to survive Malachi's disfavour than you. Consider it my penance for the trouble I've given you. Besides, when he learns what the vranakin were doing. About the etravia . . . " She shuddered. " . . . that *thing*."

"I tried to tell him. He wouldn't listen."

Suspicion returned. "You've already spoken?"

Josiri stifled a wince that would only have made matters worse. "Last night, I—"

The door opened. Not Malachi, but Izack, clad in the full armour and raiment of his rank.

"Well, aren't you a glamorous pair this fine morning?" He grinned, seemingly no worse for the early hour. "Hushed summons before break-fast, hurried in through the back door like a Sartorov. Now I find myself in the company of my favourite troublemaker, and another who I've long suspected of being rousable to mischief. An interesting day beckons."

"They're all interesting," said Erashel. "One way or another."

Josiri realigned his assumptions. Izack's presence changed everything. If this wasn't to be a reprimand for the foray into Dregmeet, then what?

"You've no notion what this is about?" he asked.

"Not a one." Izack shrugged. "But that's the soldier's life. Go here. Go there. Plant a flag. Raise a few walls. Oh, and there's always shouting. And thumping. Maybe I'm here to thump some sense into you? Heard about the mess in Dregmeet, of course. Sorry I missed it."

"Then let me tell you the rest," said Josiri.

Izack crooked an elbow against the mantelpiece and listened intently as Josiri laid out all, save his previous visit to Abbeyfields. The mention of ghosts drove the smile from Izack's lips. The grey-robed creature who had matched Ana strength for strength banished all other expression. By the time the tale turned to Elzar's intervention on Drag Hill, his face was uncharacteristically immobile.

"I see what's going on." He wagged a finger at Josiri, then at Erashel. "You're having a laugh with me. Punishment, for not enduring Zarn's pomposity. It's not very bloody funny."

"It's true, every word," said Erashel.

Thunder gathered in Izack's expression, massaged away by the passage of a meaty hand. "Somehow I knew you'd say that. What's the world coming to? I knew the vranakin had their talons in a lot of mucky business. I thought most of it tittle-tattle."

"Maybe that's how it stays secret," she replied.

"No, I don't reckon so," said Izack. "Vranakin like to make examples. If they'd that kind of power, we'd have heard long ago. They'd be running half the Republic."

"Things are stirring," murmured Josiri. "Things that should be left sleeping."

Erashel joined Izack in giving him a leery look.

"I beg your pardon?" she said.

"Something Ana said."

Izack grunted. "I'd like to have a chat with your good lady. Then I think I'd like to take a walk into Dregmeet, but with a few more bodies than you had yesterday. A few thousand more."

"I don't know that Malachi will approve."

Izack grinned. "I'm not asking permission. I swore an oath to Essamere that I'd defend this rotten little Republic. That's the glory of being a knight. Higher duty, and all that." He turned at the creak of the door. "Oh, hello. Thought you might be his lordship."

"I'm sorry to disappoint." Hawkin matched how Josiri felt far better than Izack appeared. A pang of guilt soured his spirits further. "Lord Reveque is ready. If you'll please follow me? But quietly. Much of the household is still asleep."

She led them up two flights of stairs and away towards the back of the house. A soft knock on the oaken study door, and it opened inwards to reveal a Malachi whose expression was so calm, so collected, it rang patently false. Izack filed inside, then Erashel. Josiri lingered in the passageway and drew Hawkin aside by her elbow.

"About before," he said. "I should never have put you in that position."

"It's done with." Eyes that never failed to sparkle regarded him dully. "You did what you had to. But never again, please."

Josiri followed the others. "Never" was the hardest promise to make. Hawkin remained in the corridor and pulled the door closed.

Josiri had been a frequent guest to that study in happier times. A glass or two shared at the end of a long day, in friendship or else to grease the wheels of governance. Save for the broad window that overlooked the grounds, every inch of wall boasted meticulously ordered bookshelves, furled maps and sketchbooks – a collection built up over long decades by Malachi's forebears. The study felt elevated by history where the council chamber was confined by it – knowledge wielded not as weapon or leverage, but for its own sake. It also felt uncommonly cramped when playing host to four.

Malachi retreated behind a desk that offered further clue that something was amiss. Ever a man of careful habit and fastidious penmanship, he seldom left so much as a single leaf of paper out of place. Now, documents, maps and half-written letters hid the polished wood from sight. Many were covered in thick, greasy ink-scrawl, or dark spatters that spoke to inattention.

Izack cleared his throat. "Not good manners to call an early morning tryst and leave us all hanging around. Is this about the vranakin? Because what I've been hearing—"

Malachi tapped the heel of his paper knife on the desk and looked up. "Ahrad has fallen."

Josiri suppressed a shiver that defied the crackling hearth. Erashel's lips thinned to a slash.

Izack cocked his head. "Say that again."

"The Hadari attacked this morning," said Malachi. "Castellan Noktza is dead. So are half the garrison. The Ravonn is lost, and if the Eastshires aren't overrun, they soon will be."

"Impossible," Izack snapped. "I was at Ahrad last month. I walked the walls. The shadowthorns could pound them for weeks and have nothing to show for it."

Josiri forgave his disbelief, for a part of him shared it. Ahrad, the Eskagard. The indomitable fortress. Either Malachi was deceived, or . . .

"Are you certain?" Erashel glanced at each man in turn before her gaze settled on Malachi. "This isn't something we want to be wrong about."

Malachi laughed without humour. "A squire of the 7th arrived less than an hour ago. She's been riding since dawn, changing horses at relay posts along the Silverway. She brought this letter. Lady Sarravin's seal. Her codes."

He fished a filthy scrap of paper from the corner of the desk. Izack snatched it away. He read in silence, lips twitching, then nodded grimly and offered it around.

Josiri shook his head. Each regimental commander had their own form of words to prevent false warnings being passed, but he'd quickly learned he was incapable of memorising them. Besides, if Malachi and Izack believed . . .

"So Ahrad's gone," he said.

"Who else knows?"

"Officially? We four, and perhaps half a dozen others. Unofficially? I expect half the city to know by noon. I'll issue an official proclamation as soon as Captain Darrow has the constabulary mobilised to contain any panic."

"I still don't understand how they breached the walls," said Erashel.

Izack scowled. "Sarravin's letter talks of a demon. Magic."

"Both of them terms bandied about to shape something we cannot explain," said Josiri.

"Things are stirring," muttered Erashel. "Things that should be left sleeping."

Malachi scowled. "What was that?"

Josiri shook his head. Now wasn't the time to speak of what he'd seen in Dregmeet. "What brought us to this point matters less than what we do next. Why us, Malachi? Why not the full council?"

"I don't need the Council's approval to protect the Republic. Leonast, Konor, the others . . . I've neither the time nor the patience to weather their opinions. And that's before we consider the Grand Council. I'll speak with them later, but action must come first. For that, everyone I need is in this room." He picked up a sheaf of letters from the desk and thrust them at Izack. "Authority to mobilise every regiment in the city, and those stationed at Tarvallion. I trust I can leave the chapterhouses to you?"

Izack took the letters without a glance. "I'm to take charge of this mess?"

"For now, at least."

"And your orders?"

"Bring the Hadari to battle if you can win, but save our people most of all. Cities can be rebuilt, fields re-sown." Malachi tapped a second sheaf of letters. "And keep me informed. I can't be blind. Not now. Reinforcements will come as I gather them. Thank Lumestra the harvest is done, or they'd be tilling the fields."

Izack gave a low, breathy whistle. "I said this'd be an interesting day. I bloody well hate interesting days. With your permission, First Councillor, I'll be about your business." He ruffled his sheaf of letters. "Warriors to muster, laggards to rouse, folk to shout at, and others to thump. Good day to you all."

"Lumestra ride with you," said Erashel.

"She'll need a bloody fast horse."

He yanked open the door and thumped away along the corridor.

Malachi sank into his chair and stared at the map. Josiri wondered what he saw. Fields aflame? Fortresses cast down? The dead strewn far and wide? Josiri had witnessed a little of that during the previous year's invasion. But that had been the warriors of one divided kingdom, attacking across the mountains. This was a tide of war and death that would drown all in its path. If only the border could have been sealed with the same efficiency with which he'd been caged at Branghall, but the secret of that enchantment had died with its creator.

"What about us?" he asked softly.

"Hmmm?" Malachi continued staring at the map.

Erashel drew closer. "You said everyone you needed was in this room."

He seemed hardly to hear. "It was once said that a single south-wealder's blade was worth six from the north. I hope it's true."

The words pried open old memories. "I hope you're not pinning hopes of salvation on our countrymen. Between Saran's spears, Makrov's purges and—" He remembered in time that Erashel wasn't party to the truth about Eskavord's fate. "And everything that came after, there's no army to raise. Most of what there is won't follow me, not after Eskavord. But I will try, if that's what you want."

At last, Malachi looked up. Gone were distance and indecision, replaced by determination. "That's why you're both going. Those who won't follow the Duke of Eskavord will heed the last daughter of Beral."

"Then I should stay." Josiri glanced back at Erashel and received the slightest of nods. "Erashel can manage the south. With Izack gone you'll need one of us here. The Crowmarket—"

"You're wrong, Josiri," Malachi replied. "There's something only you can do for me."

Realisation came swift and sickening. Izack was "in charge of this mess" for *now*. A safe pair of hands, but survival called for more than safety.

"No. I won't do it."

"Erashel?" Malachi produced another bundle of letters. "The *Sunrunner* sits at anchor in the estuary. She leaves with the tide and will carry you as far as Margard. Requisition what you need from there. There are troops at Ardva. Find more."

She took the letters, eyes flicking back and forth between Malachi and Josiri, the question on her lips different to the one she voiced. "So I'm to go alone?"

"That depends." Malachi's gaze never left Josiri. "Leave us to talk, would you?"

"Of course," said Erashel. "I'll see you if I see you, Josiri."

The door creaked, and then they were two.

"The Republic needs Viktor," said Malachi. "You're the only one he'll heed."

There it was, stark and sure. Not that there'd even been any doubt. "I told you I never wanted to see him again. Let him rot in the Southshires for all I care."

"And which need is greater?" asked Malachi. "Josiri Trelan's or the Republic's?"

"Viktor can do nothing Izack cannot."

Malachi shook his head. "Izack is a good man, and a canny one. You and I would both be dead otherwise. I've no doubt he'll hurt the Hadari greatly before this is done. But he lacks one thing."

"Which is?"

"He's not Viktor Akadra."

Josiri bit off a growl and spun on his heel. Viktor Akadra, the Council's Champion, the phoenix-slayer – the man who couldn't lose because he didn't know how. But victory always carried a cost borne elsewhere. But for Viktor, Josiri's mother – the dowager duchess Katya Trelan – wouldn't have taken her own life. But for Viktor, Anastacia would still be a free spirit, not shackled to a body of clay. And worst of all, Calenne. Even a year on, Josiri strove not to think of his sister, and thus spare himself the heartache. But for Viktor, she'd still be alive, rather than mingled ashes in the ruins of Eskavord. Calenne had been the last straw, one last broken promise beyond balm.

That Viktor had intended none of these fates to fall meant nothing.

Josiri clenched his fists. "Viktor took everything from me."

"That's why he'll heed you."

"He'd listen to you."

"You'd have the First Councillor leave the city? Now?"

A foolish suggestion. One that would only tempt Lamirov and the others to mischief. With Izack and Erashel gone, there wouldn't be the votes to keep them in check. "Then send Messela."

Malachi sighed. "What rank Messela holds, she does so purely because Viktor removed himself. Even if she finds him – which I doubt she can – she lacks the confidence to force the issue. And I don't trust our peers to make honest effort, let alone sway Viktor's mind. My friends are stubborn."

Josiri ignored the mixed compliment and faced Malachi once more. "Then send Kurkas."

"Same problem as Messela, only he'd save us time by refusing to go. Moreover, I was hoping I might borrow him for other business, if I may?"

"Other business?"

"Constans is determined to learn a knight's trade, and I'll sleep easier if Sidara learns the sword's art. I can think of no better tutor."

To Josiri's mind, the city held no shortage of better tutors, but perhaps none less likely to be intimidated if Constans or Sidara started throwing around their father's rank.

"If he's agreeable."

"Thank you. Now, where were we?" Malachi ticked off his fingers one at a time. "I need Elzar to muster the foundry to reinforce Izack. Rosa was at Ahrad, which means she's likely dead – if that's possible. Even if she's not, finding her takes time we don't have. Which leaves you."

"You need me here with the Crowmarket running wild! You weren't at Westernport. The vranakin aren't just killing for fun! It's a ritual. Dregmeet's sinking into the mists. Into Otherworld."

"There's always mist in Dregmeet."

"Are there always etravia?" demanded Josiri. "And there was something worse. Something that would have killed us all, but for Ana."

That shook Malachi. Though he tried to hide it behind an immobile expression, the tremor in his voice won out. "You tell me all that and say we don't need Viktor?"

"I never said that," he replied stiffly. "Only that I won't be the one to fetch him."

Malachi rose from his chair, as solemn and serious as Josiri had ever seen him. "You keep telling me north and south are all in this together. Stand by your convictions. Find him. Bring him back. Or at the very least tell me how many lives your pride is worth, so I'll know for the future."

The accusation cut deep for all its mildness, the words edged with truth. So easy – so comforting – to fall into old patterns. Half a lifetime spent hating Viktor Akadra, save for those handful of shining days where they'd fought as brothers. Frightening to dwell on the power of that hate. But Izack had been right before. There *was* duty beyond the personal.

He'd forgotten that once, and only Calenne's example had brought him to his senses. Had it been otherwise, she might still be alive. In fact, the harm Viktor had wrought upon Josiri's loved ones had only ever come to pass out of Josiri's own weakness. Because he'd lacked courage. Katya. Ana. Calenne. Calenne, most of all, with her sapphire eyes and quick temper. It took little imagination to conjure the words she'd have for him now. Malachi's would seem kind by comparison.

How many lives was his pride worth? Not even one.

"I will do as you ask."

Jeradas, 3rd Day of Wealdrust

There's little less use than a broken sword.
Save for a shield that shelters no more.

from the Vigil Oath of Essamere

Twenty-Five

Tongues of flame raced through dry timber. Clouds of choking, bitter smoke sucked air from lungs and hope from the heart. The lone figure at the kitchen's hearth vanished into their embrace.

Even as Viktor reached for her, steel glinted, and she was gone.

"Calenne!"

He lurched bolt upright. The smoke-clogged kitchen gave way to stone walls and lattice roof, cracks of sunlight brilliant through ill-fitting timbers. Blankets lay more upon the flagstoned floor than the bed. Viktor wiped sweat from his eyes, the bed's timber creaking as his weight shifted.

And deep within his soul, in the cage he'd made for it, his shadow laughed.

Cool fingers slipped around his waist.

"Hush, I'm here." The words fell softly in a room quiet save for morning birdsong. "I'm here. Was it the same dream?"

Viktor scowled. "It's always the same dream." He leaned into the embrace, fingers closing about hers, and willed his racing heart to slow. "The fire rages, and then you're gone . . ."

"But I'm not," Calenne whispered. "I'm here. And I've no mind to be anywhere else."

She leaned across his shoulder for a kiss. Tendrils of nightmare receded, and the shadow in Viktor's soul fell silent.

"And you, Lord Akadra, should be about the business of the day." Wicked asperity crept into her tone. "How you ever made a soldier by sleeping so long, I shall never understand."

She slipped from beneath the covers and padded barefoot to the battered wardrobe. Not for the first time, Viktor marvelled at how different they were. She, slender as a reed and fine of feature, with sparkling blue eyes beneath a gentle brow; he as tall and broad as she was not, with dark eyes in a swarthy face and a soldier's scars to prove his failings – the deepest of all on his left cheek, where Calenne's long-dead mother had left her mark. She but a span of summers out of girlhood, and he approaching middle-years.

Only hair dark as night offered commonality. Even there, she'd the better of him. Cropped to jawline length in commoner's fashion – and to conceal likeness to a notorious mother – it seldom strayed save in fiercest wind. Viktor's own was a bird's nest.

He bided while she dressed, elbows propped upon bundled knees. Though the nightmare was gone, its echo remained. Conscience aghast at necessary deeds. Of thousands sent to the flames to save untold others. He closed his eyes. In the darkness, Eskavord burned. So long a soldier, but one no more. That path had burned with the Grelyt Valley, burned with the remnant of Malatriant, the Tyrant Queen who'd come howling out of history to claim him as her own. A piece of Viktor had burned alongside both, but better the fire than the Dark.

That was the nature of sacrifice, to give away a piece of yourself for a greater good. Viktor didn't resent the cost to himself – the dishonour borne for deeds whose truth would never be common knowledge. Dwelling on choices made was the surest path to madness, and Viktor – who woke to fading terror each morning, and had a sliver of Dark coiling about his soul – already deemed himself closer to madness than comfort allowed. The life once lived he surrendered gladly to need.

And Calenne was right. The business of the day called.

The log split cleanly. Birchwood halves toppled from the stump to join their forebears. Another, and the sweat of honest labour banished that born of nightmare. Rhythm steadied, the rush of the axe and the dull *chonk* of falling blow blurring to strange music.

Skirts swished as Calenne sought comfier perch on the drystone wall. She picked idly at Viktor's discarded shirt, fingers tracing the stitching. "Just how much firewood do you think we need?"

"You remember last year? Snows waist-deep all about, and ice on the inside of the walls? This year, I'd rather be prepared."

"Last year, the walls were more whistling wind than stone."

"True."

He gazed back up the hill – past the thin crop-garden and the forlorn scarecrow bedecked in a fraying black surcoat – to the uneven silhouette of Tarona Watch. Decades before, the keep had stood guard over the Thrakkian border to the south, and the Valna-Ardva road that wound its way through the meadows to the north. But the floods of '76 had washed the road away, to be reinstated further north. Tarona Watch had been abandoned, and soon stripped by locals seeking stone.

Ramparts were now a jumbled tideline no taller than Viktor's knee, and the central keep a single, ramshackle storey. Mottled stone betrayed where Viktor had patched the walls, discoloured timbers where he'd repaired roofs and doors. No longer a fortress, Tarona made for an acceptable home. At least, provided one had no desire for company. It was a long walk down difficult and treacherous hillsides to reach the village of Valna, and a longer walk back. The bustling inland port of Ardva was further still. What farms the border hills possessed lay far to the west, where the ground yielded crops more nourishing than stone.

"And anyway," Viktor readied another log before the axe. "It helps me think."

She smiled. "And what weighty thoughts do you wrestle with, dear Viktor?"

"How best to restore the upper floor."

"I'm content with what we have."

So she always said. Viktor wasn't sure he believed her. She'd grown up in too much comfort for that. Now, this all seemed a grand adventure. But adventure faded. And besides, his shadow seethed in idleness, testing the bounds of its cage. Hunting quietened it; provided meat for the pot and the spit, as well as pelts for trade and barter, but it did not stir the blood or satisfy the soul. Nor did it occupy a great measure of his time. Hands without purpose only encouraged brooding thoughts, and he was already prone enough to that.

"You said that before I restored the hall," he said. "Could you return to living your whole life in one room now that we do not?"

She offered that pitying smile he'd come to know so well – the one that despaired of ever making him see reason, but somehow revelled in the failure. "Then you should at least let me help."

He returned his gaze to the logs as the old argument beckoned. "You're still not well."

"You worry too much about me."

"I've reason."

Viktor had saved Calenne's soul from Malatriant's pyre, but her body had sickened. The longest night of Viktor's life had come at winter's height, with howling wolves scrabbling at the door and a febrile, listless Calenne lost to fever. He'd left her bedside to drive away the starving pack, but had at every moment feared she'd be gone upon his return. In desperation, he'd let his shadow slip its cage and scatter the wolves – something he'd sworn never again to do.

When the thaw had come, Viktor had argued she see Ardva's physician. Argued, and lost. Calenne Trelan, who had spent her whole life in a gilded cage – longing to escape the burden of her family's history and the expectation that came alongside – feared nothing more than her brother learning that she yet lived. Viktor, who feared nothing more than losing *her*, had traded confrontation for a promise of non-exertion. And so while he laboured to build the foundations of a life together, she walked the hills and dales, or watched him at his work.

Half a year had passed thus, but Calenne was little improved. Never was it more noticeable than when sunlight revealed how pale she'd grown. She surely knew that better than Viktor did, but illness had done nothing to dim her defiance. Trelans were stubborn, even when they were Akadras.

Calenne dropped down from the wall and planted a hand on her hip. "Viktor, I rode to war for you. I traded blows with a Hadari princessa and held her to a tie ... "

Her voice tailed off as her chastisement strayed into forgotten memories. Forgotten through choice, or lost out of terror, Viktor had never determined, and had been loath to ask. He longed to forget what little he remembered of his own time under Malatriant's shadow, and could not resent Calenne for having done so.

Calenne blinked as if waking from a dream. "If I can come safe through all that, I don't see what harms modest fetching and carrying – or heaven forbid, *carpentry* – have to offer. I am not made of glass, and I won't have you treat me as such."

There it was. The defiance Viktor both loved and hated. The piece that would remain of her long after the memory of her touch and smile had faded. The piece that challenged better of them both, and had filled a void in his life he'd never known existed.

Perhaps she was right. "I don't want to lose you."

"And I won't live in a cage, even one wrought from concern." She drifted closer, dark skirts flowing across the stubbled grass. Her fingertips brushed his arm, then tightened to draw him down for a kiss. "You can't lose me, Viktor. Not now, not ever. We are—"

She stared down the overgrown cart track.

"Someone's coming."

Viktor heard it too, carrying clear through the buzz of insects and the hum of bird's wings. The soft tramp of boot. The laboured breath of someone unprepared for the hike.

Visitors didn't come to Tarona. On his rare forays into civilisation, Viktor laboured to discourage them. A chance glimpse, and rumours would spread. Calenne's secret would be for nothing, and happiness placed beyond her grasp.

"Go," he said. "I'll send them away."

"Play nicely, Viktor."

She kissed him on the cheek and walked away, her stride quickening to a run as she cleared the crest; a shadow in the sunlight, and then gone. Viktor turned again downhill, and wondered if he should return inside, take his claymore from its hooks above the hearth. Deciding against, he tugged on his shirt, retrieved the lumber axe, and marched down the hill.

Viktor waited for the intruder just beyond the vanished walls, in the dell where tangled trees drew close to an ivy-clad statue. The gangling, robed figure stared not north across the valley, but west, towards the distant sea, though what he sought there, or why, remained as mysterious as the face concealed beneath the pitted stone mask.

Viktor cared nothing for Jack, who drew worship only from rural, uncivilised folk. But he welcomed the chill air that ever hung about the statue, and the smattering of mist that never faded even under brightest sun. Not for the cold, though that was certainly welcome enough after his exertions, but because something about the dell made his shadow cower. A Forbidden Place, touched by old magic.

At last, the uninvited guest lurched into view, a staff tapping the ground ahead of his steps. Viktor let the axe fall loose. This was no thief seeking a score, nor a wolf's-head in pursuit of mischief. Best of all, he was no Council herald with summons and soldiers. No threat to be had from this man, despite the battle axe slung across his back.

A rich, red beard – plaited in the meticulous Thrakkian style – lent years to a face nearer to Calenne's age than Viktor's. A scar set diagonally across eyes and the bridge of his nose added more, barely visible though it was beneath the flame tattoo covering the right side of his face. Thick leathers and a woollen hood must have sweltered beneath the morning sun, though the traveller showed no signs of discomfort. Nor did he visibly react as his empty gaze swept across Viktor, for his eyes were white and glassy.

"Armund af Garna?" said Viktor. "What brings you to Tarona?"

Armund drew to a halt. His head regarded Viktor, though his eyes did not. "So what they're saying down in Valna is true? The high and mighty Lord Akadra *is* skulking on this hilltop?"

"A long walk for nothing if he wasn't."

"Worth the risk, to visit an old comrade. And I've time to spare. Not much call for a blind thrydaxe like myself."

He spoke jovially enough, but Viktor wondered at the truth beneath the words. He and Armund had been only brief comrades, and a battle-field had separated the strike of their steel. As for his claims of being a thrydaxe – a mercenary? Well, he'd taken no payment in either coin or promise to stand at the Battle of Davenwood – at least, not from Viktor. But "mercenary" didn't have the same connotations beyond the border as it did in the Republic. Thrakkians were fond of the bargain and the unspoken honour of the trade. Selling one's skills was a point of pride, and to do so with the balance of trade in another's favour a most generous gift.

But whatever Armund's motives, one question remained: what to do with him? Tarona's modest comforts aside, Calenne wouldn't be pleased to be away from home while Viktor entertained the unexpected guest. Better to send him away.

And yet . . .

Brief or not, comrades they had been. Armund had lost both sight and beloved twin in Calenne's defence at the Battle of Davenwood. More than that, what time Viktor and Armund had shared was unsullied by the Dark that had fallen after. Two warriors fighting for the fortunes of a land not theirs. Sending Armund away would be like sending away a piece of himself.

"If you can stagger a little further, I can manage some refreshment," said Viktor. "You must be parched."

Armund grunted. "I've had my fill of water."

"I'd not dare offer you any . . . but I do have some mead, traded for buckskin in Indrig."

Easier to trade in Thrakkian villages. Too many Tressians knew the part he'd played in Eskavord's burning. Not the truth, of course, but near enough for curses and resentment.

He laughed, a deep, warm rumble in a cold place. "See? I knew you'd not let me down."

Viktor hesitated. "Shall I guide you?"

"There's nothing wrong with my ears. Your thumping footsteps will be guidance enough."

Before long, they sat on a fallen column – the lone remnant of a cloister that had once joined the keep to a now-vanished church. Viktor poured himself a cup of mead, and handed the bottle to Armund, who took a hearty swig and gasped an appreciative sigh.

"A welcome payment for a long journey." He raised his hand high, inviting the *chink* of cup on bottle that Viktor gladly granted. "I was sorry to hear about Calenne. Those with fire like hers deserve better than a slit throat."

The old lie. The first telling had almost broken Viktor. But that had been to a brother lost in grief. Confirming it to Armund raised barely a flicker of conscience.

"Thank you."

"Still, she stood her ground. We fought the impossible fight and sent the shadowthorns howling to the border. There are worse ways to be remembered." He raised the bottle again. *"Brenæ af brenæ. Væga af væga."*

Fire from fire and death from death. The traditional Thrakkian toast, ushering spirits to the feast halls of Skanandra. Viktor raised his cup but said nothing. Fire had long since ceased to comfort him.

"Didn't think to find you up on a hilltop, drinking your life away," said Armund. "What happened to the hero's welcome?"

"It went to the deserving, I'm sure. I'm not counted among them."

"Oh, I heard that, true enough. That grief sent you mad. Funny thing, though, but I also heard something else. Eskavord concealed something rotten, and you burned it out."

Viktor gazed at him, but there were few pursuits more futile than attempting to outstare a sightless man. "You should be careful listening to stories, Armund. They'll lead you astray."

He shrugged. "I know truth when I hear it."

Which stories did he consider false? Calenne's death? His shadow, sensing dismay, clawed at the bars of its cage. Viktor walled it deeper in and swallowed his doubts. If Armund indeed suspected, or even knew, there was no one less likely to speak of it to others. Thrakkian honour was complicated, but also very simple where comrades were concerned.

"So what brings you here?" he said. "Besides your nose for mead."

"To settle a debt."

Viktor smiled without mirth. "If Josiri's sent you for my head, I must politely decline."

Again, the rumble of laughter. "Don't think I couldn't."

Politeness held Viktor back from contradiction. "Then what?"

Armund set down the bottle and unslung his axe. Moving with a sighted man's assurance, he spun the blade about and set the haft across his knees. "The debt I speak of is mine, owed to you. For ushering my sister to Skanandra when I could not."

Viktor glanced down at the axe, whose wooden haft still bore the black scars of that day. Tressians held no fate worse than the fire, but to Thrakkians it was divine.

"I was glad to do so."

"Maybe, but Anliss insists I set the ledger right."

The axe he bore was hers, wasn't it? Rescued from her pyre. "Anliss?"

Armund patted the axe-head. "Aye. She's beside Astor's forge, drinking her fill, but still she speaks to me. Always will, so long as I've this to hand. She knows what you did for her, and I'll have no peace until I've done for you in return."

Viktor held his tongue. Was this all metaphor and mysticism, or did Armund truly believe that his sister, dead a year and more, spoke to him through bond of steel?

"Tell her there is no debt."

"She won't listen. She's had me lumbering back and forth across the Southshires for months now, seeking you out." He grinned. "You're a difficult one to find, Akadra."

Viktor grunted. At first, he'd thought to live on the move, travelling from village to village and town to town, the better to watch for Malatriant's survival. Tarona had been a retreat, not a home. But then winter had come in, and Calenne had grown sick, and plans had changed. "Assuming I accept this debt exists—"

"Wise boy," said Armund, to a man ten years his senior.

"How do you intend to settle it? Other than by drinking my mead?"

"By giving you back to yourself."

Viktor blinked. "I don't follow."

"You're meant for more than this! Living alone on a hilltop, watching your life rush past in the rain. You're a warrior. You belong in battle. You deserve that folk bellow your name in praise, not whisper it like a courtesan haggling price at High Table."

The words provoked insidious stirring. Viktor tamped it down. "I've never fought for glory, only out of need."

"Glory *is* need."

"For a Thrakkian, perhaps."

"Say that's true. What if I told you there *was* need?"

"Then I'd send you to petition the reeve of Ardva."

"Hah!" snorted Armund. "She's too worried about convoys going north to trouble over the border villages."

"Which village?"

"So you *are* interested?"

Yes. Despite himself. Despite his best judgement. "I thought Thrakkians prided themselves on being straightforward."

"Valna."

Viktor frowned. He'd been in Valna two days before, and nothing had struck him terribly amiss. The people were quiet and withdrawn, yes, but southwealders always were around him. Twice bitten, and shy to invisibility. "I don't follow."

"My brother Ardothan, greedy sack of spoil that he is, has decided taking tithe from everything south of the Grelyt and north of the Goyda isn't enough for him. He's turning his eye across the border. Disri and Hadgrove paid up like good little children, but not Valna. They're to serve as example."

"Which means war between the Republic and Indrigsval."

Armund downed the last of the mead. "For a few farmers? Ardothan knows the Council won't risk that. And if they do, it'll be blood along the border."

"And how do you know this?"

"Need I lecture you about my ears again? There are still a few in my brother's court who care that he stole that throne." He shrugged. "Farmers'll still be dead, though. Unless someone steps up."

"One sword against a thane's army?"

"There'll be no more than a dozen. It's a raid, not an occupation. And it wouldn't be one sword, but one sword and one axe."

"And you think that'd be enough?"

"If it's the right sword."

Viktor's treacherous pulse quickened at the thought. He could face down a dozen Thrakkians. They'd be expecting terrified villagers, not a man who'd served as Council Champion and twice laid low a Hadari Emperor. A little blood would bring them to heel.

Then the shadow in Viktor's soul rattled the bars of its cage – a reminder why Valna's fate would have to unfold without him. "I can't do it."

"Why not? Struck by cowardice, are we?"

Viktor scowled away the insult. "Not of the sort you mean."

"Now who's not speaking plain?"

"Perhaps ... " He paused. "Perhaps the stories about me hold a meas-ure of truth. Perhaps I'm not the man I once was."

"Anliss says you are."

"I'll give you a letter for the reeve of Ardva. She's an old comrade. She'll listen."

"I don't travel as well as I used to," said Armund. "Even if I set out now, I won't reach Ardva until nightfall. Ardothan's vanaguard will be in Valna at dawn. The village will be corpses and ash long before the first wayfarer sets bum in saddle. But if we leave now, we'll be there to give proper greeting."

Corpses and ash. Viktor shook his head angrily. "You should have gone straight there."

"Why, when you're right here?"

"I said before, I can't help."

"Clinker rot! Why not?"

"Because . . . " The urge to confess – to explain – grew overpowering. "Because no aid I can give you will be worth the price. No matter what your 'sister' claims."

"I see." Armund smoothed a hand across the axe's blade. "Well, sister, you can't say I didn't try. Seems it'll be one axe and no sword."

A blind man alone? "They'll kill you."

"More likely they'll drag me to Ardothan and *he'll* kill me. But I know what I'm dying for, Akadra." Armund reslung his axe and groped for his staff where it rested against the wall. "What are you living for? The man I sought is long gone. You're but an echo."

He picked his way clear of the column and strode away, staff tapping at the ground. Calenne appeared at the hall door, though she said nothing until he was well out of sight.

"I hope you said nothing of me."

Viktor shook his head. "Your secret's safe with Armund. But no, I didn't tell him."

"I heard what he wanted. Why did you say no?"

"You know why," he growled. "Malatriant—"

"Is dead. Gone to dust, and never to return." She took his arm in hers. "She has no hold over you, Viktor."

How he wished that were true, that the shadow on his soul had never existed. That its pressure – its temptation – could be forgotten. That he could simply be himself and all he'd once stood for. Not for the Republic, for the Republic was cold and unfeeling, but for its *people*. But his shadow remained, longing to be free.

"You weren't there at the end," he said. "You didn't see how close I came. Malatriant offered me everything, and I accepted, body and soul. If it wasn't for Josiri . . ."

She scowled. "I don't believe that."

Viktor closed his eyes, the final moments of Eskavord swelling unbidden. "All that remains of Malatriant's Dark is within me, bound to my shadow. If I let it loose, there might be no putting it back. I might become everything she sought to make of me."

"But you've already let it loose, haven't you? When the snows fell and the wolves came running."

He blinked, for he'd not known she knew. "For you. Only for you."

"And I suppose the people of Valna deserve less? If your shadow worries you so much, keep it caged. Armund didn't come here seeking magic, but mettle."

"Would that it were so simple."

"Do you remember what you once told me? That too many men and women live and die longing for a moment in which to make a difference. You've just been handed such a moment, Viktor." Calenne glared, her bunched fists thrust down at her sides. "And if you'll not act, perhaps I will!"

He reached for her. "Calenne . . ."

She pulled away and retreated inside. The defiance he loved so well – that urged Viktor to be better – had blossomed, and in the challenge had found him wanting.

He stared across Tarona's overgrown courtyard. From its sentry post in the crop-garden, the surcoated scarecrow gazed back, and Viktor's shadow laughed.

Maladas, 5th Day of Wealdrust

History is an avalanche. It gathers in the distance,
the signs missed even by the vigilant. By the time the
ground shakes, all you can do is run.

from Eldor Shalamoh's "Historica"

Twenty-Six

"A good morning for it," said Armund, his axe's pommel planted on the road's flagstones, his spread hands set atop the eye.

Viktor snorted. A fiery sky might have been a good omen in Thrakkia – a reflection of Astor's forge at Skanandra – but red skies at dawn seldom portended anything good.

"Could be you change your mind before the hour's out."

Armund shrugged. "How many?"

"Looks to be a dozen."

A dozen vanaguard in heavy chain and drakon-wing helms. Cloaks of thick yellow and sea green claith – loom-woven wool whose pattern was as unique to a thane as his heraldry – guaranteed a sweltering ascent up Valna's wooded hillside. Their axes made Armund's hand-and-a-half weapon seem a toy. Splitters of shields and skulls, and impossible to stop once momentum was up. An intimidating display, and one Valna's aged militiamen had no chance of contesting.

Despite Calenne's reassurances during their bittersweet parting at Tarona, Viktor resembled every inch the scarecrow from which he'd reclaimed his surcoat. A scarecrow with a battered claymore and without armour. Valna's headman hadn't believed he stood in the presence of Lord Viktor Akadra, but the old soak had been desperate. Desperate enough to put his faith in a scarecrow and a blind man.

"There's still time to walk away," said Viktor.

Armund spat. "Bugger that. My family. My responsibility."

Viktor glanced back past Valna's ivy-covered palisade to thatched rooftops silhouetted against the dawn. A cluster of homesteads gathered around a broken-down temple and scraping a living from soil. Once, the border fortresses – or Revekah Halvor's wolf's-heads – had sheltered them from Thrakkian aggression. But the soldiers had been withdrawn, their fortresses overgrown; Halvor and her phoenixes were dead. Whatever the maps claimed, in practical terms the Republic ran no further south than the inland port of Ardva.

Valna needed a champion. If only for a day.

"I can't fight them and keep you safe," said Viktor.

"Tend to yourself, lad. Anliss watches for me from Skanandra's forge."

Again, the dead sister. Did Armund seek Valna's salvation at all, or simply a good death? Thrakkian honour was a tangle of contradictions. What if Armund had brought him there not to fight, but to stand witness?

He gripped Armund's shoulder. "Death and honour."

He nodded. "Brenæ af Brenæ, yr Væga af Væga."

Fire from fire and death from death. A promise of Skanandra for those who died well. More than ever, Viktor wondered at Armund's motives.

The vanaguards halted on the overgrown roadway. The foremost swept off her helm. A weather-beaten face stared unflinching out beneath steel grey hair.

"We come to collect tribute in the name of Ardothan, thane of Indrigsval." She spoke Tressian low-tongue thicker and slower than Armund, heavy vowels grinding against the consonants. "Stand aside, or your blood marks the first tithe."

"Still serving filth, Inkari af Üld?" growled Armund.

Her cheek twitched. "I serve the throne of Indrigsval."

"And much glory has it brought you, I'm sure. Scaring farmers for a few coins." He snorted. "You taught me better."

"I also told you never again to step within Indrigsval, and yet here you are."

"Indrigsval ends at the Grelyt," rumbled Viktor. "This is Tressia."

"The Republic has neglected the western valley. Ardothan has taken it beneath his shield."

Viktor fought to conceal disdain. Inkari had spoken prettily enough, but the underlying truth was little different to vranakin offering a merchant's shipments "protection". "Valna no longer needs your thane's generosity. It has defenders of its own."

She narrowed her eyes. "A sightless exile and a tatter-knight?"

He met the gaze. "I was – I *am* – Lord Viktor Akadra, Champion to the Council, slayer of Emperor Ceredic ... " That last wasn't entirely true, for Ceredic had died of his wounds long months after, but what did the moment call for if not bravado? " ... and the vanquisher of his son. I believe I'm ample to the task."

Signs of recognition were subtle. A hurried glance between two vanaguards. A half-step back by one, checked and reversed almost at the same moment.

Inkari's stare didn't flicker. "I heard Akadra had lost his wits."

"Perhaps I did." Viktor's shadow growled. He ignored it. "I'm feeling better."

Armund had been right about that, however muddled the Thrakkian might have been on other counts. Viktor allowed himself to enjoy the moment. A reminder of his life – his purpose – before Malatriant had torn his world apart.

"Have you not yet tallied the odds against you?" said Inkari. "We're not bond-axes, sold into service. I am a ceorla of Indrigsval, chosen by deed. With me stand vanaguards, proven and true."

The rank of ceorla marked her as a member of the thane's council. Vanaguard were that thane's chosen warriors – as close to a chapterhouse knight as a Thrakkian came. But she didn't want to fight. Cowardice? Distaste for a brigand's errand? Lingering respect? Or did she simply want the business over and done, while a brawl threatened delay?

"Enough." Viktor dragged his claymore from its slings and braced it, point down, in the moss between two flagstones. "Valna is under *my* protection. You're welcome to test me."

Armund snorted, his sightless stare not quite levelled at Inkari. "She won't face you in single combat, lad. Honour's gone and bargained away."

Inkari's face flushed. A gloved finger stabbed the air. "You'd chance to act if you wanted it otherwise, you and that sister of yours. But no, you were too busy playing at corsair, and when your father died it was Ardothan on the throne or Indrigsval swallowed up. You cast a shadow on my honour? You made yourself an exile long before Ardothan decreed you one."

Armund scowled and gripped his axe-head tight. "Maybe I'm trying to put that right."

Inkari gritted her teeth. Colour faded from her cheeks. "Only an exile would think that possible."

She stalked back towards the waiting vanguard.

"Playing at corsair?" murmured Viktor.

"It's a long story," Armund replied.

"Brenæ af Brenæ! Væga af væga!" shouted Inkari. "Kill them both!"

Axes gleamed like fire in the morning sun.

"*Væga af væga!*"

Calenne watched from among the trees, heart in her throat, as the vanguards thundered to the charge, cloaks streaming behind. Three outpaced slower companions out of hunger for the kill. The grey-haired woman hung back, two others at her side.

Nine against two. Anger growled in the pit of Calenne's stomach. If only she'd defied Viktor's decree that she carry no sword as readily as she'd ignored his insistence that she remain behind. But the chance for such defiance was in the past and her shelter beneath the eaves lay a hundred yards from Valna's gate. Even at her best, she'd never been a runner, and the winter's illness still clung close enough that her best was but a memory.

Viktor met the ragged charge head on. A thrakker tumbled to the overgrown roadway, blood pooling beneath. An axe crashed down, but he was already turning away. The blade flashed past. A sweep of the claymore drove splinters from a haft, and fingers from the axeman's hand. The pained howl and the clang of the weapon on flagstone sounded as one. Then Viktor was on the move once more and Calenne at last remembered to breathe.

Somehow she'd forgotten that death, more than anything, was his greatest gift.

A vanguard's axe whirled a tree-hewing stroke at Viktor's gut. He leapt back. Steel wasted its force on empty air. The claymore scraped up across chainmail and sliced a ragged swath from the thrakker's cloak. Off-balance, the vanguard never saw the second, which spilt her drakon-winged helm and cast her lifeless to the muddy roadside.

Then the rest of the vanguard crashed home.

An axe drove the claymore aside with a dull chime, and Calenne again forgot to breathe.

*

Viktor let the claymore fall wide and leapt forward. Bones jarred as his shoulder struck an armoured chest. The Thrakkian – axe raised high – thudded backwards onto the road.

Viktor leapt into the gap and brought down his heel on the man's throat. His shadow exulted at the rattling gurgle. It begged to be set free, to run amok. Ice crackled across the claymore as Viktor forced it back into its cage. He fell to one knee, the brilliant dawn suddenly bleak.

An axe glinted above. Stifling a curse, Viktor flung himself aside, all the while knowing he was too late.

Moments crawled by. The shadow hurled itself at the bars of its cage, begging without words to be freed – to save them both from the axeman's blade.

"Vardaga! Træger yr dogril"

The strike of Armund's axe followed hard behind his bellowed challenge to the vanaguard's parentage. The man spun away with a roar of pain, the blow meant for Viktor's skull alongside.

"Up, lad." Armund's fingers closed around Viktor's forearm and dragged him upright. "Halfway there. No getting sleepy."

"I'm fine," Viktor lied. The shadow had receded, but it remained a pressure on his soul.

He cast about. The attackers had formed a loose ring about the roadway, their prey at the centre. Fury had made them reckless; death had been their punishment. Three from Viktor's sword; two from Armund's axe. The latter seemed impossible, for the Thrakkian's eyes were as milky and masterless as ever. One kill, by chance, Viktor could have believed. Two . . . ?

Viktor looked again at Armund, this time not with his eyes, but through his shadow. There, he beheld a second figure born of crackling forge-flame – no less stocky, but finer of feature – her hand as tight about the haft of the charred axe as Armund's own.

Anliss watches for me from Skanandra's forge. The axe had been hers, fetched from the pyre beneath Davenwood's eaves. Somehow, she wielded it still.

Armund grinned. "It'll be back-to-back now, if you want to live."

Viktor glanced at Inkari, still distant from the brawl.

He dragged his claymore back up to guard. "Back-to-back it is."

*

A wounded vanaguard crawled clear of the dead, a bloody smear in his wake. Another crawled jerkily upright, one hand limp at her side, the other fast about her axe. Calenne drifted closer to the tree-line, anger at the uneven contest feeding the urge to do something – *anything*.

Thrakkers circled about Viktor and Armund, their brashness turned cold and deliberate. Abuzz with worry and frustration, Calenne reached the extent of the dawn-cast shadow and clenched her fists.

"What are you waiting for?" The grey-haired woman shoved an attendant toward the circle. "End this, and let's be gone. No . . . wait!"

She stared back downhill. There, where the Indrig–Margard road made uneven passage, a small cart led by an old man. A boy of perhaps eight or nine summers sat among bulging sacks behind the driver's perch.

"A trade," said the grey-haired thrakker. "Two lives for two lives. Bring them!"

Her companions ran down the slope. With a fleeting glance back towards Viktor, Calenne followed, ghosting between trees as fast as she dared. She flinched at every unseen strike of steel.

The old man must have been deaf, for he paid the oncoming thrakkers no heed until the boy tugged at his arm. Wheeling in alarm, he tugged an old, battered sword from beneath the bench seat.

"Back! I'll not—"

A gloved fist struck the old man's wits away before he'd chance for anything more. He fell to the road, the sword skidding away. The larger of the two thrakkers clambered onto the cart after the terrified boy.

"Leave them be!" Viktor's bellow echoed down the slope. "They've no part of this."

"Nor had you," rejoined the grey woman.

Calenne crouched in the undergrowth. *Two lives for two lives.* A slit throat for the boy if Viktor didn't surrender. If only she'd brought a sword. Like so many endeavours, disobedience was worthless if pursued by halves.

But there *was* a sword . . . fallen to the roadway from the carter's nerveless hand. She'd only to reach it. And what then? Fever had nearly carried her off scant months before. Even now, she felt more shadow than substance. But shadows could kill, if wrathful enough.

The boy yelped as the thrakker cuffed him into submission.

The grey woman folded her arms. "Lay down your sword, Akadra. They'll go free."

Calenne's knuckles whitened. Viktor would yield. Soon after, he'd be dead. All because she lacked for courage. Once upon a time, she'd led an army. How was this different?

"You are the daughter of Katya and Kevor Trelan. You were the Phoenix. Act like it."   .

Skirts whipped about her legs as Calenne ran headlong across the hillside, the prize of the fallen sword closer with every desperate stride. At any moment, she expected the grey woman to call out warning, for the thrakkers by the cart to turn. Neither came to pass. Then she knelt, the sword's grips hard beneath her fingers.

She knew something was wrong as soon as she tried to stand. Giddiness not felt since winter set the world spinning. The sword, which once she'd have lifted with ease, felt rooted to the ground. She gritted her teeth. Nausea soured her throat. Cold sweat prickled clothes suddenly closer than before. But she rose, and the sword came with her.

"Release the boy!"

The thrakkers paid her no heed. Neither so much as turned. The one on the cart reeled the boy in closer, while the other watched. Calenne flung herself forward, the carter's sword braced in both hands and her full weight behind. It shuddered as the point struck chain at the base of the nearest thrakker's spine. The links parted, and his scream split the air.

The thrakker fell, the prison of his dying flesh all but ripping the sword from Calenne's hands. She staggered against the horse, heaving for breath, unable to do more than meet the second thrakker's gaze. He froze atop the cart, eyes wide beneath the helm's eyepieces. The boy in his grasp was similarly struck, his face pale as death.

"Let . . . Let him go," gasped Calenne.

But the bloodied sword was heavier than ever. It slipped from her shaking hand and fell. A heartbeat later, Calenne did the same. Palms braced against the roadway, she fought for breath that wouldn't come, and wondered if she'd feel the axe blow that took her life.

*

"Calenne!"

Viktor's shadow seethed. His thoughts swam. She'd agreed to wait at Tarona. Except . . . Now he thought closer on the matter, he recalled no agreement. Only his instruction, and a silence taken for accord.

"Akadra? What is it?"

Confusion crowded Armund's voice, proof that however his sister's spirit guided him in battle, he yet remained blind. He couldn't see the Thrakkian moving to take Calenne's life, the boy dragged behind him like a doll.

"It doesn't matter."

Discounting the two vanguards facing Armund, there were three others – and Inkari – barring the path to Calenne. Manageable, with good fortune and a following wind, but the distance . . .? She'd be dead before he was halfway there. Armund too, if he were abandoned. Impossible. Or at least, impossible for a man alone.

An old oath – sworn at the height of summer, and renewed at winter's heart – shattered. Breath already frosting, Viktor reached down into his soul and set his shadow free.

The thrakker's scream snapped Calenne back to her senses. Axe and boy abandoned, he fell to his knees, fingers scrabbling at eyes he couldn't reach through his helm.

She understood nothing of his babble, and cared not for her lack. Nor did she care for the other screams echoing down the hillside – all edged with that same note of stark terror – or the dull, wet strike of steel into flesh. All that mattered was the feel of the sword beneath a hand that no longer shook. Anger kindled black and filled uncertain limbs.

Rising up on trembling legs, Calenne thrust.

Blood spurted over steel. The scream died.

The terrified boy scrambled behind the cart and stared at the twitching corpse. Anger bled away. Urgent fears yielded to mundane. What if he recognised her? If he started telling tales that Calenne Trelan wasn't dead in the ashes of Eskavord, as the world believed?

Too late for that now.

She offered a smile. "Nothing to fear. You're safe."

He stared blankly back. Away to Calenne's left, the carter groaned.

Even if the boy didn't recognise her, others might. One such risk was sufficient to the day. Calenne withdrew towards the trees, exhausted, but abuzz with exhilaration.

Inkari swung, but the shadow had stolen her sight. Unlike Armund, she'd no slain kin to guide her from the halls of Skanandra. Twisting her axe away, Viktor hoisted her aloft by the throat and reeled his shadow back in. It came willingly, docile – a loyal hound, repaying largesse with obedience.

"Enough," he rumbled. "Your sight will return, unless you force me to snap your neck."

A scream rang out behind, marking the final vanguard's demise. Away down the hill, Calenne vanished among the trees. Relief and frustration flooded in. A difficult conversation to come.

Inkari went still. "What are you?" Her voice was little more than a whisper.

"I'm Valna's protector. Swear to relay this to Ardothan, and you may crawl away."

After the briefest hesitation, she nodded. Viktor dropped her at his feet.

Heavy footfalls sounded. "Not killing her?"

Viktor turned. Armund stood a pace or two away, his chainmail rent at the shoulder, and his plaited beard awry. "She'll serve better as a messenger."

"Your victory. Your choice. But if my brother listened to anyone, we'd none of us be here." He shrugged. "Always wondered how you turned Davenwood around."

The words framed an unspoken question. One Viktor had no desire to answer. Despite his shadow's acquiescence, failure burned bright. Twice now he'd broken his promise not to use it. Twice he'd chanced losing himself in the Dark.

"We all made mistakes today," he replied softly. "Let us hope we can learn from them."

Twenty-Seven

Grey dawn found Sevaka hunched in the precious shelter between Vrasdavora's crooked south tower and the mountainside, eyes straining against the deluge. An unnecessary vigil – watchers concealed along the eastern roadway would sight the shadowthorns long before she did, but it distracted from a belt tightened to its last notch and the emptiness of half-rations. Among other things.

Vrasdavora's foundations had been laid down shortly after Malatriant's original overthrow, when the horrors lurking far to the south in Darkmere's bleak, angular ruins had haunted her successors' dreams. But such days were long in the past. The keep and what remained of the outer wall burrowed into the cliff as if seeking shelter from the bitter mountain rain. The subsided road they had once guarded lay as much in the valley below as on the mountainside.

"A miserable place to die," she murmured.

"Then live."

Rosa approached from the rampart stairway, every bit as sodden and windblown as Sevaka herself. But the horrific wounds taken at Ahrad were a memory, and she again a bulwark about which the dispirited soldiers had rallied.

"Easy for you to say."

"You've been avoiding me."

Sevaka scowled. "You've been busy."

And she had. The survivors from Soraved, where death had stalked the trees. Other refugees encountered on the road. Vrasdavora's thin garrison. Perhaps two thousand souls in all. All looked to Rosa for leadership. For hope in dark days. Ironic, really.

"Both can be true." Rosa splashed closer along the rampart. "You've been distant since Soraved. Talk to me. Please."

"You should have told me about the Raven."

The words should have sounded ridiculous. Rosa's guilty expression stopped them being so, and set Sevaka's heart wallowing deeper than ever.

"I don't follow," said Rosa.

"I saw you together." The accusation caught at the back of Sevaka's throat, snared by anger pent up across long and desperate days. "And then I remembered it wasn't the first time. He was at the pyre last year. Watching. Applauding. I took him for a hallucination. But he wasn't, was he? I heard he only came if you offered him a coin. Then again, I used to think you couldn't die. Now I wonder if you've been dead all along. The Raven's puppet playing me for his amusement."

"Why would he do that?"

"Why wouldn't he?" With supreme effort, she steadied herself. "Did he make you as you are?"

Rosa reached out. "Sevaka—"

She shied away. "Answer me."

Rosa's brow creased. "No. At least, he says not."

Bitter laughter hissed free. "And you believe him?"

"Not at first but . . ." She breathed deep. "He's not as the tales say. He's charming, even kind, and I think a little bit sad. No, that's not the right word. More like the world is a joke he's grown tired of. He came to Soraved to help."

"The Raven. Help. Have you any idea how mad that sounds?"

"It's only the start." She paused. "He wants me to be his queen."

"What?"

"That's why he brought his revenants to Soraved. A suitor's gift. A fraction of the dowry, he said, if I accepted his offer." A smile flickered and faded. "I refused."

Sevaka gaped, struck for words in the face of the unthinkable. But so much had changed since Ahrad. The demon at the gates. Otherworld's revenants walking ephemeral soil. So many tales turned truth, and impossibilities made inevitable. "You refused. Why?"

Again, Rosa reached for her hand. This time, Sevaka let her take it. "My place is with you, not him. Whether for a day, or for a hundred lifetimes." The smile faded. "Assuming you'll still have me?"

Sevaka hesitated. It could still be a lie. A humiliation concocted for the Raven's dubious pleasure. But if it weren't, and she walked away, then she betrayed everything she'd said and done this past year. Who cared if the Raven were laughing? The heart wanted what the heart wanted, and the days were dark enough without smothering what light remained.

Careless of the rain, Sevaka broke cover and held Rosa close. The morning lost its chill.

"Is that a yes?" murmured Rosa.

"You forsook a god for me. 'No' would seem ungrateful."

The embrace slackened. Its memory held the cold at bay. "Good, because we've work to do."

Sevaka winced. "The shadowthorns?"

A nod. "Destroying the bridge at Galda barely slowed them. They'll be at the walls before nightfall, and over them shortly after."

"Even with the constructs?"

Vrasdavora boasted twelve operational kraikons and two dozen simarka – fussed over by Proctor Maldrath. The pass was too crooked for an attacker to bring catapults to bear against the walls, and an escalade by ladder and grapnel was a foolhardy proposition with untiring constructs upon the rampart – no matter how weary the defenders.

Rosa shook her head. "Thaldvar made mention of pale-witches, and one of the silver women from Ahrad. Ashana's blessing drives out Lumestra's magic. Our constructs will be no better than statues."

"So we retreat without a fight?" Sevaka flung out a hand. "In this?"

"No. The gate's solid, and the walls are thick. We've enough ballista-shot to make the shadowthorns wary about marching past. The way I see it, the longer they're howling at us, that's thousands of swords not cutting a swathe through the Marcher Lands." Rosa shrugged. "Sometimes the calling is to die while others win elsewhere."

"So there's no hope for us?"

"Only if we keep fighting on the shadowthorns' terms. I mean to change that."

"How?"

Rosa crooked a vicious smile.

For all the thickness of Melanna's cloak – for all the depth of her hood – still the rain wormed its way through armour and cloth to the flesh beneath. An hour in the saddle felt like days, red raw and shivering. Nor were her companions at greater ease, not if the soft litany of curses and fidgeting spoke true. Warriors and plenipotentiaries reduced to sullen children by the deluge. Only Elene seemed at ease. Melanna supposed mere rain troubled her no more than the miles she'd walked barefoot where the others had ridden.

Only the steep, forested escarpment to the south offered protection against the elements; to the north, the mountainside plunged through low clouds. And away to the west – past the thin screen of rain-soaked outriders on restless horses – a lone, dark figure stood at the bridge's neck, arms folded, her threadbare hunter's green tabard sodden black, and blonde hair matted across her scalp. Alone save for the horse tethered on the far bank.

Melanna drew back her hood and shook her hair free. "How long has she been there?"

"Our outriders first glimpsed her an hour ago." Haldrane cut an inky figure atop his black mare, gloved and cloaked to the point where nothing showed of the man beneath. "Perhaps longer."

Naradna grunted. "Sweep her from the road."

"Her sword is at rest." Rare disapproval danced beneath Sera's words. "She offers to yield, and seeks surety for her followers."

The Icansae prince's horse stamped restlessly. "And is that our concern?"

"It used to be," said Melanna.

She glanced back at the leading column of Immortals, archers and shieldsmen, outriders and cataphracts, hunched and miserable against the rain, save where the lunassera's white robes added brilliance – and stared again to the west, to the sword point-down in the threadbare roadside sod. Beyond the bridge barely wide enough to take a cart – beyond the waterfall rushing from the southern crags and a frothing stream too broad for a horse to jump – the last bend before the sheer ascent to Vrasdavora. No coincidence in the meeting point, any more than the emissary's identity was happenstance. Fate's bleak humour.

"We once drew steel together. I'll speak with her."

Aeldran roused himself. "Is that wise, Ashanal?"

No, but it *was* owed. Not just by convention, but by fleeting comradeship. "She's alone."

"The trees at Soraved too seemed empty," said Naradna. "Until the revenants came."

"The Raven's gaze dwells elsewhere." Three days they'd shared a road, and Elene had spoken little. Reserved – almost timid – where Elspeth was all angry bravado. How different siblings could be. But these words, at least, she uttered with conviction. "You need not fear his wrath."

"Then kill the woman, and have done," said Naradna.

Haldrane offered a humourless chuckle. "You might find that harder than you believe, *savir.*"

Melanna wiped rain from her face to hide a wince, jealous of the mask that kept Naradna's expression as guarded as his scars. *Of course* the spymaster knew the woman's identity.

"I won't shirk from killing, if called to it." She swung from the saddle. "Haldrane, you'll speak for my father in matters where I cannot."

"Yes, *savim.*" He dismounted reluctantly, drew back his hood and stared moodily at the weeping skies.

"Elene, will you join us? You will speak for our mother."

The daughter of the moon bobbed her head.

"This is a waste of time," said Naradna, the words metallic beneath his beatific mask.

"Our warleader has spoken, brother," chided Aeldran.

Yes, how different siblings could be. Naradna had questioned at every moment of the past three days: the order of march, a sentry's watchwords – even the purpose of the pursuit itself. By contrast, Aeldran had offered nothing save support. One perceived her as an upstart to tradition, one as a warleader. One belonged to the past, the other to the future. If the rising Dark permitted any future at all.

With a last glance behind, Melanna set off for the bridge.

*

The black-robed shadowthorn's eyes widened in surprise as the hand clamped across his mouth, then lost all expression as Thaldvar's dagger took his throat. The borderer held the body close until the twitching ceased, then let it fall into the gorse. Sevaka, only a half-dozen paces distant through the trees, heard nothing. A hundred paces away down the escarpment the massed ranks of shadowthorns remained oblivious.

"Too close." Thaldvar settled at Sevaka's side, his back to the mis-shapen boulder and dagger abandoned as he fetched a dry bowstring from a pouch. Working by touch, his eyes never leaving the roadway, he bent the bow and set the string on its nocks. "Must be getting old."

"You're not alone." The sweet scent of the late-flowering gorse caught at the back of Sevaka's throat. "I've aged ten years this past week."

She eased her head around the boulder. Grey-cloaked borderers and pavissionaires – the latter without the encumbrance of their eponymous shields – took position behind rock and tree. Bows were strung and crossbows readied. Proctor Maldrath – his gold robes abandoned in favour of plain jerkin, trews and cloak – toyed nervously with an amulet in the shape of a roaring lion's head.

Bodies dotted among the gorse betrayed where other shad-owthorns had fallen foul of borderers. One cry of alarm would have brought everything to ruin, but luck had held. The kind of fortune Sevaka suspected would always favour those who had Thaldvar at their side.

On the road below, three figures passed the line of shadowthorn out-riders. One dark, one white, and another in golden scale. Three against one, and half a dozen Immortals within gallop of the bridge. Sevaka swallowed a frisson of alarm. Rosa knew the risks and her business both.

"Queen's Ashes," growled Thaldvar.

"What is it?"

"With the princessa. That's Haldrane, the Emperor's spymaster. As poisonous a serpent as ever lived." His snarl bled away into a wolf's grin. "And here he is, all unaware. Maybe Lumestra *does* love me, even in the rain."

A glance along the slope confirmed Lieutenant Gavrida's mismatched band was almost in position. Just a little longer.

"Remember why we're here," said Sevaka. "We can't afford to waste arrows."

Thaldvar grimaced. "At your command, captain."

"Princessa."

Melanna halted a dozen paces from the bridge – Haldrane and Elene a little behind, the former watchful, the latter distant. "Lady Orova. We're a long way from Eskavord, where we stood together against the Sceadotha."

"We are."

Her face could have been a mask for all it revealed.

"And now I hear the Raven fights your battles. Have you no shame?"

Orova's eyes tightened, then her mask snapped back into place. "The Raven does as he chooses. I won't be beholden to the divine."

A sour glance at Elene reinforced the message, but also offered an opening.

"Yes, we're a long way from Eskavord," said Melanna. "Further still from Tevar Flood, where I saved your life."

A flicker of consternation revealed that Haldrane hadn't known that detail. A rare lapse.

Orova's brow wrinkled. "Explain."

"The kernclaw. I drove him off." The memory felt like it belonged to another woman. "Your companion was beyond help, but I asked the Goddess to heal you. You're beholden to the divine, whether you wish it or not."

Orova advanced, leaving her embedded sword a pace behind. She flexed her hands, rainwater pooling across upturned palms and trickling away along her sleeves.

"You. You did this to me?"

Her gaze, full of black, roiling spite, set Melanna reaching for her sword. She checked the motion and cursed herself for the display of weakness.

"I saved your life. As I seek to save it now."

"I've seen the salvation you offer. At Ahrad. At Soraved. Just yesterday I saw Tregga ablaze on the horizon. You claim I consort with the Raven? You've glutted him this past week, princessa."

The accusation, true for all its necessity, spurred Melanna closer. "Only out of need. The Dark has its roots deep in your people. It must be excised, or it will claim us all."

"The Dark burned with Eskavord."

"No." Melanna sought stillness. Passion would not convince, nor anger born of shame. Only cold reason would serve. "It lives on through Lord Akadra. He is Droshna. A man-of-shadow. It spreads through him. I saw it with my own eyes. Not just at Eskavord, but after."

Orova shook her head. "You're not the first to come to me with tall tales of Lord Akadra. I try to learn from my mistakes."

"You know him well. Can you honestly say you've witnessed no change? In his allies at council? His comrades of war? He can hide what he is, but not his influence over others."

To Melanna's horror, Orova laughed. "Lord Akadra never returned from the Southshires. He could have ruled the Republic, but he walked away. He lives alone and untroubled on some godforsaken hillside. Influence over others? He has none."

Haldrane went rigid. Elene strode to Melanna's side. For the first time in their brief association, her eyes seethed with anger. White light gathered about her hands and her brow.

"My mother believes otherwise."

Orova's lip curled. "The beliefs of the witch-goddess – or her kin – do not interest me."

"Enough!" For the first time, Melanna wished there'd been a whisper of Dark about Orova. Better that, somehow, than for loyalty to blind her to the truth. "Lady Orova. You seek surety for your warriors. They will go free, provided they yield their arms. All save those tainted by the Dark, who will receive the mercy of—"

Orova shook her head. "You misunderstand, princessa. I'm not here to discuss our surrender, but yours. Once before, your father ceded battle to save your life. He'll do so again."

She spread her arms wide.

"*Savim!*"

Haldrane's cry came a heartbeat before he shoved Melanna off her feet. An arm flung to cushion her fall twisted at the wrist, sparking pain along her forearm.

A whistling chorus pierced the rain. Haldrane bellowed and slewed to the road in a spray of water, hands clutched about the arrow in his thigh.

"Haldrane!"

Even as Melanna fought to stand, Elene splashed to her knees, chest transfixed by three arrows. Pale fingers dipped to the seeping black stain about the wounds. Then she pitched forward.

As her body struck the road, it burst apart in a spray of silver dust.

An Immortal slumped across his saddle, an arrow buried in his back. Dark figures appeared on the escarpment. The sky blackened. Aeldran's shield, hoisted high above his head, bucked and shuddered.

"Treachery!" He wheeled his horse about. "Archers south!"

Another volley hissed home. Screams rang out. The whinny of panicked steeds. The cries of the dying. Barked orders as sorvidars sent men scrambling up a slope no horse could climb. Sporadic shots chased the hillside as archers of Icansae and Rhaled recovered their wits. Not one travelled the full distance, the arrows' force sapped by sodden bowstrings.

"*For Ahrad!*"

The shout hammered out of the rain, fresh arrows in its wake. A Rhalesh archer pitched forward, his arrow skittering wildly away. A havildar on the lower slope spun about, a black shaft in his shoulder. Shots thumped into shields.

Naradna galloped past, already swinging down from the saddle. Scarlet Immortals flocked to the moonsilver-etched sword and plunged into the gorse-choked rocks behind.

"*Andwar Brigantim! Icansae Brigantim!*"

The lower escarpment filled with golden scale and drawn steel. Aeldran tallied the attackers among the trees. No more than a hundred. Enough to draw blood, but little more. The first volley had killed dozens, but with surprise lost and shields set?

It was only then that Aeldran took note of *where* that first volley had fallen. Not against the golden armour of Immortals, or the rugged leathers of the shieldsmen, but against white robes running crimson with diluted blood. Aeldran's own blood ran cold at the sight, not that the enemy would dare strike at Ashana's handmaidens – though that was bad enough – but because of *why* they would do such a thing.

"The lunassera! Shield the lunassera!"

Even as he bellowed the warning, the gorse of the middle slope awoke to fury. Bronze glinted among the thorns.

Melanna staggered to her feet, lost in a fog of pain and fury. Numbed fingers found her sword's grips on the third try. The blade swept free. She turned in time to see the punch, but an age too late to avoid it.

Vision rushed red and black. Then she was on her knees once more, the sword out of reach. Grey skies darkened with Orova's shadow, the lying sword that had begged for parley again in her hand.

"Stay down, princessa. I'd rather take you whole."

Screams echoed from the east. Panicked cries. Defiance. The unmistakeable thunder of bronze claws against stone. Victims of Orova's treachery and Melanna's guilty conscience.

"Oathbreaker!" Melanna screamed.

A second punch, heavy as a horse's kick, drove her down.

"You dare?"

Orova's boot lashed out. Melanna twisted. The grazing blow set teeth rattling.

"What of Jardon Krain, who came to you with a promise of peace?" A second kick buckled Melanna's ribs and left her gasping. "Or Riego Noktza, assassinated by your demon? Or Emilia Sarravin and the soldiers of the 7th, slaughtered in the breach at Ahrad? If you seek honour in war, princessa, bring some of your own!"

Melanna rolled away from a third kick and spat blood. Orova's fingers hooked beneath her golden helm and ripped it away. Steel pressed cold at Melanna's neck.

"Yield. I'd sooner offer the Emperor his daughter than her corpse."

Trembling with pain and failure, Melanna stared down at her grime-caked hands. No. Not grime, but Elene's rain-eddied remains. And half-hidden beneath, the Daughter of the Moon's silver dagger. Purpose kindled in her lungs, hot and rich and defiant, driving back the pain.

"I've fought all my life," she gasped. "I won't stop now."

Deafened by her own scream of shame and fury, Melanna struck the sword aside and snatched up the dagger.

*

The simarka broke the vestigial shield wall at the roadway's edge. A sturdier line formed east of Aeldran, but that was of little solace for those trapped beyond. Men died beneath the swipe of bronze claws, or with their throats ripped out. Swords skittered across the lions' metal hides. The simarka fought not like men, but the beasts they resembled, caring nothing for formation or strategy, only the pursuit and slaughter of their prey, one death at a time.

"Hammers!" Aeldran bellowed. "Break them apart!"

Golden magic crackled through the rain as his words found purchase. Bronze turned cold and lifeless as its animating magic fled.

Aeldran sought Naradna among the gorse. He found his prize at the heart of a shrinking ring of scarlet and gold. A leaping simarka bowled an Immortal into the thorns, then bounded away to make another pass.

Distracted, Aeldran barely glimpsed the pouncing simarka. A desperate jerk of his arm, and his shield took the brunt. His steed screamed and plunged sideways. Thrown from the saddle, Aeldran rolled and landed heavily on hands and knees. His panicked horse scrabbled desperately away. The simarka slewed in the mud.

Aeldran scrambled to his feet. The simarka circled about, frozen sneer mocking the uselessness of Aeldran's sword.

One step. Two. The simarka gathered to the pounce. Aeldran cast aside his mangled shield, and breathed wordless prayer to Ashana.

A pale shape in torn robes slipped between them. Sera's right hand clutched her bloodied side, pierced by an arrow's splintered remnant. Her left extended towards the simarka, fingers splayed.

At once, the beast's purpose fled. Pounce dissolved into a puzzled crouch, and then a lazy sprawl suited more to a cat at the fireside. Sera held her pose a moment longer, then her legs buckled.

Aeldran caught her, too late remembering the gruesome fate promised to a man who laid hands on a lunassera. "My thanks, Ashanal."

"The princessa," she breathed. "She needs . . ."

Eyes fluttered closed behind the silver mask. Lips stuttered uneven breaths.

Aeldran stared west through the downpour, where outriders and Immortals set to watch over Melanna Saranal lay dead in the roadway. Setting down the unconscious handmaiden, he ran for his horse.

*

The silver dagger punched twice between Rosa's ribs before she staggered away. Liquid fire raged beneath her skin, the metal's kiss poison to eternal flesh.

She twisted from a third lunge and yanked at Melanna's wrist, dragging her around. She kicked the princessa's legs away. Fingers hissed and blackened as she twisted the dagger free. A flick of the wrist, and it was gone over the bridge's low parapet and into the seething stream.

"It's over. Yield."

Melanna laughed, blood bubbling on her lips. "The Goddess warned me that saving you would be the death of my dreams. I'll not beg. Do as you must."

Rosa bit back disgust. She'd nothing in common with the shadowthorn, and yet had received the answer she herself would have given. As for the business at Tevar Flood ... Did she owe the princessa her life, or for the bleak blessing of an eternal existence? Did it even matter? She hadn't sought this war. Alive, the princessa was the most valuable of hostages. Dead, she was no longer a threat – no longer a symbol.

Dead would suffice.

"Icansae Brigantim! Icansae y Saranal!"

Warned by the bellowed words and the thunder of hooves, Rosa spun around. The glittering blow meant for her head hacked into her shoulder. Teeth gritted against the pain, she back-cut at the rider. The horse reared, and the blow fell wide. The rider dropped down to shield the battered princessa, sword levelled and steady.

"Icansae y Saranal. You will not have her."

Rosa grabbed at the parapet. The pain in her shoulder was already a warm scrape as her collarbone reknitted. However impressive the shadowthorn's armour and haloed helm, he wasn't her match. Not alone. Not without silver, and the silver was gone. But as the rain quickened to fresh hoofbeats and gold gleamed against the grey, Rosa realised he wouldn't be alone for long. The gambit had failed.

"Another time, shadowthorn."

Clasping hand to chest in a salute less sardonic than intended, Rosa turned her back and set out across the bridge.

*

Thaldvar sent his last arrow winging towards shieldsmen still floundering on the slope. "She's falling back!"

Shielding her eyes from the rain, Sevaka peered at the bridge. Even as Rosa hauled herself onto the horse tethered on the western bank, a press of golden armour spilled onto the bridge.

"Maldrath! Now!" Nothing happened. Sevaka cast about for the proctor. "Maldrath!"

"Hush, child," he said testily. "Lumestra rewards the patient."

She scrambled across the scree and seized a double handful of the proctor's sodden jerkin. "Want me to move you closer to her?"

Far below, two kraikons broached the surface of the stream. Standing waist-deep among the rushing waters, they braced palms beneath the stone span and heaved.

Immortals spilled over the parapet as stone tore loose, joined in the stream's chill embrace by the arches of the disintegrating roadway. Pausing only to cast the remnants of the bridge into the massing shadowthorns, the kraikons clambered up the bank and lumbered away after Rosa's retreating steed.

"That's that, then," said Thaldvar.

"It is," Sevaka replied. "My apologies, Maldrath."

The proctor steepled his fingers and contrived a look of wounded pride.

Sevaka peered down the slope. The shadowthorns had barely made it halfway. "Tell Lieutenant Gavrida to start the retreat. We'll follow, with the simarka bringing up the rear."

Thaldvar nodded and moved away. Maldrath hesitated, then he too withdrew. After all, the plan had been Lady Roslava Orova's, not an upstart Psanneque's, and therefore not to be quibbled.

And it had been a good plan, even if it hadn't quite achieved the princessa's capture. A hundred blades and two dozen simarka had bloodied a column ten times their size for little loss in return, and had thinned the pale-witches to almost nothing. Yes, a good plan, and the first real victory since Ahrad's fall. Tomorrow would need another, but tomorrow would wait.

Twenty-Eight

[[**A** nd where are you going this fine morning?]] Anastacia's voice radiated innocence; her posture and poise contentment at being out in the sunshine. Strange to see. So far as Kurkas knew neither winter's bite nor summer's kiss offered up sensation to her porcelain skin, but for all that she was the very image of a cat basking in heavenly warmth. Elegance to match Stonecrest's slender, stone-clad façade. Modest by highblood standards, the three-storey mansion's splendour stood stark contrast to the brooding walls of Swanholt, the Akadra residence where Kurkas had served so long.

He halted at Stonecrest's modest gate and gave her the very oldest of old-fashioned looks.

"You know full well where I'm going, plant pot."

[[Don't be dull, Vladama. It doesn't suit you.]] The swirling black eyes shifted to Kurkas' left. [[You've better manners than your captain, haven't you?]]

Altiris – newly arrayed in a phoenix tabard rather more presentable than Kurkas' own – stiffened.

"Leave the boy alone."

[[Vladama, please. You make me sound like a monster.]] Dark skirts drifted across new-fallen Fade leaves. [[How are you, Altiris? I've scarcely seen you since your little misadventure.]]

He shot Kurkas a confirmatory glance, having been warned against speaking out of turn about his recovery. Receiving it, he offered a stiff bow. "I'm well, lady. Bruised and sore, but better than I've any right to be."

A musical laugh. [[I'm not a lady. I'm Anastacia – Ana to those I like. Not "lady", not "plant pot". Ana.]] She took his hand in one of hers, and patted it with the other. Dark eyes dwelled on his as if he were the only thing in the world worthy of note. [[Now, tell me where you're going.]]

"Lady, I . . ."

Altiris' throat bobbed, the lad caught between the deference owed a noblewoman, and Lord Trelan's instruction – since reinforced by Kurkas himself – that Anastacia not become involved. And then there was the crafted intimacy of touch, of the personal name. Even the perfectly balanced perfumes of lavender and jasmine – another oddity of the morning, given she was as numb to scent as to sensation. All mustered to an erosion of resolve and a temptation to indiscretion. Just because Kurkas considered himself immune to such wiles didn't render him blind to them.

Kurkas scratched his head and stared through the railings to where Brass and Kelver stood sentry in the street – the much too *empty* street. He'd known livelier curfews. Saving a period of panic the day the Council had issued proclamation of war, the city had been holding its breath. Oh, there'd been the expected departure of certain wealthy citizens to Selann and the Outer Isles – even a few to ocean-flung colonies further west – soon followed by regiments and knightly brotherhoods marching east to match the shadowthorns. Most folk were staying close to home, hoping not to be noticed. The taverns were full of gossip claiming the Council would soon order conscription. *That* was a bad sign, if true. Conscription belonged to the monarchy of old.

But the frontier wasn't Kurkas' burden until it touched on Stonecrest's bounds. Vranakin mischief? *That* was the business of the afternoon, not the morning.

He turned his attention back to Brass and Kelver. The slight twitch of Brass' shoulders spoke to scarcely contained mirth. Kurkas sighed, frustrated not just by Brass' amusement, but Anastacia's insistence on her games. It wasn't enough for her to *know*. She had to make a point of being *told* – of making someone break their promise. Better him than Altiris.

"We're bound for Abbeyfields," he said at last. "I'm tutoring Lord Reveque's kids in the art of the sword."

Anastacia let Altiris' hand fall, the boy forgotten. [[There. That wasn't so hard. The art of the sword? Such a poetic name for braining someone with a lump of metal.]]

He shrugged. "Universal language, violence. Can't hurt to speak it fluently."

[[And Altiris, I suppose, is also a tutor?]]

"He's teaching me too, lady." The lad's face flushed. "I'm of an age and height with Sidara . . . I mean the Lady Reveque . . . so we spar together."

[[It all sounds delightful. I think I'll come along. I might have insights our gallant captain does not.]]

There it was. Never a question, of course, nor a suggestion. A statement of intent.

"Ain't sure that's a good idea," said Kurkas.

[[Gainsaying the lady of the house, captain?]]

Altiris frowned. "You said you weren't a lady."

Her posture shifted from friendliness to something distinctly other.

Kurkas cleared his throat. "Altiris, you go on ahead. I'd like to speak with Lady Plant Pot."

The lad nodded, brushed a stand of wayward red hair out of his eyes and made for the gate. Anastacia a sour presence at his shoulder, Kurkas strode a dozen paces in the opposite direction, away from Brass' prying ears, and sank against a gnarled oak.

Anastacia folded her arms. [[Forgetting your place, Vladama?]]

"Don't torment the lad. It's beneath you."

[[You give lessons in dignity, as well as murder?]]

"All part of the service." He grimaced away a flash of temper. "You're not welcome up at Abbeyfields. I ain't saying it's right, but that's the way it is. You insist otherwise, it'll be trouble."

[[Afraid you'll lose out on a lucrative tutorship?]]

"Lord Trelan doesn't need you making matters worse while he's gone. Raven's Eyes, but Lady Reveque barely let me and the lad onto the grounds that first day, and watched us like a hawk every moment we were there. She barely trusts us *now*."

Anastacia folded her arms. [[You *are* forgetting your place.]]

"And what is my place? You won't retain a steward, and make no attempt to run the household, so who ends up dealing with all that? Me, that's who. Should be that with his lordship gone, you'd take on his duties at council and all the rest, but you're not doing that either. You reckon I'm forgetting *my* place? You've never shown the slightest interest in learning what yours is."

He already regretted having spoken so freely. Not because it was an appalling breach of protocol – which it was – but because Anastacia's cold, rigid stare made it impossible to forget the violence of which she was capable.

"Look, I shouldn't have—"

[[You must think me very selfish. And I am.]] To his surprise, he heard no anger, only contrition. [[This city. This world. This tangle of ephemeral threads. You were born to it. I was made for something very different. What I was and what I am ... reconciling them would drive me to tears of frustration, had I any longer that luxury. But I am trying.]]

Kurkas' mood softened. "Aggravating Lady Reveque ain't a good place to start."

[[Not long ago, you told me to seek a friend. Now you'd have it otherwise? You'd have me – who can help Sidara understand what she is – do nothing?]]

"The proctors can teach her."

[[Proctors.]] She waved the objection aside. [[Why are you tutoring her, Vladama?]]

He frowned. "Because I was asked ... And because the way things are going around here, she'll end up with a sword in her hand sooner or later. Better she knows how to wield it."

Anastacia tilted her head in victory. Sidara, of all people, had more weapons at her disposal than mere steel.

"I hate you."

[[Of course you don't, Vladama. Dregmeet scum or not, you're my friend. But you can't be right all the time.]]

Funny thing was, she sounded like she meant it. But he'd known her too long not to recognise misdirection. "And that's really all it is? You've no other stake than being 'helpful'?"

She straightened. [[Are you testing me, Vladama?]]

"Are you going to answer the question?"

She started towards the house, but after three paces checked her stride. [[This body – this *shell* Viktor Akadra entombed me within – it holds me distant from the world. From sensation. Even from myself in ways I can't wholly explain. I am smothered in gloom, numbed by it. When I touched Sidara, light broke through the clouds. For the first time in a year – *no*, for the first time since my mother sent me plummeting from Astarria – I felt like more than an echo of myself. If there's a chance she can help me regain that?]] She hung her head. [[I told you I was selfish, Vladama. Would you do different to restore your arm? Your eye? My loss outshines yours a hundredfold.]]

"Of course it does," he replied sourly. "Did you tell Lord Trelan?"

[[We didn't part on the best of terms.]]

That much Kurkas had already known. She could be lying, of course. But after a year as a phoenix, Kurkas reckoned he'd an ear for when Anastacia spoke the truth, and when she did not. When she gave away pieces of herself, as she had just then, it was truth more often than it wasn't. And she *was* right about Sidara.

"I can't sneak you into Abbeyfields," he said at last. "You'll have to climb the fence and meet us at the riverside. And if Lady Reveque discovers you—"

[[She won't. You said it yourself: she trusts you now. She'll not be watching closely.]]

The last puzzle-piece fell into place. Whimsy hadn't brought her to the gate that morning, but a balance of impatience and calculation. Long enough for Lady Reveque's lingering suspicions to subside.

"So you're using me, after all?"

[[This is Tressia, Vladama. We all use each other. That doesn't mean we're not friends.]]

He shook his head, the last anger fading into hurt. "You still don't get it, do you? Until you start putting others first, you don't have any friends."

Singlesticks met with a sharp *crack*. Scarcely had the practice swords parted when Altiris lunged to fresh attack, polished ash darting a low-low-high flurry so perfectly executed that it coaxed Kurkas to a smile.

Sidara retreated along the forested riverbank, her movements stiff, the lack of confidence testament to a sheltered upbringing. Her first parry was clean, the second came late and the third barely connected at all.

She yelped as Altiris' fourth strike tore the singlestick from her hand. Before she could reclaim it, he had the rounded "point" of the practice sword at her gambeson's throat. Like the rest of her sparring gear, the padded jacket was at least a size too large, and no amount of strap-tightening could make it otherwise. Between that and her height – Altiris' claim of parity was off by a good three inches, even without the braids coiled about her crown – she looked less the knight-in-training and more a rangy scarecrow.

Kurkas waved Altiris away. The lad delivered an approximation of a courtly bow and retreated a dozen paces to the birch tree established as one extent of the duelling ground.

"Better," said Kurkas.

Sidara, face flushed in defeat, offered a glare that was very much her mother's. "He's too strong."

"So be faster. You're fighting yourself. Your arm knows what's needed, but you do insist on thinking it through."

The scowl slid into thoughtfulness. She'd taken losing hard from the first, but her bitter moods never lasted. Kurkas had learned to neither chivvy nor indulge, but to simply offer counsel.

She stepped back. "Yes, captain."

Polite too. Never quite knew what you were getting with a nobleman's whelp. Privilege warped the brain, and never so completely as with the young.

He beckoned Altiris. "Again."

As the *clack* of singlesticks rang out anew, Kurkas withdrew deeper into the trees. "Enjoying yourself?"

Anastacia stood beside a statue of Lumestra, so motionless she might have been its twin. [[I confess, I expected more structure.]]

"Stances and grips? Stuff like that? We did a little, and you can see how fast she's picked it up." He shrugged. "As for the rest? I'm not teaching her to stand her place in a shield wall. Not sure Lady Reveque would like it if I did. She reckons her perfect daughter's never even been in a fight with other children . . . even her brother."

[[Do you believe her?]]

"I believe that *she* believes it." He raised his voice to a parade ground roar. "Elbow up, lad! Move like you've a purpose! Sorry, where was I?"

[[Lady Reveque's disapproval.]]

He stared at the house, barely visible through the trees. "How could I forget?"

Even in the riverside's seclusion, said disapproval loomed like a shadow. Sidara wasn't a problem. She'd embraced Anastacia at first sight – much to the latter's obvious discomfort, and Kurkas' amusement. But the simple truth was that even without Anastacia offering forbidden tutelage – which she so far had not – they'd already invited Sidara to deceit. Fortunately, Constans had been confined to the house as punishment for transgressions earlier that morning, so he at least remained free of conspiracy. How that was to be managed on other days, Kurkas wasn't sure.

A sharp *crack* drew his attention back to the fight. A late parry sent Sidara scrambling away in panic.

"What did I tell you?" roared Kurkas. "Be faster!"

She shot him a look of pure poison, but the next parry *was* faster. The thrust that followed sent Altiris reeling for the first time that morning. Teeth clenched and face grim with satisfaction, Sidara pursued, the singlestick a blur. Anastacia's hollow laughter danced beneath the trees.

"That's it, girl!" shouted Kurkas. "Put him in his place!"

The sticks clashed, once, twice. Altiris' stick went wide. With a cry of pure, angry delight, Sidara lunged, the point of her singlestick against Altiris' chest.

As she did, Altiris locked his free hand around her wrist, and hooked a heel behind her ankle. Triumph spiralling into alarm, she fell onto churned leaves and muddied grass. Altiris kicked away her stick and set his own at her throat.

"Do you yield, milady Reveque?"

Like his earlier bow, Altiris' attempt at a noble's clipped accent didn't quite pass muster. Nor did he take proper note of the reddening of Sidara's cheeks, or the murderous cast to her brow.

Kurkas sighed. "Now we've trouble."

He started towards the pair. Before he'd taken a second step, Sidara lashed out her foot.

"Hey!" Altiris leapt back, sparing his shin a painful encounter.

Sidara sprang to her feet. Face thunderous, she grabbed at the lad's singlestick. "You worthless, cheating southwealder!"

Altiris jerked the weapon out of reach, and earned a stinging slap across the cheek for his troubles.

"Oi! Enough!" Kurkas stepped between them. "Yes, he cheated. But what do you think we're doing here? Playing a game?"

Sidara glared. Blue eyes flickered gold, and regained their normal colour. Kurkas pretended not to notice, but his certainty slipped a notch.

Sidara shifted her gaze to the ground. "No, captain."

"Go on, over there." Kurkas pointed towards the birch. "Clear your head and we'll go again."

She stalked off. Kurkas waited until she was out of earshot and cuffed Altiris about the head.

"Ow!"

"If you're trying to impress her, this ain't the way."

"I'm just doing what you told me."

The defence was too pat, too rote. Given the chasm in rank and status – to say nothing of the fact that Sidara was a pretty enough thing, even to Kurkas' jaded and disinterested eye – it would have been stranger if Altiris *didn't* want to impress her. *And* she'd saved him from the Raven's clutches. Gratitude shaded into humiliation so easily, and humiliation in turn invited competition.

"Uh-uh. I *told* you to spar with her, not embarrass her."

Kurkas glanced towards the birch. Sidara and Anastacia were deep in conversation, the former with angry hand outflung at Altiris. Anastacia set a hand on the girl's shoulder and leaned in, her frozen lips to Sidara's ear.

"You're a good lad," said Kurkas. "I ain't forgotten what you did for Lord Trelan, but rein it in. Or Sidara gets to watch while you and *I* spar. We clear on that?"

Altiris winced. "Yes, captain."

Kurkas patted him on the back. "Good lad. I'm not telling you to *let* her win, mind. Lessons are lessons." He raised his voice. "Right! Let's try that again."

Sidara, composure restored, raised the singlestick in mock-salute and started out from the birch. Altiris went to meet her.

From the first exchange, Kurkas knew something was wrong. It wasn't just that Altiris was more hesitant – overcompensation, no doubt – and

Sidara more aggressive. No, the clincher was Anastacia's contented pose, one shoulder propped against the birch and her chin upraised in amusement.

Altiris feinted left and attacked right. Sidara stepped beyond its arc. Her back to the trees, and Altiris' to the river, she raised her stick in fresh salute.

"Do you yield, southwealder?"

Altiris halted mid-swing, brow creasing in puzzlement. "Yield? I'm not beaten."

Sidara clasped her hands together. Sunlight blazed along the river-bank, the girl a flickering shadow at its heart. Kurkas yelped and twisted away. Altiris' startled cry ended in the slap-crash of a body hitting water. Sidara's laughter danced along behind, chased on by Anastacia's soft, sardonic applause. Kurkas glowered at one, then the other. He felt no surprise. In hindsight, all was inevitable.

"I—" Altiris broke off in a chorus of gargled splutters. "I can't swim!"

Chastisement falling silent on his lips, Kurkas ran for the riverside.

Sidara beat him there. Mirth soured as the boy fought a flailing battle to stay afloat, and lost by degrees. "Help him!"

"Me?" snapped Kurkas. The backwash of magic had flung Altiris into the centre of the weed-choked channel, beyond the reach of helping hand or extended singlestick. "Just how well do you think I swim with one arm?"

Her face fell further, the horror so complete that Kurkas – who seldom entered untamed waters, but was entirely capable when he did – experienced a twinge of guilt at his deception.

Expression hardening, Sidara cast aside her singlestick, tore off her boots and gambeson, and dived into the river. She reached Altiris just as his head slipped under the surface for the third time. One arm crooked under his armpits and his head against hers, she kicked furiously for the bank.

Kurkas helped her hoist the lad to safety. As Sidara clambered up after, Altiris retched a stream of greenish water onto the mud, and collapsed, half-sitting, half-lying while his chest shuddered.

Kurkas crouched beside him. "You all right, lad?"

Altiris nodded, coughed, and nodded a second – more convincing – time.

"Good."

Kurkas clapped him on the shoulder and stepped back to regard the slimy, sodden pair. "Well, well, well. Lessons all round today. About how there's always someone ready to cheat harder . . ." He shifted his gaze from Altiris to Sidara. " . . . to the perils of wielding a weapon you don't understand."

He glanced at Anastacia, who made no more effort to involve herself in aftermath than event. Had she meant it this way? Proof that Sidara needed control over her magic if tragedies were to be avoided? Certainly she'd *claim* that as her goal. Lessons all around, save for Anastacia alone . . . and maybe for him as well, if he didn't stop expecting better of her.

Sidara glared, but aristocratic hauteur lay beyond the reach of one who resembled a bedraggled rusalka come to drag her victim into the weed-strewn depths. "I didn't mean for—"

"I said you'd good instincts," said Kurkas. "They tell you to do this, or warn you off?"

Her deepening scowl gave all the answer needed. Kurkas was glad, for he wasn't sure what he'd have done had she argued the point. Between her family's influence and what the girl herself was capable of? Well, that could turn all kinds of nasty. Out of his bloody depth, as usual, and his only anchor a plant pot of uncertain motivation. No life for an honest soldier.

Away through the trees, Abbeyfields' bell chimed noon, soon joined by the cacophony of others sweeping across the city. A reminder of challenges to come, and other depths in which to drown.

"I reckon we're done for the day," said Kurkas. "Lady Reveque, perhaps you might see to it that the guardsman is given a bath and a change of clothes? Doesn't do for a phoenix to be walking the streets looking like that."

She glanced at Altiris and winced. "Hawkin will see to it. I'll ask her."

Altiris squelched to his feet. "I thought I was coming with you. Watching your back."

"In that state?" Kurkas replied. "I don't think so."

[[Watching your back?]] Anastacia's voice, close at his shoulder without warning, set his heart skipping. [[Doing what, exactly?]]

"Never you mind."

[[I could help.]] Innocence crowded the words.

A tempting offer, had he trusted her. "Reckon I've had enough of your help today." He offered Sidara a shallow bow. "I'll be back tomorrow. Think on what you've learned this morning, for all our sakes."

Twenty-Nine

Kurkas had never known the mists so thick, nor the air so chill. As ever, there were more eyes in the alleyways than on the streets proper, but they at least offered little concern. Shorn of phoenix tabard and armour, Kurkas was just another battered soul wandering beneath the jettied eaves.

He told himself the cold kept the vranakin at bay – the darkened streets were almost deserted of all save the vaporous etravia – but recognised the sophistry of his silent claims. The sunlit city was holding its breath, Dregmeet was *waiting*. Waiting uneasily, as evidenced by pale, bluish flames flickering at stoop and windowsill. Bowls of ghostfire; burning fleenroot, duskhazel and silver dust to keep the dead from breaching sanctity of hearth and home. A custom normally observed at Midwintertide, when wronged cyraeths walked the Living Realm for a single, vengeful night. Except Midwintertide was a night of cheer, of shed sorrows cast to the flames. Not this.

More concerning was that streets Kurkas knew by heart felt *wrong* – sometimes shorter by a dozen paces, or longer by twice the tally. The familiar landmarks of tavern signs, factory gates, graffitied statues and clock towers were nowhere to be seen, or else in places at odds with memory. Heart-wrenching sobs reminded Kurkas that more than etravia walked the mists.

Should've brought the plant pot.

He pressed on, blaming the mists for senses awry, all the while knowing it was something more. Dregmeet, always tottering on Otherworld's boundary, had slipped its moorings. The muffled toll of bells brought to mind old nursery rhymes that seldom ended well for the lone, curious traveller. Tales of streets twisting back on themselves, the passage of days and nights jumbled as the sunlit world slipped away and time twisted upon itself beneath the dominion of Raven's Law. Eeriest of all was the occasional glimpse of a kraikon, frozen and lifeless as the world swirled away around it, its spark of magic suppressed by the mists.

All told, Kurkas' nerves were jangling by the time he slipped down into the Brocktree slums. They lent force to both voice and bunched fist as he hammered on peeling green paintwork.

"Come on, Kolly." He thumped the door again. "It's horrible out here."

The door opened a crack. Sweet duskhazel scent wafted out. "Vlad?" Koldra swore under his breath. "You can't be here."

"So open up before someone takes an interest?"

The door fell open, revealing a desperately unhappy Koldra. Permanently disappointed, he'd resembled a man of middle age long before his thirtieth year, two decades ago.

He hurried the door shut behind Kurkas. "What do you want?"

Kurkas glanced around the decaying room, all threadbare furniture and peeling wallpaper – a twin to the one in which he'd grown up. All it missed was his mother sitting beside the fire, sifting the day's bounty, working out what to keep and what to pass on as the Parliament's tribute. Half the keelies on Dower Street had answered to her. Blood kin or crow-cousin, they'd feared the lash of her tongue and the strike of her fist.

Most had died of sickness or quarrel long before Kurkas had fled the sunken streets. Niarla, with her crooked knife and thirst for rotgut brandy. Travor, buried alive as a groom of the grave for having the nerve to withhold tribute, and lacking the wit to conceal the theft. Sedvin, as silver-tongued a lad as any Kurkas had tumbled with, rotted inside-out by poison – the price of stealing from the wrong manor. Kurkas' broken heart had never quite mended right, and not for want of trying.

Far as he knew, Koldra was the last of them. Not a mate, exactly – the old adage about not being able to pick your family was never truer than in Dregmeet, where *everyone* was family, even when you were stealing from them – but as close as otherwise could be. Spoils shared and throats cut in good company was the best you could hope for. More like the army than most folk wanted to believe. The only friends Kurkas counted were

Lord Akadra, insofar as the gap in status allowed, and maybe – *maybe* – the plant pot. Revekah Halvor too, had she lived. After all, she was the reason he wore the phoenix.

"You know what I want," said Kurkas. "The Crowmarket's still holding southwealders. Where?"

"No one's talking. Not since Westernport. Not to me."

Same old Koldra. Not quite truth, but not quite a lie either. "Maybe, but I know that *you* know. Your keelies hear plenty they shouldn't, plying trade along Lacewalk and Nut Lane."

Not that there'd be work for them now. Hard to imagine bought and borrowed passion faring well on the mist-drowned streets. Then again, there was no accounting for taste.

"Sorry, Vlad, can't help. Not this time. If our cousins find out? I'll be floating at the docks by morning."

Our cousins. A long time in the past. Kurkas set hand on his sword. "Might still happen."

Koldra scowled. "You'd do that? To me?"

Kurkas set a purse on the sagging table. "Fifteen crowns. Same as before."

"Why do you care? Trelan's left the city. Ain't like he's riding you on this."

Kurkas stifled a sigh. Fifteen crowns was more than a hearthguard earned in a year. Ample compensation for the information he sought. Koldra seemed somehow smaller and pettier each time they spoke. Would he have been any better, had he stayed? "That's my business."

"Hah! Don't tell me you've come over all noble. Doesn't suit you, Vlad."

"Consider it a debt. Last year someone went to the fire to save my life. Sure as stone she'd be here in my place otherwise. And you, Kolly old son, would be on your knees begging her to let up on you. Her loss is your gain." He reached for the purse. "Still, if you want no part of it—"

"Wait!" Koldra licked his lips. "I'll need more. Thirty. Debts. You know how it is."

"Then you'll have to wait for the rest until I know your information's good." And until he'd chance to leverage the rest out of the safe at Stonecrest. Lord Trelan would understand.

"Don't trust me?"

"Kolly, back when we were both rassophores you once cracked me over the head and left me for the constabulary while you scurried off with my take. Six months I spent in that cell, knee-deep in salt water every time the tide washed in. Still be there if the army hadn't been desperate. So I reckon it's a bit late to be bawling about trust."

"You have it on you?"

"Guess you'll have to take my word."

"My cousin's, or the high and mighty captain's?"

"Whichever you like," said Kurkas. "So long as you tell me."

"How about I show you?"

He snorted. "You *want* to go out in that lot?"

"There's no danger, not to loyal cousins."

"I ain't so sure. The streets are all messed up. More than the streets. Reckon the old stories are coming true."

"*That's* why there's no danger," said Koldra. "Otherworld is rising. The Crowmarket is rising with it. No more hiding in the shadows. No more being hunted by the Council. An end to fat priests hoarding wealth behind church doors."

Kurkas stifled a grimace. "Yeah, yeah. Gold crowns falling like rain and eternal life for those deemed worthy. I know the stories. Kids' stuff, Kolly. Don't you ever wonder about the truth?"

"That *is* the truth," Koldra replied, eyes shining. "The Raven has returned to us."

Kurkas' gut shifted. Koldra didn't just believe old tales were coming true – he *welcomed* the idea. But what else was there in Dregmeet? Or anywhere else, for that matter? Raven's Eyes, but what else did the Republic operate on except the hope that one day old debts would come due, and old wrongs be righted? Why else did common folk tolerate the Council, save out of hope that their children might one day sit atop the pile and smother others in the dirt?

More than ever, Kurkas wished he'd shared his worries with Lord Trelan. But the business with Altiris? Then the news from Ahrad? The chance had slipped away. Whether Koldra's lead panned out or not, the Council had to know, which meant Kurkas had to tell them – even if there was little chance they'd believe.

No life for an honest soldier.

"The Raven, eh?" he said. "Say hello for me, would you? But first, show me what I came to see."

The deeper into Dregmeet they trod, the worse things became. The air grew heavy with the musty scent of yesterdays. Ravens crowded rooftop and lintel. Whenever they took wing, they left smoky, vaporous trails.

Soon, the streets were empty of all save etravia. The ghosts no longer drifted without purpose, but filed along the narrow roadways in great spectral columns, altering course only to avoid the flickering blue-white flames. Kurkas couldn't guess where they were headed, but then he himself was thoroughly lost, even though every nook and cranny, every shortcut and refuge, had been burned into his brain since his earliest years.

But worst of all was the weeping. It rose and fell with the billow of mist, lost and forlorn, at times everywhere and nowhere. Kurkas' fingers ached, locked tight about his sword's hilt.

"Better not be leading me into a prizrak nest, Kolly," he muttered.

"What's the matter?" Koldra replied. "Can't find your way?"

"You're joking, right? The only things I can see in this muck are things I'd rather not."

"It's because you ain't one of us any longer, Vlad. Not a *true* cousin."

Kurkas scowled at the back of his head. Was that true, or was Koldra simply better at covering up his fear? "That prizrak'll eat us both just as gladly. And there's more meat on you than me."

"Ain't nothing but a heartsick keelie," Koldra replied airily. "Weeping her loss into the gutter."

Kurkas shook his head and hunched his shoulders. Funny what folk believed, and what they chose not to. Prizraks were as much a part of Otherworld's myth as the etravia and the shifting streets. Men and women hollowed out by the mists, leaving a gaunt, misshapen husk wracked by hunger pains so terrible it drove them to bloody tears.

It suited Koldra to pretend otherwise. Kurkas knew better, for he'd seen one. At Trennen Sump, before storms had breached the harbour wall and drowned the place. A glimpse of fangs beneath a tattered vranakin hood. Not yet seven summers old, he'd fled back home, breathless and weeping, only to fetch the flat of his mother's hand for abandoning the precious vials she'd sent him to steal. She'd not believed either. Some things you didn't, not until they were close enough to kill.

"Here."

Koldra left the street and squeezed through a run of buckled iron railings. Kurkas followed, picking his way through the haphazard maze of moss-draped statues and headstones. Koldra halted where a second line of railings fell away across a collapsed embankment. Below, the brooding square-towered bulk of the Church of Tithes loomed over plaza and befouled fountain. Caged wagons waited in the mists, each flanked by a procession of grey-garbed vranakin and preceded by an elder cousin's tattered, drifting form.

Kurkas' heart sank. Westernport had been bad enough, but the Church of Tithes? The Parliament of Crows' own bloody nest? It'd take an army to swing that, and the Republic hadn't an army to spare.

The sonorous tolling of twin bells swept the plaza. Wagons creaked into motion, blinkered draught horses beginning the long, upward climb to the city above. Ravens flocked from the bell towers and swooped in pursuit. Hand bells clamoured across the fading echoes marked the pass of ritual advance. Too regal and deliberate for the departure of wagons whose duty had been done. This was something else. Koldra had lied.

"Where are they, Kolly?" murmured Kurkas.

"Gone. Long gone."

Kurkas turned, unable to muster surprise at the long dagger in Koldra's hand. Nor the dark shapes moving among the graves. No one to blame other than himself. Koldra hadn't known he'd be coming, but *of course* he'd had vranakin watching from the shadows, awaiting instruction and opportunity. There were a hundred ways he could have signalled them during the descent.

"So they're dead?" Kurkas replied.

"Their deaths appeased the Raven. They made this possible."

"Made *what* possible?"

"I told you: the Crowmarket is rising."

"Yeah, if you say so."

Kurkas drew his sword. Below, the plaza had all but emptied, its denizens unaware or uncaring of what unfolded atop the embankment. Koldra's vranakin were close enough now to be more than foreboding shapes. Four footpads in a half circle, knives and cudgels already to hand. Too many to fight.

Should've brought the plant pot.

"Mucky way to earn thirty crowns." Kurkas let his eye rest on each footpad in turn, searching for the weak link. "Reckon it'll be downright life-changing for at least one of you."

Koldra chuckled. "Don't be like that, Vlad. Could've slit you myself back home if that was what I wanted. We're mates, you and me, and you were always a good leg-breaker. Pay up, and you can come back to the fold."

"Generous. What if I choose otherwise?"

Koldra nodded towards the church. "Then we'll sell you on to the Parliament. Crowfather Athariss will pay a pretty price for the captain of a Privy Councillor's hearthguard."

Ransom at best, death in the middle ground and something worse than death at the extreme. What, exactly, Kurkas wasn't sure, but with Athariss' reputation and the way his luck had been breaking . . . ?

"All right, Kolly, let's hear what—"

Kurkas broke off and flung himself past Koldra. The leftmost footpad's sword came up too slow. A gasp, a tang of blood on the musty air, and Kurkas left him dying at the foot of another man's grave.

"Stop him!" shouted Koldra.

A chorus of curses and the thump of running feet chased Kurkas past the railings. Leaving the graveyard's muddy field behind, he headed uphill, threading etravia as he ran. Didn't matter how jumbled Dregmeet's streets had become. Up was out.

Kurkas' lungs burned well before he reached the next corner. The Brass Crown's sign screeched back and forth overhead. Light and mirth blazed behind the tavern's filthy windows. He passed on the locked door and scrambled up a stack of crates and dropped down into the dray yard, skidded on horse dung, and ran for the far side. The rusted lock snapped under his shoulder, and he staggered out into the alley.

Now where? Uphill. Always uphill. But not predictable. Kurkas headed left, but veered right as the alley branched, then left again beneath a crooked firestone lamp long since shorn of glass. Another right brought him out onto a narrow, cobbled road that memory tentatively identified as Clipper Street. The glimpse of a caged wagon and attendants through drifting ctravia sent Kurkas doubling back on himself, over a half-fallen wall and onto ... Marshsea Street? Yes, Marshsea Street, with its sagging, timber-framed buildings and spireless Lunastran church.

Could have been worse. Halfway, or near enough. No sign of pursuit, nor a hue and cry like the one that had harried Lord Trelan's expedition out of Westernport. Whatever profit Koldra wanted from the venture, he'd evidently sought not to share.

Kurkas propped his elbow against a wall and sucked air into aching lungs. The mists billowed, wafting heartsick sobbing into the street. Running feet drowned it out.

"There!"

Far from rested, but with limited options, Kurkas set off again. He leapt the flooded gutter at the street's edge, and dived into an alley. This time, he passed the uphill turning, and ran on to the end. He took the corner too fast, shoulder striking brick and jarring badly needed breath from lungs. Fighting for balance, he thundered on to the alley's end and out into the plaza.

Straight into the mist-haunted shadow of the Church of Tithes.

"Oh, that's just not bloody fair."

For a moment, Kurkas told himself it wasn't the church at all. But no. The squared-off towers. The tatter-winged statue sitting at the heart of the fountain. Despite his uphill flight, he was back where he'd started.

"Can't find your way Vlad? See? You're no longer vranakin at heart."

Koldra emerged from the alleyway, his footpads close behind.

"That mean the job offer's done with?"

"From the moment you slit Ravald."

The footpads closed in. Kurkas set off again, slower than before for want of legs and lungs thirty years younger. Giving the fountain a wide berth, he lurched up the slope so lately crowded with wagons and ducked into a muddy alley.

Water rushed at the far end, where the Estrina – whose artificial watercourse spilt from the Silverway to power the city's mills – boiled away. An uneven, eroded towpath clung to the near shore; the far bank was a sheer cliff, too steep for a one-armed man to climb. Upriver, slatted millwheels turned on a squeaking axle, the patter of water dedicated to the vanished goddess Endala by the flowing script scratched into timber. In the ordinary run of things the Estrina gushed into the sea further west. Who could say where it ended now, with Dregmeet muddled?

A twitch of the mists brought wailing cries.

Kurkas spun about and swung the flat of his sword onto his shoulder. "Tell you what. How about we all walk out of here, and find a bit of sunlight? I'll even stand you a round or two at the Silverway tavern. Put a bit of colour in your cheeks."

An exhausted Koldra stumbled closer. "Have some dignity, Vlad."

"Got all I need, and plenty to spare." Kurkas swung the sword off his shoulder. "Why don't you come find out, for old times' sake?"

"I don't think so." Koldra beckoned to his companions. "Take him."

The footpads came forward as a trio. More than enough to block the alley, and the treacherous footing of the old towpath promised much the same outcome as simply diving outright into the rushing waters. Still, you ran the race as best you could.

Weeping heralded the arrival of a dark shape in the mists behind Koldra. It stumbled closer, head hanging and bloody eyes downcast. Skin pale as a fish's belly and emaciated, clawed hands told Kurkas all he needed. It had been a lad of Altiris' age, before the mists had hollowed him out. Not any longer.

Kurkas cleared his throat. "Kolly, old son, you might want to turn around."

"Really, Vlad? That's the best you have?"

"Suit yourself."

Koldra narrowed his eyes. He turned in the same moment the prizrak bore him to the ground. Black talons opened his throat to sky. Two of the footpads turned at the gargling, spluttering scream.

"Queen's Ashes . . . " hissed one.

The third held his ground, vainly trying to keep Kurkas in view while also seeing what had occurred behind. "What is it?"

'It', Kurkas decided, was the situation sliding from bad to worse. Sure, Koldra was down – and good riddance – but an alley packed with three vranakin and a hungry prizrak was hardly an improvement. Monsters needed silver, not steel. Or failing that, an axe.

The prizrak clambered to its feet and bore down. A footpad swung, the blade cutting deep into the prizrak's arm. It staggered, a shrill cry parting its lips. Then it bore him to the ground and a new scream split the air.

Before he could change his mind, Kurkas leapt into the river.

Thirty

Of the many things Prazarov hated about the constabulary, sentry duty was the worst. Especially sentry duty on Dregmeet's border. And more than anything, *pointless* sentry duty. The vranakin had so many sewers, tunnels and the like to make ingress into the city proper that they seldom bothered with the Drag Hill gate.

"Relief should be here by now." Receiving no response, Prazarov raised his voice. "I said 'relief should be here by now'."

Sergeant Halledra – a ten-year veteran, and little given to indulging grievance – shot him a bored look from the other side of the archway. "Saying so ain't gonna make them show faster."

"The captain's punishing me, isn't she? Just because I looked the other way when that banker got his pockets cut in Beastmarket." The memory stung as only a bad deed in good cause could. The Freemarker tellerman had coin to spare, while the keelie had been more rib than flesh. "Unfair, that's what it is."

"Yeah? And what's my punishment for being stuck here with you?" Halledra softened her voice. "Look, Captain Darrow isn't a bad sort. She'd have let the matter slide if you'd not made such a fuss."

"I see, so now it's my—"

The deep toll of a bell set Prazarov's stomach growling. Shuffling footsteps gathered further down the mist-wreathed slope.

Halledra pushed away from the wall and cupped a hand to her mouth. "Gate's closed! Order of the Council."

A cawing torrent of black wings rushed out of the mists. Prazarov threw up a hand to shield his face as the ravens swept past, talons pluck-ing at his tabard. Then they were gone into the city.

Other figures emerged, a loose escort of vranakin grey shuffling at either side of a wagon. To the right, an old man bore a rusted iron bell-frame tucked against shoulder and hip. A strike of his hammer struck the chime anew. Escorts stiffened in anticipation. Just Dregmeet scum. A handful of masked vranakin mingled among them. Nothing to worry about, bar the number.

A wagon creaked out of the mist, drawn by an emaciated horse in ragged caparison. Crooked iron bars formed an empty cage about the wagon bed. The driver hunched over slack reins, hooded grey robes wisping at the edges. Prazarov saw no face. His heart wavered before the hood's empty gaze, overcome by the same nameless, inex-plicable dread that set his knees knocking. Instinct screamed to run. Legs refused.

A pale Halledra drew her sword. Prazarov fumbled his own attempt. Numbed fingers reclaimed the falling blade halfway to the floor.

"The Council?" The driver's voice trickled through the mist, scraping at Prazarov's soul. "This city belongs to the Parliament of Crows."

The kernclaw cast his cloak wide. The air filled with the screech of birds.

"Lumestra, bless this house with light."

Grigorad set taper to the wick. The last altar candle blazed to life, banishing gloom from the apse as the Goddess had once banished Dark from the world. Her golden statue smiled down from above the east window, the interplay of candlelight and shadow animating the kindly face. Others preferred firestone lanterns to simple flame, arguing that they were more reliable – or perhaps more fitting as they were, like the foundry's constructs, fuelled by the Goddess' magic. But Grigorad favoured flame – a simple offering for a simple house, as all churches should be. Even a church tucked away in the gardened streets of Highvale, blessed with a congregation generous in size and munificence. Even on Saint Belenzo's holy day.

He blew the taper out and set it aside. A few minutes more until bells chimed the hour. Time enough to open the doors and admit the evenhymn congregation. He retrieved his sun-staff from beside the pulpit – these days as much a support for aging bones as a symbol of office – and hobbled along the chequerboard tiles.

A scream sounded beyond the walls. Another followed. Shadows darkened the nave's stained-glass windows, rippling back and forth across the golden friezes. Running feet. The clash of steel. A body fell against the north window, head and hands dark against glass before sliding away.

Grigorad hastened to the door and heaved it open. The clamour redoubled, driven by shapes running in unseasonal mist. Greenish-white vapour trickled over Grigorad's feet and along the nave. The altar candles flickered and went out.

"What is the meaning of this?" he shouted.

A woman ran out of the mist; eyes wild, her velvet gown bloodied and torn. She fell to her knees on the marble steps and clutched at Grigorad's vestments.

"The vranakin are taking the children! They're killing anyone who objects!"

Rheumy eyes adjusted. Enough to make out bodies strewn across the church garden. Parishioners. Constables. Lazrin, the sexton, a sword used only for clearing beggars and vagrants close beside his lifeless hand. And beyond the lychgate, a caged wagon. Hands reached through the bars. Discordant, pleading sobs rose to prominence as screams faded. Grey figures moved through the murk, dragging or carrying children alongside.

Awash with horror, Grigorad stamped the butt of his staff against stone. The crystal sun at the staff's tip burst to golden light. Mist recoiled like a beast from flame. Grigorad's fear fled until only outrage remained; outrage, and a duty learned long ago on the Ravonn – one that made no exception for old bones. He pulled free of the wailing woman and strode for the gate.

A vranakin barred his path, cudgel raised. The sun-staff's flash of light swept him aside, and then no one stood between Grigorad and the wagon.

"You dare?" he roared. "In Lumestra's city? Beneath the walls of her church?"

Another vranakin came screaming from the mist. Her sword drove timber from Grigorad's staff. A flare of magic cast her from her feet. Wailing, she crawled away, one hand clasped to her mask.

Grigorad's chest heaved with unfamiliar exertion. His blood seethed with righteous fury and the magic's backwash. "Set them free!"

The sun-staff flickered. Grey robes gathered in the mists between Grigorad and the cart.

"Their old lives are done," breathed the hooded man. "They will be cousins of the Raven."

The mists grew colder. Grigorad's breathing stuttered. Outrage ebbed. A seething presence swamped his thoughts, insidious as nightmare. His knees buckled, but the grip on his staff held him upright. Sunlight vied with the cold settling in his bones.

"Lumestra commands it!"

Shapes gathered in the mists. Masked vranakin all. A circle of blades held back by light's glory.

"Lumestra belongs to the light." Something black and insectoid scuttled across the hooded man's robes and vanished beneath his sleeve. The mists shifted, carrying the sour stench of decay. "This city belongs to the Crowmarket."

The sun-stave's light guttered and died. Mist rushed in.

Thirty-One

"Reports are still arriving, but near as I can tell the mists have claimed everything between the Silverway estuary in the north and Wallmarch in the south." Vona Darrow's voice burned with frustration and, Malachi suspected, no little fear. But she maintained her ramrod-straight pose at the end of the table, helmet tucked under her arm and eyes clear. "It's gone as far east as Three Pillars. If it crosses into the Hayadra Grove it'll come rushing down Sinner's Mile, and that'll be it. And where the mist goes, so do the vranakin."

Evarn Marest brought his fist down on the table. "Raven's Eyes, but that's half the city!"

She nodded. "Not the epithet I'd have chosen in the circumstances, my lord, but you're about right."

Marest's eyes turned furtive, fearful. Leonast Lamirov's expression was a good match, as was Messela Akadra's. Rika Tarev had not yet uttered a word, though her eyes were haunted. Malachi suspected each wondered how soon the mists would reach their estates.

Only Konor Zarn seemed at ease with events, but that provoked little surprise. He was, after all, the Crowmarket's man. Not that Malachi held himself blameless in that regard. Every breath was a challenge. His stomach was sour with the knowledge that whatever witchery the Parliament of Crows had loosed, he'd played his part.

Messela leaned forward. Unplaited black hair – an unforgiveable offence against formality under less dire circumstances – tumbled past her shoulders. The summons to council had caught her partway through preparations to attend a recital of Kespid's Itharocian Tragedy. Had the herald not found her, she'd have been in her patron's box at Highvale Amphitheatre when the mists had swallowed it up. "Do we know what's happening in the mists?"

"A few desperate souls found their way out down by the docks," Darrow replied. "Didn't get much out of them beyond a lot of babble about shifting streets and having lost days in the mists – and that can't be right, because it's only been hours. Even so, it's ugly. Churches and homes ransacked with all the death and thuggery you might expect. There's also whispers of children rounded up and taken into Dregmeet."

Malachi stared into a glass emptied too soon. The decanter, empty save a dribble, sat temptingly within reach. Every crooked bargain he'd made with the Parliament of Crows, all to save his own children. How many others now paid the price? "Hostages?"

"They'll want them for cousins," said Lady Tarev. "Young enough to mould."

"Barbaric," sniffed Lord Lamirov, owner of the majority of Tressia's workhouses. "And on Saint Belenzo's feast day, of all days."

"Do you concur, captain?" said Messela.

Darrow hesitated. "I hope she's right. I don't care for the alternatives."

"And what, pray, are you doing about it, Captain Darrow?" said Lord Lamirov.

"Doing about what, my lord?"

"You command the constabulary, don't you? Or am I thinking of someone else?"

Darrow's gaze darkened. "I don't follow, *my lord.*"

"Gather your ruffians and drive the vranakin back into Dregmeet. I think I speak for everyone when I say you may be as brutal as you like."

The room fell to silence. Messela and Zarn stared mutely at the table; Lady Tarev and Lord Marest into the unknowable middle distance. Malachi caught the tightness gathering about Darrow's eyes.

"What am I doing?" Darrow set down her helmet and strode along the table, passing up the empty chairs belonging to Josiri and Izack. "Half the city lost. That means half my watch houses. Half my ruffians, as it pleases you to call them, are gone, and if anyone's seen them, they're keeping it to themselves. Perhaps you'd like to have a gander yourself, *my lord.*"

Lord Lamirov snorted. "Then request aid from the chapterhouses."

Darrow's advance quickened a hair.

Malachi cleared his throat. "Lord Lamirov will doubtless remember that the bulk of the Knights Sartorov are stationed at Fathom Rock in penance for poor decisions last year. The Hadari army lies between them and us. Essamere and Prydonis rode away the evening before last. They've barely a squire nearer than Tarvallion."

Darrow halted, a frown playing across her lips.

"Then the foundry," snapped Lord Lamirov. "Mobilise whatever simarka and kraikons there are to be had."

"The foundry's on Weirgate." Messela spoke with all the confidence lacking from her previous appearances at council. No more solid a soul than an Akadra when crisis beckoned. "There's mist for at least a dozen streets in any direction."

"It may not matter," said Darrow. "Firestone lamps fail when the mist overtakes them, and I doubt the constructs are faring better. Or is anyone in this room clinging to the belief that this is a mere fluke of weather? You might not smell it in here, but there's vranakin witchery on the air."

Lord Lamirov scowled at his knotted hands. "And the provosts?"

"Cowering in their chantry. They like torturing suspected heretics well enough, but taking a stand against *real* witchery?" Darrow shook her head. "Useless bloody lot."

"Otherworld is rising." Lady Tarev clutched tight her pendant necklace. "The Crowmarket is rising with it."

"I beg your pardon?" asked Lord Marest.

Lady Tarev stared off into the middle distance.

"Could the Hadari be part of this?" asked Messela. "Gold glitters in Dregmeet as brightly as anywhere. The shadowthorns have coin to spare."

Malachi hesitated. It'd be so easy to agree, if only to assuage his own complicity. But no. Coin alone bought no influence with the vranakin. Only a fool would offer more, and Kai Saran's actions this past week suggested the man was no fool.

He forced confidence into his voice. "The shadowthorns don't need vranakin causing mischief. We've been lax. *I've* been lax. Now we're paying the price." He stared at Zarn, who gazed disinterestedly back. "The Crowmarket are scavengers, cowards and thieves. They've seen our weakness. They're exploiting it."

Lady Tarev flinched. Darrow snorted her disgust.

Zarn remained impassive. "Then surely all you need do is show them that you – I'm sorry, that *we* – aren't so weak as they believe."

Messela nodded. "Send riders south to gather Lancras from Callastair."

"Lancras?" Lord Lamirov shook his head. "They've scarcely a hundred spurs. Their chapterhouse is an empty ruin, and their vigils more like hermit's refuges than fortresses. Why do you think we've not sent them to the border already?"

"And there's nothing to say Lancras would get here in time," said Lord Marest. "Three hours, and half the city gone. We could lose the rest by midnight."

"Which could happen whether we call for them or not," Messela replied. "Witchery abounds. What we need is fire and steel. Captain Darrow may consider every blade in my hearthguard hers to command. What say the rest of you?"

Malachi nodded, embarrassed the idea had not been his. Was his mind truly so gummed by guilt and fear? "I can't spare everyone. I've family to protect – especially now – but as for the rest?" He stood, tumultuous emotion at last settling. "Captain Darrow, you have my authority to gather whatever forces you can, wherever they may lie. I want a plan for retaking the streets – or at least containing those that remain ours – and I want it by midnight. Is that understood?"

She clasped a fist to her chest in salute and departed, glad to leave the stultifying chamber. Malachi wished he were free to do the same.

"What if this doesn't work?" asked Lord Lamirov.

"What choice do we have?" Malachi replied. "We are beset without and within. We must seize whatever options present themselves."

Lord Lamirov's chair scraped and he rose to his feet, brow furrowed. "I'll speak to my supporters in the Grand Council. Captain Darrow will have all we can provide." He made to leave but paused halfway to the door. "Josiri was right. He warned us, and we didn't listen. We . . ."

Shaking his head, he left the chamber.

Malachi shook his head at Lord Lamirov's concession, and silently lamented the times that provoked it. He glanced at Zarn, whose handsome face seemed no less perturbed at the meeting's close than at its beginning.

Seize whatever options present themselves.

"I think we might call the meeting adjourned," he said. "Konor, I'd talk to you in private, if I may."

Lord Marest and Lady Tarev departed. Malachi intercepted Messela as she reached the door, checking her with a hand to the shoulder. "Viktor would be proud. Thank you."

She dipped her head. "Leonast said it best. Josiri warned us, and we did nothing. You say Viktor would be proud? I think he'd be appalled."

Malachi let her go and eased the door to.

Zarn waited a pace away, his face crowded with suspicion. "Well, Malachi? What is it? I'd a delightful evening planned, and I'd as soon not lose more of it."

The arrogance of the man. "I need to speak to the Parliament of Crows. Tonight."

"I don't follow."

"The Crowmarket put you here to watch me. To report. I need to speak with them. Make it happen."

"Lay off the brandy, Malachi, it's addled your wits." He wagged a finger in amusement. "Or perhaps you need *more*. Tell you what, I know just the place. The girls—"

He doubled over, Malachi's fist buried in his belly.

"No more games, Konor."

Zarn steadied himself against the table. "How dare—"

Malachi hit him across the head, a year's frustration and shame behind the blow. Knuckles split. Bones jarred. Sunshine on a winter's day. Even through the pain. Even through the knowledge that the Parliament of Crows would never forgive. Some joys transcended fear. This one howled for more.

"You think I'd let them take my children?" he shouted. "My city?"

He swung again. Zarn blocked the forearm with his own. A gut-punch set black spots dancing behind Malachi's eyes. He dived, bearing Zarn backwards onto the meeting table.

Over and over they rolled, a blur of wild blows and pained grunts that left Zarn the master, and Malachi pinned beneath. Malachi's flailing foot clipped his glass, and it shattered across the floor. His hand closed about the decanter's neck.

Zarn grunted as the decanter crashed against his temple. He slid backwards, rolled off the table and collapsed against the wall. Malachi pursued, groggy but triumphant, bloodstained decanter still in hand. Bleary eyes made no mistake. Zarn's wits were clean away.

Breathing hard, Malachi snarled back self-disgust. With Zarn struck cold, he'd have to risk the mists, with no guarantee he'd come to the Church of Tithes unharmed, much less be granted audience.

He moved to set the cut-glass decanter aside. His eyes fell on Zarn's body. What use was the man now? None at all. Fire and steel to mend the problem, as Messela had said. The decanter was neither, but one good blow would carry Zarn off. One death to repay those his cousins wrought in the mist-lost streets.

He raised the decanter.

"Malachi!"

He turned, startled both by the shout, and the realisation of what he'd intended. Rika Tarev stood in the doorway, hand again on her pendant necklace.

"Leave him be," she said. "Nothing good can come of this."

"He's vranakin." He wished the words didn't make him so weary. "Nothing good can come of letting him live."

"He's a vain fool, that's all. Someone the Parliament of Crows trusted to do nothing that was not in his own interest. Who'd do nothing to curtail their power." She came closer, a tremor to voice and motion. "Sometimes all wickedness requires is a man who'll do nothing."

Malachi closed his eyes. "You don't know that."

A jerk of her hand snapped the necklace free. Rika Tarev unfurled like a blossoming flower, formal gown yielding to a black-feathered cloak; blonde plaits to auburn curls marred by a white badger's-streak.

The decanter fell from Malachi's nerveless hand and shattered on the floor. For all that he'd not seen the woman's face before, he knew it. Sevaka Psanneque's fugitive sister. The Parliament's Emissary. Rika Tarev. One and the same. No wonder the vranakin had known all that had passed at council.

"The Parliament will give you nothing," she said.

"I still have to try."

She sighed. "Then follow."

"We're here."

She ripped the blindfold away. Light rushed in, or at least its approximation. The mists shone pearlescent beneath a waning moon, lending soft glow to the ruined stones and creeping tree-limbs. Little by little, Malachi's nausea faded. Memories of the journey did not. The screech of bird voices and the rush of wind. The croaking whispers of the Emissary's cloak as she'd borne him across the city. He wanted to scream, and cast about for a reason not to.

"Where are we?"

"Essamere."

"The chapterhouse?" He stared at a roof open to the stars – a street bereft of all save drifting spirits. Even prepared for the sight by the Emissary's warning, it chilled his marrow. "I was here two days ago. This couldn't happen so quickly."

"Perhaps it didn't. Perhaps it hasn't. Perhaps it never will." She shrugged. "Otherworld has risen. Time no longer flows like a river."

Reckoning that to pursue the topic was to risk madness, Malachi sought another. "I assume Rika's dead."

"She drowned."

"An accident?"

"No."

What more could he say? How aggrieved could he be at the death of a woman he'd never known, when her imposter had held him back from murder? Who had before urged him to save Josiri's life? "Your doing?"

The Emissary grunted. "I can't. Lord Akadra saw to that. He set a shadow on my soul. It permits me to kill only when he commands."

"I don't believe you."

"He had me murder my own mother," she snarled. "What do I care for your beliefs?"

So that was how Ebigail Kiradin had died? Viktor had spoken evasively on the matter, and Malachi – like so many others – had cared only that she was dead, her dreams of rule laid in the tomb alongside.

"I'm sorry. I didn't know."

"You apologise to me?" She turned away, voice thick with disgust. "Why?"

"Someone should, don't you think? Viktor never will." Malachi stared out across the rubble. A surreal conversation for a surreal setting. "May I know your name? It's a small enough secret after all that's passed between us."

"Apara."

They sat in silence, Malachi fretfully twirling his paper knife from hand to hand as he dwelled on the conversation to come. A life once filled with myriad options reduced to two. All that remained was to embrace one, and pay the price of rejecting the other.

"He's here," said Apara.

A man more shadow than shape strode out of the mist, the foot of his gnarled raven-headed cane keeping rhythm with his steps. Of his flesh, nothing showed beneath the gold-trimmed robes save the withered hand about the cane's handle.

"Crowfather." Apara knelt, head bowed and eyes averted.

The pontiff turned his gaze on Malachi. "You know who I am?"

"I . . . " Malachi swallowed to clear a parched mouth. "I know who you claim to be. One of three cousins who struck a pact with the Raven in antiquity. An eternal existence in trade for a soul owed to Lumestra."

A thoughtful grunt. "That's an old tale, buried by ever-changing history. Not one I'd expect a devout Lumestran to have heard. Priests don't like it when their truths are challenged." His tone turned bitter. "And this land breeds priests like flies."

"I have a large library. After some legends proved themselves grounded in truth last year, I've opened my eyes to the possibilities."

"A dangerous path, Lord Reveque. It led many of my kin to the pyre."

"Ignorance burns no less hot." He stepped closer. "Inidro Krastin is long dead. He belongs to legend."

Withered lips cracked a smile. "Only in part."

The pontiff drew back his hood. Pallid skin aside, the face beneath was unremarkable save for obvious age, a man blessed with a span denied to so many, and still vigorous.

Then Malachi met his black, pupil-less eyes. His thoughts dissolved beneath a rush of desperate sorrow. In that moment, he saw his own death, and those of Lily, Sidara, Constans. He saw the city ablaze, and himself forlorn among a field of ashen corpses. An outflung hand steadied him against stone, but while the sensation lessened, it did not abate. Breaking the gaze brought relief, but the echo of fear remained. That, and the certainty that he'd but paddled on the edge of a vast, dark pool – that he'd experienced but a fraction of the terror at the pontiff's command.

Eyes held truth. Krastin or not, whatever humanity the pontiff had once possessed lay long in the past.

"I am not accustomed to being summoned, Lord Reveque. But never let it be said I am without generosity."

"I asked to speak to the Parliament."

"'Demanded', I heard. What you have to say, my siblings will hear ... if it is worth the trouble. Believe me when I say you would not find my sister so accommodating as I. She has a priest's sensibilities, and a shrill mood."

Careful not to meet Krastin's gaze, Malachi straightened. "What have you done to my city?"

"Yours? Tressia was always ours, even before Malatriant. It toiled for us, and we brought hope to those who had none. We unshackled them from priests, from a goddess who promised eternity only after lives of misery. We gave them family. But the Raven turned his back on us. Now his favour is ours once more, we unmake our error. Your kind have made poor stewards of our city, so we relieve you the burden of its western districts. You may keep the rest. For now."

He turned away. Malachi examined the words – the gift that wasn't a gift – and glimpsed hope. He'd been too long in the Crowmarket's talons not to recognise that the concession sprung not from largesse, but unreadiness to act.

"That's not good enough."

Krastin froze. "Many men have spoken to me thus over the centuries. Do you know what they offered for my forgiveness? Their kin. Their blood. Their dearest wish. All for nothing."

Something slithered beneath the words that went beyond mere threat. But Malachi had made his decision long before – even before he'd struck Konor Zarn. Two choices: stand or kneel. He'd knelt too long.

"I'm not here to beg, but to speak for my city, and my Republic." The words gathered pace, the going easier with momentum. "You and your kind will return to Dregmeet. You will give back those you have stolen."

"And if we do not?" Krastin chuckled. "You think you can drive us out, where even Malatriant could not? The Raven is my patron, boy. You would threaten me with death? It means nothing."

"Then I will find a way to give it meaning, and it will be war." Malachi drew down a steadying breath. "We will both lose. Or we can choose not to. Either way, I will do your bidding no longer."

Krastin turned, his eyes itching at Malachi's skin as they took his measure. In that moment, Malachi knew that the other could kill him, without effort and without regret.

Would Apara return his body to Abbeyfields, so that his family might at least have something to mourn? Or would he vanish, one more mystery? His heart quickened. He clenched fingers tight to slow its gallop. One life gambled against thousands was a worthy stake. Viktor would have stood his ground. Lily and Josiri too. How could he do less?

Krastin stamped his cane twice on rock, turned, and strode away.

"Think of your children, Lord Reveque. You're a bureaucrat, not a hero."

The mists swallowed him up.

Malachi stared after, unaware Apara was on her feet until her hand closed about his shoulder.

"You should heed his advice," she said softly.

Think of your children. "I intend to."

Thirty-Two

Night brought clear skies to Tarona Watch, crisp with rain to come. Calenne beheld it from the remnant of the upper floor, feet dangling out over the garden and thoughts lost to the stars. Though Tarona's keep lacked the dizzying height of her grandfather's observatory at Branghall – her old refuge after arguments with Josiri, before their ancestral home had burned – it made a passable replacement.

Viktor's silence proclaimed the coming argument as clearly as the sky promised rain. He'd spoken little since Valna, his affections distant and dutiful when offered at all. Calenne understood too well, for she was much the same, for ever putting off disagreement out of fear of seeming petty, and fuming all the while.

She flung a pebble from the wall, a scowl chasing it along. That quirk of personality had driven her and Josiri apart. That and Josiri's lies. The thought of it parting her and Viktor as well was too much to bear. Perhaps apology was owed.

A scrape of stone on the broken stair. The sound of a large man attempting silent approach. Calenne hung her head, a soft smile about her lips. Yes, they were very much the same.

"You'd make a terrible assassin."

"I settle my quarrels directly," Viktor replied. "I thought you knew that by now."

"How can we be quarrelling? You've not spoken to me since the morning."

The footsteps halted a pace or two behind, his presence impossible to miss, even unseen. "Untrue."

"You've announced intent in my presence, Viktor. It's not the same as speaking." She strove to forget that she'd done much the same, and swore she wouldn't be the first to apologise. "A wife is not a soldier to be ordered about."

"Even when she insists on behaving like one?" He sat heavily beside her and stared across the valley. "You shouldn't have become involved."

There it was. The cause laid bare. The first flicker of anger rose to meet it. "How could I not? That boy—"

"I don't fault the thought, but the deed. You could have died."

"Did I not once tell you that I am not made of glass? It remains true."

"That was before your illness."

Calenne stared down at her fingers, recalling the instinctive casting of the pebble. A week before, the throw would have been feeble. Tonight, it had cleared the garden wall. As if in lifting the sword she'd recovered something long-abandoned.

"Would you believe I'm feeling much more like myself?"

Except that wasn't quite true, was it? She felt stronger, certainly, but was unsettled by something new. An edge to her mood that went beyond annoyance at Viktor's manner. Just weariness. It would pass.

"I believe you'd tell me that were so, whether or not it truly was." He sighed. "Your recklessness forced me to some of my own. I drew upon my shadow."

"I'm sorry." Some things transcended pride. "Are you . . . ?"

"I remain myself in all ways I can measure. But the fear remains."

The fear that he wasn't his shadow's master, but its slave. That drawing upon it made him the heir of Dark that Malatriant had sought to shape him.

She took his hand, her fingers childlike atop his. "Perhaps that fear, like my illness, belongs to the past. They define us only because we permit them to. This morning? Saving that boy? I felt more myself than I have in a long time."

"As did I. And I can't for the life of me decide if that is good or bad."

"Then we'll find out together, one day at a time." She laid her head on his shoulder. "Peace?"

He hesitated. "When I saw you imperilled, I called out your name."

"You did what?" Calenne pulled away. Grit crunched under her feet as she stood. "What if someone heard?"

"What if someone recognised you?" he demanded. "It was your insistence the world think you dead. I called out to warn you. I will *not* apologise for it."

"Then why tell me?"

"Because I want no secrets between us."

"Did anyone hear?"

"No one living, save Armund. I doubt he understood. Certainly he said nothing after."

She snorted. "Too busy drowning his wits in mead, I imagine."

He rose, a twitching cheek shifting the old scar. "The truth is we must both of us be more careful. Especially after today."

Calenne held her breath, knowing it irrational to blame Viktor for a situation she'd provoked. With uttermost reluctance, the storm of her anger passed. "So I'm not the only one feeling more like myself?"

Viktor's eyes were no longer on hers, but cast north along the valley road and the soft glow of firestone lanterns.

Calenne glared. "You said Armund wouldn't be a problem."

"A blind man has no need of a lantern, much less three. Stay out of sight. I'll attend to this."

What would once have been an unremarkable hike set Josiri's lungs heaving – a reminder that the indolence of city life was a poor inheritor of his wolf's-head days, hidden though they'd been. Worse, neither companion seemed troubled by the ascent, making it impossible to ask for a pause. So instead he trudged on until the forest gave way to the open crest, and ruined walls.

"Halt and be recognised!"

Josiri ignored Erashel's soft hiss of caution. Even in starlit gloom, Viktor's outsize frame was unmistakeable, as was the claymore resting at his shoulder. Conquered emotion made fresh assault, urging Josiri back the way he'd come. Malachi's chastisement drove him on.

"We come as friends, Lord Akadra." Formality made the greeting easier, as formality should.

"Josiri?" Viktor set the claymore aside and strode to greet them. "I thought never to see you again, brother."

Lantern light gave shape to a face Josiri remembered well. A touch leaner, black hair perhaps a touch more unkempt, but undeniably Viktor. Confident. Calm. If only he'd had the sense not to so quickly offer reminder of Calenne, and the ties of betrothal that bound them both.

"You know my companions? Arlanne Keldrov, Reeve of Ardva, and Lady Erashel Beral."

"Yes and no," Viktor offered Keldrov a clasped-fist salute and Erashel a bow. "Commander Keldrov and I speak from time to time. Lady Beral I know by reputation."

Struck by the strangest feeling that there were more eyes upon him than Viktor's, Josiri gazed up at the ruined tower. He saw nothing but vines and crumbling stonework.

"Dare I ask what brings you all to my humble home?" said Viktor. "And at such an hour?"

Josiri had intended to broach the matter softly, but for all his friendliness, Viktor exuded suspicion. Moreover, every delay now cost lives. "The Republic needs you."

"So Malachi sought to convince me. You are wrong, as he was wrong."

"Ahrad has fallen." Erashel's precision carried more authority than any decree.

Viktor's expression darkened, the familiar scowl creeping into place. "Impossible."

Josiri shook his head. "The fortress is lost, the Ravonn overrun."

"When?"

"Three days. We lost two to travel, and most of another while Erashel's contacts chased you down. You're a hard man to find."

"I was meant to be." Viktor closed his eyes and offered a short, reluctant nod. "You can tell me everything inside."

Josiri.

Calenne didn't believe at first, but the lantern light didn't lie. It *was* her brother. Heavier, perhaps. His face more lined than at last sight. Blond hair cut shorter than she remembered, but more in keeping with fashion.

He'd found her.

A flutter of panic drove her deeper into imperfect concealment, chagrined at her foolishness. If only she'd done as Viktor had suggested and kept out of sight. Now it was too late. Josiri had looked straight at her. He *knew*.

The hum of conversation heading for the open door. Rational thought returned. A clutch of steady breaths helped it settle. Yes, Josiri had looked straight at her, but *looking* wasn't the same as *seeing*. Could he truly have recognised her without giving some sign, even if he meant otherwise?

Her secret remained safe.

And yet ... Would it truly be so bad were matters otherwise? It had seemed so important to vanish into the confusion of Eskavord's burning. To be free of the responsibilities and legacies of the Trelan name. But though she hated herself for it, Calenne couldn't deny a pang of loss at seeing Josiri. However his dishonesty and his unwelcome attempts to shelter her had driven them apart, he was still her brother.

Maybe none of this deception was necessary. Maybe she was free to see his smile up close. To hold him and be held in return.

No. At least, not yet. Once revealed, the truth would fly out of her control. Josiri would be angry, and neither of them were at their best when tempers were strained. Better to wait, to see if this wasn't desire, but fleeting fancy.

Still, Calenne wondered at the reason for Josiri's arrival, for nothing of his words had reached her perch. Keldrov she knew, for they'd fought as allies at Davenwood – though the nervous woman of memory matched little the confident reeve of today. But the other woman, with chestnut hair cropped closer than Calenne's own? She was a stranger, if one who'd stood closer to Josiri than a stranger should. A lover? Perhaps. Then what had become of Anastacia?

Calenne shook the puzzle away. The demon's fate was hardly her concern. And if she weren't ready to reveal herself to Josiri, a chill night beckoned. If only Viktor had sent them away!

Recognising that sentiment as entirely at odds with temptation, she picked her way quietly across stone to the shelter of the southwest corner, and drew her cloak tight against the cold.

Viktor cleared space about the dim hearth and gathered chairs from the kitchen table. Keldrov hung back by the door, arms folded across her smoke-grey tabard. A bottle of wine was fetched from the pantry as a nod towards a host's duties, and decanted to goblets. With each guest thus furnished, Viktor raised his own high.

"To old friends."

The others made murmured rejoinder, though without enthusiasm. For all Josiri's masterful attempt to conceal distaste, it was impossible to forget how they'd parted, and why. Lady Beral's gaze held little friendliness, her opinion doubtless coloured by rumours concerning Eskavord's demise. As for Keldrov, her posture belonged to a woman who'd sooner be anywhere else. But a good soldier would hardly be comfortable drinking wine while the Republic shook to the tramp of Hadari boots.

"Tell me about Ahrad," said Viktor.

Josiri looked up from his goblet. "There's not much to tell. The Hadari brought a demon against the walls. The survivors are scattered across the Eastshires. Kai Saran has emptied the Empire against us. Rhaled. Icansae. Silsaria. Corvant. Probably more."

Viktor gazed at Josiri searching for any sign that he believed Saran's demon another fragment of Malatriant's legacy. He found none, and wasn't sure whether or not to be relieved. "You should have let me kill him," he rumbled. "His daughter too."

"Well I didn't, and the moment is lost."

"Who leads the defence? Rosa?"

Lady Beral shared a glance with Josiri. "Lady Orova was at Ahrad when it fell. She's among the missing. Malachi placed Izack in command."

Rosa. Another friend lost to war. A heavy blow for a man with few worthy of the name. Viktor grimaced sorrow away. Rosa was a survivor. Missing was not the same as dead.

"Malachi. Not the Council?"

Josiri's lips twisted a wry smile. "Malachi took the decision alone, and about time too."

Sour sentiment lingered. Viktor drove back temptation to enquire. He'd left the city for a reason. "Why are you here, brother?"

Josiri stared again into his wine.

"First Councillor Reveque believes it is time for you to come home, Lord Akadra," said Lady Beral. "The Republic needs a champion."

He addressed her without blinking. "It has one in Lady Orova."

She met his stare full force, without reserve. "And if she's dead?"

"I'm flattered you think one man can make a difference."

Viktor drained his goblet, wearier than words. It wasn't that the prospect of Ahrad's fall left him cold. Far from it. The first mantra he'd been taught as a squire was that while the Eskagard stood, so did the Republic. He'd shed blood to defend it, and stacked pyres high with the bodies of those who'd challenged that duty.

Moreover, he knew the lamentable state of the Republic's deeper defences, castles and watch posts left to decay out of penny-pinching and the belief Ahrad could never fall. Tressia itself was well-fortified. His father had recognised the danger. A rare example of Hadon Akadra thinking of others save himself. The city wall he'd laid down had long been completed. But elsewhere?

"May I say something?" said Keldrov.

Viktor nodded. "Of course."

"Tomorrow, I'm marching north with every blade I can spare, and some I can't. I've told my soldiers all I know, but rumours are spreading fast, and what truth I have pales by comparison. Demons. Witches. Some are saying that the Goddess Ashana marches with the shadowthorns, beguiling honest souls to treachery." She set her empty goblet on the kitchen table and stood to attention, shoulders back and gaze level. "I've Davenwood veterans among them. A few of Captain Halvor's phoenixes, too – those who escaped the purges. One man would make a difference to them, if he's the right man. And to me."

How far she'd come since Davenwood where Viktor had placed her under Kurkas' command for fear she'd flee at the first sight of an Immortal's golden scales. "The problem is not that we won that battle, but *how* it was won."

"I don't follow." The first anger gleamed in her eyes. "If I'm honest, I don't much care. A year ago, you came to the Southshires and asked a beaten people to take up arms, because no one else could. They gave everything. This is how you'd honour that sacrifice? Skulking on a hill as the Republic drowns? I don't—"

"Arlanne. Erashel." Josiri spoke without looking up from his goblet. "Might I speak with Lord Akadra alone?"

The women shared glances united in suspicion.

Lady Beral nodded. "If that's what you want. We'll be outside."

Josiri didn't speak while they withdrew. Nor did he for some time thereafter, but sat and swirled the wine about his goblet.

Eventually, Viktor tired of the game. "It's poor manners to request a meeting, then fall asleep."

Josiri looked up. "I was just thinking how much fate hates me."

"It's kind to few."

"After all," Josiri continued as if he hadn't spoken. "Bad enough that you hounded my mother to her death. That you took my sister from me. That you burned my home. Little by little you broke me, Viktor. And now I'm to beg you to do what we both know you must? Perhaps it's not fate that hates me, but you."

Viktor winced. "That isn't true."

"And yet you make me beg."

"This isn't about you, Josiri."

"Then what is this about? You never told Rosa, and you never told me."

"I *tried* to tell you, after Eskavord. You refused to hear me."

"I was angry. I'm still angry. But I'll listen, if you'll speak."

Viktor rose and stared out the kitchen window. "My magic. It's of the Dark, as Malatriant was of the Dark. At Eskavord, she offered me her legacy. I was to be her heir. Lumestra forgive me, but I almost accepted. But for you . . . " He shook his head, striving for sundered memory. Too much of that dark day had become jumbled by distance, and from no small want of forgetting. Fire in the darkness, and a gleam of dagger's steel. "A piece of her magic resides alongside my own, and I cannot decide whether I am its jailer, or its captive. I know only that it wants to be free. I dare not let that happen."

Josiri sat back in his chair and shook his head in scorn. "Why not?"

You are to be my heir. For a heartbeat, Viktor was back in the charnel of Eskavord, Malatriant crowing her triumph.

"Have you listened to nothing I've said?" he snapped. "It comes from the Tyrant Queen."

"If I stood with my loved ones behind me and spears ahead, do you suppose I'd pass up a sword out of loathing for its previous master? For that's where we're placed. All of us."

"This isn't a sword. It's the Dark. No good can come of its use."

"Then don't use it."

"As easy as that?"

"I imagine not. But you once lectured me that living for a lost cause was sometimes necessary, no matter how difficult. I'd hate to think you'd forgotten your own lesson."

"I *am* living with my lost cause."

Josiri cast theatrically about the kitchen's confines. "Living? Clinging to a hillside, playing at farmer? This isn't you, Viktor. This isn't what you're *for*. You're a soldier, and your people need you. Not your magic, not the Dark, but *you*."

A moving argument. Powerful, but for the fact that Armund af Garna had recently wielded similar and tempted disaster. "You don't know what you're asking."

"Maybe. But despite everything, I trust you. After all, you're the only family I have left."

Was Calenne close enough to hear? Had the words brought laughter, or a smile? How strange that the closer he and Josiri came, the faster their orbits pulled them apart. Josiri had the right of it. Fate hated him. It hated them both.

"My answer must still be no."

"I see." Josiri clambered to his feet. "Malachi had to shame me into coming here. The city's a mess – the city's always a mess – and hundreds of my people are missing. Every moment I spend here makes me feel more a traitor for abandoning them! And if that weren't enough? The last thing I wanted was to speak to you again. I just wanted this done so I could get back, but I can't. Arlanne barely has a regiment, and their ears are buzzing with horrific tales of what's happening to the east. So when they march, I'm marching with them. I have to, because I can't cling to a hillside while the Republic burns."

"Josiri—"

He strode closer, eyes taut. "I'm not done. You once called me a spoilt child. A coward clinging to a worthless throne. A man without the courage of his own convictions. You were right. You forced me to do better. To *be* better. And here I am, urging you to do the same." He sighed. "I don't know whether to laugh or cry."

How to make him see? To make him understand? "What can I say?"

"Say 'yes'. Say that you'll be the Viktor Akadra I remember. The man who fights for his people. Who doesn't know how to lose."

"And if I'm not a man any longer, but his afterimage in the Dark?"

"Then I'll stop you. Whatever it costs me." Josiri shrugged. "For whatever that's worth."

So he *did* understand. Maybe Josiri was the better man, after all. A realisation that should have occasioned shame roused only pride. "More than words can convey."

For the first time, Viktor allowed himself to consider the possibility Josiri was right. That it hadn't been fortune that had kept the shadow at heel, but choice. And if he'd conquered one lapse – two, counting the wolves at Wintertide – then why not again?

And if he didn't go – if he didn't *try* – what then? How could he be worth a friendship that had somehow endured through deceit and heartbreak? How could he look Calenne in the eye – Calenne, who'd almost died defending a Republic that had only ever shown her scorn? How was he any different to his own father, who had lived his youth a hero, but his later years twisted by loss?

"You win, brother."

Josiri narrowed his eyes. "*What* do I win?"

"Allow me one last night clinging to my hillside. I'll join you at Ardva at dawn."

"Truly?"

"Have my promises been so poor they now invite question?" Viktor forced a smile. "I will fight, so long as I have your word that you'll stop me, should need arise."

He held out his hand. After brief hesitation, Josiri took it. "You have it . . . brother."

Viktor drew him into an embrace and sought solace in their moment of accord – doomed to briefness, as all such moments had ever been.

Because he knew he'd have to break Josiri's trust yet again.

Thirty-Three

The rain continued as the sun fell below the horizon. Sodden funeral pyres refused to light without the help of stinking crestis-oil. Beyond the ring of Immortals, her stride stiff and her white robes still fouled by blood, Sera moved among the flames. At each pyre, she dipped her hand to the birchwood box clutched to her chest, and scattered silver dust to sanctify the dead.

Greasy smoke billowed through the trees and away across the northern valley, bearing their spirits to an Evermoon emptied of a goddess' warmth. No songs accompanied their passing. Hearts were too full. Melanna's more than most, for were the deaths not of her making? That of Elene, her sister in moonlight, most of all. That ache ran deeper than wounds from Melanna's brawl, the pain eased and flesh knitted by the lunassera's ministrations. In all ways, it refused to yield.

She lost track of how long she stood on the span of stump-dotted mud between sullen encampment and pyre-grounds. Death in battle was a warrior's lot, but this? Orova had set a snare, and she, blinded by notions of honour, had blundered into it.

The hurt ran deeper than the tally of dead. Not least for the precision of the Tressian ambush. Fewer than a dozen handmaidens remained, and none unwounded. Too few to guarantee all but the bloodiest success at Vrasdavora's inevitable siege. Melanna found her spirit divided. The warleader mourned the strategic loss. The woman mourned the dead. Each scorned the other for dwelling on irrelevance. Only in hatred for Orova were they united, and with every flicker of flame swore revenge.

Her last observance made, Sera made her way up the hillside, her steps faltering. Careless of the indignity, Melanna ran to steady her. Bright stains oozed through silken robes as blood thwarted bandages beneath.

"I do not need your aid, Ashanal."

Sera pushed away. Beneath the silver half-mask, eyes welled with loss. Melanna let her go. How much of the defiance was born of heartache? How much from disdain for a princessa who'd led her sisters to disaster?

"I'm sorry, Sera."

A sad smile. "I blame the archers for their arrows, Ashanal, not you."

The words might have brought Melanna comfort, had she shared their sentiment.

"Melanna Saranal!"

Melanna turned her back on the pyre-grounds as Naradna's cry echoed away. Bruises protested even that slight movement. The slope behind crowded with Icansae scarlet. Not the brothers Andwar alone, but a dozen Immortals, and a handful of others whose silver torcs at throat and wrist marked them as chieftains.

Melanna's heart, already at low ebb, sank further still. "Prince Naradna."

He halted a dozen paces away. The sword, drawn with a flourish, he thrust deep into the mud. Steel shone beneath the stars.

"It has been a day of needless death," said Naradna. "The Goddess' daughter, dead. Her handmaidens, dead. Our kinsmen, dead. All because familiarity blinded you. I say you are unfit to lead, and so does my sword."

The formal challenge. Probable from the moment her father had given command of an army to a "mere" woman. Inevitable after the day's sorrows.

"She does not answer to you, Naradna Andwar." Sera's breathy words lacked Naradna's force, but none of their certainty. "She is Ashanal."

"Then let the Goddess speak in her defence," Naradna shouted. "And if the Goddess does not, let steel do so."

Voices murmured agreement. Melanna gazed about tent and firepit, taking stock of faces not hidden by helm or distance. Aeldran, holding customary position at his brother's side, seemed little enamoured of the prospect of bloodletting. In this, he was alone. Not just among the men of Icansae, but those in Rhalesh green as well. Too many old grievances at broken tradition now given chance of airing.

Or perhaps she made a convenient scapegoat. Orova had humiliated them all. Easier to seek blame without than within.

"I see the Andwar tradition of regicide flowers even in the dark." Haldrane stood apart, as was his wont, arm propped over a wooden crutch. A face pale in the firelight reminded of how much blood he'd lost before an Icansae shieldsman had stemmed the flow. "If your pride's hurting, Prince Naradna, you'll find recompense to the west."

Bitter laughter danced beneath the stars, proof that not all agreed with Naradna's challenge. It made no matter. Refusing the challenge played to the resentment of those who believed a woman could not lead.

And besides, after enduring a beating at Orova's hands, Melanna very much wanted to hear the arrogant, self-serving Icansae prince scream.

"Your sword lies, Naradna Andwar. As you lie. As your father and grandfather before you were liars. I will teach you the truth."

Vrasdavora's garrison quarters improved little with the cessation of rain and the fall of night. Darkness only added spite to the Ash Wind howling about the stones. The wind across the mountains held different character to that over the ocean. Even an open gale, its turbulent seas like plunging cliffs, lacked malice. Not here, where every gust carried keening spirits north from Darkmere's haunted ruins. Sevaka closed the door, muffling the imagined voices.

Rosa's features were unreadable in the lantern's sparking glow. Like much of the adjutant's quarters, long abandoned by a thinning garrison, "functional" was the most generous description of the lantern's condition. Castellan Paradan – in reality, a lieutenant of the 1st on his maiden command, and desperately intimidated to have the Council Champion within his walls – had offered up his own quarters. Rosa had refused.

"How is it out there?"

"Cold. Wet. But the troops seem cheerful enough. You gave them a victory."

"A victory? A few hundred dead?" Rosa stared back out the window. "The shadowthorns could lose that twenty times over and match us blade for blade."

Sevaka winced. The walls were up, and she on the outside once again. "We slaughtered the pale-witches. You should be celebrating."

"The last time we celebrated, Ahrad fell."

"There's celebrating, and there's *celebrating*." Sevaka shrugged. "Borderers are watching the road. Thaldvar talked of causing the shadowthorn pickets discomfort. We'll have warning."

"Thaldvar takes too many risks."

"This from you?" Sevaka's fingertips brushed the covers of a bed not yet slept in. She looped her arms over Rosa's shoulders. Muscles tensed beneath her forearms and gradually eased. "You ask how it is out there? I'm more concerned with how things are in here."

Rosa's hand found hers and held it tight. "They're fine, truly."

"Try again. With conviction."

The room went still. Only the sound of breathing – Rosa's deeper and more ponderous – gave challenge to the angry winds.

"She told me she saved my life."

Sevaka frowned. "What?"

"The princessa. It was her at Tevar Flood. She made me this way. When she told me . . . I lost control. The world drowned in red. I wanted to break her apart."

Sevaka doubted the words of a shadowthorn princessa held much truth. However, it wasn't what the Saranal had said, but what Rosa *believed*. "Would that have been so bad? She's the Emperor's heir."

"Perhaps not, had I chosen it. But I didn't. The decision chose me, and I was trapped in the saddle, along for the ride." She punched the wall. Dust tricked across bunched fingers. Her voice cracked, the hurt resonating in Sevaka's heart. "I'm never at my best when acting on instinct. Too arrogant, Viktor once told me, and never enough thought to consequence. I've been worse this past year. I'm drowning in anger and darkness. No wonder the Raven wants me for his queen."

Chill fingers danced along Sevaka's spine. "How can I help?"

Rosa unwound from the embrace and kissed her. "You already have. You keep me in the light."

"All being equal, I'd rather we were both elsewhere." She sighed. "I wish you saw yourself as I see you."

"I'm glad the reverse isn't true."

"Enough." Indulgence having done nothing to disperse bleak mood, Sevaka moved to the door. "I'd hoped we might take advantage of the rare moment of peace and privacy. But you need to see yourself reflected in the eyes of others, rather than your own thoughts – dark, bright or otherwise."

A duel beneath moonlight. As a girl, Melanna had thought the idea romantic. The clash of blades, honour satisfied and worth proven. Not now. Standing in the mud, with the tarnished moon a reminder of losses borne, and the air still sour with pyre-smoke.

Naradna offered no comment as the circle of Immortals and shieldsmen closed, forging an arena of flesh and bone fifteen strides across. An arena in which steel would prove truth.

Melanna gripped her sword, and wished she still bore the Goddess' blade. That a piece of Ashana would be with her in victory or defeat. But it was far to the north with her father.

Her father. What would he say? He'd certainly chide her for not nominating a champion in her stead. But then he'd gone without a champion for over a year, choosing that his own blade should speak for his honour. Beyond that? He'd urge her to win, or to die well.

"The challenge is issued and accepted." At the arena's centre, Aeldran's morose expression betrayed unhappiness. "Let the matter be decided, and Ashana show mercy upon the defeated."

He bowed and stepped clear, a gap opening up in the arena wall to accommodate him. Naradna advanced, sword held at guard. Melanna strode to meet him. The day's doubts slipped away.

Naradna sprang with a cry, sword slashing at Melanna's head. She caught the strike a span above her crossguard and drove it aside. Too easily. A test of her speed.

His second blow arrived in realisation's shadow. A low thrust, aimed to cheat the decoyed blade and pierce the scales at her waist. Melanna jerked aside and back-cut at Naradna's shoulder. Steel scraped across golden scale. The prince retreated, and the first cheers split the night sky.

Mud shifting under her feet, Melanna pressed her advantage. Her sword flashed out to left and right, seeking to lure Naradna's blade aside as she herself had been lured. He gave ground, parries smooth and measured, never once offering opening worthy of the risk, nor taking a chance of his own. He was faster than she could have believed, his blade reaching its destination before hers arrived.

Only when his back was a pace distant from the arena wall did Naradna again go on the offensive. To kinsmen's rousing cheers, he took Melanna's sword on his armoured forearm, chancing that the thick scales would hold, and lunged.

Melanna's evasion came too late. Steel pierced scale and scraped hot across her flank. As she staggered back, Naradna held the bloodied sword high, and cheers redoubled.

"Do you yield, princessa?" he sneered.

Melanna straightened, undershirt already hot and clammy about her waist. To yield was impossible, but their brief exchange had laid bare unwelcome truths. Naradna was faster. He hadn't endured a beating at Orova's hands. The longer the duel went on, the likelier her loss. Whether it ended in death or defeat, the life she'd striven for would be gone.

She sprang, the frustrations of the day spilling free as wordless cry. Naradna's sword shuddered, the force of the blow driving him back a pace. Grim delight blazed. Faster he may have been, but she was stronger. And she'd endured more to stand in that muddy circle than Naradna would ever know.

Abandoning finesse, Melanna gripped her sword in both hands and hammered at him. Naradna gave ground before the overhand first blow. A metallic hiss accompanied the second, the surprise of a man who'd seen only her slightness, and missed the strength of her roots.

The third drove him to his knees.

On the fourth, he repeated his earlier gambit, seeking to sweep the blade aside with his scaled forearm. Melanna twisted her sword as it descended. Instead of skittering across scales, her steel sliced beneath and came away red.

Naradna screamed. His counter-thrust faltered as pain scattered his balance. Before it faded, Melanna had her sword-point at the join of gorget and mask. She seized the crossguard of his sword. Resistance faded as she slid her own forward through padded silk until it met the resistance of flesh. She flung Naradna's sword away.

Cheers went silent. Others redoubled. Melanna let all fade before speaking. "Yield!"

Naradna met her gaze, eyes alive with hatred beneath the mask. "Not to you."

"Then you choose death."

"Gladly."

Reluctance boiled away. Naradna had brought this on himself. "By your deeds in the circle, you are proven a liar. May the Goddess treat you—"

"Wait!"

Aeldran broke the circle. "Spare my brother, Ashanal."

A growl of displeasure erupted about the arena.

Naradna's eyes came alive with humiliation. "No!"

Aeldran knelt before Melanna, head bowed. "You owe me your life, Ashanal. Your life, or at least your freedom. Spare my brother, and I will consider the debt paid."

Temptation remained to ram the sword home, to remove Naradna Andwar from her ever-lengthening list of woes. But ... Aeldran had spoken true. Accepting his offer brought no shame. At least, not on her. The only thing worse than to be beaten by a woman was to be spared by one. But that wasn't enough. Naradna's humiliation had to run deeper. Melanna stared at the beatific mask, the mask that spared a scarred, bitter soul from the scrutiny of his fellows.

"You may have your brother's life." Melanna let her sword fall and drew her dagger from her belt. "But his face belongs to me. I give it as a gift to the world."

Naradna made to back away. "No!"

Melanna tugged away his helm. She slit leather straps, and the golden mask came cleanly into her hands. Naradna hunched, fingers splayed in a vain attempt to conceal his scars. Except there were no scars. The mask had been a shield not against vanity, but against truth.

Naradna – who had resented her from the first – wasn't a man, but a fine-featured woman, her dark hair cropped close.

Hushed silence overtook the crowd. Melanna let the mask fall. She saw her own outrage reflected around the circle, and never stronger than upon the faces of those who'd supported Naradna's challenge. Bad enough to be a woman with pretensions to war. Worse still to wend a trail of deceit. Death would have shamed Naradna alone. Revelation tarnished Icansae entire.

Melanna despised the bigotry, but her own outrage remained. Not because of Naradna's sex, but because of her deception, and the endless lies that had made it possible. When this day was but a memory, none would recall that the Empress-to-be had vanquished unworthy challenge. They would recall only that a woman had lied.

She glared at Aeldran. "Did you know?"

He hung his head.

Mclanna turned her gaze on each chieftain in turn. None returned it. She beckoned to Sera. "Take her away. Treat her with respect, see that her needs are met, but give her no opportunity to take her own life."

"Yes, Ashanal. And what of the prince?"

Aeldran, who by complicity was as guilty as his sister? "The matter is settled. Let him do as he wishes."

Thirty-Four

Melanna found neither sleep nor solace in darkness. Her wound had long since been stitched tight, the pain reduced to numbness by bethanis tincture. She told herself both pain and anger were in the past, settled and done.

And yet ...

She'd spent her life fighting the same traditions that would now destroy Naradna. Did that call for empathy? Naradna had made herself an enemy from the very first. More, she'd dishonoured herself through deception, as Orova had dishonoured herself by promising truce as a ruse. Naradna's fate was of her own making.

Wasn't it?

Finding no answers in the dark, Melanna dressed and took station at the flaps of her tent, staring out into the renewed drizzle.

Even burdened by a makeshift crutch, Haldrane arrived at her shoulder without a whisper of sound. "Excessive introspection seldom ends well. It is poison disguised as balm."

She grunted her surprise – at humble tone as much as wisdom. Haldrane had ever been one of her staunchest critics. He, as much as any, had fought the idea of a woman taking the throne.

"Did you know about Naradna?"

Haldrane scratched his chin. "A woman in the army. Preposterous."

"I'm in no mood for jests."

"The Icansae have always been ... challenging. What agents I have among their number do not, alas, touch upon the royal family. Maggad had a gift for paranoia." He shrugged, the motion made awkward by the crutch. "You were not to know."

"Kind words for the upstart princessa?"

"For the Emperor's heir, *savim*. All else is irrelevant."

Was it truly that simple? "Is that why you took an arrow in my stead?"

"My duty and my privilege." A sardonic smile blunted humility. "I serve the Empire, and the House of Saran *is* the Empire. To protect one is to protect the other."

"Then I command your full loyalty?"

"I am dismayed you ever thought otherwise, *savim*." He crooked an eyebrow. "As for the arrow? The more I think on it, the likelier it was meant for me. I fear I have made enemies everywhere."

An understatement. Melanna could name without trying three princes of the Golden Court who would have gladly seen Haldrane dead, save for the repercussions. Men with secrets seldom appreciated those accomplished in unveiling them.

"You may be right," she replied. "Orova made claim of seeking my capture."

"To force your father's surrender?" He tucked his crutch closer. "You have always been his weakness."

She scowled. "Perhaps I remain so. We cannot pass Vrasdavora. Nor can I retreat. A siege is our only answer, but the war might well be over before it is done. My father could die a thousand deaths while the garrison starve themselves into the Raven's grasp."

"At least the Raven showed no interest in today's business."

"Orova claimed they had no alliance."

"And you believed her?"

"Once, perhaps. No more. She is as much an obstacle as the fortress and its constructs. Worse, I made her so. The Goddess warned me, and I didn't listen."

Haldrane tutted. "I counselled you against introspection. It blinds you."

"I'm not infallible, Haldrane. Not tonight."

"You number your problems in the hundreds. A garrison of flesh and blood, guarded by soldiers of magic and metal, all led by a woman who has proven herself tenacious. I see only two. The woman, and the proctor whose will drives the constructs. If they were gone ... "

Melanna shook her head. "You ask for miracles. I know these constructs. They reason well enough that the proctor need only change their
orders in challenging circumstance. And Orova is more than tenacious.
She cannot die. I don't even think she feels pain."

"The assault on a fortress is not a challenging circumstance? As for
Orova . . . " Haldrane held up fingers, and ticked them off one by one.
"Ashana's Huntsman ran her through at Ahrad. She came to Soraved by
cart. In the battle that followed, she was hardly to full vigour. Perhaps
she cannot die, as you say, but she can be removed for a time."

Hope drove back the night's chill. "How?"

"I have agents everywhere. Not all of them willing, I admit. But willing
enough. Silver burns the divine. I imagine it will harm Orova no less."

"Assassination?"

"An ugly word, more suited to pedants than princessas."

She bit back a swell of anger. First the assault on Ahrad without declaration of war. Then Elspeth's slaughter of the prisoners. Now this. "You'd
have us discard all honour?"

"Can there be honour in dealing with a woman who breaks a truce?"

Contradiction emerged from the mire. Not Melanna's, rather
Haldrane's. Lost in the tumult of the day, now dredged to the surface.
"You have agents everywhere."

"An overstatement, but in practical terms . . . ?"

"Orova told me Lord Akadra had vanished into exile and holds no
influence. I cannot help but wonder how my father's spymaster, who sees
so much, made no mention."

"So it is for a lowly functionary to gainsay a goddess?"

"If the Goddess errs, yes."

He smoothed his goatee. "I fear you overestimate my courage, *savim*."

"And I *know* you don't think me so foolish as to believe that." She tore
her gaze from the pyres. "I'll have the truth, Haldrane."

To her surprise, he offered an approving smile. "Yes, I knew. One does
not let a man like Viktor Akadra stray beyond one's sight."

"Then this is all for nothing." Melanna closed her eyes against sudden
dizziness. "The Dark has no claim on Tressia."

"Nothing?" Haldrane shook his head. "Ahrad is gone. The Republic
is in disarray. We have the opportunity to sweep Tressia from the map."

"You deceived me! You deceived my father!"

He shook his head. "A child's rationale, scrawled in bright colours against the world's murk."

"Not so! I fight for the Goddess. To free Tressia from the Dark!"

"And did you fight for the Goddess last Sommertide, when we marched on the Southshires? Did you fight to cast out the Dark? How grateful the common folk of Trelszon and Kreska and Davenwood must have felt for your largesse. A shame we never told them they died for their own good." He waved a dismissive hand. "War has ever been our way, *savim*. You know its power better than any – only the justification changes. But not mine. The Empire will never be safe while a Tressian banner flies. Plunder? Glory? The grace of the divine? I leave these to others."

She snapped her eyes open, too angry almost even to speak. "My father will hear of this."

"Your father knows."

Impossibly, the void in Melanna's stomach yawned wider. How easily she'd spoken of discarding honour. There'd been none in the endeavour from the first. "No."

"We spoke on the matter many times. You mustn't think him averse to saving the Tressians from the Dark. But he's spent his life fighting to keep the throne and the House of Saran as one. Dark or no, the Goddess offered opportunity to bind the kingdoms of the Golden Court." He shrugged. "As I said, you have always been his weakness."

Melanna clenched her fingers and sought some flaw in Haldrane's words. "Why tell me this?"

His eyebrows arched. "Because you asked, *savim*. You are the Emperor's heir. My voice, and my eyes, will ever be at your command."

Wrath boiled through the void, fed by loss and humiliation. It urged her to strike Haldrane – to banish that infuriating, conceited expression. A horrible, gnawing truth held her back: Haldrane had told her little she'd not already known, or would have seen, had she not blinded herself out of love for her father, and for a goddess who had never made claim to infallibility. For all his cynicism, Haldrane's stance wasn't without foundation. The Empire had to come first, whether for spymaster, Emperor . . . or heir.

Anger receded. Not banished, but chained. A child he'd called her, and perhaps she was. "If you wish to go on serving the Empire from this side of the mists, it would be better if I didn't hear your voice this side of dawn. Am I understood?"

Haldrane's lips parted as if to speak, then twisted to a wry smile. Offering a bow made awkward by his crutch, he limped away.

Naradna did not rise, but remained seated on the edge of the narrow bed. Having been instructed to empty it of anything with which the captive could do herself harm, Sera had taken the simple step of removing all save the barest comfort.

"Why are you here, Saranal?"

Naradna sounded more weary than defiant, a shrunken figure in silken robes. Without armour to disguise her form, Melanna recognised a woman more like her than not. Older by a few years, as Aeldran was older. Perhaps a shade darker of feature and more muscular of build. Eyes blue where her own were green. But she was otherwise no less the sister in aspect than she should have been in purpose.

Naradna snorted. "The immaculate Melanna Saranal, lost for words. It's almost worth it. I ask again: why are you here?"

The speck of sympathy bled away. "I don't know. I suppose I want to understand."

"What's to understand? You of all people shouldn't have to ask."

"You think we're the same?"

"We seek the same ends."

"You lied. You claimed to be someone you were not."

"I am Naradna. Who I was before burned alongside my elder brother."

"You killed him?"

"He died, as did so many, from my grandfather's ambition."

The unmourned King Maggad. How often it all returned to him. "Some of the tales my father told me ... some of what I saw ... I don't know why my own grandfather kept him so close."

Naradna grunted. "Ceredic was afraid. Better a tethered wolf than one running free."

"My grandfather feared nothing."

But Melanna's defence was automatic, and ill-matched memory. At the end, her grandfather had been a haunted, unsteady soul, reliant on the Golden Court more than in command over it. He'd never have understood her desires while still flesh. But perhaps now he walked immortal Evermoon, his eyes would be open to all that she was, and all she strove to be.

The expected sneer never came. "A good man should always fear a wolf. Especially one never content with his lot. My own sire died to my grandfather's paranoia, *and* two of my uncles. Victims of a plot that never existed outside delusion. Soon after, Mother died with her dagger at Grandfather's throat, cut down by his Immortals."

Naradna's eyes lost focus. Then, with swift shake of the head, she rallied. "He'd have ordered the deaths of myself and my brothers too, even though we were not of age. But Mother attempted her assassination before the Golden Court. Even in failure, she placed us plainly in the Emperor's eye, and Grandfather wasn't yet ready to challenge him. She was branded mad, and we were sent into exile at Tarrabesk. My elder brother died soon after, carried off by fever." She shrugged. "It was a simple enough matter to take his place."

"Why?"

"Why do you think?" snapped Naradna. "With his death, I became Grandfather's heir – or I would have done so, were I not a girl. I swore I would not let the Icansae throne pass to another. It was to be my revenge. Aeldran agreed."

"I'm surprised."

"I'm the elder. He's always respected that. Our retainers were loyal. They walked the bazaars, telling all who would listen that the Princessa Andwaral had succumbed to illness in her brother's place. They rejoiced that Naradna lived, though so disfigured by sickness that he never again left the estate without a mask. Eventually, Grandfather's paranoia so turned the houses of Icansae against him that he returned us to honour in exchange for a promise of support. And I set out to prove myself in the only way that has ever mattered, in the hopes that he might declare me his heir."

"Then Maggad died."

"Eventually." Naradna offered a thin smile. "He screamed for days before his heart rotted black. And better he did, or he'd be Emperor in your father's place, and you mourned as his bride of brief moonlight."

"You killed him?"

"I knew of it, and said nothing."

"Because he refused to name you his heir?" sneered Melanna.

"Because silence was a gift I owed my brother."

Melanna found the answer to be no answer at all. Aeldran had murdered Maggad, even though it put his sister's plans in jeopardy? More, she'd permitted him to do so?

"Why?"

"I know what folk say of us." Naradna folded her arms. "The Andwars are driven, by which they mean 'selfish'. Clever, by which they mean 'deceitful'. And above all, tragic – which is kinder than deeming us bleak to the point of madness. I am all those things, as were my father and my grandfather. Aeldran is not. When he learned our grandfather commissioned the attempt to assassinate your father—"

"That was Maggad?"

For a heartbeat, Melanna was back beneath the birch trees of Ashana's temple, her father's life ebbing away. She drew down a deep breath. Another memory stirred. The Icansae prince who'd been swiftest to come to their aid. Aeldran. And today. His unhappiness at the challenge . . .

Naradna nodded. "A nest of outcast vranakin dwell in the gateway slums at Bazharan. Grandfather used their talents often. My brother believes in loyalty. He would have died for the Emperor that day . . . or for his heir."

Melanna scowled, conflicted. "Poison isn't honourable."

Naradna spat. "Some people aren't worth honour."

Expedience so lately echoed by Haldrane roused quiescent anger. "I take no lessons in honour from someone who bears a name not her own."

"But it *is* my name. I made it mine." She shrugged. "What does it matter otherwise?"

"Everything. We *are* our family. Our sires and grandsires spanning back to the Empire's foundation. Back even to the Age of Kings. What you've done dishonours them all!"

"Can you even hear yourself?" Naradna laughed and shook her head. "Our sires and grandsires, as if they're all that count. What of my mother, Saranal, and hers, and her grandmother before that? Do I dishonour them? At least I remember they exist."

The accusation drove Melanna forward. "When my mother looks down from Evermoon, she sees that I live without pretence. I broke tradition and held to my path, even when swords barred my way." She halted, muscles knotted tight but determined not to give Naradna the satisfaction of a raised voice. "You've no idea what I sacrificed."

"You *are* blind." Naradna sprang to her feet, eyes gleaming. "The poor Rhalesh princessa, with no one to support her wayward dreams save her imperial father and the Goddess of Evermoon. I had only my brother. Do you know what my grandfather would have done to me had he known the truth?"

Melanna's anger curdled. Tradition decreed no specific punishment for a woman who sought war – an oversight that offered a horrifying degree of freedom for a man like Maggad Andwar. In that, at least, Naradna was correct. Melanna's father *had* been her shield, as had Ashana. She'd fought for much, but had been given far more.

"He's in no position to harm you now."

"Yes." Flat satisfaction belied Naradna's grimace. "And with mourning done, my cousins see the empty throne as theirs for the taking. *My* throne. *My* birthright. They'd never yield to a woman, but a prince, gilded with triumph? You know the power that holds. It might even break tradition once the truth stood revealed. Harder by far to remove a queen than cage a princessa. I have no desire to live out my days as a man."

The words rekindled fading anger. "All you've done is reaffirm everything tradition upholds. When men look back on this day, they won't see an heir fighting for her birthright. They'll see a liar who holds honour second to ambition. You've proved that women have no place in battle, or upon a throne. They'll wield your deception as a weapon against any who follow you."

"I should think of others?" Shoulders heaving with silent mirth, Naradna hung her head. "Two seasons since your father's coronation and your own heirdom set in stone. In all that time, you have done nothing other than for yourself." She sat heavily on the bed and leaned back, hands splayed behind as support. "A word from you would have changed it all. You said nothing. You changed nothing. You claim to have broken tradition. You *ignored* it. You cannot blame the rest of us for seeking our own paths. Honour is a privilege enjoyed by those free to indulge it."

"Wait ... *Us?*"

"You thought I was the only one?" Naradna snorted. "Armour hides much. An Immortal's helm hides more."

"You lie."

"It suits you to believe yourself remarkable, but do you really believe that in all the generations of Empire, you were unique? That when families send spears as fealty, a daughter might not take the father's place, or a sister her brother's? A warchief's gatherer sees only armour. Ample opportunity for a woman to fulfil familial duty, or to seek war out of desire."

"I'd *know.*"

"And who would tell you? The women whose families must bear the shame if they are discovered? Their comrades? You know the power of a bond forged in battle. Bodies are burned before the truth can be known." She shrugged. "And when they are not? Would our royal peers admit to knowing women fought in their ranks, or would they keep it hidden?"

Melanna grimaced. Of course the Golden Court would keep the matter suppressed. It only made the fate of the discovered women – if they existed – bleaker still. Another truth her father had held from her? Coming so close behind Haldrane's revelations about the Droshna ...

"If this is so secret, how do you know?"

"I am a deceiver," Naradna replied. "I recognise deception in others."

"How many?"

"Two or three in every hundred. I suspect the number would increase tenfold overnight, if not for tradition's weight."

"You really believe that?"

"How many boys die in battle because they're not yet ready to be men? How many families would sooner send a girl, if she'd more chance of coming home alive? How many daughters long for the chance to prove themselves a worthy inheritor?" Naradna sighed. "There are legacies beyond crowns and kingdoms, Saranal, and nothing secures them so well as a sword. Or do you consider yourself so far above the people you'd rule that you consider their wants alien to your own?"

Naradna's words held too much truth. Worse, they revealed how narrow Melanna had set her sights. As the Emperor's heir, she'd influence and power. She'd used none of it.

"You say I've failed," she murmured. "You're right. But so have you."

Naradna snorted. "A petty claim can't shield you from the truth."

"I've been blind. I *will* do better. But you? You knew this all along, and still you lied. Instead of standing tall, you hid. You should have come to me. I'd have supported you. We'd have changed things. Now? You're just a liar, proven in defeat, and no help to anyone."

"If that's what you want."

"It's what you've chosen."

Naradna leapt to her feet, face colouring and eyes narrowed to slits. For a moment, she seemed poised to pounce, even knowing death would follow. Or perhaps, Melanna allowed, that would be the point of the attack, rather than its consequence.

One heartbeat, two, and the fury slipped from Naradna's expression, if not her limbs. "So what happens now?"

"I confess I don't know. I've greater concerns than you." Melanna bottled up the day's weariness, knowing it had driven her to harshness. "I want your promise you'll not add to them."

"And why should I give it?"

"Because if you don't, I shall make it known that your brother knew who and what you were. That he is complicit in your deceptions and the death of your grandfather."

"The warchiefs will abandon him."

"I imagine so."

"You *need* him."

Melanna nodded. The men of Rhaled followed her out of fealty. Without the Princes Andwar, there remained a good chance the Icansae would slip away. "Then it's in both our interests I have your promise."

Naradna shot a murderous look and sank to the bed. When she spoke, defiance had fled her tone, leaving her sounding as weary as Melanna felt. "Everything I said of Aeldran is true, Saranal. If you harm him, you only weaken yourself."

Taking the words as agreement, Melanna left the tent. She found Sera waiting outside.

"Ashanal?"

"She is to remain a prisoner for now. She'll give no trouble."

The night air banished cobwebs from Melanna's thoughts, but their passing left her weary. *For now*. How long was that? And what would happen after?

"She told me many curious tales. I don't know which I believe, and which I don't." Melanna, careful that her words wouldn't carry to the guards, watched Sera closely. "Strangest was a claim that there are women in the army, fighting as men. I told her I didn't believe it. After all, the lunassera tend the dying and the dead. They would know, wouldn't they? *You* would know."

Sera dipped her head. Behind the mask, her face remained as inscrutable as ever. "I cannot break the confidence of the dead, Ashanal."

The answer was no answer, and yet told Melanna everything. *Women do not bear swords*. The tradition that had defined her adult life, and yet was conditional truth. How had the lunassera – demoted from bodyguards to physicians until her own rise – borne it as long as they had, knowing that other women fought and died in a manner forbidden them?

Sera had known. The Golden Court knew. Haldrane certainly did. *A woman in the army. Preposterous*. His sly joke was now twice the barb. Honour. Tradition. Just words, set aside whenever need was there, a blind eye turned to suit the beholder's needs. The world, so black and white an hour before, drowned in grey. Even Naradna, broken and misguided though she was, saw it clearer.

"Ashanal?" Sera's lips twisted. "I'm not sure what to say."

Sera, who'd lost so many sisters to the pyre. To Tressian deceit. *Honour is a privilege enjoyed by those free to indulge it*. What use was that privilege when others prospered without?

Melanna embraced her, the path ahead now shining clear beneath the moon, and went in search of Haldrane.

As had become habit, Rosa left Sevaka sleeping and took to Vrasdavora's ramparts. She threaded her way between the sentries on the east wall. Little enough to see, but it cheered her to find no slackness of watch. As when Sevaka had dragged her about the makeshift garrison earlier that night, she found faces more alert and confident than she'd any right to expect.

She completed her circuit of the rampart and made her way up the northeast tower. Along the collapsing roadway, the fires of the Hadari picket line offered reminder of the siege that would come tomorrow. So many lives offered up to the Raven, and to little purpose.

Rosa crossed to the tower's edge to stand beside the sentry. Not one of Vrasdavora's garrison, but Thaldvar. The borderer stood with one foot between the crenellations and a bottle loose in his hand.

He nodded. "Lady Orova."

"I thought you were out on the road."

"Castellan Paradan was kind enough to send soldiers to relieve us. It's been a long day. Even borderers need rest."

She nodded. It *had* been a long day, for Thaldvar's shrinking band most of all. The Tressian soldiery were all very well, but the borderers had a knack for finding firm footing. Without them, Sevaka's ambush couldn't have reached position in time. "You don't seem to be resting."

He swept the bottle out to encompass the valley. "I like to come up high when I'm nervous. Makes me feel like an eagle, rather than a mouse. The poor sentry was dead on his feet, so I offered to stand a turn." He shrugged. "Seems it's a night for restless souls."

Rosa propped herself against the rampart and folded her arms. "I seldom sleep. Not any longer. It's part of what I am."

"I'd go mad without a few hours snatched from the world."

"I think I went mad long ago."

"Who says I didn't?" He proffered the bottle, a touch unsteadily. "Care for a drink? One restless soul to another?"

"Liquor has even less grasp on my wits than sleep."

He sniffed. "This isn't liquor. It's Lasmanora whiskey. Finest in the borderlands. You don't sup it for drunkenness, but flavour." Flavour or not, the slur to his words suggested drunkenness lay near. "Consider it one last toast before things turn sour."

"You think tomorrow will go badly?"

He gave a slow, sad shake of the head. "Who said anything about tomorrow?"

"True. It could be weeks before this is done."

"And by morning, the whiskey will be gone." Thaldvar tilted his head, striking a pose common among statues of the great and the good. "Circumstance insists I offer to share, but a piece of me hopes you'll refuse."

"If that's how it is . . . " She laughed and plucked the bottle from his hand. "Why are you still here?"

He frowned. "I told you, I offered to stand watch."

Rosa took an experimental sniff. The sweet tang of peated heather summoned forth late nights and early mornings while still a squire, standing sentry at the Ravonn's watch-forts. "I don't mean that. Leave. No one will think less of you. It's not your fight."

Thaldvar shook his head. "You wouldn't believe how many times I've told myself that. Fool that I am, I stayed. Some notion of honour, I suppose. Now it's too late. We do as much as we can for as long as we're able, in the hope it repays our sins."

"You have many sins?"

"Too many to count. But there's always room for one more."

Rosa grunted, thinking back to the broken truce. "That's what I find."

She swigged from the bottle. Sweet and rich and hot with promise. But as the sweetness faded, other tastes came to the fore. Sour. Metallic. Numbness crowded in behind, seeping outward through muscle and bone.

Lungs spasmed. The bottle slipped from Rosa's fingers and shattered on stone. The world upended. She crumpled to her knees and grabbed at Thaldvar with a shuddering hand.

"What . . . Thaldvar?"

He broke her grip and stepped back. Wracked by a paroxysm of coughing, Rosa pitched forward against the rampart. A cry for help dissipated into a thin, hissing wheeze.

"I had no choice," said Thaldvar. "I'm sorry."

Hoisting her up by lifeless arms, he heaved her over the rampart and into the night.

Thirty-Five

"Captain? Captain?"

Swallowing to ease a throat bittered by inconstant sleep, Sevaka propped herself onto an elbow. "What's wrong?"

Gavrida withdrew to respectful distance, his eyes fixed straight ahead. He was pale beneath the grime, his expression drawn. "I'll wait outside while you dress."

Respect offered to a Psanneque? "Out with it, lieutenant."

"It's Commander Orova—"

"Rosa?" Instantly awake, Sevaka dragged clothes from the bedside table and pulled them on. "What's happened?"

His throat bobbed. "It's not good."

She fumbled her laces and tucked them behind her heel. "Take me."

Vrasdavora's courtyard was empty, the walls already half-manned. The rush of boots and bodies spoke to a muster underway.

Sevaka sifted the possibilities, unease mounting. Not an attack. Not without drums or buccinas. And the garrison *felt* wrong. The faces she glimpsed were more confused than alarmed. What had become of Rosa to alarm Gavrida so? He'd been at Soraved. He'd seen her resilience clearer than any.

Answers came beneath the gatehouse stables, themselves meanly occupied. A handful of draught horses, Castellan Paradan's destrier, a ring of the 11th, shields grounded and eyes outward, and . . .

Rosa lay on a bed of straw and blankets, uniform torn ragged. Black blood welled up from gashes at brow and shoulder. Her left leg was splinted and bound; her eyes, distant and sightless. A physician of the

11th, identified by his grubby white armband, knelt beside her. A curved needle and thread darted back and forth, drawing closed the puckered wound at her belly.

Sevaka bit down on her forearm. It muffled the cry, but did nothing to ease the tremor in her knees, nor the sour flutter in her stomach. One thing to hear Rosa speak of clawing her way out of a shallow grave, or of limbs re-stitched in battle's wake. Another entirely to see it. For all its initial horror, the demon's spear had been cleaner.

Pushing past the physician's assistant, she fell to her knees and grabbed Rosa's hand. "Rosa? Love? Can you hear me?"

Blue eyes settled, then twitched away, veins black and distended against scleral white. Lips muttered without sound or meaning, lost to delirium.

"Rosa?" Sevaka gripped her fingers tight. Her eyes settled on seeping wounds. "She should be healing. Why isn't she healing?"

"She's lucky to be alive, if you want to call it that." The physician tugged the needle free and began another stitch. "Castellan wanted to burn her. The lieutenant wouldn't let him."

That explained the guard. Of course Paradan hadn't understood. He knew Rosa only from a reputation no more certain than myths of demons and witchcraft.

Sevaka shot a grateful glance at Gavrida. Though of equal rank with Paradan, the other's castellanship granted seniority. That kind of quarrel ended careers. Still might, if any of them lived to worry over such things. She stared again into Rosa's glassy eyes, and saw nothing beyond lantern-light's reflection. "What happened?"

"She fell from the northeast tower. Bounced halfway down the mountainside before anyone knew. We'd never have found her, but for the borderer's warning."

"Thaldvar?" Another debt added to a lengthy list.

Gavrida nodded. "Came running down the stairs, eyes wild and full of urgency. An act."

"What do you mean?"

"In the confusion, he slipped into the chapel. He cut the proctor's throat, and that of his apprentice."

Cold crept into a knotted stomach. She'd liked Maldrath, who for all his fussiness had thrown himself willingly into the morning's escapade. Sevaka gazed down at Rosa. *Thaldvar* had done this?

"You must be mistaken."

"One of my lot heard the scream. She broke down the chapel door and caught the borderer among the remains of the lion amulets. He'd smashed them all." He scowled. "The castellan expects an attack. He's had the borderers rounded up. I'm surprised you heard nothing."

"She's always telling me I sleep like the dead," murmured Sevaka. "Paradan sent you to wake me?"

"No."

So the castellan didn't want a Psanneque underfoot? Even in this? Unfortunate, because with Rosa out of the running, Sevaka was his commander. "Thank you, lieutenant."

"I knew you'd want to know. In case ... "

"In case Rosa dies?"

Heartsick, Sevaka sought refuge in logic. With Maldrath dead, the amulets had been their only hope of controlling the garrison constructs Now the simarka would sit idle, and the kraikons would remain watchful sentries, incapable of responding to a siege's ebb and flow. It should have been the direst news of all. But try as she might, Sevaka couldn't make that leap. Not with Rosa lying thus, her eternal's vigour robbed by ...

By what? Thaldvar could answer. She drew the pain close until it hardened to fury. Paradan could wait. "Thaldvar. Where is he?"

During their rare sojourns within Vrasdavora's walls, the borderers had barracked in the garrison quarters beneath the southwest tower. They dwelled there now, bound and shackled about the circumference, their weapons stripped away and a six-man guard beyond the door. Thaldvar hung at the chamber's centre, his bound wrists suspended from the chandelier hook by thick ropes and his feet barely brushing the floor. He was naked to the waist, sweat and blood mingling atop livid bruises.

Split lips formed a grimace as the door creaked shut. "Captain."

Sevaka struck him across the face. Once. Twice. Three times. The dull smack of flesh. The gasp of pain. Each better than the last. "Why? I trusted you! *She* trusted you!"

Thaldvar hawked a bloody gobbet onto the floor. "I'd ... no choice."

"Folk always say that. It's so rarely true. What you lacked was a backbone."

Sevaka froze, fist levelled for a fourth blow. *Lacking a backbone.* Her mother's favourite derision. It tripped so easily from the tongue.

So be it. Better a little of Ebigail Kiradin's strength than none at all.

She punched him again. Thaldvar spat away a tooth.

"My brother," he gasped. "Haldrane has my brother."

Sevaka lowered her fist. "You think that's enough? After what you've done?"

He stared through tangled, greasy hair. The charming, self-deprecating man had gone. A broken, wretched soul remained. Her punches had not made him so, nor the blows inflicted by Paradan's men before they'd strung him up.

"No." Red spittle flecked the words. "But still he has my brother and his family. He promised . . . freedom if I obeyed, and death if I did not."

The Psanneque's anger ebbed. The Kiradin stoked it anew. "You were his creature all along. You all were. Never trust a borderer."

No other spoke. The borderers' hatred thickened the air.

"I thought myself free until this morning," said Thaldvar. "If my arrow had flown true . . . ? Raven curse me for the miss. His agents found me while I watched the road."

That morning. Thaldvar had drawn her eye to Haldrane. Had spoken with vehemence. She should have suspected, but at Ahrad Thaldvar had been the only welcoming face in a fortress full of disdain. They'd been comrades, maybe even friends, and it had blinded her.

Humiliation united Psanneque and Kiradin. Wrath ran cold as ice.

"The castellan will hang you for this." Sevaka slipped the dagger from her belt. The stench of blood and sweat filled her nostrils, and the Kiradin took charge. "There'll be no drop to hurl you into the mists. You'll die in agony, tongue thick in your throat and lungs burning. If you seek any kindness, tell me what you did to Rosa."

"Haldrane gave me poison. Silver dust. Fleenroot. Moonglove. I don't know what else."

Silver as a bane of magic – vicious against Lumestra's sunlight, so legend told, but potent enough against all others. Fleenroot killed the dead. Moonglove brought peace to the dying. A poison crafted for an eternal, who was all of those things, and none. That it hadn't yet killed Rosa didn't mean it wouldn't.

"An antidote. Is there one?"

"None I know. Haldrane threw in everything that offered the possibility of harm. From how he spoke, he was uncertain it would work." Thaldvar coughed. "I never wanted this."

"What you wanted is irrelevant. All that matters is what you've done."

"I chose my family over a stranger." He closed his eyes. "I don't expect you to understand."

"I chose a stranger over my family. If she dies ..." Sevaka stared at each of the borderers in turn. "Will none of you plead for his life?"

Two dozen gazes averted. No one spoke.

"There's no love for me in this room," breathed Thaldvar. "This sin is mine alone."

Sevaka nodded. The hatred she'd felt before had not been meant for her, but Thaldvar, whose betrayal marked them all. Fully in the Kiradin's grip, she felt no more sympathy for them than for him. Never trust a borderer.

She drew closer still, until her lips were level with his ear. "You don't deserve mercy."

The Kiradin slid the dagger home between his ribs. She rejoiced as the light faded from his eyes. The Psanneque wept without tears.

"You had no right!"

Castellan Paradan bore his rank on slender shoulders. A man not yet in his prime, he exuded brittle confidence, inexperience balanced by highblood privilege. Even suffused with fury, his face remained wary – fearful of the woman in the gore-slicked coat. As he should have been. Alone in his quarters he'd no support. Precisely why Sevaka had sought him there before word of Thaldvar's death spread.

"I'd every right," snapped Sevaka. "With Lady Orova sick ..." Better to say "sick" than "dying". "... command falls to me."

"Vrasdavora is a stronghold of the Tressian army, not lair to some Psanneque brigand."

Sevaka narrowed her eyes. "Thaldvar was a traitor. He died as one."

Paradan glared back. "He should have hanged."

It was all Sevaka could do to keep from laughing. The Kiradin supposed it was always thus for the weak: hiding in protocol to disguise a lack elsewhere. Her mother had tried to teach her that.

"My name doesn't matter, *lieutenant*. Only my rank."

Paradan braced knuckles on his desk and leaned closer. "You think my soldiers will follow a Psanneque?"

Sevaka stifled a wince. What influence she had came from Rosa, not her own rank.

And Rosa was . . .

Don't think it. Thinking it makes it true.

. . . dying.

"We've no time to bicker," she said. "There's an army barely a league distant. With Maldrath's death the kraikons are useless. The simarka are worse. Come noon, these walls will be swarming with shadowthorns. We have to be ready."

"Come noon, we'll be gone."

Sevaka blinked. "What?"

Paradan skirted the desk and crossed to the narrow window overlooking the part-collapsed road. "You said it yourself. The constructs will do us little good. I can't hold these walls."

"Retreat leaves the door to the Marcher Lands yawning wide!"

"And if we hold, we'll last what? A day? Two?"

Sevaka cast about for rebuttal and settled on words Rosa had spoken that morning. "Sometimes the calling is to die while others win elsewhere. Lady Orova meant to hold this place."

Paradan's expression softened. "Lady Orova is in no position to give that order. I must consider the fates of the living, not the wishes of the—"

Sevaka closed the gap. Gathering a fistful of tabard, she shoved him against the wall. "Coward!"

"Will you use the dagger on me, too?" gasped Paradan. "Will that give you the garrison's loyalty?"

The Kiradin would, had she thought it would have made any difference; the Psanneque was too forlorn to hold her back. But killing Paradan would only make truth of the lies whispered about her. Were it otherwise, rank alone would have allowed her to strip him of command. For want of authority, she needed leverage, and there was none to be had that would not make the situation worse.

The door creaked. "Apologies for the intrusion, castellan, but Sergeant Zallan—"

The Kiradin hauled Paradan around. The castellan's back was to the door before it fully opened, her lips mashed against his, smothering the grunt of protest. Hands came up to push her away. They lost urgency when Sevaka slipped her dagger-point beneath his breastplate to prick the skin.

The orderly in the doorway saw none of it. Not the dagger, nor Paradan's furious expression. He saw only what the Kiradin wanted him to see – his commander locked in passionate embrace with a Psanneque whose eyes widened in alarm at being discovered. Faced with that, he made the only natural response: he averted his eyes and shuffled away, the door falling closed behind.

Sevaka counted to ten. She stepped back and sat on the edge of the desk. A further five-count slipped away before a flushed Paradan recovered his voice.

"As a seductress, you leave much to be desired," he growled.

"You didn't see that fool's face. Surprise . . . and just a hint of scandal. Right now, I imagine he's telling a pretty tale, and if not, then soon."

"You think I care?"

There it was: the first tremor of concern. Sevaka's confidence blossomed. Leverage. "I know you do, Emil." The use of the personal name was a necessary flourish. "I met your father at one on my mother's parties. Always so proud, so desperate for patronage. What would he say if he knew about your torrid affair with a lowly Psanneque?"

"There is no affair." Ice crackled beneath the words.

"When did truth ever matter in the Republic?" She smiled. Confidence was important. "You will follow my orders – your superior's orders – as your oath to the Council dictates, or I will spend every waking moment nurturing the seed planted just now. A glance. A touch. A confidence overheard in a careless moment. Even if we never meet again, folk will know what we were to each other, even if we were really nothing at all. Consorting with a Psanneque? What will your fellow Prydonis think? What will your family?"

"You're deluded." He trembled beneath the scowl.

"Before I was a Psanneque, I was a Kiradin." Sevaka struck an imitation of her mother's disdainful smile. "My mother's whispers almost brought down the Republic. Do you *really* think I can't destroy you?"

Paradan quivered. Outrage? Fear? Sevaka couldn't tell, and barely dared breathe in case it destroyed the illusion. She'd never met the elder Lord Paradan, and she'd no intent of debasing herself with tales of shared passions with the younger. But only what Paradan *believed* mattered. The deception was everything she'd hated about her mother. But holding Vrasdavora had mattered to Rosa. Honouring that wish was worth sacrifice.

Paradan broke long before he spoke. She saw it in his eyes. "With your permission, captain, I'll inspect the defences."

"Granted, lieutenant." Sevaka smiled away relief. "We'll reconvene at dawn. If you need me before then, I'll be in my quarters . . . Unless you'd prefer I remain in yours?"

"Get out."

With sardonic tip of the head, Sevaka complied. She made it halfway to the adjutant's quarters before her legs began to shake.

Sevaka wasn't surprised to find Rosa had been moved to the bed in the adjutant's quarters – she'd given the order before seeking Thaldvar. The thin, domino-masked figure stood in lantern-shadow at the bedside was another matter. She froze in the doorway. Instinct called on her to flee, and not look back.

"Were you born in a barn?" said the Raven. "Close the door."

The gravelly voice was at odds with the thin frame, and more cultured than Sevaka had expected. Polite, almost charming. Not the grim guardian of Otherworld priests denounced from their pulpits. And her only other option was to walk away, and leave Rosa alone.

Perhaps for the last time.

The Raven offered a wry smile. "Oh, don't regard me so. This is a personal visit, not a professional one."

The door fell closed. Sevaka wondered if it would matter; if any other would see if they happened by.

"How is she?"

The Raven brushed gloved fingers across Rosa's brow. She twitched fitfully, glassy eyes seeing nothing. At least the bleeding – if it *was* blood – had ceased. Had the wounds closed, or had Rosa nothing more to give?

"The poison has made her a prisoner in her own body." He tutted. "I can't say I approve. Life? Yes, I suppose. Death? Of course. But this?"

Swallowing her fear, Sevaka pulled up a chair on the opposite side of the bed and took Rosa's hand. "Can you help her?"

"I offered aid before, and was rejected." His eyes never left Rosa's face. "Now? She'll recover in time, or she won't. It's not for me to interfere."

"You might at least sound upset," she said bitterly. "But I suppose this suits you, doesn't it? If she dies, she'll be yours."

The lantern flickered. Shadows crept closer. The Raven, who to that point could have passed for an eccentric ephemeral, suddenly filled the room – all without twitching a muscle. The urge to flee returned, and Sevaka gripped Rosa's hand tighter than ever.

"And *you* might remember that while I allow Rosa certain latitude, I take offence *very* easily." He shrugged, ephemeral aspect flowing back into place. "Or I would, if I thought that tone were meant for me."

"Why do you care?"

He shrugged. For the first time, his dark eyes left Rosa's face and bored in Sevaka's. "A suitor should be attentive to his intended's loved ones. Or do I have that wrong?"

Somehow, she met the stare without flinching. "She rejected you."

"You mistake me for a rival." He spread his hands. "Rosa chose you, and is welcome to that choice ... for however long it endures. Nothing lasts for ever."

Sevaka shivered. Nothing was less abstract than death foretold – even in haziest terms – by the Keeper of the Dead. "Not even you?"

He offered a short bow. "Not even I, Lady Kiradin."

"Don't call me that."

"Your name?"

"It's not supposed to be." She brushed a filthy blonde strand from Rosa's cheek. "And yet what's the point, if I become my mother as soon as I'm placed in a corner?"

"I'm told we all become someone else out of need." He cocked his head. "I imagine the trick lies in choosing *who*."

Sevaka closed her eyes. Echoes of her final conversation with Thaldvar washed over her. That anger was long spent, replaced by bone-hollowing weariness. Why was she even talking to the Raven? She supposed she needed to speak to *someone*, and her options were few.

"It might be I haven't the backbone to make that choice," she said. "I doubt I'll ever be free of her."

"Your mother was certainly a . . . presence to be reckoned with. Dare I ask what led you to emulate her?"

"Vrasdavora must be held."

"Ah. Death and honour. A *fine* tradition. Give the shadowthorns no satisfaction, only steel. Is that it?"

"No." So the Raven considered Vrasdavora indefensible? She looked down at Rosa. "Because it's what she'd do."

"Ah." He reclaimed his hat from the bedside table and set it on his head. The crown stopped just short of scraping the ceiling. "Well, I'm sure you know best."

She snorted. "That makes one of us."

When she looked up, the Raven had gone.

Tzadas, 6th Day of Wealdrust

Trust not the kindliness of ravens,
Nor linger 'neath the crooked tree.
A god's embrace is costly haven,
If you doubt the price, the price is thee.

Hallowsider's Nursery Rhyme

Thirty-Six

"I regret, my lord, that there's no sign of Lord Akadra." Arlanne Keldrov's cheek creased, then smoothed. A woman afraid she'd speak out of turn. "I thought he'd be here."

Josiri turned to hide his own expression. A mistake, for it granted peerless view across Ardva's uneven fortress wall, over the Grelyt River and its steep red cliffs, and out across the muster field on the far shore. The mostly *empty* muster field. Three score wayfarers among the wagons, perhaps two dozen knights in blood-red surcoats and gilded armour, a mismatched mob in militia tabards, patchwork leathers – and yes, a few phoenix tabards from Katya Trelan's time – and six companies of the 14th ordered for march beneath brooding skies.

The latter were mostly southwealders – the only such regiment in the Republic's service. The 14th had suffered greatly at Davenwood the year before, and Keldrov had recruited from the villages and towns preserved by its valour. Though the bad blood between north and south could have filled an ocean, southwealders stood ready to fight just as the 14th had fought for them. A shared history forged from division.

Little more than a thousand. Perhaps five hundred more waited on the Kreska road – all of them militia, lured forth by loyalty to the twin names of Trelan and Beral. Still, it wasn't enough. A southwealder's blade was worth six from the north? It'd have to be. Too many had died the year before. At Davenwood. At Eskavord.

Eskavord . . .

Even though the town's remains lay far to the east, hidden by Davenwood's outspread arms, Josiri could almost *see* it. The charred ruins. The desolate fields. The pervasive mist that had descended with

Wintertide, and never receded. Eskavord, the only real home he'd ever known, had become a Forbidden Place, blasted by magic and sorrow, and thick with ghost-haunted mist. Viktor's doing.

Josiri hung his head. "Viktor keeps his promises."

Erashel laid a hand on his forearm. "Perhaps no longer."

"He'll be here."

The women shared a glance. Josiri shook his head, and tried again. "There could be a dozen reasons for his delay."

Keldrov's expression betrayed unhappiness, but her tone remained level. "Dawn is long in the past. Lumestra knows we'll make little enough difference as it is. We'll make none at all if Izack's overwhelmed before we arrive. You saw the same despatch I did. Tregga's gone. The Eastshires are ablaze. Tarvallion will be next."

Tarvallion, with its slender towers and vibrant gardens. The Republic's radiant heart. And the Hadari would burn it to ash.

"Then march," Josiri replied. "I'll catch up."

"Josiri, be reasonable," said Erashel. "He's not coming."

"Does it not occur to you to wonder why? Viktor crushed Saran's dreams of conquest not far from here. Do you suppose the Emperor has forgotten?" He spoke faster, the idea taking horrible shape. "Would you chance history repeating itself, or give orders to ensure it could not?"

"Assassination?" Erashel shook her head. "The shadowthorns aren't northwealders. They'd consider that dishonourable."

Keldrov – herself a northwealder who'd endured a stream of similar asides from Erashel that past day – scowled. "We'd be fools not to think Saran's icularis aren't active in the Southshires – especially after last week's granary fire." She shot Erashel a bitter glance. "I dismissed it as the same old trouble. A few holdouts clinging to dreams of independence. Perhaps it was the Hadari. Or perhaps it was both."

Josiri's fear found new life. Viktor was a man alone, and surprise would compensate for his other talents – especially were he reluctant to use them.

"March," he repeated. "I'll see for myself."

Keldrov nodded, but her eyes held sympathy for someone clinging to a memory of a man who no longer was. "I'll give you an escort."

Josiri glanced again at the muster field. "I won't squander anyone else's time or wellbeing. Erashel, will you convey my regrets to Malachi? Tell him the Southshires has mustered all it can, and . . . " He sighed and spread his hands. "And whatever you think best about Viktor."

Erashel folded her arms. "I'll send a herald. I've no intention of returning."

"Malachi needs you."

"Malachi has a whole city. You don't. Be reasonable, Josiri. Either Viktor is dead or taken, or he's not the man you remember." She flickered a thin smile. "Either way, if we southwealders don't stick together, then what's the point?"

Josiri grimaced. "Commander Keldrov, you'll march to reinforce Izack. Lady Beral and I will see what's become of Viktor."

"And if the man you remember isn't to be found?"

The double meaning soured Josiri's gut. But the answer was the same. Distant though he'd become from his homeland, he remained a southwealder, with a southwealder's duties.

"Like I said, I'll catch you up. I'm not out of this fight."

Calenne woke to find Tarona Watch empty, as was so often the case. Viktor slept lightly, and rose with the dawn save when nightmares held him captive. But something felt different, though Calenne couldn't quite put her finger on precisely *what*. If was as if their home, and her place in it, were somehow diminished.

Ridiculous. But the sensation lingered as she dressed. By the time she departed the bedroom for the kitchen, she'd thought for little else.

"Viktor?" She peered out into the garden. A grey, miserable day. Sommertide's last gasp was slipping away. "Viktor? Are you here?"

A folded sheet of paper on the table gave shape to formless concerns. Her heart pacing a hair faster, Calenne opened it out.

I cannot sit idle while the Republic burns. But my deeds must be as unconventional as the times, and I can't risk the consequences of your involvement.

I know it's no use asking you not to be angry, and I'm sorry if this strains the bond between us.

I'm sure we'll discuss the matter upon my return.

Viktor

"Raven's Eyes, Viktor!"

That there was danger in his future seemed obvious, and perhaps on a different day Calenne would have thought well of his desire to shield her from it. But after Valna? He'd taken the avoidance of argument to heights hitherto unknown: denying her even the chance to discuss the matter. Just as Josiri had done when he'd kept secret his involvement with the wolf's-heads.

Josiri. Anger quickened to a flame. This was his fault. Even when he thought her dead he conspired to confound her happiness. Why couldn't he have let Viktor be?

Shame rushed close behind the unworthy thought. If the Republic was beset and Viktor could make a difference, then of course he should act. Holding him back suggested her love was as shallow and selfish as she sometimes feared was truth.

But to leave without word? To not even *discuss* the matter? Shame boiled into fresh anger. He'd said so little the night before, offering barely more detail than the letter, and nothing of intent. Did he really think she'd have picked up a sword and followed him into war?

She laughed bleakly. Was there a deceit more foolish than that visited upon oneself? Of course she'd have followed. If only to prove that the selfish, sheltered woman she'd been at their first meeting belonged to the past. That was their bond. She'd softened Viktor's pragmatism with compassion, and in return he'd set her free. Not only from the Council's suffocating grip and Josiri's overzealous protections, but from her own preconceptions of who and what she was. He was right not to trust her in this.

Damn Viktor anyway. He could leave her behind, but she didn't have to stay there, like some timid wife from one of Tarlev's farces. As for Viktor's course? She could follow easily enough once she reached Ardva. Subtlety seldom lay in a marching army's gift.

"Viktor? Viktor!"

Josiri's voice beyond the walls startled Calenne from rumination. She dropped the note and ran for the bedroom. She'd barely made it when the outer door crashed back on its hinges.

"Viktor!"

"He's not here." The second voice belonged to the stranger from the night before. The woman whose close-cropped hair and imperious stance matched so poorly. "We couldn't have missed him on the road."

So Viktor *hadn't* gone to join Josiri? Where was he?

Josiri growled. "There's still the other room."

Calenne scrambled for the window, chased by the thump of approaching footsteps. She made it halfway before hinges creaked. Breath souring, she forced the closest approximation of unconcern as a thundering heart would allow.

"Josiri . . ." She scrabbled for words to justify the indefensible. "Don't blame Viktor. This was my choice. He promised freedom from Katya's legacy, and I held him to it."

He glanced in her direction, then took stock of the room. "He's not here."

Still no emotion beyond urgency. But that was all right. Calenne's heart was full enough for them both – even if she couldn't quite tell one emotion from another.

"No," she replied. "I thought he'd gone to join you?"

Josiri turned away. "Erashel? I said he's not here."

"I'm not deaf." The stranger crowded the doorway and held out the letter. "It was on the table."

"Seriously? You're ignoring me?" Calenne glared at Erashel. "Both of you?"

Josiri glanced at the note. "'My involvement.' In what? And as for 'Strains the bond between us'. As if it could get any worse. What are you up to, Viktor?"

"He meant that for me!" Calenne grabbed at the note, but couldn't pull it free. Still Josiri paid her no heed. "This isn't funny!"

"That's his handwriting?" said Erashel.

"I think so."

"What do you suppose he meant by unconventional deeds?"

"Knowing Viktor, I dread to think."

Calenne scrambled back as Josiri moved towards her. In the instant before contact, dizziness swamped her senses. The room swam. A shudder of warmth overcame her, and she collapsed.

"What is it?" asked Erashel.

Calenne gazed dully up. He'd not walked past her, but *through*. How was that possible?

"I don't . . . It's nothing." Josiri shook his head like a man waking from a dream. He crossed to the wardrobe and swung it open. "He's cleaned out. Wherever he's gone, it's for a while."

"So *let* him," said Erashel. "You wanted to go home and prise our people from the vranakin. Do so."

"It's not that simple."

She strode to join him. Calenne gathered enough of her senses to crawl clear before they came into contact. It didn't help. Not with awful suspicion pricking at her thoughts.

"You know he's not been taken by the shadowthorns." Erashel's words were dim, distant, barely piercing the shroud wrapped tight about Calenne's senses. "And you know he's not in Ardva. There's nothing more you can do. What can *he* do, for that matter?"

"You don't know Viktor," said Josiri. "Once he sets his mind to something . . ."

"You *did* say he doesn't know how to lose."

"You were listening, last night?"

"Some of it. I've spent half my life in chains, Josiri. If I'd never listened at a keyhole, I'd be dead."

Josiri shrugged the reply away. "Where Viktor's concerned, it isn't a question of what he can do. It's what it will cost the rest of us. We have to find him."

They headed outside, leaving Calenne in a puddle of skirts and frayed thoughts.

He'd walked through her. Without slowing. Without the slightest hint of contact beyond that vile, crawling sensation beneath her skin – like sunshine, but without the contentment that came alongside. He'd not ignored her. He'd not heard because she wasn't there. Not all the way.

A word formed in fragmented thoughts. Cyraeth. A soul not wholly there, nor wholly gone, clinging to the world out of loss.

Breath rattling in her throat, Calenne drew up and stared at her hands. They looked real. She *felt* real. A glance at the open wardrobe set her reeling anew. In her mind's eye, she saw her dresses, her travelling clothes – even the remains of the leathers she'd worn at Davenwood.

But the wardrobe was empty.

The more Calenne picked at the thread, the faster the tapestry unfurled. The simple things. Eating, dressing, bathing. She knew she'd partaken, but could summon no recollection. Memories before Eskavord were ... sparse. Viktor, yes. Josiri, yes. Beyond that? The details of her life were fragments, viewed from without rather than within. How had she not noticed?

What had happened to her?

The day before. The thrakker. The boy. They hadn't seen her at all, had they? Just a masterless sword that killed without command. Their horrified gazes made sense now.

The wail began in the pit of her stomach and left her lungs rasping and sore. She doubled over, unable to contain shuddering, wracking sobs. And beneath it all, beneath the turbulent sea upon which she was suddenly adrift, a roiling, suffocating rage unlike any she'd ever known.

"Viktor," she gasped. "What have you made of me?"

Thirty-Seven

Thunder parted the veil of sleep, the shuddering, brooding rumble scattering gummed thoughts even as they gathered. Shadowthorn drums.

Sevaka levered herself upright in the chair. Rosa lay unmoving in the bed, asleep at last. So much for the hope of it all being nightmare. Sevaka clasped her hand, the decision made on slumber's edge coming to the fore. Strange how the hardest choice was the easiest embraced.

"Duty calls, love," she murmured. "You understand, don't you?"

Rosa offered no response. No sign, indeed, that she'd even heard. If there was to be a last moment, let this not be it. Wait another minute. Ten minutes. However long it took to fashion a last memory to hold close on the walls. But it was time she didn't have.

"You gave me the strength for this, Roslava." Sevaka laid Rosa's hand atop the blankets and kissed her brow. "Look for me come Third Dawn. I'll be waiting."

She left the adjutant's quarters, and never once looked back.

Vrasdavora's motley garrison was already thick on the battlements, sergeants bellowing latecomers into position beneath grey skies. The tabards of four regiments and two chapterhouses. The mishmash of militia and villagers with borrowed swords and bartered courage. All gathered beneath kraikons little more useful than the statues they resembled.

"Your fortress stands ready, captain." Paradan offered what seemed a genuine salute. The castellan had dressed for the occasion, a scarlet Prydonis sash looped about his army tabard. "Come what may, we'll leave the shadowthorns with scars."

Sevaka nodded. "How long do we have?"

"I've watchers at the bend. They'll bring word once the Hadari start moving."

Maybe enough time to unmake poor choices. "I need a hundred volunteers to hold the east wall. To keep the shadowthorns fixated on Vrasdavora while you make your escape."

"Captain?"

"You were right." Pride or duty. Her mother's influence, or Rosa's. In the cold watches of the night, Rosa's had won out, as it should have from the first. "Take Lady Orova. Take the wounded. Leave me a hundred swords, and those with courage enough to wield them. Get everyone else out."

Paradan's lips twisted. "You'll die."

As if anything could stop that now. "Tell the Council that Vrasdavora did not fall without a fight." She stared again to the east. "And tell Rosa I'm sorry."

Melanna watched in silence as havildars dragged the assault column into shape. Anticipation jangled beneath the drums. The taut expectation of men bound for battle.

The road, collapsed and uneven, would barely support a dozen men marching abreast. Rhalesh green mingled with Icansae scarlet – a column of shields, swords and ladders hurled as a thunderbolt against Vrasdavora's walls. More than sufficient to sweep away a few hundred Tressians. Assuming Haldrane's catspaw had done his work. But Melanna had never known the spymaster to be anything other than successful within limits he himself defined.

She lost herself in observation of the leading ranks, of willow shields locked tight. Once the assault began, the second and third ranks would hoist theirs high above the heads of the first to protect against crossbows. A flight of silver owls on emerald fields, come to claim victory for the House of Saran.

"Saranal."

Melanna stifled a scowl and glanced back. Aeldran stood a little behind – his escort of Immortals yet twenty paces distance to offer privacy. "I've no civility to spare the House of Andwar today."

"I find myself in need of your favour, all the same."

"And you think you've earned that right?"

"No. But still I must ask." He hesitated. "I regret that matters unfolded as they did."

"You regret that your sister was revealed."

"That Naradna treated you as a rival when you were not," he corrected. "I don't approve, but I refuse to judge her. You and I, we see the shape of her struggles, but cannot fully comprehend them. What she fights for, we have. Had my grandfather been more like the Emperor he sought to depose, you and she would have been as sisters. Alas, Maggad cared nothing for anyone's desires but his own. My sister and I strive to be different, but ... Alas, Andwars are not renowned for generosity of spirit, nor mercy."

"But I must be known for both?"

"That's for you to decide, Saranal. I can only make the request."

"Which is?"

"Grant me command of the assault."

Melanna blinked. She'd expected Aeldran to petition for his sister's release, but not this. "Why should I?"

"My chieftains hold me as accomplice in Naradna's deception. Whatever your scorn, theirs burns brighter. Better I prove myself before that fire consumes me. Better for us both, *savim*."

Glory to make truth of a lie. Blood washed all sins away. All failures. As for the rest? By his words, Aeldran implied what Naradna had stated plain. *If you harm him, you only weaken yourself.* If Aeldran were challenged, who could say what manner of man might take his place?

"And do you beg this as a peer of the Golden Court, or as your grandfather's assassin?"

"I am no assassin, Saranal." A frown formed in the words.

"Naradna told me you killed Maggad."

"I dreamt of his death, but I did not hasten it. Naradna refused to let his malice rule your fate as it had hers. For the longest time, she admired you."

Truth, or an attempt to instil sympathy for his imprisoned sister? Reason believed the latter; instinct the former. Melanna didn't have to ask why Naradna's admiration had soured, or why she'd refused credit for Maggad's death. *You have done nothing other than for yourself.* By inaction, Melanna had broken a faith she'd never known pledged.

"And what say you?" she asked.

"You are to be Empress, Saranal. I am your servant whether you acknowledge me or not, and it is as that servant I make my request. Name me your champion on this field, and I swear on my sister's life that you will have no cause for regret."

She turned at the sound of silk slipping across scale. Aeldran knelt, head bowed.

Champion. An honour bestowed on aspirant commoners for faithful service. It was unheard of for one of the Golden Court to put themselves so completely at another's service; to abandon all personal ambition – perhaps even life – for another's furtherment. An heir was expected to do so, of course, but this?

The possibility of deception remained. But to what end? Aeldran's declaration was tantamount to concession, placing the House of Andwar in servitude to the throne it had always coveted. So powerful and public a pact could not be broken – or betrayed. To do so might even be the Kingdom of Icansae's end.

Perhaps the House of Andwar had honour, despite the lies that had led to this place. In any case, who was she any longer to judge, she who'd stooped to assassination? Who'd withheld Ashana's death? Necessity was an excuse for them both, or for neither.

A flawed champion for a flawed princessa.

"I accept your service, Prince Aeldran," she said at last. "Open the fortress to me."

Drums redoubled to a divine roar. The first golden shields showed through the rain, scarlet dark and muddy behind.

Gavrida stomped his heels and stared beyond the parapet. "You might at least have picked a better day for it."

Sevaka glanced along the wall. Ragged uniforms of the 11th. Even what remained of the borderers. Senesta – their leader following Thaldvar's death – had muttered tersely about blood debts. Sevaka wasn't sure whether that debt was owed for Thaldvar's betrayal, or to the shadowthorns who'd forced his treachery. But ferocity had convinced. In any case, it would all be the same in a few short hours.

Even concentrated in the east, there were barely two defenders for every pace of wall. The high rampart would hide the paucity. Or so Sevaka hoped. Otherwise the shadowthorns would simply bypass Vrasdavora and harry Paradan's retreat. Once battle was joined, the gaps would show. Especially with fully half the fortress' kraikons standing guard over the north and west walls, obeying Maldrath's last command.

The Hadari column shuffled to a halt. Shields rippled; long ladders set aside. Bows were drawn and loosed. The volley fell far short of the walls, as it was meant to. A warrior's salute.

Somewhere on the battlement, a lone voice raised in song. "Bury me deep, with sword in hand."

Others picked up the refrain as the second volley hissed out. "*Come Third Dawn, my watch I'll stand.*"

Two volleys spent. One for Ashana. One for the Emperor. One for his heir yet to come.

"You should have gone west with Paradan." Between drums and song, Sevaka barely heard her own words.

"Saved my skin?" Gavrida shrugged. "My lot have been on borrowed time ever since Ahrad. We only made it this far because of you."

"Because of Rosa."

He shook his head. "Maybe after Soraved. But before? I was ready to give up. We all were. Then along comes a Psanneque – a *Psanneque* – and she holds it together better than any of us. Better than a knight of the blood. Can't turn my back on that." His voice raised to a bellow. "The 11th stands with you!"

The song dissolved into a cheer that stole Sevaka's breath. For the first time in long months, she *belonged*. For perhaps the first time in her life, she had no doubts. No hesitation. Psanneque or Kiradin, this was her place.

The third volley passed, dark rain against grey skies. Drums quickened. The shadowthorn column picked up speed. Sevaka drew her cutlass and stared along the blade. So far from the deck of the *Zephyr* and the storm-tossed expanse of the Western Ocean, but no finer place to make an end. Rosa would understand, if she recovered. At least now she'd have the chance. A hundred lives spent to safeguard hundreds more.

Sometimes the calling was to die while others won elsewhere.

Sevaka returned Gavrida's closed-fist salute and pushed to the centre of the rampart. The first quarrels hissed away. Trumpets sounded below. The Hadari broke into a run – a tall man in haloed helm and scarlet robes at the fore. Shields hauled high. Ladders levelled against the walls like a lance.

Clouds parted, spilling sunlight across the road. Sevaka's upraised cutlass blazed like fire.

"Death and honour!"

"Death and honour!"

Rosa awoke in creaking, shuddering gloom, nostrils thick with the stench of mud and sweat. Axles squeaked. Boots scuffed on stone somewhere beyond sight. Every muscle screamed and yet was numb – a raging fire behind a wall of ice. Lungs ached, no more than a thimbleful of air passing her lips with each heave. Efforts to rise occasioned nothing more than palsied twitching, so she sank back into sweat and struggled with blurred memory.

A sensation of falling. A hand about hers, and a kiss on her brow.

Sevaka?

Again, she strove to rise. Again her limbs betrayed her. Precious breath hissed away as a snarl.

"Hush." Feathered shadows gathered against canvas. The Raven loomed, hands braced atop the head of a black cane. "You've had a rough night, and more to come."

"What …" Rosa swallowed to ease a burning throat. "What happened?"

"Poison."

The face of shadowed memory took form. Thaldvar. "Where is he?"

A smile flickered beneath the domino mask. "In my keeping, courtesy of Miss Psanneque."

"I want to see her."

The smile faded. "You should rest."

Numbness grew colder and heavier. "Where is she?"

The Raven sighed. Still sitting, he twitched aside the canvas at Rosa's feet. Dark against grey clouds and shafts of reluctant sun, a broad column of men and women shuffled behind the wagon. Beyond, a handful of riders cloaked and hunched against the cold. And beyond that, two leagues distant along the pass . . .

There were no flames, just a thick, inky cloud of black smoke crawling away up the mountainside. Scarlet and emerald flags fluttered from Vrasdavora's rampart. Gold gleamed on the road beneath the walls.

"No." Rosa's fingers shuddered and failed to form a fist. "She's not . . . She isn't . . ."

"You forget to whom you're speaking." The Keeper of the Dead let the canvas fall closed. "Six hours, she held them. Three assaults, until a man named Aeldran Andwar ended her life. The same fellow who rescued the princessa at the bridge, as it happens. I confess, I didn't think she had it in her."

"No . . . It should have been me." Rosa wanted to scream. To shout. To weep. All denied her by a body that refused response. They'd only just found each other. To lose her so soon? It wasn't fair. Her heart burned; hot, cold and empty.

It wasn't fair.

"It should have been me."

He shook his head. "I warned about ephemeral smiles."

Sympathy fell flat, undermined by the tone beneath. A being grasping at alien emotion.

Rosa tried to picture Sevaka's face. She saw only darkness. "You could have helped her."

"You told me to stay away. I have respected your wishes, as a suitor should."

She'd all but screamed at him after Soraved. Had she not, Sevaka – and who could say how many more? – would still live. Selfishness of the grandest order.

"What of the Republic?"

He tutted. "Don't mistake me for a messenger pigeon." Then he shrugged. "Things are not going well. Yon fellow Izack intends to make a stand at the Rappadan. Alas that confidence alone does not win wars."

The Rappadan River, and the shining spires of Tarvallion. Treasured memories beneath starlight. Ephemeral moments lost too soon.

Sevaka.

Sorrow kindled to anger. At the shadowthorns. At the Raven. At herself.

"You're right," gasped Rosa. "I told you to stay away. No more. Stand with us and I'm yours."

He tapped the foot of his staff in time to the wagon's creak. "I will give you all that you ask, but it's not wise to frame it as a bargain."

"I don't care." Rosa's vision blurred as wrath and sorrow made feast of her body's slim reserves. But breathing came easier, even as strength faded. "Win this war – make the Hadari suffer – and I'll be your queen. I'll serve you. I'll be whatever you wish."

The Raven's lips parted, closed, and opened anew. "If that's what you desire."

The shadows bled away, and he was gone.

Thirty-Eight

An army gathered in the plaza beyond the broad palace balcony, constabulary blue joined by hearthguard from three-score noble houses. It stretched out to the scaffold-covered Vordal Tower on the square's far side – almost to the tree-lined mouth of Sinner's Mile beyond. The sight swept Malachi back to happier times, when the bells of Vordal had summoned citizens to hear the decrees of a united council or join the throng of the Guilds' Fair. Honours had been proclaimed from that balcony. Recitals and performances by the greatest artists of the age, offered in tribute to populace and goddess. All in the past, before rebellion and war had divided the Council, and ambition festered to discord.

"I reckon this is all we're getting." To Malachi's certain knowledge, Vona Darrow hadn't slept, but he'd never have read it in her clear eyes and untroubled brow. "Unless you're holding anything back?"

Malachi slipped his paper knife from his pocket and rapped it against his knuckles. Holding back? His only secrets were of shame. "No."

"There's no sense delaying, Malachi." Messela joined him at the balcony's edge. "Not unless you want to abandon hope of surprise."

Lord Lamirov stirred by the door. Like Malachi, he was unshaven – testament to a night of twisted arms and favours collected. "There'll be no surprise. The vranakin have eyes everywhere."

But not on the balcony at that moment. Rika Tarev – or Apara, as Malachi still struggled to think of her – hadn't shown. Nor had Konor Zarn or Lord Marest, who had by all accounts barricaded the doors of his mansion. Waiting to see whether the Dusk Wind carried the vranakin further into the city before pledging his fortunes.

Bracing against the impossible weight of unsought burdens, Malachi wondered what Viktor would have done in his place. "Captain Darrow? Drive the vranakin into the sea."

She offered a salute as crisp as her smile was grim. "About damn time."

Sidara waited at the riverside, gambeson buckled tight and singlestick resting against the birch. Altiris' familiar trickle of nervousness roused to a torrent. Long, brutal years on Selann had instilled a lesson that the northwealder nobility were superior by blood and birth. He'd never believed, but Sidara's surety made her seem his elder by years, though they were but months apart. Moreover, her magic had saved his life, and then set it in jeopardy. It was impossible *not* to feel diminished.

A shame she revelled in her superiority. Worse that he longed for her approval even so.

"I'm surprised the guards let a dangerous southwealder roam the grounds."

Her smile did nothing to soften the words, meant as it was for herself, and not for him. The chasm between them yawned wider.

"I have a name, Lady Reveque."

The smile broadened. "I know you do, southwealder."

"And it so happens they almost didn't," he said stiffly. "This uniform doesn't count for much if you were born south of Margard."

Sidara paused, lips parted, then scowled away whatever she'd meant to say. "Where *is* Captain Kurkas?"

No apology in the words, however much Altiris read one in her expression. "I've not seen him since yesterday. Sergeant Brass reckons he's drunk, and will turn up in his own good time."

"You don't agree?"

"I don't know." Altiris shook his head. "No. I'm worried."

"Did you ask Ana? They seem close."

"Honestly? I avoid her where I can." He glanced about. "Tell me she's not here."

"No. She said she'd make infrequent visits, so as not to offend Mother."

So as not to be caught, more like. "I see."

Sidara cocked her head. "Perhaps the captain's caught up in this business with Dregmeet. I scarcely managed two words out of

Father, but Hawkin tells me he's scrounged up hearthguard from half the city."

Altiris frowned. There'd been only two sentries at the Abbeyfields gate, where on previous days there'd been no fewer than four. "We've heard nothing at Stonecrest."

"Perhaps Father thought there wasn't anyone to be spared."

"You know what's going on?"

"Enough to know the vranakin are causing trouble, but that's hardly new. Father's worried." She scowled. "Father's always worried."

"He should be. The mists have swallowed half the city."

She paled. "I don't believe you."

"You must have seen. They end not three streets away."

"I'm not even allowed to go as far as one." Her shrug little disguised frustration, nor the longing glance towards a boundary hidden by trees. "Mother fears for me."

What little Altiris had seen of the elder Lady Reveque tended more towards anger than fear. Nonetheless, the softening of Sidara's manner did its wicked work, tempting him to undeserved sympathy.

"I'm not lying to you, lady. And it's not just the mists. Prizraks and worse. Grey men who wither with a touch."

A flicker of irritation. "I've not led so sheltered a life I've not heard the nursery rhymes."

"They're more than that, lady. I saw one. Back before I was ..." Realising his hand was pressed against his wound, Altiris hurriedly withdrew it. "I think Captain Kurkas is right in the middle of it."

Her gaze snapped back from the unseen boundary. "What do you mean?"

Altiris winced, but with the promise half-broken found little to hold him back. "Yesterday, we – he and I – were to head into Dregmeet."

"Whatever for?" A touch of asperity returned, the words not quite learned by rote. "There's nothing there but thieves and squalor."

He glared. "They're not all vranakin. Not even most of them. Just folk trying to survive. We can't all live in mansions, spending our days at swordplay and ..." He cast about for an example of how a young woman of Sidara's lineage might while away the day, but came up dry. "... discussing opera."

She hooked an eyebrow, more amused than annoyed. "We were talking about Captain Kurkas."

He pressed on, glad to have escaped. "You know the vranakin had been taking southwealders?"

"Father spoke of it a few nights ago. Mother changed the subject."

"Captain Kurkas grew up in Dregmeet. He reckoned to find out where others were being held. I was meant to go with him. But—"

"But I threw you in the river. You think something's happened to him?"

"With everything that's going on?" He shook his head. "I don't know."

Sidara stared away, her expression thoughtful. "I don't spend much time outside the grounds, but I've endured any number of Father's parties. I know how a lie sounds. Tell me the truth, Altiris."

Altiris. Not "southwealder". "Yes, lady. I fear he's come to harm."

Silence reigned, broken only by the twitter of birds in the trees and the ripple of the river.

Abbeyfields' bell chimed for eleven. Sidara straightened, features setting firm. "Let's find him."

He blinked. "Wait . . . what?"

"I said, let's find him."

Go tromping into the mists? Much less in the company of a sheltered noble like Sidara? "You said you're not allowed to leave the grounds."

"I'm not. But Constans gets out all the time. Ana got in." She shot him a withering glance. "I can climb a fence."

"It's not safe."

"Nor am I. If yesterday taught you anything, it should be that."

"Your mother . . ."

"Wants me wrapped up in wool." Bite returned to her tone, for the first time directed at elsewhere. "I should be a squire already. Father promised I could join Essamere, but Mother gainsaid him. She'll keep me here for ever."

"There's a world of difference between spreading your wings and flying into Dregmeet! We don't even know the captain's there. Even if he is, this is something for the constabulary."

"Who are never less than stretched to the limit. If all you've told me is true, do you imagine they've time for one lost soul?"

"Then send your hearthguard."

"They don't take orders from me. At best, I can make a request of Mother. I know what she'll say." She shot him a shrewd look, gold flecks among the blue. "I can't tell if you're afraid for me, or yourself."

Fair, as neither could Altiris. "I can be both."

She spread her hands in frustration then subsided to stillness. "When they brought you to me . . . I didn't want to help. Uncle Josiri pleaded, but I was afraid. Of my mother's anger. Of what I'm becoming. Then Ana said to look inside myself. At the light. It told me that I've not earned the right to do nothing, not when doing *something* might save a life. Captain Kurkas is one of the few people who comes to Abbeyfields and treats me as a person, rather than a prize. I'm not asking your permission. I'm not asking you to come. I'm telling you that I'm going into Dregmeet." She twitched a shoulder. "But I'd rather not go alone."

Habitual confidence fell away. For the first time, Altiris saw not the daughter of a noble line, but a girl his age determined to do something that terrified her.

Of course, there was a third option. He could go to the hearthguard. Even to the elder Lady Reveque. Tell them what Sidara intended. She'd be kept safe. Furious, but safe. Strange to hold the balance of power for the first time in their brief association. Stranger still to feel no temptation to use it. Or maybe not. He owed her his life. Loyalty was a small enough token of exchange.

And Kurkas *had* treated him well.

"You win."

Sidara's frown blossomed into perfect joy. "You'll come? You know I wasn't sure . . . " Her eyes widened, gaze slipping past his shoulder. "Hawkin, we were just—"

"Hush. I heard everything." The steward drew closer through the trees. Chestnut curls and long skirts worn alongside troubled expression. "Even a city girl can tread quietly when the moment calls. I thought you might need a chaperone. Turns out you need a dose of sense."

Sidara started, aghast. "Please, Hawkin. You can't tell anyone."

"Your mother trusts me. Even after my lapse. Do you know what that's worth?" Hawkin's eyes touched briefly on Altiris'. "No offence, my bonny. I'm glad you're not sitting at the Raven's hand."

Altiris nodded, knowing he could say nothing that wouldn't make matters worse.

Sidara folded her arms. She was the picture of defiance, but Altiris – who had learned a great deal that morning about reading her mood– caught the flicker of worry in her eyes. "And you'll give me away?"

"I should. Vona would in a heartbeat. Not an ounce of trust in her soul, that wife of mine." Hawkin shook her head. "I don't want you to get hurt. But I know enough of this city to know that hurt will find you, sooner or later. Just make sure it's not today. I couldn't bear that."

"Then . . . you're letting us go?"

Hawkin shook her head. "I haven't seen you, so I can't. One sniff of the mists and you'll be back, I imagine. Just make sure you don't return without her, young man. Or I'll make sure whatever Lady Lilyana does to you as punishment seems like sunshine and kittens, do you understand me?"

Despite the framing, Altiris read more challenge than threat. Better that way. Something to rise to, rather than cower beneath. "Yes, Mistress Darrow."

Thirty-Nine

The killing weight of Essamere crashed home with a thunder of galloping hooves. Zephan Tanor's arm shuddered as his lance pierced
a shadowthorn's shield. The brute slumped against his fellows, guttural
cry fading. A spear skittered off Zephan's armour. Another shattered
against his shield. Letting the lance drop, Zephan dragged free his sword
and stabbed down. A face sheeted in blood and fell away.

"*Until Death!*"

The Essamere battle cry echoed beneath grey skies, more howl than
words. Zephan spurred his destrier into the widening gap. A shieldsman
vanished screaming under a neighbour's hooves. Blood flecked the newcomer's gold and green cloak.

"Drive them into the bloody river!" bellowed Izack. "For Tregga!"

Tregga, gutted from within when traitors had opened its gates.

Zephan thrust back his spurs. He forgot the stench of sweat and blood,
and the fear that had ridden beside him on the charge. The field filled
with bodies and routed men.

Knights thundered past, plumes and cloaks streaming behind.
Zephan spurred to the pursuit, deaf to all save the rush of hooves and
the wails of the dying.

The cry of a buccina dragged him back. The falling three-note octave
that called for order.

"Show some bloody discipline!" Izack stood tall in his stirrups,
the order's banner streaming behind him. The sword and the eagle,
gold against hunter's green. "You're Essamere, not a band of drunken
thrakkers!"

Instinct drove Zephan to the second rank, among the squires yet to earn their plumes. With friends made in ten long years since taking the Vigil Oath. But that life lay behind. Instead, he walked his steed into the gap beside the chapterhouse banner. His first charge as a full knight. Against a shadowthorn shield wall bearing the stag of Silsaria, no less.

That the stag shields had come forward too soon and unsupported was no matter. Battles turned on error more than valour. The Silsarians had paid for theirs. Survivors streamed back to the golden line stretching between the caves of Sharnweald to the east and the reed-strewn Rappadan marshlands in the west.

To the east, the battle had barely begun. Wayfarers peppered the shadowthorn advance with arrows before wheeling away. Behind, overlapping lines of pavissionaires threaded the gentle rise, their hawk shields planted to form muddy walls of king's blue. Blocks of halberdiers, Prydonis foot knights and towering kraikons anchored each line. Hundreds more waited behind, ready to stiffen the defence when the shadowthorns came too close for quarrels.

Further south, great, winding serpents of the shadowthorn advance wended their way across the lowlands. Shields glittered like scales. Bodies marked where those shields had failed. Even as Zephan took his place, a ballista shot reduced a dozen men to a bloody smear. Pale-witches kept pace upon steeds of shimmering moonlight, their threat holding at bay the simarka lurking in Sharnweald's undergrowth. And behind them, grunda wagons, the calloused, leathery beasts caparisoned in silk. Shields wouldn't hold before a charging grunda, but the beasts were yet out of crossbow-shot, and so the shadowthorn shieldsmen suffered in their stead.

In the western marshes, king's blue banners of the 3rd thickened in an abandoned farm. The companies had held position since the night before – their major refusing to retreat. The emerald silks of Rhaled drew closer to the walls, driven on by ceaseless drums. And at their head, golden cataphracts, a silver crown and a sword blazing with moonfire. The Emperor himself.

"Brother." Shalan walked his steed between Zephan and his immediate neighbour. "Your lance is lost. Take mine."

Zephan sheathed his sword and he accepted the lance. The dutiful gift was echoed up and down the Essamere line as squires gave of their own arms so that knights would strike true.

Buccinas flared. Squires withdrew to the second rank.

"The Emperor's coming." Izack, still a dozen paces in front of the reforming line, wheeled his horse to make the address. Grim glee shone beneath his morose tone. "Looks like he's bringing us plenty of sport. Pale-witches, too. Remember, you can't kill their steeds except under moonlight, so aim for the doxy in the saddle!"

At least two thousand spears matched against a thousand knights and squires. Numbers alone didn't tell the tale. Heavy destriers and the folded plate of Essamere beat golden scale. Still, it would be a hard fight. And that made no account of the pale-witches riding close by. About the campfire, it was easy enough to discount rumour that their moonlight steeds were proof against ephemeral steel. Another thing entirely to see them flickering on a grey morning. Just as it was harder to forget that Saran wielded Ashana's fire. Ashana. Lunastra. A goddess loathed by many, but worshipped by Zephan's family for generations. The Lumestran church might have driven the other gods from the city of Tressia, but the Lunastran faith clung on in the provinces. More or less.

"He should have brought more!" Warden Tori Kastala shouted from beneath the banner. As mistress of Essamere's vigil in Tarvallion, she'd demanded the honour of bearing the standard. There were no safer hands.

Agreement rumbled through the ranks.

Izack accepted a fresh lance from a squire and set the pole across his shoulder. "Reckon he should. But who better than Essamere to teach the bugger a—"

"'ware right!"

To the west, the banners of the 3rd vanished from the farm, replaced by the House of Saran's spread-winged owl. The king's blue uniforms remained, now joined by emerald silks. All along the riverbank, dark, filthy figures emerged from the reeds and shook themselves into a line of shields.

Kastala spat. "Queen's Ashes!"

To the south, the line of cataphracts started forward.

The 3rd hadn't held the farm at all. They'd been overrun, their tabards and banners claimed as deception. The Silsarians hadn't erred. They'd been a lure, and now Essamere was to pay the price.

Drums shook the air. To the west, shields came forward. The first arrows flickered out from the farm. A squire screamed and toppled from her saddle. A horse reared. To the south, the cataphract line divided. The white flame of the Emperor's sword veered northeast, towards waiting pavissionaires. A man swathed in a bear cloak's thick furs led the remainder north to Essamere.

Zephan offered silent prayer to the Goddesses. For victory, and if not that then a death of which his twin families of blood and sword would be proud. To hold was to be caught between the anvil of muddy shields and the hammer of a cataphract charge. To retreat was to feel a spear in the spine. Head-on or nothing. Break the cataphract line before the shieldsmen closed.

"Canny bastard." Disdaining the hissing arrows, Izack wheeled about and snapped his visor shut. "Until Death!"

He spurred away, Kastala on his heels. The green-and-gold banner snapped and streamed behind, the eagle swooping for the kill.

"*Until Death!*"

Zephan Tanor joined his voice to the cry and rowelled his destrier.

Battles turned on error more than valour, but valour had its place.

The cataphract charge met the Knights Essamere with a crash that shook the battlefield. Horsemen spurred into gaps emptied by the strike of lance and spear. The lines mingled in a blur of gold and green.

Muscles spasmed in Kai's shield hand. *Not now.* One thing to display weakness in private. Another to do so as battle joined. Kai clenched his fist. Shaking fingers he could conceal. A seizure was another matter. Inch by tortuous inch, rebellious flesh subsided.

Elspeth's shining eyes never left the battle. "It's beautiful."

"It's necessary."

Kai wondered why he bothered. Whatever her thawing of manner, Elspeth had shown no sign of sympathy for any other than him. Nor had she accepted offer of sword and armour, despite his pleading. She faced this battle as she had every skirmish since Ahrad: barefoot, with only her much-abused white dress and the slender surety of her silver dagger.

In the distance, the brawl quickened. Unhorsed Immortals dragged knights from their saddles. The Essamere banner dipped and rose tall. The last Silsarians scrambled away, redeemed for cruelties against the Tressian populace by their offering of blood upon the field. Better to offer knaves as sacrifice than real warriors.

Unable to shake discomfort, Kai urged his horse to the canter. To the northeast, the first Tressian line crumpled as King Sard's column reached its shields. The leftmost end disintegrated, overrun by bellowing grunda and the lithe grace of the lunassera's chandirin.

The Immortals cheered, Elspeth with them.

"Cowards!" she laughed. "Why do they not stand?"

"They expected a horde," Kai replied. "When they didn't find one, they took heart. But by now they've seen Sard's rangers beneath the trees, and Corvanti shields by the river. They despair of there being any end to us. A man afraid counts every foe twice, and conjures more beyond his sight."

On the rise, the Tressian commander strove to salvage survival from defeat. Crossbows abandoned, the lines shook into a wall of blades, shields locked and halberds bristling behind.

Kai raised his sword high. Time to make an end of things. For the Goddess. And for the daughter who would follow him.

"Ashanael Brigantim!"

Elspeth reached for him, eyes wide. "No! Wait!"

Her cry came too late, his spurs already set. Churned ground rushed away beneath, shrouded by mist as sudden in onset as Elspeth's alarm. A new sound vied with drums and buccinas. A trumpet call as deep and breathy as the rumble of a thousand wagons, and yet without note or substance. The music of the open grave.

The parry saved Zephan's life at the cost of his balance. He sprawled as the cataphract hurtled past, left arm still numb from the spear-thrust that had ripped him from the saddle. He sank to his knees. The dead stared back. Cold eyes from open helms. Shadowthorn and sword-sibling, united in death.

The battle blurred away behind mist and the breathy, rumbling trumpet call. Lost were the cries of warriors beset; the clamour of steel.

As Zephan staggered to his feet, screams and silhouettes grew distant where they'd crowded close before. He knew he was dying, senses fading as Otherworld claimed his soul. Only the pain in his shoulder burned bright.

He ripped off his helm and let it fall. The air stank of sorrow.

"Amhyrador Brigantim!"

The mists parted about the tatter-cloaked cataphract. The spear dipped. Zephan clambered to his feet, sword heavy and sluggish. One last effort.

The spear-point glinted, skeins of mist trailing. Too close. Too fast.

A shape hurtled out of the mists, hooves churning the bloody ground. A sword pierced scales at the cataphract's spine. The shadowthorn toppled from the saddle, his spear falling free of a lifeless hand. His steed forged on. A glancing blow from its shoulder struck Zephan to his knees, then it was gone into the mist.

Izack sawed on his reins. "You alive, lad?"

The master of Essamere sat hunched in the saddle; helm and shield lost to the battle, armour bloodied and cloak torn. A man of stone, shoulders braced unyielding beneath the weight of the world. It demanded imitation.

Zephan stood, wincing as blessed numbness receded from his shoulder. "Yes, master."

"Don't look it." He leaned down from the saddle, hand extended. "Climb up behind. Isildi's a strong lass, she'll carry us both clear."

Zephan blinked. "Retreat?"

Izack snorted. "Retreat speaks of a battle barely lost. They've ground us to a bloody pulp. From what I saw before the mists came down, the rest of the army'll be lucky not to follow."

The world fell away as the full weight of the words sunk in. They spoke to Essamere scattered, perhaps annihilated. Unthinkable. Inevitable. The mists clung closer, tighter. Screams faded to whispering voices.

Zephan sheathed his sword and reached for Izack's hand.

The mists parted before a line of filthy shields and spears flying ragged green pennants. Trophies stripped from the Essamere dead. Horsemen loomed behind. Outriders. Swift enough to overtake a burdened steed.

Zephan drew back his hand. "Go. Leave me."

"Bugger that." Izack wheeled about to face the shadowthorns and brandished his sword. "Until ... "

The oath fell silent on lips unaccustomed to losing voice.

All around, mist darkened to shadow. Creeping, cadaverous forms pulled free of the drifting shroud. Skull masks gleamed silver. Swords blazed with black flame. And boiling above, squalling, screeching bird shapes whose wings bled into vapour.

A pale Izack fought for control of Isildi's reins. Cold hands squeezed the warmth from Zephan's heart. Until death? The dead had found them. He urged a nerveless hand to his sword. It remained unmoving, and he defenceless in the revenants' path. His whispered prayer to the Goddesses stuttered and died.

Spirits parted around him like a black tide. Gathering pace, they bore down on the shadowthorns.

The mists thickened with silvered skulls and drifting shadow. Kai's horse reared and cast him to bone-crunching impact with the battlefield's churned mud. Left and right, the cataphract line boiled away into black flame. Screams and trumpets rang out through the mists, then were drowned out by the clarion of the dead.

Terror swamped Kai's soul, hastened by recollection. The brothers Andwar, and their tales of deathless spirits at Soraved. His father's Last Ride beneath the gaping doors of Ravenscourt Temple. The ancient rites that opened Otherworld's gates to the honoured dead. Only there, ghostfires held encroaching spirits at bay. Here there was nothing. Nothing save ...

He stared into the alabaster flame of the Goddess' sword. Fear abated, drowned in moonlight. Courage rekindled.

Screaming to drown his fear, Kai plunged into the mass of shadow. A skull helm split beneath his strike, the revenant unravelling beneath. Another rode at him, blazing sword levelled like a spear. White flame met black. The latter hissed away as the revenant's sword shattered into glinting shards. A counterblow swept spirit from vaporous steed.

On Kai strode into the darkness. No fear. No hesitation. Only the white flame of the Goddess' sword, and the black that sought in vain to quench it. Shadows gathered. A knot of grinning helms and darting swords bled from the alabaster flame, only to return when it passed.

"Ashanael Brigantim!" Another helm shattered beneath Kai's strike. "I wield the Goddess' light! I fear not your darkness!"

The alabaster flame dimmed, its flicker matched to a sudden pain. Seizure gripped his chest. His veins throbbed with the remorseless, stuttering thump of his pulse. The world spun. Vision muddied, splotched red.

Kai's legs buckled. Hand clutched to his chest, he fell to one knee.

The sword's fire sputtered out.

Hissing triumph, the revenants closed, their shadow no longer distinct from the stain behind Kai's eyes. He felt himself slipping, body and spirit. A part of him bleeding into the mists. The Goddess' sword fell from numbed fingers. The sounds of battle grew more distant than ever.

"What has my sister done, that you burn so bright and brief?" A domino-masked man strode out of the mists. A hat hung loosely from his hand. A disdainful smile glimmered beneath the goatee. He squatted, dark eyes gleaming. "No greeting? I'm disappointed."

The turgid thump of Kai's pulse all but drowned the words. Pained wheeze swallowed defiant reply.

The man snapped his fingers. "What am I thinking?"

The Tressian suit rippled away into the black garb of a traditional mourning gown and its woven shawl. The man of prime years became an old woman, white of hair and lined of feature. Only the mask remained, though now its feathers shimmered behind a silken veil. An echo of the statues that guarded the Ravenscourt gate.

"I confess, I prefer the other." The Raven reached out her wizened hand. "It's time for you to come with me, Kai, son of Ceredic, son of Edric. You'll make a fine wedding gift."

Kai doubled over as the pressure about his chest tightened. Blood welled up from his eyes. It spattered across the mud, and hissed away silver. He stared, revulsed. Thoughts mired, spared from horror by weariness of sinew and bone. His last strength faded as his fingers reached the sword's grips, and he pitched forward onto an elbow.

"Yes," said the Raven. "You're ready now."

Pale, white light edged Kai's failing senses. The musky scent of spring blossoms and burning fleenroot – the cleansing fragrance of the pyre. Revenants recoiled, swallowed into mist.

The Raven rose, a scowl on her lips. "You've no business here."

Elspeth strode into sight. She bore a cataphract's upturned helm in her hands, a smoky white flame crackling and spitting within. "I swore to serve him."

"With your death?" The Raven shrank away. "You're nothing but a splinter of moonlight."

Mockery glinted. "I'm not the one recoiling from a handful of burning blossoms. You're not all here, are you, uncle? The mists came at your call, but they're already fading. A shadow of a shadow. How poetic. Or do I mean 'pathetic'?"

"I won't forget this."

"I don't care."

The Raven vanished.

Mist scattered from the battlefield. The revenants and shrieking birds went with it, leaving no trace but horrific memories, and the bodies of the slain. The shadowthorn army was gone, the dead thick upon the ground and the living set to flight. A tide of horses, men and wagons, thousands strong, streamed towards tents upon the southern hills. The Tressian lines – bowed in some places and gaping wide in others – stood silent, lost in the terrible splendour. Zephan couldn't stop shaking.

Izack dropped from Isildi's saddle and stared across the corpse-choked plain. The crop of shadowthorn dead couldn't conceal the bitter swathe of king's blue. "I don't bloody believe it."

Knots of green revealed survivors of the Essamere charge. Two-score paces to the east, the eagle-banner yet flew, Kastala's slumped corpse holding aloft in death the colours she'd borne in life. Out of every ten who had mustered to the field, perhaps two or three remained fit to fight. A dark day for Essamere.

"What happens now?" said Zephan.

Izack gave a slow shake of his head. Then he pulled himself to some semblance of the man who'd taken the field. "Now? We retreat. No one won today. Saving the Raven, of course. He must be glutted."

The Raven. It was one thing to offer prayer to the Goddesses, and another to witness Otherworld emptied to war – no matter to whose banner it marshalled. The stuff of myth and nightmare.

"I don't know that I recognise this world any longer," Zephan replied.

"Nor me, lad." Izack reached for Isildi's reins. "Nor me."

"Wake, my Emperor."

Kai lurched upright. Darkness yielded to the greys of his tent. The battlefield's embrace to that of his bed. Armour creaked alongside weary bones. Pain cobwebbed every breath, every motion. But at least he *could* breathe. Trembling fingertips traced his cheek, recalling black tears and the emptiness of unmoored spirit. The helplessness. The Raven. He bit down on his knuckles to stifle a cry.

"Hush." Elspeth stood at the tent's flaps, her back to him and arms wrapped about herself. "Devren surrendered you to my care most unwillingly. If he suspects that I mean you harm—"

"Was it real?"

"Every moment."

"And the battle?" There was no victory in the subdued camp beyond the tent's thin walls. Only despair, and snatches of mourning song.

"The Andwars spoke true. My uncle has sided with the Tressians. I drove him off, but he'll return."

Kai touched his eyes closed. "Uncle? I *saw* a woman." Only ... that wasn't true, was it? Not at first.

"The Raven is whatever he wishes," she replied. "Whatever amuses. When you are different things to different people no one has power over you, because no one truly *knows* you. But to me, the Raven will always be my uncle, because that is how my mother thought of him."

"And you?"

"I am what I have always been. What my sisters have always been. Our mother's dream of what her daughters might be. What *she* might have been, had fate taken another course." She paused. "She always claimed she and I were the most alike. Take from that what you will."

The spark of self-loathing sat ill alongside recent, selfless, deeds. "Her sword ... "

Elspeth cast a hand towards the table. Steel sat cold and dark in the gloom. "Is here."

"It failed me."

"You failed *it*. In divine hands, that blade might part the heavens. But it is only as strong as the life of he who wields it. And you . . . " She hung her head. "You are no longer among the living."

The words should have hurt. And yet Kai could barely stir himself to surprise. *What has my sister done, that you blaze so bright and brief?* The tremors he'd felt ever since Ahrad. He'd thought them a sign of age, but they were more than that. He'd been a fool to ignore them. "At my coronation. You told me you saved me!"

She turned, eyes blazing. "I strove to hold you in the balance. To make you eternal. But your soul had already splintered between ephemeral and divine. Not even the deepest obsession could hold you among the living. Only my mother's light would serve."

Kai rose from the filthy bedsheets. Knees shuddered but held. How much of the sensation was even real? "You should have told me."

"Mother commanded otherwise."

"And now?"

"Now she is in no position to forbid anything. With her light gone, I spend mine in its place."

"Why?"

"Because I promised my mother, and then I promised you. The Dark must be driven out of Tressia at your hand."

The Dark. The conceit by which he'd unified a fractured Empire. He'd used Ashana's ambitions to feed his own, never knowing the extent to which she'd used him in return. Perhaps Elspeth was right, and she the truest reflection of her mother. "What if there is no Dark to be found in Tressia?"

Elspeth turned away.

"I see," said Kai. "I am to provide Melanna with an Empire, and then fall into the mists."

"That was my mother's intent. It is not mine. However long I can sustain you, I will. But it will not last for ever."

"Nothing ever does." Anger came no more easily than surprise. Weariness, or the recognition that Ashana had not conspired to his death, only postponed it? "Why has the Raven sided with the Tressians?"

"Did you miss when I said he does little save out of amusement? His motives are mystery. And his power . . . " She shuddered. "I am the breeze that shakes the boughs. He is a hurricane. Though diminished, he should have torn me apart."

"Diminished?"

"The mists slipped away even as he laid waste your warriors. Without them, his creatures cannot walk this world."

"Do you know why?"

"I know only that I cannot do again what I did today."

"We cannot fight both the Tressians and the Raven!"

"Ghostfire holds his creatures at bay. Your sword can kill them."

The sword that had already betrayed him. That stole away his life and hastened his descent into the mists? "That's not enough!"

"It will have to be! I . . . "

Elspeth froze, motionless save for a shudder of anger. Or was it fear?

For a heartbeat, Kai thought she meant to flee his presence. Then she drew close, bare feet silent on the thick rugs of the tent floor, and set a spread hand to his chest. White light danced about her fingers, hot and cold through armour and silk. It lent strength to spent, unsteady limbs; drove back the burdens of a long and sorrowful day. She leaned into him, grey eyes earnest and pleading.

"I will give you all that I can, short of my life. But I will not perish to prove that which I already know. Challenging my uncle will be my end, and yours also."

She withdrew her hand. The glow faded. Weariness returned.

"Are my warleaders assembled?" asked Kai.

Elspeth offered a sly smile. "Even now, they argue who should command after your passing. The Raven falls distant second to ambition."

Kai laid his hands on her shoulders. "Then we should disappoint them. Go. I'll follow soon."

She bobbed her head. "Yes, my Emperor."

She withdrew without looking back, her posture straighter than before. However alike Elspeth was to her mother in character, she put Kai more and more in mind of a cat. Whatever affection she felt for him – whatever duty held her close – she would always be an observer to his life more than part of it.

His life. Whatever remained. If indeed he could truly be counted among the living.

The Goddess' sword blazed as he lifted it, though the flames were dimmer than before. The House of Saran had to go on, so it wasn't enough to hold the Raven at bay. He had to be beaten, as the Tressians had to be beaten.

Whatever it cost.

The air in the tent changed as Kai reached his decision, musty canvas yielding to damp soil and leaf rot. Shadows lengthened to crawling thorns.

You need only call my name.

He sheathed the sword.

"Jack, Lord of Fellhallow." He faltered, feeling ridiculous for addressing emptiness even though instinct warned he wasn't alone. "I accept your bargain. Vanquish the Raven – save my present – and my future is yours."

Had Jack not heard? Or did he recognise the worthlessness of the bargain he'd once proposed? Of what worth was a dead man's future?

"Jack, do you hear me?"

The air grew close and bitter, filled with the rustle and creak of brittle thorns. Hairs bristled along Kai's neck at the sense of *something* standing at his shoulder.

{{Yes,}} buzzed Jack. {{The bargain is agreed.}}

Forty

Word reached Three Pillars an hour before the motley army of constables and hearthguards. A flock of rassophores had spread their wings across shrouded skies, summoning those who owed fealty or favour. Grey-garbed bodies gathered thick on slate, the roofs a roost for vranakin of all ranks and ages. Four storeys below, yet more gathered at the mouth of alleyway and yard. They cawed defiance as uniforms descended into the plaza, swords drawn, crossbows ready and heraldry muted by mist.

Apara's raven cloak kept her cousins distant, leery of a kernclaw's fickle mood. Not Athariss. The pontiff stood at the townhouse gable, a leering, grey-draped gargoyle.

"A show of strength?" he cackled. "Lord Reveque is bold. Foolish, but bold. We'll peel them apart. Every last one."

Far below, the quartered yellow-and-black of the Karov hearthguard threaded shiftless etravia to join a line already broader and deeper than the vranakin mob it sought to contest.

"We forced him to this," said Apara.

"Do I hear criticism, cousin?" asked Athariss.

Apara flinched, her flesh crawling. "No, Crowfather."

This wasn't the Crowmarket she'd grown into. That Crowmarket had been cruel, as life was cruel, eking out survival on society's edge. It had stolen to eat. Killed to live another day. What mustered at Three Pillars was different. Hungry. Malevolent.

As the Silver Owl, she'd dallied on the edge of the mists. Stolen for challenge, or to put food in the mouths of hungry cousins. Easy to turn a blind eye when you saw so little. But as a kernclaw? She'd seen too much. Blood ritual at Westernport. The creeping horror concealed beneath an elder cousin's robes. The stolen children. One thing to become vranakin through choice; another entirely to be ripped from your kin. The Silver Owl could never have been part of that. Alas, she was gone, wrapped in the Raven's feathers and bound by the Parliament's promise to set her free from Akadra's shadow.

"We were forgotten," cackled Athariss. "Wrapped in tales of beg-gardom and decay. Something tolerated underfoot. But now the Raven's blessing flows, and a lesson must be taught. One they will not soon forget."

The words implied regret. Might even have convinced, but for the desire beneath. Apara's raven cloak cawed delight at the slaughter to come even as the shadow on her heart screamed.

"Yes, Crowfather."

The air shifted. Mist curled back from the streets, as if drawn thus by the breath of some vast, slumbering beast. The dry scent of yesterdays slipped away. Buildings shimmered and resettled as time-lost structures yielded to those of the present. Apara felt the streets reknit as the Living Realm reasserted itself.

"Crowfather? What is it?"

Athariss craned his head this way and that. Bony fingers formed to fists. "It will pass."

The mists flowed back through retangling streets. But the tension in Athariss' shoulders – his soft intake of breath – only reinforced suspi-cion. Athariss – arrogant, callous Athariss – had been *afraid*. For only a moment, perhaps, but a moment was enough.

Why?

In the plaza below, Captain Darrow clambered heavily onto a statue's pedestal with as much dignity as girth allowed. Lumestra's graven frown staring out over her shoulder, she unfolded a letter.

"By order of the Council . . . " With theatrical sigh, Darrow tucked the letter away. "We all know what it says. Come peaceably, you'll be treated well. Those who bring information leading to the return of the taken will be freed. The offer lasts until I draw my sword. After that? Lumestra help you all, because no one else will."

Darrow folded her arms and surveyed the rooftops. Apara envied her certainty, misplaced though it was. That surety went unshared by many in the captain's ranks. Hurried glances. Hands shaped to the sign of the sun. Lips moving in prayer. The mists had to be bad enough. But to see etravia drifting through the streets? To hear the wails of starving prizraks on the breeze? Nightmare made real.

The vranakin mob stared back. Unblinking and unmoving, save for the twitch of an elder cousin's robes or a kernclaw's feathered cloak.

Darrow dropped from the plinth and retook her place.

"If that's how you want it." She drew her sword. "Take back my streets!"

The line surged. The vranakin broke across the rooftops, bled away into streets and alleys. With a roar of triumph, Darrow's army pursued.

Athariss chuckled. "It begins."

The shriek of crows reached fever pitch. The first screams rang out close behind.

Sergeant Brass' hopes of a quiet evening evaporated with the doorbell's toll. Setting aside a bottle of Torianan red purloined from Stonecrest's cellar, he stomped from the kitchen. The bell tolled again as he worked the front door's latch.

"Hang on," said Brass. "Have a little patience, will you?"

Lady Reveque swept into the atrium in a swirl of black skirts and halted beneath the chandelier. Her veil did nothing to blunt a stare heightened by parallel scars part-hidden beneath.

"I want to speak to the Demon," she said icily.

Brass glanced at the Reveque carriage on the gravel drive. The carriage, and six hearthguard in the same livery. He swallowed. "If you mean Miss Psanneque . . . "

"I mean the Demon. Will you summon her, or must I have this house torn apart?"

The last thing Brass wanted to do was traipse around looking for Anastacia, who took perverse delight in employing servant's passages to stay one step ahead of her seekers. She'd been worse the last few days, her mischief more energetic to match the golden blush suffusing her porcelain skin. Then again, Lady Reveque had a reputation. The act of tearing apart the house would likely begin with him.

Hide-and-seek it was.

"If you'll just—"

Anastacia appeared at the head of the stairs. An ivory velvet dress offered perfect counterpoint to porcelain features and a wig's white curls.

[[Don't trouble yourself, Adbert. Only a rude demon would refuse audience to a serene.]] She descended the steps with measured tread. [[I must think of my reputation, mustn't I?]]

"I'm not a serene," snapped Lady Reveque.

[[But you always *dress* like a religious drab. Surely it's for a reason?]]

"Where is my daughter?"

Alabaster hands clasped to frozen lips in mock horror. [[A daughter? You have been a naughty serene, haven't you? So much for chastity.]]

She ghosted into the drawing room, Lady Reveque on her heels. Brass lumbered to the shelter of the far corner and strove to be forgotten.

"Where is she?" Lady Reveque ground out.

[[Lilyana, please. Am I a shepherd of wayward children?]] Anastacia plucked a decanter from the mantelpiece. [[May I offer you a drink? It's from Icasia. Very sweet. You could use a little of that.]]

"You've been sneaking into Abbeyfields behind my back."

Anastacia hesitated mid-pour. [[I don't *sneak* anywhere. Who told you?]]

"Hawkin. And now Sidara is missing."

[[I haven't seen her since yesterday.]]

"Hawkin says different."

Anastacia set the decanter down. The first glimmer of anger showed in her tone. [[Hawkin is mistaken.]]

"She's out of her mind with worry."

[[I don't doubt that she's out of her mind.]]

"So you haven't encouraged Sidara's fancies?" snapped Lady Reveque. "Whispered poison in her ear? My daughter is not your toy!"

[[Your daughter has a gift.]]

"Is she here?" Lady Reveque sagged. "Please. I just want her back. To be safe. Can't you understand that? Must I beg?"

Anastacia hung her head and uttered a low, hollow growl. [[Adbert, would you fetch Altiris? Maybe he can enlighten us.]]

Brass winced. "He's not been back since he left for Abbeyfields."

[[Vladama, then.]]

"No sign of him all day, lady. The lad went to Abbeyfields alone." But that wasn't all of it, was it? Brass, seeker of a quiet life and stranger to undue thought, nonetheless cared little for where those thoughts now led.

Anastacia cocked her head. [[Then I think perhaps the mystery is solved.]]

Lady Reveque scowled. "And *what* do you mean by that?"

Somehow, her frozen face contrived to leer. [[Your Sidara is such a pretty thing.]]

"Please. That boy flinches whenever he sees her."

[[Maybe she likes that. I do.]] Anastacia shook her head. [[When you cage a bird, Lilyana, you shouldn't be surprised at what happens if the door springs open.]]

Brass cleared his throat. Furious stares converged. All told, he'd rather be back at Davenwood, surrounded by bloodthirsty shadowthorns. He'd have known how to handle that.

"Altiris. This morning, he wanted me to go looking for Captain Kurkas in Dregmeet, but I was too ... tired ... from last night. Might be the boy didn't go to Abbeyfields."

"No, he was there. Sergeant Heren told me." Lady Reveque paled. The mother knew very much what the daughter might do when presented with an open door. "That doesn't mean he didn't head for Dregmeet after."

[[Or alone?]]

Lady Reveque left the room at a flat run. "I must speak to my husband."

[[Thank you for a gracious apology!]] Anastacia called after, with only a hint of mockery.

Her only reply was the creak of hinges and the slam of the front door. Beyond the walls, carriage wheels crunched on gravel and rumbled away.

[[*Ephemerals.* Why I should ever want any for friends, I'll never know.]] Anastacia poured the contents of the untouched glass back into the decanter. [[Nothing more guaranteed to make me miss liquor. Serve her right if the vranakin pick her daughter clean.]]

Perching on the arm of a chair, she clicked her fingers. Brass gaped as golden light sparked to life in her palm, weaving a young woman's likeness. The flickering figure pirouetted once – a touch unsteadily – then burst into smoke. Anastacia's head dipped, then rose, her chin tilted higher than before.

[[Adbert, my dear, close-tongued reprobate. Would there by any chance be an axe on the premises?]]

Forty-One

Vranakin hurtled past the alley's end, constables on their heels. One crow-born fled too slow. A woman in king's blue tackled him to the cobbles. Shrieking figures dropped from the rooftops. Screams split the darkness, the scent of blood close behind.

In moments, it was over. Vranakin seeped away into the misty streets, leaving the dead behind.

"At least we know why Father wanted the hearthguard," said Sidara.

Altiris glanced about. The mists were empty. Cacophony remained. A bellow of pain. Boots on cobbles. Screeching birds. The liquid, distorted toll of a church bell. Screams and the wet sound of steel on flesh. "We have to go back."

Sidara shook her head. "No. We came to find Captain Kurkas."

"And how do we do that?" snapped Altiris. With the mists rising, striking out for Dregmeet had always been a fool's errand – even with swords "borrowed" from the Reveque armoury. Seduced by Sidara's claims of noble cause, the prospect of her approval – even her smile – he'd been that fool. "We've been walking for an hour. That's Pannister Street. We're back where we started!"

"It's not my fault you're lost."

"My fault? You said you knew the way."

"I do!" Eyes flickered gold and dimmed to blue. "The streets are wrong. Everything's wrong. It's all Dregmeet now. All jumbled."

She sank against the wall, aristocratic reserve cracking.

"Lady Reveque, please . . . " The bells fell silent. Seven chimes. They'd left the Reveque estate at noon. An hour ago. More than the streets were askew. "Did you hear that? The clock's broken."

Sidara shook her head. "No. It's the mists. They're distorting everything. Can't you feel it?"

He didn't want to think about what she meant by that. Better to cling to the idea of a broken clock. "We should go back."

Sidara nodded, last resistance gone. "You win. Which way?"

Pannister Street. In theory, Three Pillars and the mists' extent were only a brisk walk – Abbeyfields a few minutes beyond that. But in theory it was afternoon, not evening as bells proclaimed.

Altiris picked his way through the two-score corpses at the alley's end. Most wore constabulary blue, a handful the mismatched garb of vranakin. Three the fox blazon and burgundy tabards of a highblood's hearthguard. One of the latter drew Altiris' eye, in defiance of his determination not to look. Withered skin and sunken eyes awoke memories of his last journey into the mists. Of green eyes blazing beneath a tattered grey hood, and insects scuttling across skin.

The colour faded from Sidara's cheeks. "Queen's Ashes. What did *that*?"

Grey shapes gathered further down the street. So much for reaching Three Pillars.

"Come on!"

They fled. A motionless kraikon passed away behind. A church's spire loomed against the darkening sky. The mists parted. A dark, feathered shape hunched over a dying constable, steel talons at his throat. Altiris froze, hand on his sword, transfixed by blazing green eyes. The scar on his belly ached. The kernclaw dissolved into a cloud of screeching, rushing wings.

"Altiris!"

Sidara slammed into him. They fell, she atop, he below. The seething flock boiled overhead. It coalesced at the head of the vranakin pursuit and staggered as a crossbow bolt hissed out of the carnage at the street's end.

King's blue uniforms thundered past. Grime spattered Altiris' face. Sidara hauled him upright and shoved him towards the churchyard. Boots scrambling on brick, he clambered over a wall and dropped onto grass. Sidara landed beside him, hair in wispy disarray and cheeks smeared with mud. She flinched at fresh screams.

Legs shaking, Altiris sank against the wall. "Thank you."

She shook her head. "We need to keep moving."

He followed through yew trees rendered macabre by enfolding mist. Sidara strode with purpose, never once looking back.

"Where—" He started as a branch brushed his sleeve. "Where are we headed?"

"I'm just trying to keep going. I'm afraid that if we stop, I'll curl up into a ball and that will be it." She twitched at a low, sonorous tolling. Not a church bell – deeper, and laden with baleful promise. "The mists have to end *somewhere*. Or maybe we'll find some of Father's hearthguard."

For the first time, Altiris saw his own fear reflected in Sidara's eyes. More than that, he had the sense that she wanted – maybe even *needed* – a voice beyond her own assuring her that all would be well.

"Lead on, milady."

Sidara's left eyelid flickered in suspicion of mockery. Then she nodded, and started along the lychpath. A wailing cry sounded beyond.

Maridov's scream stuttered as the robed figure drew him close. Carapaced shapes scuttled across withering, bloodless flesh and rusting armour. Captain Vona Darrow swallowed her horror and beckoned frantically to the constables at her back.

"Shoot! Bring the damn thing down!"

Quarrels *spacked* off the gable wall. Others thumped home. Grey robes twitched and shuddered. Maridov's body still clutched tight, the figure fell. Dust hissed away as it struck cobbles. With its fall, the other vranakin fled, a flood of turned heels running for the safety of the mists.

"Blessed Lumestra," gasped Constable Jorek. "What was that?"

Darrow edged closer, nostrils itching at the stench. Too dry for decay, but death nonetheless. Her sword twitched aside the hood, revealing a face scarcely less gaunt and rutted than the luckless Maridov's. Pallid skin clung tight to cheek and brow – the hollow features of a corpse long buried. Writhing black insects scuttled from burrows of ragged flesh and sought the shelter of gutter and cracked brick.

"Bloody disgusting is what it is."

Jorek braced his crossbow against the ground and cranked the string back into position. "Begging your pardon, captain, but this whole business is bloody disgusting."

Pinched expression belied levity. Not that the other constables looked any better. Not that Darrow *felt* any better. The streets had swallowed her makeshift army and spat out bones and blood. Knives in every shadow. Eyes on every rooftop. And with every turning, her numbers thinned. Now she'd barely a score of constables at her back. The others were still out there. She heard them fighting. She heard them *dying*. Every scrap of sound fed a temper seldom below boiling point, the anger worse for impotence.

"We let this grow," she growled. "We knew Dregmeet was trouble, but we looked the other way. Now we're paying for it."

"We offered peace, Captain Darrow," crowed a thin voice. "Refusal carries a price."

Darrow tore her gaze from the corpse and stared along the street. Two figures drew in from the alley mouth. A kernclaw and an unassuming, shrunken man in neat, gold-trimmed robes. Darrow's eyes met his. She recoiled, breathless.

Across the rooftops, the shriek and clamour of the vranakin soared to new, wild heights.

Jorek sank to his knees, crossbow abandoned. Other constables collapsed, sobbing and whimpering. Darrow flinched, seized of sudden, desperate certainty that the fear would lessen on breaking contact with those black, pupil-less eyes.

Screwing up the last of her courage, she thrust. The blade slipped between the cadaverous man's ribs. No scream. Not one drop of blood. He leaned in, teeth a rictus grin.

Darrow's gasp died on parched lips. A cold, bony hand closed about her throat. The other wrested the sword from her grip and dragged it clear of his flesh. A shimmer of black blood shone on the blade, and then hissed away silver.

The world spun. Resistance melted beneath the other's cold, black gaze.

"Hush. I will take away your fear."

*

One glimpse beyond the lychgate was enough. A glance at the shrunken figure in the gold-trimmed robes. One heartbeat of contact with those pitiless, abyssal eyes. Altiris buried his head in his hands as the tide of roiling, black terror swallowed him up and swept him away into nightmare.

Fire flickered in the smothering darkness. A flame sprung from the recollection of his father's pyre. Suddenly, Altiris was a child again, trapped in the crowd gathered before the tumbledown church of Selann's stockade, old memories woken to new life. The cold, clear gaze of Selann's reeve as he proclaimed the unproven charge of witchery. The fear in his father's eyes as the fires reached him. The bitter smell of pinewood and charring flesh.

It wasn't real. It couldn't be.

Rationale shattered beneath his father's sudden scream.

Sobbing, Altiris forced open his eyes. A shadow blotted out the greenish-white of the mists. Recognition seeped through gummed thoughts. Sidara, sword in hand and moving as if in a dream, reached for the lychgate's latch. New tears bled into old.

"Sidara?" he gasped. "No!"

"I have to try. It's Hawkin's wife." She halted, brow furrowed. Blue eyes rushed gold. "And the light wants me to."

She opened the gate and stepped uncertainly into the street.

Altiris reached for her, and stumbled as the pyre stench overtook him anew. He lost his grip on the Living Realm and sank into the black of waking nightmare. Flames danced to greet him.

"Let her go!"

A young voice. A thin voice. More than that, a familiar one, seared into memory by an impossible flash of light.

The Reveque girl.

The girl at the open lychgate was different to the one Apara remembered. Part of it was maturity's bounty – the woman sloughing off the child – but not all. There was confidence in stance and expression. Certainty. A year before, when Apara had hunted her through the darkness of the church foundry, Sidara had been terrified. Now she was merely afraid. An ocean of difference.

Apara fought the urge to shrink away.

Athariss dropped Captain Darrow to a twitching, shuddering heap. Sidara held her ground, sword in both hands and levelled in textbook high guard – horizontal at her shoulder, the point aimed between Athariss' black eyes.

He leered. "The daughter? You'll make a fine elder cousin. What better lesson for your wayward father?" His foot tapped Maridov's withered, ragged corpse. "We've lost many today. They must be replenished."

"My father will see you hanged."

"You cannot threaten a man with what he already has, child. My spirit walks with the Raven." Athariss stepped past the sobbing Darrow. "And Lord Reveque is ours already. He needs only a reminder."

The sword-point wavered. "You're lying."

Athariss took another step. "Everything we have done, he made possible. He shielded us. Protected us. Helped us offer tribute. He *is* vranakin, whatever his denials."

"You think I'd believe you?"

"I know you do." The words were measured, hypnotic.

Her shoulders slumped. The sword-point dipped.

Athariss cackled. "Perhaps I'll permit you to serve as emissary to him. Families should be together. You needn't fear death, child. It drives away all weakness."

His bony hand reached for hers.

"No!"

The sword came up in a golden arc. Athariss jerked back in a spray of black blood. He screamed and scuttled away. Hands clasped to his ruined face came away slick. Dark eyes widened in horror.

"Impossible." He stumbled through the moaning constables. Hands shook as blood welled and gushed away. The crowfather's immortality undone by the light's caress. "Impossible!"

Sidara bore down, the golden light about her shoulders driving back the mist.

"Apara!" howled Athariss.

Apara gave herself to the raven cloak. Shrieking wings flung her into Sidara's path. The girl cried out as talons raked her arm and scraped the sword away. Mantled light slipped from her shoulders.

Apara slammed the girl against brick, hand at her shoulder and talons against her throat. The iron tang of fresh blood thickened. The raven cloak shrilled its delight. The shadow in Apara's soul screamed.

"I remember you." The gold faded from Sidara's eyes, leaving them blue with defiance even as her voice ran ragged. "In the foundry. You hurt my mother."

"Kill her!" Athariss shrieked the command, his words edged with rage and pain. "Apara!"

"You know I can't!" The shadow gathered about Apara's chest, stifling her breath. Her heart pounded. "It won't let me!"

"You are vranakin! Kernclaw! Your soul belongs to the Raven, which means it belongs to me. Kill her!"

A twitch of talons would open the girl's throat to the bone. As impossible now as it had been for more than a year. But if she didn't, Athariss would give her to the mists for her failure. Madness and a prizrak's hunger. Her fate, unless Sidara died.

Apara screamed. The shadow's grip slackened.

The black clouds of Altiris' nightmare hissed away before the scream.

Sidara.

Pyre-flames guttered.

"For the Phoenix."

Altiris stuttered the words through chattering teeth. Clung to the mantra that had belonged to his parents, and now to him. Fear yielded to shame, and shame to the first trembling flame.

Jellied legs launched him through the gate. Courage faltered as he took in cowering constables and leering vranakin; Sidara pinned against the wall by a kernclaw, her right sleeve torn and matted red. Talons at her throat. The pallid, cadaverous figure sheeted in unnatural blood.

Terror gathered as dark eyes met his. Altiris drove it back the only way he knew.

"For the Phoenix!"

The words drove him on. The kernclaw leapt away, talons scraping a parry. Altiris screamed. No words. No meaning. A howl to drive out fear. Kurkas' painstaking lessons abandoned for a berserk flurry that gave no thought to defence.

The kernclaw's boot slammed into his knee. Numbed, the leg crumpled and pitched him to the cobbles. His sword skittered away.

The cadaverous man staggered closer. "Southwealders have never known when to kneel."

"Praise Lumestra," growled Captain Darrow. "But you're right."

The sword-point burst from the cadaverous man's chest in a spray of black blood and the thin hiss of his scream. Eyes bloodshot in a haggard face, Darrow wrenched the blade a quarter turn and kicked the twitching body clear. Pale hands scrabbled against cobbles. A horrible, creaking sigh of a breaking soul and they went still.

Darrow dropped to one knee, head bowed and breath rasping.

The vranakin on the rooftops fell silent. The mists dissipated. Etravia flickered. Black blood trickled between the cobbles and evaporated silver. For the briefest moment, the air lost the taste of stale memories. Stars glinted beyond the veil. Then the ghosts returned. The mists regathered, though thinner than before.

The kernclaw screamed. A mass of squalling black wings swept over Altiris, talons ripping at his face and clothes. Then she was gone, the body of the cadaverous man carried with her into the mists. Constables staggered to their feet. Some shook their heads to dispel a nightmare. Others clung to one another for support.

Altiris scrambled to where Sidara lay, her back against the wall and a bloodied arm in her lap. Scarlet gleamed where the kernclaw's talons had marked her throat.

Her lips pursed in a satisfied smile. "I'm all right."

"You're not."

Altiris tore a strip off his tunic and knotted it about her arm. Blood slicked his fingers as he worked, golden light dancing upon scarlet. He swore and tore free another strip.

Twice, she'd saved him. He could save her once.

"I showed him . . . " Sidara's voice faded. "Him and his lies."

"You did." Darrow squatted at Altiris' side, firm hands guiding his. Her eyes widened at the magic spiralling free. "Not there, boy. Higher up. Draw it tight."

He obeyed. The flow faltered. "What did she do?"

"She cut him. He didn't even blink when I struck him the first time, but her? Well, you saw. That light of hers hurt him, and badly. Soon as he was screaming, the worst of ... " She brushed halting fingers across her temple. " ... whatever that was ... Didn't seem so bad any more. And he felt my second blow, sure enough."

The memory of the pyre flickered. Altiris wound the last strip and knotted it tight. "The nightmare? You felt it too?"

"Years back, I was on the *Belligerent* when it went down. Caught below decks with the ocean rushing in. Felt it all over again when he looked at me. I couldn't breathe. Don't know how she kept her wits."

"Don't you know?" Sidara said dreamily. "I'm made of magic."

Her eyes slid closed.

Harsh voices sounded from the rooftops, rushing to a crescendo. Feet clattered on tiles.

"Captain?" A constable cupped hands to his mouth. "We've got trouble."

"When haven't we?" Darrow scowled and stood. "Get her out of here, lad."

Two vranakin came screaming out of the alleyway, serrated knives in their hands. A constable tackled one to the ground. The other died with a quarrel in his throat.

"What about you?" said Altiris.

"We'll hold the street while you slip away. She bought us a chance. We'll buy her one."

"No! We'll go together. Safety in numbers."

"Only thing numbers do on these streets is draw attention. Get her out. And if you see Lord Reveque, tell him I hope he's got a miracle in his back pocket, or the city's lost."

Darrow's expression convinced where her words did not. Flat. Hard. Bereft of hope. Offering a shaky salute, Altiris hoisted Sidara to his shoulder and staggered away.

Forty-Two

Layer by layer, the pyres grew. The work gangs sang with the hoisting of each log, the dirge's cadence darker for the onset of night and descending clouds. The chorus swelled with the voices of those who kept watch upon the walls, or offered toast to slain comrades about courtyard fires. Come dawn, the advance on the Marcher Lands would continue. But dawn was yet hours away, and the time between belonged to the victors and the dead.

Alone in the fortress chapel, Aeldran refrained from song: one last silent salute offered to those who'd drawn steel against the assault. Prince or peasant, death made equals of all. The Tressian dead lay still and cold upon pew and tile, waiting for ... For what? The embrace of stone and the darkness of the tomb, or perhaps the Light of Third Dawn? Tressian beliefs remained a peculiar mystery to Aeldran Andwar, but he none-theless revered the courage they roused. One could respect an enemy's valour even while disdaining purpose.

Take the dead woman on the pew before him, grey eyes sightless and blonde hair matted with blood both shed and stolen. Her ragged coat and torn epaulettes marked her as a sailor, as alien to the mountain fastness as was it to her. She'd no business being at Vrasdavora.

She'd fought anyway, sending three Immortals to the Raven, and twice their number to the surgeons. She'd never lost her fire, not even with her arm broken by a mace's swing. Not until Aeldran had buried his sword in her heart, and that blow had almost cost him his head. No finer companion with which to hold the wall, and no worthier foe from whom to take it.

He eased the corpse's eyes closed. "May you find whatever reward you seek," he murmured. "And know it was deserved."

Footsteps stirred Aeldran from reverie. He offered a deep bow, stifling a wince as the motion pulled on wounds recently bound. "*Savim.*"

Beneath her helm, Melanna's dark eyes revealed nothing of approval, or its lack. So very different from Naradna, whose thoughts were seldom a mystery even behind a mask. "I expected you to be basking in the glow of victory."

He offered a lopsided shrug. "Tomorrow, yes. Tonight I see only the cost."

"Your chieftains disagree. Most have already lost half their wits to drink. Mine too."

"Those who miss the lesson of sacrifice have only half their wits to begin with."

The twitch became a thin smile. "And you?"

"With my mettle proven in the assault, my position is secure." He offered a second, shallower bow. "You have my thanks, *savim.*"

She picked her way through the dead to stand at his side. "A heavy toll."

Aeldran wiped at the crusted blood on his right cheek, a gift from the woman with the grey eyes. "They fought like demons. I cannot believe they were so few."

Melanna tugged her helm clear. Black tresses slithered across her shoulders. "You respect them?"

"How can I not?" He shrugged. "How we face death is all that matters."

"Is that why you've ordered them buried, rather than burned?" Her expression was again without expression, tempting him to a misstep.

"Burial is their way, as honouring other customs used to be ours. Did I do wrong, *savim*?"

"No," Melanna said at last. "We've sacrificed too much of who we are for this war. If victory is to mean anything, we have to find our way back. This was a good start, *savir.*"

More surprising than the honorific – more surprising than to hear his own sentiment shared – was the softening of feature and tone. Years sloughed away, her imperious aspect fading. What remained was the Melanna Saranal that Aeldran had heard spoken of, but had never met. Introspective. Thoughtful. Spiritual. None of them traits admired by her detractors, but such men would only ever seek complaint. To Aeldran's mind, their value was greater than a hundred swords. After all, a sword only killed. It was a bleak realm that was founded on death alone.

"Then I have served you well?" he asked.

"Better than I'd have believed an Andwar could."

The form of words soured the compliment, even when delivered with unfamiliar levity. "Then may I request a boon?"

Suspicion glimmered. "That *is* a champion's entitlement."

He breathed deep of the chapel's sour air. Easier to climb a bowing ladder into a wall of blades than this. "Free Naradna."

Levity vanished behind the mask of the Empress-to-be. "She sought my death. Releasing her proclaims my weakness from the mountaintop."

"The woman I have respected so long never feared the whispers of jealous men."

"You should be careful investing in her. She might be nothing but fantasy."

"Perhaps, but my request remains."

Melanna pursed her lips. The sour hint of crestis oil wafted beneath the decaying roof as the first pyres were lit beyond the walls.

"I'll consider your words. But in solitude."

Aeldran bowed and withdrew from the chapel.

Crossing the courtyard, he threaded fires half-hidden by descending cloud, returning nods and drunken greetings from men of Rhaled and Icansae. That there was little segregation between the scarlet and green was cause for cheer. Rivalry and distrust set aside with battle won. But there'd be quarrels before the fires faded. Broken bones, perhaps even deaths. A cycle of belligerence burned into marrow. Allegiances born less out of love for comrades, and more from hatred of the foe.

Shaking off a drunken Immortal's offer of plundered wine, Aeldran ascended the northwest tower. Here, at least, sobriety ruled, the guardian lunassera as cold and crisp as their shard-spears.

"May I speak with my sister?"

The women shared a glance. "Surrender your sword."

Aeldran unbuckled his belt and handed it to the nearer handmaiden. The other unbarred the door and stepped aside.

The chamber was swamped in gloom, broken only by a shard of moonlight from a narrow window, the wooden frame and stained-glass sunrise far newer than the stone in which they sat. Aeldran's eyes adjusted to a room bare of all but the meanest comfort.

The door closed. A dark shape moved across the window. "Have you come to free me?"

Aeldran hesitated. "The princessa considers the matter."

She scratched at the stubble of her hair. "So she has stolen my brother, as well as my freedom."

"Not that. Never that."

"She's bewitched you."

His heart ached. "I admire her. As you once admired her. One of us should hold true to that, even as the other falls to pride."

Diffuse moonlight gave shape to his sister's scowl. To bound hands outstretched. "The window opens onto the cliff. The stones are old and worn. I know you have a dagger. Free my hands, and I'll climb."

"And if I don't?"

"Then I'll die in the valley. Broken bones bereft of a brother's love."

Aeldran stared, aghast. "You'd give yourself to the Raven out of spite?"

She glared back. "Only if you shirk duty to your elder."

"Duty?" He shook his head, anger slipping into weariness. "I held my tongue as hubris overtook you. I offered support, even when you ignored my counsel. Even to duty, there is a limit."

"I was right before. You *are* bewitched. Seduced by soft smile and silken hair."

"Wielding my love for you as a weapon against me? *That* is our grandfather talking. How many more of your words have been his? You swore to be better. Instead, you've become Maggad's heir, body, spirit and soul." He shook his head, despairing at his own words. "My sister is already dead."

Naradna slumped. "I cannot live or die at another's whim. Not again. Set me free, and I'll ask nothing more of you."

Aeldran rubbed his brow to conceal pained expression. "The princessa's ire is cooling. You need only wait."

"She will never forgive me."

"That again is our grandfather talking. He couldn't recognise forgiveness in others for he'd none of his own. I forgive you. So will the princessa."

"You don't know that."

He'd no proof to offer, only faith. And faith had never convinced Naradna of anything. "And you shouldn't judge her by your own demons, Aelia."

She flinched at the name long abandoned. Stared away into the dark. As ever guided by reckless pride, soured in the harsh tutelage of their upbringing. Aeldran scowled. For all his claims, he saw no limit to duty, not between blood. Naradna had made mistakes, but forcing her hand would only feed resentment. Coax forth the poison of their heritage until nothing of his sister remained.

With a sigh, he slid a dagger from concealment within his armoured sleeve and set it on the table. "Running is no answer. But it's not for me to choose. Stay, or seek whatever escape you wish."

Turning his back on sullen silence, Aeldran left the makeshift prison in search of wine. He was halfway across the courtyard when the mountainside shook to a booming, breathy grave-call.

The dolorous fanfare reverberated deep in Melanna's troubled soul, banishing the tangle of decisions made and yet to come. Mist gathered to smoke at the gatehouse edge, the silver of a skull helm brilliant against writhing shadow. A black flame blazed to life about the blade of its sword.

Melanna's blood slowed to an icy trickle as hollow eye sockets turned upon her. Ancient, instinctive fears woke to life. Icansae tales from Soraved assumed bleak significance. Revenants of Otherworld, set loose to the Tressian cause. The figure lunged and she dived beneath its sword. The strike of her shoulder on a battlement still stained with Tressian blood jarred sense out of stark terror.

Rolling to one knee, she swept her own sword free.

"Ashanael Brigantim!"

Her voice shook as she thrust, her blade biting deep. Sword and helm clanged on stone as the figure dissolved, the sound swallowed up by cries from the courtyard below. The anarchy of men assailed by the impossible. And above it all, the screech of circling ravens.

Shadow writhed beneath the fallen helm. Others gathered at the rampart's edge.

Heart in her throat, Melanna took the stairs three at a time. "Rhaled! To me! Ashanael!"

No response came, though there were voices aplenty. Cursing. Shrieking. Dying. Close enough to touch, and yet impossibly far away through vapour soured by Otherworld's mists. They twisted even Vrasdavora, the square-set Tressian walls become a clawed hand closing above her.

At the lower rampart, Melanna tripped on a corpse. An Icansae shieldsman, his throat ripped wide and his doublet torn bloody. Others lay close by, distorted by mist. Black fire rushed to claim her, silver leering close behind. Steel scraped. A revenant hissed to nothing and Melanna ran on, heart racing and spine prickling with the knowledge that other revenants followed close behind.

A dozen corpses slumped about a dimming fire, a Rhalesh Immortal smouldering in the ash. Three shieldsmen lay at the stairway's foot, wounds behind and swords scabbarded. In the courtyard proper, a sea of dead lapping at stone cliffs. Still the screams rang out, the defiant mingling with the dying.

"Rhaled! To me!"

No one came. No one answered. But for the screams, Melanna would have thought herself alone, drawn into Otherworld for the Raven's sport.

A circle of revenants bled out of the mists, swords levelled as they closed.

Melanna gripped her sword tight and gathered fading courage.

Light blazed. Mist recoiled before the sweet scent of spring blossom. Barely visible through the gateway, a funeral pyre crackled white. Men stood silhouetted against it, scarlet and green shoulder-to-shoulder. Revenants hissed and seethed where light yielded to darkness.

"Ashanal!"

Sera cast the last contents of her birchwood box onto the pyre and stepped to the circle's edge. A shard-spear left her hand. Pierced, the revenant nearest the gateway shrilled and dissolved into shadow, breaking the circle.

The moon slipped behind a cloud. Melanna ran for the gap.

A revenant barred her path. A wild parry checked black flame, and she hurtled on.

Melanna's boot snagged on a sightless corpse. She righted and twisted away as another revenant gathered out of the mists. The stroke meant for her skull instead scattered armoured scales about her shoulder. She spun, arm numbed by a blade cold as ice, terror reborn as the chill wormed outward from the bloodless wound.

Already off-balance, she stumbled. Shadow blotted out mist. Black flame crackled against a silver leer.

The northwest tower loomed. Or at least the jagged spire the mists had made of it. Screams rent the air, the drifting veil alive with darting shadow and black flame. The dead lay thicker with every frantic stride. Aeldran forged on, retracing steps lately taken, fear for his own life swamped by that for another's.

A thrust scattered a revenant to writhing shadow, and then the tower door was in sight. Lunassera guards stood back to back, shard-spears held in challenge to the mists. A revenant's empty helm lay on the stones nearby.

"Stay back!" said one.

"I will not leave my sister to die in a cage." Aeldran let his sword-point dip and prayed they'd listen. The night had grown dark enough without further stain. "I beg you, do not doubt my resolve."

The lunassera shared a glance. As one, they stepped aside.

Aeldran flung open the door.

"Naradna!"

The silence of drifting mist was his only answer. At the table, Aeldran's hand closed about the remnant of a severed rope. Beyond, a broken window frame sat jagged and dark.

The revenant's sword shuddered mid-sweep. Shadow dissolved into greenish-white. Helm and sword fell away. A hand dragged Melanna upright.

"Found a fight you can't win, Saranal?"

Melanna blinked at her saviour – a woman in a filthy shirt and torn trews, her face alive with savage glee. "Naradna?"

The surviving revenants drew in. Darkness gathered beneath the helm of the one Naradna had stabbed. Her shove propelled Melanna towards the gatehouse. A breathless run, and they stood beneath the pyre, flanked by terrified faces and drawn swords. Revenants crowded close at the mists' extent, their forms flowing closer as white flame flickered orange. Left and right along the roadway, pyres stood cold and dark, others blazed from white to amber in ailing refuge for the few score survivors sheltering beneath.

"I've no more duskhazel," murmured Sera. "Once it burns through . . ."

"Then we run," said a wide-eyed shieldsman. "Before it fades."

Another nodded. "If the fires hold them, we might reach the rest of the army."

"Assuming it's still there," said Melanna bleakly. "They might already be overrun. We fight."

"We'll die!"

Voices murmured agreement. Eyes darted east. Feet edged back. Too late, Melanna realised there was more scarlet than green huddled about the pyre. Too many men of Icansae who'd little reason to heed a Rhalesh princessa, warleader or no.

Naradna tucked her dagger into her boot and snatched up a corpse's spear. "I had my chance to run. I stayed." Her eyes tightened. "I am Naradna of Icansae, and I stand with the princessa. If men elect to flee while women fight, so be it."

Expressions shifted, fear yielding to shock, and then to determination as Naradna's words lent weight to rumour whispered about campfires. Whatever scorn the men of Icansae had poured upon her while drink flowed held no purchase beneath the pyre. Tradition leveraged as shame. The murmur died. Swords turned outwards. Logs spat and crackled like old leaves underfoot.

Melanna winced as sensation crawled back into a numbed arm. "How did you get free?"

"Your lunassera should have searched the room better." Naradna's stare dared to be gainsaid. "I found a dagger and slit my bonds. I'd be halfway into the valley by now, had I wanted."

"That dagger?" Melanna glanced at the blade tucked into Naradna's boot. At its serpent hilt. "Unusual to find an Icansae weapon in a Tressian fortress."

"It's of no danger to you."

Melanna recognised the deeper message and nodded.

The fire flickered, the flames more orange than white.

"Stand firm!" she cried. "Stand together! Ashanael Brigantim!"

The pyres guttered and died. The road drowned in darkness. Mist rushed in.

The dry crackling noise survived the fires' death, scratching to a crescendo over the revenants' hisses and the startled cries of fearful soldiers. Brisk wind swept the roadway, bringing with it the scent of fresh sap and withered leaves; the mustiness of the forest floor and old blossoms. Melanna stood stock still, good hand about the numbed, and both tight about her sword. The threat of the revenants, so close a heartbeat before, now seemed distant, forgotten. In its place awoke a different sensation. An unfamiliar presence.

The revenants hissed. Not in threat, but alarm. New sounds echoed. The scrape of root on stone. The rustle of dry leaves. The wet rasp of swollen timber. And beneath it all, a whispering, crackling sound like the buzz of desiccated insects.

A crack in the clouds restored wan light to the roadway. Melanna glanced at Sera, her mask a grey gleam. "What is it?"

The handmaiden shook her head, eyes aghast and lips a pale slash.

"There!" said Naradna.

A gangling, indistinct shape. Soon as seen, it was gone. Melanna had the sense of others just beyond sight, marching in time with the scritching footsteps.

Those footsteps quickened. Monstrous shapes blurred against the mists. Uneven shoulders lowered. Shieldsmen shrank back towards the pyre. Naradna scowled and gripped her spear tighter.

The clouds parted. Silver light granted shape to a nearby shadow.

The creature was hunched and gangling all at once. Had it stood straight, it would have towered over any man Melanna had ever known. Its limbs were a tangle of roots and branches, woven into a mockery of ephemeral form, caked in moss and twisted straw, and woven with thorns. The head was a misshapen knot of briars, with a jagged, creaking maw and green eyes that blazed bright beneath a lopsided, gnarled brow.

With a crackling, wheezing hiss it pounced on a revenant. Woven branches flexed like muscle around the newcomer's mouldered bones as it tore the spirit to scraps of inky darkness. Then the moon slipped behind cloud once more, and the creature was just another mist-wreathed shadow in a night overfull of them. A nightmare of fable and cautionary tale come to horrifying life.

"Blessed Goddess," breathed Naradna. "That was a strawjack."

The night erupted in a cacophony. The dull thwack of steel striking wood and the brittle rustle of trampled branches. The shrill cries of dying revenants. Sap hung sweet on the air, cloying and sickening.

Melanna's fogged thoughts writhed between fear and disbelief. Strawjacks. Whispering Ones. Demons woken from Fellhallow's ancient groves. She told herself it shouldn't have mattered. She was Ashanal, chosen of the Goddess. She'd vanquished vranakin and survived Malatriant's resurrection. But reason had little purchase in the darkness. It did little to still the tremor in her limbs.

The tumult's fading was as swift as its onset. The horrible crackling, rustling sound faded to nothing, leaving a night silent of all save Melanna's thumping heart and the hurried, febrile breaths of her companions.

When moonlight broke the clouds again, it touched on a roadway robbed of mist. Neither revenant nor strawjack graced the darkness – at least, none living. Silver masks lay strewn about, their wearers' swords inert alongside. Here and there, split timber and mangled bones marked a strawjack's demise. A lone figure stood hunched beneath Vrasdavora's gatehouse, tattered robes twitching like branches in a breeze; the smooth visage of his mask tilted in curious mockery.

{{Be not afraid, she who is to be queen,}} Jack buzzed. {{There are powers in this world greater than death, and eternities more delightful.}}

Melanna swallowed to clear ashen throat. What should have felt like salvation instead had the sensation of a poacher's snare drawing tight about her neck. Jack's gaze burrowed deep, divesting armour and cloth, skin and bone, until her naked soul shivered helpless in his sight.

Flesh writhed. Disgust awoke tremulous bravado. "What do you want of me?"

{{Nothing your father has not already promised.}} Ragged folds shifted as Jack bowed, gangling arms spread wide. {{We will see one another again.}}

A shadow passed over the moon, and he was gone. Melanna sank to her knees, her flesh itching from within. Not even the sight of survivors emerging into the light, Aeldran among them, banished the horror from her heart. It wasn't until Naradna found her voice that she'd some inkling as to why.

"Where are the bodies?" breathed Naradna. "Where are the dead?"

For of those the revenants had slain, there was no sign.

Forty-Three

Stars shone above sombre pines, the waning moon holding knightly court even as she faded. Woodsmoke mingled with salt air blown east from the distant sea. Welcome relief after months amid Tressia's squalor, ample compensation for a night with no roof save the open sky. It awoke old memories of wolf's-heads and conspiracy. They in turn reminded Josiri how much had changed, and how much had not.

Erashel fidgeted and stared into the campfire, arms looped about her knees. For all the hardships of her recent years, the Lady Beral was markedly uncomfortable away from the city's comforts. "You're *sure* he passed this way?"

"Certain," he replied, careful not to offer any quirk of expression she'd construe as amusement. "The signs are clear. Two travellers – one with an impressive stride – followed this trail a few hours back."

"Where do you suppose he's heading?"

"Indrig, I thought, avoiding the roads ... "

"More's the pity. There are taverns on the roads. Taverns *and* beds."

" ... but the further west the trail veers, the more likely it's Kellevork or Trondæ."

"A coastal fortress or a fisher village? That sounds like a man seeking a ship, which means he's running."

"*I cannot sit idle while the Republic burns.* Those aren't a deserter's words."

"They are if he's a liar."

"Not Viktor."

She shook her head. "He's desperate if he's putting faith in thrakkers."

Josiri shrugged. "My father swore Thrakkians made firm friends, so long as they owed you something."

"Mine said much the same, which is why he *never* trusted them." She offered a wry smile and hugged her legs tighter. "Always the fate of Trelans and Berals to have opinions just similar enough for contradiction."

"We're doing better lately, you and I."

Her smile adopted a little of the fire's warmth. "You *are* sure it's Viktor we're following?"

"Tell me what you hear."

She cocked her head. "The Dusk Wind in the branches. The waters of the stream."

"Nothing more?"

"No." Erashel's eyes narrowed. "What's your game?"

"No game. But these woods should be alive with birds. Nightjars, owls, kernhawks, starids. There's nothing. Something passed this way and they're hiding until its memory fades."

"And you think that's Viktor? Why?"

"Because the woods around Eskavord were always the same." He stared into the fire. "For years, I thought the town's industry had driven them off. But then I moved to the city, where larks greet every dawn and an owl's shriek every moon."

Mirth slipped away. "What really happened last year? At Eskavord. With Viktor. Not the version Malachi peddles. The truth."

Josiri hesitated, but either Viktor would join the battle for the Republic's survival and his secrets would stand revealed, or he wouldn't, and he deserved no discretion. Clambering to his feet, he leaned against a tree at the glade's edge, his back to Erashel. "Eskavord burned at Viktor's hand, as official record claims. But it was lost long before."

"The Hadari?"

"Malatriant."

"Malatriant? Be serious. She's long dead."

"So we thought. She seized Eskavord, made its people a part of her, my sister included. Nothing could be done, save the mercy of the fire. Viktor didn't hesitate. He's like an arrow in flight, no hesitation, no doubt. No matter the cost. The cost was Eskavord. The mists have held it ever since.

The locals talk of ghosts roaming the desolation. I didn't believe. Not until that day in Dregmeet."

She shook her head in disbelief, eyes clouded by fear. "And that's why the birds fall silent? Because they sense his resolve? It's a pretty tale."

"They fall silent because Viktor wields magic. Not the foundry's light. Malatriant's Dark. They're afraid of it."

Erashel's sibilant curse vanished beneath the crackle of flame. "That's not funny, Josiri."

"No. But it is the truth."

"Are you certain you *want* to find him?"

"Yes."

"Why?"

"You and I . . . We spend our lives worrying about consequence and status. Viktor belongs to a broader canvas, and yet he'd die for me, for you – for anyone – if he thought it would make a difference."

Fallen leaves crunched underfoot as Erashel drew closer. "I never thought to hear Katya Trelan's son speak thus of her killer."

Another lie, for Josiri's mother had died at her own hand. Viktor was more myth than truth, even in his own lifetime. Josiri planted an elbow against the tree and forehead against his wrist.

"I've hated him most of my life. I still do, except for when I don't. But for Viktor, Calenne would be alive, and yet I've no doubt he'd offer up his life to the Raven if it would bring her back. He tore me apart even while he showed me a better way to live. I'm trapped between admiration and rage so black it leaves me ashamed." He snorted. "And then I think, if Viktor provokes these feelings in a man he embraces as brother, what hope can there possibly be for his enemies?"

"Then why not leave him to it, for better or worse?"

"I keep asking myself that question. There's only ever one answer. It's because, despite everything Viktor's cost me, he and I *are* friends. Pathetic, isn't it?"

Her fingers tightened about his shoulder. "We can't choose those we love, Josiri, just as we can't choose those we hate. We strive to do right by one, damn the other, and hope all transpires as it should."

"Maybe you're right. It's not a lesson my parents ever taught. It seems yours did better."

"Not really. Father pledged himself to the Phoenix only when he'd no other choice. I persuaded him he'd live longer as Katya's ally than as her enemy." Her voice faded. "My reward was a slaughtered family and a cell on an exodus scow bound for Selann."

He turned without intending to, drawn by the heartbreak beneath the words. "I knew your father had changed his mind, of course, but not that you were responsible."

"Why would you?" Erashel stared off into the darkness. "Your mother's last days were full of stories. You and I were the barest of acquaintances, and you'd grief of your own."

"But you hold me responsible?"

"Exodus brought me to Lord Yordon's estate. He'd a fine opinion of his kindness, rooted little in truth. He'd set southwealders free on the fens, and hunt them with hounds for sport. He kept order through starvation, and worse. But I was lucky." Sour emphasis belied the word. "Yordon was bitter, and easily flattered. I spent my days tutoring his children, and my nights entertaining their father. I slept on Itharocian silk while others slept on straw, and I learned how to drug his wine so that I could slip away beneath the moon. I stole food for the starving, and arranged 'accidents' for the cruellest of their overseers. I bartered pieces of myself away, one inch at a time, and clung to its necessity. And all the while, I heard how Katya Trelan's children lived in luxury at Branghall. So yes, I hated you. Even after the Settlement Decree brought me home I beheld you as a spoilt child playing at statesman, ignorant of hardship and railing against shadows. It's taken me a long time to see beyond that."

Josiri tried to picture Yordon among the blur of faces that was the Grand Council. Memory found only a younger man, barely of age. "And Lord Yordon?"

"Died in his sleep the night of the Settlement Decree," Erashel replied. "His heart, I'm told."

She held his stare without blinking, without shame. Whatever mystery Yordon's death offered officialdom, it had no secrets from Erashel Beral.

"I'm sorry," he said.

She shot him a shrewd glance. "For what? Your mother's failings in rebellion, or my father's in heeding my counsel? The past is the past,

Josiri. The future is all. And with that in mind . . . " She shook her head. "It will wait. We should get some sleep."

He caught her hand as she turned away. "If I've learned anything, it's that too much goes unsaid too long. Tell me?"

"Very well." Erashel laid her free hand over his. "We need to marry, you and I."

Viktor approached the palisade gate, lingering distant enough from the fires upon its ramparts so as to not draw a sentry's notice. Beyond the harbour town, Kellevork's black stones clung to the cliffside, its forest of towers stark against the shimmering moonlit sea.

As with so much that sprang from Thrakkian hands, Kellevork was haphazard, ramshackle. Curtain walls overlapped one another in strange manner. Towers clustered too thick in some places, and too far apart in others. Worse, the upper storeys were of timber, not stone. Fire would humble long before swords breached its walls.

One regiment, supported by ballistae and mangonels, could have taken Kellevork. But then, the Thrakkians of the present preferred to settle their grievances on the open field. Kellevork belonged to the past, a bastion intended not for defence, but governance and suppression in the name of long-dead kings. That Ardothan chose to rule from Kellevork's austerity rather than Indrig's cheer reaffirmed Armund's muttered accusations. Serendipity, of the kind granted to a man of righteous intent. While Viktor was no longer so idealistic as to believe that two evils combined ever amounted to anything more than a darker, blacker one, if two serpents could be crushed with a single stomp, then so be it.

"Last chance to turn back, lad," said Armund.

"You gave me back to myself," said Viktor. "Take pride in your work."

"This isn't some grotty brawl at the village gate," he replied gloomily. "You might at least have brought an army."

"I don't have one."

"No, but Trelan did. Wouldn't have hurt to borrow it for a day or two."

Viktor shook his head. "Two days are enough to remake the world. If Ahrad is gone, the Republic needs every sword. Besides, Tressians at the gate would be . . . provocative."

"*You're* Tressian."

"I'm an outcast. Even if Ardothan claims otherwise, I doubt his peers will consider my part in this a worthy provocation. The Republic does *not* need war with the thanedoms." Even Josiri's presence would have given the air of official sanction. Better to keep him distant. And Josiri cultivated such a *fine* air of wounded indignance. A shame to waste talent like that through complicity. "And I doubt you can do this without me."

"I'm not so sure we can do this at all."

"Nor is anyone beyond that wall. Don't you want to prove them wrong?"

"It's a sickness, that's what it is." Armund shook his head. "You're a glutton for lost causes."

"Then what are you accompanying me for?"

"What else am I going to do?" Sightless eyes gazed up at the gate. "I've been running from this too long. Can't have you telling tales that Armund af Garna doesn't live up to his responsibilities, can I? Anliss will never let me hear the end of it, here or in Skanandra."

Viktor smiled at a tone less morose in the deeps than the shallows. "Shall we be about our business?"

Armund sighed and strode for the gate.

"Who goes?" A man in heavy cloak and drakonhelm stared down from the rampart, a torch blazing in his hand. "Declare yourself!"

"Armund af Garna, Thane of Indrigsval!"

A chorus of laughter shook the night sky. "Indrigsval *has* a thane. It's not you, scunner!"

Armund unslung his axe and rested the haft on the roadway. "I seek the judgement of the Cindercourt. In my name, and my sister's."

The laughter died. "That matter is settled."

"Not while my heart beats."

"A detail easily resolved."

Archers appeared at the wall, arrows nocked and bowstrings drawn.

Viktor scowled. From the outset, he'd suspected he'd have need of his shadow before the matter was settled. But to draw upon it so soon? How quickly the last resort became the first. Still, nothing was gained if they were shot down like rabid dogs . . .

"Enough!" A grey-headed woman stared down from the gate. Inkari. Sole survivor of the fight at Valna. "He has a claim, Jagraval. Let him pass."

"Ardothan won't thank you for this, Inkari."

"He's invoked Astor's law. Let him pass."

The archers withdrew at Jagraval's angry gesture. The gate creaked open.

Inkari met them in the muddy streets beyond, a vanaguard's yellow and green cloak swathed tight against the cold, and six watchful bonds-axes at her back. "You'll die here, Armund."

"Is that concern?" he replied. "Or have you found your honour at last?"

She spat. "I won't have Jagraval calling down Astor's wrath just so he can impress your brother. If Ardothan wants you dead outside of the Cindercourt, he can do it himself. Come."

Calenne's vantage among the trees afforded a splendid view as Josiri's expression slid from numb surprise to outright shock. She empathised completely, her misgivings at eavesdropping falling by the wayside at Erashel's outrageous demand.

She'd followed ever since Tarona, unseen and unremarked, trusting her brother to reunite her with Viktor. What she'd say in that event, Calenne had no notion. Even *thinking* on the horrors of her existence drenched her in panic. Easy enough to seek distraction on the road, but after nightfall, with sleep a distant comfort ...? She'd followed their conversation – and Erashel's calculated display of vulnerability – with morbid fascination.

Morbid. Her every action now was morbid.

At last, Josiri recovered his voice. "I think I must have misheard you."

"Offering to spare my blushes?" Erashel drew closer, hands clasped about his. "This isn't a romantic proposition, but a practical one."

"I am *very* much spoken for."

"As Anastacia's pet?"

He stepped back. "As her equal."

Josiri's tone didn't *quite* match the words' resolve. Much as Calenne disliked Anastacia, she'd have given a great deal for the demon to find herself present. An education for all parties, but Erashel in particular. Alas, the demon was far away, and Josiri abandoned to calculated assault.

"Even if that's true, you're the last of your family. Anastacia doesn't strike me as willing or able to provide an heir."

"Adoption is tradition older than the Republic. It serves others well enough."

"You've a duty to continue your bloodline, Josiri. As do I."

His expression darkened. "Then do so elsewhere, and leave me out of it."

Erashel's brow creased. "I don't want us to be rivals, as our parents were."

"We won't be."

"The Council won't let us be anything else!"

"You're exaggerating."

The first anger bloomed. "Lamirov will keep playing us off against one another. And our people will suffer. Or are you so naïve you believe the difficulties between north and south are done with?"

"Wedding vows won't stop that, or do you suppose they'll magically make us of one mind?"

"They send a message of unity. Our people need that more than ever. Whatever they hear, they'll *see* that the Trelans and Berals are one. You saw Ardva. The coastal villages – what's left of them. Even if the Hadari are repelled, it will take generations to undo what the Council did to us. We have to stand together. There's no better way than this, and no better time." She stepped back and held up her hands. "I knew this was a mistake. I shouldn't have said anything. Not yet."

Josiri curled his lip and stared up at Calenne, his expression so fixed, so certain, that for a moment she was convinced he saw her. She held her breath. If indeed she any longer had breath to hold. He dipped his head without a flicker of recognition.

"And am I to remain Josiri Trelan in this future of yours?"

Erashel cocked her head. "I love my people more than my name. If that's your price, I'll pay it."

"I see."

Josiri ran his hands across his face and sat down on a fallen tree.

Calenne snorted her disgust. He was considering it. He was actually *considering* it. But then, Erashel had crafted a plea perfect to exploit Josiri's weaknesses.

Duty. Responsibility. The desire to compensate for their mother's failures, and unmake her mistakes. Erashel's charms – and Calenne granted she wasn't without them – would always play distant second. And that offer to take the Trelan name – and the accompanying reminder that fidelity to Anastacia would see the bloodline die with Josiri himself? Though her brother had never spoken of a yearning for children, he'd embraced the Trelan name as fervently as Calenne herself battled to reject it. Fatherhood would be part of that.

Still, Calenne couldn't escape attendant irony. Hadn't she conspired at arranged marriage to further her own desires not once, but twice? Moreover, though she'd long held the view that Anastacia was a blight on Josiri's life, she couldn't deny the happiness the demon granted.

Was that why she felt so aggrieved? Because being so adrift in her own existence was bad enough without watching Josiri come unmoored from certainty? Because Josiri was foundering out of his depth, a neophyte in an arena for which a cloistered life had not prepared him? Or was it disgust at how methodically Erashel tempted him to betrayal, all the while claiming service to a higher duty?

Disgust boiled into anger. Calenne's hand closed about a stone. Without ever really making the decision, she let fly.

Ardothan af Garna was lighter in frame and feature than his younger brother, his hair and beard prematurely faded from flame's wrath to a mountain's snows. Alone of the Thrakkians gathered to Kellevork's great hall, he wore no armour, favouring an overcoat and tunic into which metal thread was woven at collar and cuffs.

He projected calm as Inkari made introduction. A noble ruler setting aside rancour in hospitality's name. His manner made lie of banditry and extortion, and elevated him to close company with the golden statues set in semicircle about the throne. Fidelity. Rigour. Fortitude. Generosity. Justice. Courage. Six virtues without which no thane could rule. Viktor allowed that he might even have been deceived, but for the eyes.

It wasn't just the infrequency with which Ardothan blinked, nor the fact that his eyes seldom shared common cause with his frequent smiles. Rather, it was that his gaze never lingered long in one place, darting from Armund to Inkari, to the claymore and charred axe in her keeping, to one or other of the vanguard standing close attendance in an otherwise empty hall. Not the drift of the bored or inattentive, but the mania of a mind ever in search of threat and opportunity.

More than that, Viktor deemed something amiss about the chamber itself. In his younger years, he'd accompanied his father when then elder Lord Akadra had sought treaty with one thanedom or another. Those throne rooms had been nothing less than opulent, and yet had resembled armouries as much as meeting halls. Axes had adorned every wall, gold inlay shining in blade and haft, the swirling knotwork fine beyond anything practised in Tressia. A portion of the soul lived on through the steel, or so some held, and Thrakkians liked to keep their family close, where they could. Here, the walls were bare save for tapestries, and for a soot-stained mirror above the hearth – by tradition a gateway to Skanandra, through which ancestors might view a descendant's deeds.

"You choose a late hour to seek redress, Armund," said Ardothan.

"There's never a good time to mend old mistakes."

"So it *is* as I've been told?" Ardothan sighed. "I'd hoped you'd find wisdom in exile. So much for the fruits of mercy."

"Mercy?" Armund snorted. "Exile forced Anliss to live with her shame. Death would have spared her."

"A kinslayer should feel shame, even when her axe falls astray."

"Maybe. But she died well. Her sin is absolved. Ours remain."

"I bear no sin. Our father faced the Cindercourt to answer for crimes."

"His only crimes were to be old and ailing, and to not recognise your ambition. He could barely hold an axe when he entered the circle."

Ardothan sprang to his feet, the veneer of nobility cracking as temper roiled. "He'd have sold us all to Scawmede! Our family – our history – swallowed up by a nation of churls and spendthrifts. Indrigsval would be a name on a map, remembered only in song."

"Better that than what you've made of it. Preying on the helpless? Stripping temples of their offerings? Seizing our ancestors' weapons and smelting them for your thrydaxes' blood-gold? Dress this rabble in our claith all you like, you can't conceal that mercenary stench."

Armund's gaze swept the room, though with his axe and thus his connection to Anliss' spirit in Inkari's keeping, he could've seen nothing. Expressions were impossible to read beneath visored drakonhelms, but Viktor marked which of the vanguard stiffened. Were they the mercenaries taking offence at the insult, or the true vanaguard, caring little for reminder how their honourable station had become diluted? From Inkari's bleak stare, the latter.

"I claim the right to Astor's judgement," said Armund. "For my father. For my sister. For a stolen throne. Are you afraid he'll find you wanting?"

Viktor's worries billowed to fill the ensuing silence. In theory, a thane couldn't rule without the support of his vanaguard and his landsmen, and no Thrakkian would respect a man who backed down from divine judgement. But tradition buckled under the weight of gold. If Ardothan decided its lustre eclipsed his own tarnished honour? If he decided that the risk to his position outweighed the benefit of silencing his brother's claim?

Ardothan sank onto his throne. "Inkari tells me you're a witch, Lord Akadra. And an exile."

"This would be the same woman who fled Indrigsval? A man should not be described by a coward who shies from his blade."

Inkari scowled. Ardothan's lips hooked a mirthless smile.

"She also tells me you're to serve as my brother's champion." He leaned forward, friendliness falling away. "Tell me why I should profane tradition by permitting one outcast to fight for another? What truth can that contest possibly reveal?"

"The only truth that matters."

"Is that so? Does my brother's truth extend to his own deeds? Did he tell you how our sister came to cut my throat while I slept? That but for the selflessness of my dear wife, she'd have succeeded. Armund knew her intent, and did nothing. He lacked the courage to aid one sibling, and the loyalty to warn another. His whole life, he has never chosen any side other than his own. Have you so little pride that you'll choose his?"

Armund's fingers gathered to fists. Viktor couldn't imagine what he hoped to achieve, not with his axe in Inkari's care and a dozen vanaguard between him and the throne, but knew that the attempt would unravel everything.

"Armund af Garna stood with me in need," he replied. "I pay my debts."

A little of the tension slipped from Armund's shoulders.

Ardothan smiled his wise smile. "A good answer. As to the rest . . . "

The thane hooked a finger. A vanguard howled and flung himself at Armund, his axe a brutal gleam against firelight.

Viktor's shadow slithered free almost before he gave it leave. Ice crackled across the flagstones as it closed about the vanguard and held him fast, frozen in the act of murder. The bellow of challenge choked back in terror. Horrified gasps carried across the chamber. Vanaguard inched closer, axes ready.

Ardothan stretched out a hand, restless eyes alive with triumph. "Hold."

The vanguard ceased their advance. Viktor drew back his shadow. The would-be assailant crumpled and scrambled away at Ardothan's dismissive wave.

Armund didn't even blink. "Am I missing something?"

"Nothing of note."

Viktor forced levity to conceal dismay. Their one advantage laid bare, and it gave Ardothan all the reason he'd ever need to refuse Armund's challenge. The Cindercourt was a trial of blades, not witchery. That he'd had no other choice was little consolation.

"So a coward's word is sometimes true?" Ardothan steepled his hands and tapped his forefingers against his lips. "Inkari? See that they are both fed and quartered. They face the Cindercourt at dawn tomorrow. I've nothing to fear from Astor's judgement. And I have just the champion to face you, Lord Akadra."

The stone cracked off Erashel's brow. Calenne's heart sparked to dark joy at the accompanying cry. Her laughter rippled beneath the moonlit trees, unheard by all save herself.

Josiri glanced up. "Erashel?"

She reeled, the flat of a hand clasped to her temple. "I don't know. Something hit me."

He jumped to his feet with a frown. "What? A falling branch? A bird?"

"We just talked about how there are no birds," came the acid reply.

"Then what?"

Erashel shook her head groggily. "It felt like . . . " She stared past him, eyes wide with alarm as they met Calenne's. "Josiri!"

Calenne twisted behind a tree and held her breath.

The musical scrape of a drawn sword. The hurried tread of boots on leaves. Calenne pressed her shoulders against the tree. She'd wanted to be seen, but not like this. Not caught in so childish an act. Or was it childish? Could it be so when satisfaction still burned, and yearned for more? Even for blood.

For blood? No, she didn't want to truly hurt the other woman. Just put her in her place.

Liar.

Rage boiled black beneath the fear, daring her to break cover. To beat the other woman down with fist, rock or branch. Calenne's stomach turned, knotted tight against the temper that had ruled too many thoughts and deeds since Eskavord. A deep breath helped, but with rage's passing, fear returned.

"What did you see?" said Josiri.

"She was right there," breathed Erashel. "Just for a moment. Then she was gone."

"Who?"

"I don't know. A woman. Pale. Angry. I caught only a glimpse."

Footsteps tracked closer. Josiri passed the tree to Calenne's left, Erashel to her right. Both had swords drawn. Neither paid her a second glance. She released a faltering breath.

Josiri advanced a handful of paces, made a long, slow sweep of the surrounding woods. "No one. And the undergrowth's too thick for us not to hear someone running away."

Erashel scowled, one hand still braced to her forehead. "So you don't believe me?"

"I didn't say that." He sheathed his sword. His tone was that of a man treading with exquisite care. "This doesn't have the feel of a Forbidden Place, but that doesn't mean it isn't. However, it's been a long day and we've both seen enough in the recent past to fuel tired imaginations, especially when emotions are running thin. Get some sleep. I'll wake you in a few hours." He sighed. "As to the rest? It will keep until morning. At *least* until morning."

Calenne barely noticed them leave, her existence once again in upheaval. Erashel *had* seen her, however briefly. Whatever she was – whatever she'd become – might be reversible.

There was hope.

Forty-Four

Ruined walls sprawled beneath waning moonlight, stones smeared black by the soot of spent pyres. Ahrad's middle bailey was a forest of makeshift grave markers, hummocks of fresh soil marking the defenders' last vigil in all places save one: a ring of bare grass amid the waterlogged mud, scattered with autumn leaves and ringed by stones, the dark staff of the Huntsman's spear at its heart.

No one had touched the spear since Ahrad's fall. None had even come near since Dakrash's watch had begun at dusk. Carters and provisioneers bearing supplies from the east gave the weapon as wide a berth as the makeshift road allowed. Dakrash empathised. Even looking on the weapon stole away his breath.

Not a new feeling for a miller's son tithed to war. Dakrash had felt it when he'd followed the Emperor's Immortals into the breach – for were they not heroes, pledged to the service of a mortal god? So the augurs preached at the village shrine. They did so everywhere within Corvant's borders, where Ashana was acknowledged, but deemed too distant for worship. But this? The sense of insignificance pressing down like a boot on his chest? For the first time in twenty-three winters, Dakrash understood what it was to stand in the shadow of something truly divine.

The spear that had shattered three gates. What might it do for a miller's son without wealth or prospects? Who had not yet been granted the chance to prove himself a warrior? For three nights, he'd held his post and resisted temptation, awed by half-remembered stories told by fireside at High Moon and Dark Sun – tales that warned of the grim price paid for drawing divine notice. For three nights he'd looked upon the weapon, content to dream. But as midnight approached on the fourth night and the moon shone purer than it had in days, dreams smothered fable's warning.

As watchfires and waning moon faded behind rising mist, Dakrash took his chance. Abandoning his post beside what had once been the inner gate, he passed through the graves. His heart quickened with the thickening mist, the fear as heady as the lure. Soon he stood on the ring's extent, cold air raising gooseflesh beneath leather breastplate and silk robes.

The spearhead shone with reflected moonlight, defiant of the mists. Dakrash faltered, ambition turning to ice in his veins. Licking his lips, he screwed his courage to the act. Himself a hero. A family elevated to the rank of great house by his deeds.

Setting aside his shield and his own poor ashwood spear, Dakrash stepped into the circle.

A hand erupted from the grass, scattering leaves. Streaked dark with mud, it clawed at the air and closed about the spear-staff. The ground ruptured, bucking and heaving. Withered leaves spilled away, and a naked man clawed free of loam's embrace.

Dakrash yelped and scrambled away, dreams of heroism swallowed by terror. A pale woman in a shimmering gown barred his way, a finger pressed against her lips.

"Hush. You have nothing to fear."

Dakrash's heart thundered its disagreement, but his legs locked tight and his tongue felt leaden. The woman drifted on, her being diaphanous against the mist, her expression maudlin beneath a tangle of straw-blonde hair. The man dragged his way clear of the soil. Reaching his feet, he slumped, the spear his sole support. Muscular shoulders shuddered as he strove for breath.

"I have . . . failed you, my queen."

"No. I erred. Now my brothers rouse to war, and my fears may yet shake this world apart. Will you help me mend what I have broken, old friend? I may need your strength before this is done." Mist curled up from translucent fingers as she examined her hands. "It took all I had to pull myself back together."

The man straightened. Beneath his shadowed brow, eyes smouldered to green flame. "I remain your servant. Now, and always."

They walked away into the mist, he leaning on his spear, and she more memory than being.

Only when they were lost to sight did Dakrash's legs at last obey his command.

Eyes streaming with tears he could not explain, he fled through fading mist, the memory of what he'd seen already slipping away.

Lunandas, 7th Day of Wealdrust

Pride is the spark that sets the world ablaze.
Those who seek profit by the flame
are seldom caught in its path.

from the sermons of Konor Belenzo

Forty-Five

Even with Vrasdavora's survivors reinforced from the main encampment – even with watches tripled and duskhazel ready at the fires – every scratch of shifting stone jarred Melanna from sleep. Jack's tatterdemalion silhouette loomed over all.

We will see one another again.

Melanna jerked upright, sheets falling away. Dawn gleamed about shutters and beneath the door. Grasping at the bedframe, she set her feet against the floor and strove for calm. A dream. Only a dream.

Yet still shadows crawled at vision's edge.

Melanna urged herself to stillness, lost herself in the sounds beyond the castellan's chamber. The sentry's tread. The crackle of watchfires. The Ash Wind groaning about the keep. She exhaled, the shapeless horrors of sleep falling away.

Mist thickened to a flood about her feet. Dawn's gleaming sputtered and died.

Melanna stumbled upright and fumbled the sword belt from the hook behind the door. She spun about, blade whispering from its scabbard. A cry of warning fell silent on her lips as the rear wall fell outward, stone by stone, into a mist-wreathed forest.

And there, among the trees, head bowed and weary, a figure in shimmering green, thought lost.

The remainder of the room vanished into the trees. Melanna's sword fell from numbed hands.

"Hello, Melanna," said Ashana.

*

Rosa formed a fist atop the blankets. Tremor wracked her forearm. Her brow sheeted in sweat, the salt stench as bad as the clamminess. Fingers yielded reluctantly, joints softening only after excruciating protest. That the fingers uncurled to a loose claw as soon as she relaxed her attention did nothing to stifle savage joy. The paralysis was fading. Strength would return. And then?

Then there'd be a reckoning. One tallied in the dead. Aeldran Andwar – Sevaka's slayer – foremost among them.

Beyond the cottage, the air shook to barked orders and the tramp of feet as Castellan Paradan stirred his column of beaten, humiliated soldiers to the march. They'd come for her soon; load her into the wagon for another burst of dreary miles. Away from the shadowthorns. Away from revenge.

It didn't matter. She could wait. That was an eternal's privilege.

Gritting her teeth, she bent her will upon her hand once more. Fingers curled inward.

"Aren't you looking better this morning? How do you feel?"

Rosa gasped. Her hand relaxed. The Raven was a dark presence beside the hearth. She'd not seen him arrive, but she never did. Nor did anyone else ever see him. The previous night, Paradan had made faltering report, never knowing the Keeper of the Dead stood but a pace behind, head cocked in mockery.

"Angry," she croaked.

"I'm told that's unhealthy."

"Said the God of the Dead."

He offered a sardonic smile. "I suppose I should be grateful you've recovered your usual disrespect."

"How goes the war?"

"Didn't that officious young man tell you?"

"Only guesses and rumour. *You* know where the dead lie."

He sniffed. "I don't keep score. But my efforts have not been entirely wasted. My intervention on the Toriana Plains threw the Emperor a scare. *And* I've taught his daughter not to trust stone walls."

Rosa's turgid pulse quickened. "Are they dead?"

He turned about, his attention given wholly over to examination of a poker propped against the mantelpiece. "Alas, there were complications."

"So the Raven's power isn't all that is proclaimed?"

"It is without measure," he snapped, without turning round. "Or it would be. A shower of dreary ephemerals have my mists gripped tight. You call them vranakin, I believe. All this death on the border has given weight to old rituals. They believe they've regained my favour, but all they've done is steal what isn't theirs. The harder I tug, the fiercer their response. It's the consequence of an old bargain – a *very* old bargain – and all very tedious."

"What did you get in return for your trade?"

"A blood tithe. Promises. Worship." He shrugged. "Who among us is proud of all our yesterdays?"

"A blood tithe? You mean sacrifice."

"What does it matter? They're ephemerals."

Not long before, his manner would have appalled. Not now. Ephemerals faded and died. That truth didn't care if she acknowledged it or not.

"You said complications. Plural."

He straightened, goatee twisting thoughtfully. "I can see I'll have to speak much more carefully around you. I'll have no secrets left."

"Should you have secrets from your queen?" The prospect no longer horrified. Something else that had changed.

He grunted and sat at the end of the bed. "My brother has become involved. He never could resist trying to match me. He's such an envious soul."

"Your brother."

"Jack." The Raven waved a dismissive hand. "Jerack, to the more pedantic. He intervened at Vrasdavora. Even now, his filthy little creatures will be mulching the dead. Briar, bone and rotting flesh bound to belligerence. Revolting, and *very* untidy."

A hundred tales of haunted Fellhallow vied for attention. "Why would he side with the shadowthorns?"

"Why does Jack ever do what he does? Because he wants what I have. It's pitiful, really. Imitation is flattery, yes, but to everything there are limits." Disgust darkened to a tone so barren that a piece of Rosa recoiled to hear it. "But he's never beaten me yet. He won't do so now."

The Raven sprang to his feet. He gathered Rosa's fingers and pressed them to his lips.

"Make speedy recovery, my dear Roslava. This will be a victory worth sharing."

Tears rolled down Melanna's cheeks, though she couldn't say for sure what called them forth. Joy? Anger? Fear that this was but another aspect of nightmare, come to harry her in waking aspect? Heart and soul awash, she searched for words to carry the burden and found none worthy of the deed.

"You're dead. I held you as you died."

Ashana's eyes met hers. No longer the rush-pool's crone, she was again the Goddess of cherished memory, vibrant with straw-coloured hair and pale, unblemished skin. "No woman is ever dead while she's spoken of. Her legacy abides while memory remains."

Turbulent emotion seethed to anger. Tears ran hot. "That's the best you have?"

Ashana's cheek twitched. "False hope is the province of preachers and politicians. I didn't want it to be my last gift to you." She hesitated. "I have been wrong about so much, but not about you, Melanna."

Melanna closed her heart. "Me? The weapon you level at your enemies?"

The Goddess stepped closer. "No, never think that."

Melanna backed away, her foot catching on a tree root. "How can I do otherwise? So much of what you've told me is lies! The Dark does not rule Tressia. The Droshna is one alone. He holds himself apart!"

"I didn't know." Ashana's face fell stricken. "Not then. I made a mistake."

"A mistake? You hurl my people into war, and you call it a mistake?"

"Would war not have found you otherwise?"

Melanna scowled, but could not deny the accusation, even in spite.

"But yes, I have brought war upon your people. Were that not terrible enough, I have made you complicit in my error." With a sad smile, Ashana bowed her head. "I am a poor goddess and a terrible mother, but even now one far outweighs the other."

Shock chased away the last dregs of anger. Before Ahrad, the Goddess had loomed large beyond her mortal frame. No longer. For all her seeming rejuvenation, this Ashana was but a fraction of the Goddess Melanna had known.

Anger faded to weariness. Guilt. A memory of silver dust on a muddy road. "Elene is dead."

"I know. It wasn't your fault."

"I've been so lost."

"No you haven't," said Ashana, her eyes still downcast. "You've flourished."

"I've made so many mistakes."

"Have you learned from them?"

Orova. Naradna. Even Haldrane. "I'm working on that."

"And me." She looked up. "I need your forgiveness, and your help. Withhold the former if you must, but I beg you, lend me the latter."

Melanna embraced the only mother she'd ever truly known. As they held each other close, the piece of her that always felt insignificant in the Goddess' presence slipped away. Ashana had so often claimed to be an imperfect goddess, but only now did Melanna glimpse understanding of what that meant. Wisdom earned through loss. Scars through failure. Different to Melanna's own struggles only as ephemeral and divine were different, the burden scaled to one's ability to bear it, but the weight constant to each.

"Both my help and forgiveness are yours for the asking."

Ashana pulled away, a smile trembling upon her lips. "That means more than you'll ever know."

"Then tell me, how did we come to this?"

"Because I was afraid."

Melanna blinked, caught off-guard by bluntness. "How can a goddess feel fear?"

"I wasn't always a goddess. I was born ephemeral." She shook her head, eyes unfocused. "Evermoon had no queen then, only a wanderer-king, for ever treading distant realms. Our paths tangled. We were very much in love, or so I'm told."

"How can you not *know*?"

"It belonged to a different life, and life ends. When I perished, the Wanderer sought to remake me as divine so we might pass the ages together. But you cannot steal from the Raven. When the Wanderer cheated him, the Raven cheated in return and scattered my soul across the generations. Desperate, the Wanderer drew on the Dark to reclaim me, and thought himself successful. But I remained lost – all he'd achieved was a conjuring of his own imperfect memories." Ashana's expression set hard as stone. "For all that his new queen was my twin in aspect, she was a creature of the Dark, and ruled by spite. *This* was the Ashana your ancestors worshipped – she who revelled in the spilling of blood, and whose light made wolves of men as the Dark once did before Second Dawn."

"Aunt Saramin once spun a similar tale," said Melanna. "How the Sceadotha murdered her husband in a rage, then out of grief dragged him back from Otherworld. He too went mad. I had nightmares for a week. Father was furious."

Ashana nodded. "It was no more Malatriant's husband than the Wanderer's creation was me. Only the Raven can truly return life to the dead, though he's too self-centred to bother. The rest of us can grant an eternal's existence, providing some sliver of soul holds obsession enough to endure. I did so for Roslava Orova at Tevar Flood. Some master their obsession. Others are themselves overcome."

"That's horrible."

"At least they have a chance. Those woven from the Dark know only madness. The void where the soul rests cannot be filled by another's love." She scowled. "When the Wanderer realised what he'd done, he sought me anew. Reunited, he and I overthrew Evermoon's hateful queen, but by then the love we'd shared was only a memory. We were strangers. The Wanderer resumed his journeys, and I've ever since striven to be a kinder goddess for your people."

Melanna winced. "But old ways die hard."

"Some harder than others. I thought I'd finally grasped what it was to be divine. Then I beheld the return of the Dark and glimpsed my reflection within it. She mocked my inaction, my arrogance in holding aloof from war. I saw the ruin of everything for which I'd laboured. The rest you know."

Melanna nodded. The rally of kingdoms to the Avitra Briganda – a holy war of a sort not seen in generations. Honour abandoned in search of victory.

Ashana hung her head. "After Ahrad, adrift between life and death, my fears lost their hold. I realised then what I should have from the first. The day of the Dark is done, and will never return."

"Why not?"

"Because the light will always stand against it. If not mine, then another's. And now I wonder: was it fear I heeded, or my predecessor's whispers? She's part of me still, and I part of her. Both Ashana. The dark moon and the light." She sighed. "I've never told anyone that. I keep hoping it's not true."

Few of those final words made sense to Melanna, but one truth gleamed clear. "If the war was a mistake, let it be ended. My father will listen."

Ashana shot her a shrewd look. "Will he? He's spent his life fighting the Republic. And he seeks to leave you a realm stronger than the one he inherited."

"We can try. We must."

"I wish it were that simple." Ashana stared up through the trees. "But I'm barely clinging to this life. I haven't strength to waste on follies. This ephemeral war is nothing."

Temper rekindled. "Not to the thousands who'll die before it's done."

"They'll only be the first. By interfering so plainly in ephemeral affairs, I've given licence for my brothers to do the same. The Raven and Jack have already chosen sides."

We will see one another again.

Melanna's skin crawled, the shadow of fear heavy even among the mist-draped trees. "Jack fought with us last night. Had he not, I'd be dead."

"He didn't fight *with* you. He fought *against* the Raven."

"No, he spoke of a bargain with my father."

"And I shudder to think the price. A bargain with Jack ... "

"Binds all parties?"

" ... is never as it seems," Ashana finished bleakly. "The others are already rousing. This world will crack asunder, and Third Dawn will come. At least, that's what the Tressians believe. It's more poetic than 'oblivion'. I hate poetry."

The chill air grew colder still. Third Dawn. Lumestran prophecy of a world reborn from cinders. Cold comfort to those left in the ash.

"Everyone will die," murmured Ashana. "All because I was startled by my own reflection. Please, Melanna. Help me undo the war we set in motion, before it's too late."

*

"She's mad, you know," said Naradna.

Aeldran stared down the sparsely forested slope. Melanna was barely a dark shape against the risen dawn and growing more distant with every step. "For going, or for leaving you in command?"

Naradna stiffened, armoured scales rustling atop silk, and scabbard tapping at her thigh. Only the mask was missing, a lie banished to the past. What shame Naradna Andwaral invited she now faced openly. It made it easier to read her expression. She was too accustomed to holding it secret behind gold. That would change in time, but for now Aeldran revelled in full knowledge of his sister's mind, and worries worn plain.

Only an hour before, the chieftains had acknowledged Naradna's elevation, some sullenly, others with guarded feelings. Aeldran expected most to fall into line. For those who didn't? He'd been his sister's champion long before he'd been the princessa's. He could be so again. Assuming, of course, anyone dared risk the displeasure of the third member of their group.

"Wonderful people, the mad." Haldrane leaned into his crutch. Wind set his robes dancing. "So very driven."

"What did she tell you?" asked Aeldran.

"No more than you, I imagine." The spymaster's expression hinted at deeper knowledge, but it always did. "That the Goddess calls her elsewhere. That I was to offer *Warleader* Andwaral my every support. And that we were to join our spears to the Emperor's as soon as able."

"And that was enough for the head of the icularis?" asked Naradna.

"She is the Emperor's heir. All else is irrelevant."

Aeldran grunted. Haldrane's account matched Naradna's but fell short of his own knowledge. He'd not understood much of what Melanna had told him. But his impression was that she hadn't wanted him to, and had spoken only to unburden buzzing thoughts. Aeldran cared little for those parts he *had* understood. Gods and wars and the bleakest of fates. A goddess who was but reflection, and another who feared to look upon her. Secrets held safe behind a champion's vow.

Naradna scowled. "If she *is* mad, why should any of us obey?"

Haldrane shrugged. "Because she is the Emperor's heir. All else is irrelevant."

He grinned, his eyes on hers in search of provocation's bounty. Thus,

Aeldran alone saw the sudden mist that rushed from the trees to swallow Melanna up. For a moment, he glimpsed two figures silhouetted beside her: a man in an antlered helm, hunched against a spear for support, and a woman in a long, flowing dress. Then the mists were gone, and the forest empty.

Forty-Six

Smoke from the timber and blackstone ring rushed up through the chained metal stairway, past the stone platform to dance a maddening spiral above Kellevork's keep.

Viktor had never seen so much blackstone in one place, much less set to so frivolous a use. Even in the foundry, where its wrath fuelled the smelters and its steam drove the chainways, the friable, smoky rock was hoarded. But then, Thrakkia was built on great shelves of the stuff, as plentiful below the poor soil as was the air above. Blackstone, claimed the Lumestran priests, was solidified Dark, its vapours corrupting to the faithful. It certainly burned fiercely enough, the pale blue flame leaping to join the red in a roaring crucible of justice whose walls stood four times the height of a man. By descending to do battle in the broad courtyard, a warrior proved his truth with steel, or perished a liar.

At least, that was the idea. Songs driven by pulsing drums boomed across the crackle of flame. The battlements were thick with vanaguard, thrydaxes and lowly thralls – the latter unadorned by the bright-woven claith that marked service to Ardothan or the ceorlas of his court.

Those ceorlas clustered close about Ardothan on the platform opposite, a dais of stone atop Kellevork's dungeon gate – a holdover from a time when such arenas had hosted blood sports. All were decked in gilt-edged chain and woollen cloaks that should have been unbearable so close to the fire. Then again, the trial of the Cindercourt was as much about endurance as blood. To partake in its suffering was seemly. Even Ardothan had donned armour, though his was more leather than wrought steel, save for two knotwork pauldrons anchoring a golden cloak.

Viktor's own raiment was less flamboyant: his swan surcoat worn over chainmail loaned by one of Inkari's vanaguard. Armund stood beside him on the platform, lips thoughtful beneath plaited beard; Inkari a short way distant, far enough to suggest disassociation. Around them gathered a knot of smeltpriests, their armour soot-black beneath ashen cloaks, their plain, long-hafted hammers unremarkable by Thrakkian standards.

Armund tapped the butt of his axe on stone. "At least we've drawn a crowd."

"Ardothan sent riders." Inkari shouted to be heard over the tumult of song. "Indrig, Elsbarg, Tarlsan – anywhere within reach."

"Witnesses to his justice?" said Viktor.

Her lip curled in a sneer. "It's not you they've come to see, but Ardothan's champion."

Viktor eyed the arena below, the mud already drying to dirt. "Who is he?"

Drums crashed to crescendo. Songs fell silent. A smeltpriest approached the edge of the platform and drew back her hood. Long, dark hair coiled in the cinder wind.

"The Judgement of Astor is sought," she cried. "Armund af Garna names Ardothan af Garna as a kinslayer, a stealer of birthright, and a coward. Viktor af Hadon he names his champion. Will the accused contest the Cindercourt?"

He'd have to. Tressian and Thrakkian justice at least shared the common passion of rhetoric. Having let the matter go this far, Ardothan could scarcely back down. Arrogant men never did.

"My brother is a liar!" Ardothan rose, his denial offered to the crowd, not the priest. "An exile, a vagabond, and a traitor. Astor knows this to be true."

"Have you a champion?" called the priest.

Ardothan reclaimed his throne. "I do."

The gate beneath Ardothan's throne yawned open. Two thralls staggered out into the Cindercourt, dragging taut chains. A vast shape stumbled into view, hauled by an iron collar and goaded by spears behind.

Armund rushed to the platform's edge. "Are you mad, brother?"

Below, the rangy brute reached the arena's centre. Twice Viktor's height, it was clad in rotting chainmail and pitted plate that offered little protection from the handlers' spears. Black platelets of gnarled skin shifted and cracked above forge-bright flesh. A pained bellow spilled from black, flaking lips, the outsize mannish face contorted in pain and confusion.

"Behold your folly!" Ardothan raised his arms high. "Astor sends a son to be my champion!"

The crowd roared, unaware or uncaring that the brute had chosen nothing of its fate. Viktor felt a flutter of uncertainty. Not fear. Not yet.

"What am I looking at?" he asked.

Armund stood silent, teeth bared and head bowed. When Viktor beheld him through his shadow's eyes, he saw Anliss' forge-spirit standing close by, the swirl of cinder and flame that was her face furrowed no less deeply than her twin's.

Inkari's sneer faded to unhappy awe. "We think it's a varloka."

"My friend Malachi has a copy of Gormir's *Falsang*. I've read the sagas. Varlokai are divine, yes, but no larger than a man. Gormir bested one at arm wrestling."

"So the songs tell," she said wryly. "Seems Gormir was an overcompensating braggard, even for a skald. Thralls found three when Ardothan reopened Elsbarg's mines. They were sleeping on beds of stone, surrounded by rusted blades. Two were cold and grey. This one . . . Ardothan wanted it woken."

"He's mad," rumbled Armund. "He'll roast in Skanandra's forge for this. Look at the poor scunnered thing. Astor won't forgive."

"That's tomorrow. When has Ardothan ever cared of anything beyond today?"

In the arena, the thralls laid a massive notched axe at the varloka's feet and scrambled for the safety of the dungeon gate. Cracked fingers closed about the haft.

The smeltpriest turned. Her hammer's haft thumped twice on stone. "The Cindercourt waits."

Armund scowled, his sightless eyes restless. "You can't go in there, lad. It'll pound you flat."

Viktor stared as the varloka thrashed and railed at blazing walls twice its height. So different to the florid descriptions in Gormir's *Falsang*, which had told of contemplative, measured creatures with dextrous hands and ready minds. Yet it was alike to the foundry kraikons, not just in size, but in aspect. The one the remnant of the other, fashioned by craftsmen who'd forgotten the divine creature that was inspiration's source. As a younger man, he'd sparred with a kraikon, coming away battered and broken in body and pride.

Accepting Armund's offer would have been so easy. Thrakkian honour had no claim on any save Thrakkians. But arrogant men never backed down.

"I will honour our bargain."

Viktor drew his claymore and descended into the Cindercourt.

The coastal breeze tugged at Calenne's dress and shivered at her skin. Or perhaps it didn't. Perhaps she imagined these things, as she'd plainly imagined so much of her life at Tarona. It was maddening, a night of contemplation fuelling a bleak mood as much anger as fear. Both were unfocused, suffocating, united in the urge to lash out at someone, *anyone*. As distraction. As recompense.

Beyond jumbled rocks and coarse hummocks, puddled by spent rain, Josiri and Erashel drew to a halt where the ragged, grey cliffs fell into the seething Issamar. Half a mile distant, flame leapt from Kellevork's dark walls. Gusting breeze veered north until the Ice Wind blew strong, and carried a snatch of bellicose song and the rumble of drums.

Keeping low behind the hummock ridge, Calenne scrambled closer.

"... not a Thrakkian feast day." Josiri contemplated the last of his apple core and tossed it into the white-flecked waves far below. "At least, I don't think so."

"Who can tell with thrakkers?" Erashel folded her arms. "You think it's Viktor?"

"He has a knack for raising commotion, and his trail *does* lead to Kellevork. If it *is* a feast day, they'll be friendly enough."

"And if it isn't?" Erashel sat down on an outcrop, forcing Calenne to duck lower out of sight. "I'll stay up here. One of us should keep a free hand."

Josiri stiffened. "I can take care of myself."

"I saw the border villages while you and Commander Keldrov wrestled with logistics. Fresh graves and burned farms. Let's not be reckless."

"And if some bellicose ceorla locks me up for ransom, you'll break me out?"

"Yes."

Calenne risked a glance over the hummock. Josiri stood facing Erashel, head cocked and hands loose behind his back. Wind-blown blond hair obscured much of his expression, but what remained was one Calenne had seen too often – suspicion poorly masked by polite enquiry.

"And that's all there is to it?" he asked.

Erashel frowned. "What else could it be?"

"I still haven't given you an answer."

"I can read silence. But I'm not a child, and we've other matters to worry about."

He sighed. "I understand the pragmatism at play. Honestly, I do. It's a shrewd proposal. Even flattering. But ... I've spent my life living in the shadow of tradition. What my mother expected, and what society – northwealder *and* south – demanded. It almost broke me. Even now, it threatens to do so. You've said it yourself: I'm too ready to play the outcast. If I wasn't, who knows what might be different?"

Erashel drew closer. "I can help you with that."

"I don't know that I can set aside the past as you do. I don't know that I want to. That's the difference between us. For you, the blood's more important than the name. I'm the opposite." He shrugged. "Years ago, my mother showed me our family tree. Twenty generations, stretching back through the Age of Kings. Twenty marriages, and who knows how much adoption and infidelity along the way? The Trelan name and Trelan blood likely parted long ago. But I can still honour that name."

Josiri broke off. When he spoke again, his eyes shone.

"And I love Ana. I know that shouldn't matter to a son of the first rank, but it does. For all that she can be infuriating – for all that she far eclipses me by any measure you can name – she has earned my fidelity a hundred times over. I won't turn my back on her. I'm entitled to that much selfishness."

The Ice Wind brought another burst of drums. Erashel folded her arms.

"I preferred the silence." Even now, Calenne saw her mind turning.

Erashel's wasn't the expression of a woman wrestling with rejection, but a soldier planning a new sortie even as the first failed. "But I understand. I even admire you for it, just a little. It doesn't change our situation."

"It changes everything," Josiri replied. "Secrets are corrosive. I'd rather there weren't any between us. *Especially* if you're right about the coming hours."

Erashel nodded stiffly. "Then you agree I should stay behind?"

He furrowed his brow, at last detecting subterfuge, and stared up at the sun. "I'll be back in a couple of hours, or send word. If noon rolls around and you've heard nothing ..."

"I'll come creeping to your rescue. Let's hope it's not necessary."

Josiri nodded, and set down his pack. "I'm a southwealder. Hope is my constant companion."

He strode off along the cliffs, cloak streaming in the wind. Calenne watched him go, trapped by a fold of the land that would lay her bare if Josiri glanced behind. Better to wait until he was beyond sight.

Minutes slid by. Josiri vanished around the headland path.

Time to leave.

Keeping low, Calenne sidled along the crest, only to freeze at Erashel's shout.

"I know you're there! Show yourself!"

There was no wind in the blazing circle of the Cindercourt to offer relief from the stinging ash and dry, suffocating air – only the hot rush of convection, itching at sweat-slicked skin, making trial of the slightest breath. Too like Eskavord's dying hours. Or at least, too like what little Viktor recalled.

The crash of drums heralded Thrakkian cheers. The steel stairway by which Viktor had descended rattled upward on its chains, vanishing into the swirling soot. Unless it returned, there was no exit from the ring of fire, save the gate by which the varloka had entered.

The grinding avalanche of the varloka's roar rumbled away.

Smoke parted.

Cinders swirled about the giant's axe. The air howled as Viktor hurled himself aside. Embers stung his face. He darted forward, lungs sputtering and claymore flashing at the varloka's forearm.

Bright steel sparked against calcified skin. Bone jarred at wrist and elbow. Loose chains lashed and snapped as the varloka spun around. Viktor glimpsed a red, smouldering eye. Another crusted shut by injury. Then the flat of its empty hand bowled him away.

A many-voiced cheer rolled away above the smoke.

The world spun, arrested by the thump of soot-smeared dirt. Precious breath gasped free.

The varloka bellowed its triumph.

Viktor clambered to his knees, his shadow's screams for release louder than the protests of bruised flesh. He held it tight. The rules of the Cindercourt were clear. For all that a thane's honour seemingly allowed unequal contest, to win a contest of steel through witchery ...?

Thrakkians.

The varloka closed. Larger. Stronger. Stone where he was flesh. Divine where he was ephemeral.

Regaining his feet, Viktor took measure of its weaknesses. The dragging leg. The crusted eye that rendered it blind on one side. Even the other eye, molten though it remained, flickered with madness born of agony. Whatever wit the giant had once possessed was stolen by the aeons, or by cruelties meted out at Ardothan's hand. Slim advantages. Such was a soldier's lot.

Another roar. The varloka's axe crashed down. Viktor threw himself sideways, cinders from the ungainly blade spitting at his face. The ground shook with the axe's strike. Scarcely had Viktor regained his balance when the varloka ripped the axe free and swung a blurring backhand blow.

Viktor ducked away. The wind of the axe-blade tugged at his hair. The flat struck his shoulder a bloody, glancing blow and cast him to his knees.

The varloka roared its triumph and hefted its axe high.

Viktor's shadow screamed for release, straining at its bonds.

Attention divided, half-blinded by dust and his own shadow, Viktor barely crawled from beneath the killing blow. Wiping sweat-muddled dirt from his eyes, he staggered to his feet.

A sweep of the claymore sparked against the giant's stony flesh with no sign of having done harm. Still, the varloka lurched back, surprised at the temerity of the flea come to bite at its hide, or perhaps wearied by the flurry of exertion. Fire oozed from the shifting platelets of its arm and spattered in the Cindercourt's dirt.

Viktor sucked down a ragged breath, grateful for the reprieve.

He couldn't let it strike him again. But nor could he dance about in hope of an opening. He had to end it soon, or not at all. The challenge lay in *how*.

Claymore threatening to slip from sweat-slicked fingers, Viktor backed towards the roaring flames of the Cindercourt wall.

The varloka quickened to an uneven run, the axe head dragging behind. Viktor held his ground. The world blurred behind sweat and the hot itch of skin apt to burn. Breaths foundered, unsatisfied by the choking air. Muscle ached and grew heavy. His shadow screamed.

He ignored them all.

The giant picked up speed. An avalanchine bellow revealed uneven teeth, chipped like flint. The axe came about. A wild chest-high arc, fit to scrape a shield wall into bloody oblivion.

Viktor ran. Feet stuttered on soot as he threw back his shoulders. Hip scraping against the ground, he skidded beneath the mangled axe, its passage a roar in his ears. A palm found purchase on ridged dirt. Then he was rising, the claymore in both hands and levelled like a spear.

Blind on that side, the varloka never saw its danger. The claymore's point split the rusted chainmail about its monstrous leg. Slid between the shifting, ossified platelets of its skin.

Roaring in pain and molten blood oozing from its knee, the varloka staggered blindly on, dragging the claymore from Viktor's grasp. He let it go, the giant's chains thrashing about him.

Possibly the varloka never saw the looming wall of the Cindercourt. Possibly it no longer had the wit to care. It struck the blackstone and timber trellis like a stampeding grunda. Flaming debris spattered across the giant's shoulders, the deluge quickening as the fire-weakened lattice gave way.

It fell face-first to the soot-choked floor, axe abandoned as it fought to scrabble free. Still the deluge continued, burying the giant to its shoulders. It gave a vast, booming roar and shuddered, one hand still scrabbling weakly for escape.

Viktor stumbled through the billowing soot of the wall's collapse. For the first time, a flicker of awareness came into the varloka's eyes, madness receding as the Raven reached to claim it. With it came a glimpse of the giants of Thrakkian myth, of Gormir's *Falsang*. The cleverness that birthed great works upon old hills.

In that moment, Viktor wished he wielded Lumestra's light in place of his shadow. To have the gift of healing, fit to raise the giant up. But it had never been his fortune to bring comfort. Mercy alone would have to serve.

As the crowd fell silent, he took up the varloka's axe. On the first strike, the giant's struggles slackened. On the third, the Raven took his due.

Silence reigned, broken only by the crackle of the fires.

Letting the axe fall, Viktor stepped away, breath spent and muscles locked in a quivering scream.

"Astor has spoken!" Armund roared above. "Let down the ramp! Get him out of there."

A murmur challenged the flames. Not yet a cheer, but its precursor.

"No!" Ardothan rose from his throne, quivering with fury. "The trial continues!"

The murmur rose to a growl of discontent. One thing to stack the odds. Another to defy judgement given.

"Seek your senses, brother!" said Armund. "This is ended. Astor has—"

"Throw him in!" bellowed Ardothan. "Send for my vanguard. My brother will face the Judgement of Astor."

"No!" Inkari's voice cut clear across the flames. "This is not the law!"

"Do you want to join him, Inkari af Üld?" Ardothan either didn't notice the growing malcontent of the crowd, or else was past caring. He swept up an axe from beside his throne and pointed to each of the smeltpriests in turn. "Do any of you?"

Armund made no effort to resist as the smeltpriests ushered him to the platform edge. A crack of breaking bone and a howl of pain accompanied his landing, his left ankle buckled at a horrific angle.

Viktor helped him stand as the opposite stairway ratchetted into position, offering kinder descent to drakon-helmed vanguard in sea green and yellow ... and to Ardothan himself. Twenty axes, fresh to the fight. Against a one-legged blind man, and another weary enough to drop.

Above, the crowd grew ugly, a fit match for Inkari's expression.

Viktor swallowed to ease a parched throat. "This is going well."

"Let me stand, lad." Armund pushed away. His ankle gave at once, and he sank back against Viktor. "Family, eh? Who'd have 'em?"

Calenne stood stock still behind the crest.

Had she been seen? Had she given herself away? Memory said no. Erashel and Josiri had seldom glanced behind during the morning's travel. When they had she'd taken care to hide. But was there any other possibility? Suspicion, perhaps? A refusal to accept Josiri's explanation for an attack more felt than seen? Even now, the memory of the hurled stone sparked dark satisfaction.

"He's gone," called Erashel. "We should talk. I won't hurt you."

Satisfaction soured to annoyance. How dare she? Calenne stood tall above the hummock, teeth grinding defiance. "As you wish."

To her delight, the other woman took a half-step back, hand on her sword. "So I didn't imagine you?"

"Apparently not."

"What are you?"

Calenne stared down at her hands. Grass and stone showed through flesh and sleeve, her colour washed out and hazy. A spirit caught between Otherworld and the Living Realm, fickle in sunlight. Humiliation ran sour. Maddening to have her own perception quashed by another's truth. As if she were no longer fit to judge even her own existence.

"I don't know."

Erashel's sibilant oath was lost beneath the crash of waves. She stepped closer, fingers tight about her sword. Her eyes widened. "Your face . . . You're Calenne Trelan."

Calenne flexed her fingers and let them fall to her sides. "I was."

"Blessed Lunastra."

Calenne snorted. Lunastra. Not Lumestra. The faithless moon worshipped above the radiant sun. So Erashel Beral was a heretic? The woman was riddled with deceit.

"What happened to you?"

"As if you care." Anger gorged on sorrow.

At last, Erashel let go of her sword. Her throat bobbed. "We met once, years ago. Before Zanya. I wouldn't expect you to remember. You were only a child."

Calenne's search for the memory ended like so many others, in the cloying pit that had stolen everything. People and places, yes. But events? She remembered nothing before the night Viktor had saved her life. Just snatches. Whispers. But even as she railed against the void, light gleamed elsewhere. Between bright banners contesting Davenwood and the fires of Eskavord. Her foster mother's house. A glint of steel. And a deep voice, the words indistinct. She wanted to scream.

"I won't let you use my brother."

Erashel blinked. "How long have you been following us?"

"Since you came to my home at Tarona. Since you drove Viktor away."

"Josiri wanted Viktor's help. Just as I'm trying to help *him* see a way forward."

"Liar!" Black clouds gathered. "You'll destroy him, and you don't even care!"

Calenne bore down, fists bunched and innards knotted. Erashel stumbled away. A stone skittered away, bounced once at the cliff edge, and vanished from sight. A puddle rippled beneath Calenne's boot. Just corporeal enough to count. The cliff edge beckoned. So easy. A shove, and it would be done. Lost to the waves.

Calenne blinked. No! That wasn't what she wanted. She wasn't a killer.

But she *had* killed. At Davenwood. To protect those she loved. How was this different?

It wasn't. It was necessary. Viktor would have done it.

Would he? The answer, so clear a heartbeat before, drowned in the wrathful void of missing memory. The storm in her mind gathered pace, drowning out grey daylight until all she saw was the sneer beneath Erashel's concern.

Josiri was too soft. Too trusting. He always had been.

"Calenne?" Erashel's feet found a warrior's footing on the cliff edge. Her hand closed again around her sword. "Move away. Now."

Calenne stared down at the rippling puddle. At an afterimage of herself more dream than woman. An echo of what was.

"I won't let you hurt him."

She lunged.

*

The vanaguard formed up across the Cindercourt in a ragged line, Ardothan behind. Twenty axes. One treacherous thane, flouting age-old convention. Viktor shook his head. Was it so hard to be a tyrant of conviction?

"A thousand marks for my brother's head," shouted Ardothan. "Another thousand for Akadra's. Deliver the Judgement of Astor!"

The crowd fell silent. The line came forward. Viktor set his shadow loose.

It slithered free from the smoke, hissing and howling with the heat of the fires, but also with joy at a freedom of a scope not tasted since Eskavord's final days. It snatched a vanaguard howling from his feet. Forced another to her knees. A third wailed as it coiled tight about his throat. Hands clawed madly at the Dark seething behind their eyes. Others shattered, frozen solid in his shadow's embrace.

Flagging spirit ebbed with each triumph. The weariness of day's travails, the shadow's fear of the fire – the burden of atrophied gifts long denied. They clawed at Viktor's reserves. But beneath it all, he felt the drowning sea of the Dark. The joy of it. Even as he reached out, abused flesh betrayed him. Shadow streaming from his eyes and ice crackling across his skin, he cried out and collapsed.

Teeth gritted, he held his shadow about those it had taken. Through slitted eyes, he saw Ardothan and two of his vanaguard tear free and hurtle to the charge.

"You've done your best, lad. Couldn't have asked for better." Armund stood, his axe braced as support. "My turn."

He hobbled away, sister's spirit coalescing to bright fire about him.

The first vanaguard came hasty to the fight and died the same way, cut off at the knees by the sweep of Armund's axe.

The other closed as Armund hobbled upright. Clutching tight about his last scrap of being, Viktor hurled the shadow forth. The woman spasmed, ice rushing across skin as her axe fell wide. But he could do nothing about Ardothan, who came running to the fight with eyes wilder than the varloka's.

Warned by his brother's cry, Armund twisted about, Anliss' fiery spirit moving in echo. Ardothan's axe clove his brother's charred haft in twain and hurled Armund to the ground. The ruined axe glinted and fell dark. Anliss' spirit guttered, a candleflame in a gale, and was gone.

Armund reached for the broken haft.

Ardothan kicked it away. "Astor chooses me, brother."

Armund spat. "You've betrayed Astor as you betrayed our father. As you betray our traditions. I weep for what you'll do to our people."

"Then consider it kindness that I speed you to Skanandra."

His axe came up. Viktor gritted his teeth. His shadow sputtered with his failing strength, the vanaguard pulling free.

The axe froze. Ardothan threw back his head. "Where is your praise? Your adulation? I am your thane, chosen by blood and proven in battle! You will cheer for me!"

Not one voice sounded.

"Cheer for me!" screamed Ardothan.

A harsh wind sprang up within the circle of the Cindercourt. It gathered ash and ember, streams of black soot orbiting a figure of flame at its heart. A woman's form that Viktor beheld for the first time not through his shadow, but with ephemeral sight. A likeness stuttering with the waft of flame. Anliss af Garna, freed from Skanandra's hall just long enough to right an old wrong, and deliver the judgement of a god.

The crowd's silence adopted new aspect, no longer resentment, but fear twin to that etched on Ardothan's haggard face. The surviving vanaguards fell to bended knees, eyes averted.

((Brenæ af Brenæ!)) cried the apparition. ((Væga af Væga!))

Cinders trailed behind an axe of flame.

Ardothan's head struck the ground a heartbeat before his body, the wound seared shut.

((*This* is the Judgement of Astor.))

The wind howled. The apparition dissipated. Smoke and flame leapt skyward in a great, coruscating spiral that touched the clouds. When it passed, the Cindercourt was naught but blackened timber and smouldering stone.

Calenne's palms found brief resistance, then passed clean through Erashel's shoulders.

The other fell to her knees, hands shaking and eyes wide. Ice speckled her mantle and frosted her breath. "Get . . . Get away from me!"

Calenne stared at her hands, horrified. Bitter. Angry above all. At Erashel. At herself. At a fate that had left her thus, an inconstant figment with tenuous grasp on the world. An echo of the woman she knew herself to be.

Eyes closed, she screamed her throat raw and sought identity in the darkness.

Davenwood. Eskavord. Tarona. Nothing before, and everything since felt . . . Wrong.

Again, steel glinted in the darkness. She clung to the memory, stalked headlong into the gale of her fractured being. Pace by pace, it drove her back, into confusion. The slender moorings of her being shuddered and screamed.

And then she felt it. The strength that had filled her the night before. That had billowed to life on the road beneath Valna and taken the thrakker's life. That had even brought her out of winter's fever, wolves howling at the door. Thick. Rich. Dark. Blacker than night, and so swift that she shuddered with the joy of it. Muted sensation burst to vibrancy. The rich salt of the sea. The crash of wave on stone. The cold! Gods! But the cold! It was wonderful.

The recalcitrant memory crumbled beneath her hands, broken apart and forged anew amid the billowing black. The scent of smoke, hot and bitter. Flame licking red at leaded windows. And a dagger in her hand.

The world shuddered and shook. Calenne screamed and held fast to the memory, determined that it wouldn't escape her again. When she looked up, she saw herself sat at a table, eyes unfocused as the other "her" drew close.

I couldn't save you. I couldn't save you. I'm sorry. The babble was Viktor's and hers also, so thick with emotion as to be barely recognisable as either. *I can at least spare you the fire. Forgive me.*

She slid the dagger forward. The other Calenne didn't flinch, didn't scream. She tore free of the memory, of the pooling blood, of the rasping, heaving misery echoing about the cottage walls.

Viktor had killed her.

The realisation should have provoked sorrow. Anger. *Something.* There was only emptiness. And beneath it . . . not loss, but a peculiar sense of freedom.

Viktor had *murdered* her. He'd put a blade to her throat and run her red.

And yet, if he'd done that? If she'd died in Eskavord . . . ?

How was she here?

Calenne's eyes snapped open. Her reflection in the puddle stared back. Darker, bleaker, sharper. Her, but yet not, as if pieces of her being had peeled away with the illusion of self she'd borne so long. The illusions Viktor had woven about her. *Of* her. She hadn't lost memories. She'd never possessed them. All she had was what Viktor knew. What Viktor had believed of his beloved Calenne, lost to the Dark.

She was the Dark.

Now she felt something. Laughter died as euphoria withered and cracked. Fury rode hard behind sorrow. She embraced it, let it soar. Her hands, ethereal no longer, raised Erashel to her feet.

The other woman's eyes gaped. "Calenne?"

She smiled as the last of the illusion fell away. "No."

It took no pressure at all in the end. Only the slightest shove. Then Lady Erashel Beral was gone, given to the rocks of Issamar, with nothing to mark her passing save a lingering scream.

Forty-Seven

Melanna stumbled into the ruined watchtower, glad to breathe air free of Otherworld's melancholy. Even as she gathered herself, memory faded. Only the broadest strokes remained. Afterimages of jumbled streets, familiar and yet not. A viridian sky, blazing with light and shadow. And the lost souls of the dead in sombre procession. All fading into the past, where it belonged. Only the future mattered.

"Go," said the Huntsman. "I will be waiting."

She left him in the ruins, the mist-wreathed gate billowing at his back, and began the long descent to the Hadari encampment sprawled across the plain below.

There'd been no hiding the disaster at Sharnweald, not with corpse-barges lumbering downriver with ghastly cargo, or with columns of wounded wending into Tarvallion since noon the day before. They brought with them tales of skull-helmed spirits and mists that sucked the life clean out of shadowthorns – scant comfort to any true adherent of the Lumestran creed, nor to Zephan Tanor, who owed his life to the revenants' intervention.

Church bells had rung through the night to hold those spirits at bay. Had it stopped there, Zephan wouldn't have minded. Bells brought the solace of simpler times. But it hadn't. In the Merchant's Quarter, a priest – refusing to believe that the Raven had intervened for any righteous purpose – had taken to his pulpit and blamed the day's evils, both real and exaggerated, on heretics hiding within the city. As ever, Zephan's fellow Lunastrans had borne the brunt of suspicions – the mob had razed a temple and lynched three of the congregation before the overstretched constabulary had petitioned Izack for support.

Zephan had been part of the punitive expedition. What flicker of shame he'd felt at drawing steel on civilians had faded upon sight of their terrified victims. *His* people, marked as different by the invisible line of divergent faith.

Essamere green had sent the rabble-rousers scurrying back to their houses, the call for martyrdom muted by Izack's decision to hang the priest. And then, just before dawn, orders had come down from the reeve that Tarvallion was to be abandoned.

Thus Zephan, sore from battle and bone-weary from a broken night, found himself in command of Tarvallion's Holdergate garrison. Two dozen men and women struggling to bring order to refugees blown in on a heather-scented wind. These newcomers brought rumours of their own. Not just of revenants and mist, but wood-demons that walked like men, and the war-slain dead disinterred from shallow graves. Zephan had taken to the wall as much to escape their stories as the stale press of bodies.

"I can't believe we're leaving without a fight," said Shalan. "We could hold long enough for relief."

"That's what they thought at Ahrad, and at Tregga," Zephan replied. "The city can be rebuilt."

Even as he spoke, he wondered if it was true. Tarvallion was more than a city, it was the Republic's opaline heart, where everything from the outer wall to the great cathedral of Tremora Gardens was fashioned with love and grace long-lost to Tressia itself. Tarvallion was a vision of the Republic at its best. What it was *meant* to be. Such things were not simply rebuilt.

"Not if it's cursed," Shalan replied. "Old Vannard rode out to Greyfields last night. Half those who went with him didn't come back. The lychpath trees tore 'em apart."

Zephan shot him a glare. "You know better than to spread rumours."

"Yes, sir." The squire's expression soured in hurt. "With your permission, I'll take a turn at the gate."

Zephan nodded as Shalan walked stiffly from the wall. He'd spoken harsher than he'd intended, but times were dangerous enough without feeding disquiet. That the reeve had ridden out to the swollen burial ground of Greyfields – at dead of night, atop all else – was bad enough. Worse was that the dawnlit eaves of Starik Wood were closer than at dusk the day before.

Hallowsiders knew better than to ignore such things.

Chasing away a shiver, Zephan stared down at a grubby procession beneath the gate. Most were hooded and shawled against the cold. A few led pack horses or small carts, carrying anything too precious to be left to the Hadari advance.

Shalan moved among them, two guardsmen of the 16th at his back. The Essamere tabard calmed the crowd, voices raised in dismay falling subdued.

Taking a deep breath, Zephan strove for stillness, and found more than he'd sought. The subtle heather perfumes of the breeze easing fraught nerves. A piece of him resisted, distrusting the calm. The rest drifted away on gossamer clouds.

"Demon!"

Those clouds parted before Shalan's shout, their sickly-sweet residue more alarming than the cry. Zephan ran to the rampart's inner edge just as a refugee's woollen cloak disintegrated in a storm of thrashing black fronds. The soldier to Shalan's right was on her knees, expression agape with addled wonder. The one to his left collapsed, flesh and garb slashed to ribbons.

Shalan swung at the demon's head. The wild blow tore away the tattered folds of the creature's disguise, laying bare dark stems woven to a woman's form, seething and twisting. A mask of white clay rested where the face should have been, the beatific features marred by a jagged crack running chin to brow. Behind sprouted a mane of vines abloom with black roses. Fronds lashed at shoulder and arm, dragging Shalan into a bloody embrace.

Zephan froze, reactions fogged by impossible recognition. Not a demon. A thornmaiden. A daughter of Fellhallow. He knew the tales by heart. The rhymes. The prayers. But to see one in the twisted, briared flesh . . .

Thorns burrowed beneath armour's joins. Shalan's whimpers faded. His body dropped. Screams filled the air as the crowd fled the carnage.

But not all. Refugees and soldiers fell to their knees, senses adrift on the thornmaiden's pollen. Their expressions didn't even flicker as she tore them apart. Some even smiled as their killer's dizzying, giggling laughter spiralled about them.

That sound spurred Zephan to his wits. As the thornmaiden passed beneath, he plunged from the rampart and landed atop her. Laughter turned shrill as his sword sank into briared flesh, the weight of impact driving steel deep. She staggered. Thorns lashed about Zephan's limbs and hurled him away. His head chimed on cobblestone, the dizziness of impact wedded to that of the thornmaiden's intoxicating scent.

She bore down, knocking the slack-jawed masses aside. Treacly sap pulsed from the broken fronds at her shoulder, the sword still deep in her knotted flesh. Black petals fell like rain.

{{You *hurt* me.}} There was more wonder in the tone than anger. {{Oh, we will have *so* much fun.}}

Zephan's urge to rise – to fight – floated away on sweet clouds.

{{Come. Lie with me in the green.}}

She crouched, the cracked perfection of her face level with his. Zephan felt no pain as thorned fingertips split the skin of his cheek, only a sense of loss as they withdrew.

The thornmaiden started to her feet, tendrils thrashing in alarm. Then she was gone, snatched from sight. Laughter gave way to a screech of pain, and a chorus of cracking twigs. Golden light drove the clouds from Zephan's thoughts.

"Rise up, son." A rough hand dragged Zephan to his feet. "Lumestra abhors idleness."

Zephan blinked and bowed his head as a face snapped into focus. "High Proctor, I . . . "

Tapping his sun-staff on the ground, High Proctor Ilnarov stared above Zephan's head, where the thornmaiden thrashed and railed, helpless in a kraikon's bear hug. Mouldered bone showed through torn fronds, scarlet blood mingling with sap. "Disgusting."

{{Insolent meat!}} she screamed. {{Release me!}}

Ilnarov's hand went to the lionhead amulet at his neck. "A touch tighter, if you please, Henrik."

Light sparked behind the kraikon's eyes. Metal groaned. The chorus of breaking twigs renewed. The thornmaiden howled and went silent. Kraikons might fall motionless in the mist, or if cowed by Ashana's servants, but the demons of Fellhallow had no grip upon them. Not all that was divine was equal, nor entirely holy.

"*Thank* you."

"It used to be a woman," Zephan said softly. "The Hallowsiders, we . . . *they* . . . give their criminals to the forest. Their dead. Sometimes their children. Tribute for Lord Jack and a good harvest. This is what comes back . . . "

All around, men and women shook to their senses, their eyes awash with emptiness.

Ilnarov's gaze didn't waver from the captive thornmaiden. A scholar's examination, curious and contemplative. "Fascinating. We walk with dream and nightmare. I don't know if I should rejoice or scream. I might find time for both later."

He hoisted his sun-stave to the thornmaiden's chest. Golden light blazed. She writhed, her crackling scream fading as fronds blackened to ash. Zephan shuddered, visions of old banishings rising to the fore. The ribbons on the village well. The garlands at the forest border. The sound of pipes and fiddle as spears goaded the condemned over the border.

Had he known the woman she'd been?

At the end, the thornmaiden sounded almost human. When the screams stopped, char tumbled from the kraikon's outspread hands. Zephan's sword clanged on the cobbles.

"Well," said Ilnarov. "That's done with. Keep this lot moving, would you? She won't be the last."

Melanna encountered no challenge as she made her way through the encampment, and the bright braziers of ghostfire set to hold at bay the creatures of the mists. Surrendering her sword to the Immortals standing guard, she parted the flaps of her father's tent and passed inside. Like coming home, and yet not. The fabric, the adornments. The smells and sounds of campaign. All as familiar as the rhymes she'd sung as a girl, and yet different. *She* was different. Her home, but she was a stranger, separated from the past by her father's lies.

Swallowing a sudden sense of loss, she brushed aside the inner flap.

Her father stood at a table, the map spread wide and decked with clusters of coins. Devren, as ever, was at his shoulder, sweltering beneath his bear pelt in the tent's musty air. Elspeth stood behind, arms folded.

She scowled as her gaze rose to meet Melanna's. "Oh, it's you."

Melanna's father glanced up from the map, his expression holding all the welcome Elspeth's had lacked. "Daughter. You've returned."

His smile eroded a measure of the distance haunting Melanna's thoughts. "My Emperor."

"You're very formal."

"I should be," she replied bitterly. "The mountains east of Vrasdavora are ours, but the bulk of the garrison escaped. A day, maybe two, and they'll join with the others."

"I see." The warmth faded from his expression. "How did this happen?"

She'd dwelled on what answer to give, worried over her twin failures of resolve and temper. But in the end, there was only one possible reply. "They proved themselves our better. We brought death, and they showed us courage."

Devren snorted. "Because we sent a woman."

She rounded on him, the shackles slipping from her tongue. "I had men enough in my ranks who couldn't prevail against the *women* on the walls. I wish you *had* been there, Devren. So you could have seen what I saw."

"And what, pray, is that?"

"That those who fight for survival will ever have the advantage over those who fight for lies."

"We fight for the Goddess," snapped her father. "To excise the Dark."

"There is no Dark in Tressia, Father. You've always known, and you kept it from me. As you've kept so much from me."

For the first time in the wan light of the tent, Melanna realised how grey he'd become since their last parting. A mountain still, but worn by wind and rain. Then he gathered himself in anger, no longer her father, but the Emperor she'd failed.

"I will speak with my daughter alone."

Devren's eyes flitted from Melanna to her father. Then he bowed and retreated from the tent. Elspeth followed, disdain never leaving her features. The Emperor's silence lingered. The unspoken disapproval that had haunted so much of Melanna's childhood. The sign of a line in the sand that could not easily be re-crossed. Her fault, for losing her temper.

Her father eased the moonsilver crown from his brow and laid it atop the map. "You forget your place. Devren has shared my battlefields since long before you were born. He deserves your respect."

"And I deserve *his*." She sighed. "Can we begin again?"

A muscle twitched in his cheek. "I *am* pleased to see you well, daughter. Scars and all."

Melanna traced the ridged, crusted scabs upon her cheek. Small harms, barely noticed in the taking. The worst ached beneath armour and robes – those earned brawling with Orova or duelling with Naradna.

"They'll heal."

"How do you know about the Dark?"

"I had suspicions. Haldrane confirmed them." Melanna hesitated. "So did Ashana."

His breathing quickened. "She lives?"

"She endures. She knows her mistake – the error your lies encouraged – and wants the war ended. She believes you'll refuse. I promised her otherwise."

"You accuse me of lying to the Goddess? You think I'd dare?"

"What is a lie but an omission of truth? I never realised how good you were at that."

"Truth is complicated. I don't expect you to understand."

Melanna laughed bitterly. "I understand well enough. *Women do not bear swords*. How many times have I heard those words? And now I find that our ranks are thick with women who do precisely that. Our tradition was always a lie. Can you imagine what it would have meant to know that? To know that I wasn't alone?"

"Those deceivers shame their families," he growled.

"They *fight* for their families," Melanna replied. "As for honour, are you better? This war began with a lie. Let it end with truth. Parley with the Tressians."

"Why? Because I lied to you about the Dark? Are you so vain?" His fist slammed down on the table, setting coins dancing. "This is what you wanted! A chance to prove yourself! And now you come to me in failure and *demand*? Did I raise so spoilt a child?"

Melanna's cheeks warmed. "I've nothing more to prove to you, or to the Golden Court. I realised that when I came to blows with a woman forced to a lie so she could embrace her truth. This is not about my pride!"

"Then what *is* it about?"

"Survival! The Raven stands with the Tressians, and I know you've bargained with Jack." A scowl banished the horrors of Vrasdavora back to memory. "What began as an ephemeral war is turning divine. It will consume us all. We started this, you and I. We can end it."

"This is what Ashana believes?"

"It is."

"That explains why her daughters have deserted me." He scowled. "Only Elspeth remains loyal. More loyal than my own blood, it would seem. Why doesn't the Goddess tell me herself?"

"Because she doesn't believe you'll listen! I do! Because ... " Melanna swallowed, straining to control a galloping temper. "Because you're not your lies. Because everything I know about honour, and kindness and the humility of rule, I learned from you."

He turned away, head bowed. "It seems the Goddess knows the father better than his daughter."

"Father ... "

"No!" He spun about, face tight. "You have wearied my ears with your demands and your complaints. Now you will listen. If I sue for peace – if I even withdraw – I will face accusations of weakness, and challenge after challenge from those who covet the crown. Rule of the Empire will pass to another. I will be dead, and you will have nothing. Not a throne, nor a crown. You will be a bride of brief moonlight and cast aside."

"I'll die first."

"Either way, the House of Saran will be ended. Better the whole world falls into shadow than that."

And with that, he was a stranger. A man who wore her father's face, but possessed none of his nobility. "You can't mean that."

"The Tressian Republic will fall. This is my law." He stepped closer, eyes on hers. "Will you serve me, as an heir should?"

There it was. The line in the sand. Melanna crossed it without hesitation. "No."

"Then I've no choice but to strip warleader's rank from you."

The words should have hurt, but taken alongside all else they occasioned barely a flicker of loss. "I've already set it aside. Your army marches under the command of Naradna Andwaral."

His eyes widened at the distaff surname, but only a little. A sign, perhaps, that the man she'd loved was somewhere in there still. "Then a woman's sword may yet bring me to victory. As for the rest? Go where you will, so long as it is far from my sight."

"Goodbye, Father."

Torn between sorrow and rage, Melanna strode from the tent.

It took all of Kai's fading strength to keep the tremor from treacherous knees until Melanna had gone. So many sins. So many failures. He could at least spare himself the embarrassment of weakness before his daughter. Better her hurt than his humiliation.

He reached the chair before his legs gave way entirely, half-sinking, half-falling into its embrace.

"Elspeth!"

She came at his call, a ghost passing through the tent's gloom. "My Emperor?"

"I need you." He spread his shaking fingers, appalled at their frailty. "It's worse."

"I told you it would be." She knelt beside him, fingers cold upon his hand and his brow. "Your body is wearing thin. A few days, and I'll be powerless to help."

The words echoed about the hollow of Kai's heart as his strength returned, fed by Elspeth's moonlight. A few days. Time enough to make an end of things. Especially with Jack's creatures mustering beneath the eaves of Starik Wood. Tarvallion would fall, then Tressia itself. A war that should have stretched into weeks, brought to swift victory by divine hands. A legend for the ages. Jack could have his future, as bartered – indeed, he was welcome to whatever brief span lingered past victory – but the House of Saran would go on.

Divine hands . . .

"Melanna claimed your mother wants this war ended. She says it will be the end of everything."

Elspeth snorted. "My mother delights in half-truths. You know that better than anyone. Or has she not made a walking corpse of you? She pushes us around like pieces on a gaming board, and demands we praise her manipulations. She doesn't deserve your regard."

With Elspeth's help, Kai shuffled deeper into the chair. "A daughter should speak better of her parent."

"Had the parent earned it, she would."

He examined grey eyes for irony. "Is that why you remain while your sisters depart?"

"I stay because I promised to serve you." She stood, fragile stance defying him to question her further. "It's a bargain my mother cannot annul. It's *mine*."

"So I'm your pet, as well as hers?"

"No." She frowned, offended at his poor joke. "You are my Emperor. I chose you."

Kai closed his eyes, still little the wiser to her thoughts. "You chose a stubborn old man."

"I chose . . ." Familiar defiance replaced the flash of timidity. "I chose a parent who *has* earned my regard."

Peculiar though her assertion was, it felt right – little different to Melanna claiming Ashana as a mother. A madness fit for the times. "Then tell me, daughter. What advice have you for this stubborn old man?"

"What does your heart tell you?"

The end of everything wagered against the end of his bloodline. But this wasn't the first doom Ashana had foretold, was it? Six months ago, she'd beheld a world drowning in Dark and set them all on this course. Error or lie, what was the difference? Elspeth was right. Ashana hadn't earned his regard, she'd only inherited that granted by tradition, and tradition was as flawed as she.

"That nothing has changed," he said at last. "That I should bequeath Melanna an Empire, whether she wishes it or not, and hope that one day she understands."

Elspeth smiled her delight. "Then the war continues?"

"It does."

Forty-Eight

Treadmane Street. Again. With its knackered, peeling sign and two simarka frozen mid-prowl at the crossroads and the tumbledown factory beyond.

Kurkas slumped against the twisted lamp post, its meagre blue-white ghostfire sputtering into the mist. The first dozen or so times he'd found himself opposite the old tannery the filthy cobbles had been empty. Now, they were crowded with corpses. Constables, most of them, but a few highblood colours too. A high price to confirm he'd not lost his wits. Not yet. He'd come close. His clothes were as sodden now as then. The cold burrowing in his bones urged him to lie down and rest his eyes.

Kurkas stumbled on, round and round through the impossible streets, trusting to luck stretched beyond thin. With his sword lost in the Estrina's waters and his limbs atremble, he appraised his chances of fighting corpse-eaters or crow-born as roughly that of a kitten's.

Only once had he doubted. Back an hour, a day, or a week – however long it was – a wagon had rumbled by. Kurkas had sought hurried shelter behind a crumbling wall, sluggish corpuscles roused by the sight of weeping children, hands thrust through the bars as they were borne deeper into Dregmeet. He hated himself for letting it pass without challenge, but it would have been his death to do so.

A right turn. A left. A stumble over a narrow wooden bridge more gap than plank.

Treadmane Street. Again.

Frustration welled to a growl. "You've got to be bloody kidding me!"

Kurkas knew the flash of temper was a mistake before the shout's echo faded away. Before the sound of boot on stone behind. He sighed. Maybe it wasn't all bad. Might be a *malnourished* kitten. He could win that fight, if he landed the first blow.

"Come on, then," he said. "Let's be to it."

He lurched about. His fist rose as close to a boxer's stance as he could manage.

[[Really, Vladama. That's no way to greet a lady.]] Anastacia stood on the cusp of the mists, etravia parting languidly about her. A long-handled woodsman's axe rested against her shoulder, the spatter on its blade a match for those on the sleeves of her ivory dress. [[I've already had to chastise a crow-born. I expect better manners from you.]]

Kurkas' fist fell. His jaw followed. "Plant pot?"

[[Better. But still a hair short of *actual* respect. Have you any idea how long I've been looking for you?]]

The chime of bells, distant beyond the foundry chapel's soot-choked and cracked stained-glass window, offered no clue to the passage of time. Hours tolled out of sequence, in repetition – and for heart-wrenching spans, not at all. What glimpses Altiris risked of the street granted no greater guidance than the bells. The sky was always the shiftless grey of thunder, the etravia-laced mists unyielding.

Eventually, he'd stopped looking, rising only out of need to shake loose the veil of sleep. Thoughts creaked. Senses shrieked with every whisper of movement. Had it been him alone, he'd have settled among the broken pews and slept. But doing so would rob Sidara of the slight protection offered by his presence.

She'd not stirred since he'd laid her down on an intact pew, his outer jerkin bundled as a poor pillow. The bleeding had stopped, though her bandaged arm was crusted dark with its aftermath. She resembled nothing so much as the bas-relief upon a tomb, or perhaps a rendition in oils of some princess cursed through reckless deed or a suitor's spite.

Altiris blinked, aware he'd stared at Sidara far too long, and all of it without even really seeing her. Sleep. He needed sleep. Even if the vranakin came to the chapel, he couldn't do much more than fall as a dead weight atop them.

Admitting defeat, he sat down and let his eyes fall closed.

"Altiris?"

Gummed eyes creaked open. The sour dizziness of rest taken too fleetingly rushed in. Sidara gazed down, a grubby, pale serathi with wings of stained glass behind.

Blinking furiously, Altiris hunched to a sitting position, and wiped a spatter of sleeper's drool from his cheek. "My lady Reveque? How are you feeling?"

"Tired. Hungry." She shook her head. "And it feels as though someone's tied a sack of meat to my arm. But for the throb, I'd think they had."

"Can't you heal it? After what you did for me, I'd have thought your arm was nothing."

"I've tried, but I don't think it works like that." She scowled at her arm. "I wish it did. And the light's . . . distant. Barely a glimmer. Where are we? Where's Captain Darrow?"

Altiris' gorge thickened with failure. "I don't know. She told me to leave. To get you out. I tried, but the streets kept turning back on themselves." Even that wasn't the whole truth. It missed the terror of tattered vranakin masks glimpsed through the mists. The scramble to seek concealment as they passed. "Then I saw the foundry gates. When I found no help inside, I realised I was too tired to keep going. I'm afraid I'm not much of a hero, my lady."

She sat beside him, and winced as her left hand manoeuvred the injured right into her lap. "You're doing fine."

So close, her face smudged and strained, she looked different. No longer the imperious young woman who'd taunted him by the riverside, but . . . normal. Whatever "normal" was. Had events softened her? Or had they emboldened him? "Luck had more to do with it. Luck, and Captain Darrow. Why did you do it?"

"The light wanted me to."

"It spoke to you?"

"It pushed me. It wasn't so much that it wanted me to help Captain Darrow, but to hurt the vranakin who sought to kill her. The one with the eyes." She stared down at her hands. "What do you suppose he was?"

"I don't know." Altiris shuddered away the afterimage of the pyre. Knowing it hadn't been real robbed little of its power. "He cast me into a nightmare of my father's death. I couldn't move. I couldn't even think. What did you see?"

"It doesn't matter," she replied, the lie written on pursed lips and wary eyes. "But for a moment I wasn't in control. I could *feel* the light acting through me. That should scare me, shouldn't it? That it doesn't scares me most of all."

"You've always terrified me."

Sidara glanced up. "Truly?"

"You're a daughter of the first rank. A word from you, and I'd be in the cells, or bound again for the labour camps."

"I'd never do such a thing," she said sharply.

"Wouldn't you?" He rubbed at the rose-brand hidden beneath his left sleeve. "You've never admonished an indentured servant for meeting your gaze when you wished it otherwise? That's enough, if there's an ambitious constable nearby."

"We've not had indentured servants at Abbeyfields since I was a little girl. Father freed them all when he became head of the household. He paid full wages for time served whether they chose to stay or not. Grandfather was furious, but Mother backed the decision, and that was that."

Altiris blinked. Convention aside, the monetary cost must have been staggering. "Truly?"

"That's when my grandparents moved to the house at Claveside. I didn't see them much after that."

He grunted, unwilling to abandon the point. "You still have the power to ruin my life, even if you don't use it. More than that, you perform miracles ripped straight from fable. Blessed Lumestra, but even your blood shines."

Tired eyes widened. "Is that why you called me a phoenix?"

He'd forgotten that. "*The* Phoenix, and I didn't mean you, my lady. The Phoenix of Belenzo's prophecy. It was always my father's talisman during dark times."

"You definitely called me Sidara. I heard *that*. That's not how a respectful hearthguard behaves, southwealder."

Altiris gritted his teeth. So that's how it was? "Yes, my lady Reveque."

She sank tiredly into the corner of the pew. "So we shall just have to be friends, shan't we? If you can bear that."

Altiris blinked, belatedly realising he'd misread her tone. Friends. Equity between a dregrat and a highblood. "Why wouldn't I?"

"I've not been kind to you. I've scarcely been civil. It's not becoming for a daughter of the first rank. Of any rank." She sighed. "I was jealous."

"Jealous? You have everything."

"Because you come and go as you wish. You're free of everything that binds me."

Irritation flickered. "Free to go hungry. Free to sleep in an alleyway and hope the rain holds off. An empty belly in payment for being out a heartbeat after curfew, or for meeting an overseer's eye when he wanted otherwise. I'd have given a leg to be bound as you're bound."

"I know that, and it only makes me more ashamed. I can't help how I feel, but I can stop treating you as I have."

Did she even realise the paradox of her request? They could only be equals if she chose. Even in kindness, status was leverage. But even lost to bitter exhaustion, Altiris recognised his unfairness. For all that only Sidara could decide that they were equals, they couldn't be *friends* without his choosing. And there, in the silent chapel, he realised friendship was all he'd ever sought.

"Friends it is."

She smiled. To see it made the decision worthwhile. "So, what now?"

"Can you walk?"

"I think so. At least a little. And we can't stay here. Whatever Father meant Captain Darrow to do, I think it's safe to say it didn't work." Rising, she made unsteadily for the chapel door. "If he meant it to."

Stiff muscles voiced complaint as Altiris moved to bar her path. "It's not pleasant out there."

Sidara glanced around the chapel. "Is there food in here? A path beyond the mists? Plumbing?" She twitched a wan smile. "Even if we had those things, we'll see vranakin long before we see friendly faces. We've no choice but to leave."

She eased open the door and froze.

"Queen's Ashes . . . "

Altiris steeled himself and joined her at the doorway.

Even with the forges silent, and the smelter's rivers cold and dark, the twilight glow of the mists revealed more than he wished. The constructs were bad enough. Half-finished kraikons and simarka hung from the chainway, skeletal forms trapped for ever waist-deep in the spillways of solidified metal that were to have formed their skin. Others stood as statues at the chamber's extent, chill and lifeless. For all that Altiris had spent too much of his life in fear of a kraikon's shadow – for all that he knew the constructs were nothing more than automata – he felt a pang to see them thus.

The bodies were worse.

They hung from the gantries by their heels, tethered by ropes and chains, arms and legs bound tight with black ribbon. Dozens, scores, stretching away until darkness swallowed them up. Some wore proctor's gold. Most the thick, practical drabs of men and women who laboured day and night with hissing, volatile alloys within arm's reach. Dried blood crusted every eye socket. A charm of bones and feathers the centre of every brow.

Sidara grimaced and dipped her head, the knuckles of her good hand pressed to her lips.

"I warned you."

She swallowed hard, and nodded. "You did."

Boots scraping and doubled over the banister for support, she descended the stairs. At the very bottom, she stumbled – out of weakness or horror, Altiris wasn't sure. He eased her into a sitting position on the lowest step. A simarka – this one finished – stared blankly from beside the ornate sunburst newel.

Sidara hung her head. "My father did this. At the very least, he helped it along."

"How can you say that?" Altiris couldn't settle on which surprised him more: her words, or the granite delivery. "Lord Reveque—"

"The vranakin told me. He boasted of it."

"Why believe him?"

"Because I know a lie when I hear it, and I didn't hear one." She pointed through the mists, past a knot of drifting etravia to where a gantry sat cold and dark. "Last year, a kernclaw nearly killed my mother. Right there. If Uncle Viktor hadn't saved us ... Was Father part of it, even then?"

Altiris gazed out across the horror, uncertain of what to say. "What do you believe?"

"What I believe doesn't matter." Sidara ran her hand across the simar-ka's stylised mane, fingers gentle as one fussing a flesh and blood cat. A spark of golden light flashed behind its eyes, and then was gone – lifeless bronze once more. She scowled. "It only matters what he did."

Heartbreak called for comfort a southwealder hearthguard could never have provided. But a friend? Closing his mind to the foundry's horrors, Altiris sat beside her on the stair, and jumped only a little when she rested her head on his shoulder.

Halfway along Lacewalk, Anastacia jerked to a halt beneath the jettied eaves. Kurkas, his arm slung across her shoulders for support, yelped as momentum paid cruel attention to a weary shoulder.

"Do you mind? I've only the one left."

[[I have her.]]

"What do you mean, you have her?"

[[She tried to call on her light. I saw the afterimage.]]

Kurkas stared into the distance. To his complete lack of surprise, he saw nothing. He'd quickly come to terms with the fact that Anastacia's perceptions of the mist-stolen streets were clearer than his own. For the first time since the Estrina, he'd cause to hope he might even see the sun.

"I can't believe you let the girl come running off after me."

[[I didn't know. I wasn't there. And do you know why? Because *someone* told me I shouldn't be meddling in her life, so I stayed home and read an insipid romance, like a lady of quality.]]

He snorted. "She listens to me? Now I know I'm dreaming."

[[I'm already regretting it. Now hush, before you bring half of Dregmeet down on us.]]

The sobs began so softly that Altiris didn't recognise them at first. It was only when they grew louder that his ears pricked up, the tingle between his shoulders close behind. He'd heard similar in the streets outside, and every time chose a divergent course.

Sidara sat up and stared into the darkness. "Do you hear that?"

Altiris stood and drew his sword. "It's coming closer."

"Put that away," she said. "What if it's a child?"

"Then I'll apologise." He peered at the shifting shadows away towards the loading dock. The etravia, present in number only moments before, had thinned to a handful. "Do you not have tales of prizraks in the north?"

She gasped as the first shuffled into view. Not a child. Not even anything human, not any longer. Just a pale, emaciated husk in a remnant of vranakin grey, her fingers hooked to talons. Bloody eyes met Altiris' gaze. The sob became a cold hiss spilling over needle teeth. Another parted the mists on the far side of the smelter's river. A third. A fourth.

Sidara winced. "Chapel?"

"Go."

With an ear-splitting shriek, the prizraks broke into a run, as often on all fours as feet alone. Sidara staggered as she reached the narrow landing. His shove sent her sprawling through the doorway.

Altiris spun about. His sword bit deep into pale flesh. The prizrak howled and shied away in a flurry of ragged cloth.

A second scurried up the banister on all fours. Altiris cried out as its claws opened his right cheek to the bone. A desperate thrust sent the creature wailing into the darkness, and then Altiris was through the chapel door. It crashed shut beneath Sidara's shoulder.

As Altiris joined his weight to hers, the shrieks redoubled. Timber reverberated beneath frenzied abandon.

"The window," Altiris gasped. "I'll hold them. Get down to the street."

"It's three storeys of sheer brick," she replied, breathless. "I can't climb that."

The door shuddered. Hungry cries redoubled. "Chance the fall. It's better than staying here."

Blue irises stuttered gold and fell dull. "I'm not leaving you to die."

"If there's something you can do about that, now would be good."

She didn't speak. She didn't need to. He saw the truth in her eyes. Whatever light dwelled in Sidara's blood, she'd spent too much of both on too little rest.

Impact shuddered the door open a crack. Talons scraped at the frame. Altiris hurled his shoulder at the door anew. A shriek, and the talons vanished.

"Go," he said. "While there's any chance at all."

Sidara clenched her fists. Gold light gathered briefly about her fingers and bled away.

"I'm sorry," she gasped.

A door panel splintered. Altiris' head rushed hot as talons grazed his scalp. He hunched lower, boots slipping on tiles. "Go!"

Sidara backed towards the broken window.

A scream sounded behind the door. A wet thud. Another. More followed, the accompanying shrieks now thick with pain, not hunger. A cascade of footsteps on the stairs, and they ceased entirely.

A rap of knuckles. A familiar voice. "Open this damn door!"

Altiris opened the damn door to find a sodden Kurkas propped wearily against the outer jamb, black hair greyer than at their last parting, and face markedly more lined.

"You're both in so much bloody trouble."

Behind him, on the landing proper and clad in a dress so fouled it took Altiris a moment to realise it had once been ivory white, Anastacia stood on a pile of dismembered dead. The golden light rippling beneath her frozen face contrived the image of a scowl.

[[There was a time when I flew to war arrayed in gold and silver, a sunlight spear in my hand and diamonds glittering on my brow. Kings offered me fealty. The unsullied their virtue. Now look at me. I'm a nursemaid for children, and I smell like an abattoir.]] She brought her axe down on a prizrak's corpse, splitting head neatly from body. [[I hate you all.]]

Forty-Nine

The elder cousins came to Silvane House at third bell, passing through a mansion emptied of servants and hearthguard in anticipation of their arrival. She'd wanted to run, to let the Dusk Wind carry her where it would. But defiance took courage, and Apara Rann had none. And so she sat, surrounded by gilded finery, and tried not to scream as the air crackled to ice.

"You are called to face the Parliament, cousin," said one.

"It wasn't my fault." She closed her eyes. Athariss' lifeless face stared back.

"Still you are called." Another reached out a rag-bound hand. "Will you come willingly, or must we bring you?"

She almost laughed. Even now, they presented her with a choice that was no choice at all. Her service to the Crowmarket encapsulated in one perfect moment.

You're not cut out for this. Leave while you can.

The advice of girlhood was never more apt. She wished she'd listened.

Freed from the mists to the cold afternoon air, Altiris' soul soared free. Sidara leaned on him every step of the way – though not so heavily as Kurkas did Anastacia.

As for Anastacia herself, she'd navigated the mists with her customary surety. She cut a ghoulish figure in the lantern light beyond Three Pillars. It took little effort to imagine folk cowering behind their drapes as she passed, less a serathi on a mission of mercy than a demon seeking feast. Certainly no one crossed their path, a circumstance that spoke to a curfew willingly observed – which was to the benefit of all, for there seemed to be no constables to enforce it.

At the Abbeyfields gate, Sergeant Heren sent for a cart. The final half-mile thus passed swiftly, if jarringly. Soon, Altiris stood before the grand staircase of Abbeyfields' front door, and the uncertain prospect of the elder Reveques' welcome.

Anastacia helped Kurkas from the cart and eased him against a plinth. [[I trust you can stagger the rest of the way alone, Vladama?]]

"You're leaving?" said Sidara.

[[Of course. I expect no welcome worthy of the name.]]

Kurkas snorted. He looked older and greyer than he had days before. Still on the outer cusp of his prime, but perhaps a year further removed. Altiris recalled the uneven chimes in the mists, and wondered if Kurkas had been gone a good deal longer than days. "Easier to walk away, ain't it?"

[[I've no idea what you mean.]]

"Sure you don't."

"Please stay," said Sidara. "Mother will want to thank you."

Mother, not *my parents.* Accusations about Lord Reveque's complicity had sunk deep.

[[I'm quite sure she will not.]]

"Then *I* will want to thank you. Properly."

Anastacia turned to leave. [[Then it will wait until tomorrow.]]

Light flooded the driveway. "Sidara? Blessed Lumestra."

Lady Reveque descended the stairs and flung her arms about her daughter. Fingers wended through Sidara's matted, tangled hair; arms clung tight. None of the emotional detachment tradition demanded of nobility. A woman reunited in joy with a piece of her world thought lost.

"Mother . . . " said Sidara. "My arm . . . "

Lady Reveque stepped back. Fingers traced the bloody cloth of the arm she'd trapped between them. "It must be tended. You've been fortunate."

"Yes. In my friends."

Lady Reveque's gaze touched first on Kurkas, then Altiris.

"We will talk about this." A hand snaked beneath her veil to brush away a tear. "We shall, and at some length. But only after I'm certain you'll survive the telling, and . . . "

She noted Anastacia's presence where the spill of light yielded to darkness. Hand slipping from Sidara's shoulder, she bore down, inevitable as death.

"Mother, no ... "

[[I was leaving anyway,]] said Anastacia. [[You needn't trouble yourself with the command.]]

Careless of the ruined, bloody gown, Lady Reveque embraced Anastacia with only a hair less ferocity than she had Sidara. The other went rigid, arms splayed, as one might upon discovering a spider crawling across one's leg. After a moment that strained into discomfort, Anastacia returned the embrace, but hesitatingly, with reluctance that might have been fear for the other's fragility, or might equally have been distaste.

"You returned my daughter to me," said Lady Reveque. "No demon would do such a thing."

Sidara offered a weary grin. Kurkas shook his head.

Gingerly, Anastacia pried herself clear. [[I should go.]]

"I won't hear of it." Brusqueness returned. "Not in that state. You will at the very least have clean clothes, and water to bathe. Hawkin? Hawkin!"

The steward appeared at the doorway, two maids hurrying in her wake.

"Shall I summon a physician, lady?"

Lady Reveque's attention turned on each of her unexpected guests in turn. "No. Lumestra knows the hospices have their hands full, and my years in the convent have to be useful for *something*. Hot water, Hawkin. Clean cloth. And someone help Captain Kurkas. The poor man looks dead on his feet ... " She glanced at the blood-soaked Anastacia. " ... but perhaps through the servants' door."

Hawkin bobbed her head. "Yes, lady."

Despite claims his injuries were "scrapes that would heal well enough alone", Kurkas allowed Hawkin to lead him away to the prospect of a hot bath. Anastacia crossed the threshold with all the enthusiasm of a cyraeth anticipating exorcism, but eventually followed a nervous maid deeper into the house. All of which left a none too comfortable Altiris alone at the kitchen hearth with only Sidara and her mother for company.

"Sit down, boy," said Lady Reveque. "There's a time for formality, and this isn't it. You too, Sidara. Sit."

Altiris pulled up a chair at the table as Lady Reveque set about unwinding Sidara's filthy dressings. "What a mess. You've more your father's fortunes than your mother's." Sidara flinched. Lady Reveque leaned closer. "Who did this to you? A vranakin?"

She nodded. "I'd not be here but for Altiris, and ..." Eyes wide, she rose halfway to her feet, restrained only by her mother's grip about her arm. "I must speak to Hawkin."

"She'll be back soon. Sit down."

"You don't understand. We saw Captain Darrow. She might still be lost in the mists."

"To my certain knowledge, Captain Darrow arrived at the Crossmarch watch house a little after noon today, practically carrying one of Lord Lamirov's hearthguard. She could barely stand, but refused treatment until she'd reported to your father." Again, Sidara flinched. "She told him you were wounded, but alive and in good company. I told Hawkin to take the evening off, but she wouldn't listen."

A maid returned with a bowl of steaming water, clean cloths and an assortment of physician's paraphernalia, all borne on a tray. Lady Reveque dismissed her, then set about bathing and rebinding Sidara's arm. Before long, the kitchen stank of tincture, cloying but wholesome. When all was done, she turned her attention to Altiris.

"That gash on your cheek. Is that the worst of it?"

"Bruises and sore bones, my lady. Nothing more. I too have been fortunate in my friends."

Sidara smiled.

"Good," said Lady Reveque. "But that will have to be stitched, or it'll scar."

He brushed the crust of blood and winced as she reached for the needle and thread lately used to draw Sidara's wounds closed. "I don't mind a scar."

"My daughter seems to think you're not a fool, so don't prove her wrong. Bring the chair, and look up at the light."

Sidara's brief shake of the head offered no support, so Altiris did as he was told. Proximity to Lady Reveque did nothing to lessen his unease, even though the woman lost in physician's labours was a good deal kinder in word and manner than the one he'd striven to avoid in recent days.

"It's no good, I can't see a thing." She folded back her veil, her own scars livid in the lantern light. "Better. What did this? An animal?"

"A . . . a prizrak, lady."

A thin hiss. "What days these are. Shadowthorns at the gates and horrors everywhere."

"Shadowthorns?" a young voice called from the kitchen door. "You told me I was never to use that word."

"And when have you done anything I've asked of you, Constans?"

The boy sidled into the room. Peering through his dark fringe, he beheld his battered sister with sullen disinterest. "Oh. You're back. Is she to be punished, Mother? I'm punished whenever I run off."

With a sigh, Lady Reveque drew her veil into place and set down the needle and thread. "Sidara's not a prisoner, however it may sometimes seem. I just . . . I'm afraid for you. Both of you. But there's nothing to be gained by keeping you from a world of which you must be part. Love and trust are hard to balance. You'll understand when you're older."

For all that she addressed the words to her son, Altiris sensed they were meant more for her daughter – a sidelong apology from a woman too proud to admit fault.

Constans ran a hand through his unruly black hair, one eye part-closed in sceptic appraisal. The boy remained a mystery to Altiris, having endured Kurkas' brief lessons only long enough to prove himself faster and more vicious with a singlestick than his fellow pupils.

"So she isn't to be punished?"

Sidara slid a hand over her eyes. "For pity's sake, Constans."

"Enough, both of you," said Lady Reveque. "Constans? Bed. But kindly ask Hawkin to join us, if she's done with Captain Kurkas."

Constans scowled and withdrew, having taken the measure of his mother's patience and finding it too thin to risk. Peace restored to the kitchen, Lady Reveque again turned her attention to Altiris' cheek. By the time Hawkin arrived, the matter was done, Lady Reveque's hands scrubbed clean and Altiris' nerves almost on an even keel.

"You wanted me, lady?"

"Yes. Would you send someone to tell my husband his wayward daughter is safe and well?"

"I'll go myself, if you're agreeable." Hawkin flashed a subdued smile. "I might check on Vona?"

"Yes. Yes of course."

"I imagine Father already knows," said Sidara, after Hawkin had gone.

Lady Reveque froze. "Whatever do you mean?"

"I'm sure a little bird's whispered the news in his ear. That's what vranakin do, isn't it? Trade tidings and tales."

Altiris' fleeting sense of calm dissipated. "Sidara, are you sure this is a good—"

"*Lady Reveque*," the girl's mother snapped the correction. "You forget yourself."

"Leave him alone," said Sidara. "Be angry at Father. He sold this city to the Crowmarket."

Altiris shied from the inevitable explosion. Lady Reveque stood silent and unmoving by the kitchen's stone basin, arms spear-straight at her sides.

"Young man," she said at last, in cold, quiet tones. "You have my thanks. But I will now speak with my daughter in private."

Grateful and terrified, Altiris stumbled to his feet.

"Stay." Sidara's voice halted him halfway to the door. "He knows, Mother. Sending him away won't change anything."

"You don't know that," snapped Lady Reveque.

Caught between the vying wills of mother and daughter, Altiris went still in the vain hope that he might be forgotten long enough to make his escape. It was only then he realised that Lady Reveque's retort lacked denial.

Sidara's face fell. "You already know, don't you? You know he's a vranakin."

"He's nothing of the sort! Your father's a good man. He made a difficult choice."

"What could possibly be worth what his choices have done to this city?"

"*Saving* this city! The Crowmarket helped Ebigail Kiradin take control last year. The only way to split them apart was to offer a better deal: a sympathetic ear on the Council with none of Ebigail's pride. Your father offered himself, thinking he'd never have the influence for it to matter."

Lady Reveque sagged. "Then Lord Akadra abandoned him and ruined everything."

"Uncle Viktor knew?"

"Of course not! But with him gone it all came tumbling down. Your father's held things together – kept the Crowmarket content, but also restrained them." She swallowed hard. "He thought it would grow easier, but it's only getting worse."

"It's *his* fault it's getting worse." Sidara flung out a hand. "They brag about how Malachi Reveque is just another of their playthings."

"Sometimes you can't make a decision wholly from the good. You take what life offers and do the best you can."

"Or you find another way."

"There wasn't one."

Sidara sprang to her feet, cheeks colouring. "Stop defending him!"

"I'm not defending him. I'm endeavouring to explain." Lady Reveque paused. "When has your father ever taken a decision without me?"

Sidara went deathly pale. Her good hand steadied her against the kitchen table. "The great and just Reveque line. The bedrock of the Republic. A name bound together with truth and honour, even as the other families fell to squabble and shame. One worth sacrificing dreams for. Is any of it true?"

"All of it."

Altiris' heart ached in sympathy with the pain in Lady Reveque's voice.

Sidara shook her head as if in a dream. "All of it." She looked up at Altiris, and the mother's sadness became as nothing compared to the daughter's. "Thank you for everything, Altiris. I would never have believed a southwealder more faithful than both my parents combined."

She stumbled from the kitchen.

"Sidara ..." Lady Reveque reached for her, only to have her hand brushed aside. She stood in the doorway, staring after her daughter, a broken woman suddenly years older. "So much like her mother. Too quick to judge, and too certain in that judgement."

She sank into a chair, face buried in her hands.

"Would you do me the kindness of leaving, Altiris? I need space and silence. One of the maids will find you a bedroom in which to seek your own."

Altiris was all too eager to accede. And yet he found himself halting on the threshold, his wariness of Lady Reveque worn away by her distress. "I'll say nothing of this, lady. Not to anyone. I swear I won't."

She gave a bitter laugh. "My daughter believes me a liar and a traitor. Worse, in large part she's correct. What do strangers matter?"

"Malachi?"

He blinked awake, cheek numb and gummed to the table. Thoughts gibbering their weariness, he levered himself upright. His elbow jogged a brandy glass and set amber liquid rippling. He'd not even tasted it before sleep had taken him. Too many days and nights too close to the edge, and nothing to show for it but failure.

The shapeless figure hovering half-in, half-out of the council chamber doorway resolved to familiar features. Plaited black hair, and a young face worn by recent days.

"Messela? Has there been any word from Lancras?"

"Not since this morning. I've sent a herald to remind Master Toldav of haste."

He nodded weary thanks. Lancras. Constables stripped from the Outer Isles and marines from the navy. The Republic had little else to offer. Everything else was committed, sent to reinforce Izack at Tarvallion, or lost on the march, away from his sight.

And even if the reinforcements were able to reclaim those streets, Tarvallion could already have fallen, broken apart as swiftly and brutally as Ahrad. Izack's coded reports had been guarded at best, even with their claims that dread spirits had rescued one battle from disaster. Unthinkable, a year before. Now? Now strange tales were the foundation of unfolding events. Even if they were true, why would the Raven defend the Republic against the Hadari, even while his Crowmarket undermined it from within?

"And the rest?" he asked, not wanting to know the answer. "The casualty reports from Dregmeet?"

Messela hesitated. "Lieutenant Raldan has two dozen constables watching the boundary. He claims there's as many again will be good for duty soon. It might be a handful have missed his count, but even so ... "

Even so, that left hundreds missing. Malachi had little hope they'd be found alive. And the constabulary was only a thread in the woeful tapestry.

The butcher's bill stretched far into the hundreds. Maybe thousands, when you counted the citizenry trapped in the stolen streets. Maybe even Sidara.

He crushed the thought away before misery overwhelmed.

"I spoke to the Grand Council this afternoon. They'd have torn me apart but for fear one of them would have to take my place." He forced a mirthless smile. "Who'd want that?"

Messela stepped inside and closed the door. "We're not done, Malachi. I promise you."

He snorted. "You sound like Viktor."

"Would you believe I hardly know him? If you want to know the truth, I've resented him all my life. I knew we'd always be compared, and that I'd always be judged the lesser. Maybe that's as it should be. I've never been brave, or strong." She spread her hands. "Even now, the only reason I'm here is because he chose it for me, not because I earned it. Better to be his friend than his family."

The confession said much of her reluctance at council. "I look at all I've done this last year – the mistakes I've made – and I wonder, did pride lead me here?" Malachi twitched a shrug. "My need to prove myself Viktor's equal . . . even his better?"

"You're not responsible for those the vranakin have killed."

"Am I not?" Seized by perverse desire, he almost confessed his crooked bargain. "History may judge differently."

Messela shrugged. "Let it. And there is good news alongside the bad."

He snorted. "Such as?"

"Sidara's back at Abbeyfields, hurt but mending. Word arrived a little while ago. That's why I came looking for you."

The news struck Malachi silent – giddy and breathless in a moment of perfect joy. He offered a wry smile. "You might have led with that."

"And follow good tidings with bad? It's not polite." She knelt beside him, one hand on his knee. "Go home, Malachi. See your family."

"I can't. Someone has to give Toldav his orders. If I'm not here, Leonast will do so, and matters will be worse."

"I thought you and Lord Lamirov had found common cause?"

"Not enough to trust him. It's enough to know my daughter is alive. The rest will wait."

*

The silent, kneeling crowd parted readily before Apara's escort. How many had come to the Church of Tithes out of choice, more than fear? Certainly not all. There were uninitiated among the masked vranakin; stolen children with fearful, darting eyes. Older folk, too. The wealthy citizens of Highvale shoulder to shoulder with the poor who'd scraped a living within Dregmeet's former bounds, feigning fealty in hope of survival.

The church's gates gave way to a musty interior lit by candle and sweet-scented ghostfire – for all that the Parliament of Crows welcomed the etravia to the streets, they did not do so into their own lair. There were few mourners beneath the leering, wax-crusted crow statues, and fewer faces Apara recognised. Erad was one, his averted gaze unfriendly as the grim procession passed him by. Most were elder cousins, tattered robes formless in the gloom. Apara's legs trembled with every step, but she stumbled on.

Athariss' corpse lay upon the altar, now identifiable only by its gold-edged robes. Years held at bay in life ravaged him in death, his flesh hissing to dust even as Apara had laid him on the church steps and fled into the night. Bare scraps of desiccated flesh clung to his bones, matter trickling away as eternity took revenge. Beyond the pulpits, the space where Nalka had screamed her last waited, empty and beckoning.

Krastin and Shurla stood before the dais, heads bowed.

The former looked up as she approached. "Apara. You see what your failure has wrought?"

"You should have offered the Reveque girl to the Raven," snapped Shurla.

She dropped her eyes to the cracked tiles of the floor. "I can't. You know I can't."

And yet she almost had. The shadow's grip had faltered, worn away by the mists as Krastin had promised. If she'd only been stronger, none of this would have happened.

"You will speak with respect!"

Shuddering, Apara fell to her knees, head bowed. "Yes, Crowmother."

"It wasn't her fault. Arrogance brought us to this place." Krastin ran a tender hand across Athariss' lifeless brow. "Ours. Athariss'. And Lord Reveque's. Now we are two where we should be three. The Raven's gift unmade by jealous light."

Even trammelled by fear, Apara didn't mistake the admission. That for all Darrow's sword had struck the final blow, Sidara's had sealed Athariss' fate.

"How can you speak so calmly?" hissed Shurla, too quiet for the words to carry. "Athariss is gone. Our holy grip on Otherworld falters."

"The Crowmarket's strength was never in the Raven's blessing, but in family." Not for the first time, Krastin's tone suggested unease with his sister's zealotry. "You saw the crowds beyond these walls. They *believe* in us again, as they did in old days. We need only a sign, and our family will grow, boundless with deathless promise."

Apara found it impossible not to read cynicism in his words, not with rotting forms of elder cousins standing close enough to scent their decay. For all Krastin spoke of family – for all he'd declaimed to Malachi of bringing hope to the forlorn – he was either unwilling or unable to fully share his longevity. He was eternal, whereas they were merely hollow folk who hadn't died when they should.

How many would flock to the Crowmarket if they knew that that flight ended in an elder cousin's worm-eaten existence, alive by the barest technicality, immortal in none of the ways that mattered. Were the elder cousins even aware of what they'd become? Did they care? Were they capable of caring?

A prizrak's madness might be preferable.

"The Hayadra Grove," said Krastin. "Athariss' spirit is gone, but his body holds power enough. Let the holy trees rot. Faith will falter."

Shurla nodded. "And what of her? To fail Athariss was heresy. She defied the Raven's will."

Apara shuddered as Krastin's gaze fell upon her.

"Family is forgiveness," he intoned, his words echoing through the church's gloom. "But forgiveness must be earned."

Cold hands closed about Apara's and raised her to her feet.

She swallowed. "W . . . what must I do, Crowfather?"

He stared about the church, meeting the gaze of each of the assembled cousins in turn. "Malachi Reveque has declared himself our enemy. Let him serve as a lesson to all. Not a death of shadows, but a beacon. A pyre that blazes so bright that none will doubt our resolve." His voice dropped, again the kindly grandsire, pained by the failing of his kin. "Will you give me this, Apara?"

What choice did she have? "Yes, Crowfather."

Fifty

M elanna found herself beneath the stars. Impossibly distant, they swam the inky void in graceful shoals, motion so minuscule that only ardent attention revealed it. To offer that same attention was to be lost to hypnotic splendour – to the blaze of white, and the vibrant colours of wistful clouds behind. The air hung heavy with forgotten times and broken promises.

An uneven causeway of geometric stone stretched away across the waters of a black, glimmerless river. Song danced above the rushing waters, mournful, beautiful and cold as the stars, the singers hidden in the outer darkness even as Melanna sought them.

Ashana laid a hand on her shoulder. "The river has no claim on you. I hope it never does. But it won't pass up a gift given freely."

Melanna blinked and stared down. Her feet, no longer on the firm stone of the causeway's centre, now teetered on its edge. Two strangers stared back as reflection. Ashana was no longer fair, but dark, her features sharper. Beautiful still, but the beauty of the knife, or the serpent – perfection made cruel. Melanna's own reflection bore a rich, autumnal hue in flesh and raiment alike. Even the reflection's eyes were coloured thus, the difference of texture and form marked only by the lazy swirl of ... woodgrain? The Melanna of the river was a statue, carved and polished, her limbs locked in place while her eyes screamed.

As Melanna beheld the image, the heavier her own limbs felt. Her skin grew numb. She stumbled away.

Ashana crowded close, face twisted in concern. "What did you see?"

"I don't know. It was me, but it wasn't."

The stars had lost their beauty, now cruel and cold . . . even watchful. Melanna gazed back to the gateway of mist where the Huntsman stood alone, vapour boiling to nothingness about his shoulders. Though armour and antlered helm had been restored, he bore both unsteadily. Without his spear's support he'd have fallen.

"Where are we?"

"It's never needed a name."

"It needs one now. Is this Evermoon?" Melanna shivered as she spoke the word, a frisson of reverence tempered by fear of treading sacred ground – the dwelling place of ancestors and heroes long dead.

"No." Ashana smiled as if at some private joke. "Bright Evermoon and dark Eventide are but worlds, as Aradane is a world. Each only one among many. Vaalon, Astarria, Maida . . . the others. Gears in a celestial clock. This is the face of that clock. It couldn't exist without the others, but nor would they have purpose without *it*. Otherworld exists between the gears. The river is oil that keeps them moving. Both serve as pathways through today and tomorrow, if you have the knack."

"It doesn't look like any clockface I've ever seen."

Ashana shrugged. "Of course not. It's a metaphor."

"To explain away something I don't understand?"

"To explain away something *I* don't understand." She smiled tiredly. "Not everything surrenders to our desire for answers, Melanna. The gears bite, the clock turns, and time ticks away, ushering the end."

Last Night and Third Dawn. Melanna shuddered. "Is it truly inevitable?"

"Even the inevitable can be delayed."

Ashana set off along the causeway. Melanna glanced again at the Huntsman. He'd supported when no other had. To see him worn away was harder than standing witness to his death.

"Will he be all right?"

"He'll endure," said Ashana. "He holds the gate open for our return. I'm not strong enough. Words must serve. And if they don't, then hands other than mine."

They followed the causeway, arrow-straight and unveering. Melanna closed her heart to the mournful song, to the hypnotic glory of the stars. Better to think it a dream than hark to the Goddess' tales of gears and turning worlds. It helped fend off mounting insignificance, of being a mote of dust upon a reality too vast to comprehend.

Then the causeway broadened to a craggy island, and insignificance flooded back stronger than ever.

The centre of the island fell away into a pool, the waters as black and featureless as those lapping its outer shore. Thrones clustered about, tiered in uneven circles and flanked by tall braziers. Some of the thrones were sunken, half-reclaimed by the island's stone. Others lay in ruins, backrests split or shorn away. Seven remained. One was cracked, golden light shining beneath its wounds. Another glimmered silver. A third was not stone at all, but a tangled bower woven from thorns. The fourth a plain chair, without ornament or pretension.

But Melanna's intimidation arose not from the thrones themselves, but the occupants of the three that remained.

One looked to be asleep. Dust trickled from decaying armour with every heave of a thickset frame. Corrosion clung to tarnished metallic flesh. He'd no skin to speak of, and each strand of musculature was a cable of folded iron. A torn cloak the colour of dried blood flowed from his shoulders, a many-faceted crown the colour of winter skies rested atop a mane of rust-covered wire.

Across the pool, another sat motionless, as if the tiniest flicker of movement was affront to his being. He wore a pressed waistcoat and long-sleeved suit of good cloth, almost Tressian in its design, save that there was no flamboyance to soften austerity – just as the man himself might have passed for an elderly ephemeral, but for his halo of indigo flame and empty eyes.

These two, Melanna recognised from old tales, spun by visitors to the Golden Court. Astor, Lord of the Forge and the Smelted Soul. Tzal, the Unmaker, the Forlorn. Only the third was unknown to her. In aspect a dark-haired young woman, she sat on tucked legs on a throne flanked by lissom, alabaster statues frozen in the act of beseeching her favour. Her yellow gown was as severe in cut as Tzal's raiment, though not without elegance. She too came within passing distance of human, save for her eyes, which were vivid blue-green.

Who was she? Not Endala, whom ancient Tressians had wor-shipped, for Endala was always portrayed as a woman in her prime, and serpentine below the waist. If not her, then who? Scripture named multitude false gods and demons.

Her eyes met Melanna's. She stumbled away, overcome with the urge to kneel, to flee, to beg – anything to escape attention, or dissipate the sense of worthlessness.

Ashana's hand found Melanna's shoulder, warm even in that cold, timeless place. "Be calm. You're stronger than this."

"Aren't you supposed to tell me there's nothing to fear?"

"You stand among the divine, in a place that is no place," replied Ashana. "Fear's sensible enough. But no harm will befall you."

She entered the circle of thrones.

"Ashana." Tzal's empty stare tracked her approach, his tone dry with disdain, his words threaded by a chorus of voices. "We are here, as you demanded."

"As I *requested*," said Ashana. "Where are the others?"

Astor stirred, his voice a rumble of heaving stone. "Have patience, little moon. They will come in their own time, or not at all."

The dark-haired goddess shifted on her throne.

Ashana narrowed her eyes. "Had you joined your voice to mine, they'd be here. They can't defy us all."

Tzal's indigo flames glowed richer and brighter. "Have a care, sister. I indulged your desire to meet. That is already more than you'd right to expect."

"There is an order to these affairs," rumbled Astor. "Tradition to be observed."

"We stand on a precipice," said Ashana. "What use tradition if we fall?"

Tzal snorted. "You're still ephemeral at heart."

"At least I have a heart."

"I agree with Ashana." The dark-haired goddess sat forward on her throne, her gloved hands gripping the armrests as if she expected at any moment to fall. For the first time, Melanna realised that her feet wouldn't have reached the ground even had she sat round. "The others should be here."

"It's a waste of time," growled Tzal.

"Better to waste it, Father," she replied, "than regret that we didn't when we could."

"Your opinion, daughter, matters even less than hers. You may sit upon your mother's throne, but you haven't earned it."

For all that neither Tzal nor Astor hadn't moved, Melanna had the sense that they loomed above the others, disapproval crowding out reason as night swallowed moonlight. She understood too that this wasn't the first occasion, nor would it likely be the last. With that realisation came recognition of history repeated. Not Ashana's, but her own.

How often had she stood before the Golden Court, but apart from it, ignored by old men proven in battle? They too had wielded tradition as weapon, a convention that forbade her a sword, and thus the right to challenge those who carried them. At last, Melanna understood why Ashana had supported her all these years. Why the struggle sometimes seemed more personal than it should.

And for all that Melanna felt lost in the place that was no place, her struggles with the Golden Court had taught her of tradition, and how it bound those who sought to wield it as a weapon.

"Tradition doesn't care how she came to that throne, only that she's there," said Melanna.

Her knees buckled as Tzal's baleful gaze fell upon her. "Your pet will hold her tongue, Ashana. Or I will compel her to do so."

Ashana folded her arms. "My *daughter* speaks the truth."

The deep rumble of Astor's laughter swallowed Tzal's disdainful hiss. "Let the others be called. Let them answer to the little moon, if only to spare us her disfavour."

Tzal glowered, his flames darkening to match his mood, but he nodded. Across the island, braziers burst to brilliant life. The gods sank back on their thrones, all save Ashana, who paced restlessly about the pool.

Careful not to draw too close to the island's extent, Melanna drifted away, her eyes touching again on the mist-gate and the path back to a world she understood.

"Tradition doesn't care. I shall have to remember that."

Melanna turned to find blue-green eyes boring into hers. She bowed her head. "I'm sorry. I don't know how to address you."

"I'm *supposed* to take my mother's name as I did her throne. But I'm not her, so why should I? And I've never liked my own." She smiled, her manner for the first time a match for her appearance. "So I remain a nameless lady until I choose a better. If the throne defines me, what's the point to having it?"

A little of Melanna's unease bled away. "Are they always so confrontational?"

The Nameless Lady shrugged. "They're accustomed to getting their own way."

"But not you?"

"I'm sure I'll set like stone as I get older." She glanced at Tzal, a wistful note creeping into her voice. "We all become our parents."

Melanna wondered what it would be like to have such a creature as one's sire. If only half the tales were true, Tzal was a disinterested deity at best, and a cruel one at worst. For all Ashana's flaws, she'd been fortunate to have the Goddess' guidance, and her love. What bitter soul would she have been with Tzal's flames at her back?

Braziers flickered out across the island.

"That's it," said the Nameless Lady. "But don't get your hopes up."

She drifted away, skirts flowing over stone like the tide on a beach.

The Raven stepped out of the darkness – or, at least, what Melanna presumed was the Raven – a flock of birds cawing viciously about him as they fought for perch on brazier and throne. Not the old woman of legend, but a tall man of middle-age, feather-masked, goateed and clad in a crumpled suit. For all his unfamiliarity, she'd seen him before. In the crowds beneath Ravenscourt, watching ceremonies performed in his name.

"Can't this wait?" he said, in peevish, gravelly tones. "I'm busy."

{{Be grateful for the reprieve.}} Jack lurched into view opposite. {{You're so . . . insubstantial. It's a wonder you don't fade away. Can it be you're not in full command of your kingdom, dearest brother?}}

The Raven *did* look inconstant. Old memory worn thin with passing years. Not exactly translucent, but not entirely *there*. "Run out of halfwits to tempt?"

Thorns thrashed angrily beneath the tattered robes. {{What care I for the haggler's wits, if his coin is firm?}}

"You're pathetic."

Jack crackled a mocking laugh. {{I'm winning. I will have my victory, and a queen to share my celebrations.}}

"Really?" The Raven replied languidly. "Does she know her fortune?"

{{Does it matter?}}

"What a question to ask."

For the first time, the Raven acknowledged Melanna's presence, his eyes touched briefly on hers before drifting away. Suddenly, she was back beneath Vrasdavora's walls, and Jack standing before her. *We will see one another again.* Breath ran ragged as she recalled the reflection in the black river.

Her father's bargain. Had he really done such a thing? Had he offered her to the Lord of Thorns?

No. He wouldn't. Not out of choice.

But if the war was going poorly?

The possibility crowded out all else.

Ashana stepped between the two. "We didn't summon you to endure your bickering."

"Then why, pray, are we here?" The Raven wiggled an admonishing finger. "And I wasn't summoned. I came willingly. Out of respect."

Jack straightened, robes gathered close and briars falling still. {{As did I.}}

The Raven sneered. "Of course you did."

"Enough!" Ashana's voice, so hard and cold, caused both to shrink away. Each recovered in a heartbeat, the Raven to his swagger, and Jack to his hunched, grotesque glower. "This war must end."

{{It will,}} crackled Jack. {{In glory.}}

"It ends now," she replied. "Let the ephemerals settle their own grievances."

"It's very strange." The Raven ambled closer, head tilted as if trying to catch a part of Ashana that otherwise remained hidden. "But you *look* like my little sister. You even *sound* like her. But your words ... This *is* your war, isn't it?"

Ashana scowled. "It is a mistake."

"Piffle." He locked gazes with Jack's glowering mask. "This is an opportunity. I'm grateful to you, I am, but my answer must be 'no'. Bargains have been struck and promises made. These things matter."

{{Yessss,}} said Jack. {{This will play out as it must.}}

Bitterness crowded Melanna's throat. Bargains had been struck, and she one of them.

"We could compel you," said Ashana.

The Raven shrugged. "You were only ever half a goddess, and you're worn thin. You've no leverage."

"And if it's not me alone?"

"But you *are* alone." The Raven turned, hand stretching to each occupied throne in turn, a conductor and his orchestra. "Or do you concur with our sister's demands? Astor? Tzal?"

It didn't escape Melanna's attention that he made no address to the Nameless Lady. Like the others, he considered her beneath him.

"You can't allow this!" cried Ashana.

Astor leaned forward, a spill of rust and steam hissing away from rotting armour. "I'm tired, sister. Fire runs cold, Skanandra's halls darken and my children pass into stone. If the Reckoning comes sooner, I welcome it."

Ashana glanced at the empty throne, golden light seeping through its cracked stone. "The Reckoning cannot begin until Lumestra returns."

"Then you've no cause for concern," said Tzal. "Unless you doubt the Prophecy of Third Dawn."

"Third Dawn. The Reckoning. Call it what you will. My concerns lie not in prophecy, but pragmatism. Without Lumestra, who will forge a new world from the ashes of the old when the Reckoning is done and Last Night falls?"

Tzal's lips parted in a leer. "I suppose that will depend on who emerges as the victor."

Though the words were Tzal's alone, Melanna recognised shared sentiment. They all *wanted* this, to one degree or another. The chance to usurp the absent Lumestra and fashion a new creation. Her head spun with the scale of ambition, and the unanswerable realisation that it was in its way no different to what she'd done – what her sire and grandsires had done throughout history. She'd been shaped by the throne even before it was hers. Sickening, but for the deeper horror that it soon wouldn't matter at all.

"I won't fight," said the Nameless Lady. "Not until I have to. But if it is war? No world deserves my father for a liege, much less a creator."

Ashana thrust her hands down at her side. "I won't let this happen."

{{It is already begun,}} said Jack.

Ashana stared into the inky void of the pool, lips pinched and brow set in the manner of one trying not to scream. She glanced up at Melanna, her eyes pleading.

Not knowing what else to do, Melanna nodded.

A little of Ashana's tension faded. "Lumestra or no, the Reckoning only begins when one of us murders another in an ephemeral's cause. That is prophecy. That is *tradition*. Are we agreed?"

Astor offered a weighty nod. The Raven looked on with suspicion; Jack from behind his impassive mask. The Nameless Lady flickered a smile.

Tzal waved a dismissive hand. "Why not? As you say, it is tradition."

"Then I thank you for your kind indulgence." She bobbed a curtsey, formality oozing bitter sarcasm.

The Raven snorted and departed the circle, birds cawing in his wake. Jack followed suit, the scrape of thorns on stone setting Melanna's weary nerves on edge. Tzal rose cleanly and stalked away without a word, Astor with hesitation. Only the Nameless Lady halted to offer a nod of farewell. Then even she was gone into the starlit darkness, leaving Melanna and Ashana alone.

Much to Melanna's surprise, the Goddess laughed.

"I like to tell myself it's experience that counts. That their manner would be wholly different if Lumestra were still here. But I know it's not so. Boys remain boys, even when cloaked in divine power."

"You find this amusing?" asked Melanna, too sick inside even to snarl.

"I don't, honestly I don't, but it's better to laugh than cry." Ashana perched on the edge of the silver throne, unwilling to give the whole of herself to it. "And now we at least have hope."

"They ignored you! Nothing has changed!"

"Yes, they ignored me. I always knew they would, but this had to be tried." Ashana let her head fall forward. Propping her elbows on her knees, she steepled her hands to her chin. "But something *has* changed. We know where everyone stands. If the war begins, they will fight. Whoever wins the Reckoning gets to rebuild afterwards, and none of us trust the others to do it right. Thus neither Endala's daughter nor Astor want to fight, but will if there's no other way. Tzal won't risk being the inciting murder. So this is about Jack and the Raven. Stop them, and there's no Reckoning. The clock keeps ticking."

And through it all, she a briar queen in Fellhallow. "I think ..." Melanna swallowed, not wanting to make her fears real by giving them voice. "My father has promised me to Jack."

"So you caught that? He won't have meant to. Jack's bargains always run crooked."

"Does that matter?" Melanna replied dully.

Ashana sat up straight, her gaze piercing. "Has he ever put his throne before you?"

"Never."

"There we are." She stared off into the distance. "There's still a way through this. I can see it, shining like silver, but it won't be easy. And we'll need help."

Fifty-One

"I should be furious," said Josiri. "So why is it I'm relieved to find you breathing?"

Viktor sat naked to the waist on a bench at the foot of the great hall's dais. His back and shoulders were slathered with bitter-scented salve, applied liberally by a grey-bearded thrall whose filigree wreath and white robes marked him as a healer of the antaya lodges. Greyish paste stood pale against livid burns and bruises earned less than an hour before. How Viktor smiled, Josiri couldn't conjure. But he did, a man basking in rare satisfaction amid the chamber's quiet.

"Because you're in awe," Viktor replied. "I'm told I was quite impressive."

Armund stirred on the throne, the brandished tankard odd companion for a leg splinted and bound from ankle to knee. The fragments of a charred axe hung on iron brackets behind the chair's upright. "You were, lad. A tale to rival Arkynar af Vardin. I'd offer you the throne ..." He wiped mead-sodden lips on the back of his hand and belched. "... but it's taken."

Josiri shook his head. "Erashel thought you were fleeing."

Viktor's head dipped. "And you?"

"Viktor Akadra has never been a coward. Reckless, despite his claims otherwise, but no coward. And he keeps secrets, also despite his claims otherwise."

Viktor winced. He beckoned to the antaya. "*Vaest dralla, ikna. Brenæ ist dan.*"

The old man bowed. Gathering vials and unguents, he departed the hall, leaving the three of them alone.

"I didn't know you spoke Thrakkian," said Josiri.

"That at least, is no secret. It's merely something you didn't know." Viktor clambered to his feet and drew on his shirt, wincing as cotton brushed abused flesh. "There's no great difference between Thrakkian language and the formal tongue, just as both hold common heritage with most Hadari dialects. The legacy of the Age of Kings, when all were one. Uncle Carid served as ambassador in Brinnorhill for a time, and brought back all manner of tales. Heroes, monsters, tales of doomed love and riches beyond compare. They painted the world in far brighter colours than anything to be found in the city. The chord they struck has rung through me ever since. Is that such a surprise?"

"I suppose not."

No, it chimed too well with what Josiri knew of Viktor's early life. A murdered mother and an absent father. Secret magic held close. All the reasons in the world to seek escape, if only in stories. And for all that Viktor wore the sober guise of a Tressian knight, flamboyance shone through at odd moments.

"But as to secrets. Did you have anything particular in mind?"

For all the nonchalance in Viktor's voice, there was reserve beneath. What Josiri had come to recognise as the other girding himself against unwelcome truth.

"Only the conspiracy that led you here."

Armund grunted. "Conspiracies are for feckless *caenir*. This was a noble quest, worthy of mead, and song ... and mead!"

The corner of Viktor's mouth twitched. "I didn't want it to appear that the Council was meddling in Thrakkian affairs. And you nearly spoilt that, hammering at the gates even as Armund was tossed into the Cindercourt. But it's all worked out for the best, so I forgive you."

Josiri shook his head at the outrageous reply, but couldn't shake the feeling that something else lurked just behind the truth he saw. Another secret? Or simply a morsel of fact he didn't know? "So what happens now?"

"Now, lad, you marvel at the gratitude of Armund af Garna, and the world shakes before his wrath." Armund leaned forward on his throne, the pall of drunkenness yielding to piercing sincerity. "Ardothan's pride is our providence. Normally, it'd take a day or two to gather my ceorlas, but they're all here. I've thralls stripping this mouldering ruin for whatever horses and provisions can be found. Two thousand axes. More, if you can wait while I raise the lething."

"We can't," said Viktor. "If this is to matter, we'll have to ride this afternoon. And it serves little purpose to save Tressian farmers by driving yours into battle. Two thousand will serve."

Josiri couldn't believe his ears. Two thousand must have constituted at least half of Indrigsval's warriors. "And you'll have no need of them?"

Armund grinned. "Astor himself proved me worthy. Smite Kellevork with a thunderbolt, crack its foundations, and I'll be left standing." The smile faded. "I only wish I'd be riding with you. That shadowthorn princessa owes me a pair of eyes. But Anliss is gone, and I'm a blind fool with a broken ankle. Better for us all if I'm not bouncing about in the saddle like a sack. I'll go back to Indrig, start putting things right. Better to be a thane in plain sight than behind stone walls. Inkari will pay my debts."

"You trust her?" said Viktor.

"I'm her thane," Armund replied. "To a woman like Inkari, that's worth more than all the gold in the vaults of High King Bryken."

"Then you'd better gather Lady Beral," Viktor told Josiri. "Unless you want to leave her behind."

Armund waved a dismissive hand. "Stay. Eat. Drink. I'll send a thrall."

Josiri glanced at his own tankard – like Viktor's, all but untouched. "No. It had better be me. She's not . . . Well, she doesn't have a lot of trust for your people. Let's not spoil things with avoidable tragedy. But I'll borrow a horse, if I may?"

The woman who was not Calenne passed easily through the commotion of Kellevork's outer bounds – a riot of cross-hatched claith and gruff, angular voices. She revelled in those looks that were sent her way. That most were couched in friendliness or veiled desire helped, but simply to be *acknowledged* was the greatest compliment of all. Like the stink of sweat and nightsoil – the bitter woodsmoke still clinging to the breeze – they confirmed she was part of the world, and not a ghost rushing beneath it.

Guilt at Erashel's murder faded in the press of the crowds. Calenne – for so she still considered herself, in spite of all – made no attempt to rationalise the death. That she *should* was a dim concept. Guilt belonged to an ephemeral woman, and whatever she was, she wasn't that. For all their closeness, the teeming crowds felt distant, different. They didn't matter. Specks of clamour and warmth she'd outlive. Only Viktor mattered. Viktor and Josiri.

And so she passed through the brightly coloured market stalls, smiled at children already dust in her mind's eye, and let instinct guide her deeper into Kellevork.

A wagon rumbled past the inner keep's gate, and she followed behind. An argument broke out beneath the keystone, a trio of guards in Indrigsval's sea-blown colours falling to blows with a woman in black and red. Calenne allowed herself a smile, and passed on, her breath stolen by the intricate stonework and bold canopies of the inner courtyard.

"Hold! Who goes?"

For all that she knew it shouldn't, Calenne's confidence ran cold at the vanaguard's challenge. Another piece of the Calenne-who-had-been echoing through her, and growing stronger as the helmless thrakker descended the keep stairs and struck out in her direction.

She altered course and passed through a wooden door. The dry, pungent aroma of horse dung rose to greet her, the soft champ and whinny from the stable stalls muffling the squeak of rusty hinges. She strode along the aisle, searching for an empty stall. The door creaked open.

"That's enough," said the vanaguard. "You don't belong here. That much is clear."

"I'm Lady Calenne Akadra." The Thrakkian words came as readily as the innocent tone, though she'd never used them before. "I'm looking for my husband. He's a friend to the thane."

Impossible not to know of Armund's elevation. The crowds had buzzed with it.

"Looking in the stables?"

"Not any longer. I can see he's not here."

"Maybe," said the vanaguard. "I'll send word to the great hall. Your husband can find you in the guardhouse, *if* he cares to."

A mail-clad hand closed about Calenne's wrist. The world drowned in black.

Horses screamed and reared as she lashed out. Not with a hand, or a foot, but a shadow concealed beneath the mask of her likeness. A shadow she hadn't even known was there until it gathered the thrakker up and hurled him into an empty stall. He struck a stone pillar with a sickening crunch, and lay still.

Calenne gasped, as speechless at the writhing shadow as the body at her feet. Horror receded as the horses fell silent. Horror fed on fear, on guilt, and as her shadow caressed the broken corpse, those things bled away. They belonged to the Calenne-who-had-been. The Calenne-who-was felt only exhilaration as the corpse responded to her shadow's touch, a lifeless arm jerking like a marionette at the first twitch of its strings.

Enthralled, she reached deeper. Let her shadow fill the empty flesh. A gloved hand jerked out to touch hers, fingertip to splayed fingertip.

She laughed, unable to contain a swell of childlike joy.

"Calenne?"

The shadow faded. The arm dropped. She started to her feet, absent guilt returning at a voice more familiar than her own. "Josiri?"

The stable door banged closed, let fall from a frozen hand. He stared like one lost to a dream, throat bobbing and tongue stuttering half-finished thought. "You're dead. You died. Viktor . . . "

Shame crowded Calenne's thoughts. Then anger, because she knew the shame wasn't truly hers. Both were eclipsed by joy. She stepped from the stall and the corpse hidden within.

"Viktor wanted to keep me safe. He did only what I asked."

Was that even true? Or had she parroted what Viktor believed the Calenne-who-had-been would have wanted? Had the words only ever been his, spoken by another's voice to ease troubled conscience? Did it matter, if that truth was part of her?

Eyes bright with tears, Josiri stared down his hands. "Do you really hate me that much?"

The Calenne-who-had-been spurred the Calenne-who-was closer along that aisle. She took Josiri's head in her hands, eyes welling reflected sorrow. "No. Never."

He threw his arms about her and she him. Yet for all the warmth of the embrace, it didn't touch the cold centre of her being.

"I wanted to tell you," she said.

Josiri pulled away, his face mottled and sodden with tears. "You look different."

"It's been a year, Josiri. You look different too." She offered a wavering smile. "You've eaten too well."

"Viktor . . ." He wiped his face with a grubby sleeve. "I knew he was hiding something, I just never knew which question to ask. For an honest man he lies more easily than anyone I've ever known."

Calenne drew him tight. "It doesn't matter. Not now. Let it be the past, Josiri. We're together. That's all that matters. You. Me. Viktor. Anastacia. Family, now the Beral woman is gone—"

She cursed her mistake, but it was too late. He pulled back, suspicion glinting through tears. "Erashel? What do you mean, she's gone?"

"She headed for the border after you left." She clung to the lie, willed him to believe it. "After you refused her, she didn't see any reason to stay."

"You heard all that?"

"And more. I followed you ever since Tarona."

"Last night. It was you." His brow furrowed. "What did you say to her after I left?"

"Nothing. We never spoke."

"Then how do you know why she went?"

"It was obvious!" She cast her arms wide in frustration, voice ragged. "I can't believe you! Why are you spoiling this? Can't you just be happy?"

He tilted his head, voice losing its warmth. "Why are you in the stables?"

"I was looking for you."

"No. I don't think you were."

Pushing her arm aside, he stepped past.

"Josiri, no!"

Her shadow caught him at the moment his gaze widened at the vanaguard's corpse. It hoisted him high to the rafters. Squeezing, twisting. His scrabbling hands found no purchase on its inky folds.

"You're not my sister!"

"But I am!" she screamed. "I am Calenne Akadra. I am loved! I am real!"

The world rushed black, drowned in it as her joy drowned in fury and the renewed panic of the horses. Her shadow squeezed tighter as his struggles failed, smothering the lies that were truth as they smothered his breath. Only when Josiri's effort ceased entirely did the black veil about Calenne's thoughts recede, laying bare what she'd done.

"No!"

She dropped to her knees. Josiri fell boneless beside her, throat red raw, and chest stuttering fitful breaths. Joy that he lived sputtered beneath certainty he'd never forgive, never understand. The brother she'd no choice but to love could only ever hate her for what she was, and was not.

Calenne doubled over. She'd been happy at Tarona. Happy with Viktor. Content believing the lie. Now everything was falling apart. All because someone had come creeping into their life, like a vranakin at a wedding feast, and poisoned everything.

Sorrow gave way to wrath. To resolve. Still weeping, she kissed Josiri's forehead. The last of the Calenne-who-had-been burned away. The Calenne-who-was rose to her feet and left the stables.

It all felt ... different to how Armund had expected. Not the throne, which was as hard-edged and angular as they all were. Reminder that the comforts of rule never lasted. Even if your rivals didn't get you, the Raven would, in time. Better to fill your shrinking days with deeds worthy of song.

So yes, the throne was as expected, but the rest? Reclaiming his birthright had been the dream of years, but the reality lacked something. Perhaps it was tiredness and the pain of a snapped ankle. Perhaps it was loss, with Anliss at last fully at Astor's hand, her vengeance sated in the Cindercourt. A cruel reprieve to have robbed them of final farewell, but Armund supposed she'd carry his love with her, unspoken though it was. She'd always known his mind. Infuriating and glorious, all at once.

Then perhaps it was the darkness, no longer for parting. That made sense. Too much of life's pleasure lay in the beholding. The rays of the sun dancing on the waves. Banners raised in triumph. The delicate curve of an axe well-crafted. A beautiful woman, offering a smile. Other sensations inferred these things. Warmth against skin. A victor's roar. Gentler, softer sounds and pressures. None of them the same as seeing.

Armund growled, and shook maudlin thought aside. "As if you're the first to leave his eyes behind on the field. You've glories left to come."

That was true. The angular throne was his, and he intended never to lose it. Indrigsval's treasury was his also, whatever remained after Ardothan's fancies. And beyond that, a story worth bequeathing. One that could only season with age, as all good sagas did.

And while he waited for years to pass, and family to birth and bloom, there was always mead.

He laughed softly to himself and drained his tankard.

A footstep sounded in the dark.

"Akadra? Is that you?"

No answer came, nor a second footstep to make sense of doubt.

The empty tankard loomed mournful in his thoughts. One more before lending his voice to the muster of Kellevork. A last toast to vanished sister, and a throne reclaimed. He reached out to the table, to the bell that would summon a thrall.

Another footstep. This time accompanied by a swish of cloth. Armund sought stillness and sifted the outer darkness. Unfamiliar acoustics offered up little but confusion. Too much time playing the blind man, and not enough learning his new world.

He reached for the bell. A hand closed about his. Cold. Soft. Unyielding.

"Hello, Armund."

He frowned. "I know your voice."

"I'm sure you do," she replied.

"Calenne? Calenne Trelan?" He frowned. "Can't be. You're dead."

And so she was. He heard it in her voice. The open grave and the squawk of carrion birds.

The hand withdrew, the bell with it. His voice would carry to the corridor beyond. So why was he struck by the sense it would make no difference? Maybe because Calenne – if it *was* Calenne – knew that also, and didn't care.

"You ruined everything." Footsteps drifted away to Armund's left. "We didn't have much, Viktor and I, but we had each other. We were happy. But then you set him thinking on the past, and the more I tried to make sense of it, the faster it all fell apart."

"I've no idea what you're talking about, lass. Akadra's a comrade. *We* were comrades. I lost my sight saving your life. My sister died!"

"I know you don't understand." The voice drew closer. The air crackled cold. "But you're a thrakker. You understand the importance of debts and bargains. A life for a life. Yours for mine. Maybe then things can go back to how they were."

She said the last dreamily. Heirs and sagas as yet unearned fell away into the cold, dark void.

"I won't beg," said Armund.

Her breath was a cold breeze at his ear. "I don't need you to."

Viktor heaved open a door that felt heavier than it should, the weight of the gilded timbers enhanced by a long and tiring morning. "Armund, there's a Glaiholda ceorla offering to join the muster, but . . ."

At the hall's far end, Armund sat silent on his throne. Calenne turned from his side and straightened, lips parting a bright smile.

"Calenne? When did you arrive?" He blinked. "How did you know where to come?"

She stepped from the dais and drew closer. "You think you could hide from me, Viktor? Me, of all people?"

"And you're not angry?"

"Not a bit. Disappointed, of course. But angry? No."

He frowned, his thoughts realigning. "Josiri's here. In Kellevork. If he sees you . . ."

Calenne took his hands, a flicker of pain darting behind her eyes. "We've already spoken."

"You have?"

"Just moments ago. I gave him much to think about."

That seemed inevitable. As did further argument with Josiri now he knew the truth. It would be better in the long run, especially with wider events as they were. If only she'd given him some warning. "Armund, I owe you an explanation."

Armund offered no reply other than a flex of his fingers, the knuckles white where they gripped the throne's armrests.

"I think he's asleep," said Calenne. "I'll be honest, I was about to give up on him. Perhaps we should leave him be."

If that were so, he was sleeping in the stiffest, most rigid pose Viktor had ever seen. Even Kurkas, who he'd known to slumber standing up, back braced against a tree, would have looked relaxed by comparison. Armund looked more like a man under restraint than one taking his ease. More than that, the room held a strange sensation. Not something present, but something absent, the lack so unusual that Viktor couldn't even begin to deduce its identity.

The doors crashed open. A thunder of boots admitted Josiri and Inkari at the head of a half-dozen vanaguard, the former with blood matted in his blond hair, and all with weapons readied. Josiri's cheeks were flushed with anger.

"Stand away from her, Viktor!" he shouted. "That's not Calenne."

Viktor sighed. Of all the circumstances in which to face this conversation . . . Private emotion had no place in front of strangers. Armund, perhaps, for they were bonded by battles shared. But Inkari? The vanaguards? Was this his penance for deceit, however well-meaning?

He sidestepped to set himself between Calenne and brandished steel, and turned around. "But it is, Josiri. I brought your sister out of the fires of Eskavord. I should have told you. I nearly did, that last day before you rode north. Instead I honoured her wish to be free."

"I've heard this story." Josiri tugged down the collar of his shirt. The livid bruise beneath owed nothing to intemperate emotion. "She spun it just before she sought to choke my life away."

"He's lying." Calenne clung to Viktor's arm. "He's mad with anger, and it's all my fault. I should never have asked you to deceive him."

Inkari clapped her hands. The vanaguard started forward. Viktor, weaponless, dragged Calenne behind and sought sanity in an afternoon crumbling to madness.

Josiri edged closer. "She's already killed one man, Viktor. I can show you his body. Blessed Lumestra, but I think she murdered Erashel too."

Calenne stared at him, face and voice twisted in sorrow. "Oh, Josiri. What have we come to? Take me away from this, Viktor. There's no reasoning with him."

"She has a shadow, Viktor. Like yours. She's an imposter. A demon."

"Quiet! Both of you!" The vanaguard shuddered to a halt at Viktor's bellow, wary of the man who'd bested a varloka short hours before. "Let me think. Let me explain."

Even as he spoke, Viktor realised that neither thoughts nor explanations would alter matters, for he finally realised what was wrong about the room. It was him. More precisely, it was his shadow, which was quieter than he'd known in years. Beyond quiescent, beyond cowering. It didn't want to be noticed. Why?

Arms outspread to discourage hasty action, Viktor cast his shadow upon the great hall. At once, he perceived the bonds pinning Armund to his throne, and his tongue to the roof of his mouth. He saw too the Dark billowing about Calenne, *through* Calenne – a piece of her being he'd always seen, but never recognised. Howling in despair, he lashed out at Armund's bonds, scattering them to nothing.

"She came to kill me, lad. Said I ruined everything." Armund gasped for breath and slumped on his throne. "Demon or not, she's glaikit – mad as a fish in a forge."

Viktor rounded on Calenne, about whom the Dark now flickered freely, all pretence cast aside. The pit of his stomach fell away. He felt lost, more lost than he had in years.

"What are you?"

She sank to her knees, head bowed. "Don't you know?" Her sob of despair became a bitter chuckle. "I'm your guilt. I'm what you made when you couldn't save her. Something with her face. Something you could love. I don't have her memories. I don't have a life. All I have is loss, and pain, and anger. I'm a part of you, Viktor. We are one."

Josiri looked away, face contorted in anguish. Inkari spat. Armund hung his head.

Viktor looked on his love through his shadow's eyes, and saw nothing but reflection. Calenne was not a host for the Dark, she was fashioned of it. She seethed with it. A conjuring so far-reaching, so complex, that Viktor couldn't imagine how he'd managed such a thing, let alone forgotten the striving.

A buried memory clawed to the surface. A flash of steel in a burning cottage. Blood soaking through his clothes. This wasn't Calenne. He'd killed Calenne, though Malatriant had taken her soul long before. Of course he'd driven that madness from his mind. He'd made it hers.

"We are all one in the Dark," he said softly.

"Drag it away!" said Inkari. "Throw it in the forge!"

Calenne snarled and leapt to her feet. The room rushed dark. A pulse of shadow hurled a vanaguard away. Another fell to his knees, clutching at his throat.

"No!" Viktor shouted. "No. Calenne! Look at me!"

She stopped, her shadow rigid, coiled.

"Did you want to be her?" he asked, his voice thick. "Would you be Calenne Trelan – Calenne Akadra – if only for a moment?"

The snarl slipped from her lips and her brow. "I can't."

"Look inside yourself. Look at the memories I gave you. What would she choose?"

She closed her eyes. The shadow drew back, and daylight flooded in. Arms at her sides, she stood before him, cheeks stained by tears, but her eyes unafraid.

"End this," she whispered. "Please."

Heart too full for words, he held her close. The Dark within her yielded without resistance, peeled away beneath his shadow's probing, layer by layer, inch by inch, until her Dark was his once more, and only the barest scrap of her remained.

"I love you," she said, the words little more than memory even as they were spoken.

"Of course you do," he murmured. "I never gave you any other choice."

Then the last of Calenne Akadra, the woman who had never truly existed, slipped away into shadow, and Viktor fell to his knees and wept.

Fifty-Two

By early evening, Josiri had tried and failed to bring balance to a storm-tossed heart. The only kindness was that he'd barely come to terms with "Calenne's" existence before her deceit had been revealed. The pain of a loss thought faded hadn't blossomed to greater hurt. And so he walked Kellevork's tapestried halls while the muster of Indrigsval gathered pace, his feet ushering him to a confrontation neither head nor heart wanted any part of.

In the end, Josiri found Viktor where he'd seen him last, a shirt-sleeved and silent presence in an empty hall. He sat hunched on the edge of the dais, the air cold with his brooding. But his tears? Those were long spent. Viktor Akadra was once again a rock upon which dreams foundered.

He didn't look up. "You've been avoiding me."

"I didn't know what to say," Josiri replied stiffly. "I still don't. Where would I even begin?"

Still Viktor's eyes never left the spot where "Calenne" had breathed her last. "She told me this would happen."

"Calenne?" asked Josiri, curious in spite of himself. "That *thing*?"

"Malatriant." The name shivered Josiri's spine, memories of fire and Dark rushing to the fore. "As we stood in the horrors of Eskavord, she warned me that I'd use my shadow, or would be used in return. I was so certain I could control it."

Josiri swallowed and steeled himself. "What happened to my sister? The truth."

"Everyone thought I'd lost my wits." He laughed softly. "I didn't care, because I knew I was sane. And all along—"

"Viktor!"

At last, he met Josiri's gaze. "It was all as I told you. Malatriant devoured Calenne's spirit, as she did so many others. What remained . . . I gave what kindness I could. The lie I told you of her death was the truth, and the truth that I believed was a lie."

"Speak plainly, Viktor. Just this once."

He grimaced. "I arrived in Eskavord thinking I could save Calenne, but even then her spirit was with the Raven, and what remained was a snare. Malatriant even boasted of as much, but I didn't hear her. I slew the puppet she'd made of your sister and . . . " He drew in a deep breath. "Something within me broke. When I left you – when I made an exile of myself – I left *with* Calenne, or I thought I did. Over time, my shadow made truth of that madness."

Sympathy rose unbidden. If ever Josiri had doubted Viktor's strength of feeling for Calenne, he no longer did so. Could he have killed Ana, had their situations been reversed? What would have remained of him had he done so? It might have been easier to forgive, had others not paid the price.

"Armund has people out searching for Erashel. I don't think they'll find her." Even without proof, inevitability hung heavy in Josiri's gut. If he'd insisted Erashel accompany him to Kellevork, she'd still be alive. He'd been glad for her to stay behind, the awkwardness of their parting held at bay. "You killed her, Viktor. A piece of you did."

Viktor went back to staring at the empty patch of floor. "She wasn't me. I sketched her from memory, incomplete. I've never had a mind for music, and yet she sang, sweet and clear, every morning, whenever she'd the strength." He shook his head. "She was real to me."

A pang of remorse challenged Josiri's anger. Viktor had believed Calenne Akadra his wife. What kind of hole did that leave in a man? Especially one so self-contained as Viktor.

Compassion faded. Viktor's sorrows were of his own making. That he'd spoken the truth about Calenne's death from the very first didn't make what had followed any less the lie.

"I don't know that I can forgive you for this," he said softly. "But forgiveness will have to wait. You're a terrible friend, but a good man, and the Republic needs all the good men it can find."

"A good man." Viktor rose and shook his head. "I'm of the Dark, Josiri. What if my good works are but consequences of the harm I inflict, and not the other way around?"

"Are you telling me that's so?"

"Last year, I was so *certain* I'd made an end of things. Ebigail's spiteful cabal broken. The Tyrant Queen returned to the Raven's embrace." He spread a hand in Josiri's direction. "Old wrongs put right. A man could die content with any one of those deeds. Each morning I embraced the dawn at Tarona, I knew I'd found my place in the light." He looked again at where Calenne Akadra had folded into shadow. "We know how that turned out."

Josiri grunted. "Are we to have the conversation about duty once more, Viktor? Because nothing has changed."

"Nothing has changed for you, but for me? I see the Dark clearer than ever." He strode closer, eyes fixed on Josiri's. "We fear the untrained blade for the damage it might do. This is so much more. It has been ever since Malatriant bequeathed the last of herself to me. The Dark will be used, whether I wish it or not. It will make truth of dreams and nightmares, and we might never know until it is too late. And so part of me says, let it be used! Let it serve as a weapon! One to be understood. One harnessed to the cause of light as it was when Lumestra set the stars ablaze with life and joy."

This was the man Josiri remembered. The man who'd stand alone against an army to save one life. The man whose principles challenged all around him to be more than they were. Without intending to, Josiri stood taller, straighter, and felt more the man for doing so ... until the day's tragedies took hold once more.

"You sound as though you've already decided," said Josiri.

"No. I haven't. I can't. I no longer trust myself to make that choice. How can I, after today? I reshaped a piece of the world to deceive my troubled soul, and never knew I'd done so. What if this is merely another delusion? The Dark shaping my thoughts as I shaped it?" He closed his eyes. "Even now I might be Viktor Akadra without, and the Dark within."

Josiri wished Ana were there to advise him. "You can't mean that."

Viktor sighed. "I can't be sure what I mean. All I know is that not using the Dark is no longer an option. Not while I live." He halted on the brink of collapse, and snatched Josiri's sword from its scabbard. He held it up, eyes flickering disgust at a scrap of rust. Then he reversed it, the blade in his hands and the grip extended to Josiri. "So this is the choice. I can ride north, the throng of Indrigsval at my back, and wield Dark in the cause of light. Or I can die. Here and now."

Josiri blinked. "You want *me* to kill you?"

"If that's what you deem the right course. There can be no middle ground in this, Josiri. I've sought it a year, and succeeded only in lying to myself. The Dark will be used as long as I live. There's no avoiding that."

Josiri examined words and tone for a hint of jest, and found none. Perhaps Viktor *was* mad. "I had it right before. You're a terrible friend."

"And you must be a better, for the sake of everyone."

"How dare you lay this burden on me!"

"Who else is there? I cannot trust myself, and you alone understand what's at stake." He shrugged. "If anyone is owed my life, it's you. Revenge is here, if you want it."

Josiri's hand closed around the hilt. He'd dreamed of this moment so often, or something similar enough to make no matter. Viktor Akadra, the Council Champion, the vanquisher of the Southshires, the doom of his mother, and his sister. At his mercy. His life to take. For all their conciliation, the debt of history and the sins of kith remained. They begged for the thrust that would still Viktor's heart. Lumestran edict too was brutally clear. Witches were of the Dark, and witches burned.

But what of the rest? The Republic needed Viktor. As for the Dark . . . The church derided Ana as a demon, and a witch. They'd have burned her, had fire any hope of the feast. Lumestran scorn was poor guide to truth. The wisdom of the Goddess chained tight by hierarchy and politics. And for all his failings, Viktor had never sought to do anything other than good. He'd striven for friendship, even when Josiri had offered nothing but hate in return.

"At Tarona you said you'd stop me, were it necessary," said Viktor.

Josiri shifted his grip on the sword. A promise made in part payment of an old debt. For all that he told others he hadn't earned the vanished dukedom of Eskavord, the title had been worn by a version of himself he'd sooner forget. A brittle man, defined by mistakes more than successes, who'd responded to the cage the Council had closed around him by fashioning a smaller one inside. Viktor had freed him from that. He'd helped him behold a wider world, and his place within it. How could he do less?

"I *will* stop you, if I must." He let the sword-point droop. "But that day isn't today. As for my revenge, I take it by making you redeem your mistakes."

"Then so it shall be." Viktor's lips twisted to a rueful, not-quite smile. "I barely recognise the sullen soul I found on Branghall's throne."

"Sometimes I miss those days," Josiri replied. "Life was simpler."

"Hatred is always simpler than trust. That's why love hurts so."

"Where do we go from here, you and I?"

Viktor gripped his shoulder, manner and voice restored to solidity. "North. And with all speed. We have a Republic to save."

Josiri offered a meaningful look at Viktor's tattered shirt and scuffed trews. "I sought Viktor Akadra the warrior, not the vagabond farmer of Tarona. If he's truly back, he should dress the part."

"He will."

Viktor withdrew, his stride purposeful as he stomped away. Left alone, Josiri found himself staring at the patch of floor where Calenne Akadra had perished.

He closed his eyes. Had he made the right choice? Light and Dark, black and white, necessity and sophistry. All blurred grey by failures past. The great hall stank of despair. Better to seek fresh air.

Josiri opened his eyes into a hall dancing with greenish-white mist.

"Josiri Trelan." The voice came from behind, maddening in near recognition. "We must talk, you and I."

He spun about, sword up. Features hardening, he strode forward, malice cold in blue eyes. The dry rumble of the Huntsman's growl rippled out. Mist parted before the heavy thump of his footstep. Melanna interposed herself between the two, sword scabbarded and hands held out in caution.

"Josiri, you must listen." She scoured the unfamiliar Tressian tongue for words that might convince. "For the sake of your people, you must."

He didn't slow. Didn't spare more than a glance for the antlered presence of the Huntsman at her shoulder. Courage born of anger, yes, but something more. Melanna would have expected nothing less from the man who'd broken the stockade at Davenwood, sparing her father Tressian justice.

"When have my people ever mattered to you?" he growled.

The Huntsman started forward, no less a terrifying presence for his limp. Melanna splayed a hand to his chest, offered a warning shake of the head. As he subsided, she turned her attention to Josiri once more.

How little he understood her. But then, history cast them as enemies. History, and her own deeds. Their last parting had been in friendship, but that friendship was another casualty of war, and one weightier than Melanna had realised until that moment. The honour that so many princes of the Golden Court aped without ever earning, Josiri had twice worn without effort. Kindness to a vanquished foe. Sacrifice for others. Courage in the bleakest times. Glory in victory, fortitude in defeat and honour always. He'd lived those precepts better than she.

"More than you'd ever believe," she said. "I don't want to be here. My presence will cost my people dearly. But I have no other choice."

Josiri slowed, the anger in his eyes fading. "You're not the first to stand before me today and claim paucity of choice."

"Mind your tongue," rumbled the Huntsman.

Josiri's cheek twitched. The tick betrayed that his fear of the Huntsman wasn't as controlled as he would wish, but the speed of its fading showed fear alone did not command his actions. "I don't really do that. Any respect the princessa earned, she's long since washed away with blood." He hooked a thumb over his shoulder. "Beyond those doors, there's an army of Thrakkians eager to pay a debt. I'm already wondering why I haven't called them."

"This war was a mistake," said Melanna. "If it continues, we all lose."

"Then tell your father."

"I have." She touched closed her eyes, the memory the sorest wound of recent days. "I know you've no reason to trust me, Josiri. But understand . . . Even by being here I make myself a traitor to my people."

He halted, eyes watchful more than angry. "Why should I believe you?"

"Because this is no longer a war of ephemerals."

Ashana, concealed thus far by the mists, ghosted past Melanna to stand less than a hand's breadth from Josiri's sword.

"The Raven takes your side," said Ashana. "Fellhallow flocks to Emperor Saran's banner. But the sides are not matched. The Raven is weakened. Old bargains grant the Crowmarket command of Otherworld's mists. Tressia will be overrun, the Raven will die, and the pillars of creation will come crashing down. My divine siblings will tear this world apart in hope of rebuilding it anew."

"The Crowmarket?" Josiri's eyes flickered from one to the other. "Why should I believe you any more than her?"

"Do you know me?"

"No."

"We both know that's not true. It's faint, but I feel the serathiel's embrace upon you." Ashana set her head to one side, eyes never leaving contact with his. "Say my name."

"Ashana." Josiri blinked, a man surprised by his own utterance.

She offered the faintest smile. "You see? You perceive a wider world than most. You understand divine pride. You've witnessed its full spate. It cares nothing for others. It does not crack. It does not relent. And it most certainly does not kneel." So saying, she knelt, head bowed and arms crossed with her hands at her shoulders. "I beg you, Josiri Trelan: help us end this war."

Where a Tressian muster was a thing of silent discipline, the one that filled Kellevork's outer ward was mismatched and anarchic, thick with the buzz of conversation and throaty song. Ceorlas mingled freely with the vanaguard and thrydaxes under their command, leaving little to tell them apart. The richness of armour was no guide. Most suits were heirlooms handed down the generations, the lacquer and chain repaired according to the taste of the inheritor.

The horses seemed little tamer than their masters, undocked tails and plaited manes unkempt beside the groomed perfection practised further north. Alien to a man tutored by Chapterhouse Sartorov, but Viktor didn't care. Every rider bore an axe, every quiver was filled with arrows, and despite unkempt appearance, a Thrakkian steed would outpace anything in the Republic.

And it wasn't as though Viktor himself would have passed muster on a Sartorov parade ground, not with two days' worth of stubble, and certainly not in the suit of Thrakkian armour Armund had pressed upon him. Swirling sea-gold patterns etched into the steel mimicked leaping flame. Glorious, but for the scarecrow's surcoat, but Viktor wouldn't have abandoned the Akadra swan for anything.

He descended the stairs and found Armund waiting at the foot, a young page in Indrigsval claith close by. "Does it fit?"

"Remarkably so," Viktor replied.

"It was my father's. Seems Ardothan couldn't bring himself to sell it."

Viktor frowned. "Then I can't accept the gift. It should be yours, father to son."

"Armour belongs in battle, lad, not hung as trophy." Armund tapped the puckered flesh of his burned eye socket. "My days of war are done, but if you wear that? Well, a piece of me stands with you still."

"Then all I need is a sword. Can't go showing myself up with sloppy axe-work."

"That you can't." Armund clicked his fingers. The page scurried away. "Can't rightly imagine what's in your head, lad."

"Nothing but the road ahead," Viktor lied.

Calenne – *both* Calennes, real and imagined – were millstones around his heart. And still he doubted his shadow. He worried that even when loosed it would control him, and not the other way around. That it was quiescent was little consolation. It had been quiet before.

"I'm blind, lad," said Armund. "Not stupid. But I'm grateful to you."

Viktor gazed out across the muster. "I *had* reached that conclusion."

Armund chuckled. "My gratitude only brings them together. They'll want gold in their pouches when this is done."

"They'll have it, even if I have to sell every scrap of the family estate." How Messela was to be convinced of that was another matter, but the circumstance would be unlikely to arise. The Council would pay . . . if there were a Council left to offer redress.

"Then I've two gifts left to share."

The page returned, a scabbarded sword taller than he clutched to his chest. At Armund's gesture, he knelt. Viktor took the scabbard and slid the blade free. It was perhaps an inch or two shorter than his own claymore, lost in the collapse of the Cindercourt wall, the blade a fraction wider. Golden wire bound the grips, and a stylised Lumestran sun gleamed at pommel and hilt. Flowing script chased the blade, the delicate runes Thrakkian, but the language formal Tressian. *A vo keldinel, verasalna rariath cala serathi.*

"'He who wields me shines with a serathi's radiance?'" Viktor shook his head. "I know at least one who'd contest that claim. Where did you find this?"

Armund grinned. "A weaponsmith forged it on commission for one of your knights, ten years back. Bugger died on the border, so he never paid up. The smith owed me, I owe you, we all profit from the trade. Not really a rider's weapon, but I've a feeling you'll manage." He rapped Viktor's vambrace. "Leave the past behind, lad. Forge a bright future."

Viktor smiled, the millstones a little lighter. "And is that wisdom your second gift?"

"I may have oversold the whole 'two gifts' thing." Armund patted his pocket and produced a folded scrap of paper. "Trelan asked me to give this to you."

The millstones sank deeper. Viktor took the letter.

I cannot ride with you.

    This war runs wider than we thought, and it seems my deeds must be even more unconventional than yours. Forgive me my secrets, but I can't risk the consequences of your involvement.

    I know it's no use asking you not to be angry, and I'm sorry if this strains the bond between us.

    I'm sure we'll discuss the matter upon my return.

                                  Josiri

A rebuke, but not without humour. At least, Viktor hoped so.

He laughed under his breath. "I deserved that. Do you know where he went?"

"Would you believe I never saw him leave?" Armund shrugged. "I can ask. Someone will know."

What would the answer change? The war in the north brooked no delay. Josiri, of all people, would not have turned his back on it without cause. It called for trust, and in that sphere Viktor's debts screamed fit to break the world.

"No." He slung the claymore at his back and tightened the straps. "Josiri can look after himself, and I have a war to fight."

Armund nodded and held out his hand. "Brenæ af Brenæ. Væga af Væga."

"I'll bring the fire." Viktor clasped the thanc's hand tight. "Death, I'll leave to others."

Fifty-Three

"Altiris! Altiris! Wake up!"

The strike of fist on door and Sidara's shout dragged him back to a room still heavy with night. More than night. The air's texture – its smell – were too thick, too bitter.

He lurched groggily upright. "What is it?"

"The house is on fire!"

Sleep's final veil parted. Fumbling on shirt, trews and boots, Altiris unbolted the door.

Firestone lanterns flickered. Black smoke already rushed about ornate cornices. Somewhere in the distance, flames crackled and spat.

Sidara, barefoot in nightdress and shawl, scowled. "Why was that locked?"

"Habit." One learned where an unlocked door saw you robbed, or dead.

"Habit?" She grabbed his arm. "Come *on!*"

Lady Reveque, Hawkin and Kurkas met them at the corner, the former still in full gown and the latter in shirt and trews. Constans was a pale, wide-eyed bundle carried against the captain's shoulder. The boy looked on the brink of tears.

"Never bloody ends, does it?" said Kurkas. "Where's the plant pot?"

"I don't know," said Lady Reveque, her face taut. "Hawkin?"

The steward shook her head. "She's not in her room."

Kurkas' eyepatch twitched. "Stairs! Now!"

They ran for the landing. Distant crackle billowed to a hollow roar. Smoke raced across the ceiling. Altiris spluttered, skin prickling.

Sidara lurched to a halt. "No ..."

Altiris skidded against the banister. Three storeys below, drapes, panels and furniture were all ablaze, petals of flame reaching ever higher. Dark against the horrific brilliance, two kernclaws, a man and woman, the wings of their cloaks billowing. A dozen or more vranakin advanced behind. Bodies lay still and silent in their wake.

The male kernclaw let another body fall, Sergeant Heren's craggy features recognisable even at distance. "Find them! No one escapes!"

Vranakin passed deeper into the house. Others made for the stairs. Altiris dragged Sidara from the landing's edge.

"What do we do?" said Sidara.

"We fight our way out, hide in the grounds." Altiris strove for confidence and fell short. "Captain Kurkas and I will draw them off."

"Where's your sword, lad?" said Kurkas.

Altiris put a hand to his waist and cursed. His sword – his *borrowed* sword – was back in the Reveque armoury. In the basement. None of them were armed.

"There are lanterns in the dark outside," said Hawkin. "I'd bet against it being the constabulary."

"We can't just *stay* here," snapped Altiris.

"It's happening again," murmured Lady Reveque. "I did this. The Crowmarket have come for my family."

"Lady Reveque?" Kurkas lowered Constans to the ground and turned her to face him. "*Lilyana.* This is your house. Your home. What's our best hope of getting out?"

Lady Reveque blinked, startled. "The east wing." Her voice gained confidence. "The back stairs down to the old stables, and through the grounds to the abbey. It worked before."

"So we do that. Hawkin, you know the way?"

She nodded, took two backward steps and set off.

"What about Ana?" said Sidara.

Kurkas hesitated. "We hope she can look after herself."

The raven cloak screeched its discomfort at the flames – a discomfort Apara shared. Vengeance against Malachi Reveque was all very well, even expected. Against his family? The sins of the kith repaid in blood.

But hearthguard? Servants whose only crime was to be present at the hour of vengeance?

Vranakin flocked to join the hunt. Most were young, rassophores of Erad's nest eager to prove themselves. Elder cousins drifted behind, sedate and measured, a cold presence even among the fires.

Apara shifted her gaze from a footman's glassy stare and up through the seething smoke. The fires she and Erad set had already reached the first floor, ushered on by the quiet sorcery of alchemist's powder. Soon, their wrath would shine clear across the city. A beacon, Krastin had said, and Erad had obliged. He'd always been ambitious.

"This is your chance, cousin," said Erad. "Your *last* chance. The daughter will be Athariss' bride of the grave. The others burn."

Easy for him to say. He'd not yet found himself in Sidara Reveque's path. But he was right. It *was* her chance, and she lucky to have even that.

A flicker of movement on the upper landing, scarcely visible through the smoke.

Apara's hated shadow urged her to silence. Erad hadn't seen. He didn't have to know.

She swallowed and extended a hand. "There."

Halfway along the corridor, four masked vranakin emerged from the back stairwell. For a heartbeat, they froze, as startled as their prey. Swords gleamed. Kurkas' night, already his worst for fifteen years, edged further down the rankings. Confined space? No weapon to hand? Children on the brink of panic? Oh yes, and the building was ablaze.

No life for an honest soldier.

A vranakin launched into a run. A vase crashed to the floor as Kurkas hoisted a small table from beneath the window. It broke cleanly across the vranakin's face and neck, and he dropped like a stone. His sword skidded back across the carpet, too close to his fellows to risk claiming.

Easy come, easy go.

"Back up!" Kurkas hurled a useless, splintered table leg at the oncoming vranakin. "We can't fight them here!"

Hawkin stumbled back along the corridor. Altiris was close behind, his pace steady, his back to the group and his eyes towards the enemy, daring them to close the distance.

Good lad. He'd come a long way in a few short days.

"They're behind us!" shouted Lady Reveque.

A weary glance confirmed the words. Three ahead, and at least four behind. Kurkas kicked open the nearest door. "Inside! Now!"

"No!" said Lady Reveque. "Here!"

She flung open a pair of double doors and vanished inside, Sidara on her heels. Stifling a curse, Kurkas followed. Sparing the plushly uphol-stered room the briefest of glances, he slammed the doors.

"Sidara, watch over your brother!" Shoving Constans towards his sister, Kurkas grabbed Altiris by the arm. "Right, you and me. First crow-born comes through that door gets the worst day of his damn life. We get his weapons, clear a path. Whatever it takes, and I mean *whatever*."

The boy, pale and sheened with sweat, nodded. Kurkas clapped him on the shoulder.

"Good lad. Do me proud, now." Eye on the door, he raised his voice, rising heat from the fire prickling at his lungs. "Don't suppose there's something climbable beyond that window? Drainpipe, ivy, that kind of thing?"

"No," Lady Reveque replied. "Nothing like that."

"Then what's so bloody special about this room? Begging your pardon?"

"It was my grandfather's study. He was obsessed with Hadari weaponry."

Lady Reveque clambered down from a chair, bereft wall brackets behind her, and swords clutched close. The slight curve and the double-edge to the blade marked shadowthorn heritage as plainly as the tasselled silk at the grip. But steel was steel. She gave one to Altiris, kept another for herself, and tossed the third to Kurkas. He caught it clumsily, the sluggishness an unwelcome reminder he'd not come out of the mists as whole as he'd gone in.

The doors burst open.

The first vranakin died with Kurkas' blade between his ribs. A second to a perfect fencer's lunge from Lady Reveque. A cudgel drove Altiris' sword aside, and the wielder bore the lad to the ground. Kurkas booted the vranakin clear. Others crowded the doorway.

"What are you waiting for?" he roared.

The vranakin surged, and Kurkas gave himself to the wrath of battle. He fought on as the floor smouldered, blinded by sweat and the air thick in his lungs. No thought. No fear. Just instinct and the bite of the blade; the strike of boot and elbow. He spat soot-flecked defiance with every thrust, let the pain of a missed parry and sliced flesh carry him deeper into the red.

Hawkin cried out. A flash of light vied with the first flicker of flame to hurl a vranakin against bookshelves. Loose pages fluttered, charring in the quickening fire. Distracted, Kurkas parried too late. A vranakin's blade grazed his leg, and he fell to one knee.

Lady Reveque stepped between them. The vranakin froze, eyes wide beneath the mask, as her blade plunged hilt-deep into his chest. Twisting her sword free, she let the body drop and tore away her blood-spattered veil.

"Can you stand?"

Kurkas accepted her hand and stood tall among the dead. A flash of pain trembled his wounded leg, but it held. "I'll live. Anyone else?"

"Hawkin's hurt," said Sidara.

The steward shook her head, her left arm cradled close by her right. "I'm fine."

"I can feel a simarka in the streets nearby." Sidara pinched her eyes shut. What little colour she'd regained since returning to Abbeyfields was in full retreat. "But I can't *reach* it. I can't make it listen."

"Doesn't matter," said Kurkas. "You did good."

The flash of light, twin to the one that had hurled Altiris into the river. Sidara Reveque would never be without a weapon. Anastacia had been right to teach her.

Anastacia. Where was she? Fire couldn't settle her. Wouldn't be right.

"Constans!" Lady Reveque spun on her heel, panic touching her voice. "Where's Constans?"

"Here." Altiris staggered to his feet, the cut on his cheek bleeding again. "He's over here."

The boy stood staring down at a dead vranakin. A rose-hilted dagger protruded from the corpse's bloody eye.

"He was going to kill my sister," murmured Constans.

"It's all right." Lady Reveque held him close, arms wrapped tight. "It's all right."

"We can't stay here," said Kurkas.

Lady Reveque nodded, and led Constans to the corridor. Kurkas limped after her. Flame spewed from the back landing, a gout of hot, black smoke rushing to join that streaming along the ceiling. Coughing and spluttering, Kurkas ducked into the clearer air below.

"Heads down!" he gasped. "Don't breathe it in. Back the way we came."

Grey robes gathered at the head of the main landing. Memories of the Westernport warehouse surfaced beside old fears. Kurkas glanced back at his filthy, weary company.

"Altiris? Remember what I said before, lad?"

The lad swallowed, but stepped forward. "Whatever it takes."

"That's the one. Raven's Eyes, but it's been a horrible few days."

Kurkas set off along the corridor, injured leg threatening to buckle with every step. Filthy air shimmered. Beyond the elder cousin, the landing brightened with hungry, rippling flame. The elder cousin hissed and quickened its pace, a cloud of tattered grave-clothes with hands outstretched.

"Draw it left, lad," said Kurkas. "We keep its eyes on us, and the others can slip past."

The elder cousin jerked. Its shape stiffened in consternation. Then, with a crash of breaking glass, it was gone, hurled into the night by a charred, petite figure close behind. Anastacia's dress, borrowed only hours before, was little more than a burnt and patchy covering to grimy, smeared porcelain.

"Fine time to oversleep," said Kurkas.

[[I don't sleep. I was in the west annex. Someone locked a number of doors to keep me there.]]

"The west annex?" asked Sidara.

[[Your father has . . . *had* . . . a wonderful library. Reading is one of the few pleasures I have left. I hope you weren't wanting to use the stairs. They're nothing but ash.]]

"The south wing," said Lady Reveque. "There's a lumber room above the ballroom. Even if the stairs are gone, we can get out onto the summerhouse roof and jump to the river."

Kurkas winked tears from a streaming eye. Skin crawled beneath a sweat-sodden shirt. Each breath laboured harder for lesser gain.

Vranakin, flames and poisonous air. A coin's toss to which killed them first.

"Go!" He sent Sidara staggering on.

They set off again, less fugitives running for their lives than a blind, coughing work-shift come clambering out of the mines. Constans stumbled. Anastacia gathered him beneath head and knees without missing a beat.

[[I have him! Keep going!]]

Vranakin came spluttering out of the smoke as they crossed the landing. Altiris ran one through. Kurkas grabbed the other by the throat. He dashed her skull against the wall and collapsed, slim reserves spent. Sidara pulled him onwards, though the girl's weaving gait spoke of her own struggles.

Smoke danced like desert zaifîrs about the lumber room's eaves. Sheet-draped furnishings crackled. An uneven floor spoke to the inferno raging in the ballroom below. At the far end, a filthy window, glass crazed by the heat, promised salvation.

"Just a little further," gasped Lady Reveque.

Timber shrieked high above. A flame-wreathed beam slipped its moorings and plunged through the smoke, roof tiles spilling all around.

"Look out!" Rousing to one last effort, Kurkas hurled himself at Lady Reveque and flung her clear. The falling beam hurled him into darkness.

To Altiris, Kurkas' warning and the fall of the beam came too close to think, much less act. Not so Anastacia.

[[Vladama!]]

She dropped Constans and threw herself forward, taking the beam across neck and shoulders. The impact that should have crushed Kurkas' skull instead struck him cold to the smouldering floor. The web of rafters and purlins shuddered. An ear-splitting squeal, and half the roof gave way.

Anastacia shuddered beneath the beam and the wreckage pressing down upon it, legs braced wide. An empty, angry howl from immobile lips challenged the cacophony of the roof's demise.

Her efforts held a precious circle free of burning timber while all else drowned in fire. Beyond, a portion of the floor fell away. Smoke spiralled away through gaping roof, clawing towards the moon. Flames fed anew by night air roared in triumph.

Skin blistering, Altiris pulled Sidara deeper into shelter. A weeping Constans clung to Hawkin. No room to stand. Barely even to kneel. Every breath sucked cinders into ravaged lungs.

"Mother!" shouted Sidara. "Mother, where are you?"

"I'm here! I'm all right!"

Through watering eyes, Altiris glimpsed Lady Reveque, blackened but hale, beyond the circle of flame.

Anastacia's pained howl shuddered upward in pitch. Her left foot skidded in ash. An ominous rumble ground out above. [[Sidara! Help me!]]

"How?" said Sidara. "I can't—"

Pieces clicked together in Altiris' mind. "Like throwing me into the river. Just heavier."

She clenched her fists. Her eyes stuttered gold, then blue, then gold again. Light gathered about the beam and sparked along the adjoining timbers. The descent arrested. Sliver by sliver, it reversed.

"I don't believe it," said Hawkin.

Darkness gathered beyond the fire. The air filled with the screech of crow voices. Steel shone, grasped tight by two kernclaws drawing nearer through the smoke.

Lady Reveque faced it, sword shaking in her hand.

"Mother!"

Sunlight dissipated, hurled at the kernclaws by a daughter's fear. It threw the woman against the ruins of the east wall. The man staggered, driven to his knees.

Freed, the wreckage shuddered lower. Anastacia's shoulders dipped. Constans buried his face in Hawkin's shoulder. On Kurkas' brow, blood glistened beneath a crust of soot. Altiris looked on, helpless.

[[Sidara!]]

The male kernclaw sprang to his feet and braced against another burst of golden light. He barely staggered.

[[I can't do this alone!]]

Sidara dropped to one elbow, breath rasping. "But my mother!"

Lady Reveque drew close enough to the flames that frayed skirts smouldered. "Sidara? Look at me. *Look* at me. I was wrong to hide you."

She smiled, eyes and brow atremble with contradictory emotion. "I'm so very proud."

She turned to face the kernclaw, the sword in her hand steady as stone.

"No!"

Sidara's cry dragged Apara back to her senses just as Lady Reveque threw herself at Erad, sword agleam with reflected firelight. Beyond, golden light crackled into being about the collapsing roof, but the girl's eyes never left her mother.

Head still spinning and her body one vast, vocal bruise, Apara clambered upright.

Steel shrieked as Erad's talons flickered to a parry. Once. Twice.

On the third lunge, Erad gave himself to his raven cloak. Lady Reveque struck out blindly, the storm of claws and beaks tearing at flesh and cloth. She never saw him coalesce behind. Then his talons were in her back, and it was too late for anything.

Lady Reveque toppled sideways. Her sword hit the ground a heartbeat before she did, skidding away in the leaping flames of the ballroom below. Her scream was joined by others. A daughter's. A son's. A young man with ragged voice. And something older by far.

[[I'll break every bone in your body, little crow!]]

Erad spat into the flames and turned his back. "Apara! She's still alive. Finish it. Prove yourself. Apara!"

She drew closer through spiralling smoke. Close enough to smell the blood pooling beneath Lady Reveque. Close enough to the flames that her raven cloak shrieked its fear. That she saw Sidara's accusing stare lose its golden lustre, and fade to blue with the girl's slackening strength. To see the spark of terror in the young man's expression as the wreckage lurched in new descent. To recognise the hungry gleam in Erad's eyes.

The floor buckled and cracked, fire racing out as the floor gave way. Blazing furniture tumbling into the abyss.

The shadow in Apara's soul – her leash, her jailer – screamed at her to stop, to stay back.

It was afraid. It knew. Erad was right. She'd almost bested it before. Break its hold once, and she'd be free.

But who'd be free? The Silver Owl she'd been, or the kernclaw her cousins had made of her? And free to do what? To kill and kill and kill, until she was as dead within as Erad, and as dead without as her elder cousins?

But was the alternative better? Did she even have one? Krastin's forgiveness was spent. Failure tantalised. Success appalled. And there was no road between.

She stared down at Lady Reveque, her back arched in agony, but her eyes lucid and defiant. Even dying, the better woman.

"No weakness, Apara," said Erad.

"No," she said. "No weakness."

To her surprise, the shadow in her soul – the shadow that had kept her from killing this past year – made no protest as she rammed her talons home. Even when blood gushed to soak her gloves and sleeve. Even when Erad's sightless, gasping corpse slid free and crumpled at her feet.

Floorboards fell away, tipping Lady Reveque into the flame-edged void.

"No!"

Apara dived. On the cusp of the broken floorboards, fingers closed about those of the woman she'd come to kill. Glowing timber burned her gloves, seared skin beneath. Hands slippery with sweat and blood slid apart.

"I need your other hand!"

"I'm already in the mists." The other's smoke-stained face held no fear. No anger. "I hear the choir. Please. Save my children."

Then Lady Reveque was gone into the fire, and Apara none the wiser as to which of them had let go.

"Mother!"

Sidara's heartbroken cry echoed in the pit of Apara's stomach. Even in triumph, she'd failed – the failure was worse for not recognising what was now blinding in its truth. That what had held her back from murder had not been Akadra's shadow at all, but her own conscience. All else was excuse.

You're not cut out for this. Leave while you can.

A path she should have taken long ago.

The roof screamed. The wreckage above the porcelain woman's shoulders inched downwards.

The raven cloak screamed as Apara passed through the fiery cage, its pain so bright and strident in her mind as to be inseparable from her own. Clinging desperately to consciousness, she fell to her knees beside Sidara, and cast away the cloak's burning remnant.

Dizzy with reflected agony, she barely heard the girl's banshee shriek. The punch had all the weight the girl herself lacked, and almost tipped Apara into the flames.

Breathing hard, her lungs thick and bitter with smoke, Apara held up a hand. "Let me help," she gasped.

The girl's second blow shivered to a halt in the young man's grip. "Sidara, wait."

Hawkin Darrow looked up from the boy cradled in her arms. "We've nothing to lose."

Apara closed her eyes and reached out to the mists of Otherworld, drawn close enough to touch by bloodshed. The Raven's gift. The Crowmarket's favour. The means by which kernclaws came uninvited beyond a protector's vigil. Let it serve something more than murder, just this once.

The mists fought, reluctant, but Apara had learnt much about strength that night, and brooked no quarrel. Green-white vapour mingled with smoke, the scent of yesterdays with burning wood. A roiling doorway burst into being, a dark road beckoning beyond.

"Go! If you want to live! Go!"

Suspicious faces glowered back.

[[This is coming down,]] gasped the porcelain woman. [[Be somewhere else.]]

Another creak of wreckage, and reluctance vanished. Hawkin staggered into the mists, the boy drawn behind. Sidara and the lad followed, the unconscious body of the one-armed man borne between them. Apara hesitated on the threshold, her gaze meeting that of the porcelain woman. No words were exchanged. None could have matched the baleful, endless promise of those expressionless eyes.

Apara leapt through into the deadland streets. A groaning, thunderous crash sounded at her back, fire flickering and dying in a land that had no fuel to burn. Falling to her knees, she relinquished her hold on the portal, and lay still among the drifting dead.

*

Malachi turned at the creak of the Privy Council chamber door. "Messela? Has Master Toldav finally arrived?"

He knew the answer before she spoke, framed as it was by harrowed eyes and downcast gaze.

"No," she said, her voice raw and empty. "Malachi ... Malachi, I'm so sorry."

Lumendas, 8th Day of Wealdrust

We owe allegiance to more than politicians and principalities. What binds us should always count for more than what drives us apart.

from the sermons of Konor Belenzo

Fifty-Four

"Halvor?"

Kurkas started awake, the pulsating, hammering pain of the dream persisting into reality. Such as it was. Beyond the broken stone of the collapsed wall and through the ruin of the ceiling, dark skies blazed vivid green, broken by the jagged ridges of humbled rooftops, and flights of pallid, translucent birds. Strains of a distant, mournful song rose and fell behind.

Rough, mortar-weeping stone under his hand, he reached his feet and stared out of the sunken window. Street level was little better, thick with sickly mist and the hollow stares of etravia. Cobbles yielded to broken flagstones, walls to cornices and leering caryatids. But if he tried, if he really *stared,* he glimpsed the reality behind.

The world shifted. Straight lines twisted in on themselves. Nausea squeezed out conscious thought as rubbery legs folded. Someone caught him.

"Don't fight it." The voice was impossibly near and far away all at once. "Don't try to impose your will – just accept what you see."

The supporting hands fell away. The contorted world righted itself. Balance returned. Fingers splayed against the wall, Kurkas doubled over. The headache flooded back, hammering at his thoughts. He straightened, fingers tracing puffy flesh at his brow. Memories of smoke welled behind his thoughts, just out of reach.

"Thanks," he said, turning about. "Where ... "

The words fell away into a growl as a weeping eye found her face. Auburn curls marred by a silver streak. The kernclaw from Westernport.

Ebigail Kiradin's daughter. Smoke cleared in memory. Screams. The crackle of flames. Abbeyfields ablaze and vranakin everywhere.

His fist formed and swung. She yelped and fell onto rubble, hand wiping a trickle of blood from the corner of her mouth. Anger drove Kurkas on.

"Captain, no!" Suddenly, a filthy Altiris was between them, arms outstretched. "She saved us."

"Us?"

Kurkas let his fist fall and noted new shapes in the mist. Hawkin, backed against the corner and a sleeping Constans held close. Sidara, still in filthy nightdress and housecoat, stood at the rubble-spill of the gable wall, staring out into the street.

"Lady Reveque? The plant pot?"

Altiris shook his head.

"They're gone." Sidara spoke without turning.

A tone that should have been bleak was entirely too level for Kurkas' liking. Trouble borrowed from the future. But dealing with the sorrows of a teenage girl lay far outside his experience. And Anastacia gone? That left a hole. Didn't seem right.

"The roof collapsed," murmured Altiris. "She held it up. Never seen anything like it."

"She'd a knack for that." Walling up grief and guilt, Kurkas helped the kernclaw rise. "Seems I owe an apology. What's your name?"

"Apara."

"The weather's a mite ... unusual."

She winced. "It was burn, or bring everyone through to Otherworld. The *real* Otherworld, not the echo you get in Dregmeet."

Better and better. With an effort, Kurkas walled up his fear as well. "Can we leave? Green ain't my colour."

Apara nodded. "There are ... weak points. If we can reach one, I can get us out."

"Then why haven't you?"

"You're a bit heavy, sir," said Altiris.

"Should've left me behind."

"You weren't the only problem," said Apara. "The paths ... They're not right. They're muddled. I can't follow them as I should."

"Lost your map, have you?"

She glared tiredly. "Otherworld's only as real as we think it is. That's why it looks so much like the city – at least to us. Know where you want to go and the roads attend to themselves. But it takes effort. That's why the etravia are trapped here. They lack the will to reach their reward, so they drift for ever. That or because they've no reward to find, not until Third Dawn."

He shuddered. "So you're saying you're too tired to find the way?"

"Yes, but I'm not the problem. The girl's still weak, and they're all frightened. Strong emotion muddles the paths. They're fighting me, and they don't even realise it. I thought a rest might help."

Kurkas nodded. It made as much sense as anything. Problem was, a bit of sleep wasn't going to calm Constans or Sidara, and certainly not there. And Hawkin didn't look much better. Pale and drawn, she seemed ready to bolt into the mists.

The singing dipped and faded away.

"They're back," hissed Hawkin.

Sidara dropped down off the rubble and behind the wall. As the others took cover, Kurkas squatted down beside her.

"Who's back?" he whispered.

She offered a hollow glance. "The rotting ones."

He risked a look. Perhaps halfway down the unfamiliar street, just at the point where mist swallowed all, a group of three elder cousins drifted through the paler etravia, growing closer all the time.

Kurkas ducked back and took a tally of their options. Altiris still had a sword. Apara – could she be trusted – had her talons. Not enough for one elder cousin, much less three.

"Don't suppose there's any chance of you putting a magical whammy on them?" he whispered to Sidara.

"I . . . I can't feel the light any more. It's gone. There's only emptiness."

Kurkas focused on the approaching footsteps. Closer and closer they drew, then faded away. A glance over the wall confirmed their departure. He eased a sigh of relief and joined Apara by the ruins of a leaded window. "They looking for us?"

She shot a glance towards Sidara. Her lip twitched.

Kurkas sidled to stand between them. "Tell me," he said softly.

"She helped Captain Darrow kill Crowfather Athariss."

Apara spoke so softly that Kurkas read the words on her lips more than in her voice. One of those tricks that never left you. A lifetime ago he'd made good coin spilling stolen secrets. Athariss was one of those names he'd hoped never to hear again.

"Good for her. Good for them both."

Apara scowled. "What do you think provoked all this? Darrow's probably dead by now, and the girl . . . ?"

The girl. Kurkas didn't care for the distance of the term. Made her a thing, not a person. You couldn't betray a thing. "She has a name."

"Trying to humanise her?" She shrugged. "They want to bury *Sidara* alive with Athariss' corpse. Beneath the Shaddra."

The centre of the Hayadra Grove? Kurkas grimaced. "Why there?"

"They think it'll break the power of the hayadra trees and let the whole city slide into the mists. Twin blasphemies offered to the divine sisters of light."

"If you say so."

"Krastin believes it. That's enough to doom the gi . . . *Sidara*."

Krastin. Another name he'd rather not have heard. "Then we keep moving." He stared out into the street. No sign of the elder cousins. Just the etravia, and that nerve-shivering song. "But let's be clear: I've already lost a friend today. I lose anyone else, I'll get unfriendly."

It wasn't much of a threat, not weaponless and with his head ringing like a bell.

"Don't worry, there's no taking back the choice I made."

Messela had never spent as much time in her office as she had that past day. To all appearances, it wasn't hers at all, with nothing personal to soften the bare desk and the empty shelves. However much most of her peers longed for the status brought by a suite in the palace, she'd never really accepted her own.

Through the window, black smoke spiralled against the stone ribs of Strazyn Abbey, the fires of the Reveque mansion defying all attempts to douse them. Little of Abbeyfields remained. The city waited, breath held in anticipation. Or perhaps, Messela allowed, that was transference – the empty plaza and huddled streets hunched beneath her own uncertainties.

The first decisions had been simple enough, the orders obeyed without question. Thinking on the conversations to come stole away her breath. Fighting the panic made it worse. Spasm became the coiling black fear that she'd forgotten *how* to breathe. That threatened to reach through her, and do terrible things. Clutching at the windowsill, she sought calm as her mother had taught her. The attacks always passed. The trick was recognising that in time.

Rebellious muscles eased. Parched lungs partook. Darkness bled away. Messela relaxed her grip. There. Better.

The opening of her office door threatened to set panic raging again. She stared out across the city, eyes unfocused.

"Well, where is he?" snapped Lord Lamirov.

"In the council chamber." She clung to the confidence in her reply and willed it to be truth. "I tried to send him away. '*Where would I go?*' That's what he said. I didn't have a good answer."

That wasn't all he'd said, of course. *This is all my fault. I did this.* Private words for a private moment, and not to be shared with the likes of Lamirov. Nor was the fact that Malachi had been dead drunk. He'd lost too much already to make rumour of his dignity.

"I tried the council chamber. Your hearthguards wouldn't let me in." He reached her side, a grey and peevish presence on the balcony. "Not the done thing, Messela. The palace is the constabulary's province. *And* they told me you'd dissolved the Grand Council."

"They were flapping around like gaffed fish. Most had fled to be with their families, some were panicking about how a lifetime's bribes to the vranakin seem to be for nothing. The rest were more distracting than helpful. This is ... quieter. We need quiet, Leonast. Quiet, and calm."

His eyes narrowed. "We'll see what Malachi has to say."

"Disturbing his grief gains nothing."

"Yes, well ... I feel for him, I do." A frown. The bald head dipped in thought. "Is there no chance anyone got out?"

Messela's throat tightened. "Not according to those who did."

"Damn the vranakin," Lamirov snarled. "A wife is bad enough, but to go after the children? I'll speak with Captain Darrow. If the constabulary can't keep the vranakin contained in Dregmeet, then they can at least bolster the Council's protections."

How typical, thinking of himself even now. "Captain Darrow's dead."

He drew up. "Her wounds? The physicians assured me—"

"Poison. Her lips were blue. Lieutenant Raldan says the sweet scent of seldora flower was everywhere. She went into the mists not feeling a thing."

He hissed softly. "Dark days indeed. If Malachi's not fit to govern, someone else must."

"Yes."

"I'll need your support, of course. Evarn and Konor are holed up in their mansions, Rika too, for all I know." He paused. Effect only, for he'd surely given the matter full consideration. "It's time we sought peace with the Crowmarket."

Now. The dreaded moment. Yet Messela felt nothing of that fear, none of the panic. "No."

Lamirov rounded on her. "What do you mean, no? You've read Izack's reports. Vranakin on one side, and the Hadari on the other. If we don't make peace with one, they'll squeeze us dry. The Republic will fall."

She stared through him, refusing the challenge in his eyes. He'd intimidated her from the start. The stern patriarch thrice her age. Calm. Confident. Collected. Not now. In fact, now the moment was here, she felt none of the panic that had ridden as its herald, only joy. Was this how Viktor felt when he rode into battle? Easy to see how one grew to love it.

"No, we will not kneel to the vranakin," she replied. "No, I will not support you. But you will support *me*."

Colour touched his cheeks. "Is this a joke?"

"No joke. I knew you'd use this tragedy to seize power. And I knew you'd give it away to the vranakin just as quickly—"

"How dare you!"

Messela narrowed her eyes. "I won't play that game. Your first instinct, as ever, is for yourself, and not our people."

He scowled. "And you've a solution to our woes, I suppose?"

"Not yet. But there's been too much rashness of late. We're not used to action, so speed becomes haste, and haste, horror. I won't invite more until level heads prevail."

"You've no authority."

"So you won't support me?" The smile came easily. "Did you count the number of Akadra hearthguard on station when you arrived? Everyone I have left is here. Have you more?"

Lamirov paled. "This is treason. You'll hang for this."

Treason. Confidence flickered. "You're cleverer than that, Leonast. I'm offering you the chance to emerge unsullied from whatever comes next. I'm not Ebigail Kiradin. I just want to keep things together."

"For how long?"

"Until Malachi gathers his wits, or Izack stabilises the situation in the east."

He glared, a coward trapped by his own failings. A better man would have challenged her, fearful her inexperience would cause more deaths. But Leonast Lamirov wasn't a better man, and the only death that truly troubled him was his own. "And your hearthguards?"

"Are deployed to protect Lord Reveque, nothing more." She shrugged. Lamirov knew it was a lie, but as with so much of council business, there was form to these things. "Three days, Leonast. Then I'll step aside, and you can do as you wish. To me, and to this city."

His mask of consideration did little to hide churning thoughts. Calculations. Timings. The likelihood of convincing others to dislodge her by force. The Akadra hearthguard wasn't in much better shape than others in the city, but it had a reputation.

"Very well," he said at last. "Three days."

He turned stiffly and left her office. Messela almost laughed, overtaken by the giddiness of victory. Three days. She'd expected to settle for two. Perhaps she did have a future on the Council, after all.

Then she stared out across the city again – to where the mist stole away the streets, and where the ruin of Abbeyfields blazed against the morning murk – and darkness returned.

Buildings came and went, crooked manifestations of places Kurkas knew well, and others unknown to him. Withered trees and sprawling mausolea. A sunken river, bounded by pitted and broken statues. All hurried along by the song of the etravia and the fraught, distant weeping of prizraks.

Apara led the way, Sidara limping close behind, with Hawkin and Constans shuffling along in the middle. Kurkas brought up the rear,

Altiris at his side and troubled by the slowing pace. Apara was increasingly hesitant in choosing her course.

Worse, the crumbling ruins in which he'd awoken were but a memory. Most buildings now were smooth stone, with solid doors and lantern light burning behind the windows. Or at least what passed for lantern light. Kurkas wasn't about to trust to anything burning bright green. If the elder cousins came again, there were damn all places to hide save for alleyways whose darkness set the spine tingling every bit as much as witch-lights beyond filthy glass.

"Can you handle things here for a bit?" asked Kurkas.

Altiris nodded, his face tight but his fear under control. "Long as you need, captain."

"Good lad."

Clapping Altiris on the shoulder, Kurkas lengthened his stride until he reached Hawkin and Constans. The lad was staring resolutely down at his feet, the steward's arm about his shoulder. Her other was tucked tight across her chest, the blouse stained with dry blood.

"You all right, Mistress Darrow?"

She offered a wan smile. "I'm not a soldier. I'm supposed to be interviewing a new governess for Constans this morning ... if it *is* still this morning."

He nodded and moved on. Hawkin at least seemed halfway composed, and he'd no idea how to reach Constans. Paths muddled by emotion, Apara had said. Of the two Reveque kids, Kurkas much preferred his chances of tackling Sidara.

"How're you holding up, lass?"

She offered a hollow glance. "I hurt. Inside and out."

"Altiris told me what your mother did. Worse ways to go, and worse things to die for."

She touched her eyes closed, and wiped at her cheek. Soot smudged and glistened. "She's still dead. I never even had chance to say goodbye, nor apologise for being a brat. We've done little but argue this last year. I kept wishing I was free of her. And now? Now I just want her back."

"Ain't your fault." He stared at the viridian sky, floundering even in the shallows of heartsore conversation. "Way Altiris tells it, she faced it proud. Her and the plant pot both. That's more than most can say."

"Who's Halvor?" said Sidara. "I heard you call out."

Kurkas scratched his head. "A friend of your Uncle Josiri's. She saved my life, only I couldn't return the favour." He sighed. "She chose her fate too. Seems folk keep dying to save my worthless hide. I don't like it."

"I don't think we're supposed to."

"Reckon you're right."

They walked for a time in silence, Kurkas' attention split fore and aft as he watched for pursuit. Sidara glanced behind and lowered her voice.

"My father serves the Crowmarket," she said. "The one I hurt ... Athariss, I think ... He said so. Mother confirmed it. She said he'd no other choice."

That'd explain a great deal. "Probably he doesn't. Those mangy old crows know how to twist a man."

For the first time, sorrow slipped from her expression, leaving something hard behind. "I wish I believed that."

"This is it!" Apara spun around, face framed by relief. "I can get us back from here."

Kurkas strode to join her. He saw little familiar about their surroundings. A crumbling church of a design he barely recognised, and beyond the withered churchyard, a narrow alley between timber-framed buildings. "Where?"

"Cradlesmith Alley."

He tried to match name to surroundings and failed. He shook his head. "That's in Dregmeet."

She glared. "Is that better or worse than here?"

"Good point."

Altiris beckoned. "Captain! They're here!"

Typical. Kurkas shoved Sidara towards the church's ruined porch, a pang of guilt surfacing as she stumbled. With everything else, he'd forgotten how beaten up the girl had been just a day before. Shouldn't have been moving around at all, by rights. Maybe that was why she was having trouble reaching her light. It was working overtime just keeping her upright.

"Under cover." He dragged Constans on and pointed towards the porch. "Quickly now!"

In defiance of his own orders, Kurkas headed out into the street to meet Altiris. Though he strained, he caught no sight of the elder cousins. "Where are they, lad?"

"Can't have gone far. The singing's stopped."

Kurkas grunted. The lad was paying better attention than he was. "All right. We join the others. Apara reckons she can get ... "

A thin noise, more gasp than scream, billowed forth from the church. Eyes wild, Altiris bolted across the churchyard and vanished inside. Kurkas, slowed by age and thumping headache, arrived two paces behind.

"Stay back!"

Hawkin stood on the porch's inner threshold, her arm no longer about Constans' shoulder, but tight across his neck. The other held a bloodied dagger to his throat. Apara lay gasping across a grimy pew, hands clasped to the bloodstain spreading across her lower ribcage. Sidara looked on with fury. Behind them all – behind the lopsided statue of a spread-winged raven – the viridian sky crackled and swirled through the fallen arch of a stained-glass window.

"Hawkin!" shouted Sidara.

Hawkin drew her arm tighter about Constans' neck. "Come with me, and I'll not hurt him. I promise."

Kurkas circled closer. "Starting to think your promises ain't worth much, Mistress Darrow."

She twitched the dagger, spurring a muffled cry from Constans. "We do what we have to."

Altiris stepped forward, sword raised. "Let him go."

"Can't do that, my bonny. The Parliament want Sidara, so she's coming with me."

"No," he snarled. "She's not."

Hawkin shook her head. "Not your choice, lad. Is it, Sidara?"

"You don't have to do this," said Sidara. "If you're afraid of the Crowmarket, the Council can protect you."

"How, when your father's drowning in Dregmeet? The Parliament takes what it wants. Always has. Right now it wants you."

Kurkas inched closer. Hawkin was vranakin. Equally certain was that Apara hadn't known. It made sense of the chandelier that had crushed Lady Mezar. Hawkin had been right there. Of course no one had suspected her. Who'd believe the carefree, vivacious steward had a darker side? Unless that was the only side to her, and the other a mask. Careful. Manipulative. She'd never been in any danger from the chandelier, just like she'd not been wounded during that fight at Abbeyfields – her hand was too steady for that.

"You're wasting your time," gasped Apara. "She's too . . . new. Still got the shine on it. Still believes there's a pulpit in the . . . Church of Tithes waiting . . . for her. Hope . . . the biggest lie."

"Shut your mouth, traitor!"

"They mean to kill Sidara, Hawkin," said Kurkas. "Bury her alive with a corpse for company. Can you live with that?"

Sidara paled. For all her apparent poise, Hawkin's eyes were restless, uncertain. She didn't entirely believe she'd pull this off, and that kind of uncertainty had a tendency to make itself truth. Kurkas searched for the words that would tip her over.

"Your wife's the head of the constabulary, for pity's sake."

Hawkin flinched. "Vona was dead from the moment she struck down Crowfather Athariss. I made it as kind as I could manage."

"I thought you were my friend!" Sidara's eyes crackled with golden light, then went dark with fading strength. The girl looked dead on her feet.

"Friends always leave, my bonny. You can't trust them. Only family."

Kurkas coughed. "Lad, if I get that dagger out of her hand, can you take her?"

"Count on it," said Altiris.

Kurkas' eye rested on Constans, hoping for a sign of the boy's famous wildness. A distraction. He simply stood there, face pale and eyes drawn, all resistance gone. Hard to blame the lad. A real swine of a day, and no mistake.

"No way this ends well for you, Hawkin," he said softly. "Let Constans go. We'll all be mates again. No one else has to get hurt."

No one else but Apara, who was already hurt – maybe dying. Their only way out of Otherworld.

So how did Hawkin expect to escape?

Behind her, three tattered elder cousins drifted through the shattered window. Sedate. Serene. Whether it was the three from before was impossible to tell.

Hawkin's expression became a triumphant sneer. "You're right. No one else has to die. Sidara stays. You leave."

"Let Constans go," said Sidara. "Let them all go, and I'll come with you."

Altiris started towards her. "Sidara, no!"

"Constans stays with me, so I know you'll behave." Hawkin shrugged. "I don't care about the rest."

The elder cousins were halfway across the nave. A ragged sleeve brushed a pew. Black, scuttling insects rushed away across the timber.

"This ain't the way, lass," said Kurkas.

Sidara tore her eyes off her brother's. "It's what I'm choosing, captain. Tell my father I didn't abandon my family. If anything matters to him any longer, that should mean something."

There wasn't another way, was there? Getting Constans free had always been a risk. Now it was impossible. The only choices were surrender the kids, or for them all to die. And dead men didn't effect rescues.

Throat thick and bitter, headache swamped by an impotent rage that washed everything black, Kurkas turned to Altiris. "Get Apara on her feet, lad. Get her outside. I'll be right behind."

Expression as flat and hard as Kurkas' own, the lad hauled Apara upright, his shoulder beneath hers, and stumbled out into the churchyard.

Hawkin gave a sly, triumphant smile. "No heroics, captain."

"I'm just a bluff old soldier. I leave heroics to my betters. All I have's a message." The elder cousins were close enough that their cold raised gooseflesh on Kurkas' skin. Fear burned like tinder as it met the heat of his anger. "Sidara. Constans. This ain't the end of it. And Hawkin? Same promise."

He left the church at a walk – not a run – and with every step fought the urge to look behind. Thirty yards, and the longest walk of his life.

Altiris and Apara were waiting in the street, the former staring in anguish back toward the church, the latter sitting slumped against the wall, her left hand at the wound in her chest, the other hanging loose. Only now did Kurkas note the deep slash across her right forearm, and another at her throat, the blood pulsing away over her talons' leather straps. The air stank of it.

"Paths muddled," murmured Apara. "Wasn't . . . children. Her."

Hawkin. Drawing them in circles until the odds were in her favour. Obvious in hindsight.

"Where's Sidara?" said Altiris.

"Where d'you think?" Kurkas replied heavily.

"I thought you had a plan!"

"I do!" Kurkas rounded on him, cheeks wet with tears of rage and shame. "This was it! You think I'm not sick to death of losing to these bastards? Alive, we have a chance. *They* have a chance. Dead, there's no bloody hope at all! Don't you get that?"

"No! I won't leave her to die. I can't!"

Just like that he was gone, headlong into the mists, back towards the church.

"Altiris!"

Temptation to follow rushed thick. But only a fool balanced another's recklessness with his own. Not unless all hope was gone. He crouched beside Apara.

"You still with me? Enough to get me back to Dregmeet? Somewhere *they* won't be?"

She nodded, lips pale and eyes half-lidded. "Yes."

It wasn't much, but that was all right. It'd do. He'd promises to keep. "Good."

Fifty-Five

The outriders of the southern army reached the bustling camp at noon – the vanguard as dusk purpled the western horizon. A woman rode at its head, though not the daughter Kai longed to see. This one wore her hair short. Past the ghostfires marking the camps boundary, she slowed her horse to a walk. Kai stifled a smile at Devren's soft splutter. Kai hadn't shared Melanna's warning of the princessa Andwaral's unveiling, nor had he done so when Haldrane's rider had come to camp hours before. An Emperor's privilege. For all the unwelcome surprises Kai had experienced in recent days, it felt fair to save one for his closest friend.

She slid from her saddle and knelt in the mud, head bowed as the column marched on. Behind, her brother did the same. Further back, Haldrane held a watchful peace. If asked, he'd doubtless blame the crutch for not kneeling. Truth was, Haldrane only knelt in apology for having erred.

"My Emperor," said Naradna, gaze still averted. "Vrasdavora is ours, the Greyridge shirelands taken. It was your daughter's wish we lend our strength to yours."

"And the Tressian army?"

"Escaped, my Emperor."

"So you failed?"

She hesitated. "Yes, my Emperor."

The reply buttressed a decision taken in the early hours. The warrior – the *woman* – who had sought so ardently to prove herself at Ahrad would not have passed up the opportunity to blame Melanna for the failures of the southern campaign. "And I am to understand you are to be warleader in my daughter's stead?"

Naradna raised her head. "So she instructed, my Emperor."

"And if I do not concur?"

She shared a glance with her brother and bit her lip. "Then I will serve however you think proper, so long as that service is accomplished with a sword."

He nodded, and raised his voice, letting it carry as far as failing strength would allow. "I have been blind. That the blindness was passed down from father to son is no excuse."

Conversation hushed and heads turned, the quiet rippling outwards.

"Tradition is slow to fade," said Kai, "but we can always do more to ease its passing. Women do not bear swords. That has been truth for generations. And it has been falsehood just as long. No more. The world holds lies enough. Let this one die. I name Naradna Andwaral a warleader of Empire. Rhaled recognises her claim to the throne of Icansae, and will back that claim with spears, should any offer contest."

The marcher column stuttered to stillness. Silence reigned, and never more than where Naradna knelt, open-mouthed – a woman trapped in a waking dream.

"I . . ." she stuttered.

"You have something to say, warleader?" Kai hooked an eyebrow. "You reject the honour?"

Her jaw set. An appraising expression stole over her features. Pride chanced the dream, and made it truth. "Aelia," she said. "My name is Aelia."

"Then rise," said Kai. "Subservience has its place, but I'll need boldness come the morrow. And if it is your fortune to see my daughter where I do not, please tell her that her father was possessed of some small wisdom, after all."

"Hail Aelia Andwaral, Queen of Icansae!" bellowed Aeldran. "Dotha Icansae!"

The words rushed outwards, gathering pace as other voices joined to his.

"*Dotha Icansae! Andwaral Brigantim! Dotha Icansae!*"

And Kai Saran, who had made many mistakes in recent days, knew in his heart that this could not be numbered among them.

The makeshift camp sat sullen beneath the southern eaves of Selnweald Forest. Beyond the fresh palisade, sparse banners proclaimed the presence of soldiers from a dozen regiments and two chapterhouses. Tattered cloth marked service in the chaotic retreat. Others were fresh, unmarred by smoke and bloodshed. A few hundreds, where thousands should have mustered.

"Hold fast!" bellowed a sentry. "Declare yourself!"

Saddle-sore and weary, Viktor eased his horse to a halt. At his side, Inkari did the same. The rest of the borrowed army waited a league to the south, behind a rise – and all of them better for a long day's ride than Viktor himself. A year playing at farmer had eroded so much of what he'd been.

"Lord Viktor Akadra. Where can I find Commander Keldrov?"

The sentry scowled. "I'll send word. You'll wait until then."

Not a question, and a manner that Viktor couldn't resent. With all that had happened, letting two strangers wander the camp – one a Thrakkian, and the other a vagabond in garb from either side of the border – was hardly advisable.

"Let him through." A sergeant appeared from behind the palisade, the numeral of the 14th proud blazoned on his hawk tabard. "Glad to have you with us."

"You were at Davenwood?"

"Held the line with you, lord. Be honoured to do so again."

A bright note in bleak times. Not so long ago, there'd been few more hated in the Southshires than Viktor Akadra. Proof that things could change, if the will was there. Proof that old prejudices need not hold sway, and that even a shadow might serve the light.

"And the commander?"

"Keep a straight path, lord."

Viktor thanked him and cantered into an encampment less morose than its appearance. Yes, the soldiers were filthy and tired, but a frisson burned beneath the surface. The strange alchemy of hope desired and vengeance sought, betrayed by a stiffening of the shoulders as he passed.

By salutes offered and the scrape of weapons being honed. If these were the Republic's last days – and Viktor was too much the pragmatist to completely reject the possibility – it would not easily fall, not even if all the gods mustered to the Emperor's banner.

The sergeant had spoken true, and Viktor soon dismounted before the command tent, his reins entrusted to a squire of the 14th. Saddle-weary flesh screamed joy and horror as sensation shifted, but it felt good to regain firm ground. Conversation faded as he passed inside to behold familiar faces gathered about a map. Not just Arlanne Keldrov, but . . .

"Rosa!" Viktor knew better than to embrace her in front of strangers, and settled for a shallow bow.

"Viktor."

The bow Rosa offered in return couldn't disguise her malaise. She was too pale, her skin parchment white, and her blue eyes hard. Even straw-blonde hair had dulled to grey. Then again, she'd been at Ahrad. Lumestra only knew what she'd seen since. Rosa had always taken losing hard, as a good soldier should, and the Republic had known little else in recent days.

"Lord Akadra." Keldrov offered salute and abashed expression. "I . . . wasn't sure you'd be joining us. Is she with you?"

Inkari stiffened. "*She* can speak for herself. I am Inkari af Üld af Freyd, Ceorla of Elsbarg. I bear the friendship of the Thane of Indrigsval."

Keldrov's gaze hardened. "We know of Indrigsval's 'friendship' in the south. It's that of the wolf to the flock. Or are you not the same Inkari af Üld who led the sack of Harlene?"

She bared her teeth, but subsided. "Debts are owed. Armund af Garna, Thane of Indrigsval, sends axes to settle the account."

Keldrov shook her head, perhaps recalling the long ago day where she and Armund had taken the field together.

Rosa raised an eyebrow. "How many?"

Inkari offered a wolfish smile. "Twenty reivings of his vanaguard and three sellings of thrydaxes. Two thousands, in all."

"Perhaps a little less," Viktor allowed. "They're waiting to the south. It seemed wise not to provoke . . . surprises."

"I'll warn the patrols myself. I assume you're taking command?"

"With your leave."

"How else will we see if one man *can* make a difference? Lady Orova can tell you anything you need to know. Under the circumstances . . . " She winced. "I thought you'd abandoned us. I owe you an apology."

"I gave you every reason to doubt."

"And Lord Trelan? Lady Beral?"

Through staunch effort, Viktor kept his expression motionless. "Have other matters to attend. They stand with us in spirit."

Keldrov left the reply unchallenged and glanced at Inkari. "Are you fit to ride?"

"Always."

"Then I'd like to see these two thousands for myself, if I may."

Inkari offered a stiff bow and withdrew, Keldrov close behind. Rosa stood at the table, head bowed and arms folded across her chest. A ser-athi, Kasamor Kiradin had once named her, lacking only wings and a halo of light to play the part. Not any longer. Now she was as cold and grey as the winter sea.

"Our scouts tell us that Izack's making a stand at Govanna Field," she said without looking up. "His soldiers are weary, and the Hadari will only overtake them otherwise. But the land north of here's thick with outriders and icularis. If our heralds have reached him, we've heard nothing. Saran will march with the dawn. By this time tomorrow, it'll be settled."

Viktor stared down at the map, though he knew the land well enough. Govanna marked the border between the Marcher Lands and Royal Tressia. A long march north through Selnweald Forest, or a longer one around. "How many does Izack have?"

"Hard to say. The battle at the Rappadan ended in disaster. Perhaps eight thousand? Between what Paradan rescued from Vrasdavora and what Keldrov scraped together on the journey north, we have another three and a half – maybe four."

Twelve thousand, plus the two he'd brought from Indrigsval. Respectable enough.

"And the Emperor?"

"Thirty. At least. Plus Jack's creatures."

He stared, uncertain of his hearing. "I beg your pardon?"

"The Lord of Fellhallow has declared for the shadowthorns," she said bitterly. "They drowned Tarvallion in briar without a sword drawn. The

Hadari marched straight past. There's a forest now where the city once stood. I'll be glad to offer Jack's heart to the Raven."

"I trust that's metaphor."

"I'm to be his queen," Rosa replied. "He's given me an army of revenants as dowry. A heart is a small enough price to pay."

Her heart, or Jack's? Viktor fought a growing sense of unreality. These days, the world held more surprise than certainty. "You may find it beyond reach. Jack keeps his heart well hidden, or so fable claims."

She looked up, eyes swimming with anger and loss. "Then I'll have his head, and that of the shadowthorn princessa alongside."

He stared, the map forgotten. This wasn't the woman he remembered. That Rosa had been driven, certainly. Angry, often. But the combination of wrath and distance belonged to a stranger.

"Rosa . . . What happened to you?"

Her glare shattered. Her shoulders sank. "The Hadari killed her. They poisoned me, and she died in my place."

"Killed who?"

"Sevaka."

Tone and expression spoke of a loss beyond friendship. Twin to his own, and red raw. "Sevaka? I didn't know."

She snorted. "How would you? You've been living on a hillside."

Living a lie, while those he called friend moved on in joy and sorrow. How selfish he'd been. "I'm so sorry, Rosa."

"Don't be. I've for ever to repay my sorrows." Her tone hardened, the glare back in place. "I will make the Empire a land of widows and orphans. I'll choke the mists of Otherworld with their filthy souls, and still it will only be the start."

She'd always been a creature of contradictory extremes. Guarded with her emotions, but generous with her heart. Endlessly selfless and unflinchingly proud. Merciless and kind. The strongest woman he knew, and yet the most vulnerable. In his absence, those extremes had grown pronounced. They transcended grief and mocked his selfishness for leaving, when he'd known that his friend bore a burden similar in shape to his own, if divergent in detail. Even at Tarona, he'd heard tales of the woman who could not die. He'd seen some of it for himself during the unrest of the year before.

"Rosa . . ." He drew closer. "This isn't you."

She laughed without joy. "But it *is*. A Pale Queen for the Raven King."

Viktor looked again on her pallid cheeks, her greying hair. Had grief made her thus? The poison? Or was it the Raven's doing? "Is it what you want?"

"Sevaka is dead. What else is there?"

"Life is about more than the dead. It has to be." He felt a hypocrite for saying so, given all that had led him to Selnweald. "We're soldiers, Rosa. We fight to protect those who cannot, not in service of hatred or revenge."

Again the bitter laugh. "This is the wisdom of the great Droshna, whose shadow moves an Empire to war?"

"I'm sorry?"

"That's what the princessa called you. A Droshna. A man-of-shadow. A vessel of the Dark who corrupts the Republic. All an excuse for hatred. Why should I not meet it with my own?"

Viktor fell silent at his own fears reflected. So Melanna Saranal had beheld the same future he'd feared? A new age of Dark. Was this war his fault? No. A man was responsible only for his deeds, or their lack. And his lack offered guilt enough. Empire and Republic had warred long before his birth, and would surely do so after his death.

"She's right. I am Droshna, Malatriant's heir. I hid on my hillside as much as anything else because I worried that would define me, but it doesn't have to, Rosa. No more than Sevaka's death need define you." He took her hand, the fingers cold beneath his. "What we choose matters."

She shook her head. "You really believe that?"

"I have to."

Her gaze softened. "Can you bring her back?"

Viktor's throat soured. "What do you mean?"

She stared up at him, voice and body quivering. "Sevaka. Malatriant reached beyond death. You say you're Malatriant's heir. Can you?"

Heartsick, he closed his eyes. "She's gone, Rosa." Even as Viktor spoke, he wasn't certain if he spoke of Sevaka, or Calenne. "There's nothing I can do for the dead that will not bring more misery. But the living? Those, I can help. We both can. Fight to protect, and perhaps there's still hope for you. Perhaps there's still hope for us both."

She pulled away. "That's the difference between us, Viktor. I don't care."

"You're still Essamere. You swore the Vigil Oath, a shield first and a sword second."

"That woman succumbed to shadowthorn poison. She's dead."

"Then the last of Sevaka died with her." He searched her eyes for some sign, some glimpse of the Rosa he remembered. But if it was there, grief buried it too deep. And dear to him though Rosa was, she remained but a single soul where thousands were now his concern. "Will you introduce me to my officers?"

She scowled, relief just visible beneath the disdain. "Yes, Lord Akadra."

No one challenged Zephan Tanor as he made his way along the outer defence lines. Few sentries even acknowledged his existence. If they did that, then they might also have to acknowledge the smoky shapes lurking in the mists. Better to cling close to the fires, and tell yourself that all was a nightmare. The revenants had come with dusk, without explanation and – so far – without any obvious intent. High Proctor Ilnarov had said to leave them be, and that suited Zephan just fine.

The porch lanterns of the Traitor's Pyre cast a diffuse blaze, the coaching tavern's crooked outbuildings a witch's claw reaching through the mist. Govanna lay a mile further on, the emptied buildings pressed to billets for the knights and officers of Izack's thin army. Izack had seized the tavern itself, claiming he'd a powerful thirst on the rise.

The Traitor's Pyre had been a hive of activity since before noon, with a veritable army of heralds, squires and village children who'd take a coin hurrying back and forth with orders for the army assembled to the east.

One such child burst through the door as Zephan approached, a folded scrap of paper in one hand, and a brass farthing in the other. Zephan caught the door on the backswing, shot a filthy glance at the jangling bell, and passed inside.

"Ah, Tanor! There you are. Wondered where you'd got to." Izack beckoned him over to the web of map- and parchment-strewn tables he'd arranged about the hearth. "Cold out? You're shaking like a leaf."

Zephan winced. "The mist makes everything worse."

"Here, get this down you." Izack pressed a glass of brandy into his hand. "Is the *Dauntless* in position?"

The brandy's fire did nothing to touch the cold winnowed into his soul. "Captain Kesriel has his anchors laid, but he said to remind you that a galleon makes for an easy target if it's not moving."

Kesriel had said more than that. He'd wanted to sail downriver with the wounded, and had pressed the point loudly. But the spectre of Izack's wrath had quashed all argument.

Izack waved the objection away. "Better the shadowthorns are chucking rocks at him than at the rest of us. It's the closest we've got to a fortification, so it'll have to do."

In point of fact, the *Dauntless* was a good sight better than a fortification, moored as it was broadside-on to the Silverway's southern bank. With twenty ballistae across three decks – to say nothing of the pavissionaires ferried out by longboat earlier that afternoon – it would tear any riverward advance to shreds ... at least until enemy catapults found their range.

It made for an unconventional defence, but unconventional was the watchword. The army had infantry enough but after the disaster at the Rappadan, lacked for cavalry. Together, Prydonis and Essamere mustered fewer than five hundred knights – not enough to challenge the Emperor's cataphracts. Thus Kraikons had laboured until the mists had rushed in, tirelessly digging flooded ditches to stall enemy cavalry. Meanwhile, flesh-and-blood soldiers had felled trees and stripped outbuildings to fashion barricades and sharpened stakes concealed in the thick grass of the meadowlands.

Conservative estimates from Major Gandav's wayfarers counted three shadowthorns for every man and woman mustered in the meadowlands. But Tressia's defences were too far to reach in time. When the choices were to stand and fight, or be run to ruin, you fought. Better to face them rested.

"Did you happen to see the high proctor?" said Izack, without looking up from the map.

"Not since the kraikons went dark."

"Lazy lump's probably having a nap, and good for him. Tomorrow'll be a long day. Bloody one, too. All being equal, I'd rather have Elzar's little pets at our side than the Raven's, but we are where we are." He glanced up. "Can I prevail on you for another little jaunt?"

"Of course, master."

"Torvan Mannor's preening about a mile south of here. You'll find him easily enough. The Prydonis will be singing their dirges, cheerless bunch. Tell him that if he sees our banner go forward I'll expect him to do the same. Even a coward like Mannor has one good fight in him."

He said the last jovially enough, but Zephan resolved to phrase the request otherwise. Everyone in both chapterhouses knew Izack and Mannor had been friends for years, but that seldom helped those who ended up caught between them.

"I'll take another brandy before I go."

Izack grinned. "Good lad. You're learning."

"I still say we wait. The men are tired. Why chance victory on weary shoulders?" Devren's eyes proclaimed unease at the words' impertinence, caring nothing that they were true. He'd never have spoken thus in the open air – only the tent's confines gave him courage.

And he was right, Kai allowed. The men *were* tired, the army driven to its limits by headlong advance. Added to the hundreds lost at Ahrad and the thousands along the Rappadan were those bled away by desperate bands of Tressian soldiers cut off from the retreat, or civilians gathered to valour at the sight of a homeland invaded. On top of that were garrisons established at Tregga, Vrasdavora and a score of lesser places, charged with keeping order in the conquered land, the escorts for the provisioneer trains reaching back across the border and the sizeable blockade force holding back Chapterhouse Sartorov and the garrison of Fathom Rock. Of the seventy thousands who'd crossed the border, no more than thirty-five remained beneath his banner.

And just two leagues downriver, the Tressians assembled a force a fraction of his own. Their last hope before the walls of the city, and walls alone were worthless without men to hold them.

He glanced around the table. Prince Maradan maintained a stoic, collected silence and had done ever since a knight's lance had plucked his father from the saddle at Tregga; his brother remained in the care of the lunassera while artisans laboured to weave a bindwork arm to replace one lost to a simarka's bite. Neither King Raeth nor Prince Cardivan met his gaze, but nor did they speak in Devren's support. Haldrane and Elspeth offered no comment, but in a wholly different way to Kai's peers. Their support, at least, he could count on.

"The Icansae stand ready, my Emperor." Aelia favoured each of her peers with a stare. "The Tressians look to the east and see their doom. Give me firm ground and faithful swords, and I'll forget my weariness, as will we all."

Kai grunted. Icansae pledged to support a Saran? Madness. But then what else was there in the world of late? "How long would you have me wait, old friend?"

Devren's cheek twitched. "Two days, my Emperor. What difference can two days make?"

What difference indeed? Haldrane had whispered of an uprising within the city of Tressia itself and forces thinned to breaking point. Every company of soldiers the Council scrounged from some distant garrison, Kai could match as the wounded recovered.

But what use victory if it came after he was already dead? "A few days" Elspeth had said, and one of those was already spent. Did he have even two days remaining to him? How long before he could no longer fight? If Melanna had been there to continue the campaign, it might have been different. Now his daughter's crown was the gamble, and the lives of his men the stake. Just thinking it lent squalor to glory, but what else was there?

"We attack at dawn," said Kai. "The Goddess is with us. Lord Jack is with us. What is a little weariness compared to that?"

Heads nodded around the table, the lie of Ashana's favour unquestioned. Elspeth could have gainsaid, but did not.

One by one, the warleaders filed away until only Haldrane and Elspeth remained.

"Your pardon, *savir*." Haldrane's voice didn't quite mirror the words' respect. "But is it your intention to replace all your advisors with women?"

Elspeth scowled. "Are we jealous? I could geld you. That would bring you halfway there."

Kai leaned across the table and favoured Haldrane with an

unwavering stare. "If they're apt to it. I meant what I said. Tradition is a guide to the past, it should not rule our present."

"And our future?"

Kai rose, knuckles braced against the table to steady a wave of dizziness. "Will be for Melanna to decide. Tomorrow, I secure her throne. After that . . . After that, I don't know that it matters. Now, if you'll excuse me, the air in here has grown rather stale."

Elspeth's brow flickered. "Should I come with you?"

He waved her back. "I need the wind on my face, that's all."

Kai wandered without purpose through the lanes of tents and fires, four Immortals following at respectful distance. The air *did* help his dizziness, though it was hardly fresh. No air could be sweet in an encampment the size of a small city, and it would only get staler still. But for all that, he didn't mind. Such places were more his home than the palace in Tregard, or the villa in Kinholt. The sights, the smells – memories of good times and bad. The greatest victories, and the humiliation of defeat. A warrior's life, and he'd lived it well. One last victory to open wide the Republic's gates, and it would be done. A man who lived five-score years could not achieve more.

So why did he resent it?

Melanna. It always came back to Melanna, and the fear that she was right. That the war of men was becoming one of gods, and that his every action accelerated matters. That the angry words of their parting were to be the last he'd have of her, or she of him.

Perhaps he should have told her the truth, while the chance had been there.

Lungs heaving, Kai crested the hill that marked the encampment's eastern extent and passed beyond the ghostfires. In the distance, the crumbled spires of Tarvallion stood jagged against the dusk. Too distant to make out the briars and ivy that had overtaken the city, though he saw them plainly enough in memory. He saw too the Tressians who'd been too slow to flee, black roots wound thick about their bodies and glistening red with the feast. That, he'd as soon forget.

Jack hunched out of the gathering dark, a strawjack lurching at each shoulder. There'd be more, out in the woodland gloom. How many more, Kai had never ascertained. Waving for his bodyguard to stay back, Kai held his nerve as the other drew down, and told himself that the Goddess' sword would protect him, had he the need.

Certainty lasted until the strawjack's stench reached him. Rotting flesh and fresh sap. A glint of gold beneath the wended fronds of one, and a swathe of bloodied king's blue bound tight within the other. The dead reborn in divine service. And not only the dead. He'd seen the straggling columns of men and women led into Starik Wood on clouds of thornmaiden pollen. Was that the fate Jack intended for him? A puppet dancing on vines? His soul trapped in bonds of briar, never to know Evermoon's grace?

What manner of man was he to accept such allies?

{{Tomorrow, you will have your triumph,}} crackled Jack. {{Soon after, your bargain falls due.}}

"My future?" Kai coughed away a waft of sickly sweet sap. "I wish you the joy of it."

{{I anticipate nothing but.}} He leaned closer, stooped shoulders bringing the smooth mask level with Kai's face. {{You are in need of respite? You sound like a clock winding down. Tick. Tick. Tick.}}

"I will have my victory. That's all that matters."

{{Yes. A victory. A coronation. My brother bested at his own game. A day of days.}} The sap scent thickened with Jack's laughter, the ragged hood bobbing and swaying in an invisible wind. {{There will be roses for everyone. My queen will insist, and I . . . I will be pleased to grant the favour. You will see.}}

Kai tried to picture what horror might take Jack as husband, and decided he'd as soon as not find out. "I suspect I should be glad not to."

{{Yes.}}

Skin prickling, Kai turned his back and stared out across the encampment. Far to the west, mist hung heavy on Govanna's fields.

One more day. A throne secured through victory, and a god's bargain cheated through death.

Fifty-Six

Otherworld shimmered, a hollow mirage beneath viridian skies. Tattered market canopies rose like islands out of the mist, the etravia drifting between them, patrons even in death. Beyond, a stone wall, higher than anything Kurkas had seen, and a vast fortress staring out into the fields beyond. The city with the defences it needed. Something he'd longed to see, now made real as Otherworld shifted to match his perception.

Kurkas had glimpsed living souls only once. He'd almost called out to them – would have done, but for instinct. The Tressian woman had looked almost familiar, somehow, with her dark ringlets and sweeping skirts, but her companions had been Hadari, and all three of them in furtive manner and peculiar garb. More than enough to provoke distrust. And so Kurkas had hidden until they'd passed on their own unknowable errand, and spent every moment since regretting that he'd not asked the phantasms for aid, and chanced the consequence.

He staggered to a halt and set Apara against an empty stall. Etravia gazed disinterestedly and drifted on. "Which way? Come on, lass. Can't do this without you."

Apara offered no answer save for fitful breathing. Too much blood in all the wrong places, despite his attempts at binding her up. Too little time and no chances left. She'd been a dead weight for longer than Kurkas cared to think on, the point when "dead weight" became simply "dead" drawing nearer all the time. Bad enough all by itself, but he'd no notion how to find one of her "weak points", much less open it up.

He could keep walking, of course, but what was the point?

"Just my bloody luck."

Wasn't true, of course. He'd had plenty of luck, even in the last few days. But sooner or later, fortune failed and you paid your dues. A prizrak's distant weeping reminded of payment's form. Would he even notice as the mists hollowed him out? Would he know enough to fight the hunger as it turned to madness?

Kurkas fought back self-pity. Sidara. Constans. Altiris. They needed him. But his limits lay well behind. Everything now was hope and baling twine. You put your faith in what you had. He was in Otherworld, right? Closer to the Raven than ever. Give him a coin and he'll hear you.

He fished a battered silver shilling from his pocket and pressed it to his lips.

"We're not exactly on closest terms, you and me." His cheeks warmed with ridicule, but there was something else there too. A frisson of fear that it might actually work. It might be better to be ignored. "But I've sent my share of folk your way. And I was born vranakin, for whatever that counts. So help out, would you? My old dad claimed you were the last friend a fellow could seek, and I've nowhere else to turn."

He tossed the coin into the mists. Heard it strike stone and roll away. Heartbeats crept by. Kurkas felt them go, their heaviness a reminder of the years the mists had taken from him in recent days. He chided himself for falling back on superstition. But what else was there? Nothing.

As the seconds passed, it became apparent that nothing was to be his reward. No dark shape in the mists. No beckoning hand. No flutter of wings. Not even the rising weep of a prizrak, come to end his troubles.

With a sigh, he gathered Apara back onto his shoulder. "So much for that. Walking blind, it is."

It was then that he realised one of the etravia was watching him, hand extended in beckon. She stood a short distance off, the vapour of her apparition's form twitching as the motion of her peers drew it away, the unreal cloth of a phoenix tabard fluttering on unseen breeze. She was more solid than the others, more form and less vapour. Recognition came slowly, hampered by colour washed away to greenish-white.

"Halvor? Revekah Halvor?"

The etravia turned away without reply and vanished into the street opposite the one Kurkas had thought to take. An emissary from the

Raven, guiding him home? An illusion conjured by desperate longing? Whatever. Some hope was better than none at all.

Taking a deep breath, Kurkas staggered off in pursuit.

"Apara? Apara! Stir yourself, will you?"

Apara's nightmares yielded to mist, and vicious pain edged with numbness. Was she dead? Did the dead feel pain, or just its memory?

A one-eyed shadow loomed over her. A filthy hand patted her cheek. "Made crow-born tougher in my day. Knife in the ribs was our way of saying good morning."

She knocked Kurkas' hand aside with her own left. The right was too numb to obey. Surroundings eased into focus. A vaulted roof, green skies blazing through broken spans. Walls thick with cobwebs and tellers' desks. And something glimpsed with an inner eye less tired than the outer. Beyond the cracked flagstones and the desiccated roots, a door of light and shadow, masked by sculpted timber. A way through.

"How ... did you find ... this?" she gasped.

He shrugged. "Had help, didn't I? Best shilling I ever spent." Joviality hardened. "Can you get us out of here?"

Hope burned away numbness. "Help me stand."

Every step set daggers stabbing at Apara's side, made every breath a wet rasp. Her right hand refused response as she reached the door, but her left conformed. Mists recoiled as she set her palm to the door, her faltering will rousing light to overcome shadow.

A final push, and the door bled from sight. Off-balance, she stumbled into the woken void. Kurkas grabbed her, held her upright.

"I've got you." He eyed the mists beyond the door, indistinguishable from those in which they stood. But the sky was the black of night, and not Otherworld's lurid green. "We just walk through?"

Apara nodded, too tired to speak.

A lurch, a stride, and they were through into the cold air of the high harbourside. Released from her grip, she felt the doorway fade. When she glanced behind, it was gone – crumbling red brick beneath a bowed wooden lintel. Away down the street, pale blue ghostfires danced from lamp post and sill.

"Right," said Kurkas, his voice full of sudden vigour. "I walked in endless bloody circles last time. This is your territory. Where can we get you some help?"

Apara nodded towards the nearest alley. "Through there ... Marketplace ... Shrine."

A kernclaw's screech echoed above. Daggers renewed their attention on Apara's ribs as Kurkas propped her against brick. "I'll take a gander first. We're neither of us in a state to run. Don't die on me."

Then he was gone, lost to the mists. Sounds rose to replace him. The dull thump of fist on flesh. A girl's wail. A chorus of youthful, jeering voices.

A second cry, and Apara stumbled towards the sound. Rationale became increasingly difficult through the pain. She felt only a need, a desire beyond question, that she not stand by. She'd stood by too often. If moments were seeping past, better to make them count.

The gang's ringleader paled as she rounded the corner, his meaty face frozen in horror.

"Prizrak!" shrieked a girl already scrambling away.

Not an unfair assumption, Apara supposed, bloody and filthy as she was. And fortunate. A gang of aspirant rassophores were more than her match.

The rest scattered, all save their erstwhile victim, weeping face-down in the gutter. Breath rasping, Apara helped her up. Stared into a young face harrowed by hunger and dread, bruises already forming beneath smeared silt. Just another dregrat. Even with the Crowmarket on the rise, there were those down in the mud. Always would be.

"You're not cut out for this," said Apara. "Leave while you can."

The girl scrambled away and vanished into the mists. Apara stared after, frozen by old memories. Those words. The same she'd heard as a girl. The warning she'd ignored. *Her* warning? She stuttered a pained laugh. The arrogance of ignoring an elder's advice was bad enough, but when that elder was yourself ... ?

"Oi!" Kurkas appeared at her shoulder. "Raven's Eyes, but you wander good for someone with one foot in the ... Well, you know. What's going on?"

Apara stared after the girl who might have been herself. Had she even existed? A trick of a weary mind, or a piece of the past come unmoored in the mists? Pain receded behind numbness. "Nothing . . . that matters."

He slipped his arm beneath hers. "Come on. The way's clear. Let's get you inside."

She clung to consciousness as Kurkas half-carried, half-dragged her along the alley and across the empty marketplace. Down the old stairs that belonged to another life. When she'd still been the Silver Owl. A broker and a thief, not a murderer.

"Ain't no one about," said Kurkas. "Not that I saw."

It had always been a slim hope. The shrine's keeper was likely taking advantage of the city's disorder. But at least she could rest. Apara gestured beneath the broken rafters to the stairs. "Cellar."

"All right," he replied, the words muffled. "I've got you."

She came to lying sideways on the bed, the lantern-lit cellar fuzzy to weary eyes. Where it had all gone wrong. Where she'd been given to the Raven. Full circle.

You're not cut out for this. Leave while you can. If only she'd listened to the woman . . .

To herself?

Kurkas – a dark, uncomfortable presence at the end of the bed – coughed. "No easy way to say this, but I've done all I can. Those kids . . . They come first. You understand?"

Apara swallowed. Was there anything more pathetic than a wasted life? "Go," she gasped.

He drew closer. His hand found hers. "You did good."

The far wall fell away into mist. Apara's heart fluttered in fear. A thin cry parted dry lips. The Raven was coming to claim her. The bargain falling due as her life faded.

Kurkas spun around, hand reaching for a scabbarded sword he didn't possess. A growl of defiance gave way to an awestruck stutter.

"I don't bloody believe it."

The blonde woman strode into the cellar, the mists of the gateway clinging to her shimmering skirts. Kurkas moved to bar her path and subsided, mouth agape, as her eyes met his. It wasn't so much the eyes themselves that gave him pause, but the years behind them – the sense of a billowing, divine presence unfolding from an ephemeral form perhaps half his age. She perched on the bed beside Apara and took her hand.

"This is her?"

"It is." Lord Trelan cast a suspicious eye about the cellar, only relaxing when his gaze settled on Kurkas. His expression soured as he looked upon Apara. "Doesn't look like she'll be much use to you."

"Don't question my mother," said the Hadari woman at his side. A face from the past, before fire had devoured darkness. The princessa.

Kurkas at last found his tongue. "Might've know you were part of this, shadowthorn. Always trouble when you show your face."

He started forward. Shadow shifted behind the princessa, coiling into the form of an antlered knight.

It growled.

Kurkas glared back and tried to forget that the other was a good head taller than he. "And you can shut your bloody trap, too."

The knight stepped forward.

"Captain, please." Lord Trelan took Kurkas by the arm and led him to the corner of the room. "I can see you're not having the best of days, but a little decorum wouldn't hurt."

From the look of things, Lord Trelan wasn't having the best day himself. Not a mark on him, not until you paid heed to his expression. Worries deep behind the eyes, seeking the escape of tears. For all that Lord Trelan often appeared thus – hard head and a soft heart never made an easy life – this was worse.

"Last I heard," said Kurkas, "we were at war with shadowthorns, and their heathen gods were stomping us flat. That all done with, is it?" Tiredness and heartache made the question a challenge.

The antlered knight growled. The princessa levelled an unfriendly stare. Lord Trelan glanced away. "It's complicated."

Kurkas sank against the wall, dislodging a chunk of musty plaster. "Ain't it always? Been a bugger of a week, sah. The vranakin have half the city. Lady Reveque's dead. And . . . they took the kids. Sidara and her brother. Her to bury alive, and him to keep her quiet while they do it. Altiris went after them . . . couldn't stop him." He hung his head. "Sorry, sah. Babbling."

Lord Trelan nodded. "What about Malachi? Ana?"

"Don't know about Lord Reveque. The vranakin burned Abbeyfields with us all inside, so at best he reckons his kids are in the mists along with his wife. As for the plant pot . . . " He hesitated. "She didn't make it out either. The whole bloody building came down on her."

To his amazement, Lord Trelan offered a grim smile. "Is that all? She'll be furious."

Kurkas stared. Were the other's wits as astray as his taste in company? "Did you not hear me?"

"I've stopped underestimating Ana." The smile faded. "Right now, we all need a little hope. Put yours where you will. I'm entrusting mine to her until I've reason to do otherwise."

Hope. Belatedly, Kurkas remembered why Lord Trelan had left in the first place. "Lord Akadra not with you?"

"Viktor has his battle to fight." He shot a glance at the princessa. "So do they. The Crowmarket is mine. Ours, if you're up to it."

Was it the challenge of the words, or the sympathy of the tone? Kurkas wasn't sure. But he found the strength to stand straight again, even to offer a salute. "Always. Just you and me?"

"If need be. But it won't come to that. One is a man alone. Two are a beginning."

Kurkas squinted. "You sure Lord Akadra's not coming? Because that's the kind of rot he comes out with."

"I'll settle for half Viktor's success." The grim smile returned. "We've a city to take back. Or are you too busy?"

For that manner of work? Never. And yet . . .

Kurkas glanced at Apara, lying motionless beside the woman in the shimmering dress. "What about the crow-born? She came good in the end. Deserves better than this."

Lord Trelan's lip twisted. He shared a glance with the princessa. "That's up to her."

Apara stood alone in a darkened room, no sound save for the deep, fitful pulse of a drum. She stepped forward, bare feet on polished wood, and a black skirt moulting bloody feathers behind.

"Is it that time already?" A lantern flickered to life, casting dizzying reflections across a polished marble hearth, yet the outskirts of the room remained lost to darkness. The Raven stood at the mantelpiece, elbow against the wall. "Barely a blink, and you're done."

The fear that had haunted Apara's waking moments melted away, lost in the trail of bloody feathers. Fear required hope, and hers was spent. Or perhaps fear was a thing of the body, and not the unmoored soul.

Another step. Another rush of feathers. The Raven extended a gloved hand.

Apara reached out.

"You don't have to go with him."

Darkness rushed from the adjoining corner. Plaster shrivelled and cracked beneath alabaster flame. The fire subsided, until only light remained. Light, and a woman whose gown shimmered like stars.

"Still meddling, Ashana?" the Raven asked languidly. "That'll end badly, sooner or later. This little bird was bargained to me."

Ashana ignored him. Her gaze met Apara's. "He owns only a piece of you. The rest is his only if you die. I can keep you from the mists, if you'll let me, but I'll need something in exchange."

Apara struggled to make sense of thick and syrupy thoughts. "My soul?"

The Goddess smiled as if at some private joke. "A thief."

Apara's heart leapt. A thief. The life she'd loved, before her cousins had stolen it away. A chance to reclaim what she'd squandered. "Don't let him take me. I'll steal whatever you want."

"Oh really, this is pathetic." The lantern flickered out, and the Raven was gone.

Walls fell away. A wind struck up, swirling befouled feathers beneath night-darkened trees. Apara's skin prickled as Ashana's arms closed about her, the embrace soft, welcoming. Then the trees too faded away, until Apara saw nothing but the Goddess' light.

"What do you want, little bird?"

Desire found voice. "To fly free of mist and shadow. To be the Silver Owl again."

The Goddess kissed her brow. "Then cling to that as the darkness takes you. Make it truth."

Then Ashana was gone, and Apara left alone as darkness seeped into her skin, her flesh – into even her thoughts. Through it all, she held the dream of the Silver Owl close, and made it truth.

Constable Kressick's feet hurt. He knew that made him selfish for caring about such things. So many had it worse. His colleagues from the King's Gate watch house marched off into the mists, never to return. The folk trapped in Abbeyfields while the fires took hold. First Councillor Reveque, with his family burned alive and his home a smouldering ruin. The poor sods of the army, vying with shadowthorns out in the east. By contrast, patrolling the Abbeyfields grounds was light duty, even with the possibility of vranakin lurking beneath the trees.

Of the house itself, nothing remained save for fire-blackened brick walls, and a pile of charred rubble – fruits of long and arduous labours by the district's douser brigade.

Maybe the patrol was about respect, as Lieutenant Raldan had suggested, keeping the scavengers off the slimmest of pickings. Maybe it was just the lieutenant sucking up to the Council. All Kressick knew was that his feet hurt, and that shift end was long since over.

A clatter sounded off in the darkness towards the house. Kressick turned. His lantern's light bathed the scorched rubble. "Hold! Who's there?"

No reply. Just the grind and scrape of shifting debris. Like footsteps, except there was no sign of anyone to have left them.

"I'm warning you! One chime of this bell, and there'll be a dozen others here, fit for a fight!"

A lie, as there were only five others on the grounds. One constable, and four Reveque hearthguards – for whatever they were worth. Still, Kressick slipped the bell from his belt and the wool muffler from the clapper. Six was better than none. Especially if it was vranakin come looking for trouble.

Rubble erupted. Brick and timber fragments spilled upwards and outwards, accompanied by a cascade of ash and glinting embers. And beneath the screech and scrape of the building's wretched corpse, a wordless, hollow cry that set Kressick's bones itching.

He stumbled back, coughing as ash clogged his lungs. When he righted himself, a silhouette stood knee-deep in the rubble. Lantern light set gold gleaming beneath smeared ash. What few scraps of cloth remained would have left nothing to the imagination, had they anything more than the most abstract of womanly curves to conceal.

As Kressick watched agape, she pulled one leg free of the rubble. Then the other. She stared down at her hands, at golden light guttering fingertip to fingertip. Pale fingers flexed about dark joints. They clattered across a porcelain skull, and brushed away a wig's stubble. Where they passed, a coiling mane of golden fire flowed into being.

[[Better.]]

Only then did she realise she wasn't alone. Black eyes burned into Kressick's, welling with all the anger her beatific, expressionless face concealed.

[[You. Pervert. I want clothes, armour and a sword.]]

She crunched down through rubble, implacable as an avalanche. Kressick forgot his sore feet, and fainted dead away.

Astridas, 9th Day of Wealdrust

When divinities war, there are no victors.

from Eldor Shalamoh's "Historica"

Fifty-Seven

Altiris nearly died three times since parting company with Kurkas. The first came when he slipped through the closing gateway between Otherworld and Dregmeet. He emerged into what passed for the ephemeral world on an elder cousin's tattered heels. Only a head-long dive behind a silt-clogged fountain saved him. Shoulders hunched against mossy stone and breath held close, he waited an age before the cousins and their prisoners drifted away.

The second occasion came as he followed them through the mists. Desperate not to let Sidara and her captors slip from sight, he was blind to the footpad at the alley mouth. A whisper of sound was Altiris' saviour. That, and instincts honed as a curfew-breaker on Selann. A thrust from his borrowed sword left the vranakin dead in the gutter. The fellow's tattered mask and hooded cloak did nothing to keep out the mists' cold, but offered concealment's false courage.

And as he entered the plaza beneath the Church of Tithes, Altiris Czaron almost died a third time. Not from an elder cousin's grasp, nor a vranakin blade, but from sheer, stark terror.

From the decaying churchyard to the lopsided eaves of adjoining streets, the plaza was thick with vranakin. A wagon shrouded in black cloth waited at the lychgate, sable ribbons twitching like snakes in the poor breeze. Another waited behind the hearse, its iron cage empty. At the plaza's heart, beside the rotting angel fountain, two cadaverous forms in gold-chased grey robes waited in an inky ring of kernclaws. The pontiffs. Like enough to the black-eyed man Captain Darrow had slain for Altiris to keep his gaze averted and pray not to be noticed.

The crowd swelled around Altiris, fed by the tributaries of Dregmeet's alleys. He froze, muscles rigid and throat thick with panic. Dreams of rescue died ashen. Better to run. Better still to have stayed with Kurkas. A boy playing at hero, and for what? Notions of duty? Of friendship? Neither held sway in Dregmeet.

Hawkin strode through the crowd, Constans at her side and head held high. Elder cousins drifted behind, Sidara an unsteady presence in their midst.

"See, the daughter of our esteemed First Councillor Reveque!" shouted one of the pontiffs. "A child of light who brought low Crowfather Athariss. Does she fill you with fear?"

Jeers broke out, edged with mock bird-screeches. Filth flung from gutter and gulley spattered Sidara's face and clothes. Still she staggered on, eyes ahead and face set, unflinching even when the procession halted before the fountain, and the taller of the pontiffs set knuckle beneath chin to tilt back her head.

"Rejoice, child. For you are to be Athariss' bride of the grave. To serve him as he serves the Raven, in a place where sunlight has no claim."

Sidara jerked her head free. "Do as you want with me. You can drag the city down into the mists. It won't change what you are." Her tone sharpened, the daughter's voice become an echo of her mother's, despite its weariness. "A king in the gutter is no king at all."

The pontiff snarled. The back of his withered hand drove Sidara to her knees.

"No!" Breaking free of Hawkin's grip, Constans stood between his sister and her tormentor. "Leave her alone!"

The crowd's mirth redoubled.

"Hawkin, control the whelp," snapped the second pontiff.

Expression taut, she dragged Constans away. The first pontiff's hand closed around Sidara's arm. "Come, my Lady Reveque. Your carriage awaits."

Turning, he dragged her towards the caged wagon. The hearse rumbled off as soon as the iron door slammed. And Altiris, shamed by the composure of the siblings Reveque, found courage beneath his fear. As the crowd flowed to join the cortege, so did he.

*

Malachi's bleak dreams parted to bleaker reality. Loss was a distant ache, a rumble felt in the pit of heart and gut; deep, hollow and yet unreal.

So many times in the night, he'd sworn he'd heard Lily's voice, only to stutter awake with her name on his lips, and the council chamber's darkness his only companion. She was gone, as Sidara and Constans were gone. He'd failed them, and for what? What was there left to cling to? The Republic besieged. The city swallowed up from within. His friends dead or missing. His honour bartered away. No one to blame but himself. For thinking he was equal to the task.

And Lily. Lily was lost. Their children were lost. His fault. All his fault.

Closing his eyes, he slumped back in the chair and begged for the mercy of sleep.

The faces of all those he'd failed rushed to greet him.

"Malachi?" Footsteps. The click of the door easing closed. "Malachi, are you awake?"

He creaked open his eyes. "Messela?"

"I'd hoped to give you more time, but ... " She halted at the end of the table, eyes dark-rimmed. "The vranakin are marching on the Hayadra Grove."

Bitter laughed welled up. "Trees? You're worried about a few trees?"

Her lips flickered disgust. Always further to fall. Trapped between anger and shame, Malachi stared at the table as she drew closer. "They're not 'just' trees, Malachi. They're our connection to the divine. A peace offering from Ashana to Lumestra. A symbol of hope. The city needs hope, now more than ever. We lose that, and it's over."

"It's already over. There's no one to send."

She gave an angry shake of the head. "There's Lancras. There's what remains of my hearthguard. We put out the call, others will come."

"A handful against Dregmeet? It's not enough." He leapt to his feet, chair crashing back against the floor. "How many more would you have me send to their deaths? How can you even ask?"

The room darkened as if beneath a passing cloud. Ice gathered at the windows.

"I'm not asking," snapped Messela. "This is what's going to happen."

"Then why disturb me? Just leave me alone."

"Because I thought ... " She swallowed. The shadow passed. When she spoke again, anger crackled beneath a veneer of calm. "Because I thought you deserved a chance to redeem your mistakes."

Malachi froze. She knew. Had he told her? Too much of recent days was lost behind the solace of liquor. Did it even matter what she knew? She was offering a chance to reclaim his pride. To honour the family whose name he alone now bore. Even to avenge them.

And fail, as he had so completely elsewhere?

Turning his back on Messela, he righted the chair and sat down. "Do as you wish. Leave me to my grief."

"Malachi—"

A fanfare rang out beyond the walls. Frowning, she turned for the door. It opened before she reached it, and Moldrov scurried into the room. The steward glanced hurriedly away from Malachi, his full attention offered to Messela.

"Lady, something's happening in the plaza."

If nothing else, the Vordal Tower scaffold offered excellent vantage. It had been a long time since Kurkas had seen the plaza so empty at dawn. Most days, it took a pair of pointy elbows and a bloody-minded attitude to make way without a carriage, but that morning? Between the war without and the war within, the stream of petitioners, merchants, soldiers and hangers-on had thinned almost to nothing. A few hundred folk were scattered beneath the fiery skies, scurrying about as if the end of the world were on their heels . . . which if Lord Trelan were right, might very well have been the case.

Kurkas still wasn't sure he believed the stakes, even though they'd been laid down by a goddess. That beyond the city walls, Jack o' Fellhallow and the Raven had joined the war. The Raven – weakened by the Crowmarket's grip on the mists – would surely fall, not only dooming the outnumbered Tressian army to slaughter, but the world to the fire and madness of a divine war. The only hope of stopping it lay in breaking the Crowmarket's grip on Otherworld, and even that wouldn't be the end.

Kurkas shook his head. Worrying about things he couldn't change wouldn't help anyone. The Crowmarket was his business, by blood and duty. Gods and the like? The shadowthorn princessa was welcome to all *that*.

Five storeys beneath the scaffold platform stood the assembled might of Chapterhouse Lancras, chivvied from lodgings an hour before at Lord Trelan's insistence, banners raised and trumpets sounded.

They were a sullen bunch, to Kurkas' eye. That's what happened when you took your name from the legend of a tragic hero, rather than a celebrated one. The best recruits went to Prydonis, Essamere or Sartorov, holders of noble tradition and storied victory. So the histories told, Lord Lancras had died overseas, fighting a war that couldn't be won in search of a victory no one needed. He'd lost, and for all their parade ground snap, his successors expected to lose.

And who save a glutton for punishment wore a *white* surcoat?

Kurkas allowed that his own feelings were colouring the matter. *One is a man alone. Two are a beginning.* Stirring words, but even with the Knights Lancras and the Stonecrest hearthguard mustered, they barely numbered a hundred. Enough for defiance, but not victory.

Planking creaked as Lord Trelan edged to the scaffold's extent. Every groan of timber set Kurkas' nerves jangling. How Lord Trelan managed, he couldn't conjure. The man's fear of heights was legend among his own hearthguard. But he understood symbols. To proclaim from the palace balcony was to do so as a member of the Council – a body marred by the failure of recent days. To do so from the Vordal Tower opposite? Especially when half the populace still held you an outcast, for good or for ill? Folk would listen to that.

The last fanfare faded.

"Citizens of Tressia . . . "

The plaza's acoustics gathered up Lord Trelan's words and returned them as echoes. A handful of passersby halted and craned their necks to investigate the commotion. Lord Trelan leaned further out over the varnished handrail and leaned hastily back in response to its creaked protest.

"Some of you know me, or think you do. I am Josiri Trelan, Duke of Eskavord. Southwealder. Wolf's-head. Upstart. Outcast. Troublemaker. Even traitor. I stand before you as none of those things. Not today. I stand before you as one who loves this city, and this Republic. As a man who has already lost one home, and refuses to lose another."

So much of that was lies. Kurkas knew for a fact that his master's love for the Republic wouldn't have filled a thimble. Never mind the city itself. But try as he might, Kurkas caught no dimming of passion, no tell-tale of a mistruth told. Nor, judging by the crowd slowly gathering beneath the scaffold, could any other.

"The vranakin are taking our city. They've claimed our streets. Our friends. Our family. Inch by inch, they're dragging us down. And we've let them! They took advantage of our greed. Our indolence. Our shame that they looked to the needs of the poor where we did not. I won't have it. Not in my city. Not in my home. Not while men and women fight to repel Hadari in the east. How do we face them on their return?"

He had their attention now, the plaza filling as word spread.

"We already tried!" shouted a man in constabulary blue. Lieutenant Raldan. "We were slaughtered! Where were you, Lord Trelan? Fled back to the Southshires is what I heard."

A rumble of agreement swept the crowd.

Lord Trelan gripped the handrail. "I had business in the south, it's true. It's done. I'm here now, and I will not let this stand."

"With what?" Raldan replied. "A hundred knights? The scrapings of the city's hearthguards? It's not enough."

"You're right, it's not. But this is a city of *thousands* in thrall to hundreds. Fifteen years of occupation, and my people never stopped fighting. Look at you! It's been *days*, and you're already beaten. Is Northwealder pride so weak?"

The rumble became a growl, fed by new voices. Whatever else the crowd lacked, pride wasn't in short supply. But Kurkas didn't care for the shifting mood. By making it a matter of north against south, Lord Trelan was as likely to raise an army against himself as the vranakin.

He stepped forward and lowered his mouth to Lord Trelan's ear. "Congratulations, sah. You've raised an angry mob in the heart of Tressia. Your mother'd be proud. How does it feel?"

"Strangely satisfying."

"Won't stay that way when they lynch us."

"Have faith, captain."

On the opposite side of the square, the palace gate creaked open. A double line of Swanholt hearthguard filed out, silver swans bright against black tabards. Lady Messela Akadra strode at their head.

"Hello," murmured Kurkas. "Something's happening."

"Looks so, doesn't it?"

"Wouldn't be keeping something from me, would you, sah?"

"Perish the thought."

The crowd parted as the Akadra hearthguard lined up opposite Lancras. Lady Akadra kept coming, skirting alabaster ranks until she reached the scaffold's ladder. Soon after, she stood on the platform, one alone who seemed oblivious to its creaking.

Lord Trelan bowed. "Messela. Any luck with Malachi?"

"I tried. He won't listen." She stared back at the palace's empty balcony. "You should have let me tell him."

He shook his head. "I've been where he is. He has to take the first step alone, or he's no good to anyone. This is what he needs."

"We should at least talk to Leonast. Maybe Evarn."

"At best, they'll seek advantage. At worst, they'll actively sabotage us."

Lady Akadra grimaced. "You really believe that?"

"I know we can't afford the time or the risk."

"I suppose you're right."

"We can only hope." He shrugged. "Lieutenant Raldan's playing his part well, isn't he?"

Raldan? Kurkas glared at Lord Trelan, torn between admiration and disgust. "So this is all a stitch-up?"

"Stitch-up. Politics. Theatrics. I like to think I've learned *something* this past year." A surge of disquiet drew his attention back to the crowd. "Speaking of which ... Lady Akadra, would you mind having a change of heart?"

She bobbed her head. "At your command, Lord Trelan." She turned again to the crowd and raised her voice. "Citizens ... "

Lord Trelan retreated from the scaffold's edge.

Kurkas blotted out Lady Akadra's voice and followed. "So in the small hours, when I was dragging Brass and the others out of bed, you set up all this?"

"Some of it." Lord Trelan sighed. "I don't like it, but they have to *want* to take a stand. I can order what soldiers we have into battle, but we need more than that. This city's lousy with old soldiers, coshmen, enforcers, sailors – folk who know their business when their back's against the wall.

So we show them all the reasons we can't win. Then we tell them that we can, and hope enough believe."

Lady Akadra fell silent, leaving the crowd subdued. A glance beyond the scaffold revealed why. The Swanholt hearthguard were no longer formed up in opposition to Lancras, but alongside. Even as Kurkas watched, a trickle of constabulary blue threaded through the crowd and joined the muster. One hundred became two. No longer alone, but a beginning.

"The vranakin mean to defile the Hayadra Grove," shouted Lord Trelan. "To sever our connection to Lumestra so that the mists swallow us all. A thousand swords, that's all I ask. It doesn't matter who you are. Today you fight for your home. *We* fight for our home."

The trickle of bodies became a flood. Two hundred became three, became four.

"A thousand of us went in last time. What's different?"

The challenge came not from Raldan – who, duty fulfilled, had taken his place in the growing muster – but from a Karov hearthguard captain. Thousands of eyes looked aloft to the scaffold, and Lord Trelan's hesitation became theirs.

Kurkas saw the problem at once. Theatrics aside, Lord Trelan was an honest soul and a poor liar. Much as he might want to, he couldn't claim this was anything more than a last, desperate throw of the dice. But seeing the problem and knowing its resolution were two very different dilemmas.

Amber skies turned gold.

[[Because this time, I'm coming with you.]]

Josiri stared skyward, as dumbstruck as the crowds by the figure silhouetted against the rising dawn. That he recognised Ana at once did nothing to dim his awe. Nor did it help that the armour she wore over scarlet gown had unmistakeably begun life in the Prydonis armoury, just as the fennlander's claymore strapped to her back was a close twin to Viktor's favoured weapon. Such mundane details couldn't distract from the golden wings that bore her aloft, nor flowing hair that crackled like fire.

For all that he'd glimpsed this side of her in the Westernport warehouse, that memory was a candle beside the sun. Save for the porcelain of her skin, she was again a serathi of legend, beautiful and grim, and terrible beyond words.

Below the scaffold, the crowd rippled as folk fell to their knees, objection swallowed by homage. A beat of golden wings sent Anastacia swooping a circle about the plaza. Skirts slit to the thigh and sleeves to the shoulder revealed steel beneath, and betrayed the gown as little more than a costume shaping romantic ideal, a fantasy in oils come to life. Hands reached skyward to greet her. Prayer became hymn.

Josiri watched it all, mouth agape. Theatrics? He didn't know the first thing.

"She must be bloody loving this," murmured Kurkas.

Josiri fought to contain an idiot grin, and yielded the battle. For all he'd striven to play the stalwart for Kurkas and the others, he'd been twisted by uncertainty. No longer. "I told you she'd be back."

"You also said she'd be angry, remember?"

"She's always angry."

"True."

Messela joined him at the scaffold's edge, her eyes wide and her hands clasped to her chest to hide the tremor. "I think you'll get your thousand swords now."

"Yes." What would Lilyana Reveque have said to see this?

One final circle, and Ana stepped lightly onto the scaffold. Even that small motion set the platform juddering. Josiri's heart – uncertain since he'd first set foot on the creaking timbers – quickened. Ana's wings faded as if they'd never been. Her golden hair remained – not fire, as Josiri had first thought, but sunlight. He went to speak, the arguments and insignificance forgotten in the joy of reunification, but the words wouldn't come.

[[Close your mouth, Josiri. Dignity is *so* important.]]

"I've missed you." The words did poor service to the feeling, but no others would serve.

[[Of course you have.]] She tilted her head. Gloved fingers brushed his cheek. [[It's good to see you. We *are* going after the children?]]

He nodded. "That's where it starts. It goes much deeper."

"Putting someone else first, plant pot?" said Kurkas.

[[I can always change my mind.]] The sardonic tone was familiar. The wistful note less so.

"Can you?" asked Josiri.

She shook her head. [[So much of this is my fault.]]

"Kurkas told me. You did everything you could."

[[That's not what I mean, I—]]

"Josiri." Messela pointed across the plaza to the palace balcony. "He's here."

He glanced behind and saw a dark figure against the white stone, the door open behind. Malachi. "Ana?"

Golden wings flickered back into life. Her arms looped beneath his. The crowd passed away below as a dizzying blur. Josiri pinched his eyes shut to soothe a twisted stomach and longed for the creaking scaffold. He opened them again just in time to avoid an ungainly drop onto the balcony.

"I'm never doing that again."

[[Yes, dear.]]

A beat of wings and she was gone, leaving Josiri alone with a friend who'd aged ten years in a single, short week. For all that he'd hoped to have this conversation, now it was upon him he didn't know where to begin. He should have foreseen this. He'd known Malachi had struck a deal with the Crowmarket to secure Ebigail Kiradin's downfall, but he'd been too wrapped up in his own concerns to see how deep into the mists the other had fallen – he should have at least *considered* the possibility. Perhaps he could have stopped it. Now all he could do was to pick up the pieces and strive to salvage what he could.

"Malachi . . ."

The other approached the balcony edge, his eyes fixed on crowds that paid him no heed. Mortal man couldn't compete with legend. "It's all gone, Josiri. I lectured you about responsibility and look what I've done. Look what it's cost me. All because I thought myself cleverer than I was."

"It's not over yet. I found Viktor, and . . . " He drew closer. "Sidara and Constans are *alive*, Malachi. The vranakin have them, but I swear to you I'll get them back."

He didn't believe. Not at first – Josiri read that much in his expression.

Too afraid it was some cruel joke. But the façade cracked, the first tears breaking through as he allowed himself to hope. "And Lily?"

"I'm sorry."

Malachi hung his head, resurgent joy in abeyance. "She should have run a mile the first time she heard my name."

"I doubt she'd agree." The other flinched as Josiri laid a hand on his shoulder. "Apara Rann saved your children. She said to tell you that she'd 'never have found her way back to the path' but for you. I don't know what she meant."

"It means I haven't entirely been a failure." He straightened, the first gleam of the man Josiri remembered showing beneath sorrow. His tone thickened with determination. "Messela was right. Hope is important."

"It's a start," said Josiri, embracing him. "Time to make an end of it."

Fifty-Eight

The muffled drums fell away. For the first time since dawn, silence ruled all. All along the overlapping barricades of mud and sharpened stakes, men and women stared east across the mist-draped meadowlands, searching for some clue as to what was to come.

Zephan Tanor stared with them, wishing the battle begun. The banner in his left hand was heavier than a lance, and its burden denied him a shield. But then, there were few enough lances and shields to go around. Few enough of anything, with so much abandoned in the retreat from the Rappadan.

Come dawn, the revenants had coalesced at the barricades and mud walls over the meadowlands' boundary, forming up in mimicry of ephemeral soldiers. It might have been reassuring had the cold of the grave not come with them. Worse were the reports of a stranger treading the outer defences during the night. Or more precisely, *two* strangers. One a man in tailcoated suit and battered hat, the other an old woman veiled for mourning. Sentries who'd challenged them awoke shivering, wracked with cold no fire could warm.

Twisting in his saddle, Zephan peered past the ranks of Essamere to the dark bulk of a kraikon, frozen in the act of scooping soil to a makeshift rampart ahead of the Traitor's Pyre's boundary wall. Kraikon or revenant, light or shadow. He longed for the former, but better to have horrifying allies than none at all. Especially if those allies numbered in the hundreds, as the revenants did.

To the north, the slab-sided silhouette of the *Dauntless* was more imagination than fact. Grandmaster Mannor's Knights Prydonis waited a half-mile to the south, their presence confirmed by a herald's missive barely minutes before. And in between, the overlapping barricades, manned by pavissionaires and halberdiers, by marines and proctors, by militia and farmers too tired or defiant to run.

"Buck up, Tanor," said Izack. "It's only the end of the world. No need to look glum."

"The end of the world, master?"

Izack swept an armoured gauntlet towards the column of revenant knights, formed up in mirror to the denuded Essamere formation – like them, an arrow aimed along the Govanna–Sirovo Road and into the heart of the expected shadowthorn advance. "Can't be much else when the dead are walking about, can it?"

"They're not the risen dead, master, but the Raven's servants."

He waved the objection aside. "Let 'em be what they want, so long as they hack the shadowthorns bloody. And you? Hold onto that banner. While it stands, so does Essamere. And while Essamere stands, so does the bloody Republic."

A swell of pride drove back fear, as Izack had surely meant it to do. "Yes, master."

"And the rest of you . . . " Izack rose up in his stirrups, his voice booming out over the barricades. "I don't care what brought you here, or what colours you wear. I don't give a provost's cuss if you took the silver shilling out of patriotism, out of hunger or to avoid the noose. Today, you're Essamere. You're damn well going to fight like it, or you'll answer to me."

A ragged cheer spread. Officers and sergeant bellowed for discipline. Shields locked tight.

"I don't know that Grandmaster Mannor will appreciate being recruited to Essamere," said Zephan, as Izack sank back into his saddle.

"Bugger Torvan." Izack spat into the mud. "Shouldn't have backed the wrong horse last year, should he?"

The thunder of the drums rolled anew from the east.

Drums crashed away. The third volley hissed westward towards Govanna, its arrows swallowed by mist. Kai shifted restlessly on his horse. Would the Tressians ever know that convention had been observed, or would the mist swallow sound as readily as sight? Did it even matter? The salute was tradition, a token of respect from an Emperor to his foes, and such gifts were seldom received in the spirit they were offered. Honour came from within. It accepted no other master save the self.

{{A waste of arrows,}} crackled Jack.

He lurked a short distance downhill, ragged robes clinging to his shoulders like part-moulted skin. The rest of Kai's entourage – Devren and Haldrane among them – kept a pointed distance. Elspeth regarded him with outright disgust.

Along the crest, golden cataphracts and silver lunassera surrendered to clinging mist. Banners sat limp in the stale air. Shieldsmen of Rhaled and Corvant massed behind, the Saran owl and the black tree of King Raeth joined by the badges of chiefs and headmen. Britonis mustered away to the north, where the valley floor fell away to the deep waters of the Silverway; Silsaria to the south, its left flank anchored on the eaves of Selnweald. Icansae, bloodied at Soraved and in all the days since, would come behind. Thirty-five thousand spears, marching as one along the valley.

And everywhere between, the unnerving, gangling forms of Jack's children, wiry strawjacks and lithe thornmaidens. Their crackling scratched at thought and spine.

Somewhere out in the murk, hidden in landscape rendered eerie and jumbled by Otherworld's echo, waited the outmarched Tressian army. Kai clung to the memories of dawn; Elspeth's touch, and the vigour it brought. One day more. That was all he needed. One day, and a victory to reshape the world.

"Arrows are worthless in this muck," murmured Devren. "Might as well spend them on salute."

Jack twisted about. {{You wish the mists gone?}} Gnarled fingers beckoned into the mists. {{Gwenhwyfar, attend me.}}

Arms spread, a thornmaiden dipped a curtsey. {{Father.}}

His hand brushed the crude clay of her face. {{You know what is to come?}}

{{Yes, Father.}} Her voice buzzed with breathy anticipation. {{Make me beautiful again.}}

Green buds bloomed across her shoulders and back, and among the black roses of her hair, until nary a dark petal gleamed among the white. Kai's head swam with the sweet scent of duskhazel. Gwenhwyfar turned a pirouette and pulled away, blossoms trailing behind. Elspeth's grimace deepened.

{{Oh Father. Whatever shall I give you in return?}} Gwenhwyfar spoke teasingly, as one who knew what was to come.

{{It is a father's place to be generous,}} said Jack. {{A daughter's to serve and sacrifice.}}

Fire blazed green in her mask's eyes. {{Yes, Father.}}

With a final sly glance at Kai, she danced west into the mist. Jack watched her go, the smooth expanse of his mask inscrutable.

Fresh unease gathered in the pit of Kai's stomach. "I have always considered it a father's place to protect his daughter."

Jack's laughter crackled softly through the mist. {{And yet you are so reckless with your own.}}

Kai winced beneath his helm, the last acrimonious conversation with Melanna at the forefront of his thoughts. "It's not for me to bar Melanna's path. She will understand, one day."

{{You've no need to defend yourself to me, my Emperor. I merely repay your generosity with my own.}}

Kai's unease redoubled, fed by the sense that Jack's words held meaning he'd missed. Before he unpicked the elusive thought, the Lord of Fellhallow cupped his hands, a white-blue flame springing to life against his palms.

{{Service and sacrifice.}} Melancholy tone sat ill alongside the mirth of a moment before. {{Be bright and beautiful, my daughters.}}

He brought his palms together. The fire went out.

In the distance, the screams began.

The mists boiled away. Two score raging blue-white fires dotted the middle distance. A black, wizened figure capered at the heart of each. Cries soared over drums renewed, at times wild laughter and at others heart-wrenching agony. As Zephan watched, the nearest dancer collapsed, but crawled on through grass that blackened as fire spread. Another fell and did not rise, the blue-tinted flames leaping higher and higher above her shrivelling corpse.

"Queen's Ashes," murmured Izack. "What now?"

The sweet scent of duskhazel tingled Zephan's nostrils.

The first of the Raven's revenants dissipated, cast into soot. Its neighbours at the barricade followed suit, drawn into Otherworld alongside fading mist. The contagion of unmaking raced along barricade and open field, until the mists were gone, and not one revenant remained. Soldiers cried out as their allies scattered to nothing.

Beyond the burning thornmaidens, behind a broken line of galloping outriders, the horizon gathered to golden scale. The shadowthorn line stretched north and south along the gentle hill, emerald banners giving way to midnight blue and ocean grey. Thousands upon thousands upon thousands.

"Never bloody easy, is it?" growled Izack.

Half the thornmaidens were down now, their bodies blazing bright. Others reached the foremost barricade. Cackling madly, they threw themselves at defenders struck dumb by billowing pollen. The fires spread. In the distance, catapults lurched. Blazing shot gouged bloody smears in braced shields or spattered across the Silverway's rushing waters.

Blaring trumpets joined the thunder of the drums. The golden line started forward.

"What do we do?" asked Zephan.

"We're Essamere. What do you think?" Eyes still fixed on the shadowthorn advance, Izack raised his voice. "Master Proctor? Come on, Elzar, move your idle bones!"

Ilnarov hurried over, displaying a respectable turn of speed for a man of advanced years. "The kraikons ... They're waking up."

The nearest juddered, then froze, golden sparks racing across its body.

"And that might cheer me," said Izack, "if only we'd ten times the number. Get those fires out. Smother them. Flood them. Piss on them if you have to, but get them out."

The high proctor drew himself up, the light of his sun-staff lending shape to an offended frown. "Why? Where will you be?"

"We'll get you the time to do it." Izack drew his sword and raised it to grey skies. "Essamere! Until Death!"

"*Until Death!*"

Joining his voice to the refrain, Zephan hoisted the eagle-banner high, its weight now borne aloft by something more than muscle. Izack galloped away, and the last of Essamere rode with him.

Kai urged his steed to the trot, hand loose upon the hilt of the Goddess' sword. The sword that had brought him victory after victory. The sword ushering him to a second death. Cataphracts kept pace, unflinching as the first ballista shots screamed from the distant galleon. Most went high, ploughing muddy furrows behind the advancing line. One swept a handful of Immortals from their horses, the first warriors of the morning to be spirited to Evermoon. Havildars bellowed and the lines closed up, emerald and gold implacable in advance.

He spared a glance to left and right. To Kos Devren, a long-handled mace borne alongside his emerald shield; bear cloak and ridged armour bulking him out to twice the man. To Elspeth, unarmoured and slender to the point of fragility. His oldest living friend, and the divine child who named him father. Welcome companions for his final battle. Indeed, the very finest. Save one.

Quarrels flickered out to the north. The leading ranks of the Britonisian cataphracts crumpled. Men and horses screamed as pavissionaires aboard the galleon joined their shots to those behind the makeshift barricades. A salvo of blazing stone cracked against the warship's hull as the northmost of the twin catapult batteries found its range. Fire raced across volley-ports. Burning sailors flung themselves into the Silverway's waters.

A twitch of Kai's heels quickened his horse to a canter. Arrows arced overhead, no longer a gesture of respect, but loosed to kill. Black rain shuddered against king's blue shields and earthen banks.

Far ahead, outriders wheeled away from the Tressian position, shooting backwards in the saddle as they retreated from the galloping column of knights arrayed in hunter's green. More knights came from the southwest, scarlet against grey skies, their plumes streaming in the Ash Wind. Essamere and Prydonis. Sallying forth enough though they were outnumbered three, four times over by cataphracts and lunassera.

Kai's blood stirred to fear and anticipation. A warrior's life, valour and horror balanced on the dagger's edge. All he'd known since his twelfth year. One last battle. One last chance to secure beyond question a throne for an absent daughter. The daughter he'd driven away for fear of telling her the truth. And if Ashana begrudged him that? Then perhaps Elspeth was right, and she was owed no regard, and no loyalty.

Glory in victory. Fortitude in defeat. Honour always. And family first of all.

He gripped the Goddess' sword and tore it free. Moonfire blazed beneath the miser's sky.

"Ashanael Brigantim!" he roared. "Saranal Amyradris!"

The battle thus offered to goddess and daughter, he thrust back his heels.

Prydonis struck with a crash to split the sky. The thunder of hooves yielded to the crunch of lances and the wet rip of flesh. Adulating cries became screams. Lance and spear cast riders from saddles to be trampled by those who came behind. Scarlet surcoats and gilt-edged plate blurred with emerald silk and golden scale. A moonfire sword blazed blinding at the very heart, the smell of seared flesh dancing on the wind. Torvan Mannor, red hair bright in the flame's backwash, swept a shadowthorn from the saddle and spurred on.

Then Essamere joined the unequal battle, and Zephan had no thought to spare to anything but survival. Shouting to drown his fear, he drove aside a shadowthorn spear and spurred into the gap. A clash of steel, a falling body, and Izack was at his side, howling like a starving prizrak.

"*Saran Amhyrador!*"

Fresh cataphracts crashed home. Spears bit deep. Sense drowned between the grunts and howls of vying warriors – the sour stench of sweat-mingled blood.

Moonfire blazed. Mannor pitched backwards out of his saddle. The Prydonis banner fell, its wielder sagging in the embrace of a young woman with pale skin and a blood-soaked white dress. Battle's timber shifted from defiance to reserve, and from reserve to panic. Prydonis knights shrank back from raging moonfire. Scarlet bled away, routed or dying, and the hunter's green of Essamere stood alone.

"Saran!" roared Izack. "No more hiding! Fight like a—"

A shining arc. The dull clang of metal on metal. Izack's saddle was empty, a bear-cloaked brute drawing back his mace for a second blow.

"Master!"

Zephan hauled on his reins. His destrier bucked beneath a new burden. A slender hand wended about his waist.

"Hush," breathed the pale woman. "Dream now."

Her other hand slipped beneath Zephan's open helm. The world blurred black. The banner dipped. Clinging to consciousness, he drove back his elbow. The woman yelped. Her fingers slipped away. Colour and sensation flooded back. The brute's mace chimed against Zephan's helmet. Pulsing red overwhelmed parting black. The strike of the ground drove all breath from his lungs. Thoughts and fears scattered into the grey.

When Zephan came to, the battle had moved west along the road, a trail of corpses to mark its passage. All around, dismounted knights and cataphracts hacked and tore at one another. Essamere's eagle-banner he found pinned beneath him, bloodied and torn in the fall. A shaking hand seized its stave; the other a discarded sword. Head shrieking protest, Zephan clambered up among the dead, and beheld a battle sliding to disaster.

Essamere and Prydonis fought on, a running battle of survivors scattered by the Emperor's onslaught. Reawoken kraikons succumbed again to sleep with the approach of pale-witches riding close behind. Further west, mist thickened about extinguished thornmaiden fires. The ballistae of the *Dauntless* fell sporadic as crew fought to contain the flames. And in the east, the great Hadari lines came forward across drywalled fields, the sonorous pulse of drums driving them on. Shambling, disjointed figures of strawjacks lurched alongside.

"Help ... Help me up, lad."

Zephan blinked. Izack lay among the dead barely three paces away. He'd one eye purpled and swollen shut; his right arm was twisted beneath him. "Master?"

"Bastard got lucky. Then I snapped arm and ankle on the way down."

Zephan laid aside his sword and helped the other stand. A little to the north, a dismounted cataphract stabbed a sword in their direction and bellowed a warning.

Izack clung to Zephan's shoulder. "Let's hope we bought Elzar enough time, eh?"

Zephan cast an eye towards Govanna, and the courtyard of the Traitor's Pyre. Dark patches in the returning mist betrayed the presence of revenants. Their numbers were slim. Not enough to contest the columns marching from the east.

Practically hopping, Izack retrieved a sword from the carnage, sneered at the notched blade and cast it away. "What now, lad?"

A stray steed, and they might have made it to safety, but all the horses were long fled. And besides, it wasn't them alone. Others fought on amid the carnage.

"Essamere stands." Zephan swallowed hard, willed conviction to a shaking voice and hoisted the banner high. "Essamere stands!"

He thrust the banner's foot-spike into the mud and wrestled a shield from a dead Prydonis. Izack, who'd at last found a sword worthy of his time, braced a free hand against the pole.

"Damn me if that wasn't the right answer."

They came, in ones and twos. Essamere. Prydonis. Crawling. Limping. Drawn to the banner. Drawn to the promise of vows fulfilled and death in good company.

As a loose ring of battered surcoats formed around the banner, Izack stared at the nearest column. Black trees on a dark blue field, the Corvanti ranks swollen as dismounted cataphracts joined the line. And further south, the white stags of Silsaria proud against rust fields.

Izack offered a pained grin. "Reckon you can keep up?"

Zephan regarded his master's battered body. By any reckoning, Izack was half a man at that moment. But some things you just *knew*. "No."

He grinned. "You *are* learning. All right, you worthless lot. One last brawl, and we're all owed a damn fine reward. I just hope Lumestra's watching, that's all."

His only reply was the grim silence of men and women who knew their race had been run.

At bellowed command, Corvanti spears lowered. Drums hurled them on.

A new note cut through cacophony. Not the clarion of Hadari trumpets or the deeper boom of Tressian buccinas, but the shrill of reeds, a drone roaring beneath. A sound Zephan had heard at concert, but never on a battlefield.

"There!"

A Prydonis' outstretched sword pointed to where the southern extent of the Silsarian wall folded back, desperate men scrambling away as new shields emerged from Selnweald's trees and shook themselves to order.

These were not the colours of a single regiment or warband, nor a single nation. The numerals of the 14th flew proud alongside battle-stained colours of the 1st, the 7th and the 10th. A spread-winged phoenix soared alongside the Prydonis drakon and the bull of Fellnore. At the fore, yellow and sea green pennants snapped and fluttered as the scream of pipes drove Thrakkian horsemen on, leaving the infantry far behind.

But it wasn't a Thrakkian who led the charge. Though he wore Thrakkian armour, there was no missing the sable surcoat and silver swan, no more than Zephan mistook the woman riding at his side, her Essamere garb frayed and filthy. Viktor Akadra and Roslava Orova. The Phoenix-Slayer and the Reaper of the Ravonn. A man who didn't lose, and a woman who could not die.

The pipes wailed to crescendo. Axes gleamed.

"*Væga af væga!*"

The bellow rolled across the valley like thunder. Horses quickened to the gallop.

And above it all, the sound of Izack's grim laughter. "About bloody time!"

Fifty-Nine

The mists pulled back onto a sunlit forest lost in the majesty of Fade. Of rust-coloured leaves curled tight on branch and crunching underfoot. Of that peculiar dry scent of seasonal decline, the rich verdance of Sommertide yielding to renewal's promise.

It reminded Melanna of that small, wild corner of the palace grounds where the gardeners seldom trod, but others trespassed to leave offerings of woven corn dolls. A place where brambles thrived and trees grew as they wished. She'd played there as a girl, dreaming of fetch and wisp dancing upon dark mushrooms or rustling ivy. For all that the palace had been where she'd lived, that unkempt patch of garden had been her home. Her first taste of life beyond the shelter of roof or canvas, a fascination that had survived dull lessons of deportment and protocol that had moulded the carefree girl to a princessa. She felt it again now. The desire to wander winding paths and learn their secrets.

But even without pressing need, she'd have held back. In the birdsong-haunted quiet, she felt a presence. No, not even a presence, for that implied intent. The sensation that prickled across neck and shoulder felt more like *potential*. The taste of the wind in the moments before deluge, or summer skies beneath gathering storm. Something wondrous and beautiful and dangerous beyond measure.

Even with its master away, Fellhallow remained aware.

A crunch of bracken snapped Melanna back to her senses. Apara strode past. Hard to believe the other woman had been all but dead just hours before. Now her vigour put Melanna's own to shame every bit as much as her manner irritated. Stolen glances. A tongue that moved little if not to question. The pervading sense that to not keep eyes on her was to invite misfortune. Too much like Haldrane, and without the comfort of known loyalties.

Regarding the tangle of ferns and brambles without enthusiasm, Apara spread her arms in frustration. "How are we to find anything in this?"

"Follow the paths." Ashana drifted across the mist gate's threshold, her skirts rustling fallen leaves. "In Fellhallow, all come eventually to Glandotha."

"You've spoken of nothing but urgency and waning time," said Apara. "Now you're content for us to wander?"

Ashana shrugged. "Then do as you would in Dregmeet."

"What does that even mean?" Apara stared up the boughs. "I'm no use to you here. When you said you needed a thief, I thought you'd a house in mind, maybe a palace. Walls to climb, locks to tip and the like. Not . . . Not this."

Her tone wavered. Melanna was struck by how adrift she seemed. As lost as a fish in the desert. And perhaps that was true. What little Melanna had seen of Tressia before the mists had spirited her away had left an impression of a cold, austere place, with sparse trees and gardens that grew only tombstones. Had Apara even *seen* a forest before?

Ashana smiled. "Though Fellhallow and Otherworld are opposites, they're both places where the ephemeral touches the divine. Where reality buckles to match what lies beyond. It's true in Dregmeet, and it's true here."

"I don't understand," said Melanna.

"She means we head downwards," Apara replied. "No matter which way the paths turn, we head downhill."

"You see?" said Ashana. "Your instincts do have value, even here."

Apara scowled. "A goddess' aid would be worth more."

Ashana plucked a leaf from an overhead branch and turned it over and over. "If my brothers sense I'm meddling they'll put aside their differences and vent their ire on me." The leaf crumpled beneath pale fingers. "Then I'll be forced to destroy one of them, and all will be lost."

The calm certainty sent a chill racing along Melanna's spine. Even now, the Goddess looked more absent than present, a willowy figure scarcely clinging to the world. "Could you really do that?"

"Oh yes." Ashana glanced at the mist gate, where the Huntsman stood silent vigil. "Everyone thinks I'm the nice one. I'm not. The part of me that is divine will see this world destroyed rather than allow my siblings to reshape it. But the part of me that remains ephemeral knows greatness cannot be built on selfishness and spite. I indulge her when I can, but if it's war, it's war. Find me another way. Find Jack's heart."

Melanna drew close to the Goddess, her voice soft. "I don't trust her."

"Then it's as well you're here too, isn't it?" Ashana embraced her. "Don't sleep here. Don't eat anything. Don't get caught. I'll be waiting. Look for the moonlight."

The deeper the paths wended, the closer the trees clung, and the thicker the canopy wove overhead. Sunlight became a distant gleam, blotted out by fading leaves and great lattices of plump, black vines, until only the strange luminescence of white flowers held darkness at bay.

Even clinging to the downhill paths, progress slowed. Less because the undergrowth offered hindrance – though briar and branch tore at Melanna's emerald silks even when she thought herself beyond reach – and more out of growing dread. Kin to sensation felt during that haunted night at Vrasdavora, the more Melanna denied it, the stronger it grew.

Worse was the thready, breathy pulse oozing beneath the trees like the snore of some vast, malcontent beast. She marked how leaves twitched in sympathy and told herself it was the wind. Still, the vision of the beast remained, the leaves rippling like fur as it slumbered.

Apara appeared to notice none of this, but strode on through the labyrinthine pathways. Her grey, city-dweller's garb made her seem a ghost, poorly tethered to the glory of the Fade-claimed forest. She remained watchful, at times halting to peer deeper into the trees, or to stand, head cocked, listening to some rustle of undergrowth or crackle of branch.

Even so, Melanna constantly fell behind. Each sound – each glimpse of shifting shadow – evoked half-forgotten stories. Children lured from desperate parents. Swains seduced by a gasp of thornmaiden pollen. Ancient trees mulched on travellers' bones. Unable to put such thoughts wholly from her mind, she too often found Apara waiting impatiently at a fork in the path, a sneer on her lips.

On the fourth occasion, the sneer found voice. "Is it easier to dawdle when it's not your people on the dagger's edge?"

"We're all on the dagger's edge," snapped Melanna. Her more than most, if Jack had his way. She kept one eye on a semi-distant strand of trees. Sunlight's shadow, or something moving beneath the leaves? "I thought you'd foresworn your kind?"

Grey eyes narrowed in pain. "Only the Crowmarket. I still have family. Friends."

The Crowmarket. The vranakin. Whose kernclaw had nearly killed her father with talons akin to Apara's. Melanna set the memory aside. "Haste serves no one if it gets us killed."

"There's nothing here. Just branches in the wind."

"And you know this for certain? The woman who recoils at the sight of trees?"

"I survived Dregmeet for thirty years. I know danger when it draws close." She sighed. "You won't listen. Your kind never do."

Melanna's cheeks warmed. "My kind? You know nothing of me."

"I may not have met you, but I know you. All airs and graces until you're hammering at the doors of me and mine, looking for someone who'll do what you can't ... or won't." She paused. "Like you are now."

"Ashana came to you for help, not me."

"She's not here. And I'm on unfamiliar territory, looking to steal something that probably doesn't exist from a god who most certainly does, and with only a cosseted shadowthorn for company."

"I'm a princessa of the Golden Court," Melanna replied icily. "Not some cloistered lordling dwelling on inherited glories. I'm nothing like your dusty nobility."

"You don't get a crown without trampling on others." Apara shrugged. "All shadows look the same when you're trapped beneath them."

Melanna glared, her annoyance sharpened not only by the fact that Apara's accusation wasn't so very different from Naradna's, but also by the suspicion that the other woman was right – that fear was holding her back. What *was* beyond question, was that argument only cost them time. Apara had reasons to disdain her – even to hate her. And the kernclaw's failed assassination gave Melanna all the reason she needed to distrust Apara in return. But necessity made strange alliances.

"We don't have time to—"

Apara clapped a hand over Melanna's mouth and held a finger up to her own lips. "Listen."

She heard nothing at first – at least, nothing beyond the crackle and rustle of branches that had plagued her senses since they'd left the mist gate behind. Then something louder, heavier. A rushing, intermittent creak growing steadily louder.

A heartbeat later, she saw it through the trees: a hunched, four-legged shape lumbering through the undergrowth. Its moss-draped body was like a grunda in silhouette, with a barrel-chest and a neck set low between massive shoulders. But where grundas were seldom taller than a man, this creature was the size of a house. In place of leathery grey skin, it had a strawjack's briar-woven "flesh"; where a grunda sported a curved horn on its snout, this had a pair of antlers above its vast, deep-set eyes.

Brilliant white blossoms gleamed upon a mossy back. Petals shook free with every ponderous, reverberating step, to be fought over by the thornmaidens capering in its wake. The beast lumbered on, oblivious. Melanna had no idea what the creature was, nor whether the tussle was sport or ritual.

She eased down behind an oak as the peculiar carnival lurched closer and caught the first snatches of song on the breeze, the lilting notes interrupted as one thornmaiden snatched a petal from another, and was pounced into the ferns for the deed. The first waft of pollen reached Melanna soon after, and with it the stirring, giddy compulsion to break from concealment and join the merriment. She crushed a sleeve to her nose and mouth and glanced at Apara to offer warning. None was needed. Standing in the lee of the oak, Apara had her face buried in the crook of her elbow.

The procession headed away, branches swaying uphill to mark its passage. As the song faded, the insidious pollen with it, Melanna rose. "We should keep moving."

Apara nodded, her eyes still on the broken trail of foliage. "Feel better?"

Melanna blinked at the question. "Yes. Why?"

"Always better to know there's a guard than to wonder."

It made a certain twisted sense. An ambush sprung could be fought. An ambush feared only paralysed. "They didn't look much like guards."

"I doubt anything down here looks much like anything it should." Apara stared downhill, at the maze of pathways winding beneath the dying leaves. "There are two kinds of marks. The vulnerable, and those who only *look* it."

Melanna stifled a grimace of distaste. "And which is this?"

"I don't know." For the first time, Apara smiled. "That's what makes it fun. Try to keep up."

They made better time now Melanna's nebulous fears had found expression. They encountered two more of the moss rovers during the descent, one accompanied by its own carnival of thornmaidens, and another slumped motionless in a rare sun-dappled glade, so still she couldn't tell whether it was alive or dead.

Deeper in, they sighted strawjacks too. Some shambled through the undergrowth on unknowable errands; others congregated around timeworn dolmens wreathed in black ivy, silent save for the ever-present rustling, crackling sound and swaying gently as if caught in a breeze. The more Melanna saw of the strawjacks, the more she was struck by how witless they seemed, so very unlike their thornmaiden siblings. Perhaps Jack liked his sons obedient and his daughters vicious.

They saw only one other thornmaiden, though the wind beneath the trees brought snatches of song from many more. She sat amid the roots of an ancient yew, legs tucked beneath and lithe fingers braiding the briars of her hair while luminescent flowers pulsed in time to her song.

Melanna all but stumbled into that glade, for the thornmaiden had been invisible against the yew's creased skin and garland of mistletoe. But for Apara's restraining hand, she would have done. The thornmaiden had shifted at the crackle of movement, revealing her clay mask against the darker weaving of her flesh.

When Melanna almost repeated the mistake with a strawjack grove a few minutes later, she was forced to a humbling reappraisal of her abilities. Skills honed walking the Tressian Southshires were wholly inadequate in Fellhallow, where a tree might not be a tree at all. That the briarkin were so often indistinguishable from the wider forest might have offered some comfort, if not for the fact that the city-raised Apara missed nothing.

"How do you do it?" said Melanna, grudging respect overcoming pride. "I swear I see nothing, but there's something there anyway."

Apara shrugged. "I see nothing, too. But it's a different kind of nothing. The difference between an empty space, and a space that *looks* empty. I've always known where to find eyes in the shadows. It's why they wanted me for a kernclaw."

Recollection of the birch mound flashed back. Her father's weight as they fled his assassin. "And you . . . You wanted to be a kernclaw?"

She winced. "Once. Or my cousins let me think I did. That's how it works. One decision becomes the next, and the next, and before you know it, you're doing things you never really thought you would, and you're not sure why. And all the while, a piece of you takes the credit. Better to have damned yourself than admit it was done *to* you. I've lied to myself far more than to others."

"That must be hard."

Apara laughed softly. "That's the thing. There's nothing easier when you've only bad options and worse ones."

"And which is this?"

"I don't know. I think . . . I think for the first time it might be for me to decide. At least until the Raven calls in my debts. Then I'll never choose anything else again." She slowed to a halt. "We might be here."

Melanna's heart quickened as she followed Apara into the shadow of a crooked oak and peered into a glade that, at first sight, seemed little different to the others. She could have walked the boundary of fallen leaves in a minute, no more, and there was nothing to suggest that this place was a particular seat of power. No throne. No guards. No sign of any form of life, save for the dull, breathy rumble that had by now become so familiar she barely noticed it any longer.

Indeed, the only thing that marked the glade as different was the stone circle at its heart. Melanna counted seven in all, each covered in Fellhallow's black ivy and crowned by roses. By contrast to the slab-like dolmens seen elsewhere, none were larger than a woman. The Seven Dancers of Glandotha. The Keepers of Jack's heart. At least, so they were named in legend and promised by Ashana. It felt unreal. It also felt like she'd been there before.

"Well?" she asked.

"Seven statues, and every path leads uphill." Apara swept back her hair, the badger's streak of white stark against the auburn. "If your goddess speaks truly, this is Glandotha. The heart of Fellhallow."

"She wouldn't lie. Not about this."

"I had the impression she was guessing more than she was certain."

"The heart is here." Melanna rubbed her breastbone, and realised with a start that it wasn't *her* heart that had quickened, for all that the pulse throbbed in her veins. "I can . . . I can feel it."

She made to enter the glade, then remembered recent close calls. "Do you see anything?"

"I'll keep watch."

Alert for anything out of the ordinary, Melanna broached the ferns at the glade's edge and made for the ring of dancers. Details about the stones sang out. Most notable was that there should have been eight, not seven, the missing one having been removed from the near end of the ring at some time in the past. Closer still, and she realised that, beneath the embrace of thorn and ivy, the statues appeared pristine and unmarked by time's passage.

It was then she realised that the dancers weren't stone at all, but statues of polished wood, each hewn in a woman's likeness. Two wore armour, another very little of anything at all. A fourth wore a dress more alike to Tressian styling than anything Melanna had ever donned, while a fifth's skirts bore the lace edging of a Rhalesh bridal gown. No two had much of anything in common save the tone and texture of the wood itself. Both of which were all too familiar to Melanna, for she'd seen herself reflected thus in the waters of the divine clockface.

Her head spun. She pressed a hand to her mouth to still a rush of nausea. These weren't statues. They weren't dancers. They were Jack's *brides*. Queens of Fellhallow past.

Melanna peered into the eyes of the nearest, but saw no reflection of life or soul. So Jack married his queens, then rendered them thus? Unmoving, unchanging throughout all the seasons of the world. Nothing more than trophies. The woman in front of her was little more than a girl. How had she come to her throne? Had she been tricked? Traded? Seized against her will?

That a woman would consent freely to such a fate defied belief, for of all the fates Melanna had imagined for herself in the passing years, this was bleaker by far. The traditions of the Golden Court elevated to infinity. A queen as a trophy, not a ruler.

And this was the fate her father had made for her.

Melanna's stomach spasmed and steadied. Turning from the lifeless queen, she paced to the centre of the ring, slipped her dagger free of its sheath and began to dig.

What began as calm, methodical labour quickly became frantic. Impossible to forget her bartered fate with seven regal gazes upon her, and the second heartbeat booming in her chest alongside her own. Impossible to forget Jack's creeping, crackling presence beneath the walls of Vrasdavora, or the leer in his eyes. The empty space in the ring.

Hers.

Melanna dug faster and faster, the dagger abandoned in favour of scooping away the soft loam with her hands. Nails split and fingers bled. Still she dug. Deeper. Deeper. The first she knew of her tears was when they spattered onto the soil.

"Hush." The voice was soft as silk. "You've such lovely eyes. Weeping will only spoil them."

Melanna turned. A dark-haired woman stood before the statue she'd examined, blue eyes bright and hands folded across the black lace of her bridal gown. She *was* the statue, or it her. They could have been sisters. Twins. Melanna cursed herself for being crept up on.

"My mother thought me good for nothing but scandal," said the woman. "But now I am Queen Kendrae of Fellhallow. She must feel very foolish."

Melanna clambered upright. Apara was nowhere to be seen. "How long ago was that?"

Kendrae offered a conspiratorial smile. "It doesn't matter. Time's river doesn't flow here. Not as it does out there."

Her manner was off, kin to a drunkard's. Jack's doing? Was that how he controlled her? Magic aside, there were many poisons to deaden the will, and they surely all grew in Fellhallow. "Who is Emperor? What year is it?"

"Emperor?" Kendrae giggled. "You're having a game with me."

Melanna grabbed her wrist. "How long have you been here?"

She tilted her head. "You really do have beautiful eyes."

"You'll get nothing useful out of her." The new voice came from the opposite side of the circle where a pallid Tressian woman with blonde hair and dark eyes stood before her own statue. "It must be a blessing to be so shallow. Kendrae still thinks she's his favourite. When really, of course—"

"When of course, *I'm* the only true queen," said another, this time from Melanna's right. "As you well know, Ellian."

"Really, Ilnore," sniffed Ellian. "Just because you came to him out of choice—"

"And because I've the finest hair." Ilnore frowned. "Still, *she* has beautiful hair too."

"Yes, she does," said Kendrae. "We're lucky the others are asleep."

Melanna stepped back, unease trickling to fear. "And why's that?"

Kendrae frowned. "Because—"

"Oh, you foolish girl," said Ellian. "Don't you see? Our king has chosen her. She's to be one of us."

The frown grew distinctly unfriendly. "I don't think I like that."

"Nor do I," said Ilnore. "It's crowded enough around here as it is."

"Then again," said Ellian, "our king isn't here. We *could* share her. He doesn't have to know."

The three stared at Melanna, who cast a fruitless glance beyond the glade. Where was Apara? She put a hand on her sword. Seeming not to notice, the queens drifted closer.

"So long as I get her eyes," said Kendrae.

Ellian nodded. "Agreed, if I have her hair."

Ilnore rubbed her cheek. "Then I claim her skin. The others can fight over the rest when they wake."

Melanna swallowed and drew her sword.

They were mad, that much was certain. Had they always been that way, or had madness claimed them with the passage of time? The bleak depths of her father's bargain stood clearer than ever. How long as Jack's bride before their insanity was hers also? For the first time, Melanna understood why Ashana had been so terrified of her own reflection in the Dark.

The glade's light flickered. Where the three women had stood, there were now three skeletal corpses in ragged garb, their bones woven together with vines and the stench of rotten leaf-spoil that set Melanna's head spinning.

"Don't be foolish," said Kendrae, the sweet voice macabre. "This is kindness."

A hand closed around a hank of Melanna's hair and jerked back her head. Agony racing through her scalp, she thrust at Ilnore. The point passed clean through threadbare dress and bone without making contact.

"We'll be beautiful again," said Ilnore. "You'll be free. That's fair."

Melanna pulled away, pain and torn hair a price gladly paid for freedom. Balance lost, she sprawled in the disturbed soil and scrambled away. "Apara!"

"Don't damage her hair!" hissed Ellian.

Gasping, Melanna regained her feet. Steel didn't hurt them, and she'd nothing else at her disposal. "Apara! Curse you, vranakin! Where are you?"

No answer came. Melanna bolted for the glade's far side.

Somehow, Kendrae arrived first, ragged lace drifting behind. "We don't want to hurt you. Really we don't."

Melanna ducked a grasping hand and struck out anew. Another hand tugged her ankle, and she fell. Ilnore landed atop her, grave-breath wet and pungent, her strength beyond contest as she forced Melanna's arms against the fallen leaves.

Ellian drifted close, Melanna's discarded dagger in her skeletal fingers. "Hair first. Then eyes. Then the skin. Then we'll wake the others."

She started forward.

Apara coughed. "Beg pardon, your majesties."

The queens turned. Arms still pinned in place, Melanna craned her neck.

Apara stood beside Kendrae's statue, an ornate and soil-stained wooden casket at her feet, and a small tinderbox in her taloned hand. A spark flew from the flint. The statue caught light, fire racing across its polished surface with a speed to which it had no right.

Kendrae screamed, a sound so rich with agony and madness that it jarred Melanna's bones. "What have you done! What ... "

The words bled into an ululating wail and she flung herself at Apara.

Halfway there, she burst into a swirl of thick, black smoke and smouldering vines.

The remaining queens stared, frozen in horror, as the vines about Kendrae's statue crackled and went black.

"That's two women I've burned lately," said Apara, a tightness in her voice Melanna couldn't quite read. "Want to try for three, or four? No? Then back in the statues."

The queens exchanged glances. Then they vanished as if they'd never been, leaving Melanna with the stench of the grave and kindling for a thousand nightmares. Eyes still on Kendrae's burning statue, she rose on trembling legs.

"Where were you?"

"Getting this." Gathering up the wooden box, Apara walked over and creaked open the lid. "It *is* what we came for. And since you had them distracted ... "

Melanna peered inside. There, nestling in a lining of black silk, pulsed a heart of leaf and briar, green fire flickering through the weave, and its beat marking time with the alien tremor in Melanna's own chest.

Distracted.

"Did you know?" she said, tone hard as granite. "Did you know about them?"

Apara shook her head. "I wasn't sure whether the place was vulnerable, or just looked it. I wanted to be sure."

"And I was bait?"

She snapped the box shut. "Why not? We had to know, and I bet you didn't have any alchemist's powder on your person, did you?"

Drowning in anger, disgust and lingering horror, Melanna struck her. Apara staggered, though not nearly as much as she should have. Black blood trickled from the corner of her mouth. She wiped it away with the back of her hand, brow creasing with uncertain emotion as it hissed away to nothing.

"You used me!" snapped Melanna.

"How does it feel, *princessa*?" She didn't sound triumphant, only tired. "I imagine it's a new experience."

Melanna looked again at the statues. One burning, six cold and quiet, and the one that was hers yet to be. "Burn the others."

"I'm out of alchemist's powder. We should leave before they work that out."

Still seething, Melanna turned about. There. Beyond Ilnore's statue. A gleam of moonlight through the trees. A beacon to guide them home. "This way."

Sixty

The last of Viktor's doubts fell away beneath galloping hooves. Calenne. Josiri. Self and purpose. The arithmetic of numbers and distance, of weary soldiers and Hadari spears. He beheld only battle fought on a sprawling scale he'd never seen; an army beset and the redemption of the sword.

Havildars and princes screamed at their warriors to lock shields. Arrows struck deep into the vanaguards' broad, circular shields. Thrakkian pipes screamed. The ill-made Silsarian wall shuddered. Axes bit down, and the air filled with blood.

Viktor thrust his claymore over the rim of a rust-coloured shield, silencing a challenge with steel. A spear glanced off his armoured shoulder, another from the chain peytral protecting his steed's chest. A havildar bellowed challenge and died beneath Viktor's second thrust.

"Væga af væga!" Inkari's axe swung a bloody arc and a prince's head tumbled.

Dismayed, the first rank bowed. Gaps opened up between the shields. Rosa rowelled her steed, a sword flashing in her right hand, and a borrowed vanaguard axe in her left. A Silsarian Immortal barred her path, golden shield high to fend off the sword, mace-blow angled at her horse's jaw. A twitch of heels, and her horse stepped aside. The mace wasted its force on empty air. Rosa's axe did not. The Immortal fell, his armour crimson between shoulder and neck, and then she was among the third rank, screaming like a woman possessed.

Vanaguard streamed past Viktor and howled into the gap. Hooked axe-blades snared shield rims, split helms and mangled flesh. Bowing shields broke apart.

"*Livasdri!*" came a warning bellow. "*Livasdri!*"

Gangling, crackling shapes descended on the eastern flank. Gnarled forms woven from branch and briar, nearly as tall on their misshapen legs as the riders on their horses. Thrashing fronds dragged vanguard screaming from their saddles. Axes crunched down. The sweet, musty smell of sap and heady pollen mingled with the bitter metal of spilt blood.

The underhand sweep of the claymore threw a shieldsman sprawling, and then Viktor was face to crackling face with the new-come horror. Livasdra. Strawjack. A son of Fellhallow, risen from loam and buried sins. Green fire blazed in empty eyes. The jagged slash of its mouth parted in a rustling, crackling hiss.

Branches crunched beneath the claymore's strike. Black sap oozed up over the blade. Twisted fingers wended about steel. As Viktor strove to wrest the sword free, thrashing fronds burst from the strawjack's other hand and lashed about his head. They forced their way into mouth and nostrils, and pried at his eyes.

Viktor gagged at the creature's rotten taste. Lungs already laboured by battle spasmed and strained. The claymore refused to budge, stuck fast in woody flesh and the strawjack's remorseless grasp.

He set loose his shadow.

The strawjack disintegrated in a spray of ice-crusted branches and mouldered bones. Stomach churning, Viktor ripped the masterless fronds from his mouth and spurred forward.

His shadow tore the next strawjack apart before it had chance to turn.

Two dozen paces to the west, separated from Viktor by a tide of fleeing Silsarians, Rosa's axe hacked a flurry of wet, snapping blows and another strawjack fell. Inkari's vanguard made kindling of others, their heavy, hooked blades more suited to the task than Viktor's sword.

Rosa galloped on, aiming for where an eagle-banner flew proud above a knot of battered souls and broken corpses in hunter's green. She slowed as she approached the grave of Essamere, manner cold and silent. Sword sheathed, she claimed the banner offered to her, and raised it high.

"Essamere!"

Knights cantered to her side. Bloodied orphans of the battlefield on weary horses. Newcomers in the colours of Fellnore, Prydonis and Sartorov, abandoned by the fury of the Thrakkian charge. The glory of the Republic, distilled to a hundred spurs. A force to reshape many a battle, but not that bloody valley, which had already seen the deaths of thousands, and would witness thousands more.

All this Viktor knew, and he knew that Rosa did also. But as she turned her steed to the west, where the imperial banner flew above the ruin of king's blue dead, he recognised also that she didn't care.

He spurred away from the fleeing Silsarians and the screams of slaughter. "Rosa! Wait!"

Their eyes met, her gaze bleak. Then she sprang away, banner streaming behind and her voice dolorous. "Until Death!"

"Until Death!"

The Essamere battle cry spilling from their lips, the knights of four chapterhouses galloped in her wake, rivalry forgotten in the cause of vengeance. Deaf to Viktor's bellowed orders. Deaf to all save the blood rushing in their ears, and the urging of slain comrades.

Viktor cast about the field. Bodies thickened the Selnweald approach. Most human, some not. The majority wore the rust-cloth of Silsaria or the gold of their Immortals, but sea green and yellow claith too lay bloodied among the dead – men and women who'd ridden hard to fight for coin and honour in a foreign land.

To Viktor's right, north and east from where the shield wall had broken, shrill pipes brought order to Thrakkians opposed by a thick wall of Corvanti shields. Swift-moving wayfarers traded shots with Hadari outriders as Inkari withdrew, the cloaks of the vanaguard joined by the plainer garb of mercenary thrydaxes.

Further east still, a pride of simarkas loped away from the wreckage of the southernmost Hadari catapults, leaving dead engineers in their wake. The northernmost blazed, the grassland raging with alchemist's fire cast from the *Dauntless'* ballistae.

South, Keldrov's motley regiment shook itself into a shield wall, banners raised high, and those of the 14th highest of all. More outsiders come to die in the Council's war – southwealders and phoenixes siding with one old foe against another.

A second line formed up to Keldrov's left, heavy pavissi shields planted in the mud as soldiers of the 10th readied their crossbows. A thornmaiden thrashed and died as bolts struck home. Three and a half thousand, all told. Not enough to vanquish the Icansae and Corvanti mustered on the bluffs – a host easily twice the size of Keldrov's command – but sufficient to lend caution now their catapult crews were dead and the Silsarians torn asunder.

"Typical Akadra." A limping Izack approached, supported by a stranger. "Come to take the credit now I've softened them up."

Viktor stared again at the valley. At its bounty of dead, and those who came to join them. "There'll be credit and blame enough to go around come nightfall."

"Aye." Izack shuffled to a halt, unswollen eye creasing. "Never seen anything like this. Revenants, strawjacks … Prydonis pulling their weight. If that's not the end of the world, I don't know what is."

Viktor grunted. It might not be the end of the world, but the Republic? The next few hours would see it stand or fall. Surprise was spent, and a measure of the Thrakkians' strength alongside. What remained had to be levied with care.

But where to intercede? Not to the north, where the *Dauntless* had reaped a heavy toll of the grey-clad Britonisian cataphracts and the wreckage of grunda wagons littered the riverside. Nor along Selnweald's eaves, where the balance of battle lay more in Tressian favour than anywhere else in sight.

No. The centre called. Beyond Rosa's cadre of charging knights. Beyond the blaze of emerald and gold that marked the glory of Rhaled on the march, and groves of strawjacks lurching alongside. The huddle of king's blue about the coaching inn. Men and women waiting to die behind barricades and locked shields. The fulcrum upon which the battle would turn, if deeds were sufficient. And for all that men cursed Viktor Akadra's name, none did so because his deeds were lacking.

"You'll find shelter with the 14th," he told Izack. "Tell Keldrov to send help if she can, but to take no risks."

The other scowled, pride and frustration vying for dominance. Then he clasped his uninjured hand to his chest. "I'll do that. Good hunting, Lord Akadra."

*

The Tressian shield wall shattered beneath the emerald thunderbolt. Kai hurtled on. Weakness was a memory, drowned in blood and banished by triumph's prospect. His steed vaulted the barricade, leaving dead and wounded behind. Panicked soldiers ran hither and yon against the fading blue-white flames, seeking the shelter of stone tavern and empty stables. Cataphracts ran them down, a scream for every dipped spear. The drums called to greatness – the trumpets demanded it – and Kai rode on through the spiralling duskhazel to the second Tressian line, clinging to the coaching tavern's outer courtyard.

An old man in scruffy leathers held high a blazing staff. Golden light flared against the smoke of a burning hayrick, hurling a lunassera from her ghostly chandirin. A rush of bronze sent six kraikons to contest the thunderbolt. Blades taller than a man swept Immortals from their saddles. Tressian soldiers hacked at horsemen with halberd and sword.

Another kraikon loomed, the tramp of its coming rattling teeth in Kai's jaw. He leaned low, the wind of the great sword's passage almost plucking him from the saddle. Rising, he sent moonfire blazing at the brute's chest. Steel armour ran like rain. Bronze trickled away. Golden magic sparked for the heavens and the kraikon froze, motionless.

Maces and hammers rang on bronze. Lunassera darted through the cataphracts' torn ranks, shard-spears cheating Tressian plate, the sanctity of their presence driving out the kraikons' spark. Kai cast about for Elspeth or Devren – for members of his guard. Finding none, he drove his horse on towards the hayrick and the kraikons' master. King's blue soldiers scattered before the moonfire sword. The old man held his ground.

Light flared as he raised his staff to the parry, the fires of sun and moon writhing in opposition. The clash drove the man from his feet, and the staff from his hands. Kai wheeled about to finish the deed.

The thready boom of the grave-call shuddered through his soul.

Too late, he realised that the nearest thornmaidens were dark and charred, their fires out, and duskhazel spent.

Mist rushed in, the old man lost behind a seething shroud of greenish white. The sounds of battle faded. The burning hayrick bled away into memory. There was only the mist, and grim laughter echoing within. It came from nowhere and everywhere, shifting and billowing with the vapour.

"She's coming for you," said the Raven. "My queen is so very angry. How pleased she'll be when I offer her your head."

Kai spun about in his saddle. He saw only mist. "Show yourself! Are you afraid to face me?"

"Found your honour at last, my Emperor?"

"What does the Raven know of honour?"

"Everything." The mocking chuckle turned bitter. "Let's try this again, shall we?"

Smoke bled across white. Skull helms gleamed silver.

Kai hoisted the moonfire sword high. "Ashanael Brigantim!"

"My sister can't help you," said the Raven. "She *won't* help you."

Black flame challenged white. With a scream of terror, Kai's horse hurled him from the saddle and vanished into the mist. Fighting the creak of jarred bones, Kai rose heavily to one knee, and thence to his feet.

He struck the revenant's sword aside and buried his blade in its vaporous chest. A sword fell. An empty helm rolled away. Other revenants pressed in, a noose closing tight, swords held at guard and each a perfect mirror image of the next.

"All those bargains and deceptions, and you are alone." The Raven's voice echoed about the mist. "And do you know why?"

A second revenant burst to ash, consumed by moonfire. A new circle closed tight. Silhouettes of man and horse flickered against the veil, no less distant than before.

"Should I care?" Kai bit out.

"Because sooner or later everyone comes to my keeping."

As one, the revenants' swords came up. The circle drew in.

"Until Death!"

Horses quickened to the gallop, the knights given to the madness of the charge.

Rosa abandoned herself to the wind, to a vengeance too long denied. Lances plunged deep into the cataphract rearguard and were abandoned for mace and sword. Her axe rose and fell, drawing blood with every pitiless stroke. Through it all, she held the eagle of Essamere high, so that fallen brothers and sisters might catch a glimpse from the mists and see themselves avenged.

While others faltered, Rosa forged on into a red world. A spear pierced her shoulder and ripped free. A mace-blow set the world ablur. She felt neither. There was only the brief resistance of flesh beneath the axe, and the scream summoned by its bite.

The meadowland clash of knights and cataphracts fell behind, lost to thrashing thornmaidens and the screams of their victims. The contested tavern lay ahead. Owl banners milled about the courtyard. Blackness rushed to consume them, silver death masks leering as revenants coalesced. Kraikons stood dark and desolate above the dead.

In the shadow of a burning barn, horseless Immortals vied with the revenants' flames. A slender woman – near twin to the one slain at Vrasdavora's bridge – slashed at the nearest with a silver dagger. Black flame seared her arm and she reeled away. A bear-cloaked brute caught her as she fell. His mace scattered a revenant to smoke and the mists swallowed them both.

To the west, defenders rallied beneath torn banners. To the east, rising vapour swirled about dying fires. Columns of Rhalesh shieldsmen shrank inwards as black flames seared their ranks. Thorned, grasping hands ripped revenants to shreds, skull helms and swords lifeless where they fell. Gleaming shard-spears sliced them to smoke. Others came hissing out of the mists – an endless tide in thrall to the Keeper of the Dead.

And passing through it all with as little care as a priest taking an evening's stroll, the tatter-cloaked horror of Jack o' Fellhallow, flanked by two lissom, burning women who shrieked with delight even as blue-white flames consumed them. They pressed on through the barricades and ditches, he with a creeper's stride, and they with witless caper. Where they passed, the mists recoiled, and revenants burst to mist. Shadowthorns lost their fear, shields and banners raised anew.

Rosa thrust back her spurs, steering for where she'd last seen the imperial banner. The House of Saran. The Emperor and his accursed daughter, who'd cheated her of mortal life and of a love that had made bearable an eternal's existence. Perhaps even Aeldran Andwar, were she lucky.

The Raven take them all. Sevaka would be avenged.

*

The revenant hissed its last, the helm clattering against hidden stone. Survivors drew back and pressed in anew. Muscles screaming, Kai wiped his brow. Another down. He'd lost count of how many. He'd lost all track of time. How long before Elspeth's borrowed strength ebbed? How long before the Raven tired of his game, and closed tight the ring of blades?

"Can you feel it, my Emperor?" The Raven's voice echoed about the mists. "Pieces of you are slipping away. Your army loses heart. Soon the House of Saran will be but a memory."

The revenants' swords snapped up to high guard, the blades levelled like spears at Kai's head. He circled about, gaze resting on each opponent for no more than a heartbeat.

"Melanna will be Empress!" he spat. "My line will continue!"

The Raven laughed. "Do you truly not know what you've done? You promised her to Jack. She's to be the new Queen of Fellhallow."

"No!" A cold hand closed about Kai's heart, the sensation close kin to the crippling spasms of recent days. "I offered myself! My life!"

"You offered your *future*." Beyond the circle of blades, the mists unfurled. The Raven stood, hands loose behind his back, his expression pure disdain. "Tell me, my Emperor. What is a daughter but a man's future?"

A revenant lunged. Flame raced ice-hot across Kai's ribs, scaled armour no defence against Otherworld's baleful steel. Black blood hissed away silver. A sweep of the Goddess' sword scattered the revenant to smoke.

Kai doubled over, eyes clamped shut against the pain. "No! You're lying!"

The Raven shrugged. "My brother *always* wants what I have. When I sought a queen, he *had* to have one for himself. But not for him arduous courtship, or the wooing of heart and soul. What need has he of regard when she'll be nothing but a possession of which to tire? No. He found a fool who'd trade all that he loved for a handful of ash." He spread his hands above his head. "*Do not bargain with the Lord of Fellhallow.* Someone ought to write that in nice big letters above the throne, don't you think? There's always some halfwit who tries."

The words burned at Kai's aching heart, their truth undeniable. *A father's place to be generous. A daughter's to serve and sacrifice.*

Jack's generosity with his daughters, offered in payment for Kai's own unwitting gift.

A golden future rotted away. Death was nothing beside the horror of a daughter sold. The moonfire sword slipped from nerveless fingers. Kai barely felt it go, nor the ice-hot kiss of the swords that formed a steel collar about his neck.

"Help me save her," he said. "I beg you."

The Raven tutted. "I'm afraid not."

"I'll give you anything—"

"Ah, but everything you have will be mine in time as it is. All I seek is an Emperor's head. A gift worthy of a queen."

Mists unravelled before blue-white flame and the sweet scent of dusk-hazel. Kai sank to his knees as the revenants scattered to smoke. The murk yielded to a cobbled courtyard and a toppled wagon; a stone well beneath grey skies. An imperial banner, its staff snapped and its cloth soaked red, propped limp against a wall. And bodies. So many bodies, the gold outnumbering the blue. An army brought to ruin by deception and pride.

All for nothing, and less than nothing.

A thornmaiden cackled her last and scattered to blazing blue ash. Another daughter undone by a father's ambition. The Raven stumbled away, his pallor greying as the duskhazel did its wicked work.

{{Well, brother,}} said Jack, his voice a swarm of hornets. {{Shall we make an end of this?}}

The clamour of battle rose as mist fell away. Blue-white flame hissed and spat about a woman's blackened embers. And beyond? Across cobbles choked with mud and corpses? The proud shadowthorn Emperor, face haggard and bright with tears. Rosa's heart quickened with grim joy.

She gave no thought to the Essamere banner she cast aside. She hurtled on, the axe swept back for the blow that would split Kai Saran's honourless head from his emerald-studded shoulders. For Riego Noktza and the dead of Ahrad. For the 7th. For Tregga, and Tarvallion's humbled spires. And for Sevaka. For Sevaka most of all.

"Roslava! Aid me, my queen!"

Her head jerked back at the Raven's plaintive cry. All that she was urged her to ignore it, to take the Emperor's head and have the matter done. Or almost all of her. A piece – a small piece, unfamiliar and unremarked, for it had never before demanded notice – commanded otherwise. It seized the reins, and left the rest screaming impotence.

The Raven hoved into view, a limp, huddled shape, dangling from Jack's crooked hand. {{Poor brother. Too much bartered to mortals for too little gain. I feel them clawing at the mists, tearing you apart. Allow me the kindness of sparing you its rigours.}}

Command blossomed to imperative; imperative to unshakeable desire.

With a cry as much horror as rage, Rosa brought down the axe. Jack shrieked and recoiled, his free hand clasped to the fresh scar across the mask's left eye. Frayed robes billowed in a storm of thrashing branches. As Rosa wheeled about for another blow, they snatched her up and slammed her down atop the dead.

Jack's weight settled on her spine. One foot, then another. Roots and briars burrowed into her flesh; peeling, probing, tugging at muscle.

{{Your queen? I expected something more ... durable. She seems confused. Could it be you've been less than truthful? You, the last friend to all?}} His tone turned mocking. {{I weep for your shame.}}

Rosa screamed as briar scraped against bone. Pain swirled to sick realisation. For all his claims of admiration and regard, the Raven had made her a plaything. She stared at the Emperor, his black blood seeping away.

The weight on Rosa's back shifted. The Raven slammed into the wagon and scrabbled for support. Branches wended tight about his limbs and hoisted him high.

"I had no choice," gasped the Raven. "A bargain—"

He cried out as the branches went taut.

{{Rejoice, Emperor Saran,}} said Jack. {{For the Lord of Fellhallow keeps his promises.}}

Sixty-One

The first strands of mists crept into the Hayadra Grove, spilling over the humbled walls of the old temple and gusting beneath alabaster trees. Dolorous bells and the rapt silence of massed vranakin offered welcome. The pontiffs waited at the grove's heart, heads bowed. Pallbearers approached a bier set before an open grave nestled in the Shaddra's roots. Mist curled behind, the blessing of the trees overcome by the ribbon-bound corpses they bore. The scent of damp earth permeated vapour, worm-eaten future mingled with dusty past.

Altiris averted his eyes from the suspended bodies: constables and luckless parishioners caught as the vranakin had flooded in the grove – sightless witnesses to unfolding blasphemy. Too much like the horrors of the mist-lost foundry. But then, the Hayadra Grove had horrors aplenty.

The vranakin in the grove were but half of the cortege come from Dregmeet. The rest had descended into the sunlit streets of the eastern hillside and Sinner's Mile as a caution against interference. What remained was might enough to contest an army, let alone a single soul clinging to courage's fading spark.

Kernclaws crouched among the branches, the soft cackle of their cloaks all that broke reverent silence. A ring of elder cousins barred final approach. Sidara's wagon sat within that ring, she almost a ghost already within the mist's embrace. Hawkin stood close by, Constans gagged before her, and his wrists bound.

Altiris pressed on, nerves howling at each brush of shoulder and disinterested gaze. Step by step, through the ranks of the raven-sworn and the dispossessed, past bell carriers and beggars, until he found himself at the crowd's inner edge. Two dozen paces from Sidara's wagon and as far again from the watchful pontiffs.

All of it a stroll away, and as distant as eternity.

Pallbearers set the mildewed casket on the bier, bowed and withdrew. The taller of the two pontiffs – Krastin, a name gleaned from reverent whispers – approached the body. Drawing back his hood, he stooped to kiss the withered skull.

"Rest easy, cousin. Your passing will not be for nothing."

Commotion arose to the east. Strife's clamour washing over the hill from hidden streets.

The second pontiff – Shurla – broke off from her approach to the bier. "What now?"

Krastin stood. Cold, dark eyes – twin to those Altiris remembered so well – swept the crowd and stared east. "The Council have found their courage." He planted the foot of his raven-headed cane into the sod and crooked a finger towards Sidara's cage. "Let her be wed."

Josiri abandoned all hope of order halfway up Sinner's Mile. The mob came in a rush of bodies, fuelled by hope and pride reclaimed, following the blaze of a serathi's light. Not an army of shields and martial discipline, but a tide of fists, cudgels and rusted swords that swept into the streets and left bodies in its wake.

"On!" he bellowed. "Keep moving!"

Side streets filled with shadow and steel.

"Watch the sides!" bellowed Kurkas. "Don't let them behind."

On they went, brick by brick and stone by stone.

Arrows flickered from northern rooftops. A knight collapsed, an arrow beneath his helm. A Swanholt hearthguard dropped to one knee, snapped the shaft buried in his shoulder and staggered on. A beat of sunlight wings, and the vranakin archers plunged towards cobbles. Ana spiralled away, laughter wild above the din. The sweep of her claymore caught a kernclaw mid-leap and clove him in two.

Josiri helped a wounded constable to his feet, then dropped back to where Malachi stood flanked by Brass and Jaridav's phoenix tabards. He held a sword – though he hadn't used it – and Brass was under strict instructions to keep him from the fight. Better to know that Malachi was close to danger, but protected, than to wonder what trouble he'd found. Better still if he'd stayed at the palace with Messela, but that decision was in the past.

"I keep thinking about last year," said Malachi.

Josiri recalled the confession, offered in the council chamber's privacy earlier that morning. Lady Kiradin too had clung to the Hayadra Grove, leveraging divine tradition to legitimacy. But for Malachi's fool's bargain ... "Nothing would have changed. The vranakin had their talons into Ebigail. She'd have fed them anything to keep herself afloat."

"Maybe." Malachi's eyes touched on a leather-aproned corpse. One of many citizens who'd paid steep price for courage, and more to come. "All this for my daughter."

"For us all," Josiri corrected, hoping that the words took. "The mists are bound to the Raven, the Raven to the pontiffs. Sidara can break that bond."

Bird-calls screeched. The clamour at the mob's head redoubled as more vranakin joined the fray. Josiri nodded at Brass. "Stay with him."

"Sir."

Bell-song swept through the gathering mist, mournful notes chiming mockery of a wedding carillon. Blood running cold, Josiri cupped his hands and bellowed at the skies.

"Ana! Don't wait for us! Go! Go!"

Two vranakin led Sidara down from the cart. Another set a garland of bloodied feathers about her neck. Krastin's thin, mocking laughter hissed out beneath the bells. Shurla hobbled from her post beside the grave and slid a golden ring onto the corpse's finger. A second glinted as she turned to Sidara.

"A bride of the grave. You *are* honoured."

Taking her left hand, she forced the second ring onto her finger. Sidara flung it into the grass.

Shurla crouched to retrieve it. "Tell me, Lady Reveque ... How well did defiance serve your father?" Dark eyes shifted to Constans. "What fortune do you suppose it will bring your brother?"

Sidara went still as the ring was forced upon her a second time, her eyes dull and her last resistance spent. "You'll pay for what you've done to my family."

Krastin tutted. "I will add the debt to my ledger. Prepare her!"

Altiris watched, torn, as vranakin used black ribbon to bind Sidara's arms across her chest, and her legs at ankle and knee. Part of him burned to intervene, despite the certainty of death. The rest cowered, desperate not to draw the pontiffs' gaze.

The last strand of ribbon gagged Sidara to silence. Two vranakin laid her upon the bier beside her decaying husband-to-be.

Arms outspread, Shurla turned her back on both. "In the Raven's holy name, we bind our beloved cousin Athariss to this Daughter of Light."

Six vranakin bore the bier aloft on tarnished brass handles. They processed towards the open grave, spent feathers of Sidara's garland trailing behind. The Shaddra's branches sighed in the fitful breeze.

"With the union of her last breath and his endless shadow, we renounce Lumestra's claim upon this city." Shurla's voice turned shrill with fervour. "Let all within its walls become cousin to the Raven, and servants to his loyal Parliament. Let—"

"No!"

Altiris ripped his mask clear and dragged his sword free of his cloak. Elder cousins closed ranks before him, the stench of dead flesh rank in his nostrils. A withered hand closed around his wrist. Another about his throat. Cold air turned bitter.

High above, sunlight parted the mists. Alabaster branches and golden leaves darkened to silhouette. An armoured body plunged from the heavens, swathed in sunlight. Shurla crumpled beneath its impact. Flesh folded inwards, the crackle of breaking bones and popped joints drowned out by the pontiff's agonised shriek.

Serathi.

The word hissed through the crowd, uttered with awe in some places, with fear in most.

Golden wings spread wide, Anastacia rose up from Shurla's mangled body, cocked her head and regarded Krastin with malice. Mist hissed and recoiled.

The pontiff shied from the light, fear yielding to outrage as his hands fell away and courage returned. "You can't have her!"

[[I wasn't asking.]]

The claymore gleamed. It severed Altiris' captor's wrist with a sound like brittle leaves underfoot. A second sweep of the claymore traced a red arc through the cortege, scattering Athariss' remains and pitching a wriggling Sidara onto the muddied grass.

"Defiler!" An accusing finger accompanied Krastin's shriek. "Destroy it!"

The strike of Anastacia's armoured fist drove him to his knees.

Elder cousins bore down. The first collapsed, insects scattered from her robes as claymore hewed head from body. Anastacia took wing, the sword's gleaming arc biting deep into the tattered garb of a second. The crowd surged, fear fading into the rising cacophony of bird voices, ceremony and captives forgotten.

A lasso closed about Anastacia's neck and drew tight, only to be split by a slash of steel. An elder cousin grabbed at her armoured shin and reeled off with half his head sliced away. Another grabbed her boot. A second noose tightened around her neck. A third about her wrist. Wings faltered. Inch by inch they dragged her down.

Her eyes found Altiris'. [[I thought you were a phoenix. Make yourself useful.]]

Then she was gone, sunlight drowned beneath a tide of vranakin grey.

Altiris' fingers closed around his sword. With a scream, he ran past Shurla's twitching, distended body and flung himself at the cortege's dazed survivors. Steel bit. He leapt over the falling body, a scrape of swords driving the second vranakin's crooked blade aside. The counterblow came as instinct, and then there were only the dead, the dying . . . and Sidara.

A tug pulled her gag free. His sword sliced away the worst of the ribbons. She staggered to her feet, breathing fast and shallow, her eyes wide. "Is that Ana?"

"You have to ask?"

But not for long. Whatever obsession the vranakin harboured about Sidara now paled beside outrage at Anastacia. The inner grove writhed with bodies, shadows against light.

Metal scraped on metal, and metal on stone. A porcelain hand and tattered sleeve emerged from the brawl. A vranakin spiralled away and struck a tree with a sickening thud. Others pressed forward with rope and blade.

A kernclaw held a dented breastplate aloft to shrieking cheers, and hurled it away. A gauntlet followed. An elder cousin hoisted a chunk of stone high in both hands and brought it crashing down. Anastacia's head snapped aside, daylight streaming from a jagged crack across her brow. Krastin looked on, lips hooked in malice.

"We have to help her," said Altiris. "*Please* tell me you can help her."

Sidara pursed her lips. Dismay became a scowl. Her breathing steadied. She stooped and grabbed a discarded vranakin sword. "With this, yes."

"Put that down, my bonny. Play the dutiful wife, and wait your turn."

Hawkin emerged from the mist, Constans shoved ahead and her dagger never far from his throat.

"Hawkin." Bitterness flooded Sidara's tone as she obeyed. Altiris reluctantly followed suit. "Seems only yesterday you were afraid for me. Was that all a lie?"

"This isn't what I wanted." For all the doubt in her words, Altiris found none in tone or expression. "But we all owe duty to our family."

"Your family?" snapped Altiris. "Vranakin aren't family. They're vermin. Come lean days they'll gnaw your bones."

"Only the weak go to the wall. The strong thrive."

Altiris cast a hand at an elder cousin's infested remains. "For what? To become a corpse that doesn't know it's dead? That's not prosperity. You're a free woman, Hawkin. You can choose something else."

"Freedom?" Trembling with rage, she tore back her left sleeve. The dark whorls of a rose-brand stood stark against skin. "I've never been free, not since the ships came to Disri. Sold one to another, on and on for ten years 'til the Crowmarket bought my bridle and gave me a family. What's a northwealder's life next to that?"

Altiris winced. How similar their paths had been, both of them "rescued" by the vranakin – only he'd been marked for sacrifice, and she for service. A slight difference in fortunes, and it might have been his blade at Constans' throat.

"It can be everything." He locked his eyes to Constans' and prayed the boy wasn't too far gone to fear. "I owe Sidara my life. If it's lost saving her, or her brother, I'll consider it well spent. So you have to choose."

Weaponless, he stepped closer.

"Stay back!" The first panic crowded Hawkin's eyes, and with it the suggestion that for all her claims she couldn't bring herself to harm Constans. The dagger slipped from the boy's neck and jabbed towards Altiris. "I won't tell you again!"

She doubled over as Constans drove a wiry elbow into her gut. Altiris lunged.

The rag-masked woman crumpled beneath Josiri's sword, the light gone from her eyes before she hit the roadway. The vranakin line buckled. In ones and twos, resistance melted away. A cheer growled to new heights. The mob came forward, spilling out of Sinner's Mile and plunging beneath the mist-choked trees.

Josiri ran with them.

A kernclaw boiled out of the branches. Bloody talons snatched a greatcoated sailor into oblivion. Spectral birds parted about the sweep of a pickaxe handle and reformed behind the wielder. Josiri's sword drove the kernclaw back. Brass lumbered out of the mists and finished the job with a stoic thrust and a disdainful grimace.

"Brass?" Josiri cast about for Malachi. "Where's Lord Reveque?"

He scowled. "Lost him soon as we hit the grove, sir. Don't know where he is."

Mists boiled back from the grove's centre, laying bare the seething brawl by the graveside, and a cadaverous man, arms spread wide and lips curled in a snarl of rage. "Enough!"

Black eyes gleamed in a pallid face. The day darkened.

Josiri fell to his knees, gasping for breath. The Hayadra Grove drowned beneath an inky veil, thick with keening and terrified moans.

Decaying hands burst from the ground in a spray of soil, dragging him down even as the grave-woken corpses hauled their way into the light. As Josiri reached his knees, grotesque faces stared back. Peeling lips hooked rictus smiles beneath cloudy, opalescent eyes. Plump maggots glistened in rotting, pitted flesh.

"You let us die," hissed Calenne.

"You killed us," said his mother.

"No!" Josiri clamped his eyes shut and pressed his hands to his ears. Stinking breath rushed across his cheeks. "Traitor!"

"Your bodies burned!" he screamed. "You're not real!"

He opened his eyes. The apparitions had gone, but the terror remained, chattering at his teeth and writhing like worms in his gut. It hurt to move, even to breathe. The moans of those who'd followed him up Sinner's Mile echoed about him. Through streaming eyes, he glimpsed men and women on their knees, or twitching in foetal form. Vranakin shrieked and started forward.

Only one man still stood, stumbling towards the grove's heart like one in a dream, an unbloodied sword in his hand.

Malachi.

Malachi ignored the crowd swarming about Anastacia, their heels rutting the ground as the ropes about arms and wings went taut. He cast from his mind the horror of Sidara's arms flung protectively about a twitching, mewling Constans; the sight of Altiris clutching hands to his head as Hawkin staggered away. He held his course, one foot in front of the other. The howling horror of Krastin's gaze assailed him at every step.

An elder cousin drifted to bar his path, only to retreat at a twitch of Krastin's raven-headed cane. "How is this possible? You cannot resist!"

Worthlessness and failure. Sorrow and loss. Black clouds swallowed Malachi's thoughts, seeking to stifle his soul.

"What would you show me?" he snarled. "My children dead? My wife murdered? A homeland overrun? This city swallowed through my hubris? I've seen it. You made me live it. What more can you do to me?"

With a cry born of every mistake, every loss and every bitter scrap of shame, Malachi rammed his sword between Krastin's ribs. The force drove the pontiff back until the blade shuddered deep into the Shaddra's alabaster bark. Letting go the sword, he slipped his paper knife from his pocket and rammed it deep into Krastin's left eye.

The pontiff's shriek of pain deepened to a ragged scream.

Malachi ripped the knife free and stabbed it into Krastin's right.

Black clouds dissipated, leaving weariness deeper than any Malachi had ever known. He stumbled away, bleak satisfaction fed by a rising growl: the sound of men and women pulling free from conjured fears and finding courage in the striving. The sound of hope renewed as fear bled away.

The resurgent mob reached Anastacia, Josiri at their head. Robes slackened as vranakin fell dead. A Lancras knight withered to dust in an elder cousin's grip. Anastacia ripped free of her remaining ropes, light bleeding from her brow, and snapped the cousin's neck with a gristly crack.

"This . . . changes . . . nothing," gasped Krastin.

"Oh, but it does," said Malachi. "I've made many mistakes this past year, but my worst was fighting you alone. I'm not alone. I never was. My daughter understands that. The more I tried to hold Sidara back, the more determined she was to help others. Her courage shames me. The future belongs to her kind. It will do better without you and I."

"Father!"

Fear ebbed at Sidara's desperate shout. The afterimage of his own father's pyre fading, Altiris lurched upright to see her staring off into the mists. For a heartbeat, he glimpsed a swaying Malachi Reveque standing over Krastin's hooded form. Beneath the Shaddra, Shurla thrashed in the spoil of the new-dug grave and spasmed to one knee, snarling as reknotted muscles dragged broken bones back into place. Then the mists shifted, and all were gone from sight.

Altiris grabbed Sidara's shoulders. "Hawkin? Where is she?"

"She ran," said Constans. "I hope a prizrak gets her."

The lad was pale, but had a crooked sword half his height gripped tight in both hands.

Greenish-white mist turned filthy grey with vranakin garb as newcomers stalked eastwards across the grove.

"Altiris! Sidara! Move!"

Drawn by Lord Trelan's beckoning hand, they ran headlong through the mist, ushered into a circle of worn and filthy faces. Other voices ringing through the mists spoke to a battle still raging – close or near, Altiris had no way to tell.

Sidara embraced Lord Trelan. "Uncle Josiri, my father—"

"I know," he replied. "We'll help him if we can. He'd want you to be safe."

"You two are no end of trouble, you know that?" said Kurkas.

"Sorry, captain," said Altiris.

"Eyes and sword outward, and we'll call it even. This ain't done. Constans, you stay close to me, or I'll hand you over to the vranakin myself, you hear me?"

The boy paled and took up position at the captain's side. Altiris made no move to obey, his attention stolen by Anastacia's plight. She lay awkwardly against a ruined wall at the centre of the ragged ring, wings crumpled beneath her. Light streamed from her brow, and through rents in armour and gown.

Sidara crouched beside her, and yelped as Anastacia's hand clamped her wrist.

[[Take the light. Make it yours again.]]

She blinked. "I don't understand . . . "

[[That first night we met. I stole a piece of you. I couldn't help myself. A moment of weakness, but I felt stronger than I had in years. I took more the night your mother died. It's why you can't hear the light. It's why it doesn't come at your call. I told myself I'd no choice. That I needed it to hold back the roof. But then I awoke in the rubble, as close to my old self as cold clay allowed, and I realised my want was greater than my need. Take it back.]]

Lord Trelan knelt beside them both, his eyes never leaving Anastacia's. Her fingers brushed his cheek and fell away. He bowed his head, hand shaking as it took hers. "Do as she says."

Sidara hung her head. "What happens to you?"

Anastacia hesitated. [[It doesn't matter.]]

"It matters to me."

[[Then you're a fool. Give me your other hand.]]

Sidara clasped her hands tight about Anastacia's. A burst of blinding light rushed outwards. Altiris shied away, dark spots dancing before his eyes. When they cleared, Anastacia lay still, her wings and hair faded to nothing. Sidara knelt beside her, motionless as the statue the other resembled. Eyes closed, she gathered up the broken, darkened body into embrace, tender as a girl with a favourite doll, or a mother with her child.

Altiris swallowed and reached for her. "Sidara?"

The mist thickened with vranakin. Crow voices screeched to cacophony.

*

Elder cousins circled, tattered grey robes dancing through the mist. Black blood welled from Krastin's eye sockets and hissed away silver.

"You think this will kill me? I walk with death! Even the Tyrant Queen feared us!"

"Feared you?" Malachi stumbled back, laughing without humour. "I've read the histories. The Undawning Deep. Scattered fragments of Malatriant's own Testament that generations of provosts failed to destroy. She didn't fear you. You depressed her."

"She abandoned the city to us! She fled to Darkmere!"

"And you made Tressia an open sewer. A rotting nest built on false promises of family and eternal life. Preying on desperation because you're numb to all else. She needed you as a cautionary tale, Krastin. That's all you ever were. Something to make a Tyrant Queen seem a saint."

Krastin's shaking hand ripped the paper knife from a ruined eye and hurled it away.

"Malatriant is dead," he spat. "You will beg for that same mercy."

Exhausted, Malachi sank to the ground. "You'll have nothing more from me."

Crow voices cackled to a crescendo. Bells chimed out. Malachi's skin crackled with cold as the elder cousins drifted closer.

The ground shook.

The ring of vranakin shrank inwards around Josiri's mismatched band, their confidence growing as more came shrieking to their ranks.

Josiri kept his sword steady, and his eyes forward . . . anything other than think on Ana's lifeless body. Why hadn't she told him? Pride. Selfishness. Shame. All and none, knotted deep about her soul. For all her divinity, Anastacia had always been more human than she'd cared to admit.

"She knew what was at stake," murmured Kurkas. "She made her choice."

He swallowed back bitterness. They'd failed. Tressia would fall, and the Raven perish. That the divine war would claim the vranakin soon after was of sparse comfort. "That's just it. She didn't know – not about the rest. I'd no chance to tell her."

Kurkas grimaced a reflection of Josiri's swirling emotions. He raised his voice. "Don't take this the wrong way, sah ... but retirement's looking damn good right about now."

Nervous laughter rippled at the poor joke. Josiri cast about at worried faces as the tremors quickened. Brass, lugubrious as ever. Jaridav, her hand shaking but eyes steady. Constables. Knights. Citizens with bloodied swords and filthy faces. Even a handful of vranakin, their masks torn away to mark forsaken allegiance. Rallied to the cause of light by a serathi's example. Bound to it still despite her fall. Even Constans, the boy standing straighter than some of the men, the sword steady for all it was too large for him.

All looked to him for hope. Not because he was the son of the Southshires' Phoenix. Not out of authority borrowed from Viktor, or granted by Malachi's friendship. But because he'd led them to that place. Because for all that he was a southwealder, he was one of them also, and the city his home. Strange to recognise that in the same moment all was to be stripped away.

[[*Well*, this is all very morbid.]]

Josiri's heart leapt. "Ana?"

He turned, and there she stood. Cold and dark – diminished by the light's departure, and tottering on the point of collapse. A hand *glinked* against a porcelain cheek. It traced the crack along the gold and alabaster brow and the hairless pate behind. A hollow sigh flowed.

[[So this is selflessness? I hate it.]]

Josiri embraced her amid another ripple of laughter. They didn't understand, as Josiri understood, what she'd given up. But she was *alive*.

"I thought I'd lost you."

[[It wasn't mine, Josiri,]] she said wearily. [[I couldn't keep it, however much I wanted to.]]

He glanced at Sidara, still kneeling motionless in the mud. Breathing, but otherwise lost to the world. "And now?"

[[That's up to her.]]

A bleak shadow loomed beyond the curtain of mist, hunched and distorted by bones not yet fully healed. A crooked arm reached out in accusation.

"I want their eyes!" screeched Shurla. "The girl for the grave and rest for the Raven! Let them taste his holy wrath!"

The vranakin quickened to a run, more afraid of their pontiff than the foe. Elder cousins kept pace, tattered robes streaming behind. Kernclaws flickered between the trees and over ruins, borne aloft by squalling bird forms. Fade-curled leaves fell like umber rain, shuddered from the branches by thundering feet.

Josiri turned about. "We give them nothing!" he shouted. "Not the girl! Not our fear! Nor satisfaction!"

Altiris pushed his way to the front, sword aloft. "For the Phoenix!"

"No. Not this time." Josiri laid a hand on his shoulder and raised his own blade high. "For the Republic!"

"*For the Republic!*"

The mist came alive with golden eyes.

The elder cousin froze, its rag-draped hand inches from Malachi's face, then jerked upward into the mist. Bronze arms flexed, and the kraikon ripped it in two with a sound like tearing cloth. The construct strode on, another cousin falling beneath its implacable tread.

More gathered behind, some bearing two-handed swords, others with no weapons save ponderous bronze fists. Some staggered along, mangled legs dragging behind and golden light cracking across rents in unrepaired skin. Others were more shell than sculpted form, lattices of metal bones with the barest "flesh" to hold them together. Simarka darted between. Screeches died to dust as vranakin perished beneath fangs and claws.

The broken and the unfinished, the unloved and the bleak, striding through mists that should have robbed them of life and purpose. Pulverising all in their path.

Krastin sagged against the impaling sword, his efforts to pull it free sapped by aghast wonder.

Malachi stared, his jaw slack, recognition creeping through paralysed thoughts. "Blessed Lumestra . . ."

Constructs couldn't function in the mists. That truth had made the depths of Dregmeet and the Forbidden Places of the south havens for fugitives of all creeds. Mist swallowed the light. Or at least, a *proctor's* light. But a proctor's art was but an echo of the divine. A sheen of sunlight. A memory.

Had Malachi ever doubted that Sidara wielded something more, he did so no longer.

"The foundry," gasped Altiris. "She's roused the foundry!"

The foundry, lost in the mists, its keepers slain and its children paralysed.

Until now.

Dumbstruck, he watched as the vranakin assault broke apart, shattered by the onset of sparking, lumbering kraikons, and the sleeker forms of simarka rushing beneath.

A kernclaw ducked a kraikon's pulverising fist and was dragged away screaming by a simarka's fangs. One vranakin – a vast brute of a man with a long-handled Thrakkian hammer – brought a kraikon to hands and knees with a whirling, booming blow. Another, its face an empty iron skull, scooped the fellow up without slowing and flung him from sight.

The crow-born ebbed, their anarchic right flank swept away by the half-forged horrors come lurching out of the trees. A handful fought on until Shurla fled, her cadaverous form swallowed up by the mists.

Altiris joined his voice to the rising cheer. Jaridav sank to the ground, overcome by disbelieving laughter.

"It's over," said Brass, his hand twitching to the sign of the sun even as he mopped his brow. "We damn well won."

"Not yet." Lord Trelan ran a short distance into the mists, then cried in frustration and cast down his sword. "She'll have fled back to Dregmeet. We might never find her. Not in time to break the Crowmarket's hold on the mists. We've taken back the city, but the world . . . ?"

The words, bleak as the tone that delivered them, shivered Altiris to his core. "My lord? I don't understand."

"Maybe it's better that way."

"Where's my sister?" piped up Constans. "Where's Sidara?"

Sidara strode into sight moments after the final kraikon had faded. Golden light played about her shoulders, and a pride of simarka loped at her heels. She walked slowly, carefully, as if a single misplaced step would pitch her to the ground, never to rise. Her right hand was clenched to a fist, blood dripping from the soiled bandage about her wrist. A battered sword hung loosely from her left, its tip trailing in the mud.

"Sidara!"

Turning his back on Krastin's sullen, pinioned form, Malachi held his daughter tight. A heart dragged down by fear and worry ached anew with unbearable, perfect joy. "I thought I'd lost you. I thought ... "

Words slipped away. He let them go.

"It's all right, Father," she replied. "*I'm* all right."

He stepped back, and felt no shame at tears cuffed away. "It's over. It's finally over."

She shook her head. "Not yet. Something else has to happen first."

He narrowed his eyes, suspicion dispelling happiness. Up close, Sidara looked older, so much older than when he'd seen her last, three days and a lifetime ago. And her eyes ... So hard to see those of his little girl through the gleam of gold. "What? What has to happen?"

Another simarka drew up beneath the Shaddra, this one dragging a thrashing bundle in gilt-edged robes, the flesh about her eyes torn ragged by parallel claws. Shurla. She bolted as soon as the lion opened its jaws, and crumped again as its weight bore her to the ground. Then, to Malachi's utter amazement, the simarka planted its haunches on the small of the pontiff's back, and purred.

"Thank you, Fredrik." Sidara smoothed the simarka's sculpted mane, her attention split between the captive pontiffs. "I'm going to kill them, Father. For Mother. For you. For everyone they've ever hurt, or ever used. But that's not enough. I don't want either of them to meet the Raven believing that the other has escaped. That their squalid cult endures."

Golden light rippled along her sword. Shurla screamed as it stabbed down through her neck. The mists guttered.

Krastin glared through eyes not yet fully healed, and grappled with the sword buried in his flesh. It seemed to Malachi that he should have been able to free himself long ago, until he remembered that the Shaddra was blessed, and that a divine hayadra might not be as passive as other trees. That perhaps Krastin remained trapped because the Shaddra refused to let him go.

"I curse you, Sidara Reveque," he croaked as she drew near. "In the name of the Raven and the deathless Dark that sired him, I curse you and your line to its last generation. Let them always be apart, distrusted. Alone, even in a crowd."

She smiled sadly, as if in recollection. "You threaten me with what I already have."

Her hand brushed the pommel. Light rushed across the hilt and along the blade, crackling across Krastin's flesh and severing his bond to immortality. A rush of black blood slicked the hayadra's alabaster flank and gushed away into the mud as the wound at last came due. A last stuttering, pained wheeze, and the last pontiff of the Parliament of Crows was gone. Just one more corpse in a grove strewn with them.

The last of the mist faded away, colour rushing back in as the Living Realm pulled free of Otherworld's mists. In the distance, rooftops gathered beneath watery skies.

Sidara staggered and sank against Malachi, her bloody right hand easing open and her halo fading. Her eyes dimmed, the gold become shards amid blue the mirror of her mother's. Malachi knew he should have been scared of her, and a part of him was, but the greater part was proud beyond words, and knew without doubt that Lily would have been too.

He held her close, lost in wonder to have been so swiftly and completely outgrown.

"Now is it ended?" he asked.

"Now it's ended."

Sixty-Two

There wasn't so much a threshold as a thinning, the mist gate bleeding away into the diffuse vapour Apara knew all too well. The only clue that they'd passed from Otherworld to somewhere else was that the somewhere else was nearly pitch black, and thick with a bitter, metallic scent. A mineshaft's metal rails led away into the tunnel's gloom, hazy light a dim prospect beyond the drifting etravia. Their soft, mournful song teased forth memories of happier times, insofar as Apara had ever had any.

The princessa missed her footing in the darkness, and leaned against the curved tunnel wall for support. "Where are we?"

"Dregmeet." Apara forced confidence into her voice. No sense letting the princessa see her uncertainty. The place felt familiar, but just astray enough that none of it felt quite right. "The tunnels beneath Tzalcourt. There are mine workings from the old days. They flood when the tide comes in, but they're useful for those looking to hide things. Maybe for the Raven, too."

"Let's hope it doesn't flood while we're down here," the princessa replied. "I don't swim well in the dark."

"It won't." Ashana remained a pale presence in the gloom, lit from within by moonlight while all else was dark. "We're further afield than you think. We've no choice but to be. Jack's heart is the stuff of folklore, spoken of in a hundred tales. The difficulty lay in retrieving it. The Raven is more guarded. The only piece of himself he'll let us find is one he doesn't yet know exists."

Apara swallowed a pang of frustration. Her saviour though the

Goddess had been, her oblique speech was too much like that of the Crowmarket's pontiffs for comfort. Especially with the prospect of cross-ing paths with the Raven drawing ever closer. Nor did it help that the shadowthorn princessa seemed incapable of hearing the contradiction in the Goddess' words. Still, there was pride to be taken in the business. The Silver Owl stealing from the gods – a claim worth coin, though she'd never prove it.

"How can we find a piece of the Raven that even he's ignorant of?"

Her demand drew a sour look from the princessa, but Apara was growing used to those. Just as she was used to making no dent in Ashana's serene composure.

"Because none of this has happened yet," said Ashana. "We've walked the face of the clock into tomorrow. That's why the Raven doesn't know to hide it. He's the Keeper of the Dead. His whole being looks to what was, not what will be. Death belongs to the past. Light – my light – exists everywhere that *is* everywhere."

"That's not possible," said Melanna.

"Time flows differently within the mists," Ashana replied. "Past and future are woven together. If you know the paths, they are yours to travel. How else can a journey of days become one of minutes, or one of weeks become days?"

Delivered thus, simply and without brag, outrageous claim became inevitable. Had not Apara met her younger self in Dregmeet? At what point was it better to accept that delusion was reality?

Apara nodded. "Before I left Tressia, the mists had twisted the streets back on themselves. More than the streets. I saw ... I saw a piece of my past. When I was a child, I saw that same moment as a piece of my future. I didn't recognise it, but that's what it was."

"Then the Raven – any of you – can walk in the past or the future?" said Melanna.

"We can, but our actions change nothing – that remains an ephemeral privilege," Ashana replied. "In our way, we're as separate from the flow of time as Otherworld's mists. We all experience the passage of time differently, just as the worlds of the celestial clock experience time dif-ferently. In any case, my siblings seldom bother in the attempt. It would mean admitting to error. Divine pride is a thing both rigid and fragile."

"But not yours?" asked Apara.

"No. At least ... not yet. I still remember what I was. One day, I'll be as distant and cruel as any of them. But today, I can still think like an ephemeral and perceive enough of time's passage to make this possible."

Melanna's brow creased. "If we're here, in days to come ... Does this mean we're successful? The Reckoning doesn't happen."

"When the Reckoning comes, it won't happen all at once, everywhere. It's still a war, and wars are fought over territory." Ashana stared up at the tunnel roof, a hazy arch half-seen through the dark. "The world might be ending, even as we speak."

"You mean you don't know?" said Apara.

"It might be best if you hurried."

"We don't even know what we're looking for."

"A piece of the Raven. You'll know it when you see it."

Apara bit back a retort. Etravia drifting from her path, she stalked uphill along the tunnel, footsteps guided by the harsh overspill of firestone lanterns somewhere up ahead. Either Ashana genuinely didn't know what she wanted found, or she delighted too much in playing games to say. And if a war between the gods *were* unfolding aboveground, the sooner Apara was gone – saying nothing of being parted from the Goddess' company – the better.

"She saved your life," said the princessa, drawing level. "Show some respect."

"She's using me. As she's using you."

"That's not true, she—"

A deep, grinding rumble flooded the tunnel and set Apara's teeth rattling in her jaw. The princessa halted, her eyes widening in alarm and her hand falling to her sword.

The moment of vulnerability – the loss of poise – went some way to easing Apara's frustration. "Relax, princessa. It's just the soul of the world singing. At least, that's what a priest told me. Go deep enough in Dregmeet, you'll hear it all the time."

"The soul of the world ..." Reverence mingled with suspicion in Melanna's tone.

"Not really. That's just what they call it. It's kraikons digging out new mausolea for the highbloods. I saw one of the machines once. Big as a house. Can't have the rich dumped in a pauper's grave, can we? And if the war's going badly?" She shrugged. "That means a lot more digging."

The rumble faded. The princessa's hand slackened on her sword and they pressed on until the darkened tunnel opened up into a broader cavern, awash with singing etravia and the sickly green light of Otherworld's mists.

Stuttering firestone lanterns gave shape to a simple loading terrace on Apara's right, and to an ornate archway leading beyond. On the left, the tunnel wall arced up to meet the ceiling's crooked fixtures. Too florid for an abandoned mine. A half-finished mausoleum, left to rot, its construction tunnels sealed somewhere beyond? That would fit.

Sadness thickened the air, a sense of abandonment Apara often felt when walking Dregmeet's decaying monuments. Not everything was useful for ever. Then again, with Otherworld clinging so close, who was to say how the place usually appeared? The Raven's crooked art was everywhere. Grotesques leered atop curved stone buttresses, and above decaying mosaics depicting the clash of armies. And beyond Otherworld's echo, a shimmering mirage of mismatched tile and torn posters.

The song faded. Weeping arose in its place. The manner of sorrow that left the listener heartsick and raw, if they didn't hear the hunger beneath. "Princessa . . ."

Etravia scattered as the prizrak came shrieking out of the mists. Apara glimpsed bloodied eyes beneath a tattered hood. Black claws opened her cheek to the bone as she twisted away. Balance lost, she fell, her head striking the terrace's stone floor. The pain was distant, as all pain had been since she'd woken into her new life, but the world reeled drunkenly.

Half-blind, she lashed out a boot. A crunch of bone and the prizrak dropped atop her, slashing and tearing at her face and throat. *Now* the pain demanded recognition, a score of tiny fires billowing to a blaze.

Apara brought her talons about. Prone as she was, the angle robbed the blow of force. The prizrak barely flinched, its sleeve shredded, but little else.

A cry. A gleam of steel. A fountain of dark, stinking blood. The prizrak slumped sideways, its head bouncing away into the loading gulley before coming to rest against a corroded rail. The panting princessa let her sword drop from its two-handed grip and helped Apara to her feet.

Apara's fingers traced flayed flesh as the muscle and skin of her face reknitted, the wounds healing just as those inflicted by Hawkin Darrow had before. It still seemed unreal.

She stared down at the prizrak as calmed etravia resumed their song. It had been a woman once. Possibly a vranakin, by her garb. What she herself might have been. If Kurkas had abandoned her in Otherworld. Had Krastin made good on his threats. Prizrak or eternal. Fates bound close enough to touch.

Perhaps she *did* owe the Goddess a measure of respect.

She offered the princessa a sharp nod. "Thank you."

The other wiped her sword clean on the prizrak's corpse. "What now?"

Apara cast about. "I don't know. Through the arch, perhaps. Or . . . Hold on a moment. What's this?"

She followed the loading terrace to where it joined the tunnel wall and halted at a charred mound. The embers of a fire long burned out, save that it smouldered the same green as Otherworld's skies. She felt a kinship with the remains, similar to the one she'd shared with her late, unlamented ravencloak, though immeasurably feebler. Crouching, she glimpsed the unmistakeable shape of a hand among the fragments.

Rising, she sought the princessa in the mists, but found no sign.

A hand closed about the wrist of Apara's talon-hand. Another at the base of her neck. A bellowed warning in an unfamiliar language, a shove, and she found herself up against the tiles, shoulder creaking as her assailant twisted her hand towards her shoulder blades. Torn posters fell like falling leaves.

She tried to pull free. A sharp tug on her arm, and stars burst behind her eyes. Leverage was everything. Her attacker had it, she didn't.

He shouted again, hot and urgent in her ear.

Blotting out the man's gibberish, Apara tallied options. Talons pinned against her back. No way to communicate. No way to get free without a broken arm. But broken arms healed. Even thinking it provoked nausea, but what else was there if the princessa was down, or fled?

She gritted her teeth and shifted position.

Another stream of foreign words echoed through the mists, this time in the princessa's voice. The sword's whisper silenced the man's angry reply. The pressure about Apara's wrist and neck vanished. As she pushed away from the wall, he slammed into it, hands raised level with his head and the princessa's sword-point at his chest.

Apara glared. "Took your time."

The princessa offered a lopsided shrug. "I wasn't sure whether the place was vulnerable, or just looked it."

"Hilarious." Apara made practised appraisal of the man, alert for threat. Younger than her, older than the princessa. Complexion more a match for a Tressian than Hadari. More wariness than malice in his eyes. "You understand him?"

"Mostly," replied the princessa. "It's a Britonisian commoner's dialect. His accent's appalling and his grammar's non-existent."

What was a Britonisian doing beneath Dregmeet? Was Tressia doomed to become a province of Empire? "Good to know you rub shoulders with commoners. You want to be careful. Bed down in the kennels, and who knows what you'll pick up."

"You can't rule people who can't understand you," she replied icily.

Apara grunted away her surprise. "Tell him we don't want to hurt him."

"Don't we?"

"Not unless he gives us reason."

"I doubt he will. He's not a warrior."

The fading ache in Apara's arm and shoulder begged to differ, as did her instincts. For all that the man was dressed like a steward whose employer had fallen on hard times, instinct said otherwise.

"No. He's a watchman of some kind. Maybe something more." She glanced to her right, and the doorway hidden in the crook of the smooth cavern wall. "Tell him we don't want to hurt him. Ask him what happened."

A stream of strange syllables followed, a back and forth between the princessa and the man that stuttered and faltered as they wrestled disjointed language to common purpose.

"His name's Loqueton," the princessa said at last. "He speaks of a battle here . . . against the Raven."

Apara swallowed, the mists colder than before. "Is . . . Is he still here?"

The exchange began anew. Loqueton's eyes darted to the pile of smouldering ash, two paces distant, then snapped back to the princessa's sword.

She scowled. "It's hard to follow. The words are all jumbled. But I think he's saying that there *is* no Raven any longer ... Something about a pale queen usurping him. She promised to stop ... " She paused, head canted and eyes half-closed as she sifted another burst of gibberish. "Something about mists in the streets. Maybe she didn't uphold her end of the bargain, whatever it was. I don't really understand that part. He says he was watching in case she returned."

"Then I suppose we've come for the ashes," Apara said.

But what use were ashes? The heart she understood. It was a part of Jack, and such a prize could be leveraged in all manner of ways. Blackmail was blackmail, ephemeral or divine. But ashes?

She stared at the Raven's remains. Somehow, her life was nothing but ash of late. First Abbeyfields and Lilyana Reveque, then the ghastly bride in Fellhallow ... At least she'd missed the burning this time. If the Raven was gone, maybe the Reckoning *was* raging aboveground, and he its latest casualty. How much of the city remained? How much of *Tressia* remained? The desire to see was outweighed only by apprehension over what she would behold.

The ashes shifted. A beady eye gleamed. The charred hand rolled aside, and a glossy black wing flapped free. Another spill of ash, and a bird, no larger than Apara's hand, strutted back and forth atop the embers. She pounced on the raven without thinking, fingers closed tight about its small body before it took wing. It went deathly still and shot her a glance with rather more malice than it should have been capable.

With the bird under her hand, the ashes turned dark in Apara's mind – the part of her that was still vranakin, even now, losing what fleeting kinship they'd shared. The bird, however? It felt like a part of her – or a part of who she'd *been*. Ashana had been right: she *did* know it when she saw it. She was holding the Raven, or whatever fragment remained after his queen's betrayal. Diminished. Perhaps not even fully aware. Was that why the mists lingered?

A god trapped in the palm of her hand. At her mercy.

Close her hand tight and it would repay all that had been done to her in his name. All she'd been forced to do.

But then the world would die, and everyone she knew alongside. Ashana had freed her from the Crowmarket. Strange symmetry in sparing the Raven in turn. A vranakin took everything she could, even life. The Silver Owl had the luxury of choice.

She looked up to find both the princessa's and Loqueton's eyes on her. Suspicious. Wary.

"This is what we came for."

"The bird?" replied the princessa. "You're certain?"

"It's a piece of the Raven, just like your goddess told us." Her left hand tight about the bird, Apara smoothed back the feathers of its crown and earned another baleful glare from beady eyes. "Let Loqueton go. Tell him the mists might recede once we've gone. Tell him I hope they do."

Sixty-Three

The Raven's scream reverberated through Rosa's bones. Anger and fear. Intoxicating. Dizzying. No longer able to determine whether those sensations were hers or belonged to the bleak god who had made himself her master, she knew only that she had to act. Hands braced against stone. Boots dug through grime and found purchase.

Even as she tensed, the weight on her back shifted. Jack's roots scraped at her spine. Muscles spasmed, every inch of her body afire. The Raven's scream faded beneath her own.

{{Hush,}} said Jack. {{Don't you want to be free of him?}}

The roots drew back. Rosa collapsed, wheezing, hands trembling. The blue-white blaze of a burning thornmaiden blurred. Duskhazel muddied her ragged breaths.

{{We will *all* be free of him.}}

White flame blazed beneath grey skies. Saran's sword hacked through thrashing branches. Jack screeched and flung a hand to shield his face. Moonfire sliced away a pair of crooked fingers. The weight on Rosa's back shifted as Jack staggered, his voice thick with outrage.

{{Betrayer!}}

Branches whipped back. Released, the Raven crashed against the wagon. A wheel splintered to spars beneath his falling body. His hat rolled away. Roots ripped free of Rosa's flesh, leaving her gasping. She glimpsed the Emperor stumble away, a wounded leg dragging. A black stain soured the golden scales at his waist.

"You used me!" roared Kai.

His voice was as frayed as his appearance, but his sword struck true. Bark scattered, dark with glistening sap.

{{You made a bargain. It binds us both.}} Thrashing briars tore dark rivulets across the Emperor's exposed skin and were severed in turn by white flame. {{You will have your victory, and I will have my queen.}}

"I'll die first."

{{As you wish.}} Jack lunged. The crooked fingers of his uninjured arm lengthened to talons. They plunged into Saran's chest. Golden scales swept away on a dark rush of blood. The Emperor howled. {{But the bargain endures.}}

Inch by agonising inch, Rosa reached her knees. Grasping hand found scabbarded sword.

With a wordless cry, she swung at Jack's head. He jerked, frayed robes swirling. Branches snapped, others swaying like serpents as she hacked at his leg. He screeched, sap cloying over the blade. Thrashing briars flayed Rosa's flesh to the bone and burrowed in through the welts. Blind with agony, she tore them free. Others lashed about her arms, her throat. Squeezing. Contracting. Vertebrae ground together. Nausea oozed beneath the pain.

Polite applause rippled. The Raven leaned heavily against the wagon's edge.

"Very impressive, brother." He jammed his hat on his head, weariness discarded as he rose to his full height. "But not impressive enough."

Duskhazel fires blinked out. Mist rolled in. The Ash Wind, fitful all day, roared to a sudden gale, filled with squalling, corvine shapes and thrumming black wings. The feathered storm swept over Jack, tearing deep into cloth and gnarled limb. Rosa's bonds slackened. She threw up her arms to shield her face, sight and sound buried beneath the storm.

"Can't you feel it?" Triumph roared beneath the Raven's cry. "The mists are mine again."

With a crackling moan, Jack let Saran fall and stumbled away into the mists.

Birds spiralled outwards and upwards. Grey skies darkened to brooding thunderheads. Revenants coalesced across the corpse-strewn courtyard. No longer spirits with the meanest grasp on existence, they were solid as the inevitability of death. Rosa glimpsed riders hidden deeper in the murk. Buildings shook to the grave-call's boom, and the dark host flooded east.

Screams thickened anew beneath the Raven's laughter.

Wounds reknitting, Rosa cast about for the fallen Emperor and found only a smeared black trail amid the dead. He wouldn't escape. She'd come so close. She started in pursuit.

Laughter faded. "Rosa. No. He's not important."

She halted, unable to resist the command. "Release me!" Fury flickered and ebbed, forbidden to her by the Raven's will. "What have you done to me? You're no better than him!"

A gloved hand seized her throat. Eyes blazed beneath the domino mask. "How dare you! You did this! I warned you not to make it a bargain, but you insisted. *Make the Hadari suffer. I'll serve you. I'll be whatever you wish.* I wanted a queen. An equal. You made yourself a servant. And now this ... " Releasing his grip, he spread a hand wide and clamped it shut in frustration. "This is what it is, and neither of us what we sought to be."

"You could have refused!" said Rosa.

"Don't you understand?" he snarled. "I can refuse you nothing!"

He twisted away, shoulders hunched.

Was it even true? Had she asked for this? Had he perhaps loved her, in whatever twisted way he was capable? Or was it all a game, played for hidden stakes and divine pleasure, and she just an unwitting piece upon the board? Rosa found she didn't care. That emotion belonged to another woman. Another life. Not to the Pale Queen of Otherworld. Part of her recognised the wrongness. Recoiled from it. But the spark of panic faded, smothered.

She stared down at black smoke curling from corpse-pale hands. A silver ring gleamed on her finger. Her Essamere garb was gone, replaced by a dark suit – an echo to the Raven's own, save for heavy, pleated skirts of a type she'd always loathed.

The Raven turned and took her hand, the ring's gleam hidden beneath the leather of his glove. Colour drained from the world, muted to murky grey. All around, the mist shone bright with the souls of the living. Beautiful wisps of light that flickered and faded as screams reached new heights.

"The bargain holds." He sounded sad, though Rosa no longer comprehended why. "You are the Queen of Otherworld, and also . . . and also my servant. I promised you revenge. Go. Drink your fill. But bring me my brother. He was right. This has gone on too long. Better it all ends."

The Rhalesh column stuttered to a halt. Shields rippled as rear ranks took on the duties of the front, and shields locked solid in an unbroken emerald wall. Harmonic dirge swelled beneath the wail of vanguard pipes, bellicose and mournful, a promise of forge and flame for the valiant, and death for all.

Viktor held his tongue, though he knew the thick, Thrakkian words as well as any marcher's song. Trusting his galloping steed and the press of riders to steer him true, he closed his eyes. Freed, his shadow raced before him, hungry, implacable. Cries rang out as the Hadari beheld the Dark that had loosed them to ruinous war. He felt their fear as a thing alive, writhing out of control as shadow smothered sight.

The Thrakkian song swelled to a baleful chorus. Viktor opened his eyes. Glimpsed men clutching at their eyes; rime-glinting shields cast down and spears masterless. The emerald wall gaped wide in welcome.

Viktor ripped back his shadow, and the killing began.

Moments passed in a crimson blur. The whirl and thrust of the claymore. The wet thump of axes. The chime of steel upon steel, and the desperate, bellowed orders as chieftains and havildars exhorted men to hold. The valour of men who fought for brothers of the shield and died beside them. Red deeds to conjure shame as much as pride. But Tressia had not sought this war, and Viktor's heart remained cold.

A flood of Hadari fled away east. Vanaguard spurred away in pursuit. Inkari's bellow and the shriek of pipes urged them back.

Viktor swung his bloody claymore to his shoulder and rode ahead. To the east, the resurgent mist that had already swallowed distant Govanna and the Traitor's Pyre now engulfed the leading Rhalesh columns. To the north, hummocked dead marked the demise of Britonisian shieldsmen even as the blazing *Dauntless* snapped one of her anchors and sank lower into the river. To the south, king's blue banners twitched above a drakonback's overlapping shields as the companies of the 2nd – veterans of the long border watch – marched out into an arrow-storm conjured by Corvanti bows.

Again, the centre stole Viktor's eye. The centre, where corpses marked a bloody road to divine war. A contest without quarter, fought on the border of rising mist. Smoke-wreathed spirits hacking black flame at wood-demons and torn apart in turn by the lash of frond and briar.

For all Rosa had claimed the Raven sent his servants to fight the Tressian cause, Viktor saw little sign that was so. Much the same could be said for the strawjacks, who simply tore at the spirits with the same fury offered them. All fought on without acknowledgement the shield walls grinding alongside.

Inkari clattered to a halt at Viktor's side, eyes wide beneath her winged visor. "*Volrandri* . . . It's not about us any longer, is it?"

He looked to the wounded western sky, viridian light flashing through clouds run black as night. Portent that reached beyond the wit of man and transgressed the divine.

"I don't know that it ever was."

Nor did it matter. Discipline had held the day, but it couldn't conjure swords from thin air, nor command the dead to fight. Thrakkian axes had torn one Rhalesh column to ruin, its survivors fled east to the shelter of Icansae shields. Another had already reached the Tressian lines. Two more closed through the hail of crossbow fire, shields held high.

"If the Raven will not intervene, others must," said Viktor. "Are your warriors ready?"

Broken chainmail rustled. Inkari stiffened, her lip curling. "When the thane gave his word, he gave ours."

Thrakkians. A week before, she'd tried to kill him. Today she'd die for him, if called to.

Viktor thrust the claymore to the skies. "Brenæ af Brenæ!"

"*Væga af Væga!*" The reply hammered out beneath the darkening sky. The claymore came down, and the world shook.

The sky screamed with bird voices and revenant grave-calls. Kai staggered on through corpse-choked mist. Every step tore at open wounds, blood oozing beneath ravaged armour. With every spasming pulse of his heart, he felt life ebb away, fuel for the moonfire of the Goddess' sword.

Even now, he refused to cast the blade aside. It had become a talisman. A connection to a goddess forsaken and a daughter betrayed. A fool's hope of redemption.

A knee buckled. He fell against a barricade's wreckage. Dead faces stared up in accusation. What else could they offer for a failure? For a barterer of daughters? And all for what? The dream of a throne? Worthless.

"Get up, old man." Laboured breath frosted on his lips. "Get up. Make ... Make this right."

Jack could be hurt, and that which knew pain, knew death. Surely that would end the fool's bargain? Unthinkable, to slay a god, but all was unthinkable until it was done, and legend forged.

Kai grasped at the barricade and strove to rise. Wood splintered beneath his fingers. He pitched back into the dead. The Goddess' sword flickered and slipped from his hand.

Ravens spiralled above, their dance dizzying, their mocking chorus echoing through the hollows of a dead heart. A breath caught and fluttered. Another wheezed away. Limbs disobeyed command to rise. Mist mottled and darkened.

"Here!" An urgent voice split the mists. "Warleader, it's him!"

Devren dropped to his knees, the fur of his pelt-cloak stiff and tufted with congealed blood and his lined face creased with worry. "Fight, *savir*. An Empire must have its Emperor. Girl! He needs you!"

Moonlight glimmered against golden armour and unfamiliar faces. Corvine voices crackled away. Kai's eyes slid closed.

The black flame of Rosa's sword struck the Immortal's head from his shoulders. The spark of soul flickered out through the murk of her new world, his body dull as it crumpled against his fellows. Theirs guttered and burned back bright, fear blazing to match strident cries even as they joined him in death.

Her free hand closed around a shield's rim and ripped it from the bearer's hands. A thrust between the loose rings of his leather jerkin, and his spark scattered, lost to the mists.

Inky vapour streaming behind, Rosa strode into the gap, the strike of spear and sword dull against unfeeling flesh. She heard a voice screaming, harsh and thick with joy. Her voice, and yet not. No longer a knight of Essamere, not the Council Champion. Not even the woman Sevaka had loved. A Pale Queen for a Raven King, paid court by death's dancing light. Nothing left to live for but slaughter.

Revenants flooded in. She felt them come. They were part of her as they were part of the Raven. As she was part of the Raven. Slaughter quickened, shadowthorn souls fading as death tore apart their formation from within.

Drink your fill, he'd commanded. Each death only sharpened her thirst – the woman-who-was and the queen-who-remained bound together in the need to kill. Even as the woman-who-was twisted in revulsion, the queen-who-remained cried out for more. To bathe in the reflection of sparks flown free.

"Ashanael bortha!"

A shard-spear sliced into Rosa's arm, its light blinding, searing. Howling with pain, she cast about, but saw no soul to grant the wielder shape.

The spear struck again even as flesh reknitted, glancing off a rib and punching deep into a lung. But the thrust brought the woman close – too close for the silver mask to any longer conceal the spark of her soul. That spark flickered in panic as her spear snagged on flesh. Rosa locked an arm about her neck. A greasy crack, and the hidden spark flew free. The spear's light bled away, and Rosa let the body drop.

There.

Beyond the dying sparks of the shadowthorn column, a gangling form lurching towards the safety of nearby strawjacks, the quarry she'd been loosed to claim. Ragged Jack. The King. The Coward. The faithless brother. *Her* faithless brother.

The ground trembled. Harsh song filled the sky, punctuated by the crash of axe on shield.

Screams tore Rosa's attention southeast, where souls danced like glimmerbugs against the column's grey flank. Not the work of revenants, but ephemeral riders, their own sparks blazing as those they came to kill. And at their centre, a man whose soul was black as pitch.

"Rosa?" He went still as his eyes met hers. "What has he done to you?"

Memory surfaced. The kiss of wind on skin. The exhilaration of grass rushing away beneath galloping hooves. Family, bonded by discipline and duty. The words that went alongside.

Until Death.

She stared down at her hands. Rubbed her thumb at congealed blood until the silver ring shone through. Until Death? She *was* death.

Trumpets sounded. The man was gone, swept from sight by cataphracts come late to the fray.

Jack remained.

Rosa sent revenants before her as heralds to her coming. Soul-sparks flickered and died. Banners fell. Strawjacks came shambling to protect their father, sparks as putrid as their bones. They tore the leading revenants to shreds, each a spike of pain in Rosa's thoughts, but the revenants were many, and the strawjacks few. The black flame consumed them all, and Jack was alone.

He flung up his hands, sap still dripping where an Emperor had claimed his fingers.

{{I yield,}} he crackled. Frayed robes puddled as he knelt. Breaths rasped behind the slighted mask, the fire flickering behind axe-driven scar a green spark in Rosa's grey world. {{I will discuss terms. A bargain to suit all palates.}}

Rosa drew closer, a piece of her in rapture as the sparks of battle danced and faded.

Robes parted. Thorned talons arced up at her chest. Black flame leapt in her hand and struck hand from wrist. Jack recoiled, three-fingered hand clutching at smouldering stump. The severed limb blazed and crackled at Rosa's feet, curling inwards as fire took hold.

He went still as she set the sword against his mask.

"Not this time, brother." The Raven strode serenely through the raging battle, his footsteps placed with care so as to avoid being skewered or trampled by ignorant ephemerals. "You forced the matter. Now it will be war for everyone. Damn you for forcing me to this, and damn me for the deed."

{{I beg you,}} Jack snivelled, abasing himself. {{Show pity.}}

"Everyone knows the Raven is heartless." The Raven halted and stared skyward. "I can hear them, you know. Your children, rushing to save their loving father. Even with a sword at your throat, your tongue trots a crooked path."

Revenants gathered, a black wall to blot out the battle beyond. The Raven plucked a sword from one, and held it gingerly, as if unsure of its purpose. "Should I spare him, my queen?"

How could he even ask? Why did he bother, when she could give no answer he did not desire? "No."

He hefted the sword. Gloved fingers caressed black flame. "I feel there should be more ceremony to this. An end. A beginning. It's a privilege."

A bell chimed, or what seemed a bell to Rosa's ephemeral senses. Jack's head jerked up, the thin crackle of his breath a match for watchful eyes. The bell chimed again.

"Oh really, sister," said the Raven. "You do have the worst—"

Then he and Jack were gone, and Rosa alone in a field of screams and fading lights.

Sixty-Four

The braziers around the island of thrones blazed towards the starlit sky, bringing life to the place that was no place. When the fires faded, Jack and the Raven stood on opposite sides of the dark pool, insignificant against the shroud of eternity. Neither was entirely as Melanna recalled. The Raven stood taller, straighter, his arrogance fourfold. Jack was canted over to one side, a seeping stump clutched to filthy robes.

Then again, none of the gods were quite as they'd been on Melanna's previous visit to the waters of the clockface. The Nameless Lady was older, the last of the girl gone from her countenance, and the woman she'd become garbed in a dress more austere than the one worn before. Tzal was skeletal beneath the folds of his stark suit, less an elderly man than a corpse burning with indigo flame. By contrast, Astor seemed more vigorous. Steel gleamed beneath the cracked rust of his fingers as they drummed his throne's armrest, and his eyes glowed like cinders.

And Ashana? She stood rigid beside her silver throne, apparent calm a poor mask for seething worry. Apara, standing as Melanna's mirror on the opposite side of Lumestra's empty throne, looked ready to bolt, her eyes flicking between the Raven and the distant mist gate where the Huntsman stood guard. She held the ornate wooden box – wrapped tight in a scrap of cloth to disguise its origin – tight across her chest, a talisman against divine wrath, just as Melanna held the squirming raven-shard close.

Melanna might have felt contempt for the Tressian, but for her own fear. Ashana's divine family were no less intimidating on second exposure than the first. More than that, while Melanna had Ashana to keep her safe, Apara had no such guarantor. Not one she trusted.

"What is the meaning of this?" The Raven circled the pool, his dark eyes on Jack. "I was rather in the middle of something."

{{You are nothing but a cheat. A deceiver.}} Jack clutched his wounded arm closer. {{Subverting mortals to fight your battles.}}

The Raven sniffed. "I'm not responsible for the Emperor's choices. Isn't it strange, brother, how even your allies loathe you? I can't imagine what you do to deserve it."

"Enough," said Ashana. "We didn't call you here to endure your bickering."

{{More interference, sister? Weren't you overruled when last we met?}}

"Weren't you winning?" she replied sweetly. "Things change. But no, I'm not here to call for censure. I respect the judgement of my peers, as I know you all respect me. Petitioned, I speak on behalf of others, as is my privilege and responsibility."

To Melanna, it seemed the thinnest of conceits. All present had to know this was merely another attempt to end the brothers' war. And yet, was it any different to the princes of the Golden Court remaining wilfully blind to the women who fought their battles? Sometimes, what was *said* was truth, even when it was not.

The Raven's cold gaze touched first on Melanna, then Apara. "Opportune, that she you claim as daughter is one such petitioner. The other should have come to me, had she a request. I've always been receptive to her kind. After all, we're family."

Apara flinched, the box almost falling from her grasp.

The Nameless Lady propped an elbow on her armrest and her chin on her upturned palm. Blue-green eyes gleamed amusement. "Isn't it the nature of miracles to be opportune, uncle? And the nature of divinity to smile on the impossible?"

Tzal's flames flickered darker. "It is *not* the nature of divinity to abase itself before ephemerals."

"You were outvoted, brother." Astor leaned forward with a rumble of shifting metal. "And there is no abasement. These mortals come not with demands, but bargains."

The Raven's burgeoning scowl slipped away. "Ah. That's different."

{{Is it?}} said Jack. {{And who put the idea in their heads, I wonder?}}

Melanna glanced at Ashana, who seemed not to notice the question.

"You're quibbling about the source of an idea? That's the first I've heard of you worrying over a previous owner," said the Raven. "A thing has to slip its keeper's grasp for only a moment before you spirit it away."

{{I abhor waste. The sapling cares not where it flourishes, only that it does.}}

"Indeed. What concern of mine where the idea first arose? Only the bargain matters."

Green fire flared in Jack's scarred mask, but he nodded. {{Only the bargain matters.}}

"We agreed to call you here," said Tzal stiffly. "Nothing more. If you wish to leave, we will not hold you."

"But if you do so, then you cede opportunity to bargain for what the ephemerals have brought," said the Nameless Lady. "One item, in particular, I might bid for myself."

Jack and the Raven went deathly still.

{{You would claim what is offered to me?}} crackled Jack.

"It's not yours until bartered for." Tucking her legs beneath herself, she curled up against the throne's backrest. "If you've no interest . . . ?"

{{I will hear the ephemeral's bargain.}} The words scraped through the air with reluctance of a wayward child. {{Then we will return to our own business. All of us.}}

Melanna released a breath she hadn't realised she'd been holding, though in truth the matter was far from settled.

"Your petition is accepted, Apara Rann," said Ashana. "Make your bargain."

Slowly, haltingly, Apara descended to the pool's edge as Ashana had tutored, the wooden box held out, but its lid fastened shut. She trembled as one on the point of collapse, her eyes rigidly ahead so they'd not risk glimpsing the Raven. He seemed to recognise this, and regarded her intensely, arms folded and head cocked.

"Lord Jack, Master of Fellhallow and the Living Lands . . ." Apara's wavering tone grew solid with rising confidence. "It is my wish that you make war against my homeland no longer. That the bargains struck to bring you there fall void. That there may again be peace between the Tressian Republic and august Fellhallow."

Jack issued a rasping, buzzing laugh. {{What could you possibly offer in exchange?}}

"Only this."

Laughter faded as Apara unwrapped the box from its covering and eased it open. {{That is *mine*.}}

"The sapling cares not where it flourishes," said Ashana, "only that it does."

Jack howled. A storm of briars and torn robes, he lunged for the box. Apara flinched. Indigo flame erupted from cracked stone and raced into the air. Jack shied away, crackling with anger.

Tzal's hand fell back to his throne's armrest. The fire faded. "Is dignity so far beyond you?"

Jack started forward again, then thought better of it as Tzal half-raised his hand.

{{She is a thief.}}

"So are you."

Jack's eyes blazed, but he gathered himself in. {{I will not relinquish my bride.}} Melanna's gut soured as his green eyes settled on her, the grave-stench of her predecessors heavy in her nostrils though they were far away. {{She is mine! Vouchsafed by her father's word.}}

"Did the father know his trade?" said Astor.

{{He tried to cheat me,}} Jack said sullenly. {{Everyone tries to cheat me.}}

"So he did not?"

"As if it matters!" The Nameless Lady rose to her feet, cheeks flushed and eyes bereft of mirth. "A daughter is not a possession, no matter how my own father might wish otherwise."

Tzal's flames flickered darker, but he said nothing.

{{That was the bargain. A bargain of kings. I will not break it. You may have the rest, but without a queen what use have I for a heart? That is the only bargain I offer.}}

Melanna felt Apara's gaze on her, the question in her eyes obvious for all that it was unseen. Her heart stuttered and slowed, the horror of the inevitable thick in her throat. They could refuse the counter-bargain. Seek another way. But how many more would die? By all appearances, Jack had been on the brink of defeat, and the Reckoning moments away from inevitable. How could she set her own life against that? How could she cling to the imperial throne as everything died, knowing her self-ishness had brought it to pass? The one solace was that her father had not meant to strike the bargain as he had. That counted for something.

"Apara—" she began.

"You will agree these terms, Jack," said Ashana. "You will renounce your claims, and you will let all be as it was."

{{And *why* would I do that?}}

She sighed. "Because then I will owe you a kindness. And because if you refuse . . . " Ashana's jaw set, her tone alongside. "When the two of you leave this place, I will come with you. I will spend the last of myself to help our brother tear you apart, Reckoning or no. What use is a queen to a king who no longer is?"

Jack bristled. {{All this for *her*? I don't believe you.}}

"If you deserved Melanna for your queen, you would. It's my fault as much as yours that she's in this position. I should share the burden of trade." Ashana's voice softened. "In the days of my predecessor, friend-ship existed between Fellhallow and Evermoon. You can have it again, or you can have nothing at all. Which is it to be?"

He tilted his head. {{What manner of kindness do you offer?}}

"We'll discuss it. After."

{{You'll cheat me. I am always cheated.}}

"After pledging thus before our peers?" She shook her head. "That would be foolish."

The place that was no place fell deathly silent save the buzzing crackle of Jack's breath.

{{Very well,}} he said at last. {{The bargain is agreed. Melanna Saranal will be my queen only if she chooses.}}

Melanna all but gasped. Free. She was free. "She chooses otherwise."

I will owe you a kindness. Happiness soured. She glanced at Ashana, and received no acknowledgement, nor even a smile.

Crooked fingers snatched the box from Apara's grasp. Jack held it to his chest and shied away as if clutching a child. Apara hurriedly with-drew to the relative safety of Ashana's side.

Melanna swallowed her doubts. The bargain with Jack was agreed, Ashana's price alongside, and she'd her own part to play. Step by step, she made her way down to the shore of the glimmerless pool, the raven-shard held tight. The Raven's eyes stayed on her every step of the way, threat and amusement in perfect balance. But fear remained a distant prospect, for the Raven could do no worse to her than Jack had intended.

"Lord Malgyn, Keeper of the Dead and Ruler of Otherworld. It is—"

He waved the words aside. "Yes, yes, yes. It is your wish that I remove my armies, and so on and so on. We've all enjoyed my sister's little charade – particularly the last few moments – but there's nothing that will induce me to break a bargain."

She held out the raven-shard. "There's this."

"A bird? I hate to be the one to say, *savim*, but I've no shortage of such things."

"Not like this," said Melanna. "This one is unique. It's from a day not yet come. From a world without a Raven."

He paled, domino mask and goatee stark against ash-white skin. He stared past Melanna. "Sister, you take this joke too far!"

"No joke," replied Ashana. "Even the Raven is not for ever."

He gazed at the bird, mesmerised – though Melanna couldn't say whether he found the prospect appalling or enticing. But his desire? It billowed thick around her. "How is such a thing possible?"

"Agree the bargain, and find out," Melanna replied. "It's a piece of you. The last piece. Whatever answers you seek, it holds."

He licked his lips, the corner of his mouth twitching in thought. "Your terms?"

"The war ends. Your alliance with Tressia ends." She glanced at Apara, whose gaze lay averted from the god to whom she'd been pledged. "And any debt owed you by Apara Rann is annulled. She's to be free to choose her own path."

He sighed theatrically. "The last is easily granted. Why does everyone assume I've any use for unwilling servants?" He smoothed his goatee. "As for the rest, I . . . I agree to your terms."

Melanna allowed the raven-shard to fly free. A flicker of motion, and it was gone, absorbed into the Raven's being as a raindrop claimed by the puddle.

After a brief glimmer of ecstasy, his face fell, his voice quiet as a whisper.

"Impossible! I . . . " He tapped fidgeting fingers to his lips, then closed them tight in his other hand. "I have to go. I have to *think*."

Ashana started forward, hand outstretched. "No, wait!"

He was already gone, Jack also.

Thoughts aching with the strain of preceding moments, Melanna stared sightlessly up at the stars. Was it really ended? She was free of her father's misguided promises, the divine war done and the Reckoning averted. She dared not believe, for fear it was all the whimsy of a weary mind. No, she decided, it *was* ended. Or at least, in part. An ephemeral war still raged, one she and Ashana had set in motion.

"Thank you." Apara's words shook her from reverie. "I don't know what to say. I've not exactly been a pleasant companion."

Melanna shrugged. "Someone recently pointed out that despite having every advantage, I've thought only of where I wanted to be, and not what I could do for others along the way." She stared up to where Ashana was lost in conversation with the Nameless Lady. Astor looked to be asleep, his rusty mane rising and falling in time to the swell of his armoured chest. Tzal, aloof as ever, looked on from a distance. "The throne has shaped me, and I haven't even sat in it yet. I don't want it to."

"I understand. At least, I think I do." She winced, discomfited, then looked Melanna dead in the eye. "I owe you, princessa."

"You don't owe me anything. Be free."

Apara nodded. "I can try. What comes next?"

"I must convince my father to end the war."

"We've another problem to resolve first." Ashana descended to the pool's edge, the Nameless Lady at her side. The latter offered a shallow curtsey, the mirth returned to her blue-green eyes. "The war may be ended, but neither Jack nor the Raven agreed to reclaim their minions. One last petty act."

"Actually," said the Nameless Lady. "I can help you there. One *is* the mistress of wind and waves."

Melanna eyed her warily. "And what will it cost us?"

She smiled, the years falling away until she was again the young woman Melanna had met on her last visit. "Nothing at all. My father hates generosity. His seething will be all the payment I require."

So saying, she waded into the pool, its glimmerless waters dragging at her skirts. She raised her arms high and a fierce wind whipped at the waters, spiralling about the shore and up towards the distant stars.

Sixty-Five

The gale raged, plucking at cloth and limb. White hair and dark essence streaming behind, Rosa planted her feet. Uncertain cries challenged the wind's howl, the soul-sparks of the living bright with terror. Formations broke apart and scattered. Riders plunged from panicked horses. Spectral ravens whipped to a seething funnel, drawn into a vortex of thunderous clouds.

The wind screamed to new heights. A revenant scattered into the hungry storm, streamers of black smoke sucked into the spiralling mists. The putrid flames of a strawjack's eyes guttered to grey. Then it too was gone, thrashing stems and pitted bone, swept away into the clouds. One by one, all succumbed, black blossoms twisting on unseen currents as the winds raged faster and faster, splinters of the divine dragged from an ephemeral world.

Rosa felt pieces of herself fall away. Doubt curdled, the sensation of being stretched thin overwhelming, her feet both slipping through the mud, and already somewhere distant. Trembling with effort, she bent shoulders to the storm. Pieces of the Pale Queen vanished into wind-tossed smoke. She clung to the rest and screamed.

Winds sank and the skies cleared. Rosa fell gasping to her knees, the pieces of herself almost lost to the skies rewoven to flesh and form by unfamiliar instinct. Aching eyes beheld a field robbed of the divine, but far from empty.

The heaven-bound storm had left no trace of the godly war save desiccated branches and broken stems; silver masks gleaming beneath skies woken to sunlight. But soul-sparks yet abounded, untouched and unclaimed. Tressians and shadowthorns, cast to disarray. Infantry scrambled for the solace and safety of kinsmen. Cataphracts and vana-guards for their steeds.

The Raven's final command pulsed through Rosa's thoughts. *Bring me my brother. Drink your fill.* The one was done, but the other? It was a thirst never to be slaked. It called her. It was all she had. Pent-up anger and sorrow, distilled to its essence and bound to fragmented soul.

Rising, she lost herself to the beauty of fading lights.

The men of Rhaled had endured much. The contest of shield walls. The assault of the divine. The fury of Indrigsval, and the grasp of Viktor's shadow. Now, with the air crackling in aftermath of storm, they broke. Banners were abandoned, heavy shields cast down. Voices that called for order drowned beneath the tremor of running feet.

Steadying his horse, Viktor reslung his claymore and stared across the milling field. Pockets of king's blue gathered beneath arrow-plucked banners, hoisted aloft by weary arms. The first cheers rang out as embattled countrymen recognised changing fortune in golden rivers flowing east.

Not a victory, nor anything like. Even if Rhaled's part in the battle were done, there remained spears enough to slaughter what few defenders remained. Of the troops Izack had brought to the field, perhaps two thousand remained fit to fight, and all were weary. The *Dauntless* was a sinking wreck, its filthy smoke blown north as the Ash Wind reasserted itself. And there were too many empty saddles among the Indrigsval host. Too many vanaguard and thrydaxes swept to Skanandra's mirrored forge. Even with Keldrov's force all but untouched from its fighting retreat across the valley, still the Hadari held fearsome advantage in numbers.

No, not a victory. Not yet. Maybe never.

Viktor flexed his fingers to ease aching muscles. So much to be done. The line to be formed. Keldrov's fresh soldiers to be joined to the exhausted survivors. Physicians to be harried. Words spoken to fire blood and spirit. A miracle to be mustered, if he could rouse himself to it, but how? He'd blinded an army at Davenwood, but only for a moment. This one was vaster by far – too vast for a moment to matter. His shadow alone wasn't enough. But what else was there?

Screams to the north broke his reverie, the battle that had fallen silent in all other quarters still raging along the Govanna-Sirovo road. Except it wasn't a battle, but a slaughter. A pale, vaporous figure swept across the trampled meadowlands, unbound white hair and inky darkness boiling behind like an unravelling soul. Hadari fled before her. A red wake stretched behind.

Rosa had been a soldier. A warrior. What haunted the roadside was something wholly other. It gave no account of quarry unmanned by fear, nor hands aloft in surrender. All met the blade, and their killer swept on. Already the dead escaped count. With each new corpse their killer grew wilder, her keening crueller.

Viktor had glimpsed her before, at battle's height. Lost in the struggle for survival, he'd marked only her physical deterioration. Only now did he perceive her madness, close kin to that which had claimed Calenne Akadra. Except Calenne had been a lie woven from loss. Rosa was *real*, but growing less so by the moment, a friend eaten away and something else rising in its place.

Thus Viktor, who knew better than most that humanity was lost more by degrees than by absolutes, forgot the cruel truths of battle to come.

Soldiers scattered from his path, warned by the onset of hooves and the bellows of warning.

"Rosa!"

His cry went unheeded, lost beneath the screams of her victims. Still she swept on, a bleak blossom more spirit than substance, eyes burning black in an ashen face.

"Rosa! Fight it!"

A part of Viktor rebelled his own intent. Rosa had tallied more dead in sparse minutes than he since his coming to the field. What if she were the miracle he sought? A reckoner of divine might, somehow escaped the cleansing winds.

All it would cost was what remained of her soul, and his alongside for letting it pass.

Still she swept on. A fleeing Hadari crumpled, throat open to the bone. Another rolled away beneath the hooves of Viktor's steed, torn almost in two by the blow that had taken his life.

"Rosa!"

Again she ignored him. Not a flicker of hesitation, nor a backward glance. With no other options left save ride her down, Viktor flung himself from the saddle.

Over and over they rolled, until he knelt breathless atop her. Black eyes regarded him without recognition. Lips snarled anger. A pale hand flung him away.

Viktor scrambled for footing among the dead, a chill trickle at the base of his spine. Twice Rosa's size and weighed down by plate, and still she'd flung him away. "Listen to me!"

Rosa's sword came up. Blood hissed and spat beneath black flame. "Come not between the Pale Queen and her due."

She sprang, vapour billowing behind.

Viktor shrugged his claymore free.

Buccinas boomed out. The column of march became a wall of shields, halberds and crossbows readied behind. Quarrels hissed out, pitching cataphracts and outriders from their saddles.

"Back!"

Aeldran's frustration boiled up as the wings of the doomed charge peeled away, riders pulling clear of crossbow-shot and reformed beneath their chieftains' banners.

The Icansae host, dwindled by the losses of campaign, couldn't challenge so large and disciplined a shield wall. Not without arrows, and every quiver had been empty for hours. Not without the aid of the Corvanti, and King Raeth seemed of no inclination to send his spears forward. And the Tressians were more disciplined than any he'd known. The numeral of the 14th and the spread-winged phoenix – icons whispered of grieving families after the disaster at Davenwood. For the first time, Aeldran understood how Emperor Saran's summer campaign had died.

Even as the riders fell back, buccinas sounded anew. The wall dissolved. The march resumed as it had a dozen times before, the jeers of Tressian soldiers audible even at distance.

"Raven take the Corvanti!" Aeldran thrust his unblooded sword back into its scabbard and sought Aelia – strange to think of her as such after so many careful years – among the other riders. "We need—"

He matched her stare ... northward, to where the meadowlands ran gold with routed warriors. No cry reached his ears, for the Ash Wind bore them north towards the river.

"The Emperor," he breathed. "Where is the Emperor?"

Straining eyes found no sign of the imperial standard, nor those of the foremost Rhalesh chieftains. Another glance glimpsed no suggestion of Corvanti or Silsarian shields marching to rescue disaster – only kings and princes paralysed by an army set to flight and a field choked with dead.

"Aelia. This is your moment. Your chance to prove all you have sought."

She shrugged off her helm. Eyes and voice brimmed with resignation. "They won't follow me. Not Maggad's granddaughter. Not Aelia the Liar. What regard I hold was granted by the House of Saran, and the House of Saran ... "

She fell silent, eyes on the jagged line of emerald and gold where the road met the tavern's bounds. Where the Emperor's banner had last flown. Without a word, she galloped away north.

"Rosa, please!"

Fury flushed to satisfaction as the dark man's claymore buckled beneath Rosa's strikes. He staggered, the blade flashing up to deflect another blow.

"You're a knight of Essamere. A shield first and a sword second. Look at what you've done! What would Sevaka say to see you now?"

Sevaka. The name chimed bright in her bleak heart and slid away. "Leave me alone!"

Two voices screamed the words. The Knight of Essamere and the Pale Queen.

Which was she?

Rosa found no answer in the dancing sparks, nor in her opponent's endless shadow. There was only the thirst. The dark man started forward. Her sword scraped from the claymore's steel. Plate armour buckled at the shoulder. Her opponent bellowed and lurched away, slower than before.

"Listen to me!"

Rosa swooped. Viktor flung himself aside. Steel screamed as

blades met, the throb of his wounded shoulder a drumbeat that drowned all else.

The blazing sword hacked down again and again. Even with one hand at the grips and another braced inches back from the tip, the claymore gave.

Viktor dropped to one knee and let his shadow run free.

Its embrace scarcely slowed her. He'd never expected it to.

As the black flame of her sword inched down, the shadow laid bare her withered soul. A part gleamed silver; timeless, deathless. Another was lost entirely, the void rotten black with malaise. Like enough to Calenne Akadra that Viktor's gorge thickened, but where Calenne had been nought but Dark, a spark of Rosa remained. Sunlight, tangled in tarry bonds of loss and rage, swathed in mist.

His fault, for not being there when she'd needed him. For not paying full heed when he'd finally returned. *You're a terrible friend.* Josiri's words rang truer than ever.

Driven deeper, the shadow pierced mist. Viktor recoiled, repelled by a cold even deeper than his own. For a heartbeat, he beheld a world of crooked streets and viridian skies, of squawking ravens and forsaken spirits.

The claymore jarred loose and twisted away. Black flame screamed down.

Viktor wrapped his shadow about the mists, and squeezed.

The grey world drowned in colour, soul-sparks fading into sunshine. Rosa gasped as a woman drowning, the sword falling from her hand.

She stared past Viktor to the bloodied meadowlands. Anger congealed to shame.

In memory, each dancing soul-spark gained identity. The wounded. The dying. Men with hands spread in surrender. She'd killed them all. Not a knight of Essamere, a shield first and sword second. Not a soldier, who fought for those who could not. Not even a warrior. Only a monster fit for the axe and the pyre.

She felt the Pale Queen battering at the walls Viktor had built about her. Easier to think of her as someone else. As a construct of the Raven's cursed "gift". Harder to admit that she was born of the anger that had haunted Rosa all her life. That the wall between them was thin as silk.

She tugged at the silver wedding ring. It didn't budge. A piece of her.

"Cut off my head," she whispered. "I beg you. Weight me down with silver, and bury me deep."

Viktor clambered upright, his bloodied left shoulder dipped as he embraced her. "I didn't catch you just to shove you straight back off the cliff."

Rosa pulled away, eyes averted. "You don't understand. This is what I am now."

"Then choose to be something else."

The Pale Queen writhed, fed by surging anger. "You think it's that easy?" Rosa bit out.

He dipped his head, the scar on his cheek pulled taut by a sad smile. "I know it isn't."

Aeldran found his sister stooped among the dead, ignored by the fleeing Rhalesh shieldsmen.

She stood, a green cloak bundled over her arms. The previous owner, a cataphract of the Emperor's personal guard, stared skyward with empty eyes. "Help me."

A hurried glance west confirmed no immediate danger from the reforming Tressian lines, though that would change soon enough. Hanging his shield from the saddle's horn, Aeldran dropped down. "I don't understand."

"Take this." She thrust the cloak into his hands and fumbled at the brooch holding her own. Icansae scarlet slipped from her shoulders. "The Emperor is missing. He may be dead. The army needs to see the princessa, or to think it does."

He blinked. In truth, Aelia and Melanna Saranal were not hugely alike beyond a cast of build and colouring, but once she was on horseback, with a Rhalesh cloak streaming behind and men bellowing her name? All would believe. "Aelia ... If you do this ... "

"If I do this, no one will remember the part Aelia Andwaral played in victory or defeat. If I die here, my last deeds will be forgotten. But if I don't, I'm guilty of every accusation I spat at Melanna, for I'll be thinking only of my own legend." Her lips twisted. "I need my brother's help in one last deception. Will you give it?"

One last deception, and a paradox of honour. A lie that made gift of self and so became finest truth. Aeldran spread the Rhalesh cloak wide and pinned it about his sister's shoulders.

"You need not ask, *essavim*."

Viktor glanced over his shoulder as he reached the Tressian lines. Rosa stood where he'd left her, half a mile distant and staring westward across the meadowlands. Less a woman than a mourning spirit, buffeted by the wind. Lost in a world of self-hatred and sorrow. Too much the mirror to his own recent past for comfort.

"Viktor, my boy." Shields parted and Elzar strode out – bruised, and leaning heavier on his staff than was normal. "Someone told me they'd seen you. D'you know what I said? That they must have been mistaken. *Viktor's a farmer now,* I said. *And a good one. No crop dares defy* that *scowl.*"

The self-same scowl bled away before the relentless cheer of a man more surrogate father than friend. "I got lost on the way to market, high proctor." Viktor scratched his head. "I never did have much sense of direction."

Laughter and weary smiles rewarded the words, and he was glad, for all that both were at his expense. Blood and bandages betrayed wounds taken. Averted gazes showed hope bleeding away. Empty pouches and dulled swords stood as tokens of a battle hard-fought.

One way or another, that battle would soon be done. But at least it would *be* a contest. The battered line of king's blue had been stiffened in his absence, not just by Keldrov's army, but by unhorsed Thrakkians – even a trio of kraikons and a pride of simarka. Vanaguard riders mustered on the southern flank; a draggle of knights to the northern. Inkari waited with the former. Izack sat among the latter, roped into the saddle, and a splinted arm bound across his breastplate.

Elzar drew closer, the salt-and-pepper stubble of his beard creased in concern. His words carried no further than Viktor's ears. "I'd say we've lost, but this isn't a field of winners and losers. The dead outnumber us all. Where have you been?"

Where to begin? "Making terrible mistakes."

"Your shadow?"

"In part."

Concern became annoyance. "How many times have I told you? Deeds matter more than their guiding hand. Stop letting other peoples' fears define you." His eyes flicked past Viktor's shoulder. "Hello. Seems our shadowthorn friends have found their courage."

Viktor turned and beheld a distant woman, tall in her stirrups and sword glinting in the sun. He heard snatches of words, but the Ash Wind bore most away. A gathering of shields betrayed intent. The owl of Rhaled, and the black tree of Corvant. Britonis' bleak grey sail and Silsaria's white stag. And at the centre, the scarlet serpents of Icansae.

The wind dropped. Drums growled to life. A battle cry echoed out. "*Saranal Brigantim! Ashanael Sifas!*"

"The Emperor's heir?" murmured Elzar. "I wonder what's become of old Saran?"

The Hadari at least *believed* he was still alive, or the cry would have proclaimed victory for a new Empress. Amyradris Brigantim. "That's not her," said Viktor.

Elzar squinted. "I'm sorry?"

"Her hair's too short, and she's too low in the saddle. Melanna Saranal rides as though the steed is holding her back, not bearing her forward."

"Does it matter?"

"No." Not when the Hadari line was twice as wide and three times deeper than Viktor's own. "It doesn't matter at all."

Elzar withdrew, muttering under his breath. Viktor lingered as the Hadari line came forward, not as a wall of shields, but as a tide of bodies come to sweep all away. His eyes rested again on Rosa. The piece of her he'd taken railed and writhed against his shadow, begging to be free. But the more he dwelt on it, the more it didn't feel like a piece of her at all, but something older. Apart from the world, and yet connected to everything.

A piece of the Raven? Was that even possible?

And if that were possible, what else? A horrific notion gained ground, one to test Elzar's principles of ends mattering more than means, to say nothing of his own determination. But with the prospect conjured, Viktor found it impossible to set aside.

He joined the line beneath the 14th's banner. Commander Keldrov offered formal salute. "I was wrong. One man can't make a difference. But it's an honour to fight at your side once more, Lord Akadra."

"Not Akadra." He spoke the words without thinking, the half-formed decision inevitable in hindsight. "Viktor Akadra can't win this battle."

Viktor set his back to the Hadari and held his claymore aloft. "You know my name, but I've learned the Hadari know me by another. A man-of-shadow. A Droshna. They claim the Dark runs thick in my blood." He paused. "It's true."

Expected accusations of witchcraft never sounded. Gasps of horror fell silent. On a day filled with impossible sights, one more coaxed forth little surprise. Good. At the back of the line, Elzar offered an approving nod. To the east, trumpets flared. Drums quickened.

"The Dark is my servant," shouted Viktor, "as I am the Council's servant. You've nothing to fear from it, or from me. So whatever you see, you will stand. You are soldiers of the Republic. The line that cannot be crossed. The bough that does not yield to the axe. You will hold your ground!"

He drove his claymore deep into the mud and let his shadow billow free, a cloak spread to suffocate the sky. For a moment, the stolen piece of the Raven resisted his will, but only for a moment. The merest thought, and it unravelled into a thousand gossamer fibres. Ten thousand. More. They went taut as Viktor gathered them close, the weight unbearable, inevitable.

Drums drowned beneath the thunder of hooves and running feet.

"The Hadari came to our land in fear of Viktor Droshna," he shouted, throat thick with strain. "Let them behold him now."

Aeldran's blood ran cold as shadow drowned the western skies. The Droshna. The danger warned of by goddess and Emperor, and then gainsaid by their daughter. He was real.

Aelia stiffened in her saddle and drove back her spurs. "Ashanael Brigantim!"

"Ashanael Brigantim!"

Aeldran shouted with the rest and gripped his sword until his knuckles ached. The Tressian line drew closer. Fifty yards. Thirty. Cataphracts to his left pulled ahead, red silk ribbons streaming from the pommels of their whirling swords.

Cries of alarm broke out. The whinny of panicked steeds. The crash of men falling from their saddles. Trumpets faltered. Drums fell silent. Ahead, twenty yards from the enemy shields, the cataphracts went down in a sprawl of men and horses, tripped by twitching shapes rising from the mud.

Others stumbled upright into Aeldran's path. He glimpsed blank, unfocused stares and weaponry slack in bloody hands. Then his horse twisted away, hauled by a yank of the reins more born of horror than conscious thought.

Hooves slipped on mud. Aeldran's horse slewed into a grave-woken Immortal and barged him aside. The cadaver clambered haltingly to his feet, one arm dragging with the tell-tale of a broken shoulder and his face split open to the sky.

A hand squeezed tight about Aeldran's heart as he beheld others. They filled the gap between the faltering charge and the Tressian shields, bearing between them all the colours and heraldry that had come to Govanna. Thrakkian claith. King's blue. Icansae scarlet, and more besides. All were marked by grievous wounds and shared that vacant, lifeless stare. They clung to weapons but made no move to wield them – made no move at all, save to regain their feet if struck down.

And clinging to the shoulders of each, a veil of flickering shadow, a figment of that belonging to the Droshna.

Wherever Aeldran glanced, the tale was the same. The meadowlands were thick with lurching bodies. They were infested with them. Too many to count, those slain in preceding hours roused to new and abhorrent effort.

A cage of mangled, dead flesh closing tight about the living.

At every moment, Viktor's bond with the dead threatened to unravel. Fifteen thousand empty husks hoisted aloft by the union of plundered Raven-fragment and unyielding shadow. Viktor dared not speak, not even breathe, for fear that illusion would shatter to nothing, and the Hadari realise that the dead were of no danger save to a man's resolve. They had no will of their own, no urge, no presence.

The first handful slipped away. Flashes of pain turned dark as the bodies dropped. Viktor gritted his teeth, felt mud under his knees and beneath the palms of his hands.

The rot spread. Corpses flaked away from his control. The disease rippled outwards, rushing from cadaver to cadaver. Faster and faster. Viktor's breath ran red and ragged, tinged with iron from blood shed and blood shared.

A trumpet sounded. Another. Wild. Desperate. The trample of hooves and the screams of men who could take no more. The ground shook as the Hadari retreated.

"Kill the buggers! Run them down!"

The voice, unmistakeably Izack's, rose above the din. Others joined it. Keldrov. Inkari. Thrakkians, southwealders; praises to fire and phoenix, to duty and honour. The abandon of men and women who had stared death in the eye, and now brought it as gift.

Only when the dying screams began did Viktor relinquish his grip, let the dead fall like Lumenwake blossoms. Spent, he slumped sightless.

Elzar caught him in wiry arms, held him upright as the din of slaughter reached new heights. Viktor eased a stuttering breath, and let darkness carry him off.

The madness of the rout pulled at Rosa with every step. The hedonism of victory, the horror of defeat.

She longed to join it, to indulge again that which had consumed her ever since Vrasdavora. The thought sickened, for she knew that it risked rousing the Pale Queen from her cage. But nor could she turn aside as unseen soul-sparks guttered and died. A familiar spoor danced on the air, kin to the slaughter at hand, but separate from it, as she was. It tantalised. Called to her. A hallow-wisp that drew her on over meadow and fen, and thence to a wooded copse on the Silverway's southern bank.

Shadowthorns fled her. Tressians shunned her. And so Rosa walked on in the vapour of her guttering self as those she'd once named comrades ripped dreams of conquest to wet rags. The living, the dead and she in between.

A horse skidded sideways in the mud, crushing the rider beneath him. The shadowthorn cried out, the snap of bone sounding as his sword spun away. The horse clambered up in a spray of mud and galloped off through the trees, dragging the man behind until tangled reins at last ripped free.

The maddening spoor grew stronger, thicker as Rosa approached.

Soldiers of the 14th pressed close with swords drawn, then peeled away, leery of chancing her attention. The pursuit moved on, and she was alone with that forlorn rider.

The Icansae prince. The one from the false parley at the bridge. Aeldran Andwar. He scrabbled in the mud for his sword, and howled as the broken leg folded beneath him. Rosa snatched the sword from his trembling hand and set the point at his throat. The spoor was mystery no longer, confirmed by instincts that had come with the Raven's gift. Old blood, faded with time, clinging to guilty hands. The only desire she any longer had left, begging for consummation. Maybe even the last peace of her mortality.

"You are Aeldran Andwar."

The shadowthorn's eyes went wide in a mud-spattered face. "What are you?"

"I am Death. You killed my love, so now I come for you."

Terror turned to defiance in the other's eyes. "I have killed many. A warrior's duty."

"You'd remember her. She was a naval officer, far from the sea. Her name was Sevaka Psanneque." Rosa's throat clenched, the words barely more than breath. Where was the anger now, when she needed it? "She held the wall at Vrasdavora."

His throat bobbed. His eyes never left her sword. "She died well. I will do no less."

She died well. No rancour. Even respect. Enough for the sword to grow heavy in Rosa's hand, and to clog thought with doubt.

Choose to be something else.

All her grown life, she'd been a soldier. And despite the oath she'd taken to Essamere, she'd never been a shield, only a sword. The Reaper of the Ravonn, never its defender. She'd revelled in her ability to kill. Its purity. Its simplicity. And when she'd become eternal, killing had become her world.

Sevaka was gone. She'd died well, contesting another's duty. Could Rosa say the same of all those she'd killed? How many hearts had she broken with her blade for no better reason than she could?

"What are you waiting for?" hissed Andwar. "Send me to Evermoon. Let it be done."

What was the point of death if death was the only point? It would do nothing to fill the void left by Sevaka's passing. It would only fester, until the last of what she'd loved was gone.

Rosa dropped the sword. "I give you back your life."

She walked away and felt nothing at all.

Sixty-Six

The moon was an ailing crescent against night's shroud. To the west, the fires of the Tressian sentry line granted shape to palisades thrown up with battle's ceasing, defences mustered against a counter-attack that would never come. To the east, tents clustered tight around the village of Sirovo. And between, where the lone hawthorn tree stood vigil over trampled fields, Melanna drew her cloak tight and waited as Tressian banners grew close. Her own waited a hundred yards back, her father's Immortals – *her* Immortals – unhappy to be left behind.

She'd been glad to escape the encampment, its air thick with blood, and fear, and loss. In the hours since the Huntsman had returned her to the ephemeral world, she'd walked the campfires, seen for herself the warriors staring silently at sputtering fires, voices low and bereft of song. No pyres blazed to ease the dead to Otherworld, testament to vigour drained to sickly dregs.

Haldrane's estimate of the disaster made a grim tally. Three in every five men dead or taken prisoner. Of the two remaining, one was wounded. Rhaled had suffered worst of all, whole villages robbed of their sons. But the worst – the very worst – was to tread her father's tent, and to wear its emptiness as a cloak. The unfairness of it all dragged at her heart. How could it be fair to have striven to avert one disaster, only to find another?

For all that Melanna had lived with the prospect of this day all her adult life, its burdens now were too great to bear, redoubled by the bitterness of their last parting. Worse was the knowledge that her actions had brought this sorrow to pass – first by encouraging her father's war, and then by rendering that war unwinnable through conspiracy. Haldrane's account of the battle had made that all too clear. If her father *was* dead, she'd as good as struck the blow. A world saved from the abyss was cruel consolation.

Too weary for tears, she'd lingered in her father's sanctum, seeking comfort in simple possessions. His old dagger, the blade too thinned by the whetstone's grind to serve in battle, but too lucky to throw away. The Book of Ashana, hand-copied over the course of a decade or more, the stark but graceful calligraphy revealing that an Emperor's art served more causes than war. The locket bearing Melanna's mother's likeness – that he'd left it behind said more about his hopes of victory than Melanna was ready to admit. A polished black everstone, brilliant green lights dancing within – with the tell-tale hole through which one could hear the whispers of the honoured dead – found by a bright-eyed girl in the rubble of their summer villa, and retained by her father as a keepsake of days never to return.

She hadn't wanted to leave, but she had, and ridden out to the hawthorn with but a single companion. The war council – *her* war council, until happier news proved otherwise – had argued against, but she'd brooked no objection. The Emperor was missing, likely dead; his legacy – her inheritance – stained by failure and a defeat unrivalled in living memory. The throne, once secured by a goddess' favour, hung in the balance. Weakness, even to one's subjects, was no option at all.

Fifty yards distant, the riders divided, one spurring away from the banners. Viktor Akadra. Melanna didn't need to see his face. It was inconceivable they'd send anyone else.

Naradna – now Aelia – Andwaral walked her steed to Melanna's side. It should have been Aeldran, and not his sister, who as Queen of Icansae had burdens of her own. But Aeldran drifted in the soothing embrace of bethanis to numb the pain of a leg amputated below the knee. He'd crawled a mile before the outriders had found him, and by then the limb had been beyond salvation. One broken soul among thousands. Another victim of a worthless war.

"There's still time to change your mind, *savim*."

Melanna shook her head. "I might say the same to you."

"And leave you without a champion if matters go ill?"

The rider approached, the lantern in his hand doing little to dispel the darkness about his shoulders. A shadow seen more with the heart than with the eye.

"Lord Akadra."

"Empress."

A heart barely at rest fluttered anew. "Princessa. My father is missing, not slain. Unless you know otherwise?"

He didn't answer at first, eking out her discomfort with each moment of silence. "I've had no word of his fate. He's fortunate in that."

She met his gaze. No weakness. "I understand. And our wounded?"

"Are treated better than they deserve."

"Then I would like to discuss terms of settlement."

The darkness about Akadra deepened. The air chilled. "There will be no terms. You may drain this war to the dregs for all I care. Come morning, you will."

"And how many more will die? Whatever else you are, Lord Akadra, you're not wasteful of lives."

"I've no need to be. Not when the dead march at my command."

"So I've heard, but I wonder why any of us are still alive? Perhaps the dead fear the onset of night? Or is it that your command is not all you'd have us believe?"

He offered no flicker of expression. "You of all people know what I am. You'd do well not to underestimate me."

"And you'd do well not to underestimate my..." She swallowed. "My *father's* icularis. They've already taken account of your forces. For all our losses, we outnumber you three to one, and your warriors are as weary as mine. You're formidable, Lord Akadra, as I know to my cost, but are you worth six thousand swords?"

Again Akadra fell silent. Melanna held his gaze, daring him to read the lies in her words. Haldrane had made only the vaguest assessment of the Tressian forces, and she was scarcely more confident in the tally of her own. But beneath the lies lurked a singular truth: that the day's losses would echo through the years to come. Compounding them served no one.

"What do you propose?" he said at last.

"Come morning, we will withdraw. This war can be over, if you so choose."

His eyes narrowed. "And the price?"

"We will take the Eastshires under our protection. They will become a province of Empire."

"Unacceptable."

"It's that, or lose everything east of the Tevar Flood. The Golden Court followed my father to war in hopes of claiming new territory. If I give them nothing, they will take it for themselves, and more will die. Is that what you want?"

Melanna fought to calm a racing pulse, aware that if Akadra chose to kill her, she could do little to stop him. The terms had been Haldrane's idea. To make no demand was to admit weakness, both to the Golden Court, and to the Tressian Council, and weakness invited challenge. But nor were the Eastshires so grand a prize that terms would be dismissed out of hand. They were vulnerable with Ahrad gone, and Akadra had to know that they'd be near impossible to hold, even if he refused.

"What would you have me say to those you have driven from their homes?" he snarled. "What justice do I offer to those you have slain?"

"Tell them that Melanna Saranal made herself a traitor to present this offer. That she will be fortunate to end the year with her life, let alone her throne. That may yet be their justice."

He frowned. "I don't understand."

"Lord Trelan can tell you, when next you meet."

Again, he fell silent, though this time Melanna had the impression his thoughts wandered far from that blustery stretch of meadow.

"It's ironic, isn't it?" she said. "This war began because I, and those I love most dearly, believed you a horror only fire and valour could destroy. Now I hope you have it in you to prove me wrong. That the Droshna holds less malice than an Ashanal, and offers his people more than a Legacy of Steel."

He shifted in his saddle. "I have no official standing, and can make no promises, but I will . . . recommend your offer to the Council. Were I you, I would ride soon, and ride hard." He hauled on his reins. "This will mark the third time I have shown you mercy. There will not be a fourth."

He rode off in a spray of mud. The chill of his presence remained.

Melanna exhaled to her last dreg. "You'll convey these tidings to the Golden Court? I . . . I need to be alone for a time."

Aelia nodded. "Of course, *savim*."

"How long before they challenge me?"

"They will await confirmation of your father's death. Anything less would be—"

She offered a bleak smile. "Against tradition?"

"Yes, *savim*."

The ruined cottage consisted of two tumbledown walls and a single glazed window that overlooked the wharf side and the Silverway's placid waters. But it was an island of tranquillity where the rest of the night-cloaked town rang to voices raised in jubilation and sorrow. Rosa wondered if the cottage was thought to be haunted. Certainly, it would be so after today. The window carried just enough reflection to remind her of what she'd become: a woman as much spirit as flesh, one foot in the mists and the other in the light.

Beyond the tangled, cobbled streets, a corpse-barge slipped its moorings and began the slow westward journey, bearing highblood sons and daughters on their last journey home. Misery soured to loathing. Surely half a life was better than none at all? Acknowledging the truth brought little solace. For all she walked the ephemeral world, Rosa no longer felt part of it. Which made recent resolution all the harder, but no less necessary.

She pressed a hand against the glass, fingertips guttering like candleflame.

"I have a question," said the Raven.

He stood in the ruined doorway, his customary nonchalance undercut by tension. "Go away."

He set his hat down on the floor. "No kind word?"

"Do you deserve one?"

"I suppose not."

Rosa growled and turned away. "Then ask your question, and go."

"What do you want?"

"That's your question?"

"It occurs to me that it's one I've never asked." He paused. "I've recently been privileged to glimpse how affairs will unfold. I beheld a bitter, spiteful creature railing at the world. I didn't much care for him, but he was me."

She snorted. "For the first time, I feel like we might actually have something in common."

"Strangely, I don't find that as comforting as I once might."

Rosa set her back to the window and sought a clue to his mood. "Should I care?"

"I imagine not. If it helps at all, you should consider your ... transgressions a result of my influence. However, that doesn't answer my question. What do you *want*?"

She pursed her lips, but where was the harm? He'd know soon enough, if she held to her resolve. "To fight for life more than death. To be a shield, not a sword."

"I should be offended, perhaps?" He waved at her, the swift flourish of fingers encompassing brow to heel. "I didn't want this for you. I hope you understand that."

"It doesn't matter what you wanted," she snapped. "Only what you did."

He joined her at the window and stared down at the river. "My part in your war is over, as is Jack's. Whatever happens next is for ephemerals to resolve. Which means our bargain is broken. I've not upheld my end of our agreement, so by rights I should already have returned you to how you were. But in light of our past association, I've chosen not to force the matter."

"Why would I possibly want to remain like ... Like this?"

"Even an eternal cannot accomplish what the divine can."

"The Queen of Otherworld as a champion of life?"

He shrugged. "Why not? I've always been fond of irony. The title would be purely ceremonial, of course. No influence. No subservience. No attachment. Consider it a gift."

A hand against the glass once more, Rosa closed her eyes. Free of the Raven, and yet imbued with his power. What better way to redeem past mistakes? To grow beyond what she'd been? The temptation was thick enough to taste. Only ...

Freed of the Raven's influence, her mistakes would be her own. For all he said her actions that day could be laid at his door, the claim rang hollow. The Pale Queen had done nothing that the Reaper of the Ravonn would not. Better if her mistakes went unlaced with divine power.

The windowpane shattered beneath her bunched fingers. "No. My humanity ran thin enough before. Frankly, it doesn't need the help."

"You're certain?" She'd expected anger, or disappointment, but the Raven seemed more relieved than anything. "Many would kill for what you have. As a matter of fact, three have recently come to my keeping for want of obtaining it."

"I'm sure."

"There must be something I can give you in exchange. I don't want to be like the Raven I glimpsed. He'd no room in his cold heart for anyone save himself. That isn't me. At least, I don't *want* it to be."

"Then choose to be something else."

"It's not that easy. To be human is to seek purpose. To be divine is to be trammelled by it." He shrugged. "But that doesn't mean we shouldn't try."

A shadow darkened the stoop. "Rosa?"

Rosa's breath caught at the sound of a voice more familiar than her own. One she'd despaired ever of hearing again. "Sevaka?"

It *was* her, just as she'd been at their last parting. Filthy, worn, weary and yet the most wondrous sight Rosa had ever seen. Impossible. A heart that had long abandoned joy leapt at the sight and ached anew as that joy soured to suspicion. One last bleak joke from a god who'd only ever offered misery couched in friendship.

She rounded on the Raven, voice ragged. "How dare you? Sevaka died. She's dead, and the best part of me with her."

The apparition drew closer. "It's true. I died. I walked the mists. I . . . " She shook her head. "I don't remember much about it. But I remember I held the wall. And that my last thought was of you."

Rosa stumbled back. "No. This can't be . . . "

The apparition's face creased with hurt. Certainty faltered.

"I have never lied to you, Roslava Orova," said the Raven. "Not before, and not now. What's the point of being the Keeper of the Dead if you can't bend the odd rule?"

The apparition's arms enfolded her, and doubts evaporated. No doppelganger could so perfectly match the sensation of a longed-for embrace. Not the warmth, not the touch, not the scent of a love lost. A hundred tiny details unnoticed until that moment, when Rosa needed them most. She returned the embrace, joyful tears washing away those of sorrow.

Pulling back, Rosa cradled Sevaka's head in her hands and gazed into grey eyes as bright with tears as her own.

"How?" she gasped. "How is this possible?"

The Raven curled a half-smile. "Perhaps because if the heartless Raven can be unselfish, even for a moment, then all manner of terrible things once thought inevitable may never come to pass. Or perhaps because, just once, I can choose to be a friend sooner, rather than later."

Sevaka wiped her eyes and offered him a scowl. "I am *not* a gift to ease your conscience."

"What conscience? As for the rest? Of course you're a gift, and so is Rosa. What else is love, save to be blessed with a reward of which you consider yourself unworthy, but urges you to give of yourself in exchange?" He shrugged and set his hat back onto his head. "In any case, the deed is done. I bid you good evening, ladies. May it be a long, long time before we see one another again ... but perhaps not *too* long."

Then he was gone, and they alone.

Sevaka stared at the emptiness left behind. "What do you suppose he meant by that?"

"I don't care." Rosa drew her in for a kiss, then hissed as pain creased the back of her hand.

"Rosa? What is it?"

"My hand."

Pulling free, she stared at knuckles haler of complexion than before, the lacerations from the broken windowpane bright with blood. Not the empty flesh of the Pale Queen – not even an eternal's dark ichor – but scarlet.

Kai awoke into darkness. Not the darkness of the mists, but the gloom of a shuttered lantern, haunted by the foul air of a silted river. Distant aches reminded of wounds taken. Heaviness of limbs spoke to imperfect mending; of a body fast approaching the precipice. His hand found the rough wool of a cloak, bundled as a pillow. A bear pelt spread as a blanket. No crown. No sword. Tressian song adrift beyond the walls.

Was he a prisoner again in defeat?

Muscles screaming reluctance, he rose with a creak of shifting timber.

Gold glinted, and a hand closed about his shoulder. "Hush, *savir*. We are in the very jaws of death."

"Devren?" The warleader's face grew to focus in the gloom, an expression seldom less than worried now morbidly so. "Where are we?"

"The cellar of a fisherman's hut, perhaps half a mile from Govanna."

"And the battle?"

"Done, my Emperor."

No need to enquire as to the outcome. A commoner's dwelling was hardly a victor's repose. A new pain joined the aches of unsettled bones, this one tight about Kai's heart. "How bad is it?"

"The Ashanal has walked the field. She paints a bleak picture." He wiped at stubble and looked away. "The demons of Fellhallow have abandoned us. Our warriors lie slaughtered. Those who remain have retreated to Sirovo. The Tressians whisper of the dead marshalling to their cause."

Kai kept his expression rigid, determined not to wear the burden of his heart plain upon his face. Shadows yielded to tired eyes, revealing three Immortals about the room's extent. All were filthy and bloodied, their faces crowded by the stoicism of men in denial of unpalatable truth.

"How is it we remain free?"

"Akangar and Golmund bore you here. The Ashanal mended your harms. We have abided the hours since."

"Without discovery?"

"A patrol happened by some time ago. Two men. The Ashanal cautioned us to stay silent and went to greet them. They looked inside and rode away. They saw only what she wished."

"And where is Elspeth now?"

"She left. She does not explain herself to me."

Kai grunted. "Where is my crown? My sword?"

"Jagorn has them in his keeping. They are safe."

Safe. None of them were safe, even with Elspeth watching over them as she had. The chaos of battle's aftermath had kept them hidden as much as her magic. Come morning, matters would be worse ... were he alive to see them. He was nothing but a foolish old man; no one to blame for his woes but himself. A goddess misled. A daughter betrayed. A divine bargain severed by the strike of his sword. An army broken through hubris. And if Devren's expression spoke truly, an Empire humbled where it should have triumphed. Could there be any failure more complete?

The only solace of defeat was that it freed Melanna. With the Raven unvanquished, Jack's claim on the future was spent. Or such was the hope to which Kai clung.

Drawing aside the makeshift blanket, Kai crossed to a narrow window in the far wall. He opened the filthy curtain a crack, and stared out across a river alive with barges' prow lanterns. Upstream, king's blue uniforms stood sentry before a sunken jetty. Bundled dead rattled past on hand-cart and barrow, ushered to a corpse-barge's keeping.

He let the curtain fall. "What do you counsel, old friend?"

Devren drew back his shoulders. "The fields to the east blaze with Tressian fires, but their eyes will be towards Sirovo. With a swift horse and firm purpose you can be among friends long before dawn."

If the sentries were slow to react. *If* his body didn't fail before he reached the safety of Rhalesh banners. And even if he came safely to the army, how many hours before the mists took him at last? Dead, he was a failure. A burden for ever on the House of Saran, should it long outlive him. Better simply to disappear. One more mystery in a world swollen by them.

Above, the door creaked. Stoic expressions regained purpose. Jagorn and Golmund slipped daggers from their sheaths. Devren's hand closed about his mace's haft.

Dust trickled down from the floorboards. The trapdoor creaked aside. Black boots preceded a king's blue tabard on the stairs. Akangar drew back into shadow, coiled to pounce.

"Spare me your attempts at stealth," hissed Elspeth. "It's me."

Kai sagged with relief as she descended into the cellar. "Perhaps a little warning next time, Ashanal?"

"There may not be a next time. Even now, reinforcements are dribbling in from the west. Come dawn, this riverbank will be alive with enemies. One or two I can deceive, but a patrol? A company? Even were the moon full, that would tax me." She picked at the edge of her tabard, her lip curling. "So I am forced to hide my brilliance beneath this ... this crude—"

"Then we should move, and soon," said Kai. "Devren suggests we steal horses and chance the gallop."

She shook her head. "There are too many corpse-parties on the field, and too many guards with them. Thrakkians pick over our dead like carrion. One cry of warning and you'll have an army on your heels."

"Then what else is there?" asked Devren. "The noose is closing. If the Emperor is taken, he will be paraded to the pyre. The shame of it will cling to his heir, if she lives."

Elspeth scowled. "She does. It's why I've been away so long. My mother demanded to speak with me. She offered reminder that my duty was done. I am to leave you to your fate, and carry the sword and crown to your daughter, so that an Empress may rule."

Kai closed his eyes, gave himself to the warmth kindled by her words. "Melanna lives."

"She is at Sirovo, or so Mother insists. What does it matter?"

"It is everything. You should do as the Goddess asks. My fate should not be yours."

"I cannot. I will not." She stiffened, aquiver with pride. "I promised to serve you. I will do so until the end. That was our bargain."

Kai's hand spasmed. He clenched it tight and ignored the worry in Elspeth's eyes. That end would not be long in coming. Either by Tressian blade, the spectacle of the pyre, or his own failing body, the mists would soon take him. What purpose railing against that fate without cause?

But even as the thought formed, Kai realised he *had* cause. Victory would have made unassailable Melanna's claim to the throne. Defeat left all uncertain. Even if she had the crown, and the sword ... What worth such baubles when set against an inheritance of failure? If he died, broken and feeble – if he vanished into history like a ghost – he would only further undermine her position.

Whatever came next, his path ended in the mists, but opportunity remained to ensure hers led to the throne. One last chance to blaze bright before darkness fell. Such was tradition – the same tradition Melanna had resisted all her young life. Glory to make truth of a lie. Blood spilled to wash away all sins, and all failures.

He stared out again to the bobbing lights of the river, an audacious plan taking shape. One last deed to echo through history before the mists took him.

"I will not slink away into the night. I would have my daughter know

I fought to the last. I would have our people remember my name with reverence, and the Tressians whisper it with fear." He cast his gaze about the crowded cellar, his eyes meeting each of theirs in turn. "This will be my Last Ride. There is nothing but death at the end of this road. I free you from oath and duty, but I hope you will accompany me, all the same. A man should not die alone."

Devren knelt, his grey head bowed. A ripple of gold, and the three Immortals followed suit.

"Saran Amhyrador," he said. "In life or in death, our place is at your side."

Jeradas, 10th Day of Wealdrust

Consider always that it may not be your battle to win.
A good death is worth more than gold.

from the saga of Hadar Saran

Sixty-Seven

The lock gates glided open, driven by the grind of hidden gears. The roar of the weir redoubled, and the Silverway was an inky black ribbon threading ramshackle streets, ushering the corpse-barge towards the setting sun.

The view through the cabin's filthy porthole greatly diverged from Kai's expectations. Not a bastion of stained glass and polished metal, but a squalid tangle of buildings, punctuated by the magnificence of clock towers and churches. The glories of Tressia, capital of the Republic, lay in the past . . . had they ever existed at all.

Tressia, the city of his ancestral enemies, and he now trapped within it. Worse, in the hooded garb of those enemies, for fear that warrior's silks and an easterner's aspect would spur discovery. Devren and the three Immortals waited in the bilge, concealed among the dead in anticipation of a search that had not come. The river watchman had made the briefest tour of the upper deck, skirting the tarpaulined bundles with the distaste of a man who'd seen too many such sights.

Elspeth, her army tabard exchanged for a naval coat, stood at the barge's stern with her elbow at the tiller, her expression unconcerned as she guided the craft through slime-clung wharves and the cloying, night soil stench of urban river meeting the sea.

"The watchman said there's to be a celebration tonight." Elspeth spoke as if to herself, with no flicker of expression towards the open cabin door.

Kai grunted in the gloom. A celebration meant crowds – a gift to the purpose at which he found himself. Concealment. Witness. And the one as important as the other. "Did he say where?"

Another barge slid past to starboard, towed upriver by straining carthorses. Children jeered from a crumbling embankment, flung stones spattering across the churning waters. Elspeth nudged the tiller and the barge drifted behind a broken-masted merchant hulk, moored mid-stream.

"No." She'd a wicked gleam in her eye. "I can find out. People like talking to me."

"Do so."

Fingers spasmed, the tremor a warning of waning time. Kai gripped his sword and sank back on the bench. A few hours more, and it would all be over.

Viktor sank from the saddle and into Stonecrest's gravel, his shadow as weary as his flesh. Sleep was a distant memory, devoured by the horrors of a battle won.

A battle won? Hardly that. Even without the Eastshires ceded, too many had died to claim victory. He'd considered ignoring the summons, but there was little left for him to do at Govanna that Rosa and Keldrov could not.

"Look what the cat dragged in."

Kurkas stood at the head of the stairway, the mansion's front door falling closed behind. No salute. No smile. No welcome in a face that had aged years in a few short months.

Viktor tugged his surcoat back into position and made his way up the stairs. "Captain. It's good to see you."

"Lord Trelan's waiting inside."

The expression remained impassive, Kurkas' one good eye staring straight ahead without really seeing anything. Attentive, but elsewhere. The soldier's trick, and none played it better. But always before, he'd played it for a joke. Giving shape to a distance that wasn't really distance.

"You've something you want to say to me, captain?"

The eye didn't flicker. "No, sah!"

"Say it anyway."

Silence stretched to aching eternity. Long enough for Viktor to fear he'd have to make the matter an order and undermine everything. Then, at last, the parade ground stare slipped away and shoulders drooped. The bluff soldier replaced by a disappointed friend.

"We needed you, and you weren't here."

Viktor closed his eyes. Whatever lie he told himself about the months since they'd last spoken, that truth was unassailable. So many bonds broken. Were he honest, he doubted that events would have played out greatly otherwise. He little comprehended the powers that had gathered to the war. Indeed, he scarcely understood his own, even now. But that wasn't the point, was it? He might have made a difference, and would now never know.

"I'm sorry, Vladama. It won't happen again."

The other's expression softened. "See that it doesn't. Won't end well if it's me who comes looking for you next time."

Viktor gripped Kurkas' shoulder and passed inside. Maybe the bonds weren't broken. Maybe they'd merely been tested, and he given another chance to prove himself.

A creak of the door admitted Viktor to the drawing room. Even filthy with travel and war, his face swarthy with stubble and sorrows, he looked more himself than the man Josiri had followed to Indrigsval. A piece of himself found on the battlefield, or perhaps left behind at Kellevork.

[[You're late.]] Ana, still subdued from the trials of recent days, nonetheless found strength for mockery. [[I thought ephemerals prized punctuality?]]

"I can only apologise," Viktor replied. "I'd some difficulty finding the house. Hard to believe I've never been here."

"It's fine. Malachi doesn't intend to address the crowds until dusk," said Josiri. "He wants a symbol. The sun finally set on a dark chapter of history."

The smile faded. "How is he?"

"Brittle. Lilyana's death ripped something out of him."

For all that Viktor was one of Malachi's oldest friends, he didn't yet know the full depth of the other's grief. Of his collusion with the Crowmarket. Of Hawkin's betrayal. Josiri scarcely believed the latter himself. Hard to reconcile the charming, sparkling woman he'd known with the traitor she'd been.

It would wait. It would all wait. The Parliament of Crows was gone, and those of their works that could be unmade in the process of dissolution. The streets belonged to the Council once more. Messela had led the remaining constabulary into Dregmeet to rescue those the vranakin had taken – not just the children who'd been lost to the mists, but a few dozen emaciated southwealders too. Young and old, all had been freed from their chains, though nightmares would last a lifetime.

"I sent the children to join him at the palace," Josiri continued. "They're all staying with us, as long as they need. It seemed the least I could do."

[[That *we* could do.]]

Viktor's brow twitched, then settled. "You're aware of the princessa's proposal?"

"I saw the despatch. You likely passed Malachi's herald on the road. None of us are happy, but the realities ... ?" Josiri rubbed at his brow, wearied by recollection. He'd spent his whole life trying to free an occupied Southshires, now he was party to surrendering the east. "Between the Hadari and the Crowmarket ... the troubles of last year? It'll be a generation before we've even begun to recover. I don't see we've any choice."

"The princessa said even that offer made her a traitor. She said you'd explain why."

Josiri told all. Everything Melanna had recounted when she'd come begging for his help. The Crowmarket. The Raven. Jack. A Reckoning fit to end the world and the fall of Last Night. Ashana's fears, and her folly. The deal she'd sought to strike, and presumably had. It spilled forth in disjointed torrent, ridiculous and inevitable.

When the well of Josiri's memory ran dry, Viktor stared out of the window. "You were right to keep this from me. I'd have damned the princessa and sought my own solution. In my arrogance, I'd have doomed us all. Thank you."

He frowned. "For what?"

"You saved my home."

"It's my home too." Josiri grimaced. "How can it feel so strange to say that, and yet not feel strange at all?"

"Because home isn't a place. It's who we fight for."

It was obvious when spoken aloud, as were all simple truths. Somewhere along the line, distinction between northwealder and south had ceased to matter. And with that change had come another, unrecognised until that moment. Whether their bond was friendship, the fleeting ties of family, or merely common cause that gave purpose to willing hands when all others lay idle, for the first time, Josiri knew himself to be Viktor's equal. A long way from Eskavord, across a distance measured in more than miles and months. An intoxicating revelation that brimming heart saw no way to express.

[[If you'd like to be alone to weep manly tears, I shall be relieved to withdraw,]] said Anastacia. [[Otherwise, might I suggest you leave for the palace? Malachi will be waiting.]]

Sounds of celebration raged beyond the palace walls. Within the Privy Council chamber, old ghosts hung closer than ever. Not just Ebigail Kiradin and Hadon Droshna and all the other withered old vultures Malachi had spent his career seeking to overcome, but those he'd failed, Lily foremost of all. Intellectually, Malachi understood that he was culpable for none of the woes that had haunted the Republic in recent days, but responsibility remained. Was there anything more dangerous than a man out of his depth?

Time to end all that.

"Father?" Sidara hovered in the doorway.

"You're not supposed to be in here."

Her expression took on a hint of Lily's asperity. "How else am I supposed to talk to you?"

Wasn't *that* the story of her life? One he'd authored. "Well, you're here now. Tell me."

She averted her gaze and moved for the door. "It doesn't matter."

Malachi pushed away from his chair. "Your mother ... Your mother used to lecture me for always being too busy. She worried I was becoming a stranger, and that you and Constans would wonder if I loved you at all. Never doubt it. You are my world, both of you." Grief choked away the words. He blinked back a tear, embarrassed – and yet not – to be so struck before his child. "Where's Constans?"

"In your office. Altiris is keeping an eye on him."

"Altiris? The southwealder?"

"My *friend*."

The mix of indignance and embarrassment coaxed forth a smile. "Then keep him close. A good friend is a treasure beyond price. What did you want to say?"

She rallied, as one anticipating opposition. "I'm going to be a knight, Father. I know . . . I know it's not what Mother sought for me, but I want to help people. I want to keep them safe, if I can."

"Do I hear Josiri's influence?"

"Ana's. She said I should stand firm and stop dodging the issue."

Knowing Anastacia, she'd been a good deal more blunt than that. Still, it explained where conversation had meandered after sleep had taken him the previous night. "Yes, I can imagine that."

"She also said that if I didn't learn how to control my magic, she'd take it off me again, and keep it. I *think* she was joking."

"Why take the chance?" He forced a smile. "Half the trick to life is knowing when to listen to yourself. Everyone's always telling you what you should do, or what you shouldn't. But they don't really *know*. They're just telling you what they think you need to hear, or what will get them what they want. So be a knight. Be a beacon that shines through the years to come, if that's your desire. Lumestra knows we'll need some of that. But more than that, be better than me."

He broke off, a body not yet on even keel exhausted for having spoken at such length.

She beamed and flung her arms about him. "Impossible, but I'll try."

"Then I'm sure your mother will be proud."

He held her close and promised himself he'd give a similar speech to Constans. If he'd been distant from Sidara these past few years, he'd been doubly so from his son.

A sharp knock on the door and Lord Lamirov entered, moving with cultivated affectation of wounded pride.

"I understood there was to be a meeting?"

Malachi reluctantly stepped away from his daughter. "Sidara? Perhaps you'd find your brother. I'd like you both beside me when I address the crowds. I assume there are crowds, Leonast?"

Lamirov inclined his grey head. "There are, though they don't know why they've come." His expression darkened. "But then, nor do any of us."

Sidara stifled a sneer beneath a formal curtsey and withdrew.

As she departed, the shrunken Privy Council filed in and took their seats. Messela Akadra, recently returned from overseeing the pacification of Dregmeet. The vranakin had bled away like shadows before the sun. It remained to be seen if they returned now their pontiffs were dead.

Konor Zarn, still sporting the bruises Malachi had meted out at the close of their last meeting. Another apology to offer, when he could stir himself to it. Evarn Marest, his pride worn every bit as tenuously as Lamirov's. The constabulary had practically dug him out of Windchine mansion. No Apara Rann, and thus no Rika Tarev. No Erashel Beral, who Malachi understood would not be returning from the Southshires, though Josiri had given evasive reason as to why.

And no Josiri – that would hardly have been proper. Let him find out with the decision made. One last flexing of authority, and then retirement, if not one exactly earned. Malachi would take with him all the blame for the devastation of the city, the war and the loss of the Eastshires. In exchange, Tressia would have the leader it needed, and one better than it deserved.

He took a deep breath and stared along the table. "Let us discuss the future."

The crowds offered all the concealment Kai had sought, filled with so much mingled raiment and colour that a handful of fugitives with stolen cloaks drawn tight barely elicited notice. A celebration for a war won, with all the drunkenness and cheer expected until the light of a new day brought stark tally of those lost.

Yet beneath the merriment – beneath the songs and the jugglers' whirling flames – Kai sensed melancholy, as if the Tressians already knew their loss, or else had suffered wounds he could not see. More than that, he marked few guards amid the crowds, and fewer soldiers still. He put Melanna's claims of a divine war from his thoughts. This was no night for speculation. If the Tressians lacked for swords even within their greatest city, then so much the better.

In ones and twos they crossed the plaza – Kai, Devren and the three Immortals who were companions on his Last Ride – swords concealed and eyes wary. In ones and twos they came to the servant's entrance Elspeth had spoken of, and the guard staring glassy-eyed across an empty service passage, set dreaming by her touch. A silver hand beckoned from the doorway. And then they were inside, cloaks divested, swords drawn and the door closed behind.

"Is it done?" asked Devren.

Elspeth offered a sly smile. "Nothing stirs on this floor. The servants dream, and the warriors sleep with the Raven. The doors are locked. There will be no interruptions, my Emperor. Your enemy awaits."

Kai glanced through the storage room door to the austere corridor beyond. "Devren, old friend. This is your last chance to leave."

The other man stiffened. "I have shared your victories and your disappointments for thirty years. I have feasted or starved with you as fortune decreed. I will not abandon you now."

"Then barricade the doors with whatever you can find. Return when it's done."

"Of course, *savir.*" Devren beckoned to the Immortals. "Come."

Kai unbuckled the Goddess' sword.

Elspeth watched him, eyes narrowed. "You'll need that."

He shook his head. "Devren will bring me another. This sword goes back to Melanna."

Pale lips pursed. "No. My place is at your side."

"We are dead men. I will not have you perish also."

"You swore I'd never leave your side!"

"The bargain was that you'd stay by my side until the war was done." He shook his head, the swell of weariness nothing to do with the emptiness in his bones. "The war is over, Ashanal. All that remains is a father's desperation to expunge failure in blood, and show the Golden Court that the House of Saran deserves respect. I will sacrifice much in this pursuit, but not your life. Take the sword."

"No!" The shout dropped to a thin hiss, her eyes tight with fury. "I've come this far, defied my own mother. I will not abandon you!"

"You claimed me as father. Would you defy me too?"

"Yes!"

"Then you do not comport yourself as a daughter should. Our bargain was worthless, and my last memory of you will be one of shame."

She flinched. "You cannot ask this."

"I ask nothing. This is simply how it must be." He spoke slowly, urging her to understand. "If it is to count for anything, what comes next has to be my deed, not the will of the divine."

Elspeth's glare softened, spite driven away by sorrow. A shaking hand closed around the scabbard. "Can I do nothing?"

"Lay hands upon me one last time. Grant whatever strength you can spare."

Her empty hand found his cheek and empty bones filled with moonlight. Overcome, Kai sank to his knees. For a moment, he glimpsed something beyond the storage room's drab walls. A city of shining spires, rising up above silver trees.

Then Elspeth kissed his brow, her tears hot and cold upon his forehead. The vision faded. Grey reality slid in, and with it, strength. The vigour of youth, forgotten with advancing years. One last gesture. One last deed to echo across history.

"I've given you all that I can. May it serve you well." Elspeth drew away, her movements suddenly frail and uncertain, an old woman clad in young form. "Saran Brigantim."

For a moment, she looked as though she meant to say something else. Then she was gone into the night, the sword clasped to her chest.

"Saran Brigantim," murmured Kai. "My thanks, Ashanal."

Sixty-Eight

"Josiri Trelan as First Councillor? Preposterous!" Lamirov's complexion turned an outraged shade of puce. An omen of fraught and difficult times. But in that moment Malachi found only the satisfaction of a decision well made. How loathsome to find courage in tragedy, but more so never to find it at all. It helped that it took little to imagine Lily at his side, hand on his shoulder.

"I don't believe so, Leonast," he replied. "Josiri, more than any, is responsible for the city's salvation. Even for the Republic's. You said it yourself. We should have listened to him, and we didn't. Leadership is as much about knowing when to stand aside as when to stand up. It's well past time I stood aside."

Lamirov didn't know about the bargain with the Crowmarket, but he would. Secrets always wormed their way to the surface. All the more reason to get this done before reputation and authority crumbled. Malachi would miss neither. The only reason he held on at all was to take the burden of the war settlement. Let Malachi Reveque be known as the man who'd signed away the Eastshires. Josiri Trelan, once the phoenix of the south, would surely find a way to bring them home ... Especially with Viktor as his right hand.

"Stand aside if you must," Lamirov replied. "But your replacement should be appointed by a vote – a *full* vote of a restored Council. It wouldn't be proper for Lord Trelan to act as First Councillor in the interim—"

"You have someone else in mind, Leonast?" A week before, Messela would never have dared interrupt her elder, but Malachi supposed he'd not been the only one to find courage. She sat upright and proud – a rock against which to be tested or broken. "Yourself, perhaps?"

"I am but the Republic's humble vessel. I will serve in whatever capacity—"

"I'm glad to hear it," said Malachi. Lamirov's complexion deepened further. To be interrupted once was bad enough. Twice was unthinkable. "As First Councillor, and thus the embodiment of both Councils, and therefore the Republic, I'm grateful for your support."

Lord Marest abandoned seeming examination of the tabletop. "A southwealder at the head of the Council? The people will never stand for it."

"Enough saw him fight for their future just yesterday." Malachi waved a hand towards the balcony passage and the growing roar of the crowd. "I understand he's become quite popular. Perhaps you'd like to take it up with them? You've deeds of your own to showcase, perhaps?"

Marest blanched. Messela grinned. Even Zarn offered what might have been a brief smile – a rare display of ... *something* ... from a man who'd said nothing since his arrival. A man into whom Malachi had poured all his own failings and weaknesses rather than confronting them in himself. Yes. It was well past time to stand aside. First, one last politician's deception. Had Josiri known what awaited him, he'd have found all manner of excuse for not attending. But couched as a necessary meeting of the surviving Council ... ?

"This Republic is not governed according to the will of the masses," said Lamirov.

"No. It is governed by *me*. This is not a discussion. It is not a vote. It is a decision. And if Lord Trelan has at last arrived, we can get the matter underway." He raised his voice. "Moldrov?"

The door remained resolutely closed, and the steward remarkable by his absence. Malachi stifled irritation. The man had his own woes to bear from recent days, with a brother still missing and two daughters likely dead on Govanna Field.

Messela scraped back her chair and moved for the door. "I'll go."

Messela knew something was wrong before she reached the stairway, though the shape remained elusive. It wasn't that the palace was quiet. It had been nothing but since the Grand Council's suspension, since most of the constabulary guard had lost their lives in the mists. More, it was a feeling. One that hooked deep into the darkness in her soul. Not fear. Not exhilaration. Not any emotion she could name ... just that inevitable, unutterable feeling that something was out of place.

Skirting the row of gilt-edged doors – once the guestrooms of long-dead kings, and now private offices – she continued along the landing, the unwelcome sensation growing black against her thoughts. The evening sun blazed like fire through high windows, the song and hubbub of the crowd rushing in through open lights.

A huddled shape lay at the head of the stairs.

"Moldrov?"

Gathering her skirts, Messela knelt. The steward's eyes were closed, his lips moving soundlessly. A discarded tray lay three steps further down, the carpet stained from emptied goblets. Darkness crawled tight about Messela's lungs, and she forgot how to breathe.

Outside the walls, bells chimed to mark dusk. The song of the crowd swelled.

Messela fought for breath, inch by inch reclaiming command over recalcitrant lungs. But the darkness refused to abate. It prowled about her soul, a hound awaiting command. She breathed slower, steadier, willing it back into the void between truth and imagination.

Along the landing, the door to Malachi's private office creaked open. Sidara emerged, Altiris and Constans a pace behind, the former with drawn sword and none of them at ease.

"Lady Akadra?" Sidara gripped the banister and stared down at Moldrov. "Something's wrong, isn't it? Something's coming."

Gold gleamed in the girl's eyes. The darkness slunk away. Messela found enough breath to speak. A tangible sensation scraped her thoughts. A metal-rich scent atop the palace's musty air. Blood.

"Saran Amhyrador!"

The brute rounded the landing from the south wing, sword slick with gore and murder in his eyes. Messela again forgot how to breathe. She doubled over, clutching at the banister for support as darkness clawed up through her throat. Hadari? In Tressia? In the *palace*?

Darkness gorged on fear in a bid to escape. Through blurring vision, she saw Altiris fling himself into the Hadari's path. The screech of swords. A bellow in an unfamiliar tongue. A heavy thud. The metallic scent of blood waxed stronger.

"Altiris!" shouted Sidara.

New shapes crowded the corner. Two of similar build to the one gulping his last at Altiris' feet. A scarecrow of a man in a bear cloak. And one whose tanned face was mottled grey beneath a neat beard, whose silver aura flickered whenever Messela choked back the darkness.

The strike of the bear-cloaked man's mace cast Altiris over the banister. The lad's sword thumped at Messela's feet. Then he was gone – a tangle of flailing limbs thumping down the stairs.

Sidara flung back her arms. The crowd's song drowned beneath her shriek and the stairway blazed with sunlight. Glass shattered. The banister shook beneath the mace-wielder's impact. Of the two behind him, one struck the wall with a sickening thud and a crackle of breaking bone. The other slammed sidelong into a statue, sword skidding from a nerveless hand.

The silvered man came on, sunlight parting before him like a flame in the wind.

Constans yelped and scurried away, eyes dark in a bloodless face. Sidara's scream turned bleaker as anger kindled. Golden light seethed from outstretched hands. Still the silvered man came on – as one in the teeth of a gale, but still he came.

Sidara clutched her bandaged arm and dropped to one knee.

Darkness scrabbled at Messela's throat, begging, demanding, *screaming* to be free.

For the first time in her life, she set it loose.

Broken glass shimmered gold in the dying sun and rained down upon the crowd. Josiri flung up his hands to shield his face. Song faded to cries of alarm. Screams and whimpers broke out as razor-edged glass found flesh. A girl's cry of rage ripped through the relative quiet.

Sidara.

Darkness coiled from ruined windows, swallowing sunlight and scattering icy trails across stone.

Josiri's blood ran cold, fed by memories of the year before. Of a war thought done, only for Malatriant to have wormed her way into his home. He reached for a sword he wasn't wearing. Viktor was already running for the palace entrance, his long stride eating up the terraced approach. Tearing his eyes from the seething mass of daylight and darkness, Josiri ran after him.

"Open this door!" bellowed Viktor.

The nearest constable grabbed at the handle. Wood thumped against stone.

"It's bolted." He tugged again. "It's bolted from the inside."

Viktor rammed his shoulder against the door with no more effect than the constable's tugs. The old part of the palace was as much fortress as mansion, with high-set windows and doors sealed with countersunk metal pins as a precaution against an unhappy populace. It'd take a kraikon to burst through.

"You!" Josiri stabbed a finger at the other constable. "Find a proctor. Quickly!"

He glanced left and right as the woman fled. A flat run would bring him to one of the side doors in a matter of seconds, but would do no good if they too were bolted shut. He peered up at the windows and the balcony high above. A day before, Ana had flown him there. Even today, she could probably have flung him high enough. But Ana was halfway across the city.

"We have to try another entrance," he said.

"No," Viktor replied. "We don't."

Shoving the constable aside, he laid his palms on the door. Shadow rushed across the timbers, ice crackling in its wake. Tendrils clawed and scrabbled.

Finding purchase, they heaved.

For the second time in as many minutes, Josiri shielded his face with his hands. Not against glass, but shredded timber and hunks of stone borne forth on an icy wind. When he let them fall, the door's splintered scraps hung in the archway's broken smile.

Shadow dancing like a cloak behind him, Viktor strode on.

Kai strained, awash in sunlight and shadow. Sunlight was the weaker of the two, its wielder flickering like a fading flame before the silver that glimmered about him like a moonlight shield. The magic of one goddess called to contest that of her jealous sister, and the moon outshone the sun.

But the shadow? The Dark of legend that Melanna had sworn held no grip on Tressia? It writhed and squealed before him, cold against his dying flesh; a thin, serpentine hiss in his thoughts. In place of the young woman who bore it, he beheld an icy, shifting presence, with eyes like gashes in the night sky and skin that rippled and seethed.

Sunlight buckled. The girl at its heart became a demon of cruel feature and forked tongue. Golden eyes sought submission; demanded he forswear Ashana for the tyranny of the sun. To grovel. To beg.

A piece of Kai recognised that this perception wasn't his own. He felt the cold coil of moonlight within his being – woken by the first flare of sunlight – and knew without doubt that it was feeding on his soul just as the Goddess' sword had done. Elspeth's gift – her magic, her bleakness – making tinder of the life he'd lived to grant meaning to his death.

But what meaning could his death hold if it was ushered in by madness?

He halted, the sword frozen in descent. The gold demon scrambled away on heels and hands, a fiend one moment, and the next a girl, shaking with effort and fear. Sunlight melted away, extinguished between the contest of moonlight and shadow.

Steel ripped into Kai's chest, chased by the thump of the crossguard against his ribs. He dropped his sword and sagged against the wall, the pain guttering liquid fire with every breath.

"Warn your father." The shadow demon's words crackled and spat like dark flame. "Go!"

A boy helped the golden fiend to her feet. Form bleeding and ebbing between demon and girl, she stumbled away.

Black blood gushed cold. Kai pushed away from the wall and left a smeared palm print behind. Hot metal speckled every breath. But the pain? That was distant, beyond the shimmer of moonlight. Without it, Kai knew he'd already be dead. Even with it, death would find him soon enough.

The shadow demon closed both hands about the hilt of her sword. Pain rippled outwards as she strove to free it from the prison of his flesh.

Her form decayed further, no longer more than a swirl of tattered skin and ragged cloth wrapped about shadow.

Moonlight resurgent in his soul, Kai lurched clear of the wall and clubbed her down, breaking her grip on the sword. The shadow bled away until only the woman remained.

Twisting the sword from his chest and flinging it away, Kai hoisted her high. Eyes blazing darkly into his, she spat full in his face.

"I'm not afraid of you," she gasped.

Her defiant glare never wavered. Not even when he broke her neck.

Kai cast the body aside and fell to one knee, the madness of moonlight gaining purchase alongside pain.

Devren drew level, breathing hard and his right foot dragging. The surviving Immortal followed close behind. "My Emperor—"

"Follow them!" he gasped. "Find the others!"

Was there anything worse than victory ushered in by madness? Yes. Failure. Failure was worse by far. No more hesitation. No more doubts.

Rising to his feet, Kai Saran cast the last of his soul into moonlight.

They found Altiris at the foot of the stairs, breath ragged and phoenix tabard soaked with blood. Not as bad as he'd been in the aftermath of the warehouse raid, but bad enough. In the headlong run from the gate, Josiri had seen too many others who'd had it worse. Guards and servants, some cut down without mercy, others witless without a mark on them.

Josiri crouched at the lad's side as Viktor took the stairs three at a time. "Altiris? Who did this?"

His eyes opened a slit and fell closed. "Hadari. In ... In the palace."

Not Malatriant. Not old ghosts. Never mind how they'd gotten inside. That would wait. Josiri grabbed the constable who'd followed from the front gate. "Make him comfortable."

Fingers tight about a sword claimed from a corpse in the entrance hall, Josiri set off in pursuit of Viktor.

He found him where the landing curved towards the Privy Council chamber, crouched beside Messela's body, face rigid. A bloodied sword lying close told one tale. Pale wisps of shadow rising from her body another. The wary young woman had been more like her cousin than Josiri had ever guessed. Not just in manner, but in heritage.

"She should never have been here." Viktor's murmur frosted in the air. "This was my place. Had I not left—"

A crash sounded down the corridor. A man's scream.

Shadow thickening about his mantle, Viktor took the fallen sword and strode towards the sound. The door to the council chamber crashed open beneath his boot.

Lord Marest lay dead beside the open doorway, one hand pressed to a bloody throat. Lord Lamirov was sprawled across the table, head split open and eyes glassy. A dark smear led from beneath the golden map of the old kingdom and out through the balcony passageway door.

"Saran Amhyrador!"

Two Hadari at the chamber's heart flung themselves at the doorway.

Viktor's shadow gathered up the nearest and bore him screaming away.

Josiri checked the other's mace-blow, the shock of impact shivering up his arm. The Hadari, fast beyond the suggestion of his years, spun about and struck again at Josiri's head. Hurried evasion turned a pulping blow into a grazing one that set Josiri reeling, red stars dancing behind his eyes.

Giddy with pain and nausea, he flung himself forward, weight behind one last, desperate lunge. The sword's point glanced off bone and sank deep, the Hadari's stale gasp warm on his cheek as momentum drove them both to the ground.

Josiri collapsed atop the body. Red stars turning black as the world sank into grey.

Viktor loomed above. "Brother?"

"Go." Josiri waved toward the balcony, the motion enfeebled by failing strength. "I'm all right."

Viktor ran for the balcony door. The last of the world lost its colour.

Malachi slid his arm from beneath Konor Zarn's shoulder. The other sank against the balcony's balustrade, bloodied leg buckling and good arm clutching the wound tight. Constans clung to Malachi's other hand, pale and quiet. One more horror in a week full of them.

"Not exactly how I saw my councillorship ending," murmured Zarn.

Blood bubbled over his lips, proof of wounds deeper than first thought. Malachi wondered what other details he'd missed in the whirlwind of violence.

He turned about. "Sidara? Is there any way down?"

She shook her head tiredly, giving the answer he'd always known. The balcony was a respite of seconds, no more. But even seconds were a victory now.

Malachi peered over the balustrade. The crowd seethed as constables and hearthguard forged towards the palace. Help was coming. Too late.

"I'm trying to reach a simarka," said Sidara wearily. "A kraikon. Anything. It's all so fuzzy. As soon as I make contact, it slides away."

He kissed her brow. However wondrous Sidara's gift, it remained a resource with limits. She'd been off-colour from the moment she'd burst into the council chamber, pale with lost blood and babbling about a man steeped in moonlight. There'd been no time to ask what she'd meant. Barely time to get out of the door. And now they were trapped, with no time at all.

The balcony door crashed open, and a bloodied figure strode out. But for the gleam of a moonsilver crown on his brow, Malachi would never have known him. With it, there could be no doubt. He glanced at Zarn, but the other lay still, eyes closed and barely breathing. No time. No options. Was this how Lily had felt at the end? So much left unsaid, because there'd always be another chance.

"Sidara. Keep your brother safe."

Her eyes went wide. "No, Father—"

"Get Constans away." He put his hand to her cheek and chased away a tear with his thumb. "And remember what I said. Be better than me."

She nodded, blue eyes awash.

Weaponless, he blotted out the tumult of the crowd. "Kai Saran. And to think I sought to make peace with you."

Malachi noted black blood among the red. The flicker of silver about the Emperor's wounds. A man no longer wholly alive, but not yet dead. Steeped in moonlight indeed. Steeped in something else too, by the look of his eyes. This wasn't the Kai Saran he knew from dry distance of reports, or from Josiri's accounts of the year before. The man was a shell. A vessel run dry.

He circled towards the balcony edge, and prayed that Saran would follow. A heartbeat, and he did, the heavy tread and the blood-slick sword drawing away from the door.

"Perhaps I was wrong to reject it." Saran's words gurgled and popped in his throat. "But blood washes away all failures. History will not soon forget the man who slaughtered the Tressian Council in their own lair. Your death secures my daughter's throne."

Another step. Out of the corner of his eye, Malachi saw Sidara usher Constans towards the doorway, hugging the white stone wall as they went.

"You'll never see her again," said Malachi. "There's no way out of this for you now. Only the pyre."

He chuckled, madness gleaming in bloodshot eyes. "All that remains is one last glory. My daughter will rule. Yours never will."

Weariness falling away, Saran rounded on Sidara.

"No!"

Malachi flung himself between them. No hesitation. No fear. Not even any pain as the sword punched wetly into his chest. His final certainty was that Kai Saran wouldn't live to see the pyre.

For long before his soul fell into mist, the balcony drowned in shadow.

The shadow recoiled even as it closed about Kai Saran, seared to vapour by moonlight invisible to ephemeral eyes. A year before, it would have been Viktor's death. A year before, he'd nearly died to Melanna Saranal's moonfire sword. But that had been a different man. One who'd not understood the legacy he wielded. Who'd not yet been tricked into accepting the last of Malatriant's power.

Viktor Akadra had weakened himself by for ever holding back.

Not Viktor Droshna, who blotted out his shadow's pain as soon as it began.

He parried Saran's first strike. The clash from the second split his sword a span above the hilt and drove him to his knees. The third tasted blood. A fourth hacked deep into Viktor's shoulder as he rose, casting him back to his knees.

"The Droshna," said Saran, his voice full of bleak wonder. "Fitting that you're here, in the end. After all, you brought all this to be."

Blood soaked Viktor's threadbare surcoat, stealing strength and granting only agony in exchange. But that pain was nothing beside failure. Of being absent when he'd been needed. Of all those who'd died while he'd built a false life and turned his back on duty.

Messela. Malachi. Even Rosa, in her way. His fault.

Viktor stoppered his seeping wounds with his protesting shadow. As the iron flood slowed to a trickle, he hurled the rest at Saran, smothering sight and breath even as it hissed to oblivion in the Emperor's moonlight.

Blinded, Saran howled and swung wide. His nose crunched beneath Viktor's rising fist.

The stub of Viktor's broken sword ripped a black wound across the Emperor's belly. "I brought this to be?" he bellowed. Wrath drove back the pain, conjured strength to ravaged flesh. "For years, I held back. I kept myself contained."

Shattered blade still buried in Saran's gut, Viktor struck again. And again. Knuckles split and creaked. Black blood mingled with red.

"And what good has it done my family? My friends? My city? My Republic? Those I love?"

Saran swung. Viktor stepped inside the blade's arc. Steel wasted force on empty air. The sword's hilt slammed into his flank. Ribs flexed and snapped. Breath raged like fire in a collapsing lung. His shadow howled, sparking to vapour on unseen moonlight.

Viktor drove his shoulder into Saran's chest. Back they went, past Malachi's body and the unconscious Zarn. Saran's back struck balustrade with a crack of bone. The Emperor roared, his sword falling away.

"No more!" Viktor shouted, the words raw in his throat. "No more!"

Moonlight ebbed. Viktor hoisted the dying Emperor high, ephemeral flesh lent strength by ageless shadow. He paused, aware of thousands of eyes watching him from the plaza. Then Kai Saran was gone. He made no sound until the wet thud of his landing three storeys below.

Anger ebbed, taking with it the last of Viktor's strength. Wounds reopened to full spate as the moon-seared shadow retreated into his soul. He collapsed, elbow and forehead jarring on the balustrade. Slender arms eased him the rest of the way, their owner's words all but lost beneath the sudden cheer of the crowd.

"I have you, uncle," said Sidara. "I won't lose you too."

As he sank against her, he saw Constans staring at him, eyes bright with awe.

Lunandas, 21st Day of Wealdrust

Prophecy is empty without fear.
Fear is nothing without hope.
Hope is bereft without prophecy.
The dread. The dream. The lie.
Fate turns, and the world turns also.

from Kespid's unfinished folio "The Queen's Curse"

Sixty-Nine

Melanna had hoped the cool silence of the root-bound cavern would be a balm to troubled thoughts. Hoped in vain. Doubts blossomed in the darkness. Mistakes of the past bloomed through the crystal-lit gloom, each perfect in memory. Was it some magic of the temple mound, or merely the burden of contemplation? Had her father felt thus? She wished she'd had the chance to ask him. She longed for the opportunity to say so many things, but Kai Saran had passed into legend, the hope of survival quashed first by Elspeth's arrival, and again by Haldrane's agents.

A valiant end, the Golden Court called it. Ironic, that the very tradition she despised now protected her. Those who would not respect her claim would at least honour her father's sacrifice. Just as well, for of all the kingdoms who had marched to Govanna Field, Rhaled had suffered most of all. It needed every spear on its borders, and had none to spare for intemperate friends.

A distant bell chimed. Tenth bell. The sanctum approach.

Gathering golden skirts, she knelt before the statue of Ashana. The old Ashana, not the one who was her mother. The mother who had offered only silence since Govanna.

Elspeth had offered no insight. Indeed, the Daughter of Moon had offered no words at all – only a snarl before pressing the sword into Melanna's hands and departing into the night. That sword now hung above a throne not yet claimed. Six months before, she'd defied tradition by coming armed to coronation. Now she defied it again by forsaking the sword. The imperial throne demanded a warrior, but now more than ever the *Empire* needed something more. Better to send that message from the first. The throne would not shape her as it had her father.

Shadows played across Aeldran's armour as he shifted position, a sign that he wasn't yet accustomed to the bindwork leg concealed beneath his robes. In time, when the amputation's scar had healed, the facsimile of threaded metal and moonlight might yet serve him as well as flesh and bone. But not tonight, with harms still raw. She'd argued for him to stand apart from the vigil. He'd refused, as a champion should. Just as he'd refused the scarlet of Icansae that night in favour of Rhalesh green. What the Rhalesh Immortals in the chamber made of that, Melanna couldn't guess.

Footsteps tracked across the chamber floor and halted behind.

"My princessa, you are called to coronation." Aelia knelt as she spoke, head bowed.

"And who ... " Melanna swallowed, memories thick in her throat. "Who calls me?"

"One who will guard the Empire to her last breath."

Another tradition broken, for there was no heir to call the ascendant to the throne. No one to follow, once Melanna was gone. Come that day, Aelia Andwaral, Dotha Icansae, had as worthy a claim as any. Until then, she'd agreed to serve, and thus bound the kingdoms of Rhaled and Icansae closer than ever.

"Then lead, and I will follow."

Aelia retraced her steps. Melanna followed through the temple mound, her honour guard keeping pace behind. Before long, they emerged into the gentle moonlight of the birch grove. A ring of white-cloaked guardians waited on the pool's far shore. Beyond, princes and kings of the Golden Court held vigil of their own from balcony and cloister. Their ranks were thinner than at her father's coronation, winnowed away by war and disapproval. Even now, some seethed with displeasure that a woman claimed the imperial throne, but opposition had gone no further than whispers. So far.

Demestae had sent no representative. Britonis, weeping for its losses, had dispatched only the youngest of its sons. Corvant remained true, its faith in imperial divinity unshaken. Silsaria's support she'd purchased with promises of governance over newly claimed Tressian lands. Pledges of loyalty aplenty had been issued, but the gathering told its own tale. All were waiting. Watching. Just as the Ithna'jîm and the Thrakkians were watching the humbled Empire for sign of weakness.

Eleventh bell chimed the passing of midnight and called the Goddess to temple. But if Ashana heard the call, she gave no sign. There was only the long, lonely walk to beneath the moon-dappled branches, and the hooded priestess waiting beside altar and crown.

Leaving her guards behind, Melanna trod the winding path and knelt. "I seek the Goddess' blessing."

The priestess raised the crown from its cushion of leaves – not the moonsilver crown, for that was lost to the Tressians as spoils of war – but a replica fashioned from worldly metal. It shone, though not as brightly, just as Melanna's world was duller for her father's passing.

"You will always have that," murmured the priestess. "Never doubt it."

Melanna stared up into a face as familiar as the voice. "I . . ."

"Say nothing," Ashana breathed, her face still hidden from onlookers by the folds of her hood. "No one must know. No one must even suspect."

Wonder and delight shrivelled away. Melanna bowed her head in semblance of prayer. "I don't understand."

"The kindness Jack sought of me. A simple trade. He will make no claim on you, not so long as I renounce my own. I shouldn't be here now, but I wanted to see you one last time."

"I'm not afraid of him."

Yet the words remained a lie. Even the thought of Jack invited shadow beneath the moonlight and a cold itch under her skin.

"You should be. He has pride enough for a hundred kings and loathes that he was outplayed. And . . . perhaps it is best I keep my distance. My fears almost broke this world. My love may yet prove more dangerous. Even for a goddess, knowing when to do nothing is the hardest lesson of all."

Misery flooded free. "Can I say naught to change your mind?"

"An ephemeral alter the will of the divine? Unthinkable." Arch tone faded to affection. "It is every mother's hope that her child will surpass her in happiness and wisdom. Do so, and I am content."

"And I'll be alone." Melanna hated the words, petulant and selfish as they seemed, but found no others to bear the weight of her ailing heart.

Ashana smiled. "Not so long as there's a moon in the sky." She held the crown aloft and raised her voice alongside. "The blessing is granted. As the crown passed to your father from his, so now it passes to you. The Goddess and the throne are one. May your rule be long, and her love for you never fade."

Ashana set the crown on Melanna's head. Lighter than she'd expected, and heavier also.

"Ashanael Brigantim!" shouted Aelia. "Saranal Amyradris!"

Others took up the cry. The clamour grew, joined by the thump of boot on stone. Melanna rose from unsteady knees, the elation of a moment long-sought swirling sick with the reminder of all she'd lost along the way.

"*Ashanael Brigantim! Saranal Amyradris!*"

Strength returned as Melanna made her way back along the path. The challenges of coming days did not care for what she'd lost. And for all she'd claimed otherwise, she wasn't alone. She had Sera, and the lunassera. The support of Icansae, of Haldrane's icularis, of her father's Immortals and the chieftains of Rhaled. There would be others. Those who had defied the princessa would not readily oppose an Empress.

"Congratulations, *savim*," said Aelia. "The Kingdom of Icansae stands with you."

The queen knelt, her head bowed. The ring of Rhalesh Immortals followed suit – as did Aeldran, though the discomfort of his bindwork leg must have troubled him greatly. Melanna stared past them to the temple balconies, where royalty of a dozen nations cheered her ascension. Some reluctant, others with gusto, and no few seeking to convey one while cleaving to the other. The weak and the strong; the honourable and the opportunist. A lifetime's work to tell them apart. To know which to trust, and which to watch.

She glanced back as dawn's first light touched the cloister, but Ashana was a flicker of robes beneath the temple mound, and then she was gone.

You will have to find one you can at least tolerate if this day is to mean anything.

Her father's words, spoken in that very spot, truer now than ever. Ashana had promised she would not be the last Empress. But a daughter needed a father, and an Empress a consort to share her burdens. She didn't need to trust the Golden Court entire. Just one who'd proven his loyalty.

"And do you agree with your queen's words, Prince Aeldran?" she asked.

A frown creased his brow. "My life is yours, Empress."

"Good." Extending a hand, she raised him to his feet. "Because I need you to be more than my champion."

Morning found Apara atop Seacaller's Church, lost in a sight never beheld. Oh, she'd climbed the tower many a time, risking both mouldered stairs that creaked beneath the lightest tread, and the malevolent gazes of caryatid and stone-nymph – the latter no less chilling for their thick layer of grime. If anything, they were more so, for she'd recently seen their like guarding a throne in a place that was no place. Immobile servants to a Nameless Lady. Seacaller's would never be the same again, just as Apara knew she'd never be the same again.

Nor would Dregmeet.

For the first time in Apara's life, the labyrinthine alleyways were laid bare between Drag Hill and the harbour wall. For all that she knew each step, each turning – every decaying rooftop and graffitied wall – Dregmeet was *different*. Reshaped by returning light. Or perhaps *she* was different, and Dregmeet no longer her home.

It wouldn't be anyone's home much longer. The Raven's patronage had held back the ravages of time from more than Krastin and his siblings. To the west, glimpsed through a cage of jettied eaves, the Church of Tithes crumbled inexorably inwards. One tower was gone already. The other canted as venerable buttresses crumbled. Tzalcourt was no longer a plaza, but a growing lake, fed by a dozen breaches in the neglected sea wall. Engineers scurried like ants to dam the flow, but rising waters in the sunken streets spoke to a battle lost.

Rumour claimed this as the Council's revenge, sabotage of ancient defences in the malice of victory. But it was nothing more than the passage of years reawoken to vigour.

Perhaps something would be saved. Westernport, maybe. Perhaps the Sothvane slums to the south. Apara didn't care. Already, it was hard to think of the place with any fondness. Let the sea reclaim it. Let all sink into the mud. It didn't matter. Apara Rann, the Silver Owl, would fly free.

Offering one last glance to the Church of Tithes, she did so.

The archimandrite's muttered blessing, a joining of hands – a kiss that made truth of all – and a bright chime of bells swept the Hayadra Grove. Essamere steel rippled skyward, the locked swords forming a tunnel of blades beneath bright ribbons and falling leaves. Squires barely out of childhood led the way, scattering a carpet of petals. As the brides crossed the tunnel's threshold – Rosa in hunter's green, and Sevaka in a simple white gown that dazzled like ice beneath cold morning sun – buccinas and trumpets joined the riot of carillon and cheer.

Josiri readily lent his voice to the celebration, and prayed the rain would hold off.

"A bit showy." Izack shifted against his crutch, the movement doubly awkward because the adjacent arm was bound tight in a sling. Josiri, whose head sometimes still rang with the strike of a Hadari mace, wondered how the master of Essamere could stand, much less joke. "Still, long as they've not scrimped on food and drink, you'll not be hearing me complain."

"Rosa insisted," Josiri replied. "She wanted to give folk something to celebrate. Light amid the gloom. Proof that life goes on, despite the scars."

And scars there were aplenty. Beneath the strewn petals and Fade-fallen leaves, the Hayadra Grove remained rutted and muddied. The Shaddra – under whose branches the Ladies Orova had been wed – showed no sign of recovering from the taint of Krastin's blood, her alabaster bark turning black as the stain spread.

More than that, there was the thinness of the crowd. Though invitations had delved far deeper into the Republic's social strata than was customary, nothing concealed the gaps. Between the Crowmarket and the Hadari, it was a rare and fortunate bloodline that had gone unscathed. Some families were gone entirely, their heraldry banished to history. Others hung by a thread.

Institutions had suffered deeper wounds still. The foundry was all but gone, its proctors slaughtered by vranakin and the vast majority of its constructs shattered by war. For all of Elzar's optimism, it would be years before things were set right. The constabulary and the chapter-houses had fared little better. And while most of those stolen away into Dregmeet had been freed without harm, no priest had emerged from the mists alive.

The Grand Council was depleted. The Privy Council as good as gone – beyond Josiri and Izack, only Konor Zarn still lived, and he'd sent a herald from Woldensend Manor with a letter pleading resignation.

Succession could close some gaps. Others were problematic. There were no shortage of Lamirovs and Marests to fill their forebears' empty seats. Rika Tarev had been the last official progeny of her line, though of course the Crowmarket had replaced her with an imposter long before she'd claimed her councillor's seat. Likewise, there were no more Berals. The Reveque seat now passed to Sidara, but she was too young. The Akadra reverted to Viktor ... which brought complications of its own. Not least because Viktor had been an evasive figure since Malachi's death, and was even now absent from the wedding of his oldest surviving friend.

And then there was the matter of choosing a First Councillor ...

After generations of sterility, change was coming to Tressia. It would have to, were the Republic to survive. The Parliament of Crows was gone, but their cousins clung to Dregmeet's flooding ruins. There was peace with the Hadari, but when had such peace ever lasted?

Generous of Rosa to offer distraction from uncertainty, if only for a day. All the more so, given her famous dislike of putting the personal on display. That the wedding's largesse stretched far beyond the Hayadra Grove, to every barracks, church and tavern within the city walls? That had been Sevaka's doing, financed by a tainted Kiradin fortune she'd otherwise refused to touch. One glorious day of feasting and remembrance, commemorating the victory that was no victory at all, and promising better times to come.

Tell that to the dead, and to those driven from their homes or abandoned to Hadari rule. Tarvallion lost beneath the roots of Jack's children. A quarter of the Republic lost. The greater part of its soldiers dead or wounded. Tressia didn't have swords enough to defend its holdings, let alone retake the ceded Eastshires.

The wedding procession emerged from the tunnel of swords, Sevaka beaming and Rosa wearing the rather more restrained half-smile of one striving to contain unaccustomed delight.

Embraces were shared with the foremost guests, most of whom were strangers to Josiri. In truth, he knew neither Rosa nor Sevaka well, but recognised that neither woman was entirely as he'd seen her last. Rosa's hair, once straw-blonde, was white as Sevaka's dress. Sevaka evinced subtler difference; one of manner, rather than body. Her movements held a confidence that had otherwise been absent and that couldn't wholly be ascribed to the joy of the day.

There were rumours, of course, shifting and contradictory as all soldiers' tales. But Josiri, who shared his life with a serathi and had recently walked Otherworld at a goddess' behest, was content for the world to hold some secrets, so long as they offered no harm.

"I understand you're a father now," said Izack.

"After a fashion," Josiri replied. "Constans and Sidara don't have much family, and what remains is scattered far and wide. This seemed kinder. Besides, Ana insisted."

"Did she indeed? The world *must* be ending."

"She's trying to be better. We all are. We'll have to be."

Poor Malachi. He'd tried and tried to be better, but had never quite outrun the past. If only he'd said something. But Josiri knew the power of pride more than most.

He stared across the crowd to where Kurkas held watch over a glum Constans and a brighter Sidara. Tears had been shed. More would follow – he'd walked too similar a path to believe otherwise. To lose both parents so young, and in such circumstance . . . ? But tears would pass, in time, and he'd ease their passing, if he could. Sidara would make the transition soonest – she and Ana seemed closer than ever. Constans, he suspected, would be another story. The boy had many times demanded to be returned to Abbeyfields, even though he knew it was gone.

A still visibly battered Altiris stood close by. The lad had been lucky. More than that, he'd refused Sidara's attempts to ease his wounds, claiming that he owed her enough already. They hadn't spoken for two days after that, but seemed friendly enough now.

Izack grunted. "Do yourself a favour. Pack the boy off to earn his spurs as soon as you can. May the Light shine on them both, but Lilyana coddled him and Malachi ignored him. It's a bad combination."

Such was the wisdom of Stantin Izack who, if he'd any children of his own, kept that information hidden. Still, the advice held the ring of truth. "You're not the first to tell me that. I think we might give it a while. He deserves the chance to decide what he wants to be. They both do."

"Does that extend to their names?"

"It does. Let them be Reveques as long as they wish."

"Another man would have gobbled Sidara up as his own for the prestige of it, if not the boy. The lass has a fine future ahead of her, I reckon. And then there's the wealth to be had from claiming their inheritance. You're a peculiar one, Josiri."

"You're not the first to tell me that, either."

Josiri thought back to the Indrigsval cliffside. He'd told Erashel Beral that family was about more than shared blood, but it was also about more than a shared name. Home was what you fought for. Family were those with whom you shared your life, for good or ill, in wisdom and in folly. And you didn't always get to choose them.

Coming to a decision, he tapped Izack on the shoulder. "I have to go. Please offer my congratulations."

"Gladly. Kick him up the arse for me, would you?"

Josiri wondered how long Izack had foreseen that moment. Then he shook his head and threaded his way through the crowd. As he did so, he glimpsed Apara Rann, a smile playing on her lips at her estranged sister's obvious joy, but when he looked again, she was gone.

Good luck to her. Everyone deserved a second chance.

The chime of bells was barely a whisper in the crypt, lost beneath the echo of spent memories. Stern Reveques long-dead gazed down from plinth and sepulchre, the old and the young, the cherished and the despised.

Only one tomb remained unadorned, the statue weeks from completion. Until then, only a simple inscription marked the final resting place of Malachi Reveque.

Annalor malda ani te stel. Not all strength is the sword.

Malachi slept alone, for nothing identifiable as his beloved Lilyana had been recovered from the ashes of their home. Even so, Viktor hoped that they might find one another in spirit. That would only be fair, and the return of Sevaka Psanneque – by now Sevaka *Orova* – to life and happiness offered a gleam of hope. And that Sevaka *had* returned from the mists, Viktor did not doubt, despite Rosa's claims of mistaken mourning and remarkable survival. He'd kept secrets of his own too long not to recognise them in others.

And if Sevaka had returned, what of others? Viktor strove to dwell on other matters, fearful where his hopes might lead. But there in the tunnels beneath the Hayadra Grove, surrounded by the legacy of fading families, death and hope were inextricably intertwined. Especially with the piece of the Raven he'd taken from Rosa still buried deep in his shadow. The dead. He'd raised the dead, if only in body, not soul. What the Raven took did not have to belong to him for ever. And if that were true ... ?

"I thought you'd be at the wedding. Sidara asked after you."

Josiri stood on the cusp of lantern light, more shadow than substance. Anastacia waited at his shoulder, her doll's aspect a match for the mausoleum statuary.

"I meant to be. I wanted to pay my respects here first, and somehow ... Somehow I never left. Perhaps that's as it should be. I find my mood better company for the dead than the living."

"Izack says I'm to kick you up the arse."

"How colourful."

"He's seldom anything but."

Viktor folded his arms. "You think I'm hiding."

"I wouldn't blame you. What you did at Govanna can be blamed on the Raven. But the palace? Too many saw that. If it's any consolation, I don't think anyone cares."

"They don't care that a monster walks their midst?"

"The only monster was the one who slaughtered the Council. He would have murdered Malachi's children too, before he was done. If the church provosts want you, they'll have to fight their way through half the city. Especially as those same provosts did nothing to contain the Parliament of Crows."

"And what do you think?"

"Me?" Josiri drew closer. Touching his eyes closed, he ran his fingers along the slab of Malachi's tomb. "Council business has been frantic of late, but there are still those who insist on adding to the pile. Would you believe the rector of the Hayadra Grove wanted my permission to cut down the Shaddra? He claimed the tree is poisoned beyond recovery, all because her bark is stained."

"And what did you tell him?"

"That though the Shaddra is no longer as perfect as we might wish, she remains a symbol of hope, and that the Republic needs hope more than anything in coming days." He opened his eyes, gaze unswerving as it met Viktor's. "It needs you ... brother. That much has not changed."

Viktor turned away. "It doesn't need the man I've been."

[[May I offer some advice?]] said Anastacia.

"I don't recall it being in your nature to ask permission for anything."

[[I'm just being polite. Ephemerals appreciate the illusion of choice.]]

"Indeed we do." He gave a wry shake of the head. "Say what you must."

[[If you're to skulk down here, moping over old days and lost opportunity, you might as well go back to the border and make-believe yourself another wife.]]

Even with his back to Josiri, Viktor felt him wince. "Ana, please—"

"She's right," said Viktor.

[[I'm *always* right. Eventually. It's one of immortality's many benefits.]]

"I am not, in fact, hiding. I've been thinking." He drew up to his full height. "The Council has failed this Republic time and again. I can't be part of that any longer. Watching selfishness and deceit win out over necessity for no better reason than pretence of democracy. Another round of that, and we might as well slit our own throats and have done."

"What are you proposing?"

"That we stop pretending to speak with one voice, and actually do so." Passion lent the words vigour. "Last year, you sought to install me as First Councillor. It wouldn't have worked, even had I accepted. Lamirov and his ilk would have worn me away as they did Malachi. They'd have bled me by a thousand petty cuts and left me impotent. The Republic doesn't need a First Councillor. It needs a Protector."

"You?"

Viktor turned around. "Me."

"And what's to stop you becoming everything Ebigail Kiradin sought to be?" said Josiri. "A monarch in all but name?"

"Because it won't be for ever. And because I know you'll stop me, should need arise. Just as you promised."

The anger came, as he'd known it would. "You're asking me to help you destroy the very foundation of the Republic!"

"And does that really seem so bad to you? The son of Katya Trelan? She who sought to do precisely that?"

"She didn't seek to remake the Age of Kings!"

"This is an opportunity that comes but once in ten generations. If the Council is to continue at all, it will have to be rebuilt. Why bother, when all it will bring is equivocation and pain?" Viktor spread his hands, rising anger under tight control. "We have a chance to make a Republic that serves all its people, not just the families of noble rank. We owe that to the living, you and I. The dead *demand* it of us."

Viktor held Josiri's gaze throughout, imploring him to listen, to understand. Could he not see what needed to be done? Especially now?

Josiri's lip twisted. "Ana?"

[[Oh no. I'm not touching this one.]]

His eyes shifted to Malachi's tomb. Dwelling, perhaps, on what was owed to the dead.

It wouldn't be enough. Viktor saw it plainly in his features. The reluctance he'd marked in their first meeting. Lives hung in the balance, and yet Josiri was afraid. Fear would beget refusal, and refusal, disaster. A reaffirmation of the status quo that had twice brought the Republic to the brink. The cycle would begin again.

It would take only the merest caress of shadow. Nothing so crude as the means by which Apara Rann had been dominated a year before. A nudge. A suggestion to smooth away reluctance and let necessity speak for itself. If Josiri would not act on the debt, then it fell to others to make him do so. Viktor glanced down at the tomb. Not all strength is the sword. How many times had he sworn to no longer hold back when lives lay in the balance and his sword was insufficient?

Fed by anger and frustration, the shadow slithered free. A presence so slight that even Anastacia saw nothing, or else missed its significance in the gloom. It burrowed deep and coiled tight about Josiri's reluctance. A soul in the balance, torn between principle and pragmatism. The slightest caress, and the matter would be settled. It was necessary. It was inevitable.

It was precisely what Malatriant would have done.

A chasm loomed. On one side, what Viktor had always been. On the other, what he'd sought always to reject. Frantic, he withdrew his shadow. But in the desperation of the moment, he couldn't be sure whether it was already too late.

Josiri sighed. "I've trusted you this far. I'll do so a little further. But only if you leave the dead to their dreams and walk among the living."

His decision, or one made for him? Did it even matter *why* Josiri had chosen, so long as he'd made the proper choice? Conscience commanded a heavy price, and one the Republic could ill afford. Maybe this had been necessary, as other deeds would be necessary in the months and years to come. That was a Protector's burden, and his duty.

Did it matter?

Viktor forced a smile. "Of course, brother."

No. It didn't matter at all.

Acknowledgements

Congratulations! You made it through Book 2 as well. I mean, I assume "as well", but if you borrowed *Legacy of Steel* from your local library, and your local library's anything like the one where I grew up, there's not a single first volume of a fantasy series in sight. Just one more reason for libraries to get more funding.

But I digress. This is the acknowledgements page, so acknowledgements there shall be.

First of all, a "hello" and "thanks" to Ceri Gwyther and Gareth Johnson. Ceri, for reading *Legacy of Steel* – along with damn near everything I've written – while it was in progress. Gareth hasn't read *Legacy of Steel* yet – as a Yorkshireman, he doesn't trust fancy technology and will be waiting for the printed version – but he does (partly) know how it ends. That's because over twenty-odd years he's seen the Legacy Trilogy grow from a seed to a sprawling tree, and he's cheered me on every step of the way.

Beyond that, I put the words on the page, but there's a small army makes those pages into a book. My agent, John Jarrold (for checking I'm just the right level of insane in my plotting and putting me in a place where I can do it for a living); James Long, Priyanka Krishnan and Joanna Kramer (editors with varying responsibilities and degrees of polite exasperation, but united in patience); Andy Hawes and Ilona Jasiewicz (proofreaders and copy-editors who helped me save face when it turns out I can't actually spell or sentence construct proper-like); the team at M Rules for laying out the book's innards, Larry Rostant and Charlotte Stroomer respectively for illustrating and designing another beautiful cover, Viv Mullett for breathing life into the map. Last but not least, Nazia Khatun and Angela Man for their ceaseless promotional efforts.

And, of course, endless thanks to my wife Lisa for her unflagging support, and to the pride of cats who (sometimes) leave me alone long enough to get something written.

Two down, one to go. I've a feeling we're all going to need a run-up for the last one.

About the Author

Matthew Ward is a writer, cat-servant and owner of more musical instruments than he can actually play (and considerably more than he can play *well*). He's afflicted with an obsession for old places – castles, historic cities and the London Underground chief among them – and should probably cultivate more interests to help expand out his author biography.

After a decade serving as a princial architect for Games Workshop's *Warhammer* and *Warhammer 40,000* properties, Matthew embarked on an adventure to tell stories set in worlds of his own design. He lives near Nottingham with his extremely patient wife – as well as a pride of attention-seeking cats – and writes to entertain anyone who feels there's not enough magic in the world.

Follow him on Twitter @TheTowerofStars.

Find out more about Matthew Ward and other Orbit authors by registering for the free monthly newsletter at www.orbitbooks.net.